PENGUIN CLASSICS

THE PORTABLE CONRAD

JOSEPH CONRAD (originally Konrad Korzeniowski) was born in Russian Poland in 1857 and grew up in the shadow of political unrest. His parents died when he was quite young and he was looked after by his uncle, Tadeusz Bobrowski, who was to be an enduring influence on his life. From an early age he longed to go to sea and in 1874 he travelled to Marseilles where he joined the merchant marine as an apprentice. His career as a sailor was to provide much of the material for his writing. In 1886 he became a British subject and a master mariner and in 1894, after twenty years at sea, he settled in England and devoted himself to writing. He married Jessie George in 1896 and in the same year published *Almayer's Folly.* The long subsequent series of novels, tales, essays, and reminiscences established Conrad in the front rank of creative writers. Among his many other books are *An Outcast of the Islands* (1896), *The Nigger of the "Narcissus"* (1897), *Youth* (1902), which included "Heart of Darkness," *Typhoon* (1903), *Nostromo* (1904), *The Mirror of the Sea* (1906), *The Secret Agent* (1907), *Under Western Eyes* (1911), *Chance* (1913), *Victory* (1915), *The Shadow-Line* (1917), *The Rescue* (1920), and *The Rover* (1923). His autobiography, *A Personal Record,* appeared in book form in 1912 and his unfinished novel *Suspense* was published in 1925. Joseph Conrad died in 1924.

MICHAEL GORRA is the Mary Augusta Jordan Professor of English at Smith College. His books include *After Empire: Scott, Naipaul, Rushdie,* and *The Bells in Their Silence: Travels through Germany.* For Penguin Classics he has written introductions to *The Guide* by R. K. Narayan and *The End of the Affair* by Graham Greene.

JOSEPH CONRAD

The Portable Conrad

Edited with an Introduction by

MICHAEL GORRA

PENGUIN BOOKS

PENGUIN BOOKS
Published by the Penguin Group
Penguin Group (USA) Inc., 375 Hudson Street, New York, New York 10014, U.S.A.
Penguin Group (Canada), 90 Eglinton Avenue East, Suite 700, Toronto,
Ontario, Canada M4P 2Y3 (a division of Pearson Penguin Canada Inc.)
Penguin Books Ltd, 80 Strand, London WC2R 0RL, England
Penguin Ireland, 25 St Stephen's Green, Dublin 2, Ireland (a division of Penguin Books Ltd)
Penguin Group (Australia), 250 Camberwell Road, Camberwell,
Victoria 3124, Australia (a division of Pearson Australia Group Pty Ltd)
Penguin Books India Pvt Ltd, 11 Community Centre, Panchsheel Park, New Delhi – 110 017, India
Penguin Group (NZ), 67 Apollo Drive, Rosedale, North Shore 0745,
Auckland, New Zealand (a division of Pearson New Zealand Ltd.)
Penguin Books (South Africa) (Pty) Ltd, 24 Sturdee Avenue,
Rosebank, Johannesburg 2196, South Africa

Penguin Books Ltd, Registered Offices:
80 Strand, London WC2R 0RL, England

This edition first published in Penguin Books 2007

3 5 7 9 10 8 6 4

LIBRARY OF CONGRESS CATALOGING IN PUBLICATION DATA
Conrad, Joseph, 1857–1924.
[Selections. 2007]
The portable Conrad / edited with an introduction by Michael Gorra.
p. cm.—(Penguin classics)
ISBN 978-0-14-310511-4
I. Gorra, Michael Edward. II. Title.
PR6005.O4A6 2007
823'.912—dc22 2007060130

Printed in the United States of America
Set in Sabon

Acknowledgments

My thanks to the friends and colleagues who read and responded to draft versions of my introduction: Christopher Benfey, Stephen Clingman, Jefferson Hunter, Suzanne Keen, Margery Sabin, and James Wood. J. H. Stape and Peter Lancelot Mallios provided expert advice on different aspects of Conrad scholarship. Susan C. Bourque and Charles Staelin of the Provost's Office at Smith College offered crucial material help. Bobbie Kozash and Gladys Pulido in the English Department office at Smith gave invaluable technical support. Linda Bree and Adam Hirschberg at Cambridge University Press facilitated my use of the Conrad letters. Michael Millman commissioned this project for Penguin Books; Elda Rotor, Lauren Fanelli, and Donald Homolka brought it to fruition.

Contents

Introduction

I

"I *never mean* to be slow," Joseph Conrad wrote to David Meldrum of the Blackwood publishing house in 1899, but "The stuff comes out at its own rate . . . [and] too often—alas!—I've to wait for the sentence—for the word." The process of writing involved long hours of incapacitating doubt that left him caught like a ship in a calm, an unrestful paralysis in which his mind remained "extremely active," producing "descriptions, dialogue, reflexion—everything—everything but the belief, the conviction, the only thing needed to make me put pen to paper." Days would pass without his writing a line, and Conrad would take to his bed, sick of a labor so great that it should have given "birth to masterpieces" instead of what he termed the "ridiculous mouse" his struggles would sometimes produce. His biography is full of stories about the storms through which his work made him pass. The happiest of them concerns what he called the "steady drag of 21 hours" in which he steered with care through the last pages of *Lord Jim* (1900), finishing the novel at dawn with a "cairn" of cigarette butts at his elbow. But Conrad also had a history of nervous collapse at the end of most of his major books, *Under Western Eyes* (1911) in particular, a novel that involved a prolonged psychic immersion in the Russia he both hated and feared. Few of his letters are without some plaintive or even desperate note. "My brain reduced to the size of a pea seems to rattle about in my head," he wrote to R. B. Cunninghame Graham in 1900, and if it wasn't the fight with words then it was his worries about money or housing, the illnesses of his wife and children, or the crippling attacks of gout with which his working life was spiked.

The difficulties were real. Conrad may, as his biographer Zdzislaw Najder writes, have suffered from "depression in the strict psychiatric sense of the term," but money was indeed tight, the family health poor, and the novelist was no hypochondriac, however detailed his account of his symptoms. Only he, however, would have compared the work he was doing at the time he wrote Meldrum to a species of household rodent. The previous year had seen the publication of both "Youth" and "Heart of Darkness," and the letter itself concerns the serialization of *Lord Jim*. Only Conrad would think of himself as writing slowly in the astonishing decade that began in 1897, a period that saw the publication not only of these works but also of *The Nigger of the "Narcissus"* (1897), *Nostromo* (1904), and *The Secret Agent* (1907). Yet Conrad never had what Morton Dauwen Zabel has called a sense of "fluent ease or assurance in his craft." To write at all was an achievement, a trouble that only the most strenuous of efforts could surmount.

Some of that has, doubtless, to do with the particular circumstances of Conrad's life. He was born Józef Teodor Konrad Nalecz Korzeniowski in 1857, in a part of Poland that after the partition of 1793 had fallen under Russian rule. His parents were members of the Polish gentry, and patriots—his father a poet—and before his fifth birthday the Tsarist government had sent the family into an exile, north of Moscow, that broke the health of both husband and wife. His mother died in 1865 and his father four years later, leaving the boy to the guardianship of his maternal uncle, Tadeusz Bobrowski. In 1874, facing the unacceptable possibility of Russian military service, and with an almost inexplicable hankering for the sea that he had as yet just glimpsed, the future Conrad left his Cracow home and schooling for Marseilles. There he drew upon both Bobrowski's money and his contacts to learn the trade of an officer in the merchant marine. Much about the boy's four years in France remains cloudy, and Conrad would later depict that time, in both *The Mirror of the Sea* (1906) and *The Arrow of Gold* (1919) with a degree of romantic retrospection that has made his biographers sweat. But by 1878 he had signed on to a British steamer and begun his move toward England.

Conrad's spoken English remained heavily accented—far more so than the French he had learned as a child—but in *A Personal Record* (1912) he described the language as having "adopted" him, and maintained "that if I had not known English I wouldn't have written a line for print in my life." Nevertheless he also complained, according to Ford Madox Ford, that the language was incapable of "direct statement" and that "no English word has clean edges." French seemed to him too perfectly "crystallized," but its vocabulary did at least have a limpid clarity of meaning. English words, in contrast, carried so many connotations as to be little more than "instruments for exciting blurred emotions." And some readers have, accordingly, always found his prose rather muddy—"obscure, obscure," in E. M. Forster's words, and "misty," with his sentences serving as a "smoke screen" that hides not a "jewel" but a "vapour." Yet while Conrad may have seen English as an alien medium, something he needed to wrestle with and subdue, we cannot with any precision link that tussle to his trials before the empty page. What we can do, though, is to connect both the language itself and the difficulty Conrad had *in* writing to the difficulty *of* his writing.

No one has ever thought him easy. Leave aside the anomalies of his biography: the naturalized British subject, the master mariner who left the sea in his midthirties and became a great writer in his third tongue. To his first readers the exoticism of his early material was in itself a bar. The late Victorian audience knew about imperial adventure in India and Africa, but a Borneo where the adventures never quite came off was something else entirely. Then there was the fact that Conrad stood, in Henry James's phrase, "absolutely alone as a votary of the way to do a thing that shall make it undergo most doing." There were the involutions of his syntax and what F. R. Leavis has called his "adjectival insistence." There was the elaborate framing of his tales, the nesting of one narrative within another; there was his persistent violation of chronology, the retrospection and temporal looping that make *Nostromo* seem to take two steps back for each one forward. And what could one do with the way his books seemed to dwindle off, so that at the end of *Lord Jim* we have a man waving "sadly at his butterflies"? His reviews were always strong and his reputation high, but nothing about him seemed designed for comfort, and those readers who got past Conrad's difficulties of form still had to confront his sardonic view of human endeavor and his unforgiving scrutiny of a world that does not much bear looking into.

All this ensured that his audience remained small during the years of his greatest achievement, and all this now stands among the reasons why he seems with each decade more central.

In "Heart of Darkness" Marlow sits aboard the *Nellie* and asks his listeners if they can "see the story? Do you see anything? It seems to me I am trying to tell you a dream—making a vain attempt, because no relation of a dream can convey the dream-sensation." His statement implies that words themselves can never quite capture the sensations they seek to convey, and yet it also suggests that the writer's job is nevertheless "to make you hear, to make you feel—it is, before all, to make you *see*." That is how Conrad put it in the famous preface to *The Nigger of the "Narcissus,"* and so Marlow insists as well, maintaining that his task lies in making his experience stand immanent before us, in attempting, as Edward Said has written, "to rescue meaning from his undisciplined experience." That awareness of the intractability of language—that concern with the very possibility of representation—makes Conrad an exemplary figure in the history of modernism. It is as though his individual struggle with English, his inability to take his means of expression for granted, were but an instance of the larger struggle that all writers face with language itself. It links him to such successors as James Joyce and Virginia Woolf rather than to his close friend John Galsworthy; while among artists in other media it ties him to Cézanne.

Let me quote another well-known passage as a way to clarify both Conrad's difficulty and his concern with the questions of representation and interpretation alike. Early in "Heart of Darkness" the nameless narrator of the frame-tale tells us that

> The yarns of seamen have a direct simplicity, the whole meaning of which lies within the shell of a cracked nut. But Marlow was not typical (if his propensity to spin yarns be excepted), and to him the meaning of an episode was not inside like a kernel but outside, enveloping the tale which brought it out only as a glow brings out a haze.

Conrad himself did not entirely eschew the cracked-nut method of storytelling; to cite only his successes, the term fits such tales as "An Outpost of Progress" (1897), "To-Morrow" (1902), and even the pellucid mysteries of "The Secret Sharer" (1910). But there can be little doubt that these words provide us with a kind of owner's manual, a set of instructions on the tale's proper use. They warn us that narration will not lead toward some hidden nugget of truth, some secret to be unlocked; in Ian Watt's words, "Marlow's tale will not be centered on, but surrounded by, its meaning." Still, the passage's "spectral" glow of enveloping suggestion looks so tricky to unpack that its very language has provided the terms of Forster's attack, and some of the tale's other aspects do at first seem to parry the thrust of Conrad's image.

The story is, after all, called "Heart of Darkness." It describes a journey up a great African river, and its principal action is that of penetration, of movement toward a core; a voyage into the interior of both a continent and one's own psychic being. As Said notes, the tale "draws attention to itself as a process of getting closer and closer to the center," and "process" does indeed seem the right word. For Marlow's narration concerns itself less with the physical journey than with his groping attempt to define the meaning of his own experience, and when he asks his audience if they can see the story, he is really asking himself. Once he does reach that center, however, he finds—well, something hollow. The kernel of revelation has rotted away, if indeed it ever existed. That in itself might well provide a motive for his inquiry, and yet the Inner Station's apparent absence of an inner meaning does initially appear to justify Forster's critique. But let us lean on Conrad's language just a little bit more. Not inside but outside—that's where we should look for meaning, in a murk illuminated from within. In Marlow's words, "This also . . . has been one of the dark places of the earth," and though "Heart of Darkness" may not tell us much about the Africa that is its ostensible subject, it does say a great deal about Europe, and about the enshrouding imperial system that has sent Marlow on his way.

Conrad's readers cannot be passive ones. In an early essay on Henry James he compares the act of writing "to rescue work carried out in darkness against cross gusts of wind," and he speaks of it in similarly heroic terms in the preface to *The Nigger of the "Narcissus,"* defining the writer as one who seizes "in a moment of courage, from the remorseless rush of time, a passing phase of life." His sense of his own achievement is inseparable from his sense of difficulty, as though the struggle into narrative might provide in itself a kind of victory. Reading him requires that we too undertake the "rescue work" that the creation of meaning entails. It requires, among other things, that we both fight with and parse out his imagery; that we reconstruct the sequence of a novel's action and grapple with the significance, at once proleptic and delayed, that his very violation of chronology has produced. And if we can do that, his fiction will yield a most peculiar reward. For no matter how dark his world and how miserable the fates of his characters, his books are almost never depressing. Instead we read them with an exhilarating sense of difficulties faced and met, held by the drama of the writing itself, as if we have submitted ourselves to the destructive element and kept our heads up.

II

Conrad's years at sea took him to many parts of the world, though in *A Personal Record* he would complain, prematurely, that he seemed fated never to cross the "Western Ocean"; he finally went to North America in 1923, on a triumphal visit to his publisher Frank Doubleday. From Marseilles the young man sailed for the Caribbean, and in 1878 his first British vessel, the *Mavis,* took him to Constantinople (Istanbul). Over the next dozen years he would serve on as many ships, making voyages from London to Australia and from Bombay to Dunkirk, sailing out of Bangkok and Calcutta, of Amsterdam and Port Adelaide. Ships were not always easy to find, however, and Conrad spent long months on shore, an anonymous life in lodgings broken by at least one spell of work in a portside warehouse. He became a British citizen in 1886, the same year he received his master's certificate, but his spells of unemployment grew longer as his qualifications increased. That is one reason why in 1890 this blue-water sailor sought out a very different kind of job, and found himself aboard a riverboat in the Belgian Congo.

That experience led to "Heart of Darkness," the work for which Conrad is today best known. But the part of the globe with which he's most fully identified remains that which he calls "the East," and in particular the Malay Archipelago, a region that for Conrad included Thailand, Singapore, and the great islands of what was then the Dutch East Indies. Both his first novel, *Almayer's Folly* (1895), and its successor, *An Outcast of the Islands* (1896), were set along the Berau River in eastern Borneo, a site that he visited in 1887 as the mate of a coasting steamer, the *Vidar*. Those voyages also contributed to Conrad's picture of Patusan in *Lord Jim*, and much of his shorter fiction seems inseparable from his experience of that region, from the hidden rivers of "The Lagoon" (1897) and the waterfront rivalries of "Falk" (1903), to those haunted tales of first command, "The Secret Sharer" and *The Shadow-Line* (1917). What's surprising, then, is how little time he actually passed in the islands: something under a year, and only four months with the *Vidar*. He spent more time in Australia, a place that has left almost no trace on his fiction at all.

Conrad himself claimed that if in Borneo he had not met a Eurasian named Olmeijer "it is almost certain there would never have been a line of mine in print." And even allowing for hyperbole, the fact remains that soon afterward Conrad did indeed begin to write about the man he called Kaspar Almayer, carrying the manuscript with him from England to the Congo, Australia, and on to Poland before completing it in 1894. Olmeijer managed a trading post at an upriver port on the Berau where the *Vidar* made a monthly stop, and Conrad's picture of him in *A Personal Record* suggests a man of querulous self-importance. It's a type that appears throughout his fiction, and perhaps, once given the mysteries of talent, we needn't look far to discover why such a man, and such a place, should have started Conrad off. For how, in Watt's words, "had this particular lonely derelict come to be stranded?" To the displaced Polish sailor, a man about to turn thirty and with nothing to show for it, Olmeijer's situation would have raised a "personal question of absorbing interest."

Born on Java, the fictional Almayer has moved down the food chain of colonial society, longing all the while for an Amsterdam he has never seen, his "thoughts . . . busy with gold; gold he had failed to secure; gold the others had secured—dishonestly of course." After twenty years on his isolated river he seems still marked by a restless desire for an impossible movement, and his world is full of those who have been similarly, if more successfully, washed ashore. Conrad is frequently seen as a novelist of empire, and yet he doesn't often describe the colonial administrators of a writer like Kipling. His concern lies instead with the commercial life that operates around and between the institutions of colonialism itself. So the English smugglers of "Karain" live by avoiding the Dutch customs officers, while in *Lord Jim* the port officials—the boards of enquiry, the harbor masters—prove effective substitutes for any actual government. *Almayer's Folly* defines an ad hoc society in which nobody seems to live where he might belong: the Europeans by definition, but also the Malay pirates, the Arab traders, and the Balinese prince with whom Almayer's daughter will run away. It is a vision Conrad would refine throughout the years of his great achievement, in which he would bring to light the underlying connections between diverse people and places, a vision that would lead him to *Nostromo,* the great novel of a fully globalized society. Yet even such entirely European novels as *The Secret Agent* and *Under Western Eyes* owe more than they seem to the jerkwater village of Conrad's earliest work, with its picture of human jetsam on an alien coast.

Other points of resemblance between Conrad's first books and their successors are perhaps easier to trace—and not always for the good. *An Outcast of the Islands* was written later than but set before *Almayer's Folly,* with whom it shares some characters, and in places its prose also appears to have slipped back into something other than fluency: "When he stepped off the straight and narrow path of his peculiar honesty, it was with an inward assertion of unflinching resolve to fall back again into the monotonous but safe stride of virtue as soon as his little excursion into the wayside quagmires had produced the desired effect." That's the novel's first sentence, one that seems to anticipate the memory of an action it doesn't fully describe. In both pace and vocabulary—"unflinching"—its authorship appears unmistakable, but the sentence isn't Conradian so much as what's been called "Conradese," as though it were a self-parody of the style he hasn't quite yet formed. And one can trace the pentimenti of that ungainliness in some of his greatest lines: "He was an inch, perhaps two, under six feet, powerfully built, and he advanced straight at you with a slight stoop of the shoulders, head forward, and a fixed from-under stare which made you think of a charging bull." Less than five years separate *An Outcast of the Islands* from the opening words of *Lord Jim,* and what a difference they have made! It is the same voice, but Conrad has replaced the blurred temporality of the one with a kind of quaver produced by his commas, and the nouns themselves have the punch to make one see.

Still, some aspects of these early books show that Conrad has already come into his own; when he describes the old pirate Babalatchi as a "diplomatist" we are only a step away from the terse character-defining epithets of *The Secret Agent. Almayer's Folly* got good reviews, but Conrad remained diffident, and continued to seek another command. There doesn't appear to have been a deciding moment at which he chose to leave the sea behind; one might, indeed, say that the sea left him. He had already begun *An Outcast of the Islands,* conceiving of it as a tale but soon finding that it had outgrown its initial shape. That would set a pattern. Every one of his major novels began as a story, a story forced into length by Conrad's need to explain, to circle back through time, excavating motive and pursuing its consequences. In fact, the one book that he saw as a novel from the start proved the hardest to write. In March 1896 he married Jessie George, a London typist; the oddity of their union will be clear to anyone who reads "Amy Foster." On their wedding trip Conrad began the book that after many years, interruptions, and resumptions would be published as *The Rescue* (1920), another Malay story and one characteristically set before its predecessors. But though its opening chapters went well, the narrative soon lost headway, and Conrad turned to something else. That too established a pattern, for he often worked on several stories at once, stealing time from each until the day that one of them would explode into the sole possession of his mind.

The new tale was called *The Nigger of the "Narcissus,"* an account of a voyage out of Bombay that its author described as a "shrine for the memory of men with whom I have, through many hard years lived and worked." In *Victory* (1915) Conrad would make one of his characters claim that "He who forms a tie is lost," that linking yourself to another person allows a "germ of corruption" to enter the soul. That sentiment provides a major interpretative crux in his work, an oeuvre in which it seems that every human connection must carry the heaviest of costs. Yet even in *Victory* that loss can provide a way to save the very self it threatens. For Conrad also knows such ties are necessary, and nowhere more so than on a ship like the *Narcissus,* where the safety of all requires the cooperation of each. Indeed the narrative procedures of the tale serve in themselves to dramatize Conrad's belief in the human "solidarity that knits together the loneliness of innumerable hearts . . . [and] binds men to each other." *The Nigger of the "Narcissus"* has a first-person narrator who is never named or particularized. In some places he speaks as an "I" and in others as a "we," while at certain moments Conrad offers a third-person account of a meeting between two sailors, neither of whom can be identified with any possible speaker. Fractured and choral, limited and omniscient, the tale's narrator roves as freely from person to person as in other novels Conrad will move through time, a voice manifold and yet one that defines everything about this world but his own individual place within it. He speaks for the ship. He speaks for every sailor aboard, for Belfast and Singleton and even the mutinous Donkin.

Nor is Conrad's demonstration of that solidarity limited to style alone. Halfway through, the ship's people must fight their way across a flooded deck, "swinging from belaying pin to cleat above the seas" in order to rescue the book's title figure, James Wait. I'll consider Conrad's handling of race in greater detail below, but for now will simply note his 1914 comment that "A negro in a British forecastle is a lonely being. He has no chums," not even on the polygot *Narcissus,* with its mixed crew of Cockney and Celt, Norwegian and "Russian Finn." Wait is a sick man when he joins the ship: strong enough to answer the muster and pass for able, but not strong enough to work. Some of the crew think he's shamming, and indeed he is: shamming sick as a way to hide from himself just how ill he actually is. His berth becomes the locus of all the discontent on board, with the crew divided in their view of him, and yet in that storm they act as one to save him, despite the "monstrous suspicion" that he has been "malingering heartlessly . . . in the face of our devotion." And other examples of that "solidarity" could be summoned from throughout the tale, enough to suggest the truth of Eloise Knapp Hay's claim that Conrad "could not think of men at all without thinking of the individual's immediate reliance upon, and obligations to, a politically defined community." For Conrad is never *not* political, and even in dealing with the blasts and blows of the elements themselves, he remains always concerned with the questions of social order and cohesion.

III

The first version of *The Portable Conrad* appeared in 1947, a volume edited by Morton Dauwen Zabel that served to establish a canon of Conrad's short fiction. It remained in print for sixty years, and among the Portables of its period its influence is surpassed only by Malcolm Cowley's 1946 selection from William Faulkner. Nevertheless it has today the character of a historical document, a document that bears witness not only to the state of Conrad's reputation but also to the terms of criticism itself in the middle of the twentieth century. Zabel saw Conrad as a writer for whom it was still necessary to make a case: first, because he had not yet emerged from the "probationary reaction of literary reputation" that strikes most writers after their deaths; and second, because what reputation did remain was based on a limited conception of his work. His powers of description—his ability to bring his exotic experience into the light of the fictional page—continued to command respect. Nevertheless he was admired with faint praise as an adventure writer and for his early tales of the sea.

Writing in the years immediately after the Second World War, Zabel offered a different account of Conrad's strengths, arguing that his "sense of the crisis of moral isolation" was such as to demand "a larger reference, bringing him into the highest company the English, and the European, novel provides." Nor was he alone in that claim. At almost the same moment F. R. Leavis published *The Great Tradition,* which put its weight on the books that, like *Nostromo,* were then sometimes bracketed off as "political," though Leavis himself didn't account for them in those terms. Then came a flood. Much of the scholarship in the decades that followed was on a high level, and any student of Conrad today continues both to rely on and to respond to it. The period did have its biases. It put a heavy emphasis on questions of evaluation, on sifting the "good" Conrad from the "bad," and it suffered too from a predilection for symbol hunting and psychobiography. But Conrad was far from the only novelist to receive that treatment, and Zabel's Portable can be taken as inaugurating what one might call the "heroic" phase in Conrad criticism, a phase that reached its synthesis, and its summa, in the 1979 publication of Ian Watt's *Conrad in the Nineteenth Century.*

I use that term advisedly, for it points both to the period's enormous exercise of critical intelligence and to a particular conception of Conrad's work. Zabel's own introduction provides an example. His Conrad is a writer of "tragic vision" and "tenacious endurances," someone whose greatest books define the ways in which "the individual meets his first full test of character." The Conrad protagonist must stand ready for "the signal of his destiny," and the writer himself is someone who charts "the unfathomed depths of our secret natures" and explores the "constitution of man himself." Those words speak to an elevated sense of artistic vocation, of the writer as what Lionel Trilling calls "a hero of the spirit," caught in a lonely battle with the world. One finds that sense in Joyce, and also in Faulkner, who in his Nobel Prize speech described himself as having passed his "life's work in the agony and sweat of the human spirit." And Conrad himself gives ample warrant for an appeal to the heroic. His letters are one long inventory of the obstacles he faced, and his great preface to *The Nigger of the "Narcissus"* invokes the "courage" with which the artist must snatch his truth "from the remorseless rush of time."

Part of Zabel's case depended on his persistent comparisons between Conrad and a range of other writers—predecessors like Flaubert or Turgenev, contemporaries like James or Mann—in order to suggest that he provides the hinge on which the modern novel turns. A second portion of his brief involved a "Conrad our contemporary" argument, locating him in terms of the particular concerns of the postwar era. It assigns him a totemic value as an analyst of what can only, in the language of that period, be termed "the human condition"; and as a prophet too, the man who took an anticipatory scalpel to the century's heart of darkness. Both parts of Zabel's argument hold good today, and yet it is precisely because they *are* still good that his Portable cannot be ours. For Conrad remains our contemporary. Each decade has found new things to say about him—new methods, new questions—not just because critical practice changes but also because, where Zabel's author had his antecedents and contemporaries, ours has a far-flung posterity. He has been fought with and imitated by both thriller writers and Nobel laureates—in Africa, Europe, and the Americas—and the response of his children has shaped our understanding of the whole postcolonial world.

No story has been so much a part of that changing response as "Heart of Darkness," the tale of a journey into the African interior to meet that "emissary of pity, and science, and progress," the mysterious Mr. Kurtz. The normative reading in the postwar period belongs to Albert J. Guerard, who describes the work as a "symbolic expression of Conrad's sense of isolation." Such interpretations have a long history in Conrad scholarship, with one of his first critics, Gustav Morf, accounting for the eponymous Jim's leap from the deck of the *Patna* in terms of Conrad's own guilt over leaving Poland. Guerard's argument universalizes that psychology, defining Marlow's voyage up the Congo in terms of a "night journey into the unconscious, and confrontation of an entity within the self." He admits that in its depiction of European rapacity the story does have an "important public side," but he discounts it in favor of concentrating on the work's "introspective plunge," its account of a "spiritual voyage" toward an ineffable horror. On this reading, Africa is but the incidental setting for a narrative of self-discovery, a background that serves only to heighten the drama: mood music.

The picture of the isolated individual—of "Man"—that emerged in the Conrad scholarship of the postwar period often worked in tandem with the formalist emphasis of the New Criticism to strip his work of its context, to relieve it of its moorings in the world, almost to evacuate it of content. Guerard's account of "Heart of Darkness" proved enormously persuasive, and some version of it was taught to several generations of American students. I got it myself in the twelfth grade and remember my teacher's insistence that the tale's inscrutable intentions were far too subtle for us to grasp, which didn't keep him from making us try. That kind of first encounter with Conrad was once a common experience, and yet it seems today to provide a cautionary tale about critical overreaching. It makes me think of Oscar Wilde's suggestion, in his preface to *The Picture of Dorian Gray,* that "All art is both surface and symbol. Those who go beneath the surface do so at their peril. Those who read the symbol do so at their peril." Or perhaps one should simply recall Marlow's own claim, as he tries to avoid snags and keep his boat's engine running, that "There was surface-truth enough in these things" to keep one busy.

Nothing written about Conrad since the days of Leavis and

Zabel has been so influential as Chinua Achebe's 1975 essay "An Image of Africa." If to Guerard the Congo provides but a backdrop for Marlow's voyage into the soul, for the Nigerian novelist it is central, a land with its own peoples and histories and its own claim to an autonomous place in the imagination. Yet in some sense Achebe agrees with Guerard—agrees that in "Heart of Darkness" Africa itself plays but a minimal role. Only he then turns to attack Conrad as a "bloody racist" for having written a book that treats the continent "as setting and backdrop which eliminates the African as human factor. Africa as a metaphysical battlefield devoid of all recognizable humanity, into which the wandering European enters at his peril." And however overdrawn his argument, Achebe does have a point, even as he recognizes that Conrad himself "did not originate the image of Africa which we find in this book."

Instead the tale relies on a set of commonly held European assumptions about the continent as a whole—on an "Africanist discourse," in Christopher L. Miller's phrase. For Marlow, "going up that river was like travelling back to the earliest beginnings of the world," a journey in two directions at once, both back and in, though the two coalesce when Marlow announces that the Africans "were not inhuman. Well, you know, that was the worst of it—this suspicion of their not being inhuman." And if you are man enough, he adds, you will admit the kinship you feel with them, and your desire to "go ashore for a howl and a dance." The river allows one both to underscore and to escape one's own modernity, making Africa into a primitivist metaphor for man's original state, even as it also provides an emblem for the human heart. It is the "Dark Continent," the home of "black" people to whose skin the language itself assigns a moral tinge. At the same time, as Miller notes, such a discourse takes the darkness of that skin as marking the absence of light, a sign that there's something missing. So as a boy Marlow looks at a map of Africa and thinks of it as a "blank space of delightful mystery," a blankness that provides the excuse for a land grab.

On the level of language, then, Conrad's story participates in the imperialism it appears to condemn, and I myself would argue that his reliance on that Africanist discourse matters far more than the epithet—sometimes ventriloquized, and sometimes not—

with which he describes the black sailor of the *Narcissus*. Over the years Achebe's argument has been both fought with and applauded, challenged and complicated. Conrad's earlier critics had not entirely ignored the questions of race and empire, and his later ones have continued to produce fine close readings, the best of them located at that point where formalism meets philosophy. But Achebe changed—no, broke—the interpretative paradigm. The paradox is that "Heart of Darkness" seems only the more central because of it. His attack marked out a field of investigation, making the piece into a locus of continuing debate about the relation, the inextricability, of imperialism and modernity itself. Many later readings have therefore looked at the tale with an eye for its internal contradictions, using it to explore the relation between language and ideology, to consider the limits of what can and cannot be thought in a given culture at a given time. Edward Said, for example, describes Conrad as unable to reconcile the differences between imperialism's official "idea" and its "remarkably disorienting actuality," seeing him as a willing participant in empire who nevertheless "shows its contingency, records its illusions." Marlow's narrative therefore remains inconclusive and his irony unstable, an attempt to probe the meaning of an experience that even at the end seems no more clear than the "black bank of clouds" that spreads over England itself.

Achebe's brickbat deserves much of the credit for the fact that our Conrad is more fully historicized than Zabel's, more firmly situated in his times, a man of 1900 with all its attendant blind spots and biases. But he did not work alone. Earlier scholars had already provided much of the biographical armature on which such contextual readings depend; later ones have followed that river around the sharpest of bends and up into its furthest reaches of implication. In fact Achebe presents only one aspect of Conrad's handling of empire, and to complicate the picture I want to look at another essay from the mid-1970s, another response by a writer from one of Britain's former colonies. V. S. Naipaul's 1974 "Conrad's Darkness" begins with the admission that "It has taken me a long time to come round to Conrad." The Polish writer's work had at first seemed marred by an overelaboration of method, an "unwillingness to let the story speak for itself." Yet Conrad's "originality, the news he is offering us, can go over our heads," and Naipaul soon finds that his predecessor's books have already defined the "mixed and secondhand" world into which he himself was born. He comes to realize that "Conrad . . . had been everywhere before me," and not only on the map. Indeed, to my mind Almayer's Borneo resembles the Trinidad of Naipaul's own Mr. Biswas, pieces ripped from the same tectonic plate, however far apart. And it is this sense of Conrad, not as the voice of European racism but as the most comprehensive of guides to what Naipaul calls the "deep disorder" of our times, that delimits the terrain on which the best recent criticism has staked its claim.

When Naipaul turns to "Heart of Darkness" he concentrates on Marlow's discovery, in a riverside hut, of an obscure book on navigation. One approach to "Heart of Darkness" is to focus on the dialectic the tale enacts between "civilization" and "savagery"—a dialectic summed up in Marlow's account of his own desire for a "howl and a dance." But that tattered volume suggests something far more complicated. For what is it doing in the Congo at all? "Sixty years old," heavily annotated, and with its pages "thumbed into a state of extremely dirty softness," *An Inquiry into some Points of Seamanship* seems innocent enough, and yet both its presence and its subject speak to the often appalling business of a world slowly knitting itself into one. So too does its owner, a young Russian whose "very existence" in Africa seems "improbable, inexplicable." It is, however, no more "inconceivable" than Marlow's own, and at the end of the story Conrad proffers a vision of a great "waterway leading to the uttermost ends of the earth," a vision that presents the cargo-carrying Thames—"this river"—as running out across the ocean and up into the mouth of "that river," of the Congo itself. The two become as one, a world in which the land is stitched together by water: a liquid world, through which both capital and people themselves seem perpetually to stream.

Every page that Conrad wrote at once presumes and undermines an identity between person and place, for he relies on the fixities of nineteenth-century nationalism to define his characters even as he charts a world in which they are all out of joint. Take "Typhoon" (1902), in which the steamer *Nan-Shan* moves under its Irish captain through the China Sea, carrying a freight of what we would now call guest workers, "coolies returning to their village homes." Take *Lord Jim*—not the *Patna* episode, but the later parts of the book that record the disturbances of a new order in Patusan. It is an order in which none of the participants belong to the land for which he contends, not even the tribal leader Doramin, and in which the difference between the statesman and the thief can seem but a question of getting there first. Take *Nostromo,* set in what Naipaul describes as a "half-made" Latin American republic, where the indispensable man of the people is a Genoese sailor, the funding comes from San Francisco, and the country-born tycoon is ineradicably English. To read Conrad in this way is to remember that one of the places he had been before Naipaul was London itself, that great beach of the unsettled and the lost.

In fact, it sometimes seems that the hardest thing to find in his books is a British subject at work in a part of the map splotched red. Conrad saw what would come. He charts the upheaval and restlessness produced by a world system, an incipient global society, at the very moment it comes into being. The Congo's European outposts may cloak their greed in the fiction of progress, but the imperialism Conrad describes isn't concerned with administration so much as with money, with the movement of commodities like ivory and rubber and even, in one story, potatoes. It is a system so powerful that it can either supersede governments or bend them to its will, as it does in *Nostromo,* where the Occidental Republic comes into being for the sake of the San Tomé mine. For in the "development of material interests," as that novel's Dr. Monygham says, "There is no peace and no rest," no true center and no final periphery, no border and no home.

And perhaps, with that system in mind and both Achebe's and Naipaul's essays before us, we can now weigh, and even in part recuperate, the interpretations Conrad received in the middle of the twentieth century. The critics of that period eschewed a political vocabulary, predicating their arguments instead on metaphysics or Freud, on the idea of "alienation" or an appeal to some transhistorical "human condition": a belief in certain truths that hold at all times and for all people. It's easy to see how Conrad could be read in such terms, for both his characters and he himself come to us estranged from their origins. Yet his apparent abstraction from the local, his seeming "universality," has a historical specificity of its own. It is grounded not only in the writer's own exile but also in the fact that the Poland of his birth could not be found on a map, a nation split among three states and yet with no territory of its own. It was then confirmed by his years at sea, and by the conditions of his life in England, where like Yanko in "Amy Foster" he continued to wear the "peculiar and indelible stamp" of the foreign, "separated by an immense space from his past." An argument like Naipaul's allows us to connect the Polish exile with the dislocations of British imperialism. It suggests a perspective from which *Nostromo* more closely resembles "Heart of Darkness" or *Lord Jim* than it does such other "political" novels as *The Secret Agent;* it demonstrates the degree to which Conrad's people are those who have left their ancestral worlds behind.

Achebe's essay, in turn, had such resonance precisely because it showed how Conrad's earlier critics, with their insistence on his "tragic vision" and "introspective plunge," had worked to discount the particularity of local conditions and local knowledge. He showed the way in which their terms homogenized the separate nightmares from which none of us can awake, and he demonstrated that the very idea of the "universal" itself amounted to little more than a "synonym for the . . . parochialism of Europe." For such terms have a history of their own. The claims and presumptions of Conrad's midcentury critics were characteristic of the postwar consolidation—the institutionalization—of European modernism, with its belief that the past had been superseded and with its corresponding emphasis on a few allegedly enduring truths. As such, their arguments were inseparable from and dependent upon the engirdling power of modernization itself. Conrad's readers, both then and now, stand as a part of the totalizing system that he himself defines, of the process that has placed that seaman's manual along an African river and a telephone into the last chapters of *Nostromo*. The world he describes may take its motive, its centrifugal, force from the West. Nevertheless he speaks, if not to some "human condition," then to a history in which we all increasingly share, and one that Achebe himself addresses in such books as *Arrow of God* and *No Longer at Ease*. Perhaps, indeed, Conrad's sense of his own "indelible stamp" served to confirm his "suspicion" that we are all of us "not inhuman." For the man who wrote *The Secret Agent* that double negative might be as good as it gets. He was not immune to the pressures and prejudices of his world. Nor are his critics. Yet though we might today assign a different source or valence to their universalizing claims, our predecessors were not entirely wrong to find in his work their warrant.

IV

"Heart of Darkness" will likely remain the work that Conrad's name most immediately recalls, its title so inescapably a part of our newspaper headlines that its author himself would now refuse its use. Still, its appeal isn't confined to—or by—the questions I've sketched above, for the tale also comes to us in the voice of Conrad's single most important character, "the man Marlow": the storyteller also of "Youth," the repository of the title figure's confidence in *Lord Jim,* and the intelligence picking its way through the almost trackless marsh of *Chance* (1913). "He haunts my hours of solitude," Conrad wrote, a secret sharer who seems larger than any of the works that contain him, even as he also remains just a little bit smaller. For Marlow's narration can never be identified with that of the work as a whole. The circumstances of his speech are always dramatized or framed, and with each successive use Conrad places him at a greater distance, so that his voice fills less of *Chance* than it does of *Lord Jim,* less of *Lord Jim* than of "Heart of Darkness." Even in "Youth," where he sticks close to the facts of his own life, Conrad begins with a mahogany table and a bottle of claret, with four men listening as a fifth begins to talk. Sinewy, sardonic, and with as many twists as the Congo itself, Marlow's voice speaks to us out of an experience that however deep has never allowed itself to cross the shadow-line of cynicism. In this he might stand as Conrad's better self, and perhaps, in a worldly sense, as his more successful one too.

But Conrad did not stay with Marlow. The books that followed *Lord Jim,* the great trio of "political" novels that begins with *Nostromo* and continues with *The Secret Agent* and *Under Western Eyes,* mark the point at which his work has outgrown the terms and limits of his own biography. They demonstrate his determination to try new things: to move, in midcareer, away from the ever-changing and eternal sea and into a consideration of more ambiguous public questions. Conrad did not like to be called a writer of sea stories, and he didn't want to be known as what an early reviewer called "the Kipling of the Malay Archipelago." A reputation can, however, be a hard thing to shake, and Conrad's position with both readers and reviewers alike was only just starting to seem secure when he confounded them with the South America of *Nostromo*.

That book, as he wrote to his agent, J. B. Pinker, "is a very genuine Conrad," and yet at the time almost nobody agreed with him. The three novels that now seem at the core of his achievement began to find their audience only after the Second World War, when a generation's experience of ideological combat—the Cold War, the struggles of decolonization—gave them a new resonance, as though they had been retrospectively endowed with a predictive force. Still, what attention those books got from specialists was but a corrective, a trimming of the sails. Zabel himself admired them and wrote a notable account of *Under Western Eyes*. Nevertheless his Portable scants that aspect of his subject's oeuvre, emphasizing instead the long tales of the East and the sea on which Conrad had worked in the early years of his career. Of course anthologies must often rely on short fiction, and Conrad's achievement in what Henry James called "the beautiful and blest nouvelle" is matched in English only by that of James himself. But anthologies also make canons, and Zabel's defined a midcentury bias that could admire a book like *The Secret Agent* but still see it as an exception to the general run of Conrad's work.

Once again it has required the critical movement signaled by Achebe to suggest the superficiality of the old divisions in Conrad criticism. The changes in our understanding of "Heart of Darkness" suggest something more than a shift in critical practice. In making that tale appear more central than ever, they have brought to light the degree to which, for all its variations of subject and setting, Conrad's work nevertheless remains, in the words of the preface to *The Nigger of the "Narcissus,"* all "manifold and one." Emphasizing the historical specificities of both Marlow's river journey and the language in which Conrad described it allows us to assimilate this symbolist masterpiece to his later work, to see the consistency with which, as *Nostromo* puts it, "the working of the usual public institutions presented itself to him most distinctly as a series of calamities overtaking private individuals." But Conrad did believe that one institution might avoid those calamities. His social ideal remains that of a well-officered ship: a hierarchy led by men of tested knowledge and ability, and in which each person aboard has a customary role to play. It is a community orderly, just, and inequitable—indeed orderly and just *because* inequitable—yet artificial too, the product of close quarters and confinement. It can be found on the *Narcissus,* but not on the *Patna* of *Lord Jim,* where custom has failed. On the unbounded land one will ever search for it in vain.

In 1897 Conrad wrote to his friend Cunninghame Graham that he shared his desire that people should value "faith, honour, fidelity to truth in themselves and others . . . [and] make out of these words their rule of life." There was, however, one "point of difference" between them. Cunninghame Graham had the "unwarrantable belief" that such a desire could be "realized." But Conrad himself did "not believe," and he went on to evoke a machine "evolved . . . out of a chaos of scraps" that could not be adjusted or made to do anything other than its own "horrible work . . . You can't interfere with it . . . you can't even smash it." The machine obeys no human law, and Conrad's response to that image—to that mechanism hatched of his own brain and experience—is a terminal skepticism, a sense that "nothing matters," even if he does admit "that to look at the remorseless process is sometimes amusing." One might almost say that Conrad has preferences but no principles, as if Martin Decoud in *Nostromo* were speaking for his creator when he defines a "conviction" as nothing more than "A particular view of our personal advantage either practical or emotional."

Maybe that goes too far. Conrad was a great reader of Henry James, and an account of the American writer by Richard Brodhead may serve to characterize the Polish one as well. In Brodhead's terms, James "sees the struggle for public social change as growing out of private emotional distress and as disguising the pursuit of private emotional ends." Conrad differs from his predecessor in his refusal to see the private life as a refuge, free from the calamities of "public institutions." But he places an equivalent weight on the motive force of "private distress." Or as he himself puts it, "in their own way the most ardent of revolutionaries are perhaps doing no more but seeking for peace in common with the rest of mankind—the peace of soothed vanity, of satisfied appetites, or perhaps of appeased conscience." That knowledge gives Conrad the ability to see through his own beliefs and biases without feeling the need to discard them, recognizing that, as his own, they have no more validity, but also no less, than do any other "particular" views. It is an ability that reaches its peak in the self-corroding ironies of *The Secret Agent* and *Under Western Eyes,* books far more unsettling than the almost normative tragedy of *Lord Jim*.

Still, as Zabel himself argues, what Conrad "had to say was indissociable from his way of learning to say it." Any full account of his work must also stress its extraordinary reliance on frame-tales and flashbacks, on the way he sometimes seems to begin a narrative only so that he may disrupt it. His letters show him as an effective and at times a devastating practical critic. Yet there's little in Conrad's essays that serves to lay out an aesthetic. The preface to *The Nigger of the "Narcissus"* does, admittedly, invoke the majesty of the creative act, defining it as an attempt "to render the highest kind of justice to the visible universe . . . to find in its forms, in its colours, in its light, in its shadows . . . what of each is fundamental, what is enduring and essential." The pace and the force of those words carry an inspiriting and incantatory power. But it is a credo, something comparable to D. H. Lawrence's "Why the Novel Matters" rather than to the critical manifestoes with which James or Woolf attempted to sweep the decks of their competition, to create the taste by which they would be appreciated.

The best account of Conrad's purpose comes not in anything he himself wrote but in Ford's memoir of him, which now seems a kind of primer on the writing of fiction, a guide to such things as the handling of dialogue and the introduction of minor characters. Ford writes that "we accepted without much protest" the then-pejorative term "'Impressionists' that was thrown at us." No exact corollary can be drawn between literary impressionism and the French paintings that gave the term its currency. Yet both are concerned with registering the most flickering acts of perception, the perception that precedes comprehension: the blobs of paint that resolve themselves into a cathedral, the "little sticks . . . whizzing before my nose" that Marlow in "Heart of Darkness" hasn't yet recognized as arrows. Ford argues that "we saw that Life did not narrate, but made impressions on our brains. We in turn, if we wished to produce on you an effect of life, must not narrate but render impressions." The words are cryptic, but we can clarify them by distinguishing Conrad's work from that of the other writers to whom Ford's epithet applies. Conrad's concern in his early fiction lies in defining the process, and the consequences, of his characters' growing understanding of their own perceptions, and for this purpose no better instrument than Marlow can be imagined, with his voice scored like a suite for cello. In contrast, Ford's own greatest book, *The Good Soldier,* dramatizes its narrator's absence of any understanding whatsoever, as though the impressions he receives had left, as it were, no impress. A second comparison would be to Woolf's concern with the flux and flow of a consciousness caught in what she calls an "incessant shower" of sensation. Yet Conrad isn't interested in the pulse of experience so much as in what Watt calls "the gap between impression and understanding," and his work dramatizes the process of "delayed decoding" by which we make sense of our perceptions.

Put it another way: the job Conrad gives both his characters and his readers is that of interpreting something that doesn't at first look clear, that refuses explanation or belief. Or as Jim tells Marlow, in trying to remember the moment at which he abandoned the *Patna,* "I had jumped . . . It seems." Some of that incoherence comes from the particular kind of impressions—the violent seas and more violent deaths—with which Conrad works. Rather more of it, however, grows from the belief that "Life [does] not narrate." It does not disclose its meanings with the smooth linearity of a Victorian serial, an orderly unspooling of one event after another. Such a linearity suggests that some objective value or quality of meaning inheres in the world itself, that "the remorseless rush of time" alone can be enough to make us see. To Conrad, however, that meaning does not lie so readily to hand. Life does not narrate, it produces impressions instead, and the mind's task lies in unfolding, in disentangling, whatever of the "enduring and essential" may be snatched from that undifferentiated stream of experience, as though truth were not given, but made.

One mark of Conrad's developing mastery lies in the ever-changing nature of his impressionism. In "Heart of Darkness" and *Lord Jim* he is concerned above all with Marlow's act of understanding, which stands for and indeed subsumes our own. The later books don't limit themselves that way. Halfway through *Nostromo* Conrad puts both the title figure and the gentleman-journalist Decoud aboard a boat loaded with silver. It is a foggy and moonless night, on which "no intelligence could penetrate the darkness," and when they are rammed by a steamship the two men realize that they have "nothing in common between them . . . as if they had discovered in the very shock of the collision that the loss of the lighter would not mean the same thing to them both." They may be caught by the same event, but they cannot be said to share it except in their mutual recognition that they each remain isolated within a "private vision . . . [with] no bond of conviction, of common idea." And that recognition will shape the form of Conrad's fiction itself. His work from *Nostromo* on is marked by a growing inability to rest within a single version of any event, by an insistence on the plurality of meaning that makes him swap the narration around from one point of view to another, less concerned with the perceptions of individual characters than with the reader's cumulative and many-layered impression of the book as a whole. The result can be dizzying, and often makes our judgment of individual scenes reflect the discovery of Winnie Verloc, in *The Secret Agent,* "that a simple sentence may hold several diverse meanings—mostly disagreeable."

Conrad's impressionism found its most important tool in his handling of time, his manipulation of chronology. The whole first half of *Nostromo* can be seen as one massive act of delayed decoding, in which over the course of two hundred pages Conrad's third-person narration brings us unsteadily closer to an understanding of the events we have seen in its opening pages. The book begins on a day of riot that we only later learn is in fact a day of revolution. Then it steps back some eighteen months, before retreating to an indeterminate moment in a further past, beyond which are allusions to days even more remote. We slip forward, and then back again, change continents, cross mountains, and the gears with which Conrad handles what Ford calls the "time-shift" are so perfectly meshed that the transitions seem almost invisible. Troops walk on board a steamer, and a few pages later we see them embark once more. The moment repeats itself, as though this chronicle of a Latin American republic were never quite able to get past its starting point, and when we finally do return to the riot it's only to learn that we have not yet seen it correctly. It is as if Conrad were searching for the right way to tell this story. Or perhaps that quality of endless recurrence is indeed the best way to make us see this society, to give us an impression of what one character calls its "Fifty Years of Misrule." Suppose, however, that we had started at the "beginning"—suppose Conrad had allowed the order of events to dictate the order of his narration? He would, I think, have had to start with one or another of his many characters: with an individual, not a nation. It wouldn't be the book he wants, a dispassionate analysis of a historical process that does indeed seem "indissociable from his way of learning to tell it." Yet once he has made us understand the workings of this country's "public institutions," the pulse and pause of its coups and counterrevolutions, the end can then come quickly. The novel's final chapters may define a dialectic in which the seemingly stable prosperity of the new Occidental Republic faces troubles born of that very prosperity itself, but they also ravel out in a straight line of narrative, "a series of calamities overtaking private individuals."

Conrad himself called *Nostromo* the "most anxiously meditated" of his novels, a book that carries its indirection with a kind of stately grandeur, its twisted threads stopping always just short of a snarl. *The Secret Agent* appears, in comparison, to deserve its subtitle: *A Simple Tale*. But no: it is rather one that hides its difficulties, suggesting that Conrad had learned from its predecessor the secret of a streamlined assurance. Conrad described the book as both a "new departure in *genre*," and his "first story . . . dealing with London," but he also wrote of it dismissively as a kind of tour de force, "a sustained effort in ironical treatment of a melodramatic subject." Nevertheless he prepared for it carefully, making a close study of London's anarchist milieu and of the actual 1894 explosion from which he drew his plot. Conrad devotes much of the novel to a taxonomy of different revolutionary types, from the bomb-making Professor to the wheezy "ticket-of-leave apostle" Michaelis. Yet that is not what gives the book its edge. Soon after finishing *Nostromo* he had written an essay called "Autocracy and War," an examination of the Russian empire that one reviewer described as "condemnation in the form of rhapsody," and its masterly invective would seem to have determined the subject of both *The Secret Agent* and *Under Western Eyes*. Conrad may direct an unforgiving stare at his anarchists. What drives *The Secret Agent*, however, is not its analysis of the disturbance they themselves produce, but rather its account of the disorder sparked by the attempt of a "senseless tyranny" to control them.

The novel opens in the Soho shop of Adolf Verloc, a place with "photographs of more or less undressed dancing girls" in the window and the gas-jets turned low, "either for economy's sake or for the sake of the customers." But Mr. Verloc's business is only his "ostensible business." The real work happens in the house behind, where he meets the anarchists among whom he passes as one of themselves, gathering what information he can for the foreign government that employs him. He is an indolent creature, "constitutionally averse from every superfluous exertion," but now that indolence receives a challenge. His masters want him to earn his keep, to do something that will provoke "a universal repressive legislation."

The book's opening chapters walk us through Verloc's grimy duplicitous world, and then the novel skips forward to the day of an "attempted bomb outrage in Greenwich Park," an explosion in which only the bomber himself has perished. But then Conrad dives back in time, back into Verloc's family life: a life that includes not only his wife, Winnie, but also her beloved brother, Stevie, a "sensitive" boy marked by "the vacant droop of his lower lip." That violation of chronology allows Conrad to defer the novel's climax, and yet it does something more than turn the screws of suspense. For it tells us, too, of the hopes that Winnie has placed in Verloc's apparent kindliness. Those hopes would mean little to a reader in their proper sequence, but they assume an enormous retrospective importance; as so often in Conrad, we need the end of the story to make sense of its beginning. Breaking sequence lets Conrad establish the terms on which *The Secret Agent* will conclude by making us understand that, as one police official will put it, "From a certain point of view we are here in the presence of a domestic drama," a household tragedy embedded within a tale of political terror.

From a certain point of view—though not, perhaps, from others. In this world any given event may have several diverse and disagreeable meanings—any event, and indeed any sentence. Conrad's own attraction to the anarchism he spurns manifests itself in the slippery glitter of his irony, in the perfect detonator of his prose. So he tells us repeatedly that Mr. Verloc is "no fool," that he is both "humane" and "thoroughly domesticated," and even that he "was not a debauched man. In his conduct he was respectable." It is a description at once entirely inadequate, and true. Time and again the novel echoes the preface to *The Nigger of the "Narcissus,"* with its insistence on "bringing to light the truth," making us probe beneath the surface of an affair in which "there is much . . . that does not meet the eye." Yet when Conrad does make us see, what he shows us are the remains of the Greenwich bomber: remains that, once the police have shovelled them up, resemble "what may be called the by-products of a butcher's shop with a view to an inexpensive Sunday dinner." It seems typical of this book that the inspector in charge "had not managed to get anything to eat," and *The Secret Agent* stands as Conrad's most relentless novel, a darkness visible that shares Winnie Verloc's belief "that things did not stand being looked into" even as it rubs them in our faces.

"The way of even the most justifiable revolutions is prepared by personal impulses disguised into creeds." The novel's words testify not only to Conrad's disbelief in the possibility of disinterested action but also to his equal and complementary belief that ideology is always preceded and indeed determined by "private emotional ends." And he might himself serve as an example, not only in his temperamental absence of optimism but also in the sympathy he half allows himself for questions of national struggle, as in the depiction of Garibaldi in *Nostromo* or the Polish patriot of "Prince Roman" (1911). One of the wisest things anyone has ever said about him can be found in a little 1919 essay in which T. S. Eliot presents Conrad as "the antithesis of Mr. Kipling. He is, for one thing, the antithesis of Empire (as well as of democracy) . . . Mr. Conrad has no ideas, but he has a point of view, a world; it can hardly be defined, but it pervades his work and is unmistakable." We might disagree about the absence of ideas, and almost a century's worth of criticism has gone into defining that point of view. Still, Conrad's politics can best be summarized in terms of what he himself described, in a letter to Edward Garnett, as his inability to "swallow *any* formula," an inability that makes him wear "the aspect of enemy to all mankind." But Conrad also knows that there is no escape from the world those formulae have made. In *Under Western Eyes* the student Razumov, having betrayed a man who had trusted him with his secrets and his life, tells Councillor Mikulin that he wants to be done with it all, that he wants "simply to retire." Which makes his confessor ask, softly, "Where to?" No reader of Conrad will be surprised to learn that what then happens both fulfills the literal terms of Razumov's desire and proves no retirement at all.

V

Conrad changed publishers regularly, moving in the early years of his career from Unwin to Heinemann and back again, and on to Blackwood for both the magazine and book publication of *Lord Jim* and *Youth*. He tried Harper and then Methuen, who snared him in a punitive long-term contract, before in his last years settling into an alternation of Dent and Unwin. The picture in America was simpler—a mix of houses at first, and then a steady commitment to Doubleday, where the young Alfred A. Knopf would make *Chance* a bestseller, and which collaborated with Heinemann on Conrad's first collected edition. Some of those changes grew from the attempts of his agent, J. B. Pinker, to strike the best deal in an increasingly segmented and competitve marketplace, and some came from the fact that Conrad looked to be losing the competition. He probably would have been happy to stay with Blackwood, and the lucrative serial possibilities of *Blackwood's Edinburgh Magazine,* if the publisher, who was already carrying him at a loss, hadn't refused his request for a loan.

He was never good with money, and though not improvident was certainly unthrifty, living openhanded and hand-to-mouth, a master at such costly tactics of delay as insuring his life and then borrowing on the strength of the policy. Galsworthy helped him with some regularity, there was a series of government grants, and eventually Pinker became his banker, so that Conrad's letters to him are full of requests for small and precisely calculated sums to cover one expense or another. And sometimes they weren't so small. There were long visits to Capri and Provence, and it seems typical of Conrad's bad luck that almost any trip abroad was punctuated by illness and doctors' fees. His older son, Borys, came down with pleurisy and then rheumatic fever in Geneva, while the novelist tried to finish *The Secret Agent* in something close to what that book calls "madness or despair." Jessie Conrad's chronic knee troubles, the result of a fall, would eventually necessitate a series of operations. By the time of *Under Western Eyes* Conrad's debt to Pinker amounted to £2700, and they were arguing over what and where he could publish, with the agent threatening to cut off supplies; their quarrel undoubtedly contributed to Conrad's collapse once the book itself was done.

In 1911 Conrad began to sell his manuscripts to the American collector John Quinn, and he later authorized some privately published editions of individual essays, pamphlets sold as collectors' items, thus entering into a system of patronage from which other modernists, like Joyce and Eliot, were to benefit as well. Then things changed. After his breakdown of 1910 Conrad never again attempted a "political" novel. He wrote some stories, moved house, and then, as he would do repeatedly in the years to come, he plucked an old manuscript from its drawer. Conrad had spoken of a book called *Chance* as early as 1905, though some aspects of it go back even further, to the fin de siècle invention of Marlow, and its protracted composition is perhaps responsible for its labored quality, its convolutions of narrative within narrative. Yet the book was cannily promoted, in the United States in particular, where it was serialized in the *New York Herald*. The advertising described it as "a sea story that appeals to women," and however oblique in form the novel did tell a familiar story of romantic rescue, in which an upright sea captain saves a troubled young woman from the tangles of her past. Conrad even called its two parts "The Damsel" and "The Knight." The reviews were strong, though there's some truth to Garnett's comment that "the figure of the lady on the 'jacket' . . . did more" than anything else "to bring the novel into popular favour." It was indeed popular, with sales that dwarfed Conrad's previous figures. In America, ten thousand copies went in the first week alone—and once the readers had arrived, they stayed.

"The lady on the 'jacket'" was called Flora de Barral, and if her presence got *Chance* to sell, it was perhaps because her story offered a point of contrast with its author's earlier books. The manners that interest Conrad are usually those of a ship or a port, not a drawing room, and even those novels set away from the water rely on the idea of separate spheres, in which the space given to women tends in all senses to be narrow. His repertoire of female characters is a limited one, and he portions them out, like Shakespeare, with only two or three speaking roles per book. The bit parts go to the exoticized: Jewel in *Lord Jim,* or the "barbarous and superb woman" who stretches out her arms at Kurtz's departure in "Heart of Darkness." The star turns Conrad reserves for the idealized, like the dry-eyed survivors of *Nostromo,* the Doñas Emilia and Antonia, or Natalia Haldin in *Under Western Eyes,* who owes something to his reading of Turgenev and maybe more to the ghostly memory of his own mother. Conrad does acknowledge the stakes men have in keeping such women in what Marlow calls "a beautiful world of their own," but judging the degree of irony behind those words has been a nice question for the growing body of feminist readings his work his received. In some books he recognizes that that "beautiful world" is itself a fiction; so with both Flora in *Chance* and Lena in *Victory* he takes care to show us the gap between what their men imagine them to be and the way they really are. More often, however, Conrad seems to fall under the spell himself, as he does with the conventionally sultry Rita de Lastaola in *The Arrow of Gold.* Of all his female characters, he grants only Winnie Verloc the kind of imaginative weight that places her at the book's very center.

Flora looks in spots to run her close: a fierce and loyal daughter and eventually a passionate wife, a character whose sense of her own independence is at times indistinguishable from desperation. Yet while *Chance* has its moments, nobody really thinks it one of Conrad's best books, a volume in which the story is passed like a baton from character to character and frame to frame. Too often we are reading one person's report of what a second told him a third had said, and its flaws have prompted a debate about the shape of Conrad's oeuvre, a debate most readily seen in Thomas C. Moser's 1957 analysis of his "achievement and decline." Conrad's earlier work had sometimes misfired, though few writers can equal him in having produced four great novels in a row, from *Lord Jim* to *Under Western Eyes*. Nothing from *Chance* on can match them, with the exception of the much briefer *The Shadow-Line*. Why? What happened?

Moser suggests that what gained Conrad his new popularity is also what made him go off, arguing that his "creativity" always suffered from a "near paralysis . . . when dealing with a sexual subject." During the first half of his career he managed to sidle around the issue, but in his later work he often turned to such "uncongenial" questions, to a kind of material fundamentally at odds with his temperament. Conrad's attempt to expand his range amounts, in this account, to a betrayal of his own gifts; the novelist should instead have stayed within the narrow world of men without women that so marks his early fiction. Moser's link between the "uncongenial" and "decline" risks tautology, but the problem he defines isn't simply one of the writer's admittedly uncertain handling of "sexual subject[s]." It lies, rather, in what creates that uncertainty, in the fact that Conrad "sees man as lonely and morally isolated . . . his only hope benumbing labor or, in rare cases, a little self-knowledge." It is a view that Moser believes the novelist cannot "possibly reconcile . . . with the panacea of love, wife, home, and family." The whole bent of his imagination lies away from such an affirmation, and while E. M. Forster may plead with us to "Only connect!" on this reading Conrad at his best more than half believes, in the words of *Victory,* that "He who forms a tie is lost."

Much more could be said about Conrad's picture of women. But that picture does seem to me a consistent one, from *Almayer's Folly* to the end, and we may accept Moser's estimation of Conrad's later work, its tired quality included, while disagreeing with his sense of the reason why. Going through *Chance* myself I certainly feel that the novelist has pushed his method past its breaking point—and yet I can't say it's the subject alone that has broken it. Conrad was fifty-two when he finished *Under Western Eyes:* the same age as the Dickens of *Our Mutual Friend,* his last completed novel, and older than the Woolf of *The Waves* or the

Flaubert of *A Sentimental Education*. Few novelists of his era did much of their major work after sixty, the great exception being Theodor Fontane. He had been a sickly boy, his life at sea was physically demanding, and he came back from the Congo with malaria, from whose recurring fevers he suffered. Gout often left him bedridden and lame, and at times settled like arthritis into the wrist of his writing hand. There was his family's health to worry about too, and money, and then the Great War, with Borys serving in France from 1916 on. There was, quite simply, the stress of being Conrad, something altogether different from the wildfire of being Dickens, but no less exhausting. His life had been in every sense a hard one, and I see no mystery in his failing powers.

I would tell a different story about Conrad's last years, one emphasizing something that often goes unnoticed: his disciplined professionalism. Conrad enjoyed the prosperity that *Chance* and its successors brought him—enjoyed it so much, in fact, that he still sometimes found himself briefly overdrawn. But he never forgot the saving power of what his early stories had described as the need to "get on," which by this point meant driving forward to the next page, and then to the one after that. *Victory* stands as a partial recovery from *Chance* insofar as its version of rescue ends operatically, with the heroine taking the bullet meant for her protector. The novel returns to the island settings of Conrad's first books, and it is often read as his final statement about commitment and isolation. There's little argument, however, that Conrad's most important late work is *The Shadow-Line,* a tale that he initially thought of calling "First Command": a story about a young man's unexpected appointment as master of a ship, a boat haunted by the all-but-physical presence of its malevolent late captain. In writing it Conrad drew on his own 1888 memories of taking charge of the *Otago* in Bangkok. Yet those memories are here "transposed into spiritual terms" and stretched a bit beyond the literal facts, with the voyage made more punishing than it actually was, so as to underscore the symbolic charge of the story's title, of the line that separates innocence from experience, youth from maturity. It was, he later wrote, the only subject "I found it possible to attempt at the time," and he dedicated this last masterpiece to his son Borys "and all others who like himself have crossed in early youth the shadow-line of their generation."

As the war progressed, Conrad did a few propaganda pieces for the Admiralty and finished some stories, the sublime "Warrior's Soul" among them. But in April 1917 he wrote to Garnett that he felt "broken up—or broken in two—disconnected. Impossible to start myself going impossible to concentrate to any good purpose. Is it the war—perhaps? Or the end of Conrad simply?" When later that year he began *The Arrow of Gold,* he found its germ in "The Sisters," a fragment of the 1890s, working it up into a self-consciously romantic tale of his own time in Marseilles. As a document this story of love affairs and gunrunning is both maddening and invaluable for what it appears to say about Conrad's early manhood. But as a novel it seems as densely indirect as anything in his whole body of work, and much the same can be said of *The Rescue,* another return to an abandoned manuscript. Both books depend on a "sexual subject," and it may be true that Conrad always found such material difficult. Nevertheless I would agree with Zdzislaw Najder in seeing Conrad's turn to that material "rather as a *symptom* of his weariness than as the *cause* of his decline." Invention had failed, and all he could now do was go back to the work he had once put aside.

Still, that stands in itself as a mark of his professionalism. Conrad tied the loose ends of his career. His backlist had become valuable, and he made sure that there was more of it. He began, moreover, to tend his own posterity, producing a series of brief author's notes for his collected edition: forewords at once modelled on James's prefaces to his own New York edition, and as unlike them as possible. Conrad says little about the technical difficulties he had to solve. He is instead anecdotal and concentrates above all on the originating germ of the narrative, the event or memory or bit of reading that had first set him off. These gruff avuncular notes seem, even now, to give us an image of Conrad as fully equal to any storm, as though he were the *Narcissus* itself. They mask the sense of struggle and despair to which his letters speak; they veil the turmoil of the astonishing fifteen years that had taken him from the standing start of *Almayer's Folly* through "Heart of Darkness" and on to "The Secret Sharer" and *Under Western Eyes*. Wanting a large audience, he yet never hesitated to make his work difficult, disrupting the smooth linearity of his Victorian predecessors and demanding that we face out the gusts and squalls of confusion. He showed us worlds we had not seen before, and he made technical innovation respond to the pressures of history itself. No writer of his time did more to change the stories the novel in English can tell, or indeed the way it tells them.

For Conrad there was one last tale. He had spoken for years of writing a long book about the Mediterranean in the Napoleonic era, and at his death in 1924 he left a fragment that was published the next year as *Suspense*. But he had already finished a shorter novel on the same theme, a story about an old French sailor who has come home, with a treasure, to the coast where he grew up. Most of *The Rover* (1923) is set in 1804, with a British fleet cruising just offshore, and in its hero, Jean Peyrol, Conrad gives us a man who has found calm waters after a life of storms. Some of the book recalls *Nostromo*—the money, the small boat, the islands—but Conrad has used a real place, the Giens Peninsula near Toulon, and his feel for his setting, for the interplay of sea and land, reminds me of Thomas Hardy at his best. *The Rover* was once popular, and deserves to be better known today: a delicate book, and one with a surprisingly happy ending, in which an old man finds he still has the strength to perform one great and final task.

MICHAEL GORRA

Joseph Conrad: A Chronology

1857 Józef Teodor Konrad Nałęcz Korzeniowski born 3 December at Berdyczów in a part of Poland annexed by Russia (Berdichev in present-day Ukraine). Only child of Apollo Korzeniowski and Ewelina née Bobrowska.

1861 Family moves to Warsaw. Father uses editorship of a literary journal as a cover for involvement in a nationalist, anti-Russian conspiracy. Arrested and imprisoned.

1862–67 After trial, parents sent into exile three hundred miles northeast of Moscow. The future Conrad accompanies them; both mother and son ill on the journey. In 1863, family allowed to move south, near Kiev. Ewelina dies, 18 April 1865, suffering from tuberculosis contracted in exile. First sight of the sea at Odessa, 1867.

1868–69 Apollo allowed to leave exile, settles in Austrian Ukraine at Lwów. Father and son move to Cracow, where Apollo dies, 23 May 1869. Funeral becomes a patriotic outpouring, with the boy leading a procession of thousands.

1870–73 Conrad lives with maternal grandmother, Teofila Bobrowska, in Cracow. Frequently ill; intermittent formal education, supplemented by tutors. Family tries, unsuccessfully, to get Austrian citizenship for him. In 1872, he announces his desire to go to sea.

1874–78 Based in Marseilles. First experience at sea: voyages to Martinique and Haiti. With allowance from maternal uncle, Tadeusz Bobrowski, Conrad presents himself as a young man of means. Much remains unclear about these years. Conrad would later claim to have moved in circles linked to the Spanish pretender, Don Carlos, and to have bought a share in a sailboat used for running guns. Heavily in debt, Conrad in 1878 suffers a gunshot wound to the chest. Claims to have been wounded in a duel, but Bobrowski, on arrival, learns that it was in fact a suicide attempt, though perhaps a half-hearted one.

1878–79 Conrad joins the British steamer *Mavis* as an apprentice and first arrives in Britain, 10 June. As an ordinary seaman, voyages in English coastal waters as well as the Mediterranean and Australia. Spends five months in Sydney.

1880–89 Passes exam as second mate in the British Merchant Service. Certificate as first mate follows in 1884, and as master, 1886, but he fails each of the latter two exams on his first attempt. Becomes naturalized British subject, 1886. Service, at various ranks, on a number of cargo ships. Highlights: 1881–83, second mate on the *Palestine*—the *Judea* of "Youth"; in Singapore, May 1883; 1884, sails from Bombay as second mate in the *Narcissus;* 1887, first mate in the *Vidar,* making coastal trading voyages from Singapore to Borneo and Celebes; January 1888, master of the *Otago,* his only command, sailing mostly in Australian waters. Resigns command in March 1889 and returns to Britain.

1889 Released from legal status of Russian subject; this allows him to enter Russian Poland without being liable for (having avoided) military service. Begins writing the story that would grow into *Almayer's Folly*. Plans visit to Poland and interviews for a position as a riverboat captain in the Belgian Congo.

1890 Returns to Poland for the first time since leaving for Marseilles; visits his uncle Bobrowski. Receives three-year contract from the Société Anonyme Belge pour le Commerce du Haut-Congo. Sails from Bordeaux. Six months in Africa, upriver to Stanley Falls; in charge of steamship *Roi des Belges* for a part of the journey downriver. Suffers from both dysentery and malaria.

1891–93 January 1891, returns to London. November, signs on as first mate of the *Torrens;* makes two round-trip voyages, London to Adelaide. Meets John Galsworthy, not yet a writer, but a passenger on the second voyage home in 1893.

1893–94 Visits Bobrowski in the Ukraine. Second mate of the *Adowa,* in port in Rouen, from December to January 1894. This marks the end of Conrad's professional career at sea. Bobrowski dies, 10 February 1894. Finishes *Almayer's Folly* and submits it to the London publisher T. Fisher Unwin. Novel accepted, October 1894.

1895–97 First books published: *Almayer's Folly* (1895), *An Outcast of the Islands* (1896). Marries Jessie George, 24 March 1896; the couple then spend five months in Brittany before returning to settle in Essex. Writes first short stories ("An Outpost of Progress," "The Lagoon") and begins *The Rescue,* putting it aside to start *The Nigger of the "Narcissus,"* published 1897. First meetings with Henry James, Stephen Crane, R. B. Cunninghame Graham.

1898–1903 Borys Conrad born 15 March 1898. *Tales of Unrest.* Meets Ford Madox Ford, from whom he sublets Pent Farm in Kent, and with whom he begins to collaborate (e.g., *Romance,* 1903). By the end of 1898 Conrad has written "Youth" and begun both *Lord Jim* and "The Heart of Darkness," the latter published February–April 1899 in *Blackwood's. Lord Jim* serialized there beginning in October 1899, concluding November 1900, by which time the finished book itself has appeared. Meets and after some jockeying becomes a client of the literary agent J. B. Pinker. *Youth,* a volume containing the title story, "Heart of Darkness," and "The End of the Tether," published November 1902. *Typhoon and Other Stories,* 1903. At work on *Nostromo.*

1904–7 *Nostromo* published October 1904. Jessie Conrad damages the cartilage in both knees in a fall on a London street, an injury that over the years will lead to a series of painful operations. Financial troubles. Winter 1905, writes "Autocracy and War" on Capri, and at work on short stories. February 1906, in Provence, begins short story called "Verloc," which eventually becomes *The Secret Agent* (1907). John Conrad born, 2 August 1906. *The Mirror of the Sea,* a volume of reminiscence. Both children are seriously ill in spring 1907; financial troubles. Short-lived move to Bedfordshire, but back in Kent the following year, where Conrad will be based for the rest of his life.

1908–10 *A Set of Six,* and at work on *Under Western Eyes.* September 1908, quarrels with Pinker over plans to write a series of autobiographical essays. December 1909, "The Secret Sharer." Finishes *Under Western Eyes,* January 1910, and suffers an immediate breakdown. Estranged from Pinker.

1911–14 Meets André Gide, who will later translate "Typhoon" and organize Conrad's appearance in French. *Under Western Eyes.* Resumes work on *Chance,* published in America in 1913 but delayed in Britain until January 1914: a bestseller that makes Conrad a popular success at last and ends his long period of financial difficulty. *A Personal Record* and *'Twixt Land and Sea,* both 1912, and at work on *Victory.* July 1914, Conrad travels with his family to Poland, where the outbreak of war catches them; they return to England only in December.

1915–18 *Within the Tides* and *Victory,* both 1915. Borys receives an army commission; he will eventually be attached to an artillery unit. In 1916, begins author's notes for projected collection edition; makes inspection tour of naval bases. *The Shadow-Line,* 1917. October 1918, Borys in hospital, suffering from shell shock.

1919–22 *The Arrow of Gold.* Stage version of *Victory* opens in London; at work on dramatization of *The Secret Agent.* Sells film rights to *Lord Jim* and three other novels and moves house one last time, to Oswalds, near Canterbury. *The Rescue,* 1920. *Notes on Life and Letters,* 1921. Collected edition begins to appear in both Britain and America. Pinker dies, February 1922. Brief London run of dramatized *The Secret Agent.*

1923–24 Makes American promotional tour, his only visit to the United States, April–June 1923. *The Rover,* 1923. Declines offer of a knighthood, 1924. Dies of a heart attack, 3 August 1924, at home.

1925–26 *Suspense* (unfinished) and *Tales of Hearsay,* both 1925; *Last Essays,* 1926.

In preparing this chronology I am indebted to two sources in particular: *Joseph Conrad: A Chronicle,* by Zdzislaw Najder, translated by Halina Carroll Najder (New Brunswick, NJ: Rutgers University Press, 1983); and the *Oxford Reader's Companion to Conrad,* edited by Owen Knowles and Gene Moore (Oxford: Oxford University Press, 2000).

I
A Calm and a Storm

Any selection from Conrad's fiction should offer its readers three things: the East, an initiation, and a spell of bad weather. These are the regularly recurring features of his maritime tales, and "The Secret Sharer" contains all three, with the bad weather coming in the form of a breathless calm, something potentially as dangerous to a ship under sail as any knock of the wind. The story has always been taken as quintessentially "Conradian," a work that places its nameless narrator at what he himself describes as "the threshhold of a . . . passage" in which he must measure his "fitness for a long and arduous enterprise." Certainly its dramatic situation, the relation between that narrator and the homicidal Leggatt, finds an echo in many of Conrad's other works. His pages are full of secret sharers: of the guilty who whisper into our ears and claim, in the words of *Lord Jim,* to be "one of us." In this tale, that kinship is underlined by the physical resemblance between the two men, one so marked that some readers have taken Leggatt's very presence as a projection of the narrator's own inner life. But Conrad always needs to be understood literally before he can be read symbolically, even if the uncanny similarity of the two does echo such fantastical nineteenth-century stories of doubling as E. T. A. Hoffmann's "The Sandman" or Robert Louis Stevenson's "Strange Case of Dr. Jekyll and Mr. Hyde."

Conrad wrote the piece in December 1909, interrupting his halting progress on *Under Western Eyes* to do so, and in many ways they are the same story. Each tells us about a young man into whose rule-bound life a murderer suddenly breaks, a murderer who begs his sympathy and shelter. The two versions reach different conclusions, and to Conrad the almost farcical details of this narrator's attempt to keep Leggatt hidden must have seemed like a release from the relentless quality of his Russian narrative. But Conrad had a more particular purpose as well, and one that marks "The Secret Sharer" as a conscious return to the world of his earlier work. He wrote it after a visit from an English sea captain who had spent his career in the Malay Archipelago, and who told him that his work was popular "out there." His fellow sailors had been reading his books and wondering "who [the] devil has been around taking notes." That made Conrad decide they should "have some more of the stories they like." In writing he used his own 1888 experience in assuming command of the *Otago,* as he later would for *The Shadow-Line.* Not that he was visited by a Leggatt. The narrator's feelings on assuming command do, however, seem taken from Conrad's own life, and so are some details of the ending, which draw upon "a bit of manoeuvering of mine" that had given his first mate "an unforgettable scare."

Conrad once said that he had written "two Storm-Pieces" and "two Calm-pieces"; the ones *not* included here are "Typhoon" and *The Shadow-Line,* respectively. *The Nigger of the "Narcissus"* has always had a special place in the Conrad canon. It stands as his first unequivocal masterpiece, and its preface is contemporary with the tale itself, a statement of principle that looks to the future as much as to the work at hand. Conrad modeled the book's journey on his own 1884 service aboard a ship of that name, which he had joined as second mate for a passage from Bombay to Dunkirk. But he relied on his experience of other ships too, and though one member of the *Narcissus*'s crew did die on the voyage, no secure identification can be made between James Wait, the black sailor of the story, and anyone actually aboard. Different readers will have their favorite moments here: the nighttime mustering of the crew in the tale's first pages; the great storm through which the *Narcissus* passes, one of Conrad's best pieces of kinetic description; or perhaps the gestures toward mutiny that follow. To me nothing seems finer than the book's last pages, in which its narrator describes the crew's end as a coherent unit, and in doing so separates himself from the rest of them. The *Narcissus* makes port, and its men—heroes at sea but clumsy and anonymous on land—stand "swaying irresolute" on the London streets. Then they vanish in the sunshine. "I never saw them again," the narrator tells us. But Conrad has made us see them, and hear them, and know them, in what he described as the book by which "I am willing to stand or fall."

He began the tale in the summer of 1896, and it was serialized in the *New Review* from August to December 1897, with the preface appearing there at the end of the last installment. Conrad relied on magazine publication as an important source of income, but he can't be called a serial novelist in the manner of Dickens or even Hardy. He found it almost impossible to plan a story in advance, the regular deadlines were hard to manage, and with this work in particular he felt that "The installment plan ruins it." Conrad almost invariably revised the magazine versions of his fiction before they appeared in cloth, though in this case those revisions were not as extensive as with some later volumes, such as *The Secret Agent*. Book publication, by Heinemann, coincided with the end of the serial; an American edition under the title *The Children of the Sea* had appeared the month before. The preface made its first book appearance in an American printing of 1914, but had to wait until 1921 in Britain.

I have chosen the text prepared by Cedric Watts for his 1988 Penguin edition of the novel, to which I refer interested readers. It is based on a comparison of Heinemann's first British trade edition of 1897 with that publisher's 1921 version, the last that Conrad himself saw through the press. "The Secret Sharer" first appeared in *Harper's Magazine* (August–September 1910), and then as one of three stories in *'Twixt Land and Sea* (Dent, 1912). The copy text is taken from the Kent edition of Conrad's works (Doubleday, Page, 1925), which used corrected plates from his first collected edition, the "Sun-Dial Edition" of 1920–28.

THE SECRET SHARER

An Episode from the Coast

I

On my right hand there were lines of fishing-stakes resembling a mysterious system of half-submerged bamboo fences, incomprehensible in its division of the domain of tropical fishes, and crazy of aspect as if abandoned for ever by some nomad tribe of fishermen now gone to the other end of the ocean; for there was no sign of human habitation as far as the eye could reach. To the left a group of barren islets, suggesting ruins of stone walls, towers, and blockhouses, had its foundations set in a blue sea that itself looked solid, so still and stable did it lie below my feet; even the track of light from the westering sun shone smoothly, without that animated glitter which tells of an imperceptible ripple. And when I turned my head to take a parting glance at the tug which had just left us anchored outside the bar, I saw the straight line of the flat shore joined to the stable sea, edge to edge, with a perfect and unmarked closeness, in one levelled floor half brown, half blue under the enormous dome of the sky. Corresponding in their insignificance to the islets of the sea, two small clumps of trees, one on each side of the only fault in the impeccable joint, marked the mouth of the river Meinam we had just left on the first preparatory stage of our homeward journey; and, far back on the inland level, a larger and loftier mass, the grove surrounding the great Paknam pagoda, was the only thing on which the eye could rest from the vain task of exploring the monotonous sweep of the horizon. Here and there gleams as of a few scattered pieces of silver marked the windings of the great river; and on the nearest of them, just within the bar, the tug steaming right into the land became lost to my sight, hull and funnel and masts, as though the impassive earth had swallowed her up without an effort, without a tremor. My eye followed the light cloud of her smoke, now here, now there, above the plain, according to the devious curves of the stream, but always fainter and farther away, till I lost it at last behind the mitre-shaped hill of the great pagoda. And then I was left alone with my ship, anchored at the head of the Gulf of Siam.

She floated at the starting-point of a long journey, very still in an immense stillness, the shadows of her spars flung far to the eastward by the setting sun. At that moment I was alone on her decks. There was not a sound in her—and around us nothing moved, nothing lived, not a canoe on the water, not a bird in the air, not a cloud in the sky. In this breathless pause at the threshold of a long passage we seemed to be measuring our fitness for a long and arduous enterprise, the appointed task of both our existences to be carried out, far from all human eyes, with only sky and sea for spectators and for judges.

There must have been some glare in the air to interfere with one's sight, because it was only just before the sun left us that my roaming eyes made out beyond the highest ridge of the principal islet of the group something which did away with the solemnity of perfect solitude. The tide of darkness flowed on swiftly; and with tropical suddenness a swarm of stars came out above the shadowy earth, while I lingered yet, my hand resting lightly on my ship's rail as if on the shoulder of a trusted friend. But, with all that multitude of celestial bodies staring down at one, the comfort of quiet communion with her was gone for good. And there were also disturbing sounds by this time—voices, footsteps forward; the steward flitted along the main deck, a busily ministering spirit; a hand-bell tinkled urgently under the poop-deck. . . .

I found my two officers waiting for me near the supper table, in the lighted cuddy. We sat down at once, and as I helped the chief mate, I said:

"Are you aware that there is a ship anchored inside the islands? I saw her mastheads above the ridge as the sun went down."

He raised sharply his simple face, overcharged by a terrible growth of whisker, and emitted his usual ejaculations: "Bless my soul, sir! You don't say so!"

My second mate was a round-cheeked, silent young man, grave beyond his years, I thought; but as our eyes happened to meet I detected a slight quiver on his lips. I looked down at once. It was not my part to encourage sneering on board my ship. It must be said, too, that I knew very little of my officers. In consequence of certain events of no particular significance, except to myself, I had been appointed to the command only a fortnight before. Neither did I know much of the hands forward. All these people had been together for eighteen months or so, and my position was that of the only stranger on board. I mention this because it has some bearing on what is to follow. But what I felt most was my being a stranger to the ship; and if all the truth must be told, I was somewhat of a stranger to myself. The youngest man on board (barring the second mate), and untried as yet by a position of the fullest responsibility, I was willing to take the adequacy of the others for granted. They had simply to be equal to their tasks; but I wondered how far I should turn out faithful to that ideal conception of one's own personality every man sets up for himself secretly.

Meantime the chief mate, with an almost visible effect of collaboration on the part of his round eyes and frightful whiskers, was trying to evolve a theory of the anchored ship. His dominant trait was to take all things into earnest consideration. He was of a painstaking turn of mind. As he used to say, he "liked to account to himself" for practically everything that came in his way, down to a miserable scorpion he had found in his cabin a week before. The why and the wherefore of that scorpion—how it got on board and came to select his room rather than the pantry (which was a dark place and more what a scorpion would be partial to), and how on earth it managed to drown itself in the inkwell of his writing desk—had exercised him infinitely. The ship within the islands was much more easily accounted for; and just as we were about to rise from table he made his pronouncement. She was, he doubted not, a ship from home lately arrived. Probably she drew too much water to cross the bar except at the top of spring tides. Therefore she went into that natural harbour to wait for a few days in preference to remaining in an open roadstead.

"That's so," confirmed the second mate, suddenly, in his slightly hoarse voice. "She draws over twenty feet. She's the Liverpool ship *Sephora* with a cargo of coal. Hundred and twenty-three days from Cardiff."

Sephora - Daughter of Moses

We looked at him in surprise.

"The tugboat skipper told me when he came on board for your letters, sir," explained the young man. "He expects to take her up the river the day after tomorrow."

After thus overwhelming us with the extent of his information he slipped out of the cabin. The mate observed regretfully that he "could not account for that young fellow's whims." What prevented him telling us all about it at once, he wanted to know.

I detained him as he was making a move. For the last two days the crew had had plenty of hard work, and the night before they had very little sleep. I felt painfully that I—a stranger—was doing something unusual when I directed him to let all hands turn in without setting an anchor-watch. I proposed to keep on deck myself till one o'clock or thereabouts. I would get the second mate to relieve me at that hour.

"He will turn out the cook and the steward at four," I concluded, "and then give you a call. Of course at the slightest sign of any sort of wind we'll have the hands up and make a start at once."

He concealed his astonishment. "Very well, sir." Outside the cuddy he put his head in the second mate's door to inform him of my unheard-of caprice to take a five hours' anchor-watch on myself. I heard the other raise his voice incredulously—"What? The Captain himself?" Then a few more murmurs, a door closed, then another. A few moments later I went on deck.

My strangeness, which had made me sleepless, had prompted that unconventional arrangement, as if I had expected in those solitary hours of the night to get on terms with the ship of which I knew nothing, manned by men of whom I knew very little more. Fast alongside a wharf, littered like any ship in port with a tangle of unrelated things, invaded by unrelated shore people, I had hardly seen her yet properly. Now, as she lay cleared for sea, the stretch of her main-deck seemed to me very fine under the stars. Very fine, very roomy for her size, and very inviting. I descended the poop and paced the waist, my mind picturing to myself the coming passage through the Malay Archipelago, down the Indian Ocean, and up the Atlantic. All its phases were familiar enough to me, every characteristic, all the alternatives which were likely to face me on the high seas—everything! . . . except the novel responsibility of command. But I took heart from the reasonable thought that the ship was like other ships, the men like other men, and that the sea was not likely to keep any special surprises expressly for my discomfiture.

Arrived at that comforting conclusion, I bethought myself of a cigar and went below to get it. All was still down there. Everybody at the after end of the ship was sleeping profoundly. I came out again on the quarter-deck, agreeably at ease in my sleeping-suit on that warm breathless night, barefooted, a glowing cigar in my teeth, and, going forward, I was met by the profound silence of the fore end of the ship. Only as I passed the door of the forecastle I heard a deep, quiet, trustful sigh of some sleeper inside. And suddenly I rejoiced in the great security of the sea as compared with the unrest of the land, in my choice of that untempted life presenting no disquieting problems, invested with an elementary moral beauty by the absolute straightforwardness of its appeal and by the singleness of its purpose.

The riding-light in the fore-rigging burned with a clear, untroubled, as if symbolic, flame, confident and bright in the mysterious shades of the night. Passing on my way aft along the other side of the ship, I observed that the rope side-ladder, put over, no doubt, for the master of the tug when he came to fetch away our letters, had not been hauled in as it should have been. I became annoyed at this, for exactitude in small matters is the very soul of discipline. Then I reflected that I had myself peremptorily dismissed my officers from duty, and by my own act had prevented the anchor-watch being formally set and things properly attended to. I asked myself whether it was wise ever to interfere with the established routine of duties even from the kindest of motives. My action might have made me appear eccentric. Goodness only knew how that absurdly whiskered mate would "account" for my conduct, and what the whole ship thought of that informality of their new captain. I was vexed with myself.

Not from compunction certainly, but, as it were mechanically, I proceeded to get the ladder in myself. Now a side-ladder of that sort is a light affair and comes in easily, yet my vigorous tug, which should have brought it flying on board, merely recoiled upon my body in a totally unexpected jerk. What the devil! . . . I was so astounded by the immovableness of that ladder that I remained stock-still, trying to account for it to myself like that imbecile mate of mine. In the end, of course, I put my head over the rail.

The side of the ship made an opaque belt of shadow on the

darkling glassy shimmer of the sea. But I saw at once something elongated and pale floating very close to the ladder. Before I could form a guess a faint flash of phosphorescent light, which seemed to issue suddenly from the naked body of a man, flickered in the sleeping water with the elusive, silent play of summer lightning in a night sky. With a gasp I saw revealed to my stare a pair of feet, the long legs, a broad livid back immersed right up to the neck in a greenish cadaverous glow. One hand, awash, clutched the bottom rung of the ladder. He was complete but for the head. A headless corpse! The cigar dropped out of my gaping mouth with a tiny plop and a short hiss quite audible in the absolute stillness of all things under heaven. At that I suppose he raised up his face, a dimly pale oval in the shadow of the ship's side. But even then I could barely make out down there the shape of his black-haired head. However, it was enough for the horrid, frost-bound sensation which had gripped me about the chest to pass off. The moment of vain exclamations was past, too. I only climbed on the spare spar and leaned over the rail as far as I could, to bring my eyes nearer to that mystery floating alongside.

As he hung by the ladder, like a resting swimmer, the sea-lightning played about his limbs at every stir; and he appeared in it ghastly, silvery, fish-like. He remained as mute as a fish, too. He made no motion to get out of the water, either. It was inconceivable that he should not attempt to come on board, and strangely troubling to suspect that perhaps he did not want to. And my first words were prompted by just that troubled incertitude.

"What's the matter?" I asked in my ordinary tone, speaking down to the face upturned exactly under mine.

"Cramp," it answered, no louder. Then slightly anxious, "I say, no need to call any one."

"I was not going to," I said.

"Are you alone on deck?"

"Yes."

I had somehow the impression that he was on the point of letting go the ladder to swim away beyond my ken—mysterious as he came. But, for the moment, this being appearing as if he had risen from the bottom of the sea (it was certainly the nearest land to the ship) wanted only to know the time. I told him. And he, down there, tentatively: "I suppose your captain's turned in?"

"I am sure he isn't," I said.

He seemed to struggle with himself, for I heard something like the low, bitter murmur of doubt. "What's the good?" His next words came out with a hesitating effort.

"Look here, my man. Could you call him out quietly?"

I thought the time had come to declare myself.

"*I* am the captain."

I heard a "By Jove!" whispered at the level of the water. The phosphorescence flashed in the swirl of the water all about his limbs, his other hand seized the ladder.

"My name's Leggatt."

The voice was calm and resolute. A good voice. The self-possession of that man had somehow induced a corresponding state in myself. It was very quietly that I remarked:

"You must be a good swimmer."

"Yes. I've been in the water practically since nine o'clock. The question for me now is whether I am to let go this ladder and go on swimming till I sink from exhaustion, or—to come on board here."

I felt this was no mere formula of desperate speech, but a real alternative in the view of a strong soul. I should have gathered from this that he was young; indeed, it is only the young who are ever confronted by such clear issues. But at the time it was pure intuition on my part. A mysterious communication was established already between us two—in the face of that silent, darkened tropical sea. I was young, too; young enough to make no comment. The man in the water began suddenly to climb up the ladder, and I hastened away from the rail to fetch some clothes.

Before entering the cabin I stood still, listening in the lobby at the foot of the stairs. A faint snore came through the closed door of the chief mate's room. The second mate's door was on the hook, but the darkness in there was absolutely soundless. He, too, was young and could sleep like a stone. Remained the steward, but he was not likely to wake up before he was called. I got a sleeping-suit out of my room and, coming back on deck, saw the naked man from the sea sitting on the main-hatch, glimmering white in the darkness, his elbows on his knees and his head in his hands. In a moment he had concealed his damp body in a sleeping-suit of the same grey-stripe pattern as the one I was wearing and followed me like my double on the poop. Together we moved right aft, barefooted, silent.

"What is it?" I asked in a deadened voice, taking the lighted lamp out of the binnacle, and raising it to his face.

"An ugly business."

He had rather regular features; a good mouth; light eyes under somewhat heavy, dark eyebrows; a smooth, square forehead; no growth on his cheeks; a small, brown moustache, and a well-shaped, round chin. His expression was concentrated, meditative, under the inspecting light of the lamp I held up to his face; such as a man thinking hard in solitude might wear. My sleeping-suit was just right for his size. A well-knit young fellow of twenty-five at most. He caught his lower lip with the edge of white, even teeth.

"Yes," I said, replacing the lamp in the binnacle. The warm, heavy tropical night closed upon his head again.

"There's a ship over there," he murmured.

"Yes, I know. The *Sephora*. Did you know of us?"

"Hadn't the slightest idea. I am the mate of her—" He paused and corrected himself. "I should say I *was*."

"Aha! Something wrong?"

"Yes. Very wrong indeed. I've killed a man."

"What do you mean? Just now?"

"No, on the passage. Weeks ago. Thirty-nine south. When I say a man—"

"Fit of temper," I suggested, confidently.

The shadowy, dark head, like mine, seemed to nod imperceptibly above the ghostly grey of my sleeping-suit. It was, in the night, as though I had been faced by my own reflection in the depths of a sombre and immense mirror.

"A pretty thing to have to own up to for a Conway boy," murmured my double, distinctly.

"You're a Conway boy?"

"I am," he said, as if startled. Then, slowly . . . "Perhaps you too—"

It was so; but being a couple of years older I had left before he joined. After a quick interchange of dates a silence fell; and I thought suddenly of my absurd mate with his terrific whiskers and the "Bless my soul—you don't say so" type of intellect. My double gave me an inkling of his thoughts by saying: "My father's a parson in Norfolk. Do you see me before a judge and jury on that charge? For myself I can't see the necessity. There are fellows that an angel from heaven— And I am not that. He was one of those creatures that are just simmering all the time with a silly sort of wickedness. Miserable devils that have no business to live at all. He wouldn't do his duty and wouldn't let anybody else do theirs. But what's the good of talking! You know well enough the sort of ill-conditioned snarling cur—"

He appealed to me as if our experiences had been as identical as our clothes. And I knew well enough the pestiferous danger of such a character where there are no means of legal repression. And I knew well enough also that my double there was no homicidal ruffian. I did not think of asking him for details, and he told me the story roughly in brusque, disconnected sentences. I needed no more. I saw it all going on as though I were myself inside that other sleeping-suit.

"It happened while we were setting a reefed foresail, at dusk. Reefed foresail! You understand the sort of weather. The only sail we had left to keep the ship running; so you may guess what it had been like for days. Anxious sort of job, that. He gave me some of his cursed insolence at the sheet. I tell you I was overdone with this terrific weather that seemed to have no end to it. Terrific, I tell you—and a deep ship. I believe the fellow himself was half crazed with funk. It was no time for gentlemanly reproof, so I turned round and felled him like an ox. He up and at me. We closed just as an awful sea made for the ship. All hands saw it coming and took to the rigging, but I had him by the throat, and went on shaking him like a rat, the men above us yelling, 'Look out! look out!' Then a crash as if the sky had fallen on my head. They say that for over ten minutes hardly anything was to be seen of the ship—just the three masts and a bit of the forecastle head and of the poop all awash driving along in a smother of foam. It was a miracle that they found us, jammed together behind the forebits. It's clear that I meant business, because I was holding him by the throat still when they picked us up. He was black in the face. It was too much for them. It seemed they rushed us aft together, gripped as we were, screaming 'Murder!' like a lot of lunatics, and broke into the cuddy. And the ship running for her life, touch and go all the time, any minute her last in a sea fit to turn your hair grey only a-looking at it. I understand that the skipper, too, started raving like the rest of them. The man had been deprived of sleep for more than a week, and to have this sprung on him at the height of a furious gale nearly drove him out of his mind. I wonder they didn't fling me overboard after getting the carcass of their precious ship-mate out of my fingers. They had rather a job to separate us, I've been told. A sufficiently fierce story to make an old judge and a respectable jury sit up a bit. The first thing I heard when I came to myself was the maddening howling of that endless gale, and on that the voice of the old man. He was hanging on to my bunk, staring into my face out of his sou'wester.

"'Mr. Leggatt, you have killed a man. You can act no longer as chief mate of this ship.'"

His care to subdue his voice made it sound monotonous. He rested a hand on the end of the skylight to steady himself with, and all that time did not stir a limb, so far as I could see. "Nice little tale for a quiet tea-party," he concluded in the same tone.

One of my hands, too, rested on the end of the skylight; neither did I stir a limb, so far as I knew. We stood less than a foot from each other. It occurred to me that if old "Bless my soul—you don't say so" were to put his head up the companion and catch sight of us, he would think he was seeing double, or imagine himself come upon a scene of weird witchcraft; the strange captain having a quiet confabulation by the wheel with his own grey ghost. I became very much concerned to prevent anything of the sort. I heard the other's soothing undertone.

"My father's a parson in Norfolk," it said. Evidently he had forgotten he had told me this important fact before. Truly a nice little tale.

"You had better slip down into my stateroom now," I said, moving off stealthily. My double followed my movements; our bare feet made no sound; I let him in, closed the door with care, and, after giving a call to the second mate, returned on deck for my relief.

"Not much sign of any wind yet," I remarked when he approached.

"No, sir. Not much," he assented, sleepily, in his hoarse voice, with just enough deference, no more, and barely suppressing a yawn.

"Well, that's all you have to look out for. You have got your orders."

"Yes, sir."

I paced a turn or two on the poop and saw him take up his position face forward with his elbow in the ratlines of the mizzen-rigging before I went below. The mate's faint snoring was still going on peacefully. The cuddy lamp was burning over the table on which stood a vase with flowers, a polite attention from the ship's provision merchant—the last flowers we should see for the next three months at the very least. Two bunches of bananas hung from the beam symmetrically, one on each side of the rudder-casing. Everything was as before in the ship—except that two of her captain's sleeping-suits were simultaneously in use, one motionless in the cuddy, the other keeping very still in the captain's stateroom.

It must be explained here that my cabin had the form of the capital letter L the door being within the angle and opening into the short part of the letter. A couch was to the left, the bed-place to the right; my writing-desk and the chronometers' table faced the door. But any one opening it, unless he stepped right inside, had no view of what I call the long (or vertical) part of the letter. It contained some lockers surmounted by a bookcase; and a few clothes, a thick jacket or two, caps, oilskin coat, and such like, hung on hooks. There was at the bottom of that part a door opening into my bath-room, which could be entered also directly from the saloon. But that way was never used.

The mysterious arrival had discovered the advantage of this particular shape. Entering my room, lighted strongly by a big bulkhead lamp swung on gimbals above my writing-desk, I did not see him anywhere till he stepped out quietly from behind the coats hung in the recessed part.

"I heard somebody moving about, and went in there at once," he whispered.

I, too, spoke under my breath.

"Nobody is likely to come in here without knocking and getting permission."

He nodded. His face was thin and the sunburn faded, as though he had been ill. And no wonder. He had been, I heard presently, kept under arrest in his cabin for nearly seven weeks. But there was nothing sickly in his eyes or in his expression. He was not a bit like me, really; yet, as we stood leaning over my bed-place, whispering side by side, with our dark heads together and our backs to the door, anybody bold enough to open it stealthily would have been treated to the uncanny sight of a double captain busy talking in whispers with his other self.

"But all this doesn't tell me how you came to hang on to our side-ladder," I inquired, in the hardly audible murmurs we used, after he had told me something more of the proceedings on board the *Sephora* once the bad weather was over.

"When we sighted Java Head I had had time to think all those matters out several times over. I had six weeks of doing nothing else, and with only an hour or so every evening for a tramp on the quarter-deck."

He whispered, his arms folded on the side of my bed-place, staring through the open port. And I could imagine perfectly the manner of this thinking out—a stubborn if not steadfast operation; something of which I should have been perfectly incapable.

"I reckoned it would be dark before we closed with the land," he continued, so low that I had to strain my hearing, near as we were to each other, shoulder touching shoulder almost. "So I asked to speak to the old man. He always seemed very sick when he came to see me—as if he could not look me in the face. You know, that foresail saved the ship. She was too deep to have run long under bare poles. And it was I that managed to set it for him. Anyway, he came. When I had him in my cabin—he stood by the door looking at me as if I had the halter round my neck already—I asked him right away to leave my cabin door unlocked at night while the ship was going through Sunda Straits. There would be the Java coast within two or three miles, off Angier Point. I wanted nothing more. I've had a prize for swimming my second year in the Conway."

"I can believe it," I breathed out.

"God only knows why they locked me in every night. To see some of their faces you'd have thought they were afraid I'd go about at night strangling people. Am I a murdering brute? Do I look it? By Jove! if I had been he wouldn't have trusted himself like that into my room. You'll say I might have chucked him aside and bolted out, there and then—it was dark already. Well, no. And for the same reason I wouldn't think of trying to smash the door. There would have been a rush to stop me at the noise, and I did not mean to get into a confounded scrimmage. Somebody else might have got killed—for I would not have broken out only to get chucked back, and I did not want any more of that work. He refused, looking more sick than ever. He was afraid of the men, and also of that old second mate of his who had been sailing with him for years—a grey-headed old humbug; and his steward, too, had been with him devil knows how long—seventeen years or more—a dogmatic sort of loafer who hated me like poison, just because I was the chief mate. No chief mate ever made more than one voyage in the *Sephora,* you know. Those two old chaps ran the ship. Devil only knows what the skipper wasn't afraid of (all his nerve went to pieces altogether in that hellish spell of bad weather we had)—of what the law would do to him—of his wife, perhaps. Oh, yes! she's on board. Though I don't think she would have meddled. She would have been only too glad to have me out of the ship in any way. The 'brand of Cain' business, don't you see. That's all right. I was ready enough to go off wandering on the face of the earth—and that was price enough to pay for an Abel of that sort. Anyhow, he wouldn't listen to me. 'This thing must take its course. I represent the law here.' He was shaking like a leaf. 'So you won't?' 'No!' 'Then I hope you will be able to sleep on that,' I said, and turned my back on him. 'I wonder that *you* can,' cries he, and locks the door.

"Well, after that, I couldn't. Not very well. That was three weeks ago. We have had a slow passage through the Java Sea; drifted about Carimata for ten days. When we anchored here they thought, I suppose, it was all right. The nearest land (and that's five miles) is the ship's destination; the consul would soon set about catching me; and there would have been no object in bolting to these islets there. I don't suppose there's a drop of water on them. I don't know how it was, but to-night that steward, after bringing me my supper, went out to let me eat it, and left the door unlocked. And I ate it—all there was, too. After I had finished I strolled out on the quarter-deck. I don't know that I meant to do anything. A breath of fresh air was all I wanted, I believe. Then a sudden temptation came over me. I kicked off my slippers and was in the water before I had made up my mind fairly. Somebody heard the splash and they raised an awful hullabaloo. 'He's gone! Lower the boats! He's committed suicide! No, he's swimming.' Certainly I was swimming. It's not so easy for a swimmer like me to commit suicide by drowning. I landed on the nearest islet before the boat left the ship's side. I heard them pulling about in the dark, hailing, and so on, but after a bit they gave up. Everything quieted down and the anchorage became as still as death. I sat down on a stone and began to think. I felt certain they would start searching for me at daylight. There was no place to hide on those stony things—and if there had been, what would have been the good? But now I was clear of that ship, I was not going back. So after a while I took off all my clothes, tied them up in a bundle with a stone inside, and dropped them in the deep water on the outer side of that islet. That was suicide enough for me. Let them think what they liked, but I didn't mean to drown myself. I meant to swim till I sank—but that's not the same thing. I struck out for another of these little islands, and it was from that one that I first saw your riding-light. Something to swim for. I went on easily, and on the way I came upon a flat rock a foot or two above water. In the daytime, I dare say, you might make it out with a glass from your poop. I scrambled up on it and rested myself for a bit. Then I made another start. That last spell must have been over a mile."

His whisper was getting fainter and fainter, and all the time he stared straight out through the porthole, in which there was not even a star to be seen. I had not interrupted him. There was something that made comment impossible in his narrative, or perhaps in himself; a sort of feeling, a quality, which I can't find a name for. And when he ceased, all I found was a futile whisper: "So you swam for our light?"

"Yes—straight for it. It was something to swim for. I couldn't see any stars low down because the coast was in the way, and I couldn't see the land, either. The water was like glass. One might have been swimming in a confounded thousand-feet deep cistern with no place for scrambling out anywhere; but what I didn't like was the notion of swimming round and round like a crazed bullock before I gave out; and as I didn't mean to go back . . . No. Do you see me being hauled back, stark naked, off one of these little islands by the scruff of the neck and fighting like a wild beast? Somebody would have got killed for certain, and I did not want any of that. So I went on. Then your ladder—"

"Why didn't you hail the ship?" I asked, a little louder.

He touched my shoulder lightly. Lazy footsteps came right over our heads and stopped. The second mate had crossed from the other side of the poop and might have been hanging over the rail, for all we knew.

"He couldn't hear us talking—could he?" My double breathed into my very ear, anxiously.

His anxiety was an answer, a sufficient answer, to the question I had put to him. An answer containing all the difficulty of that situation. I closed the porthole quietly, to make sure. A louder word might have been overheard.

"Who's that?" he whispered then.

"My second mate. But I don't know much more of the fellow than you do."

And I told him a little about myself. I had been appointed to take charge while I least expected anything of the sort, not quite a fortnight ago. I didn't know either the ship or the people. Hadn't had the time in port to look about me or size anybody up. And as to the crew, all they knew was that I was appointed to take the ship home. For the rest, I was almost as much of a stranger on board as himself, I said. And at the moment I felt it most acutely. I felt that it would take very little to make me a suspect person in the eyes of the ship's company.

He had turned about meantime; and we, the two strangers in the ship, faced each other in identical attitudes.

"Your ladder—" he murmured, after a silence. "Who'd have thought of finding a ladder hanging over at night in a ship anchored out here! I felt just then a very unpleasant faintness. After the life I've been leading for nine weeks, anybody would have got out of condition. I wasn't capable of swimming round as far as your rudder-chains. And, lo and behold! there was a ladder to get hold of. After I gripped it I said to myself, 'What's the good?' When I saw a man's head looking over I thought I would swim away presently and leave him shouting—in whatever language it was. I didn't mind being looked at. I—I liked it. And then you speaking to me so quietly—as if you had expected me—made me hold on a little longer. It had been a confounded lonely time—I don't mean while swimming. I was glad to talk a little to somebody that didn't belong to the *Sephora*. As to asking for the captain, that was a mere impulse. It could have been no use, with all the ship knowing about me and the other people pretty certain to be round here in the morning. I don't know—I wanted to be seen, to talk with somebody, before I went on. I don't know what I would have said. . . . 'Fine night, isn't it?' or something of the sort."

"Do you think they will be round here presently?" I asked with some incredulity.

"Quite likely," he said, faintly.

He looked extremely haggard all of a sudden. His head rolled on his shoulders.

"H'm. We shall see then. Meantime get into that bed," I whispered. "Want help? There."

It was a rather high bed-place with a set drawers underneath. This amazing swimmer really needed the lift I gave him by seizing his leg. He tumbled in, rolled over on his back, and flung one arm across his eyes. And then, with his face nearly hidden, he must have looked exactly as I used to look in that bed. I gazed upon my other self for a while before drawing across carefully the two green serge curtains which ran on a brass rod. I thought for a moment of pinning them together for greater safety, but I sat down on the couch, and once there I felt unwilling to rise and hunt for a pin. I would do it in a moment. I was extremely tired, in a peculiarly intimate way, by the strain of stealthiness, by the effort of whispering and the general secrecy of this excitement. It was three o'clock by now and I had been on my feet since nine, but I was not sleepy; I could not have gone to sleep. I sat there, fagged out, looking at the curtains, trying to clear my mind of the confused sensation of being in two places at once, and greatly bothered by an exasperating knocking in my head. It was a relief to discover suddenly that it was not in my head at all, but on the outside of the door. Before I could collect myself the words "Come in" were out of my mouth, and the steward entered with a tray, bringing my morning coffee. I had slept, after all, and I was so frightened that I shouted, "This way! I am here, steward," as though he had been miles away. He put down the tray on the table next to the couch and only then said, very quietly, "I can see you are here, sir." I felt him give me a keen look, but I dared not meet his eyes just then. He must have wondered why I had drawn the curtains of my bed before going to sleep on the couch. He went out, hooking the door open as usual.

I heard the crew washing decks above me. I knew I would have been told at once if there had been any wind. Calm, I thought, and I was doubly vexed. Indeed, I felt dual more than ever. The steward reappeared suddenly in the doorway. I jumped up from the couch so quickly that he gave a start.

"What do you want here?"

"Close your port, sir—they are washing decks."

"It is closed," I said, reddening.

"Very well, sir." But he did not move from the doorway and returned my stare in an extraordinary, equivocal manner for a time. Then his eyes wavered, all his expression changed, and in a voice unusually gentle, almost coaxingly:

"May I come in to take the empty cup away, sir?"

"Of course!" I turned my back on him while he popped in and out. Then I unhooked and closed the door and even pushed the bolt. This sort of thing could not go on very long. The cabin was as hot as an oven, too. I took a peep at my double, and discovered that he had not moved, his arm was still over his eyes; but his chest heaved; his hair was wet; his chin glistened with perspiration. I reached over him and opened the port.

"I must show myself on deck," I reflected.

Of course, theoretically, I could do what I liked, with no one to say nay to me within the whole circle of the horizon; but to lock my cabin door and take the key away I did not dare. Directly I put my head out of the companion I saw the group of my two officers, the second mate barefooted, the chief mate in long india-rubber boots, near the break of the poop, and the steward half-way down the poop-ladder talking to them eagerly. He happened to catch sight of me and dived, the second ran down on the main-deck shouting some order or other, and the chief mate came to meet me, touching his cap.

There was a sort of curiosity in his eye that I did not like. I don't know whether the steward had told them that I was "queer" only, or downright drunk, but I know the man meant to have a good look at me. I watched him coming with a smile which, as he got into point-blank range, took effect and froze his very whiskers. I did not give him time to open his lips.

"Square the yards by lifts and braces before the hands go to breakfast."

It was the first particular order I had given on board that ship;

and I stayed on deck to see it executed, too. I had felt the need of asserting myself without loss of time. That sneering young cub got taken down a peg or two on that occasion, and I also seized the opportunity of having a good look at the face of every foremast man as they filed past me to go to the after braces. At breakfast time, eating nothing myself, I presided with such frigid dignity that the two mates were only too glad to escape from the cabin as soon as decency permitted; and all the time the dual working of my mind distracted me almost to the point of insanity. I was constantly watching myself, my secret self, as dependent on my actions as my own personality, sleeping in that bed, behind the door which faced me as I sat at the head of the table. It was very much like being mad, only it was worse because one was aware of it.

I had to shake him for a solid minute, but when at last he opened his eyes it was in the full possession of his senses, with an inquiring look.

"All's well so far," I whispered. "Now you must vanish into the bath-room."

He did so, as noiseless as a ghost, and then I rang for the steward, and facing him boldly, directed him to tidy up my stateroom while I was having my bath—"and be quick about it." As my tone admitted of no excuses, he said, "Yes, sir," and ran off to fetch his dust-pan and brushes. I took a bath and did most of my dressing, splashing, and whistling softly for the steward's edification, while the secret sharer of my life stood drawn up bolt upright in that little space, his face looking very sunken in daylight, his eyelids lowered under the stern, dark line of his eyebrows drawn together by a slight frown.

When I left him there to go back to my room the steward was finishing dusting. I sent for the mate and engaged him in some insignificant conversation. It was, as it were, trifling with the terrific character of his whiskers; but my object was to give him an opportunity for a good look at my cabin. And then I could at last shut, with a clear conscience, the door of my stateroom and get my double back into the recessed part. There was nothing else for it. He had to sit still on a small folding stool, half smothered by the heavy coats hanging there. We listened to the steward going into the bath-room out of the saloon, filling the water-bottles there, scrubbing the bath, setting things to rights, whisk, bang, clatter—out again into the saloon—turn the key—click. Such was my scheme for keeping my second self invisible. Nothing better could be contrived under the circumstances. And there we sat; I at my writing-desk ready to appear busy with some papers, he behind me out of sight of the door. It would not have been prudent to talk in daytime; and I could not have stood the excitement of that queer sense of whispering to myself. Now and then, glancing over my shoulder, I saw him far back there, sitting rigidly on the low stool, his bare feet close together, his arms folded, his head hanging on his breast—and perfectly still. Anybody would have taken him for me.

I was fascinated by it myself. Every moment I had to glance over my shoulder. I was looking at him when a voice outside the door said:

"Beg pardon, sir."

"Well!" . . . I kept my eyes on him, and so when the voice outside the door announced, "There's a ship's boat coming our way, sir," I saw him give a start—the first movement he had made for hours. But he did not raise his bowed head.

"All right. Get the ladder over."

I hesitated. Should I whisper something to him? But what? His immobility seemed to have been never disturbed. What could I tell him he did not know already? . . . Finally I went on deck.

II

The skipper of the *Sephora* had a thin red whisker all round his face, and the sort of complexion that goes with hair of that colour; also the particular, rather smeary shade of blue in the eyes. He was not exactly a showy figure; his shoulders were high, his stature but middling—one leg slightly more bandy than the other. He shook hands, looking vaguely around. A spiritless tenacity was his main characteristic, I judged. I behaved with a politeness which seemed to disconcert him. Perhaps he was shy. He mumbled to me as if he were ashamed of what he was saying; gave his name (it was something like Archbold—but at this distance of years I hardly am sure), his ship's name, and a few other particulars of that sort, in the manner of a criminal making a reluctant and doleful confession. He had had terrible weather on the passage out—terrible—terrible—wife aboard, too.

By this time we were seated in the cabin and the steward brought in a tray with a bottle and glasses. "Thanks! No." Never took liquor. Would have some water, though. He drank two tumblerfuls. Terrible thirsty work. Ever since daylight had been exploring the islands round his ship.

"What was that for—fun?" I asked, with an appearance of polite interest.

"No!" He sighed. "Painful duty."

As he persisted in his mumbling and I wanted my double to hear every word, I hit upon the notion of informing him that I regretted to say I was hard of hearing.

"Such a young man, too!" he nodded, keeping his smeary blue, unintelligent eyes fastened on me. "What was the cause of it—some disease?" he inquired, without the least sympathy and as if he thought that, if so, I'd got no more than I deserved.

"Yes; disease," I admitted in a cheerful tone which seemed to shock him. But my point was granted, because he had to raise his voice to give me his tale. It is not worth while to record that version. It was just over two months since all this had happened, and he had thought so much about it that he seemed completely muddled as to its bearings, but still immensely impressed.

"What would you think of such a thing happening on board your ship? I've had the *Sephora* for these fifteen years. I am a well-known shipmaster."

He was densely distressed—and perhaps I should have sympathised with him if I had been able to detach my mental vision from the unsuspected sharer of my cabin as though he were my second self. There he was on the other side of the bulkhead, four or five feet from us, no more, as we sat in the saloon. I looked politely at Captain Archbold (if that was his name), but it was the other I saw, in a grey sleeping-suit, seated on a low stool, his bare feet close together, his arms folded, and every word said between us falling into the ears of his dark head bowed on his chest.

"I have been at sea now, man and boy, for seven-and-thirty years, and I've never heard of such a thing happening in an English ship. And that it should be my ship. Wife on board, too."

I was hardly listening to him.

"Don't you think," I said, "that the heavy sea which, you told me, came aboard just then might have killed the man? I have seen the sheer weight of a sea kill a man very neatly, by simply breaking his neck."

"Good God!" he uttered, impressively, fixing his smeary blue eyes on me. "The sea! No man killed by the sea ever looked like that." He seemed positively scandalized at my suggestion. And as I gazed at him, certainly not prepared for anything original on his part, he advanced his head close to mine and thrust his tongue out at me so suddenly that I couldn't help starting back.

After scoring over my calmness in this graphic way he nodded wisely. If I had seen the sight, he assured me, I would never forget it as long as I lived. The weather was too bad to give the corpse a proper sea burial. So next day at dawn they took it up on the poop, covering its face with a bit of bunting; he read a short prayer, and then, just as it was, in its oilskins and long boots, they launched it amongst those mountainous seas that seemed ready every moment to swallow up the ship herself and the terrified lives on board of her.

"That reefed foresail saved you," I threw in.

"Under God—it did," he exclaimed fervently. "It was by a special mercy, I firmly believe, that it stood some of those hurricane squalls."

"It was the setting of that sail which—" I began.

"God's own hand in it," he interrupted me. "Nothing less could have done it. I don't mind telling you that I hardly dared give the order. It seemed impossible that we could touch anything without losing it, and then our last hope would have been gone."

The terror of that gale was on him yet. I let him go on for a bit, then said, casually—as if returning to a minor subject:

"You were very anxious to give up your mate to the shore people, I believe?"

He was. To the law. His obscure tenacity on that point had in it something incomprehensible and a little awful; something, as it were, mystical, quite apart from his anxiety that he should not be suspected of "countenancing any doings of that sort." Seven-and-thirty virtuous years at sea, of which over twenty of immaculate command, and the last fifteen in the *Sephora*, seemed to have laid him under some pitiless obligation.

Socratic Irony

"And you know," he went on, groping shamefacedly amongst his feelings, "I did not engage that young fellow. His people had some interest with my owners. I was in a way forced to take him on. He looked very smart, very gentlemanly, and all that. But do you know—I never liked him, somehow. I am a plain man. You see, he wasn't exactly the sort for the chief mate of a ship like the *Sephora*."

I had become so connected in thoughts and impressions with the secret sharer of my cabin that I felt as if I, personally, were being given to understand that I, too, was not the sort that would have done for the chief mate of a ship like the *Sephora*. I had no doubt of it in my mind.

"Not at all the style of man. You understand," he insisted, superfluously, looking hard at me.

I smiled urbanely. He seemed at a loss for a while.

"I suppose I must report a suicide."

"Beg pardon?"

"Sui-cide! That's what I'll have to write to my owners directly I get in."

"Unless you manage to recover him before to-morrow," I assented, dispassionately. . . . "I mean, alive."

He mumbled something which I really did not catch, and I turned my ear to him in a puzzled manner. He fairly bawled:

"The land—I say, the mainland is at least seven miles off my anchorage."

"About that."

My lack of excitement, of curiosity, of surprise, of any sort of pronounced interest, began to arouse his distrust. But except for the felicitous pretence of deafness I had not tried to pretend anything. I had felt utterly incapable of playing the part of ignorance properly, and therefore was afraid to try. It is also certain that he had brought some ready-made suspicions with him, and that he viewed my politeness as a strange and unnatural phenomenon. And yet how else could I have received him? Not heartily! That was impossible for psychological reasons, which I need not state here. My only object was to keep off his inquiries. Surlily? Yes, but surliness might have provoked a point-blank question. From its novelty to him and from its nature, punctilious courtesy was the manner best calculated to restrain the man. But there was the danger of his breaking through

The good/evil doubles

my defence bluntly. I could not, I think, have met him by a direct lie, also for psychological (not moral) reasons. If he had only known how afraid I was of his putting my feeling of identity with the other to the test! But, strangely enough—(I thought of it only afterwards)—I believe that he was not a little disconcerted by the reverse side of that weird situation, by something in me that reminded him of the man he was seeking—suggested a mysterious similitude to the young fellow he had distrusted and disliked from the first.

However that might have been, the silence was not very prolonged. He took another oblique step.

"I reckon I had no more than a two-mile pull to your ship. Not a bit more."

"And quite enough, too, in this awful heat," I said.

Another pause full of mistrust followed. Necessity, they say, is mother of invention, but fear, too, is not barren of ingenious suggestions. And I was afraid he would ask me point-blank for news of my other self.

"Nice little saloon, isn't it?" I remarked, as if noticing for the first time the way his eyes roamed from one closed door to the other. "And very well fitted out, too. Here, for instance," I continued, reaching over the back of my seat negligently and flinging the door open, "is my bath-room."

He made an eager movement, but hardly gave it a glance. I got up, shut the door of the bath-room, and invited him to have a look round, as if I were very proud of my accommodation. He had to rise and be shown round, but he went through the business without any raptures whatever.

"And now we'll have a look at my stateroom," I declared, in a voice as loud as I dared to make it, crossing the cabin to the starboard side with purposely heavy steps.

He followed me in and gazed around. My intelligent double had vanished. I played my part.

"Very convenient—isn't it?"

"Very nice. Very comf . . ." He didn't finish and went out brusquely as if to escape from some unrighteous wiles of mine. But it was not to be. I had been too frightened not to feel vengeful; I felt I had him on the run, and I meant to keep him on the run. My polite insistence must have had something menacing in it, because he gave in suddenly. And I did not let him off a single item; mate's room, pantry, store-rooms, the very sail-locker which was also under the poop—he had to look into them all. When at last I showed him out on the quarter-deck he drew a long, spiritless sigh, and mumbled dismally that he must really be going back to his ship now. I desired my mate, who had joined us, to see the captain's boat.

The man of whiskers gave a blast on the whistle which he used to wear hanging round his neck, and yelled, "*Sephora*'s away!" My double down there in my cabin must have heard, and certainly could not feel more relieved than I. Four fellows came running out from somewhere forward and went over the side, while my own men, appearing on deck too, lined the rail. I escorted my visitor to the gangway ceremoniously, and nearly overdid it. He was a tenacious beast. On the very ladder he lingered, and in that unique, guiltily conscientious manner of sticking to the point:

"I say . . . you . . . you don't think that—"

I covered his voice loudly:

"Certainly not. . . . I am delighted. Good-bye."

I had an idea of what he meant to say, and just saved myself by the privilege of defective hearing. He was too shaken generally to insist, but my mate, close witness of the parting, looked mystified and his face took on a thoughtful cast. As I did not want to appear as if I wished to avoid all communication with my officers, he had the opportunity to address me.

"Seems a very nice man. His boat's crew told our chaps a very extraordinary story, if what I am told by the steward is true. I suppose you had it from the captain, sir?"

"Yes. I had a story from the captain."

"A very horrible affair—isn't it, sir?"

"It is."

"Beats all these tales we hear about murders in Yankee ships."

"I don't think it beats them. I don't think it resembles them in the least."

"Bless my soul—you don't say so! But of course I've no acquaintance whatever with American ships, not I, so I couldn't go against your knowledge. It's horrible enough for me. . . . But the queerest part is that those fellows seemed to have some idea the man was hidden aboard here. They had really. Did you ever hear of such a thing?"

the struggle of evil over good.

"Preposterous—isn't it?"

We were walking to and fro athwart the quarter-deck. No one of the crew forward could be seen (the day was Sunday), and the mate pursued:

"There was some little dispute about it. Our chaps took offence. 'As if we would harbour a thing like that,' they said. 'Wouldn't you like to look for him in our coal-hole?' Quite a tiff. But they made it up in the end. I suppose he did drown himself. Don't you, sir?"

"I don't suppose anything."

"You have no doubt in the matter, sir?"

"None whatever."

I left him suddenly. I felt I was producing a bad impression, but with my double down there it was most trying to be on deck. And it was almost as trying to be below. Altogether a nerve-trying situation. But on the whole I felt less torn in two when I was with him. There was no one in the whole ship whom I dared take into my confidence. Since the hands had got to know his story, it would have been impossible to pass him off for any one else, and an accidental discovery was to be dreaded now more than ever. . . .

The steward being engaged in laying the table for dinner, we could talk only with our eyes when I first went down. Later in the afternoon we had a cautious try at whispering. The Sunday quietness of the ship was against us; the stillness of air and water around her was against us; the elements, the men were against us—everything was against us in our secret partnership; time itself—for this could not go on forever. The very trust in Providence was, I suppose, denied to his guilt. Shall I confess that this thought cast me down very much? And as to the chapter of accidents which counts for so much in the book of success, I could only hope that it was closed. For what favourable accident could be expected?

"Did you hear everything?" were my first words as soon as we took up our position side by side, leaning over my bed-place.

He had. And the proof of it was his earnest whisper, "The man told you he hardly dared to give the order."

I understood the reference to be to that saving foresail.

"Yes. He was afraid of it being lost in the setting."

"I assure you he never gave the order. He may think he did, but he never gave it. He stood there with me on the break of the poop after the maintopsail blew away, and whimpered about our last hope—positively whimpered about it and nothing else—and the night coming on! To hear one's skipper go on like that in such weather was enough to drive any fellow out of his mind. It worked me up into a sort of desperation. I just took it into my own hands and went away from him, boiling, and— But what's the use telling you? *You* know! . . . Do you think that if I had not been pretty fierce with them I should have got the men to do anything? Not it! The bo's'n perhaps? Perhaps! It wasn't a heavy sea—it was a sea gone mad! I suppose the end of the world will be something like that; and a man may have the heart to see it coming once and be done with it—but to have to face it day after day— I don't blame anybody. I was precious little better than the rest. Only—I was an officer of that old coal-wagon, anyhow—"

"I quite understand," I conveyed that sincere assurance into his ear. He was out of breath with whispering; I could hear him pant slightly. It was all very simple. The same strung-up force which had given twenty-four men a chance, at least, for their lives, had, in a sort of recoil, crushed an unworthy mutinous existence.

But I had no leisure to weigh the merits of the matter—footsteps in the saloon, a heavy knock. "There's enough wind to get under way with, sir." Here was the call of a new claim upon my thoughts and even upon my feelings.

"Turn the hands up," I cried through the door. "I'll be on deck directly."

I was going out to make the acquaintance of my ship. Before I left the cabin our eyes met—the eyes of the only two strangers on board. I pointed to the recessed part where the little camp-stool awaited him and laid my finger on my lips. He made a gesture—somewhat vague—a little mysterious, accompanied by a faint smile, as if of regret.

This is not the place to enlarge upon the sensations of a man who feels for the first time a ship move under his feet to his own independent word. In my case they were not unalloyed. I was not wholly alone with my command; for there was the stranger in my cabin. Or rather, I was not completely and wholly with her. Part of me was absent. That mental feeling of being in two places at once affected me physically as if the mood of secrecy had pene-

The final destruction of evil.

trated my very soul. Before an hour had elapsed since the ship had begun to move, having occasion to ask the mate (he stood by my side) to take a compass bearing of the Pagoda, I caught myself reaching up to his ear in whispers. I say I caught myself, but enough had escaped to startle the man. I can't describe it otherwise than by saying that he shied. A grave, preoccupied manner, as though he were in possession of some perplexing intelligence, did not leave him henceforth. A little later I moved away from the rail to look at the compass with such a stealthy gait that the helmsman noticed it—and I could not help noticing the unusual roundness of his eyes. These are trifling instances, though it's to no commander's advantage to be suspected of ludicrous eccentricities. But I was also more seriously affected. There are to a seaman certain words, gestures, that should in given conditions come as naturally, as instinctively as the winking of a menaced eye. A certain order should spring on to his lips without thinking; a certain sign should get itself made, so to speak, without reflection. But all unconscious alertness had abandoned me. I had to make an effort of will to recall myself back (from the cabin) to the conditions of the moment. I felt that I was appearing an irresolute commander to those people who were watching me more or less critically.

And, besides, there were the scares. On the second day out, for instance, coming off the deck in the afternoon (I had straw slippers on my bare feet) I stopped at the open pantry door and spoke to the steward. He was doing something there with his back to me. At the sound of my voice he nearly jumped out of his skin, as the saying is, and incidentally broke a cup.

"What on earth's the matter with you?" I asked astonished.

He was extremely confused. "Beg your pardon, sir. I made sure you were in your cabin."

"You see I wasn't."

"No, sir. I could have sworn I had heard you moving in there not a moment ago. It's most extraordinary . . . very sorry, sir."

I passed on with an inward shudder. I was so identified with my secret double that I did not even mention the fact in those scanty, fearful whispers we exchanged. I suppose he had made some slight noise of some kind or other. It would have been miraculous if he hadn't at one time or another. And yet, haggard as he appeared, he looked always perfectly self-controlled, more than calm—almost invulnerable. On my suggestion he remained almost entirely in the bath-room, which, upon the whole, was the safest place. There could be really no shadow of an excuse for any one ever wanting to go in there, once the steward had done with it. It was a very tiny place. Sometimes he reclined on the floor, his legs bent, his head sustained on one elbow. At others I would find him on the camp-stool, sitting in his grey sleeping-suit and with his cropped dark hair like a patient, unmoved convict. At night I would smuggle him into my bed-place, and we would whisper together, with the regular footfalls of the officer of the watch passing and repassing over our heads. It was an infinitely miserable time. It was lucky that some tins of fine preserves were stowed in a locker in my stateroom; hard bread I could always get hold of; and so he lived on stewed chicken, paté de foie gras, asparagus, cooked oysters, sardines—on all sorts of abominable sham delicacies out of tins. My early morning coffee he always drank; and it was all I dared do for him in that respect.

Every day there was the horrible manœuvering to go through so that my room and then the bath-room should be done in the usual way. I came to hate the sight of the steward, to abhor the voice of that harmless man. I felt that it was he who would bring on the disaster of discovery. It hung like a sword over our heads.

The fourth day out, I think (we were then working down the east side of the Gulf of Siam, tack for tack, in light winds and smooth water)—the fourth day, I say, of this miserable juggling with the unavoidable, as we sat at our evening meal, that man, whose slightest movement I dreaded, after putting down the dishes ran up on deck busily. This could not be dangerous. Presently he came down again; and then it appeared that he had remembered a coat of mine which I had thrown over a rail to dry after having been wetted in a shower which had passed over the ship in the afternoon. Sitting stolidly at the head of the table I became terrified at the sight of the garment on his arm. Of course he made for my door. There was no time to lose.

"Steward," I thundered. My nerves were so shaken that I could not govern my voice and conceal my agitation. This was the sort of thing that made my terrifically whiskered mate tap his forehead with his forefinger. I had detected him using that gesture while talking on deck with a confidential air to the carpenter. I was too far to hear a word, but I had no doubt that this pantomime could only refer to the strange new captain.

"Yes, sir," the pale-faced steward turned resignedly to me. It was this maddening course of being shouted at, checked without rhyme or reason, arbitrarily chased out of my cabin, suddenly called into it, sent flying out of his pantry on incomprehensible errands, that accounted for the growing wretchedness of his expression.

"Where are you going with that coat?"

"To your room, sir."

"Is there another shower coming?"

"I'm sure I don't know, sir. Shall I go up again and see, sir?"

"No! never mind."

My object was attained, as of course my other self in there would have heard everything that passed. During this interlude my two officers never raised their eyes off their respective plates; the lip of that confounded cub, the second mate, quivered visibly.

I expected the steward to hook my coat on and come out at once. He was very slow about it; but I dominated my nervousness sufficiently not to shout after him. Suddenly I became aware (it could be heard plainly enough) that the fellow for some reason or other was opening the door of the bath-room. It was the end. The place was literally not big enough to swing a cat in. My voice died in my throat and I went stony all over. I expected to hear a yell of surprise and terror, and made a movement, but had not the strength to get on my legs. Everything remained still. Had my second self taken the poor wretch by the throat? I don't know what I could have done next moment if I had not seen the steward come out of my room, close the door, and then stand quietly by the sideboard.

"Saved," I thought. "But, no! Lost! Gone! He was gone!"

I laid my knife and fork down and leaned back in my chair. My head swam. After a while, when sufficiently recovered to speak in a steady voice, I instructed my mate to put the ship round at eight o'clock himself.

"I won't come on deck," I went on. "I think I'll turn in, and unless the wind shifts I don't want to be disturbed before midnight. I feel a bit seedy."

"You did look middling bad a little while ago," the chief mate remarked without showing any great concern.

They both went out, and I stared at the steward clearing the table. There was nothing to be read on that wretched man's face. But why did he avoid my eyes I asked myself. Then I thought I should like to hear the sound of his voice.

"Steward!"

"Sir!" Startled as usual.

"Where did you hang up that coat?"

"In the bath-room, sir." The usual anxious tone. "It's not quite dry yet, sir."

For some time longer I sat in the cuddy. Had my double vanished as he had come? But of his coming there was an explanation, whereas his disappearance would be inexplicable. . . . I went slowly into my dark room, shut the door, lighted the lamp, and for a time dared not turn round. When at last I did I saw him standing bolt-upright in the narrow recessed part. It would not be true to say I had a shock, but an irresistible doubt of his bodily existence flitted through my mind. Can it be, I asked myself, that he is not visible to other eyes than mine? It was like being haunted. Motionless, with a grave face, he raised his hands slightly at me in a gesture which meant clearly, "Heavens! what a narrow escape!" Narrow indeed. I think I had come creeping quietly as near insanity as any man who has not actually gone over the border. That gesture restrained me, so to speak.

The mate with the terrific whiskers was now putting the ship on the other tack. In the moment of profound silence which follows upon the hands going to their stations I heard on the poop his raised voice: "Hard alee!" and the distant shout of the order repeated on the main-deck. The sails, in that light breeze, made but a faint fluttering noise. It ceased. The ship was coming round slowly; I held my breath in the renewed stillness of expectation; one wouldn't have thought that there was a single living soul on her decks. A sudden brisk shout, "Mainsail haul!" broke the spell, and in the noisy cries and rush overhead of the men running away with the main-brace we two, down in my cabin, came together in our usual position by the bed-place.

He did not wait for my question. "I heard him fumbling here and just managed to squat myself down in the bath," he whispered to me. "The fellow only opened the door and put his arm in to hang the coat up. All the same—"

"I never thought of that," I whispered back, even more appalled than before at the closeness of the shave, and marvelling at that something unyielding in his character which was carrying him through so finely. There was no agitation in his whisper. Whoever was being driven distracted, it was not he. He was sane. And the proof of his sanity was continued when he took up the whispering again.

"It would never do for me to come to life again."

It was something that a ghost might have said. But what he was alluding to was his old captain's reluctant admission of the theory of suicide. It would obviously serve his turn—if I had understood at all the view which seemed to govern the unalterable purpose of his action.

"You must maroon me as soon as ever you can get amongst these islands off the Cambodge shore," he went on.

"Maroon you! We are not living in a boy's adventure tale," I protested. His scornful whispering took me up.

"We aren't indeed! There's nothing of a boy's tale in this. But there's nothing else for it. I want no more. You don't suppose I am afraid of what can be done to me? Prison or gallows or whatever they may please. But you don't see me coming back to explain such things to an old fellow in a wig and twelve respectable tradesmen, do you? What can they know whether I am guilty or not—or of *what* I am guilty, either? That's my affair. What does the Bible say? 'Driven off the face of the earth.' Very well. I am off the face of the earth now. As I came at night so I shall go."

"Impossible!" I murmured. "You can't."

"Can't? . . . Not naked like a soul on the Day of Judgment. I shall freeze on to this sleeping-suit. The Last Day is not yet—and . . . you have understood thoroughly. Didn't you?"

I felt suddenly ashamed of myself. I may say truly that I understood—and my hesitation in letting that man swim away from my ship's side had been a mere sham sentiment, a sort of cowardice.

"It can't be done now till next night," I breathed out. "The ship is on the off-shore tack and the wind may fail us."

"As long as I know that you understand," he whispered. "But of course you do. It's a great satisfaction to have got somebody to understand. You seem to have been there on purpose." And in the same whisper, as if we two whenever we talked had to say things to each other which were not fit for the world to hear, he added, "It's very wonderful."

We remained side by side talking in our secret way—but sometimes silent or just exchanging a whispered word or two at long intervals. And as usual he stared through the port. A breath of wind came now and again into our faces. The ship might have been moored in dock, so gently and on an even keel she slipped through the water, that did not murmur even at our passage, shadowy and silent like a phantom sea.

At midnight I went on deck, and to my mate's great surprise put the ship round on the other tack. His terrible whiskers flitted round me in silent criticism. I certainly should not have done it if it had been only a question of getting out of that sleepy gulf as quickly as possible. I believe he told the second mate, who relieved him, that it was a great want of judgment. The other only yawned. That intolerable cub shuffled about so sleepily and lolled against the rails in such a slack, improper fashion that I came down on him sharply.

"Aren't you properly awake yet?"

"Yes, sir! I am awake."

"Well, then, be good enough to hold yourself as if you were. And keep a look-out. If there's any current we'll be closing with some islands before daylight."

The east side of the gulf is fringed with islands, some solitary, others in groups. On the blue background of the high coast they seem to float on silvery patches of calm water, arid and grey, or dark green and rounded like clumps of evergreen bushes, with the larger ones, a mile or two long, showing the outlines of ridges, ribs of grey rock under the dank mantle of matted leafage. Unknown to trade, to travel, almost geography, the manner of life they harbour is an unsolved secret. There must be villages—settlements of fishermen at least—on the largest of them, and some communication with the world is probably kept up by native craft. But all that forenoon, as we headed for them, fanned along by the faintest of breezes, I saw no sign of man or canoe in the field of the telescope I kept on pointing at the scattered group.

At noon I gave no orders for a change of course, and the mate's whiskers became much concerned and seemed to be offering themselves unduly to my notice. At last I said:

"I am going to stand right in. Quite in—as far as I can take her."

The stare of extreme surprise imparted an air of ferocity also to his eyes, and he looked truly terrific for a moment.

"We're not doing well in the middle of the gulf," I continued, casually. "I am going to look for the land breezes to-night."

"Bless my soul! Do you mean, sir, in the dark amongst the lot of all them islands and reefs and shoals?"

"Well—if there are any regular land breezes at all on this coast one must get close inshore to find them, mustn't one?"

"Bless my soul!" he exclaimed again under his breath. All that afternoon he wore a dreamy, contemplative appearance which in him was a mark of perplexity. After dinner I went into my stateroom as if I meant to take some rest. There we two bent our dark heads over a half-unrolled chart lying on my bed.

"There," I said. "It's got to be Koh-ring. I've been looking at it ever since sunrise. It has got two hills and a low point. It must be inhabited. And on the coast opposite there is what looks like the mouth of a biggish river—with some town, no doubt, not far up. It's the best chance for you that I can see."

"Anything. Koh-ring let it be."

He looked thoughtfully at the chart as if surveying chances and distances from a lofty height—and following with his eyes his own figure wandering on the blank land of Cochin-China, and then passing off that piece of paper clean out of sight into uncharted regions. And it was as if the ship had two captains to plan her course for her. I had been so worried and restless running up and down that I had not had the patience to dress that day. I had remained in my sleeping-suit, with straw slippers and a soft floppy hat. The closeness of the heat in the gulf had been most oppressive, and the crew were used to see me wandering in that airy attire.

"She will clear the south point as she heads now," I whispered into his ear. "Goodness only knows when, though, but certainly after dark. I'll edge her in to half a mile, as far as I may be able to judge in the dark—"

"Be careful," he murmured, warningly—and I realised suddenly that all my future, the only future for which I was fit, would perhaps go irretrievably to pieces in any mishap to my first command.

I could not stop a moment longer in the room. I motioned him to get out of sight and made my way on the poop. That unplayful cub had the watch. I walked up and down for a while thinking things out, then beckoned him over.

"Send a couple of hands to open the two quarter-deck ports," I said mildly.

He actually had the impudence, or else so forgot himself in his wonder at such an incomprehensible order, as to repeat:

"Open the quarter-deck ports! What for, sir?"

"The only reason you need concern yourself about is because I tell you to do so. Have them opened wide and fastened properly."

He reddened and went off, but I believe made some jeering remark to the carpenter as to the sensible practice of ventilating a ship's quarter-deck. I know he popped into the mate's cabin to impart the fact to him because the whiskers came on deck, as it were by chance, and stole glances at me from below—for signs of lunacy or drunkenness, I suppose.

A little before supper, feeling more restless than ever, I rejoined, for a moment, my second self. And to find him sitting so quietly was surprising, like something against nature, inhuman.

I developed my plan in a hurried whisper.

"I shall stand in as close as I dare and then put her round. I will presently find means to smuggle you out of here into the sail-locker, which communicates with the lobby. But there is an opening, a sort of square for hauling the sails out, which gives straight on the quarter-deck and which is never closed in fine weather, so as to give air to the sails. When the ship's way is deadened in stays and all the hands are aft at the main-braces you will have a clear road to slip out and get overboard through the open quarter-deck port. I've had them both fastened up. Use a rope's end to lower yourself into the water so as to avoid a splash—you know. It could be heard and cause some beastly complication."

He kept silent for a while, then whispered, "I understand."

"I won't be there to see you go," I began with an effort. "The rest . . . I only hope I have understood, too."

"You have. From first to last"—and for the first time there seemed to be a faltering, something strained in his whisper. He caught hold of my arm, but the ringing of the supper bell made me start. He didn't, though; he only released his grip.

After supper I didn't come below again till well past eight o'clock. The faint, steady breeze was loaded with dew; and the wet, darkened sails held all there was of propelling power in it. The night, clear and starry, sparkled darkly, and the opaque, lightless patches shifting slowly against the low stars were the drifting islets. On the port bow there was a big one more distant and shadowily imposing by the great space of sky it eclipsed.

On opening the door I had a back view of my very own self looking at a chart. He had come out of the recess and was standing near the table.

"Quite dark enough," I whispered.

He stepped back and leaned against my bed with a level, quiet glance. I sat on the couch. We had nothing to say to each other. Over our heads the officer of the watch moved here and there. Then I heard him move quickly. I knew what that meant. He was making for the companion; and presently his voice was outside my door.

"We are drawing in pretty fast, sir. Land looks rather close."

"Very well," I answered. "I am coming on deck directly."

I waited till he was gone out of the cuddy, then rose. My double moved too. The time had come to exchange our last whispers, for neither of us was ever to hear each other's natural voice.

"Look here!" I opened a drawer and took out three sovereigns. "Take this anyhow. I've got six and I'd give you the lot, only I must keep a little money to buy some fruit and vegetables for the crew from native boats as we go through Sunda Straits."

He shook his head.

"Take it," I urged him, whispering desperately. "No one can tell what—"

He smiled and slapped meaningly the only pocket of the sleeping-jacket. It was not safe, certainly. But I produced a large old silk handkerchief of mine, and tying the three pieces of gold in a corner, pressed it on him. He was touched, I suppose, because he took it at last and tied it quickly round his waist under the jacket, on his bare skin.

Our eyes met; several seconds elapsed, till, our glances still mingled, I extended my hand and turned the lamp out. Then I passed through the cuddy, leaving the door of my room wide open. . . . "Steward!"

He was still lingering in the pantry in the greatness of his zeal, giving a rub-up to a plated cruet stand the last thing before going to bed. Being careful not to wake up the mate, whose room was opposite, I spoke in an undertone.

He looked round anxiously. "Sir!"

"Can you get me a little hot water from the galley?"

"I am afraid, sir, the galley fire's been out for some time now."

"Go and see."

He flew up the stairs.

"Now," I whispered, loudly, into the saloon—too loudly, perhaps, but I was afraid I couldn't make a sound. He was by my side in an instant—the double captain slipped past the stairs—through a tiny dark passage . . . a sliding door. We were in the sail-locker, scrambling on our knees over the sails. A sudden thought struck me. I saw myself wandering barefooted, bareheaded, the sun beating on my dark poll. I snatched off my floppy hat and tried hurriedly in the dark to ram it on my other self. He dodged and fended off silently. I wonder what he thought had come to me before he understood and suddenly desisted. Our hands met gropingly, lingered united in a steady, motionless clasp for a second. . . . No word was breathed by either of us when they separated.

I was standing quietly by the pantry door when the steward returned.

"Sorry, sir. Kettle barely warm. Shall I light the spirit-lamp?"

"Never mind."

I came out on deck slowly. It was now a matter of conscience to shave the land as close as possible—for now he must go overboard whenever the ship was put in stays. Must! There could be no going back for him. After a moment I walked over to leeward and my heart flew into my mouth at the nearness of the land on the bow. Under any other circumstances I would not have held on a minute longer. The second mate had followed me anxiously.

I looked on till I felt I could command my voice.

"She will weather," I said then in a quiet tone.

"Are you going to try that, sir?" he stammered out incredulously.

I took no notice of him and raised my tone enough to be heard by the helmsman.

"Keep her good full."

"Good full, sir."

The wind fanned my cheek, the sails slept, the world was silent. The strain of watching the dark loom of the land grow bigger and denser was too much for me. I had shut my eyes—because the ship must go closer. She must! The stillness was intolerable. Were we standing still?

When I opened my eyes the second view started my heart with a thump. The black southern hill of Koh-ring seemed to hang right over the ship like a towering fragment of the everlasting night. On that enormous mass of blackness there was not a gleam to be seen, not a sound to be heard. It was gliding irresistibly towards us and yet seemed already within reach of the hand. I saw the vague figures of the watch grouped in the waist, gazing in awed silence.

"Are you going on, sir?" inquired an unsteady voice at my elbow.

I ignored it. I had to go on.

"Keep her full. Don't check her way. That won't do now," I said warningly.

"I can't see the sails very well," the helmsman answered me, in strange, quavering tones.

Was she close enough? Already she was, I won't say in the shadow of the land, but in the very blackness of it, already swallowed up as it were, gone too close to be recalled, gone from me altogether.

"Give the mate a call," I said to the young man who stood at my elbow as still as death. "And turn all hands up."

My tone had a borrowed loudness reverberated from the height of the land. Several voices cried out together: "We are all on deck, sir."

Then stillness again, with the great shadow gliding closer, towering higher, without a light, without a sound. Such a hush had fallen on the ship that she might have been a bark of the dead floating in slowly under the very gate of Erebus.

"My God! Where are we?"

It was the mate moaning at my elbow. He was thunderstruck, and as it were deprived of the moral support of his whiskers. He clapped his hands and absolutely cried out, "Lost!"

"Be quiet," I said, sternly.

He lowered his tone, but I saw the shadowy gesture of his despair. "What are we doing here?"

"Looking for the land wind."

He made as if to tear his hair, and addressed me recklessly.

"She will never get out. You have done it, sir. I knew it'd end in something like this. She will never weather, and you are too close now to stay. She'll drift ashore before she's round. O my God!"

I caught his arm as he was raising it to batter his poor devoted head, and shook it violently.

"She's ashore already," he wailed, trying to tear himself away.

"Is she? . . . Keep good full there!"

"Good full, sir," cried the helmsman in a frightened, thin, child-like voice.

I hadn't let go the mate's arm and went on shaking it. "Ready about, do you hear? You go forward"—shake—"and stop there"—shake—"and hold your noise"—shake—"and see these head-sheets properly overhauled"—shake, shake—shake.

And all the time I dared not look towards the land lest my heart should fail me. I released my grip at last and he ran forward as if fleeing for dear life.

I wondered what my double there in the sail-locker thought of this commotion. He was able to hear everything—and perhaps he was able to understand why, on my conscience, it had to be thus close—no less. My first order "Hard alee!" re-echoed ominously under the towering shadow of Koh-ring as if I had shouted in a mountain gorge. And then I watched the land intently. In that smooth water and light wind it was impossible to feel the ship coming-to. No! I could not feel her. And my second self was making now ready to slip out and lower himself overboard. Perhaps he was gone already . . . ?

The great black mass brooding over our very mastheads began to pivot away from the ship's side silently. And now I forgot the secret stranger ready to depart, and remembered only that I was a total stranger to the ship. I did not know her. Would she do it? How was she to be handled?

I swung the mainyard and waited helplessly. She was perhaps stopped, and her very fate hung in the balance, with the black mass of Koh-ring like the gate of the everlasting night towering over her taffrail. What would she do now? Had she way on her yet? I stepped to the side swiftly, and on the shadowy water I could see nothing except a faint phosphorescent flash revealing the glassy smoothness of the sleeping surface. It was impossible to tell—and I had not learned yet the feel of my ship. Was she moving? What I needed was something easily seen, a piece of paper, which I could throw overboard and watch. I had nothing on me. To run down for it I didn't dare. There was no time. All at once my strained, yearning stare distinguished a white object floating within a yard of the ship's side. White on the black water. A phosphorescent flash passed under it. What was that thing? . . . I recognised my own floppy hat. It must have fallen off his head . . . and he didn't bother. Now I had what I wanted—the saving mark for my eyes. But I hardly thought of my other self, now gone from the ship, to be hidden for ever from all friendly faces, to be a fugitive and a vagabond on the earth, with no brand of the curse on his sane forehead to stay a slaying hand . . . too proud to explain.

And I watched the hat—the expression of my sudden pity for his mere flesh. It had been meant to save his homeless head from the dangers of the sun. And now—behold—it was saving the ship, by serving me for a mark to help out the ignorance of my strangeness. Ha! It was drifting forward, warning me just in time that the ship had gathered sternway.

"Shift the helm," I said in a low voice to the seaman standing still like a statue.

The man's eyes glistened wildly in the binnacle light as he jumped round to the other side and spun round the wheel.

I walked to the break of the poop. On the overshadowed deck all hands stood by the forebraces waiting for my order. The stars ahead seemed to be gliding from right to left. And all was so still in the world that I heard the quiet remark, "She's round," passed in a tone of intense relief between two seamen.

"Let go and haul."

The foreyards ran round with a great noise, amidst cheery cries. And now the frightful whiskers made themselves heard giving various orders. Already the ship was drawing ahead. And I was alone with her. Nothing! no one in the world should stand now between us, throwing a shadow on the way of silent knowledge and mute affection, the perfect communion of a seaman with his first command.

Walking to the taffrail, I was in time to make out, on the very edge of a darkness thrown by a towering black mass like the very

Erebus - Hell

gateway of Erebus—yes, I was in time to catch an evanescent glimpse of my white hat left behind to mark the spot where the secret sharer of my cabin and of my thoughts, as though he were my second self, had lowered himself into the water to take his punishment: a free man, a proud swimmer striking out for a new destiny.

PREFACE TO

THE NIGGER OF THE "NARCISSUS"

A work that aspires, however humbly, to the condition of art should carry its justification in every line. And art itself may be defined as a single-minded attempt to render the highest kind of justice to the visible universe, by bringing to light the truth, manifold and one, underlying its every aspect. It is an attempt to find in its forms, in its colours, in its light, in its shadows, in the aspects of matter and in the facts of life, what of each is fundamental, what is enduring and essential—their one illuminating and convincing quality—the very truth of their existence. The artist, then, like the thinker or the scientist, seeks the truth and makes his appeal. Impressed by the aspect of the world the thinker plunges into ideas, the scientist into facts—whence, presently, emerging they make their appeal to those qualities of our being that fit us best for the hazardous enterprise of living. They speak authoritatively to our common-sense, to our intelligence, to our desire of peace or to our desire of unrest; not seldom to our prejudices, sometimes to our fears, often to our egotism—but always to our credulity. And their words are heard with reverence, for their concern is with weighty matters: with the cultivation of our minds and the proper care of our bodies; with the attainment of our ambitions; with the perfection of the means and the glorification of our precious aims.

It is otherwise with the artist.

Confronted by the same enigmatical spectacle the artist descends within himself, and in that lonely region of stress and strife, if he be deserving and fortunate, he finds the terms of his appeal. His appeal is made to our less obvious capacities: to that part of our nature which, because of the warlike conditions of existence, is necessarily kept out of sight within the more resisting and hard qualities—like the vulnerable body within the steel armour. His appeal is less loud, more profound, less distinct, more stirring—and sooner forgotten. Yet its effect endures for ever. The changing wisdom of successive generations discards ideas, questions facts, demolishes theories. But the artist appeals to that part of our being which is not dependent on wisdom: to that in us which is a gift and not an acquisition—and, therefore, more permanently enduring. He speaks to our capacity for delight and wonder, to the sense of mystery surrounding our lives; to our sense of pity, and beauty, and pain; to the latent feeling of fellowship with all creation—and to the subtle but invincible, conviction of solidarity that knits together the loneliness of innumerable hearts: to the solidarity in dreams, in joy, in sorrow, in aspirations, in illusions, in hope, in fear, which binds men to each other, which binds together all humanity—the dead to the living and the living to the unborn.

It is only some such train of thought, or rather of feeling, that can in a measure explain the aim of the attempt, made in the tale which follows, to present an unrestful episode in the obscure lives of a few individuals out of all the disregarded multitude of the bewildered, the simple and the voiceless. For, if there is any part of truth in the belief confessed above, it becomes evident that there is not a place of splendour or a dark corner of the earth that does not deserve, if only a passing glance of wonder and pity. The motive, then, may be held to justify the matter of the work; but this preface, which is simply an avowal of endeavour, cannot end here—for the avowal is not yet complete.

Fiction—if it at all aspires to be art—appeals to temperament. And in truth it must be, like painting, like music, like all art, the appeal of one temperament to all the other innumerable temperaments whose subtle and resistless power endows passing events with their true meaning, and creates the moral, the emotional atmosphere of the place and time. Such an appeal, to be effective, must be an impression conveyed through the senses; and, in fact, it cannot be made in any other way, because temperament, whether individual or collective, is not amenable to persuasion. All art, therefore, appeals primarily to the senses, and the artistic aim when expressing itself in written words must also make its appeal through the senses, if its high desire is to reach the secret spring of responsive emotions. It must strenuously aspire to the plasticity of sculpture, to the colour of painting, and to the magic suggestiveness of music—which is the art of arts. And it is only through complete, unswerving devotion to the perfect blending of form and substance; it is only through an unremitting, never-discouraged care for the shape and ring of sentences that an approach can be made to plasticity, to colour; and the light of magic suggestiveness may be brought to play for an evanescent instant over the commonplace surface of words: of the old, old words, worn thin, defaced by ages of careless usage.

The sincere endeavour to accomplish that creative task, to go as far on that road as his strength will carry him, to go undeterred by faltering, weariness or reproach, is the only valid justification for the worker in prose. And if his conscience is clear, his answer to those who, in the fulness of a wisdom which looks for immediate profit, demand specifically to be edified, consoled, amused; who demand to be promptly improved, or encouraged, or frightened, or shocked, or charmed, must run thus:—My task which I am trying to achieve is, by the power of the written word, to make you hear, to make you feel—it is, before all, to make you *see*. That—and no more, and it is everything. If I succeed, you shall find there according to your deserts: encouragement, consolation, fear, charm—all you demand; and, perhaps, also that glimpse of truth for which you have forgotten to ask.

To snatch in a moment of courage, from the remorseless rush of time, a passing phase of life is only the beginning of the task. The task approached in tenderness and faith is to hold up unquestioningly, without choice and without fear, the rescued fragment before all eyes and in the light of a sincere mood. It is to show its vibration, its colour, its form; and through its movement, its form, and its colour, reveal the substance of its truth—disclose its inspiring secret: the stress and passion within the core of each convincing moment. In a single-minded attempt of that kind, if one be deserving and fortunate, one may perchance attain to such clearness of sincerity that at last the presented vision of regret or pity, of terror or mirth, shall awaken in the hearts of the beholders that feeling of unavoidable solidarity; of the solidarity in mysterious origin, in toil, in joy, in hope, in uncertain fate, which binds men to each other and all mankind to the visible world.

It is evident that he who, rightly or wrongly, holds by the convictions expressed above cannot be faithful to any one of the temporary formulas of his craft. The enduring part of them—the truth which each only imperfectly veils—should abide with him as the most precious of his possessions, but they all: Realism, Romanticism, Naturalism, even the unofficial sentimentalism (which, like the poor, is exceedingly difficult to get rid of); all these gods must, after a short period of fellowship, abandon him—even on the very threshold of the temple—to the stammerings of his conscience and to the outspoken consciousness of the difficulties of his work. In that uneasy solitude the supreme cry of Art for Art, even, loses the exciting ring of its apparent immortality. It sounds far off. It has ceased to be a cry, and is heard only as a whisper, often incomprehensible, but at times, and faintly, encouraging.

Sometimes, stretched at ease in the shade of a roadside tree, we watch the motions of a labourer in a distant field, and after a time, begin to wonder languidly as to what the fellow may be at. We watch the movements of his body, the waving of his arms, we see him bend down, stand up, hesitate, begin again. It may add to the charm of an idle hour to be told the purpose of his exertions. If we know he is trying to lift a stone, to dig a ditch, to uproot a stump, we look with a more real interest at his efforts; we are disposed to condone the jar of his agitation upon the restfulness of the landscape; and even, if in a brotherly frame of mind, we may bring ourselves to forgive his failure. We understood his object, and, after all, the fellow has tried, and perhaps he had not the strength, and perhaps he had not the knowledge. We forgive, go on our way—and forget.

And so it is with the workman of art. Art is long and life is short, and success is very far off. And thus, doubtful of strength to travel so far, we talk a little about the aim—the aim of art, which, like life itself, is inspiring, difficult—obscured by mists. It is not in the clear logic of a triumphant conclusion; it is not in the unveiling of one of those heartless secrets which are called the Laws of Nature. It is not less great, but only more difficult.

To arrest, for the space of a breath, the hands busy about the work of the earth, and compel men entranced by the sight of distant goals to glance for a moment at the surrounding vision of form and colour, of sunshine and shadows; to make them pause for a look, for a sigh, for a smile—such is the aim, difficult and evanescent, and reserved only for a very few to achieve. But sometimes, by the deserving and the fortunate, even that task is accomplished. And when it is accomplished—behold!—all the truth of life is there: a moment of vision, a sigh, a smile—and the return to an eternal rest.

THE NIGGER OF THE "NARCISSUS"

A Tale of the Sea

I

Mr. Baker, chief mate of the ship *Narcissus,* stepped in one stride out of his lighted cabin into the darkness of the quarter-deck. Above his head, on the break of the poop, the night-watchman rang a double stroke. It was nine o'clock. Mr. Baker, speaking up to the man above him, asked—"Are all the hands aboard, Knowles?"

The man limped down the ladder, then said reflectively:—

"I think so, sir. All our old chaps are there, and a lot of new men has come. . . . . They must be all there."

"Tell the boatswain to send all hands aft," went on Mr. Baker; "and tell one of the youngsters to bring a good lamp here. I want to muster our crowd."

The main deck was dark aft, but halfway from forward, through the open doors of the forecastle, two streaks of brilliant light cut the shadow of the quiet night that lay upon the ship. A hum of voices was heard there, while port and starboard, in the illuminated doorways, silhouettes of moving men appeared for a moment, very black, without relief, like figures cut out of sheet tin. The ship was ready for sea. The carpenter had driven in the last wedge of the main-hatch battens, and, throwing down his maul, had wiped his face with great deliberation, just on the stroke of five. The decks had been swept, the windlass oiled and made ready to heave up the anchor; the big tow-rope lay in long bights along one side of the main deck, with one end carried up and hung over the bows, in readiness for the tug that would come paddling and hissing noisily, hot and smoky, in the limpid, cool quietness of the early morning. The captain was ashore, where he had been engaging some new hands to make up his full crew; and, the work of the day over, the ship's officers had kept out of the way, glad of a little breathing-time. Soon after dark the few liberty-men and the new hands began to arrive in shore-boats rowed by white-clad Asiatics, who clamoured fiercely for payment before coming alongside the gangway-ladder. The feverish and shrill babble of Eastern language struggled against the masterful tones of tipsy seamen, who argued against brazen claims and dishonest hopes by profane shouts. The resplendent and bestarred peace of the East was torn into squalid tatters by howls of rage and shrieks of lament raised over sums ranging from five annas to half a rupee; and every soul afloat in Bombay Harbour became aware that the new hands were joining the *Narcissus*.

Gradually the distracting noise had subsided. The boats came no longer in splashing clusters of three or four together, but dropped alongside singly, in a subdued buzz of expostulation cut short by a "Not a pice more! You go to the devil!" from some man staggering up the accommodation-ladder—a dark figure, with a long bag poised on the shoulder. In the forecastle the newcomers, upright and swaying amongst corded boxes and bundles of bedding, made friends with the old hands, who sat one above another in the two tiers of bunks, gazing at their future shipmates with glances critical but friendly. The two forecastle lamps were turned up high, and shed an intense hard glare; shore-going hard hats were pushed far on the backs of heads, or rolled about on the deck amongst the chain-cables; white collars, undone, stuck out on each side of red faces; big arms in white sleeves gesticulated; the growling voices hummed steady amongst bursts of laughter and hoarse calls. "Here, sonny, take that bunk! . . . . Don't you do it! . . . . What's your last ship? . . . . I know her. . . . . Three years ago, in Puget Sound . . . . This here berth leaks, I tell you! . . . . Come on; give us a chance to swing that chest! . . . . Did you bring a bottle, any of you shore toffs? . . . . Give us a bit of 'baccy. . . . . I know her; her skipper drank himself to death. . . . . He was a dandy boy! . . . . Liked his lotion inside, he did! . . . . No! . . . . Hold your row, you chaps! . . . . I tell you, you came on board a hooker, where they get their money's worth out of poor Jack, by——! . . . ."

A little fellow, called Craik and nicknamed Belfast, abused the ship violently, romancing on principle, just to give the new hands something to think over. Archie, sitting aslant on his sea-chest, kept his knees out of the way, and pushed the needle steadily through a white patch in a pair of blue trousers. Men in black jackets and stand-up collars, mixed with men bare-footed, bare-armed, with coloured shirts open on hairy chests, pushed against one another in the middle of the forecastle. The group swayed, reeled, turning upon itself with the motion of a scrimmage, in a haze of tobacco smoke. All were speaking together, swearing at every second word. A Russian Finn, wearing a yellow shirt with pink stripes, stared upwards, dreamy-eyed, from under a mop of tumbled hair. Two young giants with smooth, baby faces—two Scandinavians—helped each other to spread their bedding, silent, and smiling placidly at the tempest of good-humoured and meaningless curses. Old Singleton, the oldest able seaman in the ship, sat apart on the deck right under the lamps, stripped to the waist, tattooed like a cannibal chief all over his powerful chest and enormous biceps. Between the blue and red patterns his white skin gleamed like satin; his bare back was propped against the heel of the bowsprit, and he held a book at arm's length before his big, sunburnt face. With his spectacles and a venerable white beard, he resembled a learned and savage patriarch, the incarnation of barbarian wisdom serene in the blasphemous turmoil of the world. He was intensely absorbed, and, as he turned the pages an expression of grave surprise would pass over his rugged features. He was reading "Pelham." The popularity of Bulwer Lytton in the forecastles of Southern-going ships is a wonderful and bizarre phenomenon. What ideas do his polished and so curiously insincere sentences awaken in the simple minds of the big children who people those dark and wandering places of the earth? What meaning can their rough, inexperienced souls find in the elegant verbiage of his pages? What excitement?—what forgetfulness?—what appeasement? Mystery! Is it the fascination of the incomprehensible?—is it the charm of the impossible? Or are those beings who exist beyond the pale of life stirred by his tales as by an enigmatical disclosure of a resplendent world that exists within the frontier of infamy and filth, within that border of dirt and hunger, of misery and dissipation, that comes down on all sides to the water's edge of the incorruptible ocean, and is the only thing they know of life, the only thing they see of surrounding land—those life-long prisoners of the sea? Mystery!

Singleton, who had sailed to the southward since the age of twelve, who in the last forty-five years had lived (as we had calculated from his papers) no more than forty months ashore—old Singleton, who boasted, with the mild composure of long years well spent, that generally from the day he was paid off from one ship till the day he shipped in another he seldom was in a condition to distinguish daylight—old Singleton sat unmoved in the clash of voices and cries, spelling through "Pelham" with slow labour, and lost in an absorption profound enough to resemble a trance. He breathed regularly. Every time he turned the book in his enormous and blackened hands the muscles of his big white arms rolled slightly under the smooth skin. Hidden by the white moustache, his lips, stained with tobacco-juice that trickled down the long beard, moved in inward whisper. His bleared eyes gazed fixedly from behind the glitter of black-rimmed glasses. Opposite to him, and on a level with his face, the ship's cat sat on the barrel of the windlass in the pose of a crouching chimera, blinking its green eyes at its old friend. It seemed to meditate a leap on to the old man's lap over the bent back of the ordinary seaman who sat at Singleton's feet. Young Charley was lean and long-necked. The ridge of his backbone made a chain of small hills under the old shirt. His face of a street-boy—a face precocious, sagacious, and ironic, with deep downward folds on each side of the thin, wide mouth—hung low over his bony knees. He was learning to make a lanyard knot with a bit of an old rope. Small drops of perspiration stood out on his bulging forehead; he sniffed strongly from time to time, glancing out of the corners of his restless eyes at the old seaman, who took no notice of the puzzled youngster muttering at his work.

The noise increased. Little Belfast seemed, in the heavy heat of the forecastle, to boil with facetious fury. His eyes danced; in the crimson of his face, comical as a mask, the mouth yawned black, with strange grimaces. Facing him, a half-undressed man held his sides, and, throwing his head back, laughed with wet eyelashes. Others stared with amazed eyes. Men sitting doubled up in the upper bunks smoked short pipes, swinging bare brown feet above the heads of those who, sprawling below on sea-chests, listened, smiling stupidly or scornfully. Over the white rims of berths stuck out heads with blinking eyes; but the bodies were lost in the gloom of those places, that resembled narrow niches for coffins in a white-washed and lighted mortuary. Voices buzzed louder. Archie, with compressed lips, drew himself in, seemed to shrink into a smaller space, and sewed steadily, industrious and dumb. Belfast shrieked like an inspired Dervish:—". . . . So I seez to him, boys, seez I, 'Beggin' yer pardon, sorr,' seez I to that second mate of that steamer—'beggin' your-r-r pardon, sorr, the Board of Trade must 'ave been drunk when they granted you your certificate!' 'What do you say, you——!' seez he, comin' at me like a mad bull . . . . all in his white clothes; and I up with my tarpot and capsizes it all over his blamed lovely face and his lovely jacket. . . . 'Take that!' seez I. 'I am a sailor, anyhow, you nosing, skipper-licking, useless, sooperfloos bridge-stanchion, you! That's the kind of man I am!' shouts I. . . . . You should have seed him skip, boys! Drowned, blind with tar, he was! So . . . ."

"Don't 'ee believe him! He never upset no tar; I was there!" shouted somebody. The two Norwegians sat on a chest side by side, alike and placid, resembling a pair of love-birds on a perch, and with round eyes stared innocently; but the Russian Finn, in the racket of explosive shouts and rolling laughter, remained motionless, limp and dull, like a deaf man without a backbone. Near him Archie smiled at his needle. A broad-chested, slow-eyed newcomer spoke deliberately to Belfast during an exhausted lull in the noise:—"I wonder any of the mates here are alive yet with such a chap as you on board! I concloode they ain't that bad now, if you had the taming of them, sonny."

"Not bad! Not bad!" screamed Belfast. "If it wasn't for us sticking together. . . . . Not bad! They ain't never bad when they ain't got a chawnce, blast their black 'arts. . . . ." He foamed, whirling his arms, then suddenly grinned and, taking a tablet of black tobacco out of his pocket, bit a piece off with a funny show of ferocity. Another new hand—a man with shifty eyes and a yellow hatchet face, who had been listening open-mouthed in the shadow of the midship locker—observed in a squeaky voice:—"Well, it's a 'omeward trip, anyhow. Bad or good, I can do it hall on my 'ed—s'long as I get 'ome. And I can look after my rights! I will show 'em!" All the heads turned towards him. Only the ordinary seaman and the cat took no notice. He stood with arms akimbo, a little fellow with white eyelashes. He looked as if he had known all the degradations and all the furies. He looked as if he had been cuffed, kicked, rolled in the mud; he looked as if he had been scratched, spat upon, pelted with unmentionable filth . . . . and he smiled with a sense of security at the faces around. His ears were bending down under the weight of his battered hard hat. The torn tails of his black coat flapped in fringes about the calves of his legs. He unbuttoned the only two buttons that remained and every one saw he had no shirt under it. It was his deserved misfortune that those rags which nobody could possibly be supposed to own looked on him as if they had been stolen. His neck was long and thin; his eyelids were red: rare hairs hung about his jaws: his shoulders were peaked and drooped like the broken wings of a bird; all his left side was caked with mud which showed that he had lately slept in a wet ditch. He had saved his inefficient carcass from violent destruction by running away from an American ship where, in a moment of forgetful folly, he had dared to engage himself; and he had knocked about for a fortnight ashore in the native quarter, cadging for drinks, starving, sleeping on rubbish-heaps, wandering in sunshine: a startling visitor from a world of nightmares. He stood repulsive and smiling in the sudden silence. This clean white forecastle was his refuge; the place where he could be lazy; where he could wallow, and lie and eat—and curse the food he ate; where he could display his talents for shirking work, for cheating, for cadging; where he could find surely some one to wheedle and some one to bully—and where he would be paid for doing all this. They all knew him. Is there a spot on earth where such a man is unknown, an ominous survival testifying to the eternal fitness of lies and impudence? A taciturn long-armed shellback, with hooked fingers, who had been lying on his back smoking, turning in his bed to examine him dispassionately, then, over his head, sent a long jet of clear saliva towards the door. They all knew him! He was the man that cannot steer, that cannot splice, that dodges the work on dark nights; that, aloft, holds on frantically with both arms and legs, and swears at the wind, the sleet, the darkness; the man who curses the sea while others work. The man who is the last out and the first in when all hands are called. The man who can't do most things and won't do the rest. The pet of philanthropists and self-seeking landlubbers. The sympathetic and deserving creature that knows all about his rights, but knows nothing of courage, of endurance, and of the unexpressed faith, of the unspoken loyalty that knits together a ship's company. The independent offspring of the ignoble freedom of the slums full of disdain and hate for the austere servitude of the sea.

Some one cried at him: "What's your name?"—"Donkin," he said, looking round with a cheerful effrontery.—"What are you?" asked another voice.—"Why, a sailor like you, old man," he replied, in a tone that meant to be hearty but was impudent.—"Blamme if you don't look a blamed sight worse than a broken-down fireman," was the comment in a convinced mutter. Charley lifted his head and piped in a cheeky voice: "He is a man and a sailor"—then wiping his nose with the back of his hand bent down industriously over his bit of rope. A few laughed. Others stared doubtfully. The ragged newcomer was indignant.—"That's a fine way to welcome a chap into a fo'c'sle," he snarled. "Are you men or a lot of 'artless cannybals?"—"Don't take your shirt off for a word, shipmate," called out Belfast, jumping up in front, fiery, menacing, and friendly at the same time.—"Is that 'ere bloke blind?" asked the indomitable scarecrow, looking right and left with affected surprise. "Can't 'ee see I 'aven't got no shirt?"

He held both his arms out crosswise and shook the rags that hung over his bones with dramatic effect.

"'Cos why?" he continued very loud. "The bloody Yankees been tryin' to jump my guts hout 'cos I stood up for my rights like a good 'un. I ham a Henglishman, I ham. They set upon me an' I 'ad to run. That's why. A'n't yer never seed a man 'ard up? Yah! What kind of blamed ship is this? I'm dead broke. I 'aven't got nothink. No bag, no bed, no blanket, no shirt—not a bloomin' rag but what I stand in. But I 'ad the 'art to stand hup agin' them Yankees. 'As any of you 'art enough to spare a pair of old pants for a chum?"

He knew how to conquer the naïve instincts of that crowd. In a moment they gave him their compassion, jocularly, contemptuously, or surlily; and at first it took the shape of a blanket thrown at him as he stood there with the white skin of his limbs showing his human kinship through the black fantasy of his rags. Then a pair of old shoes fell at his muddy feet. With a cry:—"From under," a rolled-up pair of trousers, heavy with tar stains, struck him on the shoulder. The gust of their benevolence sent a wave of sentimental pity through their doubting hearts. They were touched by their own readiness to alleviate a shipmate's misery. Voices cried:—"We will fit you out, old man." Murmurs: "Never seed seech a hard case. . . . . Poor beggar . . . . . I've got an old singlet. . . . . Will that be of any use to you? . . . . Take it, matey. . . . ." Those friendly murmurs filled the forecastle. He pawed around with his naked foot, gathering the things in a heap and looked about for more. Unemotional Archie perfunctorily contributed to the pile an old cloth cap with the peak torn off. Old Singleton, lost in the serene regions of fiction, read on unheeding. Charley, pitiless with the wisdom of youth, squeaked:—"If you want brass buttons for your new unyforms I've got two for you." The filthy object of universal charity shook his fist at the youngster.—"I'll make you keep this 'ere fo'c'sle clean, young feller," he snarled viciously. "Never you fear. I will learn you to be civil to an able seaman, you hignorant hass." He glared harmfully, but saw Singleton shut his book, and his little beady eyes began to roam from berth to berth.—"Take that bunk by the door there—it's pretty fair," suggested Belfast. So advised, he gathered the gifts at his feet, pressed them in a bundle against his breast, then looked cautiously at the Russian Finn, who stood on one side with an unconscious gaze, contemplating, perhaps, one of those weird visions that haunt men of his race. "Get out of my road, Dutchy," said the victim of Yankee brutality. The Finn did not move—did not hear. "Get out, blast ye," shouted the other, shoving him aside with his elbow. "Get out, you blanked deaf and dumb fool. Get out." The man staggered, recovered himself, and gazed at the speaker in silence.—"Those damned furriners should be kept hunder," opined the amiable Donkin to the forecastle. "If you don't teach 'em their place they put on you like hanythink." He flung all his worldly possessions into the empty bed-place, gauged with another shrewd look the risks of the proceeding, then leaped up to the Finn, who stood pensive and dull.—"I'll teach you to swell around," he yelled. "I'll plug your eyes for you, you blooming square-head." Most of the men were now in their bunks and the two had the forecastle clear to themselves. The development of the destitute Donkin aroused interest. He danced all in tatters before the amazed Finn, squaring from a distance at the heavy, unmoved face. One or two men cried encouragingly: "Go it, Whitechapel!" settling themselves luxuriously in their beds to survey the fight. Others shouted: "Shut yer row! . . . . Go an' put yer 'ed in a bag!. . . . ." The hubbub was recommencing. Suddenly many heavy blows struck with a handspike on the deck above boomed like discharges of small cannon through the forecastle. Then the boatswain's voice rose outside the door with an authoritative note in its drawl:—"D'ye hear, below there? Lay aft! Lay aft to muster all hands!"

There was a moment of surprised stillness. Then the forecastle floor disappeared under men whose bare feet flopped on the planks as they sprang clear out of their berths. Caps were rooted for amongst tumbled blankets. Some, yawning, buttoned waistbands. Half-smoked pipes were knocked hurriedly against woodwork and stuffed under pillows. Voices growled:—"What's up? . . . . Is there no rest for us?" Donkin yelped:—"If that's the way of this ship, we'll 'ave to change hall that. . . . . You leave me alone. . . . . I will soon. . . . ." None of the crowd noticed him. They were lurching in twos and threes through the doors, after the manner of merchant Jacks who cannot go out of a door fairly, like mere landsmen. The votary of change followed them. Singleton, struggling into his jacket, came last, tall and fatherly, bearing high his head of weatherbeaten sage on the body of an old athlete. Only Charley remained alone in the white glare of the empty place, sitting between the two rows of iron links that stretched into the narrow gloom forward. He pulled hard at the strands in a hurried endeavour to finish his knot. Suddenly he started up, flung the rope at the cat, and skipped after the black tom that went off leaping sedately over chain compressors, with the tail carried stiff and upright, like a small flag pole.

Outside the glare of the steaming forecastle the serene purity of the night enveloped the seamen with its soothing breath, with its tepid breath flowing under the stars that hung countless above the mastheads in a thin cloud of luminous dust. On the town side the blackness of the water was streaked with trails of light which undulated gently on the slight ripples, similar to filaments that float rooted to the shore. Rows of other lights stood away in straight lines as if drawn up on parade between towering buildings; but on the other side of the harbour sombre hills arched high their black spines, on which, here and there, the point of a star resembled a spark fallen from the sky. Far off, Byculla way, the electric lamps at the dock gates shone on the end of lofty standards with a glow blinding and frigid like captive ghosts of some evil moons. Scattered all over the dark polish of the roadstead, the ships at anchor floated in perfect stillness under the feeble gleam of their riding-lights, looming up, opaque and bulky, like strange and monumental structures abandoned by men to an everlasting repose.

Before the cabin door Mr. Baker was mustering the crew. As they stumbled and lurched along past the mainmast, they could see aft his round, broad face with a white paper before it, and beside his shoulder the sleepy head, with dropped eyelids, of the boy, who held, suspended at the end of his raised arm, the luminous globe of a lamp. Even before the shuffle of naked soles had ceased along the decks, the mate began to call over the names. He called distinctly in a serious tone befitting this roll-call to unquiet loneliness, to inglorious and obscure struggle, or to the more trying endurance of small privations and wearisome duties. As the chief mate read out a name, one of the men would answer: "Yes, sir!" or "Here!" and, detaching himself from the shadowy mob of heads visible above the blackness of starboard bulwarks, would step bare-footed into the circle of light, and in two noiseless strides pass into the shadows on the port side of the quarter-deck. They answered in divers tones: in thick mutters, in clear, ringing voices; and some, as if the whole thing had been an outrage on their feelings, used an injured intonation: for discipline is not ceremonious in merchant ships, where the sense of hierarchy is weak, and where all feel themselves equal before the unconcerned immensity of the sea and the exacting appeal of the work.

Mr. Baker read on steadily:—"Hanssen—Campbell—Smith—Wamibo. Now, then, Wamibo. Why don't you answer? Always got to call your name twice." The Finn emitted at last an uncouth grunt, and, stepping out, passed through the patch of light, weird and gaudy, with the face of a man marching through a dream. The mate went on faster:—"Craik—Singleton—Donkin. . . . . O Lord!" he involuntarily ejaculated as the incredibly dilapidated figure appeared in the light. It stopped: it uncovered pale gums and long, upper teeth in a malevolent grin.—"Is there anythink wrong with me, Mister Mate?" it asked, with a flavour of insolence in the forced simplicity of its tone. On both sides of the deck subdued titters were heard.—"That'll do. Go over," growled Mr. Baker, fixing the new hand with steady blue eyes. And Donkin vanished suddenly out of the light into the dark group of mustered men, to be slapped on the back and to hear flattering whispers. Round him men muttered to one another:—"He ain't afeard, he'll give sport to 'em, see if he don't. . . . . Reg'lar Punch and Judy show. . . . . Did ye see the mate start at him? . . . . Well! Damme, if I ever! . . . ."

The last man had gone over, and there was a moment of silence while the mate peered at his list.—"Sixteen, seventeen," he muttered. "I am one hand short, bosun," he said aloud. The big westcountryman at his elbow, swarthy and bearded like a gigantic Spaniard, said in a rumbling bass:—"There's no one left forward, sir. I had a look round. He ain't aboard, but he may turn up before daylight."—"Ay. He may or he may not," commented the mate; "can't make out that last name. It's all a smudge. . . . . That will do, men. Go below."

The indistinct and motionless group stirred, broke up, began to move forward.

"Wait!" cried a deep, ringing voice.

All stood still. Mr. Baker, who had turned away yawning, spun round open-mouthed. At last, furious, he blurted out:—"What's this? Who said 'Wait'? What . . . ."

But he saw a tall figure standing on the rail. It came down and pushed through the crowd, marching with a heavy tread towards the light on the quarter-deck. Then again the sonorous voice said with insistence:—"Wait!" The lamplight lit up the man's body. He was tall. His head was away up in the shadows of lifeboats that stood on skids above the deck. The whites of his eyes and teeth gleamed distinctly, but the face was indistinguishable. His hands were big and seemed gloved.

Mr. Baker advanced intrepidly. "Who are you? How dare you . . . ." he began.

The boy, amazed like the rest, raised the light to the man's face. It was black. A surprised hum—a faint hum that sounded like the suppressed mutter of the word "Nigger"—ran along the deck and escaped out into the night. The nigger seemed not to hear. He balanced himself where he stood in a swagger that marked time. After a moment he said calmly:—"My name is Wait—James Wait."

"Oh!" said Mr. Baker. Then, after a few seconds of smouldering silence, his temper blazed out. "Ah! Your name is Wait. What of that? What do you want? What do you mean, coming shouting here?"

The nigger was calm, cool, towering, superb. The men had approached and stood behind him in a body. He overtopped the tallest by half a head. He said: "I belong to the ship." He enunciated distinctly, with soft precision. The deep, rolling tones of his voice filled the deck without effort. He was naturally scornful, unaffectedly condescending, as if from his height of six foot three he had surveyed all the vastness of human folly and had made up his mind not to be too hard on it. He went on:—"The captain shipped me this morning. I couldn't get aboard sooner. I saw you all aft as I came up the ladder, and could see directly you were mustering the crew. Naturally I called out my name. I thought you had it on your list, and would understand. You misapprehended." He stopped short. The folly around him was confounded. He was right as ever, and as ever ready to forgive. The disdainful tones had ceased, and, breathing heavily, he stood still, surrounded by all these white men. He held his head up in the glare of the lamp—a head vigorously modelled into deep shadows and shining lights—a head powerful and misshapen with a tormented and flattened face—a face pathetic and brutal: the tragic, the mysterious, the repulsive mask of a nigger's soul.

Mr. Baker, recovering his composure, looked at the paper close. "Oh, yes; that's so. All right, Wait. Take your gear forward," he said.

Suddenly the nigger's eyes rolled wildly, became all whites. He put his hand to his side and coughed twice, a cough metallic, hollow, and tremendously loud; it resounded like two explosions in a vault; the dome of the sky rang to it, and the iron plates of the ship's bulwarks seemed to vibrate in unison; then he marched off forward with the others. The officers lingering by the cabin door could hear him say: "Won't some of you chaps lend a hand with my dunnage? I've got a chest and a bag." The words, spoken sonorously, with an even intonation, were heard all over the ship, and the question was put in a manner that made refusal impossible. The short, quick shuffle of men carrying something heavy went away forward, but the tall figure of the nigger lingered by the main hatch in a knot of smaller shapes. Again he was heard asking: "Is your cook a coloured gentleman?" Then a disappointed and disapproving "Ah! h'm!" was his comment upon the information that the cook happened to be a mere white man. Yet, as they went all together towards the forecastle, he condescended to put his head through the galley door and boom out inside a magnificent "Good evening, doctor!" that made all the saucepans ring. In the dim light the cook dozed on the coal locker in front of the captain's supper. He jumped up as if he had been cut with a whip, and dashed wildly on deck to see the backs of several men going away laughing. Afterwards, when talking about that voyage he used to say:—"The poor fellow had scared me. I thought I had seen the devil." The cook had been seven years in the ship with the same captain. He was a serious-minded man with a wife and three children, whose society he enjoyed on an average one month out of twelve. When on shore he took his family to church twice every Sunday. At sea he went to sleep every evening with his lamp turned up full, a pipe in his mouth, and an open Bible in his hand. Some one had always to go during the night to put out the light, take the book from his hand, and the pipe from between his teeth. "For"—Belfast used to say, irritated and complaining—"some night, you stupid cookie, you'll swallow your ould clay, and we will have no cook."—"Ah! sonny, I am ready for my Maker's call . . . . wish you all were," the other would answer with a benign serenity that was altogether imbecile and touching. Belfast outside the galley door danced with vexation. "You holy fool! I don't want you to die," he howled, looking up with furious, quivering face and tender eyes. "What's the hurry? you blessed wooden-headed ould heretic, the divvle will have you soon enough. Think of Us . . . . of Us . . . . of Us!" And he would go away, stamping, spitting aside, disgusted and worried; while the other, stepping out, saucepan in hand, hot, begrimed, and placid, watched with a superior, cock-sure smile the back of his "queer little man" reeling in a rage. They were great friends.

Mr. Baker, lounging over the after-hatch, sniffed the humid night in the company of the second mate.—"Those West India niggers run fine and large—some of them . . . . Ough! . . . . Don't they? A fine, big man that, Mr. Creighton. Feel him on a rope. Hey? Ough! I will take him into my watch, I think." The second mate, a fair, gentlemanly young fellow, with a resolute face and a splendid physique, observed quietly that it was just about what he expected. There could be felt in his tone some slight bitterness which Mr. Baker very kindly set himself to argue away. "Come, come, young man," he said, grunting between words. "Come! Don't be too greedy. You had that big Finn in your watch all the voyage. I will do what's fair. You may have those two young Scandinavians and I . . . . Ough! . . . . I get the nigger, and will take that . . . . Ough! that cheeky costermonger chap in a black frock-coat. I'll make him . . . . Ough! . . . . make him toe the mark, or my . . . . Ough! . . . . name isn't Baker. Ough! Ough! Ough!"

He grunted thrice—ferociously. He had that trick of grunting so between his words and at the end of sentences. It was a fine, effective grunt that went well with his menacing utterance, with his heavy, bull-necked frame, his jerky, rolling gait; with his big, seamed face, his steady eyes, and sardonic mouth. But its effect had been long ago discounted by the men. They liked him; Belfast—who was a favourite, and knew it—mimicked him, not quite behind his back. Charley—but with greater caution—imitated his walk. Some of his sayings became established, daily quotations in the forecastle. Popularity can go no farther! Besides, all hands were ready to admit that on a fitting occasion the mate could "jump down a fellow's throat in a reg'lar Western Ocean style."

Now he was giving his last orders. "Ough! . . . . You, Knowles! Call all hands at four, I want . . . . Ough! . . . . to heave short before the tug comes. Look out for the captain. I am going to lay down in my clothes. . . . . Ough! . . . . Call me when you see the boat coming. Ough! Ough! . . . . The old man is sure to have something to say when he comes aboard," he remarked to Creighton. "Well, good-night. . . . . Ough! A long day before us to-morrow. . . . . Ough! . . . . Better turn in now. Ough! Ough!"

Upon the dark deck a band of light flashed, then a door slammed, and Mr. Baker was gone into his neat cabin. Young Creighton stood leaning over the rail, and looked dreamily into the night of the East. And he saw in it a long country lane, a lane of waving leaves and dancing sunshine. He saw stirring boughs of old trees outspread, and framing in their arch the tender, the caressing blueness of an English sky. And through the arch a girl in a clear dress, smiling under a sunshade, seemed to be stepping out of the tender sky.

At the other end of the ship the forecastle, with only one lamp burning now, was going to sleep in a dim emptiness traversed by loud breathings, by sudden short sighs. The double row of berths yawned black, like graves tenanted by uneasy corpses. Here and there a curtain of gaudy chintz, half drawn, marked the resting-place of a sybarite. A leg hung over the edge very white and lifeless. An arm stuck straight out with a dark palm turned up, and thick fingers half closed. Two light snores, that did not synchronise, quarrelled in funny dialogue. Singleton stripped again—the old man suffered much from prickly heat—stood cooling his back in the doorway, with his arms crossed on his bare and adorned chest. His head touched the beam of the deck above. The nigger, half undressed, was busy casting adrift the lashing of his box, and spreading his bedding in an upper berth. He moved about in his socks, tall and noiseless, with a pair of braces beating about his heels. Amongst the shadows of stanchions and bowsprit, Donkin munched a piece of hard ship's bread, sitting on the deck with upturned feet and restless eyes; he held the biscuit up before his mouth in the whole fist, and snapped his jaws at it with a raging face. Crumbs fell between his outspread legs. Then he got up.

"Where's our water-cask?" he asked in a contained voice.

Singleton, without a word, pointed with a big hand that held a short smouldering pipe. Donkin bent over the cask, drank out of the tin, splashing the water, turned round and noticed the nigger looking at him over the shoulder with calm loftiness. He moved up sideways.

"There's a blooming supper for a man," he whispered bitterly. "My dorg at 'ome wouldn't 'ave it. It's fit enouf for you an' me. 'Ere's a big ship's fo'c'sle! . . . . Not a blooming scrap of meat in the kids. I've looked in all the lockers. . . . ."

The nigger stared like a man addressed unexpectedly in a foreign language. Donkin changed his tone:—"Giv' us a bit of 'baccy, mate," he breathed out confidentially, "I 'aven't 'ad smoke or chew for the last month. I am rampin' mad for it. Come on, old man."

"Don't be familiar," said the nigger. Donkin started and sat down on a chest near by, out of sheer surprise. "We haven't kept pigs together," continued James Wait in a deep undertone. "Here's your tobacco." Then, after a pause, he asked:—"What ship?"—"*Golden State,*" muttered Donkin indistinctly, biting the tobacco. The nigger whistled low.—"Ran?" he said curtly. Donkin nodded: one of his cheeks bulged out.—"In course I ran," he mumbled. "They booted the life hout of one Dago chap on the passage 'ere, then started on me. I cleared hout 'ere."—"Left your dunnage behind?"—"Yes, dunnage and money," answered Donkin, raising his voice a little; "I got nothink. No clothes, no bed. A bandy-legged little Hirish chap 'ere 'as give me a blanket. . . . . Think I'll go an' sleep in the fore topmast staysail tonight."

He went on deck trailing behind his back a corner of the blanket. Singleton, without a glance, moved slightly aside to let him pass. The nigger put away his shore togs and sat in clean working clothes on his box, one arm stretched over his knees. After staring at Singleton for some time he asked without emphasis:—"What kind of ship is this? Pretty fair? Eh?"

Singleton didn't stir. A long while after he said, with unmoved face:—"Ship! . . . . Ships are all right. It is the men in them!"

He went on smoking in the profound silence. The wisdom of half a century spent in listening to the thunder of the waves had spoken unconsciously through his old lips. The cat purred on the windlass. Then James Wait had a fit of roaring, rattling cough, that shook him, tossed him like a hurricane, and flung him panting with staring eyes headlong on his sea-chest. Several men woke up. One said sleepily out of his bunk: "'Struth! what a blamed row!"—"I have a cold on my chest," gasped Wait.—"Cold! you call it," grumbled the man; "should think 'twas something more. . . ."—"Oh! you think so," said the nigger upright and loftily scornful again. He climbed into his berth and began coughing persistently while he put his head out to glare all round the forecastle. There was no further protest. He fell back on the pillow, and could be heard there wheezing regularly like a man oppressed in his sleep.

Singleton stood at the door with his face to the light and his back to the darkness. And alone in the dim emptiness of the sleeping forecastle he appeared bigger, colossal, very old; old as Father Time himself, who should have come there into this place as quiet as a sepulchre to contemplate with patient eyes the short victory of sleep, the consoler. Yet he was only a child of time, a lonely relic of a devoured and forgotten generation. He stood, still strong, as ever unthinking; a ready man with a vast empty past and with no future, with his childlike impulses and his man's passions already dead within his tattooed breast. The men who could understand his silence were gone—those men who knew how to exist beyond the pale of life and within sight of eternity. They had been strong, as those are strong who know neither doubts nor hopes. They had been impatient and enduring, turbulent and devoted, unruly and faithful. Well-meaning people had tried to represent those men as whining over every mouthful of their food; as going about their work in fear of their lives. But in truth they had been men who knew toil, privation, violence, debauchery—but knew not fear, and had no desire of spite in their hearts. Men hard to manage, but easy to inspire; voiceless men—but men enough to scorn in their hearts the sentimental voices that bewailed the hardness of their fate. It was a fate unique and their own; the capacity to bear it appeared to them the privilege of the chosen! Their generation lived inarticulate and indispensable, without knowing the sweetness of affections or the refuge of a home—and died free from the dark menace of a narrow grave. They were the everlasting children of the mysterious sea. Their successors are the grown-up children of a discontented earth. They are less naughty, but less innocent; less profane, but perhaps also less believing; and if they had learned how to speak they have also learned how to whine. But the others were strong and mute: they were effaced, bowed and enduring, like stone caryatides that hold up in the night the lighted halls of a resplendent and glorious edifice. They are gone now—and it does not matter. The sea and the earth are unfaithful to their children: a truth, a faith, a generation of men goes—and is forgotten, and it does not matter! Except, perhaps, to the few of those who believed the truth, confessed the faith—or loved the men.

A breeze was coming. The ship that had been lying tide-rode swung to a heavier puff; and suddenly the slack of the chain cable between the windlass and the hawse-pipe clinked, slipped forward an inch, and rose gently off the deck with a startling suggestion as of unsuspected life that had been lurking stealthily in the iron. In the hawse-pipe the grinding links sent through the ship a sound like a low groan of a man sighing under a burden. The strain came on the windlass, the chain tautened like a string, vibrated—and the handle of the screw-brake moved in slight jerks. Singleton stepped forward.

Till then he had been standing meditative and unthinking, reposeful and hopeless, with a face grim and blank—a sixty-year-old child of the mysterious sea. The thoughts of all his lifetime could have been expressed in six words, but the stir of those things that were as much part of his existence as his beating heart called up a gleam of alert understanding upon the sternness of his aged face. The flame of the lamp swayed, and the old man, with knitted and bushy eyebrows, stood over the brake, watchful and motionless in the wild saraband of dancing shadows. Then the ship, obedient to the call of her anchor, forged ahead slightly and eased the strain. The cable relieved, hung down, and after swaying imperceptibly to and fro dropped with a loud tap on the hard wood planks. Singleton seized the high lever, and, by a violent throw forward of his body, wrung out another half-turn from the brake. He recovered himself, breathed largely, and remained for awhile glaring down at the powerful and compact engine that squatted on the deck at his feet, like some quiet monster—a creature amazing and tame.

"You . . . . hold!" he growled at it masterfully, in the incult tangle of his white beard.

II

Next morning, at daylight, the *Narcissus* went to sea.

A slight haze blurred the horizon. Outside the harbour the measureless expanse of smooth water lay sparkling like a floor of jewels, and as empty as the sky. The short black tug gave a pluck to windward, in the usual way, then let go the rope, and hovered for a moment on the quarter with her engines stopped; while the slim, long hull of the ship moved ahead slowly under lower topsails. The loose upper canvas blew out in the breeze with soft round contours, resembling small white clouds snared in the maze of ropes. Then the sheets were hauled home, the yards hoisted, and the ship became a high and lonely pyramid, gliding, all shining and white, through the sunlit mist. The tug turned short round and went away towards the land. Twenty-six pairs of eyes watched her low broad stern crawling languidly over the smooth swell between the two paddle-wheels that turned fast, beating the water with fierce hurry. She resembled an enormous and aquatic blackbeetle, surprised by the light, overwhelmed by the sunshine, trying to escape with ineffectual effort into the distant gloom of the land. She left a lingering smudge of smoke on the sky, and two vanishing trails of foam on the water. On the place where she had stopped a round black patch of soot remained, undulating on the swell—an unclean mark of the creature's rest.

The *Narcissus* left alone, heading south, seemed to stand resplendent and still upon the restless sea, under the moving sun. Flakes of foam swept past her sides; the water struck her with flashing blows; the land glided away, slowly fading; a few birds screamed on motionless wings over the swaying mastheads. But soon the land disappeared, the birds went away; and to the west the pointed sail of an Arab dhow running for Bombay, rose triangular and upright above the sharp edge of the horizon, lingered, and vanished like an illusion. Then the ship's wake, long and straight, stretched itself out through a day of immense solitude. The setting sun, burning on the level of the water, flamed crimson below the blackness of heavy rain clouds. The sunset squall, coming up from behind, dissolved itself into the short deluge of a hissing shower. It left the ship glistening from trucks to waterline, and with darkened sails. She ran easily before a fair monsoon, with her decks cleared for the night; and, moving along with her, was heard the sustained and monotonous swishing of the waves, mingled with the low whispers of men mustered aft for the setting of watches; the short plaint of some block aloft; or, now and then, a loud sigh of wind.

Mr. Baker, coming out of his cabin, called out the first name sharply before closing the door behind him. He was going to take charge of the deck. On the homeward trip, according to an old custom of the sea, the chief officer takes the first night-watch—from eight till midnight. So Mr. Baker, after he had heard the last "Yes, sir!" said moodily, "Relieve the wheel and look-out"; and climbed with heavy feet the poop ladder to windward. Soon after Mr. Creighton came down, whistling softly, and went into the cabin. On the doorstep the steward lounged, in slippers, meditative, and with his shirt-sleeves rolled up to the armpits. On the main deck the cook, locking up the galley doors, had an altercation with young Charley about a pair of socks. He could be heard saying impressively, in the darkness amidships: "You don't deserve a kindness. I've been drying them for you, and now you complain about the holes—and you swear, too! Right in front of me! If I hadn't been a Christian—which you ain't, you young ruffian—I would give you a clout on the head. . . . . Go away!" Men in couples or threes stood pensive or moved silently along the bulwarks in the waist. The first busy day of a homeward passage was sinking into the dull peace of resumed routine. Aft, on the high poop, Mr. Baker walked shuffling; grunted to himself in the pauses of his thoughts. Forward, the look-out man, erect between the flukes of the two anchors, hummed an endless tune, keeping his eyes fixed dutifully ahead in a vacant stare. A multitude of stars coming out into the clear night peopled the emptiness of the sky. They glittered, as if alive above the sea; they surrounded the running ship on all sides; more intense than the eyes of a staring crowd, and as inscrutable as the souls of men.

The passage had begun; and the ship, a fragment detached from the earth, went on lonely and swift like a small planet. Round her the abysses of sky and sea met in an unattainable frontier. A great circular solitude moved with her, ever changing and ever the same, always monotonous and always imposing. Now and then another wandering white speck, burdened with life, appeared far off—disappeared; intent on its own destiny. The sun looked upon her all day, and every morning rose with a burning, round stare of undying curiosity. She had her own future; she was alive with the lives of those beings who trod her decks; like that earth which had given her up to the sea, she had an intolerable load of regrets and hopes. On her lived timid truth and audacious lies; and, like the earth, she was unconscious, fair to see—and condemned by men to an ignoble fate. The august loneliness of her path lent dignity to the sordid inspiration of her pilgrimage. She drove foaming to the southward, as if guided by the courage of a high endeavour. The smiling greatness of the sea dwarfed the extent of time. The days raced after one another, brilliant and quick like the flashes of a lighthouse, and the nights, eventful and short, resembled fleeting dreams.

The men had shaken into their places, and the half-hourly voice of the bells ruled their life of unceasing care. Night and day the head and shoulders of a seaman could be seen aft by the wheel, outlined high against sunshine or starlight, very steady above the stir of revolving spokes. The faces changed, passing in rotation. Youthful faces, bearded faces, dark faces: faces serene, or faces moody, but all akin with the brotherhood of the sea; all with the same attentive expression of eyes, carefully watching the compass or the sails. Captain Allistoun, serious, and with an old red muffler round his throat, all day long pervaded the poop. At night, many times he rose out of the darkness of the companion, such as a phantom above a grave, and stood watchful and mute under the stars, his night-shirt fluttering like a flag—then, without a sound, sank down again. He was born on the shores of the Pentland Firth. In his youth he attained the rank of harpooner in Peterhead whalers. When he spoke of that time his restless grey eyes became still and cold, like the loom of ice. Afterwards he went into the East Indian trade for the sake of change. He had commanded the *Narcissus* since she was built. He loved his ship, and drove her unmercifully; for his secret ambition was to make her accomplish some day a brilliantly quick passage which would be mentioned in nautical papers. He pronounced his owner's name with a sardonic smile, spoke but seldom to his officers, and reproved errors in a gentle voice, with words that cut to the quick. His hair was iron-grey, his face hard and of the colour of pump-leather. He shaved every morning of his life—at six—but once (being caught in a fierce hurricane eighty miles south-west of Mauritius) he had missed three consecutive days. He feared naught but an unforgiving God, and wished to end his days in a little house, with a plot of ground attached—far in the country—out of sight of the sea.

He, the ruler of that minute world, seldom descended from the Olympian heights of his poop. Below him—at his feet, so to speak—common mortals led their busy and insignificant lives. Along the main deck Mr. Baker grunted in a manner bloodthirsty and innocuous; and kept all our noses to the grindstone, being—as he once remarked—paid for doing that very thing. The men working about the deck were healthy and contented—as most seamen are, when once well out to sea. The true peace of God begins at any spot a thousand miles from the nearest land; and when He sends there the messengers of His might it is not in terrible wrath against crime, presumption, and folly, but paternally, to chasten simple hearts—ignorant hearts that know nothing of life, and beat undisturbed by envy or greed.

In the evening the cleared decks had a resposeful aspect, resembling the autumn of the earth. The sun was sinking to rest, wrapped in a mantle of warm clouds. Forward, on the end of the spare spars, the boatswain and the carpenter sat together with crossed arms; two men friendly, powerful, and deep-chested. Beside them the short, dumpy sailmaker—who had been in the Navy—related, between the whiffs of his pipe, impossible stories about Admirals. Couples tramped backwards and forwards, keeping step and balance without effort, in a confined space. Pigs grunted in the big pigstye. Belfast, leaning thoughtfully on his elbow, above the bars, communed with them through the silence of his meditation. Fellows with shirts open wide on sunburnt breasts sat upon the mooring bits, and all up the steps of the forecastle ladders. By the foremast a few discussed in a circle the characteristics of a gentleman. One said:—"It's money as does it." Another maintained:—"No, it's the way they speak." Lame Knowles stumped up with an unwashed face (he had the distinction of being the dirty man of the forecastle), and, showing a few yellow fangs in a shrewd smile, explained craftily that he "had seen some of their pants." The backsides of them—he had observed—were thinner than paper from constant sitting down in offices, yet otherwise they looked first-rate and would last for years. It was all appearance. "It was," he said, "bloomin' easy to be a gentleman when you had a clean job for life." They disputed endlessly, obstinate and childish; they repeated in shouts and with inflamed faces their amazing arguments; while the soft breeze, eddying down the enormous cavity of the foresail, that stood out distended above their bare heads, stirred the tumbled hair with a touch passing and light like an indulgent caress.

They were forgetting their toil, they were forgetting themselves. The cook approached to hear, and stood by, beaming with the inward consciousness of his faith, like a conceited saint unable to forget his glorious reward; Donkin, solitary and brooding over his wrongs on the forecastle-head, moved closer to catch the drift of the discussion below him; he turned his sallow face to the sea, and his thin nostrils moved, sniffing the breeze, as he lounged negligently by the rail. In the glow of sunset faces shone with interest, teeth flashed, eyes sparkled. The walking couples stood still suddenly, with broad grins; a man, bending over a washtub, sat up, entranced, with the soapsuds flecking his wet arms. Even the three petty officers listened leaning back, comfortably propped and with superior smiles. Belfast left off scratching the ear of his favourite pig, and, open mouthed, tried with eager eyes to have his say. He lifted his arms, grimacing and baffled. From a distance Charley screamed at the ring:—"I know about gentlemen morn'n any of you. I've been hintymate with 'em . . . . I've blacked their boots." The cook, craning his neck to hear better, was scandalised. "Keep your mouth shut when your elders speak, you impudent young heathen—you." "All right, old Hallelujah, I'm done," answered Charley, soothingly. At some opinion of dirty Knowles, delivered with an air of supernatural cunning, a ripple of laughter ran along, rose like a wave, burst with a startling roar. They stamped with both feet; they turned their shouting faces to the sky; many, spluttering, slapped their thighs; while one or two, bent double, gasped, hugging themselves with both arms like men in pain. The carpenter and the boatswain, without changing their attitude, shook with laughter where they sat; the sailmaker, charged with an anecdote about a Commodore, looked sulky; the cook was wiping his eyes with a greasy rag; and lame Knowles, astonished at his own success, stood in their midst showing a slow smile.

Suddenly the face of Donkin leaning high-shouldered over the after-rail became grave. Something like a weak rattle was heard through the forecastle door. It became a murmur; it ended in a sighing groan. The washerman plunged both his arms into the tub abruptly; the cook became more crestfallen than an exposed backslider; the boatswain moved his shoulders uneasily; the carpenter got up with a spring and walked away—while the sailmaker seemed mentally to give his story up, and began to puff at his pipe with sombre determination. In the blackness of the doorway a pair of eyes glimmered white, and big, and staring. Then James Wait's head protruding, became visible, as if suspended between the two hands that grasped a doorpost on each side of the face. The tassel of his blue woollen nightcap, cocked forward, danced gaily over his left eyelid. He stepped out in a tottering stride. He looked powerful as ever, but showed a strange and affected unsteadiness in his gait; his face was perhaps a trifle thinner, and his eyes appeared rather startling prominent. He seemed to hasten the retreat of departing light by his very presence; the setting sun dipped sharply, as though fleeing before our nigger; a black mist emanated from him; a subtle and dismal influence; a something cold and gloomy that floated out and settled on all the faces like a mourning veil. The circle broke up. The joy of laughter died on stiffened lips. There was not a smile left among all the ship's company. Not a word was spoken. Many turned their backs, trying to look unconcerned; others, with averted heads, sent half-reluctant glances out of the corners of their eyes. They resembled criminals conscious of misdeeds more than honest men distracted by doubt; only two or three stared frankly, but stupidly, with lips slightly open. All expected James Wait to say something, and, at the same time, had the air of knowing beforehand what he would say. He leaned his back against the doorpost, and with heavy eyes swept over us a glance domineering and pained, like a sick tyrant overawing a crowd of abject but untrustworthy slaves.

No one went away. They awaited in fascinated dread. He said ironically, with gasps between the words:—

"Thank you . . . . chaps. You . . . . are nice . . . . and . . . . quiet . . . . you are! Yelling so . . . . before . . . . the door . . . ."

He made a longer pause, during which he worked his ribs in an exaggerated labour of breathing. It was intolerable. Feet were shuffled. Belfast let out a groan; but Donkin above blinked his red eyelids with invisible eyelashes, and smiled bitterly over the nigger's head.

The nigger went on again with surprising ease. He gasped no more, and his voice rang, hollow and loud, as though he had been talking in an empty cavern. He was contemptuously angry.

"I tried to get a wink of sleep. You know I can't sleep o' nights. And you come jabbering near the door here like a blooming lot of old women. . . . . You think yourselves good shipmates. Do you? . . . . Much you care for a dying man!"

Belfast spun away from the pigstye. "Jimmy," he cried tremulously, "if you hadn't been sick I would——"

He stopped. The nigger waited awhile, then said, in a gloomy tone:—"You would. . . . . What? Go an' fight another such one as yourself. Leave me alone. It won't be for long. I'll soon die. . . . . It's coming right enough!"

Men stood around very still, breathing lightly, and with exasperated eyes. It was just what they had expected, and hated to hear, that idea of a stalking death, thrust at them many times a day like a boast and like a menace by this obnoxious nigger. He seemed to take a pride in that death which, so far, had attended only upon the ease of his life; he was overbearing about it, as if no one else in the world had ever been intimate with such a companion; he paraded it unceasingly before us with an affectionate persistence that made its presence indubitable, and at the same time incredible. No man could be suspected of such monstrous friendship! Was he a reality—or was he a sham—this ever-expected visitor of Jimmy's? We hesitated between pity and mistrust, while, on the slightest provocation, he shook before our eyes the bones of his bothersome and infamous skeleton. He was for ever trotting him out. He would talk of that coming death as though it had been already there, as if it had been walking the deck outside, as if it would presently come in to sleep in the only empty bunk; as if it had sat by his side at every meal. It interfered daily with our occupations, with our leisure, with our amusements. We had no songs and no music in the evening, because Jimmy (we all lovingly called him Jimmy, to conceal our hate of his accomplice) had managed, with that prospective decease of his, to disturb even Archie's mental balance. Archie was the owner of the concertina; but after a couple of stinging lectures from Jimmy he refused to play any more. He said:—"Yon's an uncanny joker. I dinna ken what's wrang wi' him, but there's something verra wrang, verra wrang. It's nae manner of use asking me. I won't play." Our singers became mute because Jimmy was a dying man. For the same reason no chap—as Knowles remarked—could "drive in a nail to hang his few poor rags upon," without being made aware of the enormity he committed in disturbing Jimmy's interminable last moments. At night, instead of the cheerful yell, "One bell! Turn out! Do you hear there? Hey! hey! hey! Show leg!" the watches were called man by man, in whispers, so as not to interfere with Jimmy's, possibly, last slumber on earth. True, he was always awake, and managed, as we sneaked out on deck, to plant in our backs some cutting remark that, for the moment, made us feel as if we had been brutes, and afterwards made us suspect ourselves of being fools. We spoke in low tones within the fo'c'sle as though it had been a church. We ate our meals in silence and dread, for Jimmy was capricious with his food, and railed bitterly at the salt meat, at the biscuits, at the tea, as at articles unfit for human consumption—"let alone for a dying man!" He would say:—"Can't you find a better slice of meat for a sick man who's trying to get home to be cured—or buried? But there! If I had a chance, you fellows would do away with it. You would poison me. Look at what you have given me!" We served him in his bed with rage and humility, as though we had been the base courtiers of a hated prince; and he rewarded us by his unconciliating criticism. He had found the secret of keeping for ever on the run the fundamental imbecility of mankind; he had the secret of life, that confounded dying man, and he made himself master of every moment of our existence. We grew desperate, and remained submissive. Emotional little Belfast was for ever on the verge of assault or on the verge of tears. One evening he confided to Archie:—"For a ha'penny I would knock his ugly black head off—the skulking dodger!" And the straightforward Archie pretended to be shocked! Such was the infernal spell which that casual St. Kitt's nigger had cast upon our guileless manhood! But the same night Belfast stole from the galley the officers' Sunday fruit pie, to tempt the fastidious appetite of Jimmy. He endangered not only his long friendship with the cook but also—as it appeared—his eternal welfare. The cook was overwhelmed with grief; he did not know the culprit but he knew that wickedness flourished; he knew that Satan was abroad amongst those men, whom he looked upon as in some way under his spiritual care. Whenever he saw three or four of us standing together he would leave his stove, to run out and preach. We fled from him; and only Charley (who knew the thief) affronted the cook with a candid gaze which irritated the good man. "It's you, I believe," he groaned, sorrowful, and with a patch of soot on his chin. "It's you. You are a brand for the burning! No more of YOUR socks in my galley." Soon, unofficially, the information was spread about that, should there be another case of stealing, our marmalade (an extra allowance: half a pound per man) would be stopped. Mr. Baker ceased to heap jocular abuse upon his favourites, and grunted suspiciously at all. The captain's cold eyes, high up on the poop, glittered mistrustful, as he surveyed us trooping in a small mob from halyards to braces for the usual evening pull at all the ropes. Such stealing in a merchant ship is difficult to check, and may be taken as a declaration by men of their dislike for their officers. It is a bad symptom. It may end in God knows what trouble. The *Narcissus* was still a peaceful ship, but mutual confidence was shaken. Donkin did not conceal his delight. We were dismayed.

Then illogical Belfast reproached our nigger with great fury. James Wait, with his elbow on the pillow, choked, gasped out:—"Did I ask you to bone the dratted thing? Blow your blamed pie. It has made me worse—you little Irish lunatic, you!" Belfast, with scarlet face and trembling lips, made a dash at him. Every man in the forecastle rose with a shout. There was a moment of wild tumult. Some one shrieked piercingly:—"Easy, Belfast! Easy! . . . ." We expected Belfast to strangle Wait without more ado. Dust flew. We heard through it the nigger's cough, metallic and explosive like a gong. Next moment we saw Belfast hanging over him. He was saying plaintively:—"Don't! Don't, Jimmy! Don't be like that. An angel couldn't put up with ye—sick as ye are." He looked round at us from Jimmy's bedside, his comical mouth twitching, and through tearful eyes; then he tried to put straight the disarranged blankets. The unceasing whisper of the sea filled the forecastle. Was James Wait frightened, or touched, or repentant? He lay on his back with a hand to his side, and as motionless as if his expected visitor had come at last. Belfast fumbled about his feet, repeating with emotion:—"Yes. We know. Ye are bad, but . . . . just say what ye want done, and . . . . We all know ye are bad—very bad. . . . ." No! Decidely James Wait was not touched or repentant. Truth to say, he seemed rather startled. He sat up with incredible suddenness and ease. "Ah! You think I am bad, do you?" he said gloomily, in his clearest baritone voice (to hear him speak sometimes you would never think there was anything wrong with that man). "Do you? . . . . Well, act according! Some of you haven't sense enough to put a blanket shipshape over a sick man. There! Leave it alone! I can die anyhow!" Belfast turned away limply with a gesture of discouragement. In the silence of the forecastle, full of interested men, Donkin pronounced distinctly:—"Well, I'm blowed!" and sniggered. Wait looked at him.

He looked at him in a quite friendly manner. Nobody could tell what would please our incomprehensible invalid: but for us the scorn of that snigger was hard to bear.

Donkin's position in the forecastle was distinguished but unsafe. He stood on the bad eminence of a general dislike. He was left alone; and in his isolation he could do nothing but think of the gales of the Cape of Good Hope and envy us the possession of warm clothing and waterproofs. Our sea-boots, our oilskin coats, our well-filled sea-chests, were to him so many causes for bitter meditation: he had none of those things, and he felt instinctively that no man, when the need arose, would offer to share them with him. He was impudently cringing to us and systematically insolent to the officers. He anticipated the best results, for himself, from such a line of conduct—and was mistaken. Such natures forget that under extreme provocation men will be just—whether they want to be so or not. Donkin's insolence to long-suffering Mr. Baker became at last intolerable to us, and we rejoiced when the mate, one dark night, tamed him for good. It was done neatly, with great decency and decorum, and with little noise. We had been called—just before midnight—to trim the yards, and Donkin—as usual—made insulting remarks. We stood sleepily in a row with the forebrace in our hands waiting for the next order, and heard in the darkness a scuffly trampling of feet, an exclamation of surprise, sounds of cuffs and slaps, suppressed, hissing whispers:—"Ah! Will you!" . . . . "Don't! . . . . Don't!" . . . . "Then behave." . . . . "Oh! Oh! . . . ." Afterwards there were soft thuds mixed with the rattle of iron things as if a man's body had been tumbling helplessly amongst the main-pump rods. Before we could realise the situation, Mr. Baker's voice was heard very near and a little impatient:—"Haul away, men! Lay back on that rope!" And we did lay back on the rope with great alacrity. As if nothing had happened, the chief mate went on trimming the yards with his usual and exasperating fastidiousness. We didn't at the time see anything of Donkin, and did not care. Had the chief officer thrown him overboard, no man would have said as much as "Hallo! he's gone!" But, in truth, no great harm was done—even if Donkin did lose one of his front teeth. We perceived this in the morning, and preserved a ceremonious silence: the etiquette of the forecastle commanded us to be blind and dumb in such a case, and we cherished the decencies of our life more than ordinary landsmen respect theirs. Charley, with unpardonable want of *savoir vivre,* yelled out:—" 'Ave you been to your dentyst? . . . . Hurt ye, didn't it?" He got a box on the ear from one of his best friends. The boy was surprised, and remained plunged in grief for at least three hours. We were sorry for him, but youth requires even more discipline than age. Donkin grinned venomously. From that day he became pitiless; told Jimmy that he was a "black fraud"; hinted to us that we were an imbecile lot, daily taken in by a vulgar nigger. And Jimmy seemed to like the fellow!

Singleton lived untouched by human emotions. Taciturn and unsmiling, he breathed amongst us—in that alone resembling the rest of the crowd. We were trying to be decent chaps, and found it jolly difficult; we oscillated between the desire of virtue and the fear of ridicule; we wished to save ourselves from the pain of remorse, but did not want to be made the contemptible dupes of our sentiment. Jimmy's hateful accomplice seemed to have blown with his impure breath undreamt-of subtleties into our hearts. We were disturbed and cowardly. That we knew. Singleton seemed to know nothing, understand nothing. We had thought him till then as wise as he looked, but now we dared, at times, suspect him of being stupid—from old age. One day, however, at dinner, as we sat on our boxes round a tin dish that stood on the deck within the circle of our feet, Jimmy expressed his general disgust with men and things in words that were particularly disgusting. Singleton lifted his head. We became mute. The old man, addressing Jimmy, asked:—"Are you dying?" Thus interrogated, James Wait appeared horribly startled and confused. We all were startled. Mouths remained open; hearts thumped; eyes blinked; a dropped tin fork rattled in the dish; a man rose as if to go out, and stood still. In less than a minute Jimmy pulled himself together.—"Why? Can't you see I am?" he answered shakily. Singleton lifted a piece of soaked biscuit ("his teeth"—he declared—"had no edge on them now") to his lips.—"Well, get on with your dying," he said with venerable mildness; "don't raise a blamed fuss with us over that job. We can't help you." Jimmy fell back in his bunk, and for a long time lay very still wiping the perspiration off his chin. The dinner-tins were put away quickly. On deck we discussed the incident in whispers. Some showed a chuckling exultation. Many looked grave. Wamibo, after long periods of staring dreaminess, attempted abortive smiles; and one of the young Scandinavians, much tormented by doubt, ventured in the second dog-watch to approach Singleton (the old man did not encourage us much to speak to him) and ask sheepishly:—"You think he will die?" Singleton looked up.—"Why, of course he will die," he said deliberately. This seemed decisive. It was promptly imparted to every one by him who had consulted the oracle. Shy and eager, he would step up and with averted gaze recite his formula:—"Old Singleton says he will die." It was a relief! At last we knew that our compassion would not be misplaced, and we could again smile without misgivings—but we reckoned without Donkin. Donkin "didn't want to 'ave no truck with 'em dirty furriners." When Neillssen came to him with the news: "Singleton says he will die," he answered him by a spiteful "And so will you—you fat-headed Dutchman. Wish you Dutchmen were hall dead—'stead comin' takin' our money hinto your starvin' country." We were appalled. We perceived that after all Singleton's answer meant nothing. We began to hate him for making fun of us. All our certitudes were going; we were on doubtful terms with our officers; the cook had given us up for lost; we had overheard the boatswain's opinion that "we were a crowd of softies." We suspected Jimmy, one another, and even our very selves. We did not know what to do. At every insignificant turn of our humble life we met Jimmy overbearing and blocking the way, arm-in-arm with his awful and veiled familiar. It was a weird servitude.

It began a week after leaving Bombay and came on us stealthily like any other great misfortune. Every one had remarked that Jimmy from the first was very slack at his work; but we thought it simply the outcome of his philosophy of life. Donkin said:—"You put no more weight on a rope than a bloody sparrer." He disdained him. Belfast, ready for a fight, exclaimed provokingly:—"You don't kill yourself, old man!"—"Would YOU?" he retorted with extreme scorn—and Belfast retired. One morning, as we were washing decks, Mr. Baker called to him:—"Bring your broom over here, Wait." He strolled languidly. "Move yourself! Ough!" grunted Mr. Baker; "what's the matter with your hind legs?" He stopped dead short. He gazed slowly with eyes that bulged out, with an expression audacious and sad.—"It isn't my legs," he said, "it's my lungs." Everybody listened.—"What's . . . . Ough! . . . .

What's wrong with them?" inquired Mr. Baker. All the watch stood around on the wet deck, grinning, and with brooms or buckets in their hands. He said mournfully:—"Going—or gone. Can't you see I'm a dying man? I know it!" Mr. Baker was disgusted.—"Then why the devil did you ship aboard here?"—"I must live till I die—mustn't I?" he replied. The grins became audible.—"Go off the deck—get out of my sight," said Mr. Baker. He was nonplussed. It was an unique experience. James Wait, obedient, dropped his broom, and walked slowly forward. A burst of laughter followed him. It was too funny. All hands laughed. . . . . They laughed! . . . . Alas!

He became the tormentor of all our moments; he was worse than a nightmare. You couldn't see that there was anything wrong with him; a nigger does not show. He was not very fat—certainly—but then he was no leaner than other niggers we had known. He coughed often, but the most prejudiced person could perceive that, mostly, he coughed when it suited his purpose. He wouldn't, or couldn't, do his work—and he wouldn't lie-up. One day he would skip aloft with the best of them, and next time we would be obliged to risk our lives to get his limp body down. He was reported, he was examined; he was remonstrated with, threatened, cajoled, lectured. He was called into the cabin to interview the captain. There were wild rumours. It was said he had cheeked the old man; it was said he had frightened him. Charley maintained that the "skipper, weepin', 'as giv' 'im 'is blessin' an' a pot of jam." Knowles had it from the steward that the unspeakable Jimmy had been reeling against the cabin furniture; that he had groaned; that he had complained of general brutality and disbelief; and had ended by coughing all over the old man's meteorological journals which were then spread on the table. At any rate, Wait returned forward supported by the steward, who, in a pained and shocked voice, entreated us:—"Here! Catch hold of him, one of you. He is to lie-up." Jimmy drank a tin mugful of coffee, and, after bullying first one and then another, went to bed. He remained there most of the time, but when it suited him would come on deck and appear amongst us. He was scornful and brooding; he looked ahead upon the sea; and no one could tell what was the meaning of that black man sitting apart in a meditative attitude and as motionless as a carving.

He refused steadily all medicine; he threw sago and cornflour overboard till the steward got tired of bringing it to him. He asked for paregoric. They sent him a big bottle; enough to poison a wilderness of babies. He kept it between his mattress and the deal lining of the ship's side; and nobody ever saw him take a dose. Donkin abused him to his face, jeered at him while he gasped; and the same day Wait would lend him a warm jersey. Once Donkin reviled him for half an hour; reproached him with the extra work his malingering gave to the watch; and ended by calling him "a black-faced swine." Under the spell of our accursed perversity we were horror-struck. But Jimmy positively seemed to revel in that abuse. It made him look cheerful—and Donkin had a pair of old sea boots thrown at him. "Here, you East-end trash," boomed Wait, "you may have that."

At last Mr. Baker had to tell the captain that James Wait was disturbing the peace of the ship. "Knock discipline on the head—he will, Ough," grunted Mr. Baker. As a matter of fact, the starboard watch came as near as possible to refusing duty, when ordered one morning by the boatswain to wash out their forecastle. It appears Jimmy objected to a wet floor—and that morning we were in a compassionate mood. We thought the boatswain a brute, and, practically, told him so. Only Mr. Baker's delicate tact prevented an all-fired row: he refused to take us seriously. He came bustling forward, and called us many unpolite names, but in such a hearty and seamanlike manner that we began to feel ashamed of ourselves. In truth, we thought him much too good a sailor to annoy him willingly; and after all Jimmy might have been a fraud—probably was! The forecastle got a clean up that morning; but in the afternoon a sick-bay was fitted up in the deck-house. It was a nice little cabin opening on the deck, and with two berths. Jimmy's belongings were transported there, and then—notwithstanding his protests—Jimmy himself. He said he couldn't walk. Four men carried him on a blanket. He complained that he would have to die there alone, like a dog. We grieved for him, and were delighted to have him removed from the forecastle. We attended him as before. The galley was next door, and the cook looked in many times a day. Wait became a little more cheerful. Knowles affirmed having heard him laugh to himself in peals one day. Others had seen him walking about on deck at night. His little place, with the door ajar on a long hook, was always full of tobacco smoke. We spoke through the crack cheerfully, sometimes abusively, as we passed by, intent on our work. He fascinated us. He would never let doubt die. He overshadowed the ship. Invulnerable in his promise of speedy corruption he trampled on our self-respect, he demonstrated to us daily our want of moral courage; he tainted our lives. Had we been a miserable gang of wretched immortals, unhallowed alike by hope and fear, he could not have lorded it over us with a more pitiless assertion of his sublime privilege.

III

Meantime the *Narcissus,* with square yards, ran out of the fair monsoon. She drifted slowly, swinging round and round the compass, through a few days of baffling light airs. Under the patter of short warm showers, grumbling men whirled the heavy yards from side to side; they caught hold of the soaked ropes with groans and sighs, while their officers, sulky and dripping with rain water, unceasingly ordered them about in wearied voices. During the short respites they looked with disgust into the smarting palms of their stiff hands, and asked one another bitterly:—"Who would be a sailor if he could be a farmer?" All the tempers were spoilt, and no man cared what he said. One black night, when the watch, panting in the heat and half-drowned with the rain, had been through four mortal hours hunted from brace to brace, Belfast declared that he would "chuck going to sea for ever and go in a steamer." This was excessive, no doubt. Captain Allistoun, with great self-control, would mutter sadly to Mr. Baker:—"It is not so bad—not so bad," when he had managed to shove, and dodge, and manœuvre his smart ship through sixty miles in twenty-four hours. From the doorstep of the little cabin, Jimmy, chin in hand, watched our distasteful labours with insolent and melancholy eyes. We spoke to him gently—and out of his sight exchanged sour smiles.

Then, again, with a fair wind and under a clear sky, the ship went on piling up the South Latitude. She passed outside Madagascar and Mauritius without a glimpse of land. Extra lashings were put on the spare spars. Hatches were looked to. The steward in his leisure moments and with a worried air tried to fit washboards to the cabin doors. Stout canvas was bent with care. Anxious eyes looked to the westward, towards the cape of storms. The ship began to dip into a south-west swell, and the softly luminous sky of low latitudes took on a harder sheen from day to day above our heads: it arched high above the ship, vibrating and pale, like an immense dome of steel, resonant with the deep voice of freshening gales. The sunshine gleamed cold on the white curls of black waves. Before the strong breath of westerly squalls the ship, with reduced sail, lay slowly over, obstinate and yielding. She drove to and fro in the unceasing endeavour to fight her way through the invisible violence of the winds; she pitched headlong into dark smooth hollows; she struggled upwards over the snowy ridges of great running seas; she rolled, restless, from side to side, like a thing in pain. Enduring and valiant, she answered to the call of men; and her slim spars waving for ever in abrupt semicircles, seemed to beckon in vain for help towards the stormy sky.

It was a bad winter off the Cape that year. The relieved helmsmen came off flapping their arms, or ran stamping hard and blowing into swollen, red fingers. The watch on deck dodged the sting of cold sprays or, crouching in sheltered corners, watched dismally the high and merciless seas boarding the ship time after time in unappeasable fury. Water tumbled in cataracts over the forecastle doors. You had to dash through a waterfall to get into your damp bed. The men turned in wet and turned out stiff to face the redeeming and ruthless exactions of their glorious and obscure fate. Far aft, and peering watchfully to windward, the officers could be seen through the mist of squalls. They stood by the weather-rail, holding on grimly, straight and glistening in their long coats; then, at times, in the disordered plunges of the hard-driven ship, they appeared high up, attentive, tossing violently above the grey line of a clouded horizon, and in motionless attitudes.

They watched the weather and the ship as men on shore watch the momentous chances of fortune. Captain Allistoun never left the deck, as though he had been part of the ship's fittings. Now and then the steward, shivering, but always in shirt sleeves, would struggle towards him with some hot coffee, half of which the gale blew out of the cup before it reached the master's lips. He drank what was left gravely in one long gulp, while heavy sprays pattered loudly on his oilskin coat, the seas swishing broke about his high boots; and he never took his eyes off the ship. He watched her every motion; he kept his gaze riveted upon her as a loving man who watches the unselfish toil of a delicate woman upon the slender thread of whose existence is hung the whole meaning and joy of the world. We all watched her. She was beautiful and had a weakness. We loved her no less for that. We admired her qualities aloud, we boasted of them to one another, as though they had been our own, and the consciousness of her only fault we kept buried in the silence of our profound affection. She was born in the thundering peal of hammers beating upon iron, in black eddies of smoke, under a grey sky, on the banks of the Clyde. The clamorous and sombre stream gives birth to things of beauty that float away into the sunshine of the world to be loved by men. The *Narcissus* was one of that perfect brood. Less perfect than many perhaps, but she was ours, and, consequently, incomparable. We were proud of her. In Bombay, ignorant landlubbers alluded to her as that "pretty grey ship." Pretty! A scurvy meed of commendation! We knew she was the most magnificent sea-boat ever launched. We tried to forget that, like many good sea-boats, she was at times rather crank. She was exacting. She wanted care in loading and handling, and no one knew exactly how much care would be enough. Such are the imperfections of mere men! The ship knew, and sometimes would correct the presumptuous human ignorance by the wholesome discipline of fear. We had heard ominous stories about past voyages. The cook (technically a seaman, but in reality no sailor)—the cook, when unstrung by some misfortune, such as the rolling over of a saucepan, would mutter gloomily while he wiped the floor:—"There! Look at what she has done! Some voy'ge she will drown all hands! You'll see if she won't." To which the steward, snatching in the galley a moment to draw a breath in the hurry of his worried life, would remark philosophically:—"Those that see won't tell, anyhow. I don't want to see it." We derided those fears. Our hearts went out to the old man when he pressed her hard so as to make her hold her own, hold to every inch gained to windward; when he made her, under reefed sails, leap obliquely at enormous waves. Then men, knitted together aft into a ready group by the first sharp order of an officer coming to take charge of the deck in bad weather:—

"Keep handy the watch," stood admiring her valiance. Their eyes blinked in the wind; their dark faces were wet with drops of water more salt and bitter than human tears; beards and moustaches, soaked, hung straight and dripping like fine seaweed. They were fantastically misshapen; in high boots, in hats like helmets, and swaying clumsily, stiff and bulky in glistening oilskins, they resembled men strangely equipped for some fabulous adventure. Whenever she rose easily to a towering green sea, elbows dug ribs, faces brightened, lips murmured:—"Didn't she do it cleverly," and all the heads turning like one watched with sardonic grins the foiled wave go roaring to leeward, white with the foam of a monstrous rage. But when she had not been quick enough and, struck heavily, lay over trembling under the blow, we clutched at ropes, and looking up at the narrow bands of drenched and strained sails waving desperately aloft, we thought in our hearts:—"No wonder. Poor thing!"

The thirty-second day out of Bombay began inauspiciously. In the morning a sea smashed one of the galley doors. We dashed in through lots of steam and found the cook very wet and indignant with the ship:—"She's getting worse every day. She's trying to drown me in front of my own stove!" He was very angry. We pacified him, and the carpenter, though washed away twice from there, managed to repair the door. Through that accident our dinner was not ready till late, but it didn't matter in the end because Knowles, who went to fetch it, got knocked down by a sea and the dinner went over the side. Captain Allistoun, looking more hard and thin-lipped than ever, hung on to full topsails and foresail, and would not notice that the ship, asked to do too much, appeared to lose heart altogether for the first time since we knew her. She refused to rise, and bored her way sullenly through the seas. Twice running, as though she had been blind or weary of life, she put her nose deliberately into a big wave and swept the decks from end to end. As the boatswain observed with marked annoyance, while we were splashing about in a body to try and save a worthless wash-tub:—"Every blooming thing in the ship is going overboard this afternoon." Venerable Singleton broke his habitual silence and said with a glance aloft:—"The old man's in a temper with the weather, but it's no good bein' angry with the winds of heaven." Jimmy had shut his door, of course. We knew he was dry and comfortable within his little cabin, and in our absurd way were pleased one moment, exasperated the next, by that certitude. Donkin skulked shamelessly, uneasy and miserable. He grumbled:—"I'm perishin' with cold houtside in bloomin' wet rags, an' that 'ere black sojer sits dry on a blamed chest full of bloomin' clothes; blank his black soul!" We took no notice of him; we hardly gave a thought to Jimmy and his bosom friend. There was no leisure for idle probing of hearts. Sails blew adrift. Things broke loose. Cold and wet, we were washed about the deck while trying to repair damages. The ship tossed about, shaken furiously, like a toy in the hand of a lunatic. Just at sunset there was a rush to shorten sail before the menace of a sombre hail cloud. The hard gust of wind came brutal like the blow of a fist. The ship relieved of her canvas in time received it pluckily: she yielded reluctantly to the violent onset; then, coming up with a stately and irresistible motion, brought her spars to windward in the teeth of the screeching squall. Out of the abysmal darkness of the black cloud overhead white hail streamed on her, rattled on the rigging, leaped in handfuls off the yards, rebounded on the deck—round and gleaming in the murky turmoil like a shower of pearls. It passed away. For a moment a livid sun shot horizontally the last rays of sinister light between the hills of steep, rolling waves. Then a wild night rushed in—stamped out in a great howl that dismal remnant of a stormy day.

There was no sleep on board that night. Most seamen remember in their life one or two such nights of a culminating gale. Nothing seems left of the whole universe but darkness, clamour, fury—and the ship. And like the last vestige of a shattered creation she drifts, bearing an anguished remnant of sinful mankind, through the distress, tumult, and pain of an avenging terror. No one slept in the forecastle. The tin oil-lamp suspended on a long string, smoking, described wide circles; wet clothing made dark heaps on the glistening floor; a thin layer of water rushed to and fro. In the bed-places men lay booted, resting on elbows and with open eyes. Hung-up suits of oilskin swung out and in, lively and disquieting like reckless ghosts of decapitated seamen dancing in a tempest. No one spoke and all listened. Outside the night moaned and sobbed to the accompaniment of a continuous loud tremor as of innumerable drums beating far off. Shrieks passed through the air. Tremendous dull blows made the ship tremble while she rolled under the weight of the seas toppling on her deck. At times she soared up swiftly as if to leave this earth for ever, then during interminable moments fell through a void with all the hearts on board of her standing still, till a frightful shock, expected and sudden, started them off again with a big thump. After every dislocating jerk of the ship, Wamibo, stretched full length, his face on the pillow, groaned slightly with the pain of his tormented universe. Now and then, for the fraction of an intolerable second, the ship, in the fiercer burst of a terrible uproar, remained on her side, vibrating and still, with a stillness more appalling than the wildest motion. Then upon all those prone bodies a stir would pass, a shiver of suspense. A man would protrude his anxious head and a pair of eyes glistened in the sway of light, glaring wildly. Some moved their legs a little as if making ready to jump out. But several, motionless on their backs and with one hand gripping hard the edge of the bunk, smoked nervously with quick puffs, staring upwards; immobilised in a great craving for peace.

At midnight, orders were given to furl the fore and mizen topsails. With immense efforts men crawled aloft through a merciless buffeting, saved the canvas, and crawled down almost exhausted, to bear in panting silence the cruel battering of the seas. Perhaps for the first time in the history of the merchant service the watch, told to go below, did not leave the deck, as if compelled to remain there by the fascination of a venomous violence. At every heavy gust men, huddled together, whispered to one another:—"It can blow no harder"—and presently the gale would give them the lie with a piercing shriek, and drive their breath back into their throats. A fierce squall seemed to burst asunder the thick mass of sooty vapours; and above the wrack of torn clouds glimpses could be caught of the high moon rushing backwards with frightful speed over the sky, right into the wind's eye. Many hung their heads, muttering that it "turned their inwards out" to look at it. Soon the clouds closed up, and the world again became a raging, blind darkness that howled, flinging at the lonely ship salt sprays and sleet.

About half-past seven the pitchy obscurity round us turned a ghastly grey, and we knew that the sun had risen. This unnatural and threatening daylight, in which we could see one another's wild eyes and drawn faces, was only an added tax on our endurance. The horizon seemed to have come on all sides within arm's length of the ship. Into that narrowed circle furious seas leaped in, struck, and leaped out. A rain of salt, heavy drops flew aslant like mist. The main-topsail had to be goose-winged, and with stolid resignation every one prepared to go aloft once more; but the officers yelled, pushed back, and at last we understood that no more men would be allowed to go on the yard than were absolutely necessary for the work. As at any moment the masts were likely to be jumped out or blown overboard, we concluded that the captain didn't want to see all his crowd go over the side at once. That was reasonable. The watch then on duty, led by Mr. Creighton, began to struggle up the rigging. The wind flattened them against the ratlines; then, easing a little, would let them ascend a couple of steps; and again, with a sudden gust, pin all up the shrouds the whole crawling line in attitudes of crucifixion. The other watch plunged down on the main deck to haul up the sail. Men's heads bobbed up as the water flung them irresistibly from side to side. Mr. Baker grunted encouragingly in our midst, spluttering and blowing amongst the tangled ropes like an energetic porpoise. Favoured by an ominous and untrustworthy lull, the work was done without any one being lost either off the deck or from the yard. For the moment the gale seemed to take off, and the ship, as if grateful for our efforts, plucked up heart and made better weather of it.

At eight the men off duty, watching their chance, ran forward over the flooded deck to get some rest. The other half of the crew remained aft for their turn of "seeing her through her trouble," as they expressed it. The two mates urged the master to go below. Mr. Baker grunted in his ear:—"Ough! surely now . . . . Ough! . . . . confidence in us . . . . nothing more to do . . . . she must lay it out or go. Ough! Ough!" Tall young Mr. Creighton smiled down at him cheerfully:—". . . . She's right as a trivet! Take a spell, sir." He looked at them stonily with bloodshot, sleepless eyes. The rims of his eyelids were scarlet, and he moved his jaw unceasingly with a slow effort, as though he had been masticating a lump of india-rubber. He shook his head. He repeated:—"Never mind me. I must see it out—I must see it out," but he consented to sit down for a moment on the skylight, with his hard face turned unflinchingly to windward. The sea spat at it—and, stoical, it streamed with water as though he had been weeping. On the weather side of the poop the watch, hanging on to the mizen rigging and to one another, tried to exchange encouraging words. Singleton, at the wheel, yelled out:—"Look out for yourselves!" His voice reached them in a warning whisper. They were startled.

A big, foaming sea came out of the mist; it made for the ship, roaring wildly, and in its rush it looked as mischievous and discomposing as a madman with an axe. One or two, shouting, scrambled up the rigging; most, with a convulsive catch of the breath, held on where they stood. Singleton dug his knees under the wheel-box, and carefully eased the helm to the headlong pitch of the ship, but without taking his eyes off the coming wave. It towered close-to and high, like a wall of green glass topped with snow. The ship rose to it as though she had soared on wings, and for a moment rested poised upon the foaming crest, as if she had been a great sea-bird. Before we could draw breath a heavy gust struck her, another roller took her unfairly under the weather bow, she gave a toppling lurch, and filled her decks. Captain Allistoun leaped up, and fell; Archie rolled over him, screaming:—"She will rise!" She gave another lurch to leeward; the lower deadeyes dipped heavily; the men's feet flew from under them, and they hung kicking above the slanting poop. They could see the ship putting her side in the water, and shouted all together:—"She's going!" Forward the forecastle doors flew open, and the watch below were seen leaping out one after another, throwing their arms up; and, falling on hands and knees, scrambled aft on all fours along the high side of the deck, sloping more than the roof of a house. From leeward the seas rose, pursuing them; they looked wretched in a hopeless struggle, like vermin fleeing before a flood; they fought up the weather ladder of the poop one after another, half naked and staring wildly; and as soon as they got up they shot to leeward in clusters, with closed eyes, till they brought up heavily with their ribs against the iron stanchions of the rail; then, groaning, they rolled in a confused mass. The immense volume of water thrown forward by the last scend of the ship had burst the lee door of the forecastle. They could see their chests, pillows, blankets, clothing, come out floating upon the sea. While they struggled back to windward they looked in dismay. The straw beds swam high, the blankets, spread out, undulated; while the chests, waterlogged and with a heavy list, pitched heavily, like dismasted hulks, before they sank; Archie's big coat passed with outspread arms, resembling a drowned seaman floating with his head under water. Men were slipping down while trying to dig their fingers into the planks; others, jammed in corners, rolled enormous eyes. They all yelled unceasingly:—"The masts! Cut! Cut! . . . ." A black squall howled low over the ship, that lay on her side with the weather yard-arms pointing to the clouds; while the tall masts, inclined nearly to the horizon, seemed to be of an unmeasurable length. The carpenter let go his hold, rolled against the skylight, and began to crawl to the cabin entrance, where a big axe was kept ready for just such an emergency. At that moment the topsail sheet parted, the end of the heavy chain racketed aloft, and sparks of red fire streamed down through the flying sprays. The sail flapped once with a jerk that seemed to tear our hearts out through our teeth, and instantly changed into a bunch of fluttering narrow ribbons that tied themselves into knots and became quiet along the yard. Captain Allistoun struggled, managed to stand up with his face near the deck, upon which men swung on the ends of ropes, like nest robbers upon a cliff. One of his feet was on somebody's chest; his face was purple; his lips moved. He yelled also; he yelled, bending down:—"No! No!" Mr. Baker, one leg over the binnacle-stand, roared out:—"Did you say no? Not cut?" He shook his head madly. "No! No!" Between his legs the crawling carpenter heard, collapsed at once, and lay full length in the angle of the skylight. Voices took up the shout—"No! No!" Then all became still. They waited for the ship to turn over altogether, and shake them out into the sea; and upon the terrific noise of wind and sea not a murmur of remonstrance came out from those men, who each would have given ever so many years of life to see "them damned sticks go overboard!" They all believed it their only chance; but a little hard-faced man shook his grey head and shouted "No!" without giving them as much as a glance. They were silent, and gasped. They gripped rails, they had wound ropes'-ends under their arms; they clutched ringbolts, they crawled in heaps where there was foothold; they held on with both arms, hooked themselves to anything to windward with elbows, with chins, almost with their teeth; and some, unable to crawl away from where they had been flung, felt the sea leap up, striking against their backs as they struggled upwards. Singleton had stuck to the wheel. His hair flew out in the wind; the gale seemed to take its life-long adversary by the beard and shake his old head. He wouldn't let go, and, with his knees forced between the spokes, flew up and down like a man on a bough. As Death appeared unready, they began to look about. Donkin, caught by one foot in a loop of some rope, hung, head down, below us, and yelled, with his face to the deck:—"Cut! Cut!" Two men lowered themselves cautiously to him; others hauled on the rope. They caught him up, shoved him into a safer place, held him. He shouted curses at the master, shook his fist at him with horrible blasphemies, called upon us in filthy words to "Cut! Don't mind that murdering fool! Cut, some of you!" One of his rescuers struck him a back-handed blow over the mouth; his head banged on the deck, and he became suddenly very quiet, with a white face, breathing hard, and with a few drops of blood trickling from his cut lip. On the lee side another man could be seen stretched out as if stunned; only the washboard prevented him from going over the side. It was the steward. We had to sling him up like a bale, for he was paralysed with fright. He had rushed up out of the pantry when he felt the ship go over, and had rolled down helplessly, clutching a china mug. It was not broken. With difficulty we tore it from him, and when he saw it in our hands he was amazed. "Where did you get that thing?" he kept on asking, in a trembling voice. His shirt was blown to shreds; the ripped sleeves flapped like wings. Two men made him fast, and, doubled over the rope that held him, he resembled a bundle of wet rags. Mr. Baker crawled along the line of men, asking:—"Are you all there?" and looking them over. Some blinked vacantly, others shook convulsively; Wamibo's head hung over his breast; and in painful attitudes, cut by lashings, exhausted with clutching, screwed up in corners, they breathed heavily. Their lips twitched, and at every sickening heave of the overturned ship they opened them wide as if to shout. The cook, embracing a wooden stanchion, unconsciously repeated a prayer. In every short interval of the fiendish noises around he could be heard there, without cap or slippers, imploring in that storm the Master of our lives not to lead him into temptation. Soon he also became silent. In all that crowd of cold and hungry men, waiting wearily for a violent death, not a voice was heard; they were mute, and in sombre thoughtfulness listened to the horrible imprecations of the gale.

Hours passed. They were sheltered by the heavy inclination of the ship from the wind that rushed in one long unbroken moan above their heads, but cold rain showers fell at times into the uneasy calm of their refuge. Under the torment of that new infliction a pair of shoulders would writhe a little. Teeth chattered. The sky was clearing, and bright sunshine gleamed over the ship. After every burst of battering seas, vivid and fleeting rainbows arched over the drifting hull in the flick of sprays. The gale was ending in a clear blow, which gleamed and cut like a knife. Between two bearded shellbacks Charley, fastened with somebody's long muffler to a deck ringbolt, wept quietly, with rare tears wrung out by bewilderment, cold, hunger, and general misery. One of his neighbours punched him in the ribs, asking roughly:—"What's the matter with your cheek? In fine weather there's not holding you, youngster." Turning about with prudence he worked himself out of his coat and threw it over the boy. The other man closed up, muttering:—" 'Twill make a bloomin' man of you, sonny." They flung their arms over and pressed against him. Charley drew his feet up and his eyelids dropped. Sighs were heard, as men, perceiving that they were not to be "drowned in a hurry," tried easier positions. Mr. Creighton, who had hurt his leg, lay amongst us with compressed lips. Some fellows belonging to his watch set about securing him better. Without a word or a glance he lifted his arms one after another to facilitate the operation, and not a muscle moved in his stern, young face. They asked him with solicitude:—"Easier now, sir?" He answered with a curt:—"That'll do." He was a hard young officer, but many of his watch used to say they liked him well enough because he had "such a gentlemanly way of damning us up and down the deck." Others, unable to discern such fine shades of refinement, respected him for his smartness. For the first time since the ship had gone on her beam ends Captain Allistoun gave a short glance down at his men. He was almost upright—one foot against the side of the skylight, one knee on the deck; and with the end of the vang round his waist swung back and forth with his gaze fixed ahead, watchful, like a man looking out for a sign. Before his eyes the ship, with half her deck below water, rose and fell on heavy seas that rushed from under her flashing in the cold sunshine. We began to think she was wonderfully buoyant—considering. Confident voices were heard shouting:—"She'll do, boys!" Belfast exclaimed with fervour:—"I would giv' a month's pay for a draw at a pipe!" One or two, passing dry tongues on their salt lips, muttered something about a "drink of water." The cook, as if inspired, scrambled up with his breast against the poop water-cask and looked in. There was a little at the bottom. He yelled, waving his arms, and two men began to crawl backwards and forwards with the mug. We had a good mouthful all round. The master shook his head impatiently, refusing. When it came to Charley one of his neighbours shouted:—"That bloomin' boy's asleep." He slept as though he had been dosed with narcotics. They let him be. Singleton held to the wheel with one hand while he drank, bending down to shelter his lips from the wind. Wamibo had to be poked and yelled at before he saw the mug held before his eyes. Knowles said sagaciously:—"It's better'n a tot o' rum." Mr. Baker grunted:—"Thank ye." Mr. Creighton drank and nodded. Donkin gulped greedily, glaring over the rim. Belfast made us laugh when with grimacing mouth he shouted:—"Pass it this way. We're all taytottlers here." The master, presented with the mug again by a crouching man, who screamed up at him:—"We all had a drink, captain," groped for it without ceasing to look ahead, and handed it back stiffly as though he could not spare half a glance away from the ship. Faces brightened. We shouted to the cook:—"Well done, doctor!" He sat to leeward, propped by the water-cask and yelled back abundantly, but the seas were breaking in thunder just then, and we only caught snatches that sounded like: "Providence" and "born again." He was at his old game of preaching. We made friendly but derisive gestures at him, and from below he lifted one arm, holding on with the other, moved his lips; he beamed up to us, straining his voice—earnest, and ducking his head before the sprays.

Suddenly some one cried:—"Where's Jimmy?" and we were appalled once more. On the end of the row the boatswain shouted hoarsely:—"Has any one seed him come out?" Voices exclaimed dismally:—"Drowned—is he? . . . . No! In his cabin! . . . . Good

Lord! . . . . Caught like a bloomin' rat in a trap. . . . . Couldn't open his door . . . . Aye! She went over too quick and the water jammed it . . . . Poor beggar! . . . . No help for 'im. . . . . Let's go and see . . . ." "Damn him, who could go?" screamed Donkin.—"Nobody expects you to," growled the man next to him; "you're only a thing."—"Is there half a chance to get at 'im?" inquired two or three men together. Belfast untied himself with blind impetuosity, and all at once shot down to leeward quicker than a flash of lightning. We shouted all together with dismay; but with his legs overboard he held and yelled for a rope. In our extremity nothing could be terrible; so we judged him funny kicking there, and with his scared face. Some one began to laugh, and, as if hysterically infected with screaming merriment, all those haggard men went off laughing, wild-eyed, like a lot of maniacs tied up on a wall. Mr. Baker swung off the binnacle-stand and tendered him one leg. He scrambled up rather scared, and consigning us with abominable words to the "divvle." "You are . . . . Ough! You're a foul-mouthed beggar, Craik," grunted Mr. Baker. He answered, stuttering with indignation:—"Look at 'em, sorr. The bloomin' dirty images! laughing at a chum going overboard. Call themselves men, too." But from the break of the poop the boatswain called out:—"Come along," and Belfast crawled away in a hurry to join him. The five men, poised and gazing over the edge of the poop, looked for the best way to get forward. They seemed to hesitate. The others, twisting in their lashings, turning painfully, stared with open lips. Captain Allistoun saw nothing; he seemed with his eyes to hold the ship up in a superhuman concentration of effort. The wind screamed loud in sunshine; columns of spray rose straight up; and in the glitter of rainbows bursting over the trembling hull the men went over cautiously, disappearing from sight with deliberate movements.

They went swinging from belaying-pin to cleat above the seas that beat the half-submerged deck. Their toes scraped the planks. Lumps of green cold water toppled over the bulwark and on their heads. They hung for a moment on strained arms, with the breath knocked out of them, and with closed eyes—then, letting go with one hand, balanced with lolling heads, trying to grab some rope or stanchion further forward. The long-armed and athletic boatswain swung quickly, gripping things with a fist hard as iron, and remembering suddenly snatches of the last letter from his "old woman." Little Belfast scrambled rageously, muttering "cursed nigger." Wamibo's tongue hung out with excitement; and Archie, intrepid and calm, watched his chance to move with intelligent coolness.

When above the side of the house, they let go one after another, and falling heavily, sprawled, pressing their palms to the smooth teak wood. Round them the backwash of waves seethed white and hissing. All the doors had become trap-doors, of course. The first was the galley door. The galley extended from side to side, and they could hear the sea splashing with hollow noise in there. The next door was that of the carpenter's shop. They lifted it, and looked down. The room seemed to have been devastated by an earthquake. Everything in it had tumbled on the bulkhead facing the door, and on the other side of that bulkhead there was Jimmy, dead or alive. The bench, a half-finished meat-safe, saws, chisels, wire rods, axes, crowbars, lay in a heap besprinkled with loose nails. A sharp adze stuck up with a shining edge that gleamed dangerously down there like a wicked smile. The men clung to one another peering. A sickening, sly lurch of the ship nearly sent them overboard in a body. Belfast howled "Here goes!" and leaped down. Archie followed cannily, catching at shelves that gave way with him, and eased himself in a great crash of ripped wood. There was hardly room for three men to move. And in the sunshiny blue square of the door, the boatswain's face, bearded and dark, Wamibo's face, wild and pale, hung over—watching.

Together they shouted: "Jimmy! Jim!" From above the boatswain contributed a deep growl: "You . . . . Wait!" In a pause, Belfast entreated: "Jimmy, darlin', are ye aloive?" The boatswain said: "Again! All together, boys!" All yelled excitedly. Wamibo made noises resembling loud barks. Belfast drummed on the side of the bulkhead with a piece of iron. All ceased suddenly. The sound of screaming and hammering went on thin and distinct—like a solo after a chorus. He was alive. He was screaming and knocking below us with the hurry of a man prematurely shut up in a coffin. We went to work. We attacked with desperation the abominable heap of things heavy, of things sharp, of things clumsy to handle. The boatswain crawled away to find somewhere a flying end of a rope; and Wamibo, held back by shouts:—

"Don't jump! . . . . Don't come in here, muddle-head!"—remained glaring above us—all shining eyes, gleaming fangs, tumbled hair; resembling an amazed and half-witted fiend gloating over the extraordinary agitation of the damned. The boatswain adjured us to "bear a hand," and a rope descended. We made things fast to it and they went up spinning, never to be seen by man again. A rage to fling things overboard possessed us. We worked fiercely, cutting our hands, and speaking brutally to one another. Jimmy kept up a distracting row; he screamed piercingly, without drawing a breath, like a tortured woman; he banged with hands and feet. The agony of his fear wrung our hearts so terribly that we longed to abandon him, to get out of that place deep as a well and swaying like a tree, to get out of his hearing, back on the poop where we could wait passively for death in incomparable repose. We shouted to him to "shut up, for God's sake." He redoubled his cries. He must have fancied we could not hear him. Probably he heard his own clamour but faintly. We could picture him crouching on the edge of the upper berth, letting out with both fists at the wood, in the dark, and with his mouth wide open for that unceasing cry. Those were loathsome moments. A cloud driving across the sun would darken the doorway menacingly. Every movement of the ship was pain. We scrambled about with no room to breathe, and felt frightfully sick. The boatswain yelled down at us:—"Bear a hand! Bear a hand! We two will be washed away from here directly if you ain't quick!" Three times a sea leaped over the high side and flung bucketfuls of water on our heads. Then Jimmy, startled by the shock, would stop his noise for a moment—waiting for the ship to sink, perhaps—and began again, distressingly loud, as if invigorated by the gust of fear. At the bottom the nails lay in a layer several inches thick. It was ghastly. Every nail in the world, not driven firmly somewhere, seemed to have found its way into that carpenter's shop. There they were, of all kinds, the remnants of stores from seven voyages. Tin-tacks, copper tacks (sharp as needles), pump nails, with big heads, like tiny iron mushrooms; nails without any heads (horrible); French nails polished and slim. They lay in a solid mass more inabordable than a hedgehog. We hesitated, yearning for a shovel, while Jimmy below us yelled as though he had been flayed. Groaning, we dug our fingers in, and very much hurt, shook our hands, scattering nails and drops of blood. We passed up our hats full of assorted nails to the boatswain, who, as if performing a mysterious and appeasing rite, cast them wide upon a raging sea.

We got to the bulkhead at last. Those were stout planks. She was a ship, well finished in every detail—the *Narcissus* was. They were the stoutest planks ever put into a ship's bulkhead—we thought—and then we perceived that, in our hurry, we had sent all the tools overboard. Absurd little Belfast wanted to break it down with his own weight, and with both feet leaped straight up like a springbok, cursing the Clyde shipwrights for not scamping their work. Incidentally he reviled all North Britain, the rest of the earth, the sea—and all his companions. He swore, as he alighted heavily on his heels, that he would never, never any more associate with any fool that "hadn't savee enough to know his knee from his elbow." He managed by his thumping to scare the last remnant of wits out of Jimmy. We could hear the object of our exasperated solicitude darting to and fro under the planks. He had cracked his voice at last, and could only squeak miserably. His back or else his head rubbed the planks, now here, now there, in a puzzling manner. He squeaked as he dodged the invisible blows. It was more heartrending even than his yells. Suddenly Archie produced a crowbar. He had kept it back; also a small hatchet. We howled with satisfaction. He struck a mighty blow and small chips flew at our eyes. The boatswain above shouted:—"Look out! Look out there. Don't kill the man. Easy does it!" Wamibo, maddened with excitement, hung head down and insanely urged us:—"Hoo! Strook 'im! Hoo! Hoo!" We were afraid he would fall in and kill one of us and, hurriedly, we entreated the boatswain to "shove the blamed Finn overboard." Then, all together, we yelled down at the planks:—"Stand from under! Get forward," and listened. We only heard the deep hum and moan of the wind above us, the mingled roar and hiss of the seas. The ship, as if overcome with despair, wallowed lifelessly, and our heads swam with the unnatural motion. Belfast clamoured:—"For the love of God, Jimmy, where are ye? . . . . Knock! Jimmy darlint! . . . . Knock! You bloody black beast! Knock!" He was as quiet as a dead man inside a grave; and, like men standing above a grave, we were on the verge of tears—but with vexation, the strain, the fatigue; with the great longing to be done with it, to get away, and lay down to rest somewhere where we could see our danger and breathe. Archie shouted:—"Gi'e me room!" We crouched behind him, guarding our heads, and he struck time after time in the joint of the planks. They cracked. Suddenly the crowbar went halfway in through a splintered oblong hole. It must have missed Jimmy's head by less than an inch. Archie withdrew it quickly, and that infamous nigger rushed at the hole, put his lips to it, and whispered "Help" in an almost extinct voice; he pressed his head to it, trying madly to get out through that opening one inch wide and three inches long. In our disturbed state we were absolutely paralysed by his incredible action. It seemed impossible to drive him away. Even Archie at last lost his composure. "If ye don't clear oot I'll drive the crowbar thro' your head," he shouted in a determined voice. He meant what he said, and his earnestness seemed to make an impression on Jimmy. He disappeared suddenly, and we set to prising and tearing at the planks with the eagerness of men trying to get at a mortal enemy, and spurred by the desire to tear him limb from limb. The wood split, cracked, gave way. Belfast plunged in head and shoulders and groped viciously. "I've got 'im! Got 'im," he shouted. "Oh! There! . . . . He's gone; I've got 'im! . . . . Pull at my legs! . . . . Pull!" Wamibo hooted unceasingly. The boatswain shouted directions:—"Catch hold of his hair, Belfast; pull straight up, you two! . . . . Pull fair!" We pulled fair. We pulled Belfast out with a jerk, and dropped him with disgust. In a sitting posture, purple-faced, he sobbed despairingly:—"How can I hold on to 'is blooming short wool?" Suddenly Jimmy's head and shoulders appeared. He stuck halfway, and with rolling eyes foamed at our feet. We flew at him with brutal impatience, we tore the shirt off his back, we tugged at his ears, we panted over him; and all at once he came away in our hands as though somebody had let go his legs. With the same movement, without a pause, we swung him up. His breath whistled, he kicked our upturned faces, he grasped two pairs of arms above his head, and he squirmed up with such precipitation that he seemed positively to escape from our hands like a bladder full of gas. Streaming with perspiration, we swarmed up the rope, and, coming into the blast of cold wind, gasped like men plunged into icy water. With burning faces we shivered to the very marrow of our bones. Never before had the gale seemed to us more furious, the sea more mad, the sunshine more merciless and mocking, and the position of the ship more hopeless and appalling. Every movement of her was ominous of the end of her agony and of the beginning of ours. We staggered away from the door, and, alarmed by a sudden roll, fell down in a bunch. It appeared to us that the side of the house was more smooth than glass and more slippery than ice. There was nothing to hang on to but a long brass hook used sometimes to keep back an open door. Wamibo held on to it and we held on to Wamibo, clutching our Jimmy. He had completely collapsed now. He did not seem to have the strength to close his hand. We stuck to him blindly in our fear. We were not afraid of Wamibo letting go (we remembered that the brute was stronger than any three men in the ship), but we were afraid of the hook giving way, and we also believed that the ship had made up her mind to turn over at last. But she didn't. A sea swept over us. The boatswain spluttered:—"Up and away. There's a lull. Away aft with you, or we will all go to the devil here." We stood up surrounding Jimmy. We begged him to hold up, to hold on, at least. He glared with his bulging eyes, mute as a fish, and with all the stiffening knocked out of him. He wouldn't stand; he wouldn't even as much as clutch at our necks; he was only a cold black skin loosely stuffed with soft cotton wool; his arms and legs swung jointless and pliable; his head rolled about; the lower lip hung down, enormous and heavy. We pressed round him, bothered and dismayed; sheltering him we swung here and there in a body; and on the very brink of eternity we tottered all together with concealing and absurd gestures, like a lot of drunken men embarrassed with a stolen corpse.

Something had to be done. We had to get him aft. A rope was tied slack under his armpits, and, reaching up at the risk of our lives, we hung him on the foresheet cleet. He emitted no sound; he looked as ridiculously lamentable as a doll that had lost half its sawdust, and we started on our perilous journey over the main deck, dragging along with care that pitiful, that limp, that hateful burden. He was not very heavy, but had he weighed a ton he could not have been more awkward to handle. We literally passed him from hand to hand. Now and then we had to hang him up on a handy belaying-pin, to draw a breath and reform the line. Had the pin broken he would have irretrievably gone into the Southern

Ocean, but he had to take his chance of that; and after a little while, becoming apparently aware of it, he groaned slightly, and with a great effort whispered a few words. We listened eagerly. He was reproaching us with our carelessness in letting him run such risks: "Now, after I got myself out from there," he breathed out weakly. "There" was his cabin. And he got himself out. We had nothing to do with it apparently! . . . . No matter. . . . . We went on and let him take his chances, simply because we could not help it; for though at that time we hated him more than ever—more than anything under heaven—we did not want to lose him. We had so far saved him; and it had become a personal matter between us and the sea. We meant to stick to him. Had we (by an incredible hypothesis) undergone similar toil and trouble for an empty cask, that cask would have become as precious to us as Jimmy was. More precious, in fact, because we would have had no reason to hate the cask. And we hated James Wait. We could not get rid of the monstrous suspicion that this astounding blackman was shamming sick, had been malingering heartlessly in the face of our toil, of our scorn, of our patience—and now was malingering in the face of our devotion—in the face of death. Our vague and imperfect morality rose with disgust at his unmanly lie. But he stuck to it manfully—amazingly. No! It couldn't be. He was at all extremity. His cantankerous temper was only the result of the provoking invincibleness of that death he felt by his side. Any man may be angry with such a masterful chum. But, then, what kind of men were we—with our thoughts! Indignation and doubt grappled within us in a scuffle that trampled upon the finest of our feelings. And we hated him because of the suspicion; we detested him because of the doubt. We could not scorn him safely—neither could we pity him without risk to our dignity. So we hated him, and passed him carefully from hand to hand. We cried, "Got him?"—"Yes. All right. Let go." And he swung from one enemy to another, showing about as much life as an old bolster would do. His eyes made two narrow white slits in the black face. He breathed slowly, and the air escaped through his lips with a noise like the sound of bellows. We reached the poop ladder at last, and it being a comparatively safe place, we lay for a moment in an exhausted heap to rest a little. He began to mutter. We were always incurably anxious to hear what he had to say. This time he mumbled peevishly, "It took you some time to come. I began to think the whole smart lot of you had been washed overboard. What kept you back? Hey? Funk?" We said nothing. With sighs we started again to drag him up. The secret and ardent desire of our hearts was the desire to beat him viciously with our fists about the head; and we handled him as tenderly as though he had been made of glass. . . . .

The return on the poop was like the return of wanderers after many years amongst people marked by the desolation of time. Eyes were turned slowly in their sockets glancing at us. Faint murmurs were heard. "Have you got 'im after all?" The well-known faces looked strange and familiar; they seemed faded and grimy; they had a mingled expression of fatigue and eagerness. They seemed to have become much thinner during our absence, as if all these men had been starving for a long time in their abandoned attitudes. The captain, with a round turn of a rope on his wrist, and kneeling on one knee, swung with a face cold and stiff; but with living eyes he was still holding the ship up, heeding no one, as if lost in the unearthly effort of that endeavour. We fastened up James Wait in a safe place. Mr. Baker scrambled along to lend a hand. Mr. Creighton, on his back, and very pale, muttered, "Well done," and gave us, Jimmy and the sky, a scornful glance, then closed his eyes slowly. Here and there a man stirred a little, but most remained apathetic, in cramped positions, muttering between shivers. The sun was setting. A sun enormous, unclouded and red, declining low as if bending down to look into their faces. The wind whistled across long sunbeams that, resplendent and cold, struck full on the dilated pupils of staring eyes without making them wink. The wisps of hair and the tangled beards were grey with the salt of the sea. The faces were earthy, and the dark patches under the eyes extended to the ears, smudged into the hollows of sunken cheeks. The lips were livid and thin, and when they moved it was with difficulty, as though they had been glued to the teeth. Some grinned sadly in the sunlight, shaking with cold. Others were sad and still. Charley, subdued by the sudden disclosure of the insignificance of his youth, darted fearful glances. The two smooth-faced Norwegians resembled decrepid children, staring stupidly. To leeward, on the edge of the horizon, black seas leaped up towards the glowing sun. It sank slowly, round and blazing, and the crests of waves splashed on the edge of the luminous circle. One of the Norwegians appeared to catch sight of it, and, after giving a violent start, began to speak. His voice, startling the others, made them stir. They moved their heads stiffly, or turning with difficulty, looked at him with surprise, with fear, or in grave silence. He chattered at the setting sun, nodding his head, while the big seas began to roll across the crimson disc; and over miles of turbulent waters the shadows of high waves swept with a running darkness the faces of men. A crested roller broke with a loud hissing roar, and the sun, as if put out, disappeared. The chattering voice faltered, went out together with the light. There were sighs. In the sudden lull that follows the crash of a broken sea a man said wearily. "Here's that blooming Dutchman gone off his chump." A seaman, lashed by the middle, tapped the deck with his open hand with unceasing quick flaps. In the gathering greyness of twilight a bulky form was seen rising aft, and began marching on all fours with the movements of some big cautious beast. It was Mr. Baker passing along the line of men. He grunted encouragingly over every one, felt their fastenings. Some, with half-open eyes, puffed like men oppressed by heat; others mechanically and in dreamy voices answered him, "Aye! aye! sir!" He went from one to another grunting, "Ough! . . . . See her through it yet;" and unexpectedly, with loud angry outbursts, blew up Knowles for cutting off a long piece from the fall of the relieving tackle. "Ough!——Ashamed of yourself——Relieving tackle——Don't you know better!——Ough!——Able seaman! Ough!" The lame man was crushed. He muttered, "Get som'think for a lashing for myself, sir."—"Ough! Lashing——yourself. Are you a tinker or a sailor——What? Ough!——May want that tackle directly——Ough!——More use to the ship than your lame carcass. Ough!——Keep it!——Keep it, now you've done it." He crawled away slowly, muttering to himself about some men being "worse than children." It had been a comforting row. Low exclamations were heard: "Hallo . . . . Hallo." . . . . Those who had been painfully dozing asked with convulsive starts, "What's up? . . . . What is it?" The answers came with unexpected cheerfulness: "The mate is going bald-headed for lame Jack about something or other." "No!". . . . "What 'as he done?" Some one even chuckled. It was like a whiff of hope, like a reminder of safe days. Donkin, who had been stupefied with fear, revived suddenly and began to shout:—"'Ear 'im; that's the way they tawlk to hus. Vy donch 'ee 'it 'imone ov yer? 'It 'im. 'It 'im! Comin' the mate hover hus. We are as good men as 'ee. We're hall goin' to 'ell now. We 'ave been starved in this rotten ship, an' now we're goin' to be drowned for them black-'earted bullies! 'It 'im!" He shrieked in the deepening gloom, he blubbered and sobbed, screaming:—"'It 'im! 'It 'im!" The rage and fear of his disregarded right to live tried the steadfastness of hearts more than the menacing shadows of the night that advanced through the unceasing clamour of the gale. From aft Mr. Baker was heard:—"Is one of you men going to stop him—must I come along?" "Shut up!" . . . . "Keep quiet!" cried various voices, exasperated, trembling with cold.—"You'll get one across the mug from me directly," said an invisible seaman, in a weary tone, "I won't let the mate have the trouble." He ceased and lay still with the silence of despair. On the black sky the stars, coming out, gleamed over an inky sea that, speckled with foam, flashed back at them the evanescent and pale light of a dazzling whiteness born from the black turmoil of the waves. Remote in the eternal calm they glittered hard and cold above the uproar of the earth; they surrounded the vanquished and tormented ship on all sides: more pitiless than the eyes of a triumphant mob, and as unapproachable as the hearts of men.

The icy south wind howled exultingly under the sombre splendour of the sky. The cold shook the men with a resistless violence as though it had tried to shake them to pieces. Short moans were swept unheard off the stiff lips. Some complained in mutters of "not feeling themselves below the waist"; while those who had closed their eyes, imagined they had a block of ice on their chests. Others, alarmed at not feeling any pain in their fingers, beat the deck feebly with their hands—obstinate and exhausted. Wamibo stared vacant and dreamy. The Scandinavians kept on a meaningless mutter through chattering teeth. The spare Scotchmen, with determined efforts, kept their lower jaws still. The West-country men lay big and stolid in an invulnerable surliness. A man yawned and swore in turns. Another breathed with a rattle in his throat. Two elderly hard-weather shellbacks, fast side by side, whispered dismally to one another about the landlady of a boarding-house in Sunderland, whom they both knew. They extolled her motherliness and her liberality; they tried to talk about the joint of beef and the big fire in the downstairs kitchen. The words dying faintly on their lips, ended in light sighs. A sudden voice cried into the cold night, "Oh Lord!" No one changed his position or took any notice of the cry. One or two passed, with a repeated and vague gesture, their hand over their faces, but most of them kept very still. In the benumbed immobility of their bodies they were excessively wearied by their thoughts, that rushed with the rapidity and vividness of dreams. Now and then, by an abrupt and startling exclamation, they answered the weird hail of some illusion; then, again, in silence contemplated the vision of known faces and familiar things. They recalled the aspect of forgotten shipmates and heard the voice of dead and gone skippers. They remembered the noise of gaslit streets, the steamy heat of tap-rooms, or the scorching sunshine of calm days at sea.

Mr. Baker left his insecure place, and crawled, with stoppages, along the poop. In the dark and on all fours he resembled some carnivorous animal prowling amongst corpses. At the break, propped to windward of a stanchion, he looked down on the main deck. It seemed to him that the ship had a tendency to stand up a little more. The wind had eased a little, he thought, but the sea ran as high as ever. The waves foamed viciously, and the lee side of the deck disappeared under a hissing whiteness as of boiling milk, while the rigging sang steadily with a deep vibrating note, and, at every upward swing of the ship, the wind rushed with a long-drawn clamour amongst the spars. Mr. Baker watched very still. A man near him began to make a blabbing noise with his lips, all at once and very loud, as though the cold had broken brutally through him. He went on:—"Ba—ba—ba—brrr—brr—ba—ba."—"Stop that!" cried Mr. Baker, groping in the dark. "Stop it!" He went on shaking the leg he found under his hand.—"What is it, sir?" called out Belfast, in the tone of a man awakened suddenly; "we are looking after that 'ere Jimmy."—"Are you? Ough! Don't make that row then. Who's that near you?"—"It's me—the boatswain, sir," growled the West-country man; "we are trying to keep life in that poor devil."—"Aye, aye!" said Mr. Baker. "Do it quietly, can't you."—"He wants us to hold him up above the rail," went on the boatswain, with irritation, "says he can't breathe here under our jackets."—"If we lift 'im, we drop 'im overboard," said another voice, "we can't feel our hands with cold."—"I don't care. I am choking!" exclaimed James Wait in a clear tone.—"Oh, no, my son," said the boatswain, desperately, "you don't go till we all go on this fine night."—"You will see yet many a worse," said Mr. Baker, cheerfully.—"It's no child's play, sir!" answered the boatswain. "Some of us further aft, here, are in a pretty bad way."—"If the blamed sticks had been cut out of her she would be running along on her bottom now like any decent ship, an' giv' us all a chance," said some one, with a sigh.—"The old man wouldn't have it . . . . much he cares for us," whispered another.—"Care for you!" exclaimed Mr. Baker, angrily. "Why should he care for you? Are you a lot of women passengers to be taken care of? We are here to take care of the ship—and some of you ain't up to that. Ough! . . . . What have you done so very smart to be taken care of? Ough! . . . . Some of you can't stand a bit of breeze without crying over it."—"Come, sorr. We ain't so bad," protested Belfast, in a voice shaken by shivers; "we ain't . . . . brrr . . . ."—"Again," shouted the mate, grabbing at the shadowy form: "again! . . . . Why, you're in your shirt! What have you done?"—"I've put my oilskin and jacket over that half-dead nayggur—and he says he chokes," said Belfast, complainingly.—"You wouldn't call me nigger if I wasn't half dead, you Irish beggar!" boomed James Wait, vigorously.—"You . . . . brrr . . . . You wouldn't be white if you were ever so well . . . . I will fight you . . . . brrrr . . . . in fine weather . . . . brrr . . . . with one hand tied behind my back . . . . brrrrrr . . . ."—"I don't want your rags—I want air," gasped out the other faintly, as if suddenly exhausted.

The sprays swept over whistling and pattering. Men disturbed in their peaceful torpor by the pain of quarrelsome shouts, moaned, muttering curses. Mr. Baker crawled off a little way to leeward where a water-cask loomed up big, with something white against it. "Is it you. Podmore?" asked Mr. Baker. He had to repeat the question twice before the cook turned, coughing feebly.—"Yes, sir. I've been praying in my mind for a quick deliverance; for I am prepared for any call. . . . . I——"—"Look here, cook," interrupted Mr. Baker, "the men are perishing with cold."—"Cold!" said the cook, mournfully: "they will be warm enough before long."—

"What?" asked Mr. Baker, looking along the deck into the faint sheen of frothing water.—"They are a wicked lot," continued the cook solemnly, but in an unsteady voice, "about as wicked as any ship's company in this sinful world! Now, I"—he trembled so that he could hardly speak; his was an exposed place, and in a cotton shirt, a thin pair of trousers, and with his knees under his nose, he received, quaking, the flicks of stinging, salt drops; his voice sounded exhausted—"now, I—any time . . . . My eldest youngster, Mr. Baker . . . . a clever boy . . . . last Sunday on shore before this voyage he wouldn't go to church, sir. Says I, 'You go and clean yourself, or I'll know the reason why!' What does he do? . . . . Pond, Mr. Baker—fell into the pond in his best rig, sir! . . . . Accident? . . . . 'Nothing will save you, fine scholar though you are!' says I. . . . . Accident! . . . . I whopped him, sir, till I couldn't lift my arm. . . . ." His voice faltered. "I whopped 'im!" he repeated, rattling his teeth; then, after a while, let out a mournful sound that was half a groan, half a snore. Mr. Baker shook him by the shoulders. "Hey! Cook! Hold up, Podmore! Tell me—is there any fresh water in the galley tank? The ship is lying along less, I think; I would try to get forward. A little water would do them good. Hallo! Look out! Look out!" The cook struggled.—"Not you, sir—not you!" He began to scramble to windward. "Galley! . . . . my business!" he shouted.—"Cook's going crazy now," said several voices. He yelled:—"Crazy, am I? I am more ready to die than any of you, officers incloosive—there! As long as she swims I will cook! I will get you coffee."—"Cook, ye are a gentleman!" cried Belfast. But the cook was already going over the weather ladder. He stopped for a moment to shout back on the poop:—"As long as she swims I will cook!" and disappeared as though he had gone overboard. The men who had heard sent after him a cheer that sounded like a wail of sick children. An hour or more afterwards some one said distinctly: "He's gone for good."—"Very likely," assented the boatswain; "even in fine weather he was as smart about the deck as a milch-cow on her first voyage. We ought to go and see." Nobody moved. As the hours dragged slowly through the darkness Mr. Baker crawled back and forth along the poop several times. Some men fancied they had heard him exchange murmurs with the master, but at that time the memories were incomparably more vivid than anything actual, and they were not certain whether the murmurs were heard now or many years ago. They did not try to find out. A mutter more or less did not matter. It was too cold for curiosity, and almost for hope. They could not spare a moment or a thought from the great mental occupation of wishing to live. And the desire of life kept them alive, apathetic and enduring, under the cruel persistence of wind and cold; while the bestarred black dome of the sky revolved slowly above the ship, that drifted, bearing their patience and their suffering, through the stormy solitude of the sea.

Huddled close to one another, they fancied themselves utterly alone. They heard sustained loud noises, and again bore the pain of existence through long hours of profound silence. In the night they saw sunshine, felt warmth, and suddenly, with a start, thought that the sun would never rise upon a freezing world. Some heard laughter, listened to songs; others, near the end of the poop, could hear loud human shrieks, and, opening their eyes, were surprised to hear them still, though very faint, and far away. The boatswain said:—"Why, it's the cook, hailing from forward, I think." He hardly believed his own words or recognised his own voice. It was a long time before the man next to him gave a sign of life. He punched hard his other neighbour and said:—"The cook's shouting!" Many did not understand, others did not care; the majority further aft did not believe. But the boatswain and another man had the pluck to crawl away forward to see. They seemed to have been gone for hours, and were very soon forgotten. Then suddenly men that had been plunged in a hopeless resignation became as if possessed with a desire to hurt. They belaboured one another with fists. In the darkness they struck persistently anything soft they could feel near, and, with a greater effort than for a shout, whispered excitedly:—"They've got some hot coffee. . . . . Bosun got it. . . . ." "No! . . . . Where?" . . . . "It's coming! Cook made it." James Wait moaned. Donkin scrambled viciously, caring not where he kicked, and anxious that the officers should have none of it. It came in a pot, and they drank in turns. It was hot, and while it blistered the greedy palates, it seemed incredible. The men sighed out parting with the mug:—"How 'as he done it?" Some cried weakly:—"Bully for you, doctor!"

He had done it somehow. Afterwards Archie declared that the thing was "meeraculous." For many days we wondered, and it was the one ever-interesting subject of conversation to the end of the voyage. We asked the cook, in fine weather, how he felt when he saw his stove "reared up on end." We inquired, in the north-east trade and on serene evenings, whether he had to stand on his head to put things right somewhat. We suggested he had used his bread-board for a raft, and from there comfortably had stoked his grate; and we did our best to conceal our admiration under the wit of fine irony. He affirmed not to know anything about it, rebuked our levity, declared himself, with solemn animation, to have been the object of a special mercy for the saving of our unholy lives. Fundamentally he was right, no doubt; but he need not have been so offensively positive about it—he need not have hinted so often that it would have gone hard with us had he not been there, meritorious and pure, to receive the inspiration and the strength for the work of grace. Had we been saved by his recklessness or his agility, we could have at length become reconciled to the fact; but to admit our obligation to anybody's virtue and holiness alone was as difficult for us as for any other handful of mankind. Like many benefactors of humanity, the cook took himself too seriously, and reaped the reward of irreverence. We were not ungrateful, however. He remained heroic. His saying—*the* saying of his life—became proverbial in the mouths of men as are the sayings of conquerors or sages. Later on, whenever one of us was puzzled by a task and advised to relinquish it, he would express his determination to persevere and to succeed by the words:—"As long as she swims I will cook!"

The hot drink helped us through the bleak hours that precede the dawn. The sky low by the horizon took on the delicate tints of pink and yellow like the inside of a rare shell. And higher, where it glowed with a pearly sheen, a small black cloud appeared, like a forgotten fragment of the night set in a border of dazzling gold. The beams of light skipped on the crests of waves. The eyes of men turned to the eastward. The sunlight flooded their weary faces. They were giving themselves up to fatigue as though they had done for ever with their work. On Singleton's black oilskin coat the dried salt glistened like hoar frost. He hung on by the wheel, with open and lifeless eyes. Captain Allistoun, unblinking, faced the rising sun. His lips stirred, opened for the first time in twenty-four hours, and with a fresh firm voice he cried, "Wear ship!"

The commanding sharp tones made all these torpid men start like a sudden flick of a whip. Then again, motionless where they lay, the force of habit made some of them repeat the order in hardly audible murmurs. Captain Allistoun glanced down at his crew, and several, with fumbling fingers and hopeless movements, tried to cast themselves adrift. He repeated impatiently, "Wear ship. Now then, Mr. Baker, get the men along. What's the matter with them?"—"Wear ship. Do you hear there?—Wear ship!" thundered out the boatswain suddenly. His voice seemed to break through a deadly spell. Men began to stir and crawl.—"I want the fore-topmast stay-sail run up smartly," said the master, very loudly; "if you can't manage it standing up you must do it lying down—that's all. Bear a hand!"—"Come along! Let's give the old girl a chance," urged the boatswain.—"Aye! aye! Wear ship!" exclaimed quavering voices. The forecastle men, with reluctant faces, prepared to go forward. Mr. Baker pushed ahead grunting on all fours to show the way, and they followed him over the break. The others lay still with a vile hope in their hearts of not being required to move till they got saved or drowned in peace.

After some time they could be seen forward appearing on the forecastle head, one by one in unsafe attitudes; hanging on to the rails; clambering over the anchors; embracing the cross-head of the windlass or hugging the fore-capstan. They were restless with strange exertions, waved their arms, knelt, lay flat down, staggered up, seemed to strive their hardest to go overboard. Suddenly a small white piece of canvas fluttered amongst them, grew larger, beating. Its narrow head rose in jerks—and at last it stood distended and triangular in the sunshine.—"They have done it!" cried the voices aft. Captain Allistoun let go the rope he had round his wrist and rolled to leeward headlong. He could be seen casting the lee main braces off the pins while the backwash of waves splashed over him.—"Square the main yard!" he shouted up to us—who stared at him in wonder. We hesitated to stir. "The main brace, men. Haul! haul anyhow! Lay on your backs and haul!" he screeched, half drowned down there. We did not believe we could move the main yard, but the strongest and the less discouraged tried to execute the order. Others assisted half-heartedly. Singleton's eyes blazed suddenly as he took a fresh grip of the spokes. Captain Allistoun fought his way up to windward.—

"Haul men! Try to move it! Haul, and help the ship." His hard face worked suffused and furious. "Is she going off, Singleton?" he cried.—"Not a move yet, sir," croaked the old seaman in a horribly hoarse voice.—"Watch the helm, Singleton," spluttered the master. "Haul men! Have you no more strength than rats? Haul, and earn your salt." Mr. Creighton, on his back, with a swollen leg and a face as white as a piece of paper, blinked his eyes; his bluish lips twitched. In the wild scramble men grabbed at him, crawled over his hurt leg, knelt on his chest. He kept perfectly still, setting his teeth without a moan, without a sigh. The master's ardour, the cries of that silent man inspired us. We hauled and hung in bunches on the rope. We heard him say with violence to Donkin, who sprawled abjectly on his stomach,—"I will brain you with this belaying-pin if you don't catch hold of the brace," and that victim of men's injustice, cowardly and cheeky, whimpered:—"Are you goin' ter murder hus now?" while with sudden desperation he gripped the rope. Men sighed, shouted, hissed meaningless words, groaned. The yards moved, came slowly square against the wind, that hummed loudly on the yard-arms.—"Going off, sir," shouted Singleton, "she's just started."—"Catch a turn with that brace. Catch a turn!" clamoured the master. Mr. Creighton, nearly suffocated and unable to move, made a mighty effort, and with his left hand managed to nip the rope.—"All fast!" cried some one. He closed his eyes as if going off into a swoon, while huddled together about the brace we watched with scared looks what the ship would do now.

She went off slowly as though she had been weary and disheartened like the men she carried. She paid off very gradually, making us hold our breath till we choked, and as soon as she had brought the wind abaft the beam she started to move, and fluttered our hearts. It was awful to see her, nearly overturned, begin to gather way and drag her submerged side through the water. The dead-eyes of the rigging churned the breaking seas. The lower half of the deck was full of mad whirlpools and eddies; and the long line of the lee rail could be seen showing black now and then in the swirls of a field of foam as dazzling and white as a field of snow. The wind sang shrilly amongst the spars; and at every slight lurch we expected her to slip to the bottom sideways from under our backs. When dead before it she made the first distinct attempt to stand up, and we encouraged her with a feeble and discordant howl. A great sea came running up aft and hung for a moment over us with a curling top; then crashed down under the counter and spread out on both sides into a great sheet of bursting froth. Above its fierce hiss we heard Singleton's croak:—"She is steering!" He had both his feet now planted firmly on the grating, and the wheel spun fast as he eased the helm.—"Bring the wind on the port quarter and steady her!" called out the master, staggering to his feet, the first man up from amongst our prostrate heap. One or two screamed with excitement:—"She rises!" Far away forward, Mr. Baker and three others were seen erect and black on the clear sky, lifting their arms, and with open mouths as though they had been shouting all together. The ship trembled, trying to lift her side, lurched back, seemed to give up with a nerveless dip, and suddenly with an unexpected jerk swung violently to windward, as though she had torn herself out from a deadly grasp. The whole immense volume of water, lifted by her deck, was thrown bodily across to starboard. Loud cracks were heard. Iron ports breaking open thundered with ringing blows. The water topped over the starboard rail with the rush of a river falling over a dam. The sea on deck, and the seas on every side of her, mingled together in a deafening roar. She rolled violently. We got up and were helplessly run or flung about from side to side. Men, rolling over and over, yelled,—"The house will go!"—"She clears herself!" Lifted by a towering sea she ran along with it for a moment, spouting thick streams of water through every opening of her wounded sides. The lee braces having been carried away or washed off the pins, all the ponderous yards on the fore swung from side to side and with appalling rapidity at every roll. The men forward were seen crouching here and there with fearful glances upwards at the enormous spars that whirled about over their heads. The torn canvas and the ends of the broken gear streamed in the wind like wisps of hair. Through the clear sunshine, over the flashing turmoil and uproar of the seas, the ship ran blindly, dishevelled and headlong, as if fleeing for her life; and on the poop we spun, we tottered about, distracted and noisy. We all spoke at once in a thin babble; we had the aspect of invalids and the gestures of maniacs. Eyes shone, large and haggard, in smiling, meagre faces that seemed to have been dusted over with powdered chalk. We stamped, clapped our hands, feeling ready to jump and do anything; but in reality hardly able to keep on our feet. Captain Allistoun, hard and slim, gesticulated madly from the poop at Mr. Baker: "Steady these fore-yards! Steady them the best you can!" On the main deck, men excited by his cries, splashed, dashing aimlessly here and there with the foam swirling up to their waists. Apart, far aft, and alone by the helm, old Singleton had deliberately tucked his white beard under the top button of his glistening coat. Swaying upon the din and tumult of the seas, with the whole battered length of the ship launched forward in a rolling rush before his steady old eyes, he stood rigidly still, forgotten by all, and with an attentive face. In front of his erect figure only the two arms moved crosswise with a swift and sudden readiness, to check or urge again the rapid stir of circling spokes. He steered with care.

IV

On men reprieved by its disdainful mercy, the immortal sea confers in its justice the full privilege of desired unrest. Through the perfect wisdom of its grace they are not permitted to meditate at ease upon the complicated and acrid savour of existence, lest they should remember and, perchance, regret the reward of a cup of inspiring bitterness, tasted so often, and so often withdrawn from before their stiffening but reluctant lips. They must without pause justify their life to the eternal pity that commands toil to be hard and unceasing, from sunrise to sunset, from sunset to sunrise; till the weary succession of nights and days tainted by the obstinate clamour of sages, demanding bliss and an empty heaven, is redeemed at last by the vast silence of pain and labour, by the dumb fear and the dumb courage of men obscure, forgetful, and enduring.

The master and Mr. Baker coming face to face stared for a moment, with the intense and amazed looks of men meeting unexpectedly after years of trouble. Their voices were gone, and they whispered desperately at one another.—"Any one missing?" asked Captain Allistoun.—"No. All there."—"Anybody hurt?"—"Only the second mate."—"I will look after him directly. We're lucky."—"Very," articulated Mr. Baker, faintly. He gripped the rail and rolled bloodshot eyes. The little grey man made an effort to raise his voice above a dull mutter, and fixed his chief mate with a cold gaze, piercing like a dart.—"Get sail on the ship," he said, speaking authoritatively, and with an inflexible snap of his thin lips. "Get sail on her as soon as you can. This is a fair wind. At once, sir—Don't give the men time to feel themselves. They will get done up and stiff, and we will never . . . . We must get her along now" . . . . He reeled to a long heavy roll; the rail dipped into the glancing hissing water. He caught a shroud, swung helplessly against the mate . . . . "now we have a fair wind at last.——Make——sail." His head rolled from shoulder to shoulder. His eyelids began to beat rapidly. "And the pumps——pumps, Mr. Baker." He peered as though the face within a foot of his eyes had been a half a mile off. "Keep the men on the move to——to get her along," he mumbled in a drowsy tone, like a man going off into a doze. He pulled himself together suddenly. "Mustn't stand. Won't do," he said with a painful attempt at a smile. He let go his hold, and, propelled by the dip of the ship, ran aft unwillingly, with small steps, till he brought up against the binnacle stand. Hanging on there he looked up in an objectless manner at Singleton, who, unheeding him, watched anxiously the end of the jib-boom—"Steering gear works all right?" he asked. There was a noise in the old seaman's throat, as though the words had been rattling there together before they could come out.—"Steers . . . . like a little boat," he said at last, with hoarse tenderness, without giving the master as much as half a glance—then, watchfully, spun the wheel down, steadied, flung it back again. Captain Allistoun tore himself away from the delight of leaning against the binnacle, and began to walk the poop, swaying and reeling to preserve his balance. . . .

The pump-rods, clanking, stamped in short jumps, while the fly-wheels turned smoothly, with great speed, at the foot of the mainmast, flinging back and forth with a regular impetuosity two limp clusters of men clinging to the handles. They abandoned themselves, swaying from the hip with twitching faces and stony eyes. The carpenter, sounding from time to time, exclaimed mechanically: "Shake her up! Keep her going!" Mr. Baker could not speak, but found his voice to shout; and under the goad of his objurgations, men looked to the lashings, dragged out new sails; and thinking themselves unable to move, carried heavy blocks aloft—

overhauled the gear. They went up the rigging with faltering and desperate efforts. Their heads swam as they shifted their hold, stepped blindly on the yards like men in the dark; or trusted themselves to the first rope to hand with the negligence of exhausted strength. The narrow escapes from falls did not disturb the languid beat of their hearts; the roar of the seas seething far below them sounded continuous and faint like an indistinct noise from another world; the wind filled their eyes with tears, and with heavy gusts tried to push them off from where they swayed in insecure positions. With streaming faces and blowing hair they flew up and down between sky and water, bestriding the ends of yard-arms, crouching on foot-ropes, embracing lifts to have their hands free, or standing up against chain ties. Their thoughts floated vaguely between the desire of rest and the desire of life, while their stiffened fingers cast off head-earrings, fumbled for knives, or held with tenacious grip against the violent shocks of beating canvas. They glared savagely at one another, made frantic signs with one hand while they held their life in the other, looked down on the narrow strip of flooded deck, shouted along to leeward: "Light-to!" .... "Haul out!" .... "Make fast!" Their lips moved, their eyes started, furious and eager with the desire to be understood, but the wind tossed their words unheard upon the disturbed sea. In an unendurable and unending strain they worked like men driven by a merciless dream to toil in an atmosphere of ice or flame. They burnt and shivered in turns. Their eyeballs smarted as if in the smoke of a conflagration; their heads were ready to burst with every shout. Hard fingers seemed to grip their throats. At every roll they thought: Now I must let go. It will shake us all off—and thrown about aloft they cried wildly: "Look out there—catch the end." .... "Reeve clear" .... "Turn this block. ...." They nodded desperately; shook infuriated faces. "No! No! From down up." They seemed to hate one another with a deadly hate. The longing to be done with it all gnawed their breasts, and the wish to do things well was a burning pain. They cursed their fate, contemned their life, and wasted their breath in deadly imprecations upon one another. The sailmaker, with his bald head bared, worked feverishly, forgetting his intimacy with so many admirals. The boatswain, climbing up with marlinspikes and bunches of spunyarn rovings, or kneeling on the yard and ready to take a turn with the midship-stop, had acute and fleeting visions of his old woman and the youngsters in a moorland village. Mr. Baker, feeling very weak, tottered here and there, grunting and inflexible, like a man of iron. He waylaid those who, coming from aloft, stood gasping for breath. He ordered, encouraged, scolded. "Now then—to the main topsail now! Tally on to that gantline. Don't stand about there!"—"Is there no rest for us?" muttered voices. He spun round fiercely, with a sinking heart.—"No! No rest till the work is done. Work till you drop. That's what you're here for." A bowed seaman at his elbow gave a short laugh.—"Do or die," he croaked bitterly, then spat into his broad palms, swung up his long arms, and grasping the rope high above his head sent out a mournful, wailing cry for a pull all together. A sea boarded the quarter-deck and sent the whole lot sprawling to leeward. Caps, handspikes floated. Clenched hands, kicking legs, with here and there a spluttering face, stuck out of the white hiss of foaming water. Mr. Baker, knocked down with the rest, screamed—"Don't let go that rope! Hold on to it! Hold!" And sorely bruised by the brutal fling, they held on to it, as though it had been the fortune of their life. The ship ran, rolling heavily, and the topping crests glanced past port and starboard flashing their white heads. Pumps were freed. Braces were rove. The three topsails and foresail were set. She spurted faster over the water, outpacing the swift rush of waves. The menacing thunder of distanced seas rose behind her—filled the air with the tremendous vibrations of its voice. And devastated, battered, and wounded she drove foaming to the northward, as though inspired by the courage of a high endeavour. . . .

The forecastle was a place of damp desolation. They looked at their dwelling with dismay. It was slimy, dripping; it hummed hollow with the wind, and was strewn with shapeless wreckage like a half-tide cavern in a rocky and exposed coast. Many had lost all they had in the world, but most of the starboard watch had preserved their chests; thin streams of water trickled out of them, however. The beds were soaked; the blankets spread out and saved by some nail squashed under foot. They dragged wet rags from evil-smelling corners, and, wringing the water out, recognised their property. Some smiled stiffly. Others looked round blank and mute. There were cries of joy over old waistcoats, and groans of sorrow over shapeless things found amongst the black splinters of smashed bed boards. One lamp was discovered jammed under the bowsprit. Charley whimpered a little. Knowles stumped here and there, sniffing, examining dark places for salvage. He poured dirty water out of a boot, and was concerned to find the owner. Those who, overwhelmed by their losses, sat on the forepeak hatch, remained elbows on knees, and, with a fist against each cheek, disdained to look up. He pushed it under their noses. "Here's a good boot. Yours?" They snarled, "No—get out." One snapped at him, "Take it to hell out of this." He seemed surprised. "Why? It's a good boot," but remembering suddenly that he had lost every stitch of his clothing, he dropped his find and began to swear. In the dim light cursing voices clashed. A man came in and, dropping his arms, stood still, repeating from the doorstep, "Here's a bloomin' old go! Here's a bloomin' old go!" A few rooted anxiously in flooded chests for tobacco. They breathed hard, clamoured with heads down. "Look at that, Jack!" . . . . "Here! Sam! Here's my shore-going rig spoilt for ever." One blasphemed tearfully holding up a pair of dripping trousers. No one looked at him. The cat came out from somewhere. He had an ovation. They snatched him from hand to hand, caressed him in a murmur of pet names. They wondered where he had "weathered it out"; disputed about it. A squabbling argument began. Two men came in with a bucket of fresh water, and all crowded round it; but Tom, lean and mewing, came up with every hair astir and had the first drink. A couple of men went aft for oil and biscuits.

Then in the yellow light and in the intervals of mopping the deck they crunched hard bread, arranging to "worry through somehow." Men chummed as to beds. Turns were settled for wearing boots and having the use of oilskin coats. They called one another "old man" and "sonny" in cheery voices. Friendly slaps resounded. Jokes were shouted. One or two stretched on the wet deck, slept with heads pillowed on their bent arms, and several, sitting on the hatch, smoked. Their weary faces appeared through a thin blue haze, pacified and with sparkling eyes. The boatswain put his head through the door. "Relieve the wheel, one of you"—he shouted inside—"it's six. Blamme if that old Singleton hasn't been there more'n thirty hours. You are a fine lot." He slammed the door again. "Mate's watch on deck," said some one. "Hey, Donkin, it's your relief!" shouted three or four together. He had crawled into an empty bunk and on wet planks lay still. "Donkin, your wheel." He made no sound. "Donkin's dead," guffawed some one. "Sell 'is bloomin' clothes," shouted another. "Donkin, if ye don't go to the bloomin' wheel they will sell your clothes—d'ye hear?" jeered a third. He groaned from his dark hole. He complained about pains in all his bones, he whimpered pitifully. "He won't go," exclaimed a contemptuous voice, "your turn, Davies." The young seaman rose painfully squaring his shoulders. Donkin stuck his head out, and it appeared in the yellow light, fragile and ghastly. "I will giv' yer a pound of tobaccer," he whined in a conciliating voice, "so soon as I draw it from haft. I will—s'elp me. . . . ." Davies swung his arm backhanded and the head vanished. "I'll go," he said, "but you will pay for it." He walked unsteady but resolute to the door. "So I will," yelped Donkin, popping out behind him. "So I will—s'elp me . . . . a pound . . . . three bob the chawrge." Davies flung the door open. "You will pay my price . . . . in fine weather," he shouted over his shoulder. One of the men unbuttoned his wet coat rapidly, threw it at his head. "Here, Taffy—take that, you thief!" "Thank you!" he cried from the darkness above the swish of rolling water. He could be heard splashing; a sea came on board with a thump. "He's got his bath already," remarked a grim shellback. "Aye, aye!" grunted others. Then, after a long silence, Wamibo made strange noises. "Hallo, what's up with you?" said one grumpily. "He says he would have gone for Davy," explained Archie, who was the Finn's interpreter generally. "I believe him!" cried voices . . . . "Never mind, Dutchy . . . . You'll do, muddlehead . . . . Your turn will come soon enough . . . . You don't know when ye're well off." They ceased, and all together turned their faces to the door. Singleton stepped in, made two paces, and stood swaying slightly. The sea hissed, flowed roaring past the bows, and the forecastle trembled, full of a deep rumour; the lamp flared, swinging like a pendulum. He looked with a dreamy and puzzled stare, as though he could not distinguish the still men from their restless shadows. There were awe-struck murmurs:—"Hallo, hallo" . . . . "How does it look outside now, Singleton?" Those who sat on the hatch lifted their eyes in silence, and the next oldest seaman in the ship (those two understood one another, though they hardly exchanged three words in a day) gazed up at his friend attentively for a moment, then taking a short clay pipe out of his mouth, offered it without a word. Singleton put out his arm towards it, missed, staggered, and suddenly fell forward, crashing down, stiff and headlong like an uprooted tree. There was a swift rush. Men pushed, crying:—"He's done!" . . . . "Turn him over!" . . . . "Stand clear there!" Under a crowd of startled faces bending over him he lay on his back, staring upwards in a continuous and intolerable manner. In the breathless silence of a general consternation, he said in a grating murmur:—"I am all right," and clutched with his hands. They helped him up. He mumbled despondently:—"I am getting old . . . . old."—"Not you," cried Belfast, with ready tact. Supported on all sides, he hung his head.—"Are you better?" they asked. He glared at them from under his eyebrows with large black eyes, spreading over his chest the bushy whiteness of a beard long and thick.—"Old! old!" he repeated sternly. Helped along, he reached his bunk. There was in it a slimy soft heap of something that smelt, like does at dead low water a muddy foreshore. It was his soaked straw bed. With a convulsive effort he pitched himself on it, and in the darkness of the narrow place could be heard growling angrily, like an irritated and savage animal uneasy in its den:—"Bit of breeze . . . . small thing . . . . can't stand up . . . . old!" He slept at last. He breathed heavily, high-booted, sou'wester on head, and his oilskin clothes rustled, when with a deep sighing groan he turned over. Men conversed about him in quiet concerned whispers. "This will break 'im up" . . . . "Strong as a horse" . . . . "Aye. But he ain't what he used to be." . . . . In sad murmurs they gave him up. Yet at midnight he turned out to duty as if nothing had been the matter, and answered to his name with a mournful "Here!" He brooded alone more than ever, in an impenetrable silence and with a saddened face. For many years he had heard himself called "Old Singleton," and had serenely accepted the qualification, taking it as a tribute of respect due to a man who through half a century had measured his strength against the favours and the rages of the sea. He had never given a thought to his mortal self. He lived unscathed, as though he had been indestructible, surrendering to all the temptations, weathering many gales. He had panted in sunshine, shivered in the cold; suffered hunger, thirst, debauch; passed through many trials—known all the furies. Old! It seemed to him he was broken at last. And like a man bound treacherously while he sleeps, he woke up fettered by the long chain of disregarded years. He had to take up at once the burden of all his existence, and found it almost too heavy for his strength. Old! He moved his arms, shook his head, felt his limbs. Getting old . . . . and then? He looked upon the immortal sea with the awakened and groping perception of its heartless might; he saw it unchanged, black and foaming under the eternal scrutiny of the stars; he heard its impatient voice calling for him out of a pitiless vastness full of unrest, of turmoil, and of terror. He looked afar upon it, and he saw an immensity tormented and blind, moaning and furious, that claimed all the days of his tenacious life, and, when life was over, would claim the worn-out body of its slave.

This was the last of the breeze. It veered quickly, changed to a black south-easter, and blew itself out, giving the ship a famous shove to the northward into the joyous sunshine of the trade. Rapid and white she ran homewards in a straight path, under a blue sky and upon the plain of a blue sea. She carried Singleton's completed wisdom, Donkin's delicate susceptibilities, and the conceited folly of us all. The hours of ineffective turmoil were forgotten; the fear and anguish of these dark moments were never mentioned in the glowing peace of fine days. Yet from that time our life seemed to start afresh as though we had died and had been resuscitated. All the first part of the voyage, the Indian Ocean on the other side of the Cape, all that was lost in a haze, like an ineradicable suspicion of some previous existence. It had ended—then there were blank hours; a livid blurr—and again we lived! Singleton was possessed of sinister truth; Mr. Creighton of a damaged leg; the cook of fame—and shamefully abused the opportunities of his distinction. Donkin had an added grievance. He went about repeating with insistence:—" 'E said 'e would brain me—did yer 'ear? They hare goin' to murder hus now for the least little thing." We began at last to think it was rather awful. And we were conceited! We boasted of our pluck, of our capacity for work, of our energy. We remembered honourable episodes: our devotion, our indomitable perseverance—and were proud of them as though they had been the outcome of our unaided impulses. We remembered our danger, our toil—and conveniently forgot our horrible scare. We decried our officers—who had done nothing—and listened to the fascinating Donkin. His care for our rights, his disinterested concern for our dignity, were not discouraged by the invariable contumely of our words, by the disdain of our looks. Our contempt for him was unbounded—and we could not but listen with interest to that consummate artist. He told us we were good men— a "bloomin' condemned lot of good men." Who thanked us? Who took any notice of our wrongs? Didn't we lead a "dorg's loife for two poun' ten a month?" Did we think that miserable pay enough to compensate us for the risk to our lives and for the loss of our clothes? "We've lost hevery rag!" he cried. He made us forget that he, at any rate, had lost nothing of his own. The younger men listened, thinking—this 'ere Donkin's a long-headed chap, though no kind of man, anyhow. The Scandinavians were frightened at his audacities: Wamibo did not understand; and the older seamen thoughtfully nodded their heads making the thin gold earrings glitter in the fleshy lobes of hairy ears. Severe, sun-burnt faces were propped meditatively on tattooed forearms. Veined, brown fists held in their knotted grip the dirty white clay of smouldering pipes. They listened, impenetrable, broad-backed, with bent shoulders, and in grim silence. He talked with ardour, despised and irrefutable. His picturesque and filthy loquacity flowed like a troubled stream from a poisoned source. His beady little eyes danced, glancing right and left, ever on the watch for the approach of an officer. Sometimes Mr. Baker going forward to take a look at the head sheets would roll with his uncouth gait through the sudden stillness of the men; or Mr. Creighton limped along, smooth-faced, youthful, and more stern than ever, piercing our short silence with a keen glance of his clear eyes. Behind his back Donkin would begin again darting stealthy, sidelong looks.—" 'Ere's one of 'em. Some of yer 'as made 'im fast that day. Much thanks yer got for hit. Ain't 'ee a-drivin' yer wusse'n hever? . . . . Let 'im slip hoverboard . . . . Vy not? It would 'ave been less trouble. Vy not?" He advanced confidentially, backed away with great effect; he whispered, he screamed, waved his miserable arms no thicker than pipe-stems—stretched his lean neck—spluttered—squinted. In the pauses of his impassioned orations the wind sighed quietly aloft, the calm sea unheeded murmured in a warning whisper along the ship's side. We abominated the creature and could not deny the luminous truth of his contentions. It was all so obvious. We were indubitably good men; our deserts were great and our pay small. Through our exertions we had saved the ship and the skipper would get the credit of it. What had he done? we wanted to know. Donkin asked:—"What 'ee could do without hus?" and we could not answer. We were oppressed by the injustice of the world, surprised to perceive how long we had lived under its burden without realising our unfortunate state, annoyed by the uneasy suspicion of our undiscerning stupidity. Donkin assured us it was all our "good 'eartedness," but we would not be consoled by such shallow sophistry. We were men enough to courageously admit to ourselves our intellectual shortcomings; though from that time we refrained from kicking him, tweaking his nose, or from accidentally knocking him about, which last, after we had weathered the Cape, had been rather a popular amusement. Davies ceased to talk at him provokingly about black eyes and flattened noses. Charley, much subdued since the gale, did not jeer at him. Knowles deferentially and with a crafty air propounded questions such as:— "Could we all have the same grub as the mates? Could we all stop ashore till we got it? What would be the next thing to try for if we got that?" He answered readily with contemptuous certitude; he strutted with assurance in clothes that were much too big for him as though he had tried to disguise himself. These were Jimmy's clothes mostly—though he would accept anything from anybody; but nobody, except Jimmy, had anything to spare. His devotion to Jimmy was unbounded. He was for ever dodging in the little cabin, ministering to Jimmy's wants, humoring his whims, submitting to his exacting peevishness, often laughing with him. Nothing could keep him away from the pious work of visiting the sick, especially when there was some heavy hauling to be done on deck. Mr. Baker had on two occasions jerked him out from there by the scruff of the neck to our inexpressible scandal. Was a sick chap to be left without attendance? Were we to be ill-used for attending a shipmate?—"What?" growled Mr. Baker, turning menacingly at the mutter, and the whole half-circle like one man stepped back a pace. "Set the topmast stunsail. Away aloft, Donkin, overhaul the gear," ordered the mate inflexibly. "Fetch the sail along; bend the down-haul clear. Bear a hand." Then, the sail set, he would go slowly aft and stand looking at the compass for a long time, careworn, pensive, and breathing hard as if stifled by the taint of unaccountable ill-will that pervaded the ship. "What's up amongst them?" he thought. "Can't make out this hanging back and growling. A good crowd, too, as they go nowadays." On deck the men exchanged bitter words, suggested by a silly exasperation against something unjust and irremediable that would not be denied, and would whisper into their ears long after Donkin had ceased speaking. Our little world went on its curved and unswerving path carrying a discontented and aspiring population. They found comfort of a gloomy kind in an interminable and conscientious analysis of their unappreciated worth; and inspired by Donkin's hopeful doctrines they dreamed enthusiastically of the time when every lonely ship would travel over a serene sea, manned by a wealthy and well-fed crew of satisfied skippers.

It looked as if it would be a long passage. The south-east trades, light and unsteady, were left behind; and then, on the equator and under a low grey sky, the ship, in close heat, floated upon a smooth sea that resembled a sheet of ground glass. Thunder squalls hung on the horizon, circled round the ship, far off and growling angrily, like a troop of wild beasts afraid to charge home. The invisible sun, sweeping above the upright masts, made on the clouds a blurred stain of rayless light, and a similar patch of faded radiance kept pace with it from east to west over the unglittering level of the waters. At night, through the impenetrable darkness of earth and heaven, broad sheets of flame waved noiselessly; and for half a second the becalmed craft stood out with its masts and rigging, with every sail and every rope distinct and black in the centre of a fiery outburst, like a charred ship enclosed in a globe of fire. And, again, for long hours she remained lost in a vast universe of night and silence where gentle sighs wandering here and there like forlorn souls, made the still sails flutter as in sudden fear, and the ripple of a beshrouded ocean whisper its compassion afar—in a voice mournful, immense, and faint. . . .

When the lamp was put out, and through the door thrown wide open, Jimmy, turning on his pillow, could see vanishing beyond the straight line of top-gallant rail, the quick, repeated visions of a fabulous world made up of leaping fire and sleeping water. The lightning gleamed in his big sad eyes that seemed in a red flicker to burn themselves out in his black face, and then he would lay blinded and invisible in the midst of an intense darkness. He could hear on the quiet deck soft footfalls, the breathing of some man lounging on the doorstep; the low creak of swaying masts; or the calm voice of the watch-officer reverberating aloft, hard and loud, amongst the unstirring sails. He listened with avidity, taking a rest in the attentive perception of the slightest sound from the fatiguing wanderings of his sleeplessness. He was cheered by the rattling of blocks, reassured by the stir and murmur of the watch, soothed by the slow yawn of some sleepy and weary seaman settling himself deliberately for a snooze on the planks. Life seemed an indestructible thing. It went on in darkness, in sunshine, in sleep; tireless, it hovered affectionately round the imposture of his ready death. It was bright, like the twisted flare of lightning, and more full of surprises than the dark night. It made him safe, and the calm of its overpowering darkness was as precious as its restless and dangerous light.

But in the evening, in the dog-watches, and even far into the first night-watch, a knot of men could always be seen congregated before Jimmy's cabin. They leaned on each side of the door, peacefully interested and with crossed legs; they stood astride the doorstep discoursing, or sat in silent couples on his sea-chest; while against the bulwark along the spare topmast, three or four in a row stared meditatively, with their simple faces lit up by the projected glare of Jimmy's lamp. The little place, repainted white, had, in the night, the brilliance of a silver shrine where a black idol, reclining stiffly under a blanket, blinked its weary eyes and received our homage. Donkin officiated. He had the air of a demonstrator showing a phenomenon, a manifestation bizarre, simple, and meritorious, that, to the beholders, should be a profound and an everlasting lesson. "Just look at 'em, 'ee knows what's what—never fear!" he exclaimed now and then, flourishing a hand hard and fleshless like the claw of a snipe. Jimmy, on his back, smiled with reserve and without moving a limb. He affected the languor of extreme weakness, so as to make it manifest to us that delay in hauling him out from his horrible confinement, and then that night spent on the poop among our selfish neglect of his needs, had "done for him." He rather liked to talk about it, and of course we were always interested. He spoke spasmodically, in fast rushes with long pauses between, as a tipsy man walks. . . . . "Cook had just given me a pannikin of hot coffee. . . . . Slapped it down there, on my chest—banged the door to. . . . . I felt a heavy roll coming; tried to save my coffee, burnt my fingers . . . . and fell out of my bunk. . . . . She went over so quick. . . . . Water came in through the ventilator. . . . . I couldn't move the door . . . . dark as a grave . . . . tried to scramble up into the upper berth. . . . . Rats . . . . a rat bit my finger as I got up. . . . . I could hear him swimming below me. . . . . I thought you would never come . . . . I thought you were all gone overboard . . . . of course . . . . Could hear nothing but the wind. . . . . Then you came . . . . to look for the corpse, I suppose. A little more and . . . ."

"Man! But ye made a rare lot of noise in here," observed Archie, thoughtfully.

"You chaps kicked up such a confounded row above. . . . . Enough to scare any one. . . . . I didn't know what you were up to. . . . . Bash in the blamed planks . . . . my head. . . . . Just what a silly, scary gang of fools would do. . . . . Not much good to me anyhow. . . . . Just as well . . . . drown. . . . . Pah."

He groaned, snapped his big white teeth, and gazed with scorn. Belfast lifted a pair of dolorous eyes, with a broken-hearted smile, clenched his fists stealthily; blue-eyed Archie caressed his red whiskers with a hesitating hand; the boatswain at the door stared a moment, and brusquely went away with a loud guffaw. Wamibo dreamed. . . . . Donkin felt all over his sterile chin for the few rare hairs, and said, triumphantly, with a sidelong glance at Jimmy:—"Look at 'im! Wish I was 'arf has 'ealthy has 'e his—I do." He jerked a short thumb over his shoulder towards the after end of the ship. "That's the blooming way to do 'em!" he yelped, with forced heartiness. Jimmy said:—"Don't be a dam' fool," in a pleasant voice. Knowles, rubbing his shoulder against the doorpost, remarked shrewdly:—"We can't all go an' be took sick—it would be mutiny.—"Mutiny—gawn!" jeered Donkin; "there's no bloomin' law against bein' sick."—"There's six weeks' hard for refoosing dooty," argued Knowles. "I mind I once seed in Cardiff the crew of an overloaded ship—leastways she weren't overloaded, only a fatherly old gentleman with a white beard and an umbreller came along the quay and talked to the hands. Said as how it was crool hard to be drownded in winter just for the sake of a few pounds more for the owner—he said. Nearly cried over them—he did; and he had a square mainsail coat, and a gaff-topsail hat too—all proper. So they chaps they said they wouldn't go to be drownded in winter—depending upon that 'ere Plimsoll man to see 'em through the court. They thought to have a bloomin' lark and two or three days' spree. And the beak giv' 'em six weeks—coss the ship warn't overloaded. Anyways they made it out in court that she wasn't. There wasn't one overloaded ship in Penarth Dock at all. 'Pears that old coon he was only on pay and allowance from some kind people, under orders to look for overloaded ships, and he couldn't see no further than the length of his umbreller. Some of us in the boarding-house, where I live when I'm looking for a ship in Cardiff, stood by to duck that old weeping spunger in the dock. We kept a good look out, too—but he topped his boom directly he was outside the court. . . . . Yes. They got six weeks' hard. . . . ."

They listened, full of curiosity, nodding in the pauses their rough pensive faces. Donkin opened his mouth once or twice, but restrained himself. Jimmy lay still with open eyes and not at all interested. A seaman emitted the opinion that after a verdict of atrocious partiality "the bloomin' beaks go an' drink at the skipper's expense." Others assented. It was clear, of course. Donkin said:—"Well, six weeks hain't much trouble. You sleep hall night in, reg'lar, in chokey. Do it hon my 'ead." "You are used to it ainch'ee, Donkin?" asked somebody. Jimmy condescended to laugh. It cheered up every one wonderfully. Knowles, with surprising mental agility, shifted his ground. "If we all went sick what would become of the ship? eh?" He posed the problem and grinned all round.—"Let 'er go to 'ell," sneered Donkin. "Damn'er. She ain't yourn."—"What? Just let her drift?" insisted Knowles in a tone of unbelief.—"Aye! Drift, an' be blowed," affirmed Donkin with fine recklessness. The other did not see it—meditated.—"The stores would run out," he muttered, "and . . . . never get anywhere . . . . and what about pay-day?" he added with greater assurance.—"Jack likes a good pay-day," exclaimed a listener on the doorstep. "Aye, because then the girls put one arm round his neck an' t'other in his pocket, an' call him ducky.

Don't they, Jack?"—"Jack, you're a terror with the gals."—"He takes three of 'em in tow to once, like one of 'em Watkinses two-funnel tugs waddling away with three schooners behind."—"Jack, you're a lame scamp."—"Jack, tell us about that one with a blue eye and a black eye. Do."—"There's plenty of girls with one black eye along the Highway by . . . ."—"No, that's a speshul one—come Jack." Donkin looked severe and disgusted; Jimmy very bored; a grey-haired sea-dog shook his head slightly, smiling at the bowl of his pipe, discreetly amused. Knowles turned about bewildered; stammered first at one, then at another.—"No! . . . . I never! . . . . can't talk sensible sense midst you. . . . . Always on the kid." He retired bashfully—muttering and pleased. They laughed hooting in the crude light, around Jimmy's bed, where on a white pillow his hollowed black face moved to and fro restlessly. A puff of wind came, made the flame of the lamp leap, and outside, high up, the sails fluttered, while near by the block of the foresheet struck a ringing blow on the iron bulwark. A voice far off cried, "Helm up!" another, more faint, answered, "Hard-up, sir!" They became silent—waited expectantly. The grey-haired seaman knocked his pipe on the doorstep and stood up. The ship leaned over gently and the sea seemed to wake up, murmuring drowsily. "Here's a little wind comin'," said some one very low. Jimmy turned over slowly to face the breeze. The voice in the night cried loud and commanding:—"Haul the spanker out." The group before the door vanished out of the light. They could be heard tramping aft while they repeated with varied intonations:—"Spanker out!" . . . . "Out spanker, sir!" Donkin remained alone with Jimmy. There was a silence. Jimmy opened and shut his lips several times as if swallowing draughts of fresher air; Donkin moved the toes of his bare feet and looked at them thoughtfully.

"Ain't you going to give them a hand with the sail?" asked Jimmy.

"No. Hif six ov 'em hain't 'nough beef to set that blamed, rotten spanker, they hain't fit to live," answered Donkin in a bored, faraway voice, as though he had been talking from the bottom of a hole. Jimmy considered the conical, fowl-like profile with a queer kind of interest; he was leaning out of his bunk with the calculating, uncertain expression of a man who reflects how best to lay hold of some strange creature that looks as though it could sting or bite. But he said only:—"The mate will miss you—and there will be ructions."

Donkin got up to go. "I will do for 'im hon some dark night, see hif I don't," he said over his shoulder.

Jimmy went on quickly:—"You're like a poll-parrot, like a screechin' poll-parrot." Donkin stopped and cocked his head attentively on one side. His big ears stood out, transparent and veined, resembling the thin wings of a bat.

"Yuss?" he said, with his back towards Jimmy.

"Yes! Chatter out all you know—like . . . . like a dirty white cockatoo."

Donkin waited. He could hear the other's breathing, long and slow; the breathing of a man with a hundredweight or so on the breast-bone. Then he asked calmly:—"What do I know?"

"What? . . . . What I tell you . . . . not much. What do you want . . . . to talk about my health so . . . ."

"Hit's a blooming himposyshun. A bloomin', stinkin', first-class himposyshun—but hit don't tyke me hin. Not hit."

Jimmy kept still. Donkin put his hands in his pockets, and in one slouching stride came up to the bunk.

"I talk—what's the hodds. They hain't men here—sheep they hare. A driven lot of sheep. I 'old you hup . . . . Vy not? You're well hoff."

"I am . . . . I don't say anything about that. . . . ."

"Well. Let 'em see hit. Let 'em larn what a man can do. I ham a man, I know hall about yer. . . . ." Jimmy threw himself further away on the pillow; the other stretched out his skinny neck, jerked his bird face down at him as though pecking at the eyes. "I ham a man. I've seen the hinside of every chokey in the Colonies rather'n give hup my rights. . . . ."

"You are a jail-prop," said Jimmy weakly.

"I ham . . . . an' proud of it too. You! You 'aven't the bloomin' nerve—so you hinventyd this 'ere dodge. . . . ." He paused; then with marked afterthought accentuated slowly;—"Yer ain't sick—hare yer?"

"No," said Jimmy firmly. "Been out of sorts now and again this year," he mumbled with a sudden drop in his voice.

Donkin closed one eye, amicable and confidential. He whispered:—"Ye 'ave done hit afore—aven'tchee?" Jimmy smiled—

then as if unable to hold back he let himself go:—"Last ship—yes. I was out of sorts on the passage. See? It was easy. They paid me off in Calcutta, and the skipper made no bones about it either. . . . . I got my money all right. Laid up fifty-eight days! The fools! O Lord! The fools! Paid right off." He laughed spasmodically. Donkin chummed giggling. Then Jimmy coughed violently. "I am as well as ever," he said, as soon as he could draw breath.

Donkin made a derisive gesture. "In course," he said profoundly, "hany one can see that."—"They don't," said Jimmy, gasping like a fish.—"They would swallow any yarn," affirmed Donkin.—"Don't you let on too much" admonished Jimmy in an exhausted voice—"Your little gyme? Eh?" commented Donkin jovially. Then with sudden disgust: "Yer hall for yerself, s'long has ye're right. . . . ."

So charged with egoism James Wait pulled the blanket up to his chin and lay still for awhile. His heavy lips protruded in an everlasting black pout. "Why are you so hot on making trouble?" he asked without much interest.

" 'Cos hit's a bloomin' shayme. We hare put hon . . . . bad food, bad pay . . . . I want hus to kick up a bloomin' row; a blamed 'owling row that would make 'em remember! Knocking people habout . . . . brain hus . . . . hindeed! Ain't we men?" His altruistic indignation blazed. Then he said calmly:—"I've been a-hairing ov yer clothes."—"All right," said Jimmy languidly, "bring them in."—"Giv' us the key of your chest, I'll put 'em away for yer," said Donkin with friendly eagerness.—"Bring 'em in, I will put them away myself," answered James Wait with severity. Donkin looked down, muttering. . . . . "What d'you say? What d'you say?" inquired Wait anxiously.—"Nothink. The night's dry, let 'em 'ang out till the morning," said Donkin, in a strangely trembling voice, as though restraining laughter or rage. Jimmy seemed satisfied.—"Give me a little water for the night in my mug—there," he said. Donkin took a stride over the doorstep.—"Git it yerself," he replied in a surly tone. "You can do it, hunless you *hare* sick."—"Of course I can do it," said Wait, "only . . . ."—"Well, then, do it," said Donkin viciously, "if yer can look hafter yer clothes, yer can look hafter yerself." He went on deck without a look back.

Jimmy reached out for the mug. Not a drop. He put it back

gently with a faint sigh—and closed his eyes. He thought:—That lunatic Belfast will bring me some water if I ask. Fool. I am very thirsty. . . . . It was very hot in the cabin, and it seemed to turn slowly round, detach itself from the ship, and swing out smoothly into a luminous, arid space where a black sun shone, spinning very fast. A place without any water! No water! A policeman with the face of Donkin drank a glass of beer by the side of an empty well, and flew away flapping vigorously. A ship whose mastheads protruded through the sky and could not be seen, was discharging grain, and the wind whirled the dry husks in spirals along the quay of a dock with no water in it. He whirled along with the husks—very tired and light. All his inside was gone. He felt lighter than the husks—and more dry. He expanded his hollow chest. The air streamed in carrying away in its rush a lot of strange things that resembled houses, trees, people, lamp-posts. . . . . No more! There was no more air—and he had not finished drawing his long breath. But he was in gaol! They were locking him up. A door slammed. They turned the key twice, flung a bucket of water over him—Phoo! What for?

He opened his eyes, thinking the fall had been very heavy for an empty man—empty—empty. He was in his cabin. Ah! All right! His face was streaming with perspiration, his arms heavier than lead. He saw the cook standing in the doorway, a brass key in one hand and a bright tin hook-pot in the other.

"I have been locking up for the night," said the cook, beaming benevolently. "Eight-bells just gone. I brought you a pot of cold tea for your night's drinking, Jimmy. I sweetened it with some white cabin sugar, too. Well—it won't break the ship."

He came in, hung the pot on the edge of the bunk, asked perfunctorily, "How goes it?" and sat down on the box.—"H'm," grunted Wait inhospitably. The cook wiped his face with a dirty cotton rag, which, afterwards, he tied round his neck.—"That's how them firemen do in steamboats," he said serenely, and much pleased with himself. "My work is as heavy as theirs—I'm thinking—and longer hours. Did you ever see them down the stokehold? Like fiends they look—firing—firing—firing—down there."

He pointed his forefinger at the deck. Some gloomy thought darkened his shining face, fleeting, like the shadow of a travelling cloud over the light of a peaceful sea. The relieved watch tramped noisily forward, passing in a body across the sheen of the doorway. Some one cried, "Good night!" Belfast stopped for a moment and looked in at Jimmy, quivering and speechless as if with repressed emotion. He gave the cook a glance charged with dismal foreboding, and vanished. The cook cleared his throat. Jimmy stared upwards and kept as still as a man in hiding.

The night was clear, with a gentle breeze. The ship heeled over a little, slipping quietly over a sombre sea towards the inaccessible and festal splendour of a black horizon pierced by points of flickering fire. Above the mastheads the resplendent curve of the Milky Way spanned the sky like a triumphal arch of eternal light, thrown over the dark pathway of the earth. On the forecastle head a man whistled with loud precision a lively jig, while another could be heard faintly, shuffling and stamping in time. There came from forward a confused murmur of voices, laughter—snatches of song. The cook shook his head, glanced obliquely at Jimmy, and began to mutter. "Aye. Dance and sing. That's all they think of. I am surprised the Providence don't get tired. . . . . They forget the day that's sure to come . . . . but you. . . . ."

Jimmy drank a gulp of tea, hurriedly, as though he had stolen it, and shrank under his blanket, edging away towards the bulkhead. The cook got up, closed the door, then sat down again and said distinctly:—

"Whenever I poke my galley fire I think of you chaps—swearing, stealing, lying, and worse—as if there was no such thing as another world. . . . . Not bad fellows, either, in a way," he conceded slowly; then, after a pause of regretful musing, he went on in a resigned tone:—"Well, well. They will have a hot time of it. Hot! Did I say? The furnaces of one of them White Star boats ain't nothing to it."

He kept very quiet for a while. There was a great stir in his brain; an addled vision of bright outlines; an exciting row of rousing songs and groans of pain. He suffered, enjoyed, admired, approved. He was delighted, frightened, exalted—like on that evening (the only time in his life—twenty-seven years ago; he loved to recall the number of years) when as a young man he had—through keeping bad company—become intoxicated in an East-end music-hall. A tide of sudden feeling swept him clean out of his body. He soared. He contemplated the secret of the hereafter. It commended itself to him. It was excellent; he loved it, himself, all hands, and Jimmy. His heart overflowed with tenderness, with comprehension, with the desire to meddle, with anxiety for the soul of that black man, with the pride of possessed eternity, with the feeling of might. Snatch him up in his arms and pitch him right into the middle of salvation . . . . the black soul—blacker—body—rot—Devil. No! Talk—strength—Samson. . . . . There was a great din as of cymbals in his ears; he flashed through an ecstatic jumble of shining faces, lilies, prayer-books, unearthly joy, white shirts, gold harps, black coats, wings. He saw flowing garments, clean shaved faces, a sea of light—a lake of pitch. There were sweet scents, a smell of sulphur—red tongues of flame licking a white mist. An awesome voice thundered! . . . . It lasted three seconds.

"Jimmy!" he cried in an inspired tone. Then he hesitated. A spark of human pity glimmered yet through the infernal fog of his supreme conceit.

"What?" said James Wait, unwillingly. There was a silence. He turned his head just the least bit, and stole a cautious glance. The cook's lips moved inaudibly; his face was rapt, his eyes turned up. He seemed to be mentally imploring deck beams, the brass hook of the lamp, two cockroaches.

"Look here," said Wait, "I want to go to sleep. I think I could."

"This is no time for sleep!" exclaimed the cook, very loud. He had prayerfully divested himself of the last vestige of his humanity. He was a voice—a fleshless and sublime thing, as on that memorable night—the night when he went over the sea to make coffee for perishing sinners. "This is not time for sleeping," he repeated with exaltation. "*I* can't sleep."

"Don't care damn," said Wait, with factitious energy. "I can. Go an' turn in."

"Swear . . . . in the very jaws! . . . . In the very jaws! Don't you see the fire . . . . don't you feel it? Blind, chock-full of sin! I can see it for you. I can't bear it. I hear the call to save you. Night and day. Jimmy let me save you!" The words of entreaty and menace broke out of him in a roaring torrent. The cockroaches ran away. Jimmy perspired, wriggling stealthily under his blanket. The cook yelled. . . . . "Your days are numbered! . . . ."—"Get out of this," boomed Wait, courageously.—"Pray with me! . . . ."—"I won't! . . . ." The little cabin was as hot as an oven. It contained an immensity of fear and pain; an atmosphere of shrieks and moans; prayers vociferated like blasphemies and whispered curses. Outside, the men called by Charley, who informed them in tones of delight that there was a row going on in Jimmy's place, pushed before the closed door, too startled to open it. All hands were there. The watch below had jumped out on deck in their shirts, as after a collision. Men running up, asked:—"What is it?" Others said:—"Listen!" The muffled screaming went on:—"On your knees! On your knees!"—"Shut up!"—"Never! You are delivered into my hands. . . . . Your life has been saved. . . . . Purpose. . . . . Mercy. . . . . Repent."—"You are a crazy fool! . . . ."—"Account of you . . . . you . . . . Never sleep in this world, if I . . . ."—"Leave off."—"No! . . . . stokehold . . . . only think! . . . ." Then an impassioned screeching babble where words pattered like hail.—"No!" shouted Jim.—"Yes. You are! . . . . No help. . . . . Everybody says so."—"You lie!"—"I see you dying this minnyt . . . . before my eyes . . . . as good as dead now."—"Help!" shouted Jimmy, piercingly.—"Not in this valley. . . . . look upwards," howled the other.—"Go away! Murder! Help!" clamoured Jimmy. His voice broke. There were moanings, low mutters, a few sobs.

"What's the matter now?" said a seldom-heard voice.—"Fall back, men! Fall back, there!" repeated Mr. Creighton sternly, pushing through.—"Here's the old man," whispered some.—"The cook's in there, sir," exclaimed several, backing away. The door clattered open; a broad stream of light darted out on wondering faces; a warm whiff of vitiated air passed. The two mates towered head and shoulders above the spare, grey-headed man who stood revealed between them, in shabby clothes, stiff and angular, like a small carved figure, and with a thin, composed face. The cook got up from his knees. Jimmy sat high in the bunk, clasping his drawn-up legs. The tassel of the blue nightcap almost imperceptibly trembled over his knees. They gazed astonished at his long, curved back, while the white corner of one eye gleamed blindly at them. He was afraid to turn his head, he shrank within himself; and there was an aspect astounding and animal-like in the perfection of his expectant immobility. A thing of instinct—the unthinking stillness of a scared brute.

"What are you doing here?" asked Mr. Baker, sharply.—"My duty," said the cook, with ardour.—"Your . . . . what?" began the mate. Captain Allistoun touched his arm lightly.—"I know his caper," he said, in a low voice. "Come out of that, Podmore," he ordered, aloud.

The cook wrung his hands, shook his fists above his head, and his arms dropped as if too heavy. For a moment he stood distracted and speechless.—"Never," he stammered. "I . . . . he . . . . I."—"What—do—you—say?" pronounced Captain Allistoun. "Come out at once—or . . . ."—"I am going," said the cook, with a hasty and sombre resignation. He strode over the doorstep firmly—hesitated—made a few steps. They looked at him in silence.—"I make you responsible!" he cried desperately, turning half round. "That man is dying. I make you . . . ."—"You there yet?" called the master in a threatening tone.—"No, sir," he exclaimed hurriedly in a startled voice. The boatswain led him away by the arm; some one laughed; Jimmy lifted his head for a stealthy glance, and in one unexpected leap sprang out of his bunk; Mr. Baker made a clever catch and felt him very limp in his arms; the group at the door grunted with surprise.—"He lies," gasped Wait, "he talked about black devils—he is a devil—a white devil—I am all right." He stiffened himself, and Mr. Baker, experimentally, let him go. He staggered a pace or two; Captain Allistoun watched him with a quiet and penetrating gaze; Belfast ran to his support. He did not appear to be aware of any one near him; he stood silently for a moment, battling single-handed with a legion of nameless terrors, amidst the eager looks of excited men who watched him far off, utterly alone in the impenetrable solitude of his fear. Heavy breathings stirred the darkness. The sea gurgled through the scuppers as the ship heeled over to a short puff of wind.

"Keep him away from me," said James Wait at last in his fine baritone voice, and leaning with all his weight on Belfast's neck. "I've been better this last week . . . . I am well . . . . I was going back to duty . . . . to-morrow—now if you like—Captain." Belfast hitched his shoulders to keep him upright.

"No," said the master, looking at him fixedly.

Under Jimmy's armpit Belfast's red face moved uneasily. A row of eyes gleaming stared on the edge of light. They pushed one another with elbows, turned their heads, whispered. Wait let his chin fall on his breast and, with lowered eyelids, looked round in a suspicious manner.

"Why not?" cried a voice from the shadows, "the man's all right, sir."

"I am all right," said Wait with eagerness. "Been sick . . . . better . . . . turn-to now." He sighed.—"Howly Mother!" exclaimed Belfast with a heave of the shoulders, "stand up, Jimmy."—"Keep away from me then," said Wait, giving Belfast a petulant push, and reeling fetched against the door-post. His cheek-bones glistened as though they had been varnished. He snatched off his nightcap, wiped his perspiring face with it, flung it on the deck. "I am coming out," he said without stirring.

"No. You don't," said the master curtly. Bare feet shuffled, disapproving voices murmured all round; he went on as if he had not heard:—"You have been skulking nearly all the passage and now you want to come out. You think you are near enough to the pay-table now. Smell the shore, hey?"

"I've been sick . . . . now—better," mumbled Wait glaring in the light.—"You have been shamming sick," retorted Captain Allistoun with severity; "Why . . . ." he hesitated for less than half a second. "Why, anybody can see that. There's nothing the matter with you, but you choose to lie-up to please yourself—and now you shall lie-up to please me. Mr. Baker, my orders are that this man is not to be allowed on deck to the end of the passage."

There were exclamations of surprise, triumph, indignation. The dark group of men swung across the light. "What for?" "Told you so . . . ." "Bloomin' shame . . . ."—"We've got to say something habout that," screeched Donkin from the rear.—"Never mind, Jim—we will see you righted," cried several together. An elderly seaman stepped to the front. "D'ye mean to say, sir," he asked ominously, "that a sick chap ain't allowed to get well in this 'ere hooker?" Behind him Donkin whispered excitedly amongst a staring crowd where no one spared him a glance, but Captain Allistoun shook a forefinger at the angry bronzed face of the speaker.—"You—you hold your tongue," he said warningly.—"This isn't the way," clamoured two or three younger men.—"Hare we bloomin' masheens?" inquired Donkin in a piercing tone, and dived under the elbows of the front rank.—"Soon show 'im we ain't boys . . . ."—"The man's a man if he is black."—"We ain't goin' to work this bloomin' ship shorthanded if Snowball's all right . . . ."—"He says he is."—"Well then, strike, boys, strike!"—"That's the bloomin' ticket." Captain Allistoun said sharply to the second mate: "Keep quiet, Mr. Creighton," and stood composed in the tumult, listening with profound attention to mixed growls and screeches, to every exclamation and every curse of the sudden outbreak. Somebody slammed the cabin door to with a kick: the darkness full of menacing mutters leaped with a short clatter over the streak of light, and the men became gesticulating shadows that growled, hissed, laughed excitedly. Mr. Baker whispered:—"Get away from them, sir." The big shape of Mr. Creighton hovered silently about the slight figure of the master.—"We have been hymposed upon all this voyage," said a gruff voice, "but this 'ere fancy takes the cake."—"That man is a shipmate."—"Are we bloomin' kids?"—"The port watch will refuse duty." Charley carried away by his feelings whistled shrilly, then yelped:—"Giv' us our Jimmy!" This seemed to cause a variation in the disturbance. There was a fresh burst of squabbling uproar. A lot of quarrels were set going at once.—"Yes"—"No."—"Never been sick."—"Go for them to once."—"Shut yer mouth, youngster—this is men's work."—"Is it?" muttered Captain Allistoun bitterly. Mr. Baker grunted: "Ough! They're gone silly. They've been simmering for the last month."—"I did notice," said the master.—"They have started a row amongst themselves now," said Mr. Creighton with disdain, "better get aft, sir. We will soothe them."—"Keep your temper, Creighton," said the master. And the three men began to move slowly towards the cabin door.

In the shadows of the fore rigging a dark mass stamped, eddied, advanced, retreated. There were words of reproach, encouragement, unbelief, execration. The elder seamen, bewildered and angry, growled their determination to go through with something or other; but the younger school of advanced thought exposed their and Jimmy's wrongs with confused shouts, arguing amongst themselves. They clustered round that moribund carcass, the fit emblem of their aspirations, and encouraging one another they swayed, they tramped on one spot, shouting that they would not be "put upon." Inside the cabin, Belfast, helping Jimmy into his bunk, twitched all over in his desire not to miss all the row, and with difficulty restrained the tears of his facile emotion. James Wait, flat on his back under the blanket, gasped complaints.—"We will back you up, never fear," assured Belfast, busy about his feet.—"I'll come out to-morrow morning——take my chance——you fellows must——" mumbled Wait. "I come out to-morrow——skipper or no skipper." He lifted one arm with great difficulty, passed a hand over his face; "Don't you let cook . . . ." he breathed out.—"No, no," said Belfast, turning his back on the bunk. "I will put a head on him if he comes near you."—"I will smash his mug!" exclaimed faintly Wait, enraged and weak; "I don't want to kill a man, but . . . ." He panted fast like a dog after a run in sunshine. Some one just outside the door shouted, "He's as fit as any ov us!" Belfast put his hand on the door-handle.—"Here!" called James Wait hurriedly and in such a clear voice that the other spun round with a start. James Wait, stretched out black and deathlike in the dazzling light, turned his head on the pillow. His eyes stared at Belfast, appealing and impudent. "I am rather weak from lying-up so long," he said distinctly. Belfast nodded. "Getting quite well now," insisted Wait.—"Yes. I noticed you getting better this . . . . last month," said Belfast looking down. "Hallo! What's this?" he shouted and ran out.

He was flattened directly against the side of the house by two men who lurched against him. A lot of disputes seemed to be going on all round. He got clear and saw three indistinct figures standing alone in the fainter darkness under the arched foot of the mainsail, that rose above their heads like a convex wall of a high edifice. Donkin hissed:—"Go for them . . . . it's dark!" The crowd took a short run aft in a body—then there was a check. Donkin, agile and thin, flitted past with his right arm going like a windmill—and then stood still suddenly with his arm pointing rigidly above his head. The hurtling flight of some small heavy object was heard; it passed between the heads of the two mates, bounded heavily along the deck, struck the after hatch with a ponderous and deadened blow. The bulky shape of Mr. Baker grew distinct. "Come to your senses, men!" he cried, advancing at the arrested crowd. "Come back, Mr. Baker!" called the master's quiet voice. He obeyed unwillingly. There was a minute of silence, then a deafening hubbub arose. Above it Archie was heard energetically:—"If you do oot ageen I wull tell!" There were shouts. "Don't!"

"Drop it!"—"We ain't that kind!" The black cluster of human forms reeled against the bulwark, back again towards the house. Shadowy figures could be seen tottering, falling, leaping up. Ring-bolts rang under stumbling feet.—"Drop it!" "Let me!"—"No!"—"Curse you . . . . hah!" Then sounds as of some one's face being slapped; a piece of iron fell on the deck; a short scuffle, and some one's shadowy body scuttled rapidly across the main hatch before the shadow of a kick. A raging voice sobbed out a torrent of filthy language . . . . —"Throwing things—good God!" grunted Mr. Baker in dismay.—"That was meant for me," said the master quietly; "I felt the wind of that thing; what was it—an iron belaying-pin?"—"By Jove!" muttered Mr. Creighton. The confused voices of men talking amidships mingled with the wash of the sea, ascended between the silent and distended sails—seemed to flow away into the night, further than the horizon, higher than the sky. The stars burned steadily over the inclined mastheads. Trails of light lay on the water, broke before the advancing hull, and, after she had passed, trembled for a long time as if in awe of the murmuring sea.

Meantime the helmsman, anxious to know what the row was about, had let go the wheel, and, bent double, ran with long stealthily footsteps to the break of the poop. The *Narcissus,* left to herself, came up gently to the wind without any one being aware of it. She gave a slight roll, and the sleeping sails woke suddenly, coming all together with a mighty flap against the masts, then filled again one after another in a quick succession of loud reports that ran down the lofty spars, till the collapsed mainsail flew out last with a violent jerk. The ship trembled from trucks to keel; the sails kept on rattling like a discharge of musketry; the chain sheets and loose shackles jingled aloft in a thin peal; the gin blocks groaned. It was as if an invisible hand had given the ship an angry shake to recall the men that peopled her decks to the sense of reality, vigilance, and duty.—"Helm up!" cried the master sharply. "Run aft, Mr. Creighton, and see what that fool there is up to."—"Flatten in the head sheets. Stand by the weather fore-braces," growled Mr. Baker. Startled men ran swiftly repeating the orders. The watch below, abandoned all at once by the watch on deck, drifted towards the forecastle in two and threes, arguing noisily as they went.—"We shall see to-morrow!" cried a loud voice, as if to cover with a menacing hint an inglorious retreat. And then only orders were heard, the falling of heavy coils of rope, the rattling of blocks. Singleton's white head flitted here and there in the night, high above the deck, like the ghost of a bird.—"Going off, sir!" shouted Mr. Creighton from aft.—"Full again."—"All right . . . ."—"Ease off the head sheets. That will do the braces. Coil the ropes," grunted Mr. Baker, bustling about.

Gradually the tramping noises, the confused sound of voices died out, and the officers, coming together on the poop, discussed the events. Mr. Baker was bewildered and grunted; Mr. Creighton was calmly furious; but Captain Allistoun was composed and thoughtful. He listened to Mr. Baker's growling argumentation, to Creighton's interjected and severe remarks, while looking down on the deck he weighed in his hand the iron belaying-pin—that a moment ago had just missed his head—as if it had been the only tangible fact of the whole transaction. He was one of those commanders who speak little, seem to hear nothing, look at no one—and know everything, hear every whisper, see every fleeting shadow of their ship's life. His two big officers towered above his lean, short figure; they talked over his head; they were dismayed, surprised, and angry, while between them the little quiet man seemed to have found his taciturn serenity in the profound depths of a larger experience. Lights were burning in the forecastle; now and then a loud gust of babbling chatter came from forward, swept over the decks, and became faint, as if the unconscious ship, gliding gently through the great peace of the sea, had left behind and for ever the foolish noise of turbulent mankind. But it was renewed again and again. Gesticulating arms, profiles of heads with open mouths appeared for a moment in the illuminated squares of doorways; black fists darted—withdrew. . . . . "Yes. It was most damnable to have such an unprovoked row sprung on one," assented the master. . . . . A tumult of yells rose in the light, abruptly ceased. . . . . He didn't think there would be any further trouble just then. . . . . A bell was struck aft, another, forward, answered in a deeper tone, and the clamour of ringing metal spread round the ship in a circle of wide vibrations that ebbed away into the immeasurable night of an empty sea. . . . . Didn't he know them! Didn't he! In past years. Better men, too. Real men to stand by one in a tight place. Worse than devils too sometimes—downright, horned devils. Pah! This—nothing. A miss as good as a mile. . . . . The wheel was being relieved in the usual way.—"Full and by," said, very loud, the man going off.—"Full and by," repeated the other, catching hold of the spokes.—"This head wind is my trouble," exclaimed the master, stamping his foot in sudden anger; "head wind! all the rest is nothing." He was calm again in a moment. "Keep them on the move to-night, to-night, gentlemen; just to let them feel we've got hold all the time—quietly, you know. Mind you keep your hands off them, Creighton. To-morrow I will talk to them like a Dutch Uncle. A crazy crowd of tinkers! Yes, tinkers! I could count the real sailors amongst them on the fingers of one hand. Nothing will do but a row—if—you—please." He paused. "Did you think I had gone wrong there, Mr. Baker?" He tapped his forehead, laughed short. "When I saw him standing there, three parts dead and so scared—black amongst the gaping lot—no grit to face what's coming to us all—the notion came to me all at once, before I could think. Sorry for him—like you would be for a sick brute. If ever creature was in a mortal funk to die! . . . . I thought I would let him go out in his own way. Kind of impulse. It never came into my head, those fools. . . . . H'm! Stand to it now—of course." He stuck the belaying-pin in his pocket, seemed ashamed of himself, then sharply:—"If you see Podmore at his tricks again tell him I will have him put under the pump. Had to do it once before. The fellow breaks out like that now and then. Good cook tho'." He walked away quickly, came back to the companion. The two mates followed him through the starlight with amazed eyes. He went down three steps, and changing his tone, spoke with his head near the deck:—"I shan't turn in to-night, in case anything; just call out if . . . . Did you see the eyes of that sick nigger, Mr. Baker? I fancied he begged me for something. What? Past all help. One lone black beggar amongst the lot of us, and he seemed to look through me into the very hell. Fancy, this wretched Podmore! Well, let him die in peace. I am master here after all. Say what I like. Let him be. He might have been half a man once . . . . Keep a good look-out!" He disappeared down below, leaving his mates facing one another, and more impressed than if they had seen a stone image shed a miraculous tear of compassion over the incertitudes of life and death. . . . .

In the blue mist spreading from twisted threads that stood upright in the bowls of pipes, the forecastle appeared as vast as a hall. Between the beams a heavy cloud stagnated; and the lamps surrounded by halos burned each at the core of a purple glow in two lifeless flames without rays. Wreaths drifted in denser wisps. Men sprawled about on the deck, sat in negligent poses or, bending a knee, drooped with one shoulder against a bulkhead. Lips moved, eyes flashed, waving arms made sudden eddies in the smoke. The murmur of voices seemed to pile itself higher and higher as if unable to run out quick enough through the narrow doors. The watch below in their shirts, and striding on long white legs, resembled raving somnambulists; while now and then one of the watch on deck would rush in, looking strangely over-dressed, listen a moment, fling a rapid sentence into the noise and run out again; but a few remained near the door, fascinated, and with one ear turned to the deck.—"Stick together, boys," roared Davis. Belfast tried to make himself heard. Knowles grinned in a slow, dazed way. A short fellow with a thick clipped beard kept on yelling periodically:—"Who's afeard? Who's afeard?" Another one jumped up, excited, with blazing eyes, sent out a string of unattached curses and sat down quietly. Two men discussed familiarly, striking one another's breast in turn, to clinch arguments. Three others, with their heads in a bunch, spoke all together with a confidential air, and at the top of their voices. It was a stormy chaos of speech where intelligible fragments tossing, struck the ear. One could hear:—"In the last ship"—"Who cares? Try it on any one of us if——." "Knock under"—"Not a hand's turn"—"He says he is all right"—"I always thought"—"Never mind. . . . ." Donkin, crouching all in a heap against the bowsprit, hunched his shoulder-blades as high as his ears, and hanging a peaked nose, resembled a sick vulture with ruffled plumes. Belfast, straddling his legs, had a face red with yelling, and with arms thrown up, figured a Maltese cross. The two Scandinavians, in a corner, had the dumbfounded and distracted aspect of men gazing at a cataclysm. And, beyond the light, Singleton stood in the smoke, monumental, indistinct, with his head touching the beam; like a statue of heroic size in the gloom of a crypt.

He stepped forward, impassive and big. The noise subsided like a broken wave; but Belfast cried once more with uplifted arms:—

"The man is dying I tell ye!" then sat down suddenly on the hatch and took his head between his hands. All looked at Singleton, gazing upwards from the deck, staring out of dark corners, or turning their heads with curious glances. They were expectant and appeased as if that old man, who looked at no one, had possessed the secret of their uneasy indignations and desires, a sharper vision, a clearer knowledge. And indeed standing there amongst them, he had the uninterested appearance of one who had seen multitudes of ships, had listened many times to voices such as theirs, had already seen all that could happen on the wide seas. They heard his voice rumble in his broad chest as though the words had been rolling towards them out of a rugged past. "What do you want to do?" he asked. No one answered. Only Knowles muttered—"Aye, aye," and somebody said low:—"It's a bloomin' shame." He waited, made a contemptuous gesture:—"I have seen rows aboard ship before some of you were born," he said slowly, "for something or nothing; but never for such a thing."—"The man is dying, I tell ye," repeated Belfast woefully, sitting at Singleton's feet.—"And a black fellow, too," went on the old seaman, "I have seen them die like flies." He stopped, thoughtful, as if trying to recollect gruesome things, details of horrors, hecatombs of niggers. They looked at him fascinated. He was old enough to remember slavers, bloody mutinies, pirates perhaps; who could tell through what violences and terrors he had lived! What would he say? He said—"You can't help him; die he must." He made another pause. His moustache and beard stirred. He chewed words, mumbled behind tangled white hairs; incomprehensible and exciting, like an oracle behind a veil. . . . .—"Stop ashore——sick.——Instead——bringing all this head wind. Afraid. The sea will have her own.——Die in sight of land. Always so. They know it——long passage——more days, more dollars.——You keep quiet.——What do you want? Can't help him." He seemed to wake up from a dream. "You can't help yourselves," he said austerely, "Skipper's no fool. He has something in his mind. Look out—I say! I know 'em!" With eyes fixed in front he turned his head from right to left, from left to right, as if inspecting a long row of astute skippers.—"He said 'e would brain me!" cried Donkin in a heartrending tone. Singleton peered downwards with puzzled attention, as though he couldn't find him.—"Damn you!"

he said vaguely, giving it up. He radiated unspeakable wisdom, hard unconcern, the chilling air of resignation. Round him all the listeners felt themselves somehow completely enlightened by their disappointment, and, mute, they lolled about with the careless ease of men who can discern perfectly the irremediable aspect of their existence. He, profound and unconscious, waved his arm once, and strode out on deck without another word.

Belfast was lost in a round-eyed meditation. One or two vaulted heavily into upper berths, and, once there, sighed; others dived head first inside lower bunks—swift, and turning round instantly upon themselves, like animals going into lairs. The grating of a knife scraping burnt clay was heard. Knowles grinned no more. Davies said, in a tone of ardent conviction:—"Then our skipper's looney." Archie muttered:—"My faith! we haven't heard the last of it yet!" Four bells were struck.—"Half our watch below is gone!" cried Knowles in alarm, then reflected. "Well, two hours' sleep is something towards a rest," he observed consolingly. Some already pretended to slumber; and Charley, sound asleep, suddenly said a few slurred words in an arbitrary, blank voice.—"This blamed boy has worrums!" commented Knowles from under a blanket, and in a learned manner. Belfast got up and approached Archie's berth.—"We pulled him out," he whispered sadly.—"What?" said the other, with sleepy discontent.—"And now we will have to chuck him overboard," went on Belfast, whose lower lip trembled.—"Chuck what?" asked Archie.—"Poor Jimmy," breathed out Belfast.—"He be blowed!" said Archie with untruthful brutality, and sat up in his bunk; "It's all through him. If it hadn't been for me, there would have been murder on board this ship!"—"'Tain't his fault, is it?" argued Belfast, in a murmur; "I've put him to bed . . . . an' he ain't no heavier than an empty beef-cask," he added, with tears in his eyes. Archie looked at him steadily, then turned his nose to the ship's side with determination. Belfast wandered about as though he had lost his way in the dim forecastle, and nearly fell over Donkin. He contemplated him from on high for awhile. "Ain't ye going to turn in?" he asked. Donkin looked up hopelessly.—"That black-'earted Scotch son of a thief kicked me!" he whispered from the floor, in a tone of utter desolation.—"And a good job, too!" said Belfast, still very depressed; "You were as near hanging as damn-it to-night, sonny. Don't you play any of your murthering games around my Jimmy! You haven't pulled him out. You just mind! 'Cos if I start to kick you"—he brightened up a bit—"if I start to kick you, it will be Yankee fashion—to break something!" He tapped lightly with his knuckles the top of the bowed head. "You moind, me bhoy!" he concluded, cheerily. Donkin let it pass.—"Will they split on me?" he asked, with pained anxiety.—"Who—split?" hissed Belfast, coming back a step. "I would split your nose this minyt if I hadn't Jimmy to look after! Who d'ye think we are?" Donkin rose and watched Belfast's back lurch through the doorway. On all sides invisible men slept, breathing calmly. He seemed to draw courage and fury from the peace around him. Venomous and thin-faced, he glared from the ample misfit of borrowed clothes as if looking for something he could smash. His heart leaped wildly in his narrow chest. They slept! He wanted to wring necks, gouge eyes, spit on faces. He shook a dirty pair of meagre fists at the smoking lights. "Ye're no men!" he cried, in a deadened tone. No one moved. "Yer 'aven't the pluck of a mouse!" His voice rose to a husky screech. Wamibo darted out a dishevelled head, and looked at him wildly. "Ye're sweepings ov ships! I 'ope you will hall rot before you die!" Wamibo blinked, uncomprehending but interested. Donkin sat down heavily; he blew with force through quivering nostrils, he ground and snapped his teeth, and, with the chin pressed hard against the breast, he seemed busy gnawing his way through it, as if to get at the heart within. . . . .

In the morning the ship, beginning another day of her wandering life, had an aspect of sumptuous freshness, like the spring-time of the earth. The washed decks glistened in a long clear stretch; the oblique sunlight struck the yellow brasses in dazzling splashes, darted over the polished rods in lines of gold, and the single drops of salt water forgotten here and there along the rail were as limpid as drops of dew, and sparkled more than scattered diamonds. The sails slept, hushed by a gentle breeze. The sun, rising lonely and splendid in the blue sky, saw a solitary ship gliding close-hauled on the blue sea.

The men pressed three deep abreast of the mainmast and opposite the cabin-door. They shuffled, pushed, had an irresolute mien and stolid faces. At every slight movement Knowles lurched heavily on his short leg. Donkin glided behind backs, restless and anxious, like a man looking for an ambush. Captain Allistoun came out suddenly. He walked to and fro before the front. He was grey, slight, alert, shabby in the sunshine, and as hard as adamant. He had his right hand in the side-pocket of his jacket, and also something heavy in there that made folds all down the side. One of the seamen cleared his throat ominously.—"I haven't till now found fault with you men," said the master, stopping short. He faced them with his worn, steely gaze, that by an universal illusion looked straight into every individual pair of the twenty pairs of eyes before his face. At his back Mr. Baker, gloomy and bull-necked, grunted low; Mr. Creighton, fresh as paint, had rosy cheeks and a ready, resolute bearing. "And I don't now," continued the master; "but I am here to drive this ship and keep every man-jack aboard of her up to the mark. If you knew your work as well as I do mine, there would be no trouble. You've been braying in the dark about 'See to-morrow morning!' Well, you see me now. What do you want?" He waited, stepping quickly to and fro, giving them searching glances. What did they want? They shifted from foot to foot, they balanced their bodies; some, pushing back their caps, scratched their heads. What did they want? Jimmy was forgotten; no one thought of him, alone forward in his cabin, fighting great shadows, clinging to brazen lies, chuckling painfully over his transparent deceptions. No, not Jimmy; he was more forgotten than if he had been dead. They wanted great things. And suddenly all the simple words they knew seemed to be lost for ever in the immensity of their vague and burning desire. They knew what they wanted, but they could not find anything worth saying. They stirred on one spot, swinging, at the end of muscular arms, big tarry hands with crooked fingers. A murmur died out.—"What is it—food?" asked the master, "you know the stores had been spoiled off the Cape."—"We know that, sir," said a bearded shell-back in the front rank.—"Work too hard—eh? Too much for your strength?" he asked again. There was an offended silence.—"We don't want to go shorthanded, sir," began at last Davies in a wavering voice, "and this 'ere black— . . . ."—"Enough!" cried the master. He stood scanning them for a moment, then walking a few steps this way and that began to storm at them, coldly, in gusts violent and cutting like gales of those icy seas that had known his youth.—"Tell you what's the matter? Too big for your boots. Think yourselves damn good men. Know half your work. Do half your duty. Think it too much. If you did ten times as much it wouldn't be enough."—"We did our best by her, sir," cried some one with shaky exasperation.—"Your best," stormed on the master; "You hear a lot on shore, don't you? They don't tell you there your best isn't much to boast of. I tell you—your best is no better than bad. You can do no more? No, I know, and say nothing. But you stop your caper or I will stop it for you. I am ready for you! Stop it!" He shook a finger at the crowd. "As to that man," he raised his voice very much; "as to that man," if he puts his nose out on deck without my leave I will clap him in irons. There!" The cook heard him forward, ran out of the galley lifting his arms, horrified, unbelieving, amazed, and ran in again. There was a moment of profound silence during which a bow-legged seaman, stepping aside, expectorated decorously into the scupper. "There is another thing," said the master calmly. He made a quick stride and with a swing took an iron belaying-pin out of his pocket. "This!" His movement was so unexpected and sudden that the crowd stepped back. He gazed fixedly at their faces, and some at once put on a surprised air as though they had never seen a belaying-pin before. He held it up. "This is my affair. I don't ask you any questions, but you all know it; it has got to go where it came from." His eyes became angry. The crowd stirred uneasily. They looked away from the piece of iron, they appeared shy, they were embarrassed and shocked as though it had been something horrid, scandalous, or indelicate, that in common decency should not have been flourished like this in broad daylight. The master watched them attentively. "Donkin," he called out in a short, sharp tone.

Donkin dodged behind one, then behind another, but they looked over their shoulders and moved aside. The ranks kept on opening before him, closing behind, till at last he appeared alone before the master as though he had come up through the deck. Captain Allistoun moved close to him. They were much of a size, and at short range the master exchanged a deadly glance with the beady eyes. They wavered.—"You know this," asked the master.—"No, I don't," answered the other with cheeky trepidation.—"You are a cur. Take it," ordered the master. Donkin's arms seemed glued to his thighs; he stood, eyes front, as if drawn on parade. "Take it," repeated the master, and stepped closer; they breathed on one another. "Take it," said Captain Allistoun again, making a menacing gesture. Donkin tore away one arm from his side.—"Vy hare yer down hon me?" he mumbled with effort and as if his mouth had been full of dough.—"If you don't . . . ." began the master. Donkin snatched at the pin as though his intention had been to run away with it, and remained stock still holding it like a candle. "Put it back where you took it from," said Captain Allistoun, looking at him fiercely. Donkin stepped back opening wide eyes. "Go, you blackguard, or I will make you," cried the master, driving him slowly backwards by a menacing advance. He dodged, and with the dangerous iron tried to guard his head from a threatening fist. Mr. Baker ceased grunting for a moment.—"Good! By Jove," murmured appreciatively Mr. Creighton in the tone of a connoisseur.—"Don't tech me," snarled Donkin, backing away.—"Then go. Go faster."—"Don't yer 'it me. . . . . I will pull yer hup afore the magistryt. . . . . I'll show yer hup." Captain Allistoun made a long stride, and Donkin, turning his back fairly, ran off a little, then stopped and over his shoulder showed yellow teeth.—"Further on, fore-rigging," urged the master, pointing with his arm.—"Hare yer goin' to stand by and see me bullied," screamed Donkin at the silent crowd that watched him. Captain Allistoun walked at him smartly. He started off again with a leap, dashed at the fore-rigging, rammed the pin into its hole violently. "I will be heven with yer yet," he screamed at the ship at large and vanished beyond the foremast. Captain Allistoun spun round and walked back aft with a composed face, as though he already forgotten the scene. Men moved out of his way. He looked at no one.—"That will do, Mr. Baker. Send the watch below," he said quietly. "And you men try to walk straight for the future," he added in a calm voice. He looked pensively for a while at the backs of the impressed and retreating crowd. "Breakfast, steward," he called in a tone of relief through the cabin door.—"I didn't like to see you—Ough!—give that pin to that chap, sir," observed Mr. Baker; "he could have bust—Ough!—bust your head like an eggshell with it."—"O! he!" muttered the master absently. "Queer lot," he went on in a low voice. "I suppose it's all right now. Can never tell tho', nowadays, with such a . . . . Years ago; I was a young master then—one China voyage I had a munity; real munity, Baker. Different men tho'. I knew what they wanted: they wanted to broach cargo and get at the liquor. Very simple. . . . . We knocked them about for two days, and when they had enough—gentle as lambs. Good crew. And a smart trip I made." He glanced aloft at the yards braced sharp up. "Head wind day after day," he exclaimed bitterly. "Will we never get a decent slant this passage?"—"Ready, sir," said the steward, appearing before them as if by magic with a stained napkin in his hand.—"Ah! All right. Come along, Mr. Baker—it's late—with all this nonsense."

V

A heavy atmosphere of oppressive quietude pervaded the ship. In the afternoon men went about washing clothes and hanging them out to dry in the unprosperous breeze with the meditative languor of disenchanted philosophers. Very little was said. The problem of life seemed too voluminous for the narrow limits of human speech, and by common consent it was abandoned to the great sea that had from the beginning enfolded it in its immense grip; to the sea that knew all, and would in time infallibly unveil to each the wisdom hidden in all the errors, the certitude that lurks in doubts, the realm of safety and peace beyond the frontiers of sorrow and fear. And in the confused current of impotent thoughts that set unceasingly this way and that through bodies of men, Jimmy bobbed up on the surface, compelling attention, like a black buoy chained to the bottom of a muddy stream. Falsehood triumphed. It triumphed through doubt, through stupidity, through pity, through sentimentalism. We set ourselves to bolster it up, from compassion, from recklessness, from a sense of fun. Jimmy's steadfastness to his untruthful attitude in the face of the inevitable truth had the proportions of a colossal enigma—of a manifestation grand and incomprehensible that at times inspired a wondering awe; and there was also, to many, something exquisitely droll in fooling him thus to the top of his bent. The latent egoism of tenderness to suffering appeared in the developing anxiety not to see him die. His obstinate non-recognition of the only certitude whose approach we could watch from day to day was as disquieting as the failure of some law of nature. He was so utterly wrong about himself that one could not but suspect him of having access to some source of supernatural knowledge. He was absurd to the point of inspiration. He was unique, and as fascinating as only something inhuman could be; he seemed to shout his denials already from beyond the awful border. He was becoming immaterial like an apparition; his cheekbones rose, the forehead slanted more; the face was all hollows, patches of shade; and the fleshless head resembled a disinterred black skull, fitted with two restless globes of silver in the sockets of eyes. He was demoralising. Through him we were becoming highly humanised, tender, complex, excessively decadent: we understood the subtlety of his fear, sympathised with all his repulsions, shrinkings, evasions, delusions—as though we had been over-civilised, and rotten, and without any knowledge of the meaning of life. We had the air of being initiated in some infamous mysteries; we had the profound grimaces of conspirators, exchanged meaning glances, significant short words. We were inexpressibly vile and very much pleased with ourselves. We lied to him with gravity, with emotion, with unction, as if performing some moral trick with a view to an eternal reward. We made a chorus of affirmation to his wildest assertions, as though he had been a millionaire, a politician, or a reformer—and we a crowd of ambitious lubbers. When we ventured to question his statements we did it after the manner of obsequious sycophants, to the end that his glory should be augmented by the flattery of our dissent. He influenced the moral tone of our world as though he had it in his power to distribute honours, treasures, or pain; and he could give us nothing but his contempt. It was immense; it seemed to grow gradually larger, as his body day by day shrank a little more, while we looked. It was the only thing about him—of him—that gave the impression of durability and vigour. It lived within him with an unquenchable life. It spoke through the eternal pout of his black lips; it looked at us through the profound impertinence of his large eyes, that stood far out of his head like the eyes of crabs. We watched them intently. Nothing else of him stirred. He seemed unwilling to move, as if distrustful of his own solidity. The slightest gesture must have disclosed to him (it could not surely be otherwise) his bodily weakness, and caused a pang of mental suffering. He was chary of movements. He lay stretched out, chin on blanket, in a kind of sly, cautious immobility. Only his eyes roamed over faces; his eyes disdainful, penetrating and sad.

It was at that time that Belfast's devotion—and also his pugnacity—secured universal respect. He spent every moment of his spare time in Jimmy's cabin. He tended him, talked to him; was as gentle as a woman, as tenderly gay as an old philanthropist, as sentimentally careful of his nigger as a model slave-owner. But outside he was irritable, explosive as gunpowder, sombre, suspicious, and never more brutal than when most sorrowful. With him it was a tear and a blow: a tear for Jimmy, a blow for any one who did not seem to take a scrupulously orthodox view of Jimmy's case. We talked about nothing else. The two Scandinavians, even, discussed the situation—but it was impossible to know in what spirit, because they quarrelled in their own language. Belfast suspected one of them of irreverence, and in this incertitude thought that there was no option but to fight them both. They became very much terrified by his truculence, and henceforth lived amongst us, dejected, like a pair of mutes. Wamibo never spoke intelligibly, but he was as smileless as an animal—seemed to know much less about it all than the cat—and consequently was safe. Moreover he had belonged to the chosen band of Jimmy's rescuers, and was above suspicion. Archie was silent generally, but often spent an hour or so talking to Jimmy quietly with an air of proprietorship. At any time of the day and often through the night some man could be seen sitting on Jimmy's box. In the evening, between six and eight, the cabin was crowded, and there was an interested group at the door. Every one stared at the nigger.

He basked in the warmth of our interest. His eyes gleamed ironically, and in a weak voice he reproached us with our cowardice. He would say, "If you fellows had stuck out for me I would be now on deck." We hung our heads. "Yes, but if you think I am going to let them put me in irons just to show you sport. . . . Well, no. . . . It ruins my health, this lying up, it does. You don't care." We were as abashed as if it had been true. His superb impudence carried all before it. We would not have dared to revolt. We didn't want to really. We wanted to keep him alive till home—to the end of the voyage.

Singleton as usual held aloof, appearing to scorn the insignificant events of an ended life. Once only he came along, and unexpectedly stopped in the doorway. He peered at Jimmy in profound silence, as if desirous to add that black image to the crowd of Shades that peopled his old memory. We kept very quiet, and for a long time Singleton stood there as though he had come by appointment to call for some one, or to see some important event. James Wait lay perfectly still, and apparently not aware of the gaze scrutinising him with a steadiness full of expectation. There was a sense of tussle in the air. We felt the inward strain of men watching a wrestling bout. At last Jimmy with perceptible apprehension turned his head on the pillow.—"Good evening," he said in a conciliating tone.—"H'm," answered the old seaman, grumpily. For a moment longer he looked at Jimmy with severe fixity, then suddenly went away. It was a long time before any one spoke in the little cabin, though we all breathed more freely as men do after an escape from some dangerous situation. We all knew the old man's ideas about Jimmy, and nobody dared to combat them. They were unsettling, they caused pain; and, what was worse, they might have been true for all we knew. Only once did he condescend to explain them fully, but the impression was lasting. He said that Jimmy was the cause of head winds. Mortally sick men—he maintained—linger till the first sight of land, and then die; and Jimmy knew that the land would draw his life from him. It is so in every ship. Didn't we know it? He asked us with austere contempt; what did we know? What would we doubt next? Jimmy's desire encouraged by us and aided by Wamibo's (he was a Finn—wasn't he? Very well!) by Wamibo's spells delayed the ship in the open sea. Only lubberly fools couldn't see it. Whoever heard of such a run of calms and head winds? It wasn't natural . . . . We could not deny that it was strange. We felt uneasy. The common saying, "more days, more dollars," did not give the usual comfort because the stores were running short. Much had been spoiled off the Cape, and we were on half allowance of biscuit. Peas, sugar and tea had been finished long ago. Salt meat was giving out. We had plenty of coffee but very little water to make it with. We took up another hole in our belts and went on scraping, polishing, painting the ship from morning to night. And soon she looked as though she had come out of a band-box; but hunger lived on board of her. Not dead starvation, but steady, living hunger that stalked about the decks, slept in the forecastle; the tormentor of waking moments, the disturber of dreams. We looked to windward for signs of change. Every few hours of night and day we put her round with the hope that she would come up on that tack at last! She didn't. She seemed to have forgotten the way home; she rushed to and fro, heading north-west, heading east; she ran backwards and forwards, distracted, like a timid creature at the foot of a wall. Sometimes, as if tired to death, she would wallow languidly for a day in the smooth swell of an unruffled sea. All up the swinging masts the sails thrashed furiously through the hot stillness of the calm. We were weary, hungry, thirsty; we commenced to believe Singleton, but with unshaken fidelity dissembled to Jimmy. We spoke to him with jocose allusiveness, like cheerful accomplices in a clever plot; but we looked to the westward over the rail with mournful eyes for a sign of hope, for a sign of fair wind; even if its first breath should bring death to our reluctant Jimmy. In vain! The universe conspired with James Wait. Light airs from the northward sprang up again; the sky remained clear; and round our weariness the glittering sea, touched by the breeze, basked voluptuously in the great sunshine, as though it had forgotten our life and trouble.

Donkin looked out for a fair wind along with the rest. No one knew the venom of his thoughts now. He was silent, and appeared thinner, as if consumed slowly by an inward rage at the injustice of men and of fate. He was ignored by all and spoke to no one, but his hate for every man looked out through his eyes. He talked with the cook only, having somehow persuaded the good man that he—Donkin—was a much calumniated and persecuted person. Together they bewailed the immorality of the ship's company. There could be no greater criminals than we, who by our lies conspired to send the soul of a poor ignorant black man to everlasting perdition. Podmore cooked what there was to cook, remorsefully, and felt all the time that by preparing the food of such sinners he imperilled his own salvation. As to the Captain—he had lived with him for seven years, he said, and would not have believed it possible that such a man . . . . "Well. Well . . . . There it is . . . . Can't get out of it. Judgment capsized all in a minute . . . . Struck in all his pride . . . . More like a sudden visitation than anything else." Donkin, perched sullenly on the coal-locker, swung his legs and concurred. He paid in the coin of spurious assent for the privilege to sit in the galley; he was disheartened and scandalised; he agreed with the cook; could find no words severe enough to criticise our conduct; and when in the heat of reprobation he swore at us, Podmore, who would have liked to swear also if it hadn't been for his principles, pretended not to hear. So Donkin, unrebuked, cursed enough for two, cadged for matches, borrowed tobacco, and loafed for hours, very much at home before the stove. From there he could hear us on the other side of the bulkhead, talking to Jimmy. The cook knocked the pots about, slammed the oven door, muttered prophecies of damnation for all the ship's company; and Donkin, who did not admit of any hereafter, except for purposes of blasphemy, listened, concentrated and angry, gloating fiercely over a called-up image of infinite torment—like men gloat over the accursed images of cruelty and revenge, of greed, and of power. . . . .

On clear evenings the silent ship, under the cold sheen of the dead moon, took on the false aspect of passionless repose resembling the winter of the earth. Under her a long band of gold barred the black disc of the sea. Footsteps echoed on her quiet decks. The moonlight clung to her like a frosted mist, and the white sails stood out in dazzling cones as of stainless snow. In the magnificence of the phantom rays the ship appeared pure like a vision of ideal beauty, illusive like a tender dream of serene peace. And nothing in her was real, nothing was distinct and solid but the heavy shadows that filled her decks with their unceasing and noiseless stir; the shadows blacker than the night and more restless than the thoughts of men.

Donkin prowled spiteful and alone amongst the shadows, thinking that Jimmy too long delayed to die. That evening, just before dark, land had been reported from aloft, and the master, while adjusting the tubes of the long glass, had observed with quiet bitterness to Mr. Baker that, after fighting our way inch by inch to the Western Islands, there was nothing to expect now but a spell of calm. The sky was clear and the barometer high. The light breeze dropped with the sun, and an enormous stillness, forerunner of a night without wind, descended upon the heated waters of the ocean. As long as daylight lasted, the hands collected on the forecastle-head watched on the eastern sky the island of Flores, that rose above the level expanse of the sea with irregular and broken outlines like a sombre ruin upon a vast and deserted plain. It was the first land seen for nearly four months. Charley was excited, and in the midst of general indulgence took liberties with his betters. Men strangely elated without knowing why, talked in groups, and pointed with bare arms. For the first time that voyage Jimmy's sham existence seemed for a moment forgotten in the face of a solid reality. We had got so far anyhow. Belfast discoursed, quoting imaginary examples of short homeward passages from the Islands. "Them smart fruit schooners do it in five days," he affirmed. "What do you want?—only a good little breeze." Archie maintained that seven days was the shortest passage, and they disputed amicably with insulting words. Knowles declared he could already smell home from there, and with a heavy list on his short leg laughed fit to split his sides. A group of grizzled sea-dogs looked out for a time in silence and with grim absorbed faces. One said suddenly—"'Tain't far to London now."—"My first night ashore, blamme if I haven't steak and onions for supper . . . . and a pint of bitter," said another.—"A barrel ye mean," shouted some one.—"Ham an' eggs three times a day. That's the way I live!" cried an excited voice. There was a stir, appreciative murmurs; eyes began to shine; jaws champed; short nervous laughs were heard. Archie smiled with reserve all to himself. Singleton came up, gave a negligent glance, and went down again without saying a word, indifferent, like a man who had seen Flores an incalculable number of times. The night travelling from the East blotted out of the limpid sky the purple stain of the high land. "Dead calm," said somebody quietly. The murmur of lively talk suddenly wavered, died out; the clusters broke up; men began to drift away one by one, descending the ladders slowly and with serious faces as if sobered by that reminder of their dependence upon the invisible. And when the big yellow moon ascended gently above the sharp rim of the clear horizon it found the ship wrapped up in a breathless silence; a fearless ship that seemed to sleep profoundly, dreamlessly, on the bosom of the sleeping and terrible sea.

Donkin chafed at the peace—at the ship—at the sea that stretching away on all sides merged into the illimitable silence of all creation. He felt himself pulled up sharp by unrecognised grievances. He had been physically cowed, but his injured dignity remained indomitable, and nothing could heal his lacerated feelings. Here was land already—home very soon—a bad pay-day—no clothes—more hard work. How offensive all this was. Land. The land that draws away life from sick sailors. That nigger there had money—clothes—easy times; and would not die. Land draws life away . . . . He felt tempted to go and see whether it did. Perhaps already . . . . It would be a bit of luck. There was money in the beggar's chest. He stepped briskly out of the shadows into the moonlight, and, instantly, his craving, hungry face from sallow became livid. He opened the door of the cabin and had a shock. Sure enough, Jimmy was dead! He moved no more than a recumbent figure with clasped hands, carved on the lid of a stone coffin. Donkin glared with avidity. Then Jimmy, without stirring, blinked his eyelids, and Donkin had another shock. Those eyes were rather startling. He shut the door behind his back with gentle care, looking intently the while at James Wait as though he had come in there at great risk to tell some secret of startling importance. Jimmy did not move but glanced languidly out of the corners of his eyes.—"Calm?" he asked.—"Yuss," said Donkin, very disappointed, and sat down on the box.

Jimmy breathed with composure. He was used to such visits at all times of night or day. Men succeeded one another. They spoke in clear voices, pronounced cheerful words, repeated old jokes, listened to him; and each, going out, seemed to leave behind a little of his own vitality, surrender some of his own strength, renew the assurance of life—the indestructible thing! He did not like to be alone in his cabin, because, when he was alone, it seemed to him as if he hadn't been there at all. There was nothing. No pain. Not now. Perfectly right—but he couldn't enjoy his healthful repose unless some one was by to see it. This man would do as well as anybody. Donkin watched him stealthily.—"Soon home now," observed Wait.—"Why d'yer whisper?" asked Donkin with interest, "can't yer speak hup?" Jimmy looked annoyed and said nothing for a while; then in a lifeless unringing voice:—"Why should I shout? You ain't deaf that I know."—"Oh! I can 'ear right enough," answered Donkin in a low tone, and looked down. He was thinking sadly of going out when Jimmy spoke again.—"Time we did get home . . . . to get something decent to eat . . . .

I am always hungry." Donkin felt angry all of a sudden.—"What habout me," he hissed, "I am 'ungry too an' got ter work. You, 'ungry!"—"Your work won't kill you," commented Wait, feebly; "there's a couple of biscuits in the lower bunk there—you may have one. I can't eat them." Donkin dived in, groped in the corner, and when he came up again his mouth was full. He munched with ardour. Jimmy seemed to doze with open eyes. Donkin finished his hard bread and got up.—"You're not going?" asked Jimmy, staring at the ceiling.—"No," said Donkin impulsively, and instead of going out leaned his back against the closed door. He looked at James Wait, and saw him long, lean, dried up, as though all his flesh had shrivelled on his bones in the heat of a white furnace; the meagre fingers of one hand moved lightly upon the edge of the bunk playing an endless tune. To look at him was irritating and fatiguing; he could last like this for days; he was outrageous—belonging wholly neither to death nor life, and perfectly invulnerable in his apparent ignorance of both. Donkin felt tempted to enlighten him.—"What hare yer thinkin' of?" he asked surlily. James Wait had a grimacing smile that passed over the deathlike impassiveness of his bony face, incredible and frightful as would, in a dream, have been the sudden smile of a corpse.

"There is a girl," whispered Wait . . . . "Canton Street girl—— She chucked a third engineer of a Rennie boat——for me. Cooks oysters just as I like . . . . She says——she would chuck——any toff——for a coloured gentleman . . . . That's me. I am kind to wimmen," he added a shade louder.

Donkin could hardly believe his ears. He was scandalised.—"Would she? Yer wouldn't be hany good to 'er," he said with unrestrained disgust. Wait was not there to hear him. He was swaggering up the East India Dock Road; saying kindly, "Come along for a treat," pushing glass swing-doors, posing with superb assurance in the gaslight above a mahogany counter.—"D'yer think yer will hever get ashore?" asked Donkin angrily. Wait came back with a start.—"Ten days," he said promptly, and returned at once to the regions of memory that know nothing of time. He felt untired, calm, and as if safely withdrawn within himself beyond the reach of every grave incertitude. There was something of the immutable quality of eternity in the slow moments of his complete restfulness. He was very quiet and easy amongst his vivid reminiscences which he mistook joyfully for images of an undoubted future. He cared for no one. Donkin felt this vaguely like a blind man may feel in his darkness the fatal antagonism of all the surrounding existences, that to him shall for ever remain irrealisable, unseen and enviable. He had a desire to assert his importance, to break, to crush; to be even with everybody for everything; to tear the veil, unmask, expose, leave no refuge—a perfidious desire of truthfulness! He laughed in a mocking splutter and said:

"Ten days. Strike me blind if I hever! . . . . You will be dead by this time to-morrow p'r'aps. Ten days!" He waited for a while. "D'ye 'ear me? Blamme if yer don't look dead halready."

Jimmy must have been collecting his strength for he said almost aloud—"You're a stinking, cadging liar. Every one knows you." And sitting up, against all probability, startled his visitor horribly. But very soon Donkin recovered himself. He blustered. "What? What? Who's a liar? You hare—the crowd hare—the skipper—heverybody. I haint! Putting on hairs! Who's yer?" He nearly choked himself with indignation. "Who's yer to put on hairs," he repeated trembling. " 'Ave one—'ave one, says 'ee—an' cawn't heat 'em 'isself. Now I'll 'ave both. By Gawd—I will! Yer nobody!"

He plunged into the lower bunk, rooted in there and brought to light another dusty biscuit. He held it up before Jimmy—then took a bite defiantly.

"What now?" he asked with feverish impudence. "Yer may take one—says yer. Why not giv' me both? No. I'm a mangy dorg. One fur a mangy dorg. I'll tyke both. Can yer stop me? Try. Come on. Try."

Jimmy was clasping his legs and hiding his face on the knees. His shirt clung to him. Every rib was visible. His emaciated back was shaken in repeated jerks by the panting catches of his breath.

"Yer won't? Yer can't! What did I say?" went on Donkin fiercely. He swallowed another dry mouthful with a hasty effort. The other's silent helplessness, his weakness, his shrinking attitude exasperated him. "Ye're done!" he cried. "Who's yer to be lied to; to be waited on 'and an' foot like a bloomin' hymperor. Yer nobody. Yer no one at all!" he spluttered with such a strength of unerring conviction that it shook him from head to foot in coming out, and left him vibrating like a released string.

Jimmy rallied again. He lifted his head and turned bravely at

Donkin, who saw a strange face, an unknown face, a fantastic and grimacing mask of despair and fury. Its lips moved rapidly; and hollow, moaning, whistling sounds filled the cabin with a vague mutter full of menace, complaint and desolation, like the far-off murmur of a rising wind. Wait shook his head; rolled his eyes; he denied, cursed, menaced—and not a word had the strength to pass beyond the sorrowful pout of those black lips. It was incomprehensible and disturbing; a gibberish of emotions, a frantic dumb show of speech pleading for impossible things, threatening a shadowy vengeance. It sobered Donkin into a scrutinising watchfulness.

"Yer can't holler. See? What did I tell yer?" he said slowly after a moment of attentive examination. The other kept on headlong and unheard, nodding passionately, grinning with grotesque and appalling flashes of big white teeth. Donkin, as if fascinated by the dumb eloquence and anger of that black phantom, approached, stretching his neck out with distrustful curiosity; and it seemed to him suddenly that he was looking only at the shadow of a man crouching high in the bunk on the level with his eyes.—"What? What?" he said. He seemed to catch the shape of some words in the continuous panting hiss. "Yer will tell Belfast! Will yer? Hare yer a bloomin' kid?" He trembled with alarm and rage. "Tell yer gran'mother! Yer afeard! Who's yer ter be afeard more'n hanyone?" His passionate sense of his own importance ran away with a last remnant of caution. "Tell an' be damned! Tell, if yer can!" he cried. "I've been treated worser'n a dorg by your blooming back-lickers. They 'as set me on, honly to turn aginst me. I ham the honly man 'ere. They clouted me, kicked me—an' yer laffed—yer black, rotten hincumbrance, you! You will pay fur it. They giv' yer their grub, their water—yer will pay fur hit to me, by Gawd! Who haxed me ter 'ave a drink of water? They put their bloomin' rags on yer that night, an' what did they giv' ter me—a clout on the bloomin' mouth—blast their . . . . S'elp me! . . . . Yer will pay fur hit with yer money. Hi'm goin' ter 'ave it in a minyte; has soon has ye're dead, yer bloomin' useless fraud. That's the man I ham. An' ye're a thing—a bloody thing. Yah—you corpse!"

He flung at Jimmy's head the biscuit he had been all the time clutching hard, but it only grazed, and striking with a loud crack the bulkhead beyond burst like a hand-grenade into flying pieces. James Wait, as though wounded mortally, fell back on the pillow.

His lips ceased to move and the rolling eyes became quiet and stared upwards with an intense and steady persistence. Donkin was surprised; he sat suddenly on the chest, and looked down, exhausted and gloomy. After a moment he began to mutter to himself, "Die, you beggar—die. Somebody'll come in . . . . I wish I was drunk . . . . Ten days . . . . Hoysters . . . ." He looked up and spoke louder. "No . . . . No more for yer . . . . no more bloomin' gals that cook hoysters . . . . Who's yer? Hit's my turn now . . . . I wish I was drunk; I would soon giv' you a leg up haloft. That's where yer will go. Feet furst, through a port . . . . Splash! Never see yer hany more. Hoverboard! Good 'nuff fur yer."

Jimmy's head moved slightly and he turned his eyes to Donkin's face; a gaze unbelieving, desolated and appealing, of a child frightened by the menace of being shut up alone in the dark. Donkin observed him from the chest with hopeful eyes; then without rising he tried the lid. Locked. "I wish I was drunk," he muttered and getting up listened anxiously to the distant sound of footsteps on the deck. They approached—ceased. Some one yawned interminably just outside the door, and the footsteps went away shuffling lazily. Donkin's fluttering heart eased its pace, and when he looked towards the bunk again Jimmy was staring as before at the white beam.—"Ow d'yer feel now?" he asked.—"Bad," breathed out Jimmy.

Donkin sat down patient and purposeful. Every half-hour the bells spoke to one another ringing along the whole length of the ship. Jimmy's respiration was so rapid that it couldn't be counted, so faint that it couldn't be heard. His eyes were terrified as though he had been looking at unspeakable horrors; and by his face one could see that he was thinking of abominable things. Suddenly with an incredibly strong and heart-breaking voice he sobbed out:

"Overboard! . . . . I! . . . . My God!"

Donkin writhed a little on the box. He looked unwillingly. Jimmy was mute. His two long bony hands smoothed the blanket upwards, as though he had wished to gather it all up under his chin. A tear, a big solitary tear, escaped from the corner of his eye and, without touching the hollow cheek, fell on the pillow. His throat rattled faintly.

And Donkin, watching the end of that hateful nigger, felt the anguishing grasp of a great sorrow on his heart at the thought that he himself, some day, would have to go through it all—just like this—perhaps! His eyes became moist. "Poor beggar," he murmured. The night seemed to go by in a flash; it seemed to him he could hear the irremediable rush of precious minutes. How long would this blooming affair last? Too long surely. No luck. He could not restrain himself. He got up and approached the bunk. Wait did not stir. Only his eyes appeared alive and his hands continued their smoothing movement with a horrible and tireless industry. Donkin bent over.

"Jimmy," he called low. There was no answer, but the rattle stopped. "D'yer see me?" he asked trembling. Jimmy's chest heaved. Donkin, looking away, bent his ear to Jimmy's lips, and heard a sound like the rustle of a single dry leaf driven along the smooth sand of a beach. It shaped itself.

"Light . . . . the lamp . . . . and . . . . go," breathed out Wait.

Donkin, instinctively, glanced over his shoulder at the blazing flame; then, still looking away, felt under the pillow for a key. He got it at once and for the next few minutes was shakily but swiftly busy about the box. When he got up, his face—for the first time in his life—had a pink flush—perhaps of triumph.

He slipped the key under the pillow again, avoiding to glance at Jimmy, who had not moved. He turned his back squarely from the bunk, and started to the door as though he were going to walk a mile. At his second stride he had his nose against it. He clutched the handle cautiously, but at that moment he received the irresistible impression of something happening behind his back. He spun round as though he had been tapped on the shoulder. He was just in time to see Jimmy's eyes blaze up and go out at once, like two lamps overturned together by a sweeping blow. Something resembling a scarlet thread hung down his chin out of the corner of his lips—and he had ceased to breathe.

Donkin closed the door behind him gently but firmly. Sleeping men, huddled under jackets, made on the lighted deck shapeless dark mounds that had the appearance of neglected graves. Nothing had been done all through the night and he hadn't been missed. He stood motionless and perfectly astounded to find the world outside as he had left it; there was the sea, the ship—sleeping men; and he wondered absurdly at it, as though he had expected to find the men dead, familiar things gone for ever: as though, like a wanderer returning after many years, he had expected to see bewildering changes. He shuddered a little in the penetrating freshness of the air, and hugged himself forlornly. The declining moon drooped sadly in the western board as if withered by the cold touch of a pale dawn. The ship slept. And the immortal sea stretched away, immense and hazy, like the image of life, with a glittering surface and lightless depths; promising, empty, inspiring—terrible. Donkin gave it a defiant glance and slunk off noiselessly as if judged and cast out by the august silence of its might.

Jimmy's death, after all, came as a tremendous surprise. We did not know till then how much faith we had put in his delusions. We had taken his chances of life so much at his own valuation that his death, like the death of an old belief, shook the foundations of our society. A common bond was gone; the strong, effective and respectable bond of a sentimental lie. All that day we mooned at our work, with suspicious looks and a disabused air. In our hearts we thought that in the matter of his departure Jimmy had acted in a perverse and unfriendly manner. He didn't back us up, as a shipmate should. In going he took away with himself the gloomy and solemn shadow in which our folly had posed, with humane satisfaction, as a tender arbiter of fate. And now we saw it was no such thing. It was just common foolishness; a silly and ineffectual meddling with issues of majestic import—that is, if Podmore was right. Perhaps he was? Doubt survived Jimmy; and, like a community of banded criminals disintegrated by a touch of grace, we were profoundly scandalised with each other. Men spoke unkindly to their best chums. Others refused to speak at all. Singleton only was not surprised. "Dead—is he? Of course," he said, pointing at the island right abeam: for the calm still held the ship spell-bound within sight of Flores. Dead—of course. *He* wasn't surprised. Here was the land, and there, on the forehatch and waiting for the sailmaker—there was that corpse. Cause and effect. And for the first time that voyage, the old seaman became quite cheery and garrulous, explaining and illustrating from the stores of experience how, in sickness, the sight of an island (even a very small one) is generally more fatal than the view of a continent. But he couldn't explain why.

Jimmy was to be buried at five, and it was a long day till then—a day of mental disquiet and even of physical disturbance. We took no interest in our work and, very properly, were rebuked for it. This, in our constant state of hungry irritation, was exasperating. Donkin worked with his brow bound in a dirty rag, and looked so ghastly that Mr. Baker was touched with compassion at the sight of this plucky suffering.—"Ough! You, Donkin! Put down your work and go lay-up this watch. You look ill."—"Hi ham, sir—in my 'ead," he said in a subdued voice, and vanished speedily. This annoyed many, and they thought the mate "bloomin' soft to-day." Captain Allistoun could be seen on the poop watching the sky cloud over from the south-west, and it soon got to be known about the decks that the barometer had begun to fall in the night, and that a breeze might be expected before long. This, by a subtle association of ideas, led to violent quarreling as to the exact moment of Jimmy's death. Was it before or after "that 'ere glass started down?" It was impossible to know, and it caused much contemptuous growling at one another. All of a sudden there was a great tumult forward. Pacific Knowles and good-tempered Davies had come to blows over it. The watch below interfered with spirit, and for ten minutes there was a noisy scrimmage round the hatch, where, in the balancing shade of the sails, Jimmy's body, wrapped up in a white blanket, was watched over by the sorrowful Belfast, who, in his desolation, disdained the fray. When the noise had ceased, and the passions had calmed into surly silence, he stood up at the head of the swathed body, and lifting both arms on high, cried with pained indignation:—"You ought to be ashamed of yourselves! . . . ." We were.

Belfast took his bereavement very hard. He gave proofs of unextinguishable devotion. It was he, and no other man, who would help the sailmaker to prepare what was left of Jimmy for a solemn surrender to the insatiable sea. He arranged the weights carefully at the feet: two holystones, an old anchor-shackle without its pin, some broken links of a worn-out stream cable. He arranged them this way, then that. "Bless my soul! you aren't afraid he will chafe his heel?" said the sailmaker, who hated the job. He pushed the needle, puffing furiously, with his head in a cloud of tobacco smoke; he turned the flaps over, pulled at the stitches, stretched at the canvas.—"Lift his shoulders . . . . Pull to you a bit . . . . So—o—o. Steady." Belfast obeyed, pulled, lifted, overcome with sorrow, dropping tears on the tarred twine.—"Don't you drag the canvas too taut over his poor face, Sails," he entreated tearfully.—"What are you fashing yourself for? He will be comfortable enough," assured the sailmaker, cutting the thread after the last stitch, that came about the middle of Jimmy's forehead. He rolled up the remaining canvas, put away the needles. "What makes you take on so?" he asked. Belfast looked down at the long package of grey sailcloth.—"I pulled him out," he whispered, "and he did not want to go. If I had sat up with him last night he would have kept alive for me . . . . but something made me tired." The sailmaker took vigorous draws at his pipe and mumbled:—"When I . . . . West India Station . . . . In the *Blanche* frigate . . . . Yellow Jack . . . . sewed in twenty men a day . . . . Portsmouth—Devonport men—townies—knew their fathers, mothers—sisters—the whole boiling of 'em. Thought nothing of it. And these niggers like this one—you don't know where it comes from. Got nobody. No use to nobody. Who will miss him?"—"I do—I pulled him out," mourned Belfast dismally.

On two planks nailed together, and apparently resigned and still under the folds of the Union Jack with a white border, James Wait, carried aft by four men, was deposited slowly, with his feet pointing at an open port. A swell had set in from the westward, and following on the roll of the ship, the red ensign, at half-mast, darted out and collapsed again on the grey sky, like a tongue of flickering fire; Charley tolled the bell; and at every swing to starboard the whole vast semi-circle of steely waters visible on that side seemed to come up with a rush to the edge of the port, as if impatient to get at our Jimmy. Every one was there but Donkin, who was too ill to come; the Captain and Mr. Creighton stood bareheaded on the break of the poop; Mr. Baker, directed by the master, who had said to him gravely:—"You know more about the prayer book than I do," came out of the cabin door quickly and a little embarrassed. All the caps went off. He began to read in a low tone, and with his usual harmlessly menacing utterance, as though he had been for the last time reproving confidentially that dead seaman at his feet. The men listened in scattered groups; they leaned on the fife rail, gazing on the deck; they held their chins in their hands thoughtfully, or, with crossed arms and one knee slightly bent, hung their heads in an attitude of upright meditation. Wamibo dreamed. Mr. Baker read on, grunting reverently at the turn of every page. The words, missing the unsteady hearts of men, rolled out to wander without a home upon the heartless sea; and James Wait, silenced for ever, lay uncritical and passive under the hoarse murmur of despair and hopes.

Two men made ready and waited for those words that send so many of our brothers to their last plunge. Mr. Baker began the passage. "Stand by," muttered the boatswain. Mr. Baker read out: "To the deep," and paused. The men lifted the inboard end of the planks, the boatswain snatched off the Union Jack, and James Wait did not move.—"Higher," muttered the boatswain angrily. All the heads were raised; every man stirred uneasily, but James Wait gave no sign of going. In death and swatched up for all eternity, he yet seemed to hang on to the ship with the grip of an undying fear. "Higher! Lift!" whispered the boatswain fiercely.—"He won't go," stammered one of the men shakily, and both appeared ready to drop everything. Mr. Baker waited, burying his face in the book, and shuffling his feet nervously. All the men looked profoundly disturbed; from their midst a faint humming noise spread out—growing louder. . . . . "Jimmy!" cried Belfast in a wailing tone, and there was a second of shuddering dismay.

"Jimmy, be a man!" he shrieked passionately. Every mouth was wide open, not an eyelid winked. He stared wildly, twitching all over; he bent his body forward like a man peering at an horror. "Go!" he shouted, and leaped off with his arm thrown out. "Go, Jimmy!—Jimmy, go! Go!" His fingers touched the head of the body, and the grey package started reluctantly to, all at once, whizz off the lifted planks with the suddenness of a flash of lightning. The crowd stepped forward like one man; a deep Ah—h—h! came out vibrating from the broad chests. The ship rolled as if relieved of an unfair burden; the sails flapped. Belfast, supported by Archie, gasped hysterically; and Charley, who anxious to see Jimmy's last dive, leaped headlong on the rail, was too late to see anything but the faint circle of a vanishing ripple.

Mr. Baker, perspiring abundantly, read out the last prayer in a deep rumour of excited men and fluttering sails. "Amen!" he said in an unsteady growl, and closed the book.

"Square the yards!" thundered a voice above his head. All hands gave a jump; one or two dropped their caps; Mr. Baker looked up surprised. The master, standing on the break of the poop, pointed to the westward. "Breeze coming," he said, "square the yards. Look alive, men!" Mr. Baker crammed the book hurriedly into his pocket.—"Forward, there—let go the foretack!" he hailed joyfully, bareheaded and brisk; "Square the foreyard, you port-watch!"—"Fair wind—fair wind," muttered the men going to the braces.—"What did I tell you?" mumbled old Singleton, flinging down coil after coil with hasty energy; "I knowed it—he's gone, and here it comes."

It came with the sound of a lofty and powerful sigh. The sails filled, the ship gathered way, and the waking sea began to murmur sleepily of home to the ears of men.

That night, while the ship rushed foaming to the Northward before a freshening gale, the boatswain unbosomed himself to the petty officers' berth:—"The chap was nothing but trouble," he said, "from the moment he came aboard—d'ye remember—that night in Bombay? Been bullying all that softy crowd—cheeked the old man—we had to go fooling all over a half-drowned ship to save him. Dam' nigh a mutiny all for him—and now the mate abused me like a pickpocket for forgetting to dab a lump of grease on them planks. So I did, but you ought to have known better, too, than to leave a nail sticking up—hey, Chips?" "And you ought to have known better than to chuck all my tools overboard for 'im, like a skeary greenhorn," retorted the morose carpenter. "Well—he's gone after 'em now," he added in an unforgiving tone. "On the China Station, I remember once, the Admiral he says to me . . . ." began the sailmaker.

A week afterwards the *Narcissus* entered the chops of the Channel.

Under the white wings she skimmed low over the blue sea like a great tired bird speeding to its nest. The clouds raced with her mastheads; they rose astern enormous and white, soared to the zenith, flew past, and falling down the wide curve of the sky seemed to dash headlong into the sea—the clouds swifter than the ship, more free, but without a home. The coast to welcome her stepped out of space into the sunshine. The lofty headlands trod masterfully into the sea; the wide bays smiled in the light; the shadows of homeless clouds ran along the sunny plains, leaped over valleys, without a check darted up the hills, rolled down the slopes; and the sunshine pursued them with patches of running brightness. On the brows of dark cliffs white lighthouses shone in pillars of light. The Channel glittered like a blue mantle shot with gold and starred by the silver of the capping seas. The *Narcissus* rushed past the headlands and the bays. Outward-bound vessels crossed her track, lying over, and with their masts stripped for a slogging fight with the hard sou'wester. And, inshore, a string of smoking steamboats waddled, hugging the coast, like migrating and amphibious monsters, distrustful of the restless waves.

At night the headlands retreated, the bays advanced into one unbroken line of gloom. The lights of the earth mingled with the lights of heaven; and above the tossing lanterns of a trawling fleet a great lighthouse shone steadily, such as an enormous riding light burning above a vessel of fabulous dimensions. Below its steady glow, the coast, stretching away straight and black, resembled the high side of an indestructible craft riding motionless upon the immortal and unresting sea. The dark land lay alone in the midst of waters, like a mighty ship bestarred with vigilant lights—a ship carrying the burden of millions of lives—a ship freighted with dross and with jewels, with gold and with steel. She towered up immense and strong, guarding priceless traditions and untold suffering, sheltering glorious memories and base forgetfulness, ignoble virtues and splendid transgressions. A great ship! For ages had the ocean battered in vain her enduring sides; she was there when the world was vaster and darker, when the sea was great and mysterious, and ready to surrender the prize of fame to audacious men. A ship mother of fleets and nations! The great flagship of the race; stronger than the storms! and anchored in the open sea.

The *Narcissus,* heeling over to off-shore gusts, rounded the South Foreland, passed through the Downs, and, in tow, entered the river. Shorn of the glory of her white wings, she wound obediently after the tug through the maze of invisible channels. As she passed them the red-painted light-vessels, swung at their moorings, seemed for an instant to sail with great speed in the rush of tide, and the next moment were left hopelessly behind. The big buoys on the tails of banks slipped past her sides very low, and, dropping in her wake, tugged at their chains like fierce watch-dogs. The reach narrowed; from both sides the land approached the ship. She went steadily up the river. On the riverside slopes the houses appeared in groups—seemed to stream down the declivities at a run to see her pass, and, checked by the mud of the foreshore, crowded on the banks. Further on, the tall factory chimneys appeared in insolent bands and watched her go by, like a straggling crowd of slim giants, swaggering and upright under the black plummets of smoke, cavalierly aslant. She swept round the bends; an impure breeze shrieked a welcome between her stripped spars; and the land, closing in, stepped between the ship and the sea.

A low cloud hung before her—a great opalescent and tremulous cloud, that seemed to rise from the steaming brows of millions of men. Long drifts of smoky vapours soiled it with livid trails; it throbbed to the beat of millions of hearts, and from it came an immense and lamentable murmur—the murmur of millions of lips praying, cursing, sighing, jeering—the undying murmur of folly, regret, and hope exhaled by the crowds of the anxious earth. The *Narcissus* entered the cloud; the shadows deepened; on all sides there was the clang of iron, the sound of mighty blows, shrieks, yells. Black barges drifted stealthily on the murky stream. A mad jumble of begrimed walls loomed up vaguely in the smoke, bewildering and mournful, like a vision of disaster. The tugs, panting furiously, backed and filled in the stream, to hold the ship steady at the dock-gates; from her bows two lines went through the air whistling, and struck at the land viciously, like a pair of snakes. A bridge broke in two before her, as if by enchantment; big hydraulic capstans began to turn all by themselves, as though animated by a mysterious and unholy spell. She moved through a narrow lane of water between two low walls of granite, and men with check-ropes in their hands kept pace with her, walking on the broad flagstones. A group waited impatiently on each side of the vanished bridge: rough heavy men in caps; sallow-faced men in high hats; two bareheaded women; ragged children, fascinated, and with wide eyes. A cart coming at a jerky trot pulled up sharply. One of the women screamed at the silent ship—"Hallo, Jack!" without looking at any one in particular, and all hands looked at her from the forecastle head.—"Stand clear! Stand clear of that rope!" cried the dockmen, bending over stone posts. The crowd murmured, stamped where they stood.—"Let go your quarter-checks! Let go!" sang out a ruddy-faced old man on the quay. The ropes splashed heavily falling in the water, and the *Narcissus* entered the dock.

The stony shores ran away right and left in straight lines, enclosing a sombre and rectangular pool. Brick walls rose high above the water—soulless walls, staring through hundreds of windows as troubled and dull as the eyes of over-fed brutes. At their base monstrous iron cranes crouched, with chains hanging from their long necks, balancing cruel-looking hooks over the decks of lifeless ships. A noise of wheels rolling over stones, the thump of heavy things falling, the racket of feverish winches, the grinding of strained chains, floated on the air. Between high buildings the dust of all the continents soared in short flights; and a penetrating smell of perfumes and dirt, of spices and hides, of things costly and of things filthy, pervaded the space, made for it an atmosphere precious and disgusting. The *Narcissus* came gently into her berth; the shadows of soulless walls fell upon her, the dust of all the continents leaped upon her deck, and a swarm of strange men, clambering up her sides, took possession of her in the name of the sordid earth. She had ceased to live.

A toff in a black coat and high hat scrambled with agility, came up to the second mate, shook hands, and said:—"Hallo, Herbert." It was his brother. A lady appeared suddenly. A real lady, in a black dress and with a parasol. She looked extremely elegant in the midst of us, and as strange as if she had fallen there from the sky. Mr. Baker touched his cap to her. It was the master's wife. And very soon the Captain, dressed very smartly and in a white shirt, went with her over the side. We didn't recognise him at all till, turning on the quay, he called to Mr. Baker:—"Remember to wind up the chronometers to-morrow morning." An underhand lot of seedy-looking chaps with shifty eyes wandered in and out of the forecastle looking for a job—they said.—"More likely for something to steal," commented Knowles cheerfully. Poor beggars. Who cared? Weren't we home! But Mr. Baker went for one of them who had given him some cheek, and we were delighted. Everything was delightful.—"I've finished aft, sir," called out Mr. Creighton.—"No water in the well, sir," reported for the last time the carpenter, sounding-rod in hand. Mr. Baker glanced along the decks at the expectant groups of men, glanced aloft at the yards.—"Ough! That will do, men," he grunted. The groups broke up. The voyage was ended.

Rolled-up beds went flying over the rail; lashed chests went sliding down the gangway—mighty few of both at that. "The rest is having a cruise off the Cape," explained Knowles enigmatically to a dock-loafer with whom he had struck a sudden friendship. Men ran, calling to one another, hailing utter strangers to "lend a hand with the dunnage," then with sudden decorum approached the mate to shake hands before going ashore.—"Good-bye, sir," they repeated in various tones. Mr. Baker grasped hard palms, grunted in a friendly manner at every one, his eyes twinkled.—"Take care of your money, Knowles. Ough! Soon get a nice wife if you do." The lame man was delighted.—"Good-bye, sir," said Belfast with emotion, wringing the mate's hand, and looked up with swimming eyes. "I thought I would take 'im ashore with me," he went on plaintively. Mr. Baker did not understand, but said kindly:—"Take care of yourself, Craik," and the bereaved Belfast went over the rail mourning and alone.

Mr. Baker in the sudden peace of the ship moved about solitary and grunting, trying door handles, peering into dark places, never done—a model chief mate! No one waited for him ashore. Mother dead; father and two brothers, Yarmouth fishermen, drowned together on the Dogger Bank; sister married and unfriendly. Quite a lady. Married to the leading tailor of a little town, and its leading politician, who did not think his sailor brother-in-law quite respectable enough for him. Quite a lady, quite a lady, he thought, sitting down for a moment's rest on the quarter-hatch. Time enough to go ashore and get a bit, and sup, and a bed somewhere. He didn't like to part with a ship. No one to think about then. The darkness of a misty evening fell, cold and damp, upon the deserted deck; and Mr. Baker sat smoking, thinking of all the successive ships to whom through many long years he had given the best of a seaman's care. And never a command in sight. Not once!—"I haven't somehow the cut of a skipper about me," he meditated placidly, while the shipkeeper (who had taken possession of the galley), a wizened old man with bleared eyes, cursed him in whispers for "hanging about so."—"Now, Creighton," he pursued the unenvious train of thought, "quite a gentleman . . . . swell friends . . . . will get on. Fine young fellow . . . . a little more experience." He got up and shook himself. "I'll be back first thing to-morrow morning for the hatches. Don't you let them touch anything before I come, shipkeeper," he called out. Then, at last, he also went ashore—a model chief mate!

The men scattered by the dissolving contact of the land came together once more in the shipping office.—"The *Narcissus* pays off," shouted outside a glazed door a brass-bound old fellow with a crown and the capitals B. T. on his cap. A lot trooped in at once but many were late. The room was large, white-washed, and bare; a counter surmounted by a brass-wire grating fenced off a third of the dusty space, and behind the grating a pasty-faced clerk, with his hair parted in the middle, had the quick, glittering eyes and the vivacious, jerky movements of a caged bird. Poor Captain Allistoun also in there, and sitting before a little table with piles of gold and notes on it, appeared subdued by his captivity. Another Board of Trade bird was perching on a high stool near the door: an old bird that did not mind the chaff of elated sailors. The crew of the *Narcissus,* broken up into knots, pushed in the corners. They had new shore togs, smart jackets that looked as if they had been shaped with an axe, glossy trousers that seemed made of crumpled sheet-iron, collarless flannel shirts, shiny new boots. They tapped on shoulders, button-holed one another, asked:—"Where did you sleep last night?" whispered gaily, slapped their thighs, stamped, with bursts of subdued laughter. Most had clean radiant faces; only one or two were dishevelled and sad; the two young Norwegians looked tidy, meek, and altogether of a promising material for the kind ladies that patronise the Scandinavian Home. Wamibo, still in his working clothes, dreamed, upright and burly in the middle of the room, and, when Archie came in, woke up for a smile. But the wide-awake clerk called out a name, and the paying-off business began.

One by one they came up to the pay-table to get the wages of their glorious and obscure toil. They swept the money with care into broad palms, rammed it trustfully into trousers' pockets, or, turning their backs on the table, reckoned with difficulty in the hollow of their stiff hands.—"Money right? Sign the release. There—there," repeated the clerk, impatiently. "How stupid those sailors are!" he thought. Singleton came up, venerable—and uncertain as to daylight; brown drops of tobacco juice maculated his white beard; his hands, that never hesitated in the great light of the open sea, could hardly find the small pile of gold in the profound darkness of the shore. "Can't write?" said the clerk, shocked. "Make a mark, then." Singleton painfully sketched in a heavy cross, blotted the page. "What a disgusting old brute," muttered the clerk. Somebody opened the door for him, and the partriarchal seaman passed through unsteadily, without as much as a glance at any of us.

Archie had a pocket-book. He was chaffed. Belfast, who looked wild, as though he had already luffed up through a public-house or two, gave signs of emotion and wanted to speak to the Captain privately. The master was surprised. They spoke through the wires, and we could hear the Captain saying:—"I've given it up to the Board of Trade." "I should 've liked to get something of his," mumbled Belfast. "But you can't, my man. It's given up, locked and sealed, to the Marine Office," expostulated the master; and Belfast stood back, with drooping mouth and troubled eyes. In a pause of the business we heard the master and the clerk talking. We caught "James Wait—deceased—found no papers of any kind—no relations—no trace—the Office must hold his wages then." Donkin entered. He seemed out of breath, was grave, full of business. He went straight to the desk, talked with animation to the clerk, who thought him an intelligent man. They discussed the account, dropping h's against one another as if for a wager—very friendly. Captain Allistoun paid. "I give you a bad discharge," he said, quietly. Donkin raised his voice:—"I don't want your bloomin' discharge—keep it. I'm goin' ter 'ave a job hashore." He turned to us. "No more bloomin' sea fur me," he said, aloud. All looked at him. He had better clothes, had an easy air, appeared more at home than any of us; he stared with assurance, enjoying the effect of his declaration. "Yuss. I 'ave friends well hoff. That's more'n yer got. But I ham a man. Yer shipmates for all that. Who's comin' fur a drink?"

No one moved. There was a silence; a silence of blank faces and stony looks. He waited a moment, smiled bitterly, and went to the door. There he faced round once more. "Yer won't? Yer bloomin' lot of 'ypocrites. No? What 'ave I done to yer? Did I bully yer? Did I hurt yer? Did I? . . . . Yer won't drink? . . . . No! . . . . Then may yer die of thirst, hevery mother's son of yer! Not one of yer 'as the sperrit of a bug. Ye'rr the scum of the world. Work and starve!"

He went out, and slammed the door with such violence that the old Board of Trade bird nearly fell off his perch.

"He's mad," said Archie. "No! No! He's drunk," insisted Belfast, lurching about, and in a maudlin tone. Captain Allistoun sat smiling thoughtfully at the cleared pay-table.

Outside, on Tower Hill, they blinked, hesitated clumsily, as if blinded by the strange quality of the hazy light, as if discomposed by the view of so many men; and they who could hear one another in the howl of gales seemed deafened and distracted by the dull roar of the busy earth.—"To the Black Horse! To the Black Horse!" cried some. "Let us have a drink together before we part." They crossed the road, clinging to one another. Only Charley and Belfast wandered off alone. As I came up I saw a red-faced, blowsy woman, in a grey shawl, and with dusty, fluffy hair, fall on Charley's neck. It was his mother. She slobbered over him:—"O, my boy! My boy!"—"Leggo of me," said Charley. "Leggo, mother!" I was passing him at the time, and over the untidy head of the blubbering woman he gave me a humorous smile and a glance ironic, courageous, and profound, that seemed to put all my knowledge of life to shame. I nodded and passed on, but heard him say again, good-naturedly:—"If you leggo of me this minyt—ye shall 'ave a bob for a drink out of my pay." In the next few steps I came upon Belfast. He caught my arm with tremulous enthusiasm.—"I couldn't go wi' 'em," he stammered, indicating by a nod our noisy crowd, that drifted slowly along the other sidewalk. "When I think of Jimmy. . . . . Poor Jim! When I think of him I have no heart for drink. You were his chum, too . . . . but I pulled him out . . . . didn't I? Short wool he had. . . . . Yes. And I stole the blooming pie. . . . . He wouldn't go. . . . . He wouldn't go for nobody." He burst into tears. "I never touched him—never—never!" he sobbed. "He went for me like . . . . like . . . . a lamb."

I disengaged myself gently. Belfast's crying fits generally ended in a fight with some one, and I wasn't anxious to stand the brunt of his inconsolable sorrow. Moreover, two bulky policemen stood near by, looking at us with a disapproving and incorruptible gaze.—"So long!" I said, and went off.

But at the corner I stopped to take my last look at the crew of the *Narcissus*. They were swaying irresolute and noisy on the broad flagstones before the Mint. They were bound for the Black Horse where men, in fur caps, with brutal faces and in shirt sleeves, dispense out of varnished barrels the illusions of strength, mirth, happiness; the illusion of splendour and poetry of life, to the paid-off crews of southern-going ships. From afar I saw them discoursing, with jovial eyes and clumsy gestures, while the sea of life thundered into their ears ceaseless and unheeded. And swaying about there on the white stones, surrounded by the hurry and clamour of men, they appeared to be creatures of another kind—lost, alone, forgetful, and doomed; they were like castaways, like reckless and joyous castaways, like mad castaways making merry in the storm and upon an insecure ledge of a treacherous rock. The roar of the town resembled the roar of topping breakers, merciless and strong, with a loud voice and cruel purpose; but overhead the clouds broke; a flood of sunshine streamed down the walls of grimy houses. The dark knot of seamen drifted in sunshine. To the left of them the trees in Tower Gardens sighed, the stones of the Tower gleaming, seemed to stir in the play of light, as if remembering suddenly all the great joys and sorrows of the past, the fighting prototypes of these men; press-gangs; mutinous cries; the wailing of women by the riverside, and the shouts of men welcoming victories. The sunshine of heaven fell like a gift of grace on the mud of the earth, on the remembering and mute stones, on greed, selfishness; on the anxious faces of forgetful men. And to the right of the dark group the stained front of the Mint, cleansed by the flood of light, stood out for a moment, dazzling and white, like a marble palace in a fairy tale. The crew of the *Narcissus* drifted out of sight.

I never saw them again. The sea took some, the steamers took others, the graveyards of the earth will account for the rest. Singleton has no doubt taken with him the long record of his faithful work into the peaceful depths of an hospitable sea. And Donkin, who never did a decent day's work in his life, no doubt earns his living by discoursing with filthy eloquence upon the right of labour to live. So be it! Let the earth and the sea each have its own.

A gone shipmate, like any other man, is gone for ever; and I never saw one of them again. But at times the spring-flood of memory sets with force up the dark River of the Nine Bends. Then on the waters of the forlorn stream drifts a ship—a shadowy ship manned by a crew of Shades. They pass and make a sign, in a shadowy hail. Haven't we, together and upon the immortal sea, wrung out a meaning from our sinful lives? Good-bye, brothers! You were a good crowd. As good a crowd as ever fisted with wild cries the beating canvas of a heavy foresail; or tossing aloft, invisible in the night, gave back yell for yell to a westerly gale.

II

Three Stories

Conrad's major novels from *Lord Jim* on all began as short stories. Even *Nostromo,* his "largest canvas," was at first planned as a piece on the scale of "Karain." Most of these early versions have been lost, but for *Lord Jim* we do have the book's originating germ, an 1898 sketch that Conrad then put aside while he wrote "Heart of Darkness." He started up again in 1899, but the novel had been appearing in *Blackwood's* for some months before he had any conception of its final length, and much of the concluding Patusan sequence was evidently a late addition. That compositional history has led some critics to discount the book's second half and has even made them doubt Conrad's suitability for the novel as a form, as though he should always have written short. The idea seems to me absurd—and yet much of what is most original about Conrad's novels, *Lord Jim* in particular, can indeed be explained by reference to the pre-Chekhovian European story. The frame-tales, the hints of the inexplicable, the startling shifts in point of view, the speaking voice of a wise man musing over the experience of others, the sense of extremes and even of violence so at odds with the norms of English realism: all these have their place in the tradition of short narratives that in German are called *Novellen.* They are the kinds of tales one finds in Heinrich von Kleist and Nikolai Gogol, in Prosper Mérimée and even in Turgenev's *A Sportsman's Sketches. Lord Jim* is the most obvious case in which Conrad blew the features of such a tale up to novel length, but I think one can find them too in *Under Western Eyes.*

In Britain the short story has always seemed a latecomer, something that had fully arrived only at the moment that Conrad himself appeared, ready to take advantage of it. It had gotten an early foothold in America, with Hawthorne and Poe, but though the

Victorian masters wrote many journalistic sketches, they produced few short stories as such. That began to change in the last decades of the nineteenth century, when the rise of the general-interest magazine created a steady market for the form, a market fed—and fed on—by writers as different as Henry James and Arthur Conan Doyle. Once over the hump of *Almayer's Folly*, Conrad focused in the early years of his career on short or mid-length fiction. Most of his best stories come from right around the turn of the century: pieces like "Youth," "An Outpost of Progress," and the first two of the works I've included here. A number of his strongest long tales date from this period as well, such as "Heart of Darkness" and "Typhoon." From *Nostromo* on, however, Conrad would put the best of himself into his novels. There are exceptions, "The Secret Sharer" among them. But after the *Typhoon* volume most of his short things are either honorable potboilers or first attempts at material that, as with "The Informer" (1906), he would later develop in a novel.

I've selected these stories with an eye to variety and have excluded some favorites, such as "Youth," in the attempt to minimize any thematic repetition in this volume as a whole. As it happens, though, all three of them present us with a first-person narrative set within the frame of the tale as a whole. In "The Warrior's Soul" that frame is of the lightest, a few sentences only. In "Karain," though, Conrad inserts the title character's account into a longer and more complex narrative in the voice of an English trader. In a classic essay Walter Benjamin defines two different kinds of storytellers: first, "the resident tiller of the soil," the person who knows all "the local tales and traditions"; and second, the wanderer returned from afar, whose type is the "trading seaman." Many of Conrad's narrators are just such wanderers, the principal speaker of "Karain" included. That sailor's understanding of this "Eastern" tale does, however, remain limited, and Conrad's consciously exoticized work tells us far more than any of its characters themselves can know. "The Warrior's Soul" also depends on a speaker who has come back from afar, an old Russian officer remembering his part in the events of 1812. In its anecdotal form the tale seems deliberately old-fashioned, a return to the period at which such a narrator might have spoken, and yet written in 1916 it owes its mood to the slaughter then going on in

France. The middle story here, "Amy Foster," stands, in contrast, as an example of Benjamin's second type: a story told by a country doctor who knows all the buried secrets of his community. Its title character has often been taken as a fictional portrait of Jessie Conrad, and in reading it does seem impossible to take the struggles of her shipwrecked husband, Yanko, as anything but a metaphoric account of Konrad Korzeniowski's own.

"Karain" was Conrad's first contribution to *Blackwood's,* where it was published in November 1897, appearing the next year in *Tales of Unrest* (Unwin). The text given here is that of the Kent edition of 1925. "Amy Foster" came out in the *Illustrated London News* for December 1901, and then in *Typhoon* (Heinemann, 1903). I've used the version in Paul Kirschner's careful 1992 Penguin edition of that collection. "The Warrior's Soul" first appeared in *Land & Water* (March 1917) but was not collected until the posthumous publication of *Tales of Hearsay* (Unwin, 1925); the text is once again drawn from the Kent edition.

KARAIN: A MEMORY

I

We knew him in those unprotected days when we were content to hold in our hands our lives and our property. None of us, I believe, has any property now, and I hear that many, negligently, have lost their lives; but I am sure that the few who survive are not yet so dim-eyed as to miss in the befogged respectability of their newspapers the intelligence of various native risings in the Eastern Archipelago. Sunshine gleams between the lines of those short paragraphs—sunshine and the glitter of the sea. A strange name wakes up memories; the printed words scent the smoky atmosphere of to-day faintly, with the subtle and penetrating perfume as of land breezes breathing through the starlight of bygone nights; a signal fire gleams like a jewel on the high brow of a sombre cliff; great trees, the advanced sentries of immense forests, stand watchful and still over sleeping stretches of open water; a line of white surf thunders on an empty beach, the shallow water foams on the reefs; and green islets scattered through the calm of noonday lie upon the level of a polished sea, like a handful of emeralds on a buckler of steel.

There are faces too—faces dark, truculent, and smiling; the frank audacious faces of men barefooted, well armed and noiseless. They thronged the narrow length of our schooner's decks with their ornamented and barbarous crowd, with the variegated colours of checkered sarongs, red turbans, white jackets, embroideries; with the gleam of scabbards, gold rings, charms, armlets, lance blades, and jewelled handles of their weapons. They had an independent bearing, resolute eyes, a restrained manner; and we seem yet to hear their soft voices speaking of battles, travels, and escapes; boasting with composure, joking quietly; sometimes in well-bred murmurs extolling their own valour, or generosity; or celebrating with loyal enthusiasm the virtues of their ruler. We remember the faces, the eyes, the voices, we see again the gleam of silk and metal; the murmuring stir of that crowd, brilliant, festive, and martial; and we seem to feel the touch of friendly brown hands that, after one short grasp, return to rest on a chased hilt. They were Karain's people—a devoted following. Their movements hung on his lips; they read their thoughts in his eyes; he murmured to them nonchalantly of life and death, and they accepted his words humbly, like gifts of fate. They were all free men, and when speaking to him said, "Your slave." On his passage voices died out as though he had walked guarded by silence; awed whispers followed him. They called him their war-chief. He was the ruler of three villages on a narrow plain; the master of an insignificant foothold on the earth—of a conquered foothold that, shaped like a young moon, lay ignored between the hills and the sea.

From the deck of our schooner, anchored in the middle of the bay, he indicated by a theatrical sweep of his arm along the jagged outline of the hills the whole of his domain; and the ample movement seemed to drive back its limits, augmenting it suddenly into something so immense and vague that for a moment it appeared to be bounded only by the sky. And really, looking at that place, landlocked from the sea and shut off from the land by the precipitous slopes of mountains, it was difficult to believe in the existence of any neighbourhood. It was still, complete, unknown, and full of a life that went on stealthily with a troubling effect of solitude; of a life that seemed unaccountably empty of anything that would stir the thought, touch the heart, give a hint of the ominous sequence of days. It appeared to us a land without memories, regrets, and hopes; a land where nothing could survive the coming of the night, and where each sunrise, like a dazzling act of special creation, was disconnected from the eve and the morrow.

Karain swept his hand over it. "All mine!" He struck the deck with his long staff; the gold head flashed like a falling star; very close behind him a silent old fellow in a richly embroidered black jacket alone of all the Malays around did not follow the masterful gesture with a look. He did not even lift his eyelids. He bowed his head behind his master, and without stirring held hilt up over his right shoulder a long blade in a silver scabbard. He was there on duty, but without curiosity, and seemed weary, not with age, but with the possession of a burdensome secret of existence. Karain, heavy and proud, had a lofty pose and breathed calmly. It was our first visit, and we looked about curiously.

The bay was like a bottomless pit of intense light. The circular sheet of water reflected a luminous sky, and the shores enclosing it made an opaque ring of earth floating in an emptiness of transparent blue. The hills, purple and arid, stood out heavily on the sky: their summits seemed to fade into a coloured tremble as of ascending vapour; their steep sides were streaked with the green of narrow ravines; at their foot lay rice-fields, plantain-patches, yellow sands. A torrent wound about like a dropped thread. Clumps of fruit-trees marked the villages; slim palms put their nodding heads together above the low houses; dried palm-leaf roofs shone afar, like roofs of gold, behind the dark colonnades of tree-trunks; figures passed vivid and vanishing; the smoke of fires stood upright above the masses of flowering bushes; bamboo fences glittered, running away in broken lines between the fields. A sudden cry on the shore sounded plaintive in the distance, and ceased abruptly, as if stifled in the downpour of sunshine. A puff of breeze made a flash of darkness on the smooth water, touched our faces, and became forgotten. Nothing moved. The sun blazed down into a shadowless hollow of colours and stillness.

It was the stage where, dressed splendidly for his part, he strutted, incomparably dignified, made important by the power he had to awaken an absurd expectation of something heroic going to take place—a burst of action or song—upon the vibrating tone of a wonderful sunshine. He was ornate and disturbing, for one could not imagine what depth of horrible void such an elaborate front could be worthy to hide. He was not masked—there was too much life in him, and a mask is only a lifeless thing; but he presented himself essentially as an actor, as a human being aggressively disguised. His smallest acts were prepared and unexpected, his speeches grave, his sentences ominous like hints and complicated like arabesques. He was treated with a solemn respect accorded in the irreverent West only to the monarchs of the stage, and he accepted the profound homage with a sustained dignity seen nowhere else but behind the footlights and in the condensed falseness of some grossly tragic situation. It was almost impossible to remember who he was—only a petty chief of a conveniently isolated corner of Mindanao, where we could in comparative safety break the law against the traffic in firearms and ammunition with the natives. What would happen should one of the moribund Spanish gun-boats be suddenly galvanized into a flicker of active life did not trouble us, once we were inside the bay—so completely did it appear out of the reach of a meddling world; and besides, in those days we were imaginative enough to look with a kind of joyous equanimity on any chance there was of being quietly hanged somewhere out of the way of diplomatic remonstrance. As to Karain, nothing could happen to him unless what happens to all—failure and death; but his quality was to appear clothed in the illusion of unavoidable success. He seemed too effective, too necessary there, too much of an essential condition for the existence of his land and his people, to be destroyed by anything short of an earthquake. He summed up his race, his country, the elemental force of ardent life, of tropical nature. He had its luxuriant strength, its fascination; and, like it, he carried the seed of peril within.

In many successive visits we came to know his stage well—the purple semicircle of hills, the slim trees leaning over houses, the yellow sands, the streaming green of ravines. All that had the crude and blended colouring, the appropriateness almost excessive, the suspicious immobility of a painted scene; and it enclosed so perfectly the accomplished acting of his amazing pretences that the rest of the world seemed shut out forever from the gorgeous spectacle. There could be nothing outside. It was as if the earth had gone on spinning, and had left that crumb of its surface alone in space. He appeared utterly cut off from everything but the sunshine, and that even seemed to be made for him alone. Once when asked what was on the other side of the hills, he said, with a meaning smile, "Friends and enemies—many enemies; else why should I buy your rifles and powder?" He was always like this—word-perfect in his part, playing up faithfully to the mysteries and certitudes of his surroundings. "Friends and enemies"—nothing else. It was impalpable and vast. The earth had indeed rolled away from under his land, and he, with his handful of people, stood surrounded by a silent tumult as of contending shades. Certainly no sound came from outside. "Friends and enemies!" He might have added, "and memories," at least as far as he himself was concerned; but he neglected to make that point then. It made itself later on, though; but it was after the daily performance—in the wings, so to speak, and with the lights out. Meantime he filled the stage with barbarous dignity. Some ten years ago he had led his people—a scratch lot of wandering Bugis—to the conquest of the bay, and now in his august care they had forgotten all the past, and had lost all concern for the future. He gave them wisdom, advice, reward, punishment, life or death, with the same serenity of attitude and voice. He understood irrigation and the art of war—the qualities of weapons and the craft of boat-building. He could conceal his heart; had more endurance; he could swim longer, and steer a canoe better than any of his people; he could shoot straighter, and negotiate more tortuously than any man of his race I knew. He was an adventurer of the sea, an outcast, a ruler—and my very good friend. I wish him a quick death in a stand-up fight, a death in sunshine; for he had known remorse and power, and no man can demand more from life. Day after day he appeared before us, incomparably faithful to the illusions of the stage, and at sunset the night descended upon him quickly, like a falling curtain. The seamed hills became black shadows towering high upon a clear sky; above them the glittering confusion of stars resembled a mad turmoil stilled by a gesture; sounds ceased, men slept, forms vanished—and the reality of the universe alone remained—a marvellous thing of darkness and glimmers.

II

But it was at night that he talked openly, forgetting the exactions of his stage. In the daytime there were affairs to be discussed in state. There were at first between him and me his own splendour, my shabby suspicions, and the scenic landscape that intruded upon the reality of our lives by its motionless fantasy of outline and colour. His followers thronged round him; above his head the broad blades of their spears made a spiked halo of iron points, and they hedged him from humanity by the shimmer of silks, the gleam of weapons, the excited and respectful hum of eager voices. Before sunset he would take leave with ceremony, and go off sitting under a red umbrella, and escorted by a score of boats. All the paddles flashed and struck together with a mighty splash that reverberated loudly in the monumental amphitheatre of hills. A broad stream of dazzling foam trailed behind the flotilla. The canoes appeared very black on the white hiss of water; turbaned heads swayed back and forth; a multitude of arms in crimson and yellow rose and fell with one movement; the spearmen upright in the bows of canoes had variegated sarongs and gleaming shoulders like bronze statues; the muttered strophes of the paddlers' song ended periodically in a plaintive shout. They diminished in the distance; the song ceased; they swarmed on the beach in the long shadows of the western hills. The sunlight lingered on the purple crests, and we could see him leading the way to his stockade, a burly bareheaded figure walking far in advance of a straggling *cortège,* and swinging regularly an ebony staff taller than himself. The darkness deepened fast; torches gleamed fitfully, passing behind bushes; a long hail or two trailed in the silence of the evening; and at last the night stretched its smooth veil over the shore, the lights, and the voices.

Then, just as we were thinking of repose, the watchmen of the schooner would hail a splash of paddles away in the starlit gloom of the bay; a voice would respond in cautious tones, and our serang, putting his head down the open skylight, would inform us without surprise, "That Rajah, he coming. He here now." Karain appeared noiselessly in the doorway of the little cabin. He was simplicity itself then; all in white; muffled about his head; for arms only a kriss with a plain buffalo-horn handle, which he would politely conceal within a fold of his sarong before stepping over the threshold. The old sword-bearer's face, the worn-out and mournful face so covered with wrinkles that it seemed to look out through the meshes of a fine dark net, could be seen close above his shoulders. Karain never moved without that attendant, who stood or squatted close at his back. He had a dislike of an open space behind him. It was more than a dislike—it resembled fear, a nervous preoccupation of what went on where he could not see. This, in view of the evident and fierce loyalty that surrounded him, was inexplicable. He was there alone in the midst of devoted men; he was safe from neighbourly ambushes, from fraternal ambitions; and yet more than one of our visitors had assured us that their ruler could not bear to be alone. They said, "Even when he eats and sleeps there is always one on the watch near him who has strength and weapons." There was indeed always one near him, though our informants had no conception of that watcher's strength and weapons, which were both shadowy and terrible. We knew, but only later on, when we had heard the story. Meantime we noticed that, even during the most important interviews, Karain would often give a start, and interrupting his discourse, would sweep his arm back with a sudden movement, to feel whether the old fellow was there. The old fellow, impenetrable and weary, was always there. He shared his food, his repose, and his thoughts; he knew his plans, guarded his secrets; and, impassive behind his master's agitation, without stirring the least bit, murmured above his head in a soothing tone some words difficult to catch.

It was only on board the schooner, when surrounded by white faces, by unfamiliar sights and sounds, that Karain seemed to forget the strange obsession that wound like a black thread through the gorgeous pomp of his public life. At night we treated him in a free and easy manner, which just stopped short of slapping him on the back, for there are liberties one must not take with a Malay. He said himself that on such occasions he was only a private gentleman coming to see other gentlemen whom he supposed as well born as himself. I fancy that to the last he believed us to be emissaries of Government, darkly official persons furthering by our illegal traffic some dark scheme of high statecraft. Our denials and protestations were unavailing. He only smiled with discreet politeness and inquired about the Queen. Every visit began with that inquiry; he was insatiable of details; he was fascinated by the holder of a sceptre the shadow of which, stretching from the westward over the earth and over the seas, passed far beyond his own hand's-breadth of conquered land. He multiplied questions; he could never know enough of the Monarch of whom he spoke with wonder and chivalrous respect—with a kind of affectionate awe! Afterwards, when we had learned that he was the son of a woman who had many years ago ruled a small Bugis state, we came to suspect that the memory of his mother (of whom he spoke with enthusiasm) mingled somehow in his mind with the image he tried to form for himself of the far-off Queen whom he called Great, Invincible, Pious, and Fortunate. We had to invent details at last to satisfy his craving curiosity; and our loyalty must be pardoned, for we tried to make them fit for his august and resplendent ideal. We talked. The night slipped over us, over the still schooner, over the sleeping land, and over the sleepless sea that thundered amongst the reefs outside the bay. His paddlers, two trustworthy men, slept in the canoe at the foot of our side-ladder. The old confidant, relieved from duty, dozed on his heels, with his back against the companion-doorway; and Karain sat squarely in the ship's wooden armchair, under the slight sway of the cabin lamp, a cheroot between his dark fingers, and a glass of lemonade before him. He was amused by the fizz of the thing, but after a sip or two would let it get flat, and with a courteous wave of his hand ask for a fresh bottle. He decimated our slender stock; but we did not begrudge it to him, for, when he began, he talked well. He must have been a great Bugis dandy in his time, for even then (and when we knew him he was no longer young) his splendour was spotlessly neat, and he dyed his hair a light shade of brown. The quiet dignity of his bearing transformed the dim-lit cuddy of the schooner into an audience-hall. He talked of inter-island politics with an ironic and melancholy shrewdness. He had travelled much, suffered not a little, intrigued, fought. He knew native Courts, European Settlements, the forests, the sea, and, as he said himself, had spoken in his time to many great men. He liked to talk with me because I had known some of these men: he seemed to think that I could understand him, and, with a fine confidence, assumed that I, at least, could appreciate how much greater he was himself. But he preferred to talk of his native country—a small Bugis state on the island of Celebes. I had visited it some time before, and he asked eagerly for news. As men's names came up in conversation he would say, "We swam against one another when we were boys"; or, "We hunted the deer together—he could use the noose and the spear as well as I." Now and then his big dreamy eyes would roll restlessly; he frowned or smiled, or he would become pensive, and, staring in silence, would nod slightly for a time at some regretted vision of the past.

His mother had been the ruler of a small semi-independent state on the sea-coast at the head of the Gulf of Boni. He spoke of her with pride. She had been a woman resolute in affairs of state and of her own heart. After the death of her first husband, undismayed by the turbulent opposition of the chiefs, she married a rich trader, a Korinchi man of no family. Karain was her son by that second marriage, but his unfortunate descent had apparently nothing to do with his exile. He said nothing as to its cause, though once he let slip with a sigh, "Ha! my land will not feel any more the weight of my body." But he related willingly the story of his wanderings, and told us all about the conquest of the bay. Alluding to the people beyond the hills, he would murmur gently, with a careless wave of the hand, "They came over the hills once to fight us, but those who got away never came again." He thought for a while, smiling to himself. "Very few got away," he added, with proud serenity. He cherished the recollections of his successes; he had an exulting eagerness for endeavour; when he talked, his aspect was warlike, chivalrous, and uplifting. No wonder his people admired him. We saw him once walking in daylight amongst the houses of the settlement. At the doors of huts groups of women turned to look after him, warbling softly, and with gleaming eyes; armed men stood out of the way, submissive and erect; others approached from the side, bending their backs to address him humbly; an old woman stretched out a draped lean arm—"Blessings on thy head!" she cried from a dark doorway; a fiery-eyed man showed above the low fence of a plantain-patch a streaming face, a bare breast scarred in two places, and bellowed out pantingly after him, "God give victory to our master!" Karain walked fast, and with firm long strides; he answered greetings right and left by quick piercing glances. Children ran forward between the houses, peeped fearfully round corners; young boys kept up with him, gliding between bushes; their eyes gleamed through the dark leaves. The old sword-bearer, shouldering the silver scabbard, shuffled hastily at his heels with bowed head, and his eyes on the ground. And in the midst of a great stir they passed swift and absorbed, like two men hurrying through a great solitude.

In his council hall he was surrounded by the gravity of armed chiefs, while two long rows of old headmen dressed in cotton stuffs squatted on their heels, with idle arms hanging over their knees. Under the thatch roof supported by smooth columns, of which each one had cost the life of a straight-stemmed young palm, the scent of flowering hedges drifted in warm waves. The sun was sinking. In the open courtyard suppliants walked through the gate, raising, when yet far off, their joined hands above bowed heads, and bending low in the bright stream of sunlight. Young girls, with flowers in their laps, sat under the wide-spreading boughs of a big tree. The blue smoke of wood fires spread in a thin mist above the high-pitched roofs of houses that had glistening walls of woven reeds, and all round them rough wooden pillars under the sloping eaves. He dispensed justice in the shade; from a high seat he gave orders, advice, reproof. Now and then the hum of approbation rose louder, and idle spearmen that lounged listlessly against the posts, looking at the girls, would turn their heads slowly. To no man had been given the shelter of so much respect, confidence, and awe. Yet at times he would lean forward and appear to listen as for a far-off note of discord, as if expecting to hear some faint voice, the sound of light footsteps; or he would start half up in his seat, as though he had been familiarly touched on the shoulder. He glanced back with apprehension; his aged follower whispered inaudibly at his ear; the chiefs turned their eyes away in silence, for the old wizard, the man who could command ghosts and send evil spirits against enemies, was speaking low to their ruler. Around the short stillness of the open place the trees rustled faintly, the soft laughter of girls playing with the flowers rose in clear bursts of joyous sound. At the end of upright spear-shafts the long tufts of dyed horse-hair waved crimson and filmy in the gust of wind; and beyond the blaze of hedges the brook of limpid quick water ran invisible and loud under the drooping grass of the bank, with a great murmur, passionate and gentle.

After sunset, far across the fields and over the bay, clusters of torches could be seen burning under the high roofs of the council shed. Smoky red flames swayed on high poles, and the fiery blaze flickered over faces, clung to the smooth trunks of palm-trees, kindled bright sparks on the rims of metal dishes standing on fine floor-mats. That obscure adventurer feasted like a king. Small groups of men crouched in tight circles round the wooden platters; brown hands hovered over snowy heaps of rice. Sitting upon a rough couch apart from the others, he leaned on his elbow with inclined head; and near him a youth improvised in a high tone a song that celebrated his valour and wisdom. The singer rocked himself to and fro, rolling frenzied eyes; old women hobbled about with dishes, and men, squatting low, lifted their heads to listen gravely without ceasing to eat. The song of triumph vibrated in the night, and the stanzas rolled out mournful and fiery like the thoughts of a hermit. He silenced it with a sign, "Enough!" An owl hooted far away, exulting in the delight of deep gloom in dense foliage; overhead lizards ran in the attap thatch, calling softly; the dry leaves of the roof rustled; the rumour of mingled voices grew louder suddenly. After a circular and startled glance, as of a man waking up abruptly to the sense of danger, he would throw himself back, and under the downward gaze of the old sorcerer take up, wide-eyed, the slender thread of his dream. They watched his moods; the swelling rumour of animated talk subsided like a wave on a sloping beach. The chief is pensive. And above the spreading whisper of lowered voices only a light rattle of weapons would be heard, a single louder word distinct and alone, or the grave ring of a big brass tray.

III

For two years at short intervals we visited him. We came to like him, to trust him, almost to admire him. He was plotting and preparing a war with patience, with foresight—with a fidelity to his purpose and with a steadfastness of which I would have thought him racially incapable. He seemed fearless of the future, and in his plans displayed a sagacity that was only limited by his profound ignorance of the rest of the world. We tried to enlighten him, but our attempts to make clear the irresistible nature of the forces which he desired to arrest failed to discourage his eagerness to strike a blow for his own primitive ideas. He did not understand us, and replied by arguments that almost drove one to desperation by their childish shrewdness. He was absurd and unanswerable. Sometimes we caught glimpses of a sombre, glowing fury within him—a brooding and vague sense of wrong, and a concentrated lust of violence which is dangerous in a native. He raved like one inspired. On one occasion, after we had been talking to him late in his campong, he jumped up. A great, clear fire blazed in the grove; lights and shadows danced together between the trees; in the still night bats flitted in and out of the boughs like fluttering flakes of denser darkness. He snatched the sword from the old man, whizzed it out of the scabbard, and thrust the point into the earth. Upon the thin, upright blade the silver hilt, released, swayed before him like something alive. He stepped back a pace, and in a deadened tone spoke fiercely to the vibrating steel: "If there is virtue in the fire, in the iron, in the hand that forged thee, in the words spoken over thee, in the desire of my heart, and in the wisdom of thy makers,—then we shall be victorious together!" He drew it out, looked along the edge. "Take," he said over his shoulder to the old sword-bearer. The other, unmoved on his hams, wiped the point with a corner of his sarong, and returning the weapon to its scabbard, sat nursing it on his knees without a single look upwards. Karain, suddenly very calm, reseated himself with dignity. We gave up remonstrating after this, and let him go his way to an honourable disaster. All we could do for him was to see to it that the powder was good for the money and the rifles serviceable, if old.

But the game was becoming at last too dangerous; and if we, who had faced it pretty often, thought little of the danger, it was decided for us by some very respectable people sitting safely in countinghouses that the risks were too great, and that only one more trip could be made. After giving in the usual way many misleading hints as to our destination, we slipped away quietly, and after a very quick passage entered the bay. It was early morning, and even before the anchor went to the bottom the schooner was surrounded by boats.

The first thing we heard was that Karain's mysterious sword-bearer had died a few days ago. We did not attach much importance to the news. It was certainly difficult to imagine Karain without his inseparable follower; but the fellow was old, he had never spoken to one of us, we hardly ever had heard the sound of his voice; and we had come to look upon him as upon something inanimate, as a part of our friend's trappings of state—like that sword he had carried, or the fringed red umbrella displayed during an official progress. Karain did not visit us in the afternoon as usual. A message of greeting and a present of fruit and vegetables came off for us before sunset. Our friend paid us like a banker, but treated us like a prince. We sat up for him till midnight. Under the stern awning bearded Jackson jingled an old guitar and sang, with an execrable accent, Spanish love-songs; while young Hollis and I, sprawling on the deck, had a game of chess by the light of a cargo lantern. Karain did not appear. Next day we were busy unloading, and heard that the Rajah was unwell. The expected invitation to visit him ashore did not come. We sent friendly messages, but, fearing to intrude upon some secret council, remained on board. Early on the third day we had landed all the powder and rifles, and also a six-pounder brass gun with its carriage which we had subscribed together for a present for our friend. The afternoon was sultry. Ragged edges of black clouds peeped over the hills, and invisible thunderstorms circled outside, growling like wild beasts. We got the schooner ready for sea, intending to leave next morning at daylight. All day a merciless sun blazed down into the bay, fierce and pale, as if at white heat. Nothing moved on the land. The beach was empty, the villages seemed deserted; the trees far off stood in unstirring clumps, as if painted; the white smoke of some invisible bush-fire spread itself low over the shores of the bay like a settling fog. Late in the day three of Karain's chief men, dressed in their best and armed to the teeth, came off in a canoe, bringing a case of dollars. They were gloomy and languid, and told us they had not seen their Rajah for five days. No one had seen him! We settled all accounts, and after shaking hands in turn and in profound silence, they descended one after another into their boat, and were paddled to the shore, sitting close together, clad in vivid colours, with hanging heads: the gold embroideries of their jackets flashed dazzlingly as they went away gliding on the smooth water, and not one of them looked back once. Before sunset the growling clouds carried with a rush the ridge of hills, and came tumbling down the inner slopes. Everything disappeared; black whirling vapours filled the bay and in the midst of them the schooner swung here and there in the shifting gusts of wind. A single clap of thunder detonated in the hollow with a violence that seemed capable of bursting into small pieces the ring of high land, and a warm deluge descended. The wind died out. We panted in the close cabin; our faces streamed; the bay outside hissed as if boiling; the water fell in perpendicular shafts as heavy as lead; it swished about the deck, poured off the spars, gurgled, sobbed, splashed, murmured in the blind night. Our lamp burned low.

Hollis, stripped to the waist, lay stretched out on the lockers, with closed eyes and motionless like a despoiled corpse; at his head Jackson twanged the guitar, and gasped out in sighs a mournful dirge about hopeless love and eyes like stars. Then we heard startled voices on deck crying in the rain, hurried footsteps overhead, and suddenly Karain appeared in the doorway of the cabin. His bare breast and his face glistened in the light; his sarong, soaked, clung about his legs; he had his sheathed kriss in his left hand; and wisps of wet hair, escaping from under his red kerchief, stuck over his eyes and down his cheeks. He stepped in with a headlong stride and looking over his shoulder like a man pursued. Hollis turned on his side quickly and opened his eyes. Jackson clapped his big hand over the strings and the jingling vibration died suddenly. I stood up.

"We did not hear your boat's hail!" I exclaimed.

"Boat! The man's swum off," drawled out Hollis from the locker. "Look at him!"

He breathed heavily, wild-eyed, while we looked at him in silence. Water dripped from him, made a dark pool, and ran crookedly across the cabin floor. We could hear Jackson, who had gone out to drive away our Malay seamen from the doorway of the companion; he swore menacingly in the patter of a heavy shower, and there was a great commotion on deck. The watchmen, scared out of their wits by the glimpse of a shadowy figure leaping over the rail, straight out of the night as it were, had alarmed all hands.

Then Jackson, with glittering drops of water on his hair and beard, came back looking angry, and Hollis, who, being the youngest of us, assumed an indolent superiority, said without stirring, "Give him a dry sarong—give him mine; it's hanging up in the bathroom." Karain laid the kriss on the table, hilt inwards, and murmured a few words in a strangled voice.

"What's that?" asked Hollis, who had not heard.

"He apologizes for coming in with a weapon in his hand," I said, dazedly.

"Ceremonious beggar. Tell him we forgive a friend . . . on such a night," drawled out Hollis. "What's wrong?"

Karain slipped the dry sarong over his head, dropped the wet one at his feet, and stepped out of it. I pointed to the wooden armchair—his armchair. He sat down very straight, said "Ha!" in a strong voice; a short shiver shook his broad frame. He looked over his shoulder uneasily, turned as if to speak to us, but only stared in a curious blind manner, and again looked back. Jackson bellowed out, "Watch well on deck there!" heard a faint answer from above, and reaching out with his foot slammed-to the cabin door.

"All right now," he said.

Karain's lips moved slightly. A vivid flash of lightning made the two round sternports facing him glimmer like a pair of cruel and phosphorescent eyes. The flame of the lamp seemed to wither into brown dust for an instant, and the looking-glass over the little sideboard leaped out behind his back in a smooth sheet of livid light. The roll of thunder came near, crashed over us; the schooner trembled, and the great voice went on, threatening terribly, into the distance. For less than a minute a furious shower rattled on the decks. Karain looked slowly from face to face, and then the silence became so profound that we all could hear distinctly the two chronometers in my cabin ticking along with unflagging speed against one another.

And we three, strangely moved, could not take our eyes from him. He had become enigmatical and touching, in virtue of that mysterious cause that had driven him through the night and through the thunderstorm to the shelter of the schooner's cuddy. Not one of us doubted that we were looking at a fugitive, incredible as it appeared to us. He was haggard, as though he had not slept for weeks; he had become lean, as though he had not eaten for days. His cheeks were hollow, his eyes sunk, the muscles of his chest and arms twitched slightly as if after an exhausting contest. Of course it had been a long swim off to the schooner; but his face showed another kind of fatigue, the tormented weariness, the anger and the fear of a struggle against a thought, an idea—against something that cannot be grappled, that never rests—a shadow, a nothing, unconquerable and immortal, that preys upon life. We knew it as though he had shouted it at us. His chest expanded time after time, as if it could not contain the beating of his heart. For a moment he had the power of the possessed—the power to awaken in the beholders wonder, pain, pity, and a fearful near sense of things invisible, of things dark and mute, that surround the loneliness of mankind. His eyes roamed about aimlessly for a moment, then became still. He said with effort—

"I came here . . . I leaped out of my stockade as after a defeat. I ran in the night. The water was black. I left him calling on the edge of black water . . . I left him standing alone on the beach. I swam . . . he called out after me . . . I swam . . ."

He trembled from head to foot, sitting very upright and gazing straight before him. Left whom? Who called? We did not know. We could not understand. I said at all hazards—

"Be firm."

The sound of my voice seemed to steady him into a sudden rigidity, but otherwise he took no notice. He seemed to listen, to expect something for a moment, then went on—

"He cannot come here—therefore I sought you. You men with white faces who despise the invisible voices. He cannot abide your unbelief and your strength."

He was silent for a while, then exclaimed softly—

"Oh! the strength of unbelievers!"

"There's no one here but you—and we three," said Hollis, quietly. He reclined with his head supported on elbow and did not budge.

"I know," said Karain. "He has never followed me here. Was not the wise man ever by my side? But since the old wise man, who knew of my trouble, has died, I have heard the voice every night. I shut myself up—for many days—in the dark. I can hear the sorrowful murmurs of women, the whisper of the wind, of the running waters; the clash of weapons in the hands of faithful men, their footsteps—and his voice! . . . Near . . . So! In my ear! I felt him near . . . His breath passed over my neck. I leaped out without a cry. All about me men slept quietly. I ran to the sea. He ran by my side without footsteps, whispering, whispering old words—whispering into my ear in his old voice. I ran into the sea; I swam off to you, with my kriss between my teeth. I, armed, I fled before a breath—to you. Take me away to your land. The wise old man has died, and with him is gone the power of his words and charms. And I can tell no one. No one. There is no one here faithful enough and wise enough to know. It is only near you, unbelievers, that my trouble fades like a mist under the eye of day."

He turned to me.

"With you I go!" he cried in a contained voice. "With you, who know so many of us. I want to leave this land—my people . . . and him—there!"

He pointed a shaking finger at random over his shoulder. It was hard for us to bear the intensity of that undisclosed distress. Hollis stared at him hard. I asked gently—

"Where is the danger?"

"Everywhere outside this place," he answered, mournfully. "In every place where I am. He waits for me on the paths, under the trees, in the place where I sleep—everywhere but here."

He looked round the little cabin, at the painted beams, at the tarnished varnish of bulkheads; he looked round as if appealing to all its shabby strangeness, to the disorderly jumble of unfamiliar things that belong to an inconceivable life of stress, of power, of endeavour, of unbelief—to the strong life of white men, which rolls on irresistible and hard on the edge of outer darkness. He stretched out his arms as if to embrace it and us. We waited. The wind and rain had ceased, and the stillness of the night round the schooner was as dumb and complete as if a dead world had been laid to rest in a grave of clouds. We expected him to speak. The necessity within him tore at his lips. There are those who say that a native will not speak to a white man. Error. No man will speak to his master; but to a wanderer and a friend, to him who does not come to teach or to rule, to him who asks for nothing and accepts all things, words are spoken by the camp fires, in the shared solitude of the sea, in riverside villages, in resting places surrounded by forests—words are spoken that take no account of race or colour. One heart speaks—another one listens; and the earth, the sea, the sky, the passing wind and the stirring leaf, hear also the futile tale of the burden of life.

He spoke at last. It is impossible to convey the effect of his story. It is undying, it is but a memory, and its vividness cannot be made clear to another mind, any more than the vivid emotions of a dream. One must have seen his innate splendour, one must have known him before—looked at him then. The wavering gloom of the little cabin; the breathless stillness outside, through which only the lapping of water against the schooner's sides could be heard; Hollis's pale face, with steady dark eyes; the energetic head of Jackson held up between two big palms, and with the long yellow hair of his beard flowing over the strings of the guitar lying on the table; Karain's upright and motionless pose, his tone—all this made an impression that cannot be forgotten. He faced us across the table. His dark head and bronze torso appeared above the tarnished slab of wood, gleaming and still as if cast in metal. Only his lips moved, and his eyes glowed, went out, blazed again, or stared mournfully. His expressions came straight from his tormented heart. His words sounded low, in a sad murmur as of running water; at times they rang loud like the clash of a war-gong—or trailed slowly like weary travellers—or rushed forward with the speed of fear.

IV

This is, imperfectly, what he said—

"It was after the great trouble that broke the alliance of the four states of Wajo. We fought amongst ourselves, and the Dutch watched from afar till we were weary. Then the smoke of their fire-ships was seen at the mouth of our rivers, and their great men came in boats full of soldiers to talk to us of protection and peace. We answered with caution and wisdom, for our villages were burnt, our stockades weak, the people weary, and the weapons blunt. They came and went; there had been much talk, but after they went away everything seemed to be as before, only their ships remained in sight from our coast, and very soon their traders came amongst us under a promise of safety. My brother was a Ruler, and one of those who had given the promise. I was young then, and had fought in the war, and Pata Matara had fought by my side. We had shared hunger, danger, fatigue, and victory. His eyes saw my danger quickly, and twice my arm had preserved his life. It was his destiny. He was my friend. And he was great amongst us—one of those who were near my brother, the Ruler. He spoke in council, his courage was great, he was the chief of many villages round the great lake that is in the middle of our country as the heart is in the middle of a man's body. When his sword was carried into a campong in advance of his coming, the maidens whispered wonderingly under the fruit-trees, the rich men consulted together in the shade, and a feast was made ready with rejoicing and songs. He had the favour of the Ruler and the affection of the poor. He loved war, deer hunts, and the charms of women. He was the possessor of jewels, of lucky weapons, and of men's devotion. He was a fierce man; and I had no other friend.

"I was the chief of a stockade at the mouth of the river, and collected tolls for my brother from the passing boats. One day I saw a Dutch trader go up the river. He went up with three boats, and no toll was demanded from him, because the smoke of Dutch war-ships stood out from the open sea, and we were too weak to forget treaties. He went up under the promise of safety, and my brother gave him protection. He said he came to trade. He listened to our voices, for we are men who speak openly and without fear; he counted the number of our spears, he examined the trees, the running waters, the grasses of the bank, the slopes of our hills. He went up to Matara's country and obtained permission to build a house. He traded and planted. He despised our joys, our thoughts, and our sorrows. His face was red, his hair like flame, and his eyes pale, like a river mist; he moved heavily, and spoke with a deep voice; he laughed aloud like a fool, and knew no courtesy in his speech. He was a big, scornful man, who looked into women's faces and put his hand on the shoulders of free men as though he had been a noble-born chief. We bore with him. Time passed.

"Then Pata Matara's sister fled from the campong and went to live in the Dutchman's house. She was a great and wilful lady: I had seen her once carried high on slaves' shoulders amongst the people, with uncovered face, and I had heard all men say that her beauty was extreme, silencing the reason and ravishing the heart of the beholders. The people were dismayed; Matara's face was blackened with that disgrace, for she knew she had been promised to another man. Matara went to the Dutchman's house, and said, 'Give her up to die—she is the daughter of chiefs.' The white man refused and shut himself up, while his servants kept guard night and day with loaded guns. Matara raged. My brother called a council. But the Dutch ships were near, and watched our coast greedily. My brother said, 'If he dies now our land will pay for his blood. Leave him alone till we grow stronger and the ships are gone.' Matara was wise; he waited and watched. But the white man feared for her life and went away.

"He left his house, his plantations, and his goods! He departed, armed and menacing, and left all—for her! She had ravished his heart! From my stockade I saw him put out to sea in a big boat. Matara and I watched him from the fighting platform behind the pointed stakes. He sat cross-legged, with his gun in his hands, on the roof at the stern of his prau. The barrel of his rifle glinted aslant before his big red face. The broad river was stretched under him—level, smooth, shining, like a plain of silver; and his prau, looking very short and black from the shore, glided along the silver plain and over into the blue of the sea.

"Thrice Matara, standing by my side, called aloud her name with grief and imprecations. He stirred my heart. It leaped three times; and three times with the eye of my mind I saw in the gloom within the enclosed space of the prau a woman with streaming hair going away from her land and her people. I was angry—and sorry. Why? And then I also cried out insults and threats. Matara said, 'Now they have left our land their lives are mine. I shall follow and strike—and, alone, pay the price of blood.' A great wind was sweeping towards the setting sun over the empty river. I cried, 'By your side I will go!' He lowered his head in sign of assent. It was his destiny. The sun had set, and the trees swayed their boughs with a great noise above our heads.

"On the third night we two left our land together in a trading prau.

"The sea met us—the sea, wide, pathless, and without voice. A sailing prau leaves no track. We went south. The moon was full; and, looking up, we said to one another, 'When the next moon shines as this one, we shall return and they will be dead.' It was fifteen years ago. Many moons have grown full and withered and I have not seen my land since. We sailed south; we overtook many praus; we examined the creeks and the bays; we saw the end of our coast, of our island—a steep cape over a disturbed strait, where drift the shadows of shipwrecked praus and drowned men clamour in the night. The wide sea was all round us now. We saw a great mountain burning in the midst of water; we saw thousands of islets scattered like bits of iron fired from a big gun; we saw a long coast of mountain and lowlands stretching away in sunshine from west to east. It was Java. We said, 'They are there; their time is near, and we shall return or die cleansed from dishonour.'

"We landed. Is there anything good in that country? The paths run straight and hard and dusty. Stone campongs, full of white faces, are surrounded by fertile fields, but every man you meet is a slave. The rulers live under the edge of a foreign sword. We ascended mountains, we traversed valleys; at sunset we entered villages. We asked everyone, 'Have you seen such a white man?' Some stared; others laughed; women gave us food, sometimes, with fear and respect, as though we had been distracted by the visitation of God; but some did not understand our language, and some cursed us, or, yawning, asked with contempt the reason of our quest. Once, as we were going away, an old man called after us, 'Desist!'

"We went on. Concealing our weapons, we stood humbly aside before the horsemen on the road; we bowed low in the courtyards of chiefs who were no better than slaves. We lost ourselves in the fields, in the jungle; and one night, in a tangled forest, we came upon a place where crumbling old walls had fallen amongst the trees, and where strange stone idols—carved images of devils with many arms and legs, with snakes twined round their bodies, with twenty heads and holding a hundred swords—seemed to live and threaten in the light of our camp fire. Nothing dismayed us. And on the road, by every fire, in resting places, we always talked of her and of him. Their time was near. We spoke of nothing else. No! not of hunger, thirst, weariness, and faltering heart. No! we spoke of him and her! Of her! And we thought of them—of her! Matara brooded by the fire. I sat and thought and thought, till suddenly I could see again the image of a woman, beautiful, and young, and great and proud, and tender, going away from her land and her people. Matara said, 'When we find them we shall kill her first to cleanse the dishonour—then the man must die.' I would say, 'It shall be so; it is your vengeance.' He stared long at me with his big sunken eyes.

"We came back to the coast. Our feet were bleeding, our bodies thin. We slept in rags under the shadow of stone enclosures; we prowled, soiled and lean, about the gateways of white men's courtyards. Their hairy dogs barked at us, and their servants shouted from afar, 'Begone!' Low-born wretches, that keep watch over the streets of stone campongs, asked us who we were. We lied, we cringed, we smiled with hate in our hearts, and we kept looking here, looking there for them—for the white man with hair like flame, and for her, for the woman who had broken faith, and therefore must die. We looked. At last in every woman's face I thought I could see hers. We ran swiftly. No! Sometimes Matara would whisper, 'Here is the man,' and we waited, crouching. He came near. It was not the man—those Dutchmen are all alike. We suffered the anguish of deception. In my sleep I saw her face, and was both joyful and sorry. . . . Why? . . . I seemed to hear a whisper near me. I turned swiftly. She was not there! And as we trudged wearily from stone city to stone city I seemed to hear a light footstep near me. A time came when I heard it always, and I was glad. I thought, walking dizzy and weary in sunshine on the hard paths of white men—I thought, She is there—with us! . . . Matara was sombre. We were often hungry.

"We sold the carved sheaths of our krisses—the ivory sheaths with golden ferules. We sold the jewelled hilts. But we kept the blades—for them. The blades that never touch but kill—we kept the blades for her. . . . Why? She was always by our side. . . . We starved. We begged. We left Java at last.

"We went West, we went East. We saw many lands, crowds of strange faces, men that live in trees and men who eat their old people. We cut rattans in the forest for a handful of rice, and for a living swept the decks of big ships and heard curses heaped upon our heads. We toiled in villages; we wandered upon the seas with the Bajow people, who have no country. We fought for pay; we hired ourselves to work for Goram men, and were cheated; and under the orders of rough white faces we dived for pearls in barren bays, dotted with black rocks, upon a coast of sand and desolation. And everywhere we watched, we listened, we asked. We asked traders, robbers, white men. We heard jeers, mockery, threats—words of wonder and words of contempt. We never knew rest; we never thought of home, for our work was not done. A year passed, then another. I ceased to count the number of nights, of moons, of years. I watched over Matara. He had my last handful of rice; if there was water enough for one he drank it; I covered him up when he shivered with cold; and when the hot sickness came upon him I sat sleepless through many nights and fanned his face. He was a fierce man, and my friend. He spoke of her with fury in the daytime, with sorrow in the dark; he remembered her in health, in sickness. I said nothing; but I saw her every day—always! At first I saw only her head, as of a woman walking in the low mist on a river bank. Then she sat by our fire. I saw her! I looked at her! She had tender eyes and a ravishing face. I murmured to her in the night. Matara said sleepily sometimes, 'To whom are you talking? Who is there?' I answered quickly, 'No one' . . . It was a lie! She never left me. She shared the warmth of our fire, she sat on my couch of leaves, she swam on the sea to follow me. . . . I saw her! . . . I tell you I saw her long black hair spread behind her upon the moonlit water as she struck out with bare arms by the side of a swift prau. She was beautiful, she was faithful, and in the silence of foreign countries she spoke to me very low in the language of my people. No one saw her; no one heard her; she was mine only! In daylight she moved with a swaying walk before me upon the weary paths; her figure was straight and flexible like the stem of a slender tree; the heels of her feet were round and polished like shells of eggs; with her round arm she made signs. At night she looked into my face. And she was sad! Her eyes were tender and frightened; her voice soft and pleading. Once I murmured to her, 'You shall not die,' and she smiled . . . ever after she smiled! . . . She gave me courage to bear weariness and hardships. Those were times of pain, and she soothed me. We wandered patient in our search. We knew deception, false hopes; we knew captivity, sickness, thirst, misery, despair. . . . Enough! We found them! . . ."

He cried out the last words and paused. His face was impassive, and he kept still like a man in a trance. Hollis sat up quickly, and spread his elbows on the table. Jackson made a brusque movement, and accidentally touched the guitar. A plaintive resonance filled the cabin with confused vibrations and died out slowly. Then Karain began to speak again. The restrained fierceness of his tone seemed to rise like a voice from outside, like a thing unspoken but heard; it filled the cabin and enveloped in its intense and deadened murmur the motionless figure in the chair.

"We were on our way to Atjeh, where there was war; but the vessel ran on a sandbank, and we had to land in Delli. We had earned a little money, and had bought a gun from some Selangore traders; only one gun, which was fired by the spark of a stone: Matara carried it. We landed. Many white men lived there, planting tobacco on conquered plains, and Matara . . . But no matter. He saw him! . . . The Dutchman! . . . At last! . . . We crept and watched. Two nights and a day we watched. He had a house—a big house in a clearing in the midst of his fields; flowers and bushes grew around; there were narrow paths of yellow earth between the cut grass, and thick hedges to keep people out. The third night we came armed, and lay behind a hedge.

"A heavy dew seemed to soak through our flesh and made our very entrails cold. The grass, the twigs, the leaves, covered with drops of water, were gray in the moonlight. Matara, curled up in the grass, shivered in his sleep. My teeth rattled in my head so loud that I was afraid the noise would wake up all the land. Afar, the watchmen of white men's houses struck wooden clappers and hooted in the darkness. And, as every night, I saw her by my side. She smiled no more! . . . The fire of anguish burned in my breast, and she whispered to me with compassion, with pity, softly—as women will; she soothed the pain of my mind; she bent her face over me—the face of a woman who ravishes the hearts and silences the reason of men. She was all mine, and no one could see her—no one of living mankind! Stars shone through her bosom, through her floating hair. I was overcome with regret, with tenderness, with sorrow. Matara slept . . . Had I slept? Matara was shaking me by the shoulder, and the fire of the sun was drying the grass, the bushes, the leaves. It was day. Shreds of white mist hung between the branches of trees.

"Was it night or day? I saw nothing again till I heard Matara breathe quickly where he lay, and then outside the house I saw her. I saw them both. They had come out. She sat on a bench under the wall, and twigs laden with flowers crept high above her head, hung over her hair. She had a box on her lap, and gazed into it, counting the increase of her pearls. The Dutchman stood by looking on; he smiled down at her; his white teeth flashed; the hair on his lip was like two twisted flames. He was big and fat, and joyous, and without fear. Matara tipped fresh priming from the hollow of his palm, scraped the flint with his thumb-nail, and gave the gun to me. To me! I took it . . . O fate!

"He whispered into my ear, lying on his stomach, 'I shall creep close and then amok . . . let her die by my hand. You take aim at the fat swine there. Let him see me strike my shame off the face of the earth—and then . . . you are my friend—kill with a sure shot.' I said nothing; there was no air in my chest—there was no air in the world. Matara had gone suddenly from my side. The grass nodded. Then a bush rustled. She lifted her head.

"I saw her! The consoler of sleepless nights, of weary days; the companion of troubled years! I saw her! She looked straight at the place where I crouched. She was there as I had seen her for years—a faithful wanderer by my side. She looked with sad eyes and had smiling lips; she looked at me . . . Smiling lips! Had I not promised that she should not die!

"She was far off and I felt her near. Her touch caressed me, and her voice murmured, whispered above me, around me, 'Who shall be thy companion, who shall console thee if I die?' I saw a flowering thicket to the left of her stir a little . . . Matara was ready . . . I cried aloud—'Return!'

"She leaped up; the box fell; the pearls streamed at her feet. The big Dutchman by her side rolled menacing eyes through the still sunshine. The gun went up to my shoulder. I was kneeling and I was firm—firmer than the trees, the rocks, the mountains. But in front of the steady long barrel the fields, the house, the earth, the sky swayed to and fro like shadows in a forest on a windy day. Matara burst out of the thicket; before him the petals of torn flowers whirled high as if driven by a tempest. I heard her cry; I saw her spring with open arms in front of the white man. She was a woman of my country and of noble blood. They are so! I heard her shriek of anguish and fear—and all stood still! The fields, the house, the earth, the sky stood still—while Matara leaped at her with uplifted arm. I pulled the trigger, saw a spark, heard nothing; the smoke drove back into my face, and then I could see Matara roll over head first and lie with stretched arms at her feet. Ha! A sure shot! The sunshine fell on my back colder than the running water. A sure shot! I flung the gun after the shot. Those two stood over the dead man as though they had been bewitched by a charm. I shouted at her, 'Live and remember!' Then for a time I stumbled about in a cold darkness.

"Behind me there were great shouts, the running of many feet; strange men surrounded me, cried meaningless words into my face, pushed me, dragged me, supported me . . . I stood before the big Dutchman; he stared as if bereft of his reason. He wanted to know, he talked fast, he spoke of gratitude, he offered me food, shelter, gold—he asked many questions. I laughed in his face. I said, 'I am a Korinchi traveller from Perak over there, and know nothing of that dead man. I was passing along the path when I heard a shot, and your senseless people rushed out and dragged me here.' He lifted his arms, he wondered, he could not believe, he could not understand, he clamoured in his own tongue! She had her arms clasped round his neck, and over her shoulder stared back at me with wide eyes. I smiled and looked at her; I smiled and waited to hear the sound of her voice. The white man asked her suddenly, 'Do you know him?' I listened—my life was in my ears! She looked at me long, she looked at me with unflinching eyes, and said aloud, 'No! I never saw him before.' . . . What! Never before? Had she forgotten already? Was it possible? Forgotten already—after so many years—so many years of wandering, of companionship, of trouble, of tender words! Forgotten already! . . . I tore myself out from the hands that held me and went away without a word . . . They let me go.

"I was weary. Did I sleep? I do not know. I remember walking upon a broad path under a clear starlight; and that strange country seemed so big, the rice-fields so vast, that, as I looked around, my head swam with the fear of space. Then I saw a forest. The joyous starlight was heavy upon me. I turned off the path and entered the forest, which was very sombre and very sad."

V

Karain's tone had been getting lower and lower, as though he had been going away from us, till the last words sounded faint but clear, as if shouted on a calm day from a very great distance. He moved not. He stared fixedly past the motionless head of Hollis, who faced him, as still as himself. Jackson had turned sideways, and with elbow on the table shaded his eyes with the palm of his hand. And I looked on, surprised and moved; I looked at that man, loyal to a vision, betrayed by his dream, spurned by his illusion, and coming to us unbelievers for help—against a thought. The silence was profound; but it seemed full of noiseless phantoms, of things sorrowful, shadowy, and mute, in whose invisible presence the firm, pulsating beat of the two ship's chronometers ticking off steadily the seconds of Greenwich Time seemed to me a protection and a relief. Karain stared stonily; and looking at his rigid figure, I thought of his wanderings, of that obscure Odyssey of revenge, of all the men that wander amongst illusions; of the illusions as restless as men; of the illusions faithful, faithless; of the illusions that give joy, that give sorrow, that give pain, that give peace; of the invincible illusions that can make life and death appear serene, inspiring, tormented, or ignoble.

A murmur was heard; that voice from outside seemed to flow out of a dreaming world into the lamp-light of the cabin. Karain was speaking.

"I lived in the forest.

"She came no more. Never! Never once! I lived alone. She had forgotten. It was well. I did not want her; I wanted no one. I found an abandoned house in an old clearing. Nobody came near. Sometimes I heard in the distance the voices of people going along a path. I slept; I rested; there was wild rice, water from a running stream—and peace! Every night I sat alone by my small fire before the hut. Many nights passed over my head.

"Then, one evening, as I sat by my fire after having eaten, I looked down on the ground and began to remember my wanderings. I lifted my head. I had heard no sound, no rustle, no footsteps—but I lifted my head. A man was coming towards me across the small clearing. I waited. He came up without a greeting and squatted down into the firelight. Then he turned his face to me. It was Matara. He stared at me fiercely with his big sunken eyes. The night was cold; the heat died suddenly out of the fire, and he stared at me. I rose and went away from there, leaving him by the fire that had no heat.

"I walked all that night, all next day, and in the evening made up a big blaze and sat down—to wait for him. He had not come into the light. I heard him in the bushes here and there, whispering, whispering. I understood at last—I had heard the words before, 'You are my friend—kill with a sure shot.'

"I bore it as long as I could—then leaped away, as on this very night I leaped from my stockade and swam to you. I ran—I ran crying like a child left alone and far from the houses. He ran by my side, without footsteps, whispering, whispering—invisible and heard. I sought people—I wanted men around me! Men who had not died! And again we two wandered. I sought danger, violence, and death. I fought in the Atjeh war, and a brave people wondered at the valiance of a stranger. But we were two; he warded off the blows . . . Why? I wanted peace, not life. And no one could see him; no one knew—I dared tell no one. At times he would leave me, but not for long; then he would return and whisper or stare. My heart was torn with a strange fear, but could not die. Then I met and old man.

"You all knew him. People here called him my sorcerer, my servant and sword-bearer; but to me he was father, mother, protection, refuge and peace. When I met him he was returning from a pilgrimage, and I heard him intoning the prayer of sunset. He had gone to the holy place with his son, his son's wife, and a little child; and on their return, by the favour of the Most High, they all died: the strong man, the young mother, the little child—they died; and the old man reached his country alone. He was a pilgrim serene and pious, very wise and very lonely. I told him all. For a time we lived together. He said over me words of compassion, of wisdom, of prayer. He warded from me the shade of the dead. I begged him for a charm that would make me safe. For a long time he refused; but at last, with a sigh and a smile, he gave me one. Doubtless he could command a spirit stronger than the unrest of my dead friend, and again I had peace; but I had become restless, and a lover of turmoil and danger. The old man never left me. We travelled together. We were welcomed by the great; his wisdom and my courage are remembered where your strength, O white men, is forgotten! We served the Sultan of Sula. We fought the Spaniards. There were victories, hopes, defeats, sorrow, blood, women's tears . . . What for? . . . We fled. We collected wanderers of a warlike race and came here to fight again. The rest you know. I am the ruler of a conquered land, a lover of war and danger, a fighter and a plotter. But the old man has died, and I am again the slave of the dead. He is not here now to drive away the reproachful shade—to silence the lifeless voice! The power of his charm has died with him. And I know fear; and I hear the whisper, 'Kill! kill! kill!' . . . Have I not killed enough? . . ."

For the first time that night a sudden convulsion of madness and rage passed over his face. His wavering glances darted here and there like sacred birds in a thunderstorm. He jumped up, shouting—

"By the spirits that drink blood: by the spirits that cry in the night: by all the spirits of fury, misfortune, and death, I swear—some day I will strike into every heart I meet—I . . ."

He looked so dangerous that we all three leaped to our feet, and Hollis, with the back of his hand, sent the kriss flying off the table. I believe we shouted together. It was a short scare, and the next moment he was again composed in his chair, with three white men standing over him in rather foolish attitudes. We felt a little ashamed of ourselves. Jackson picked up the kriss, and, after an inquiring glance at me, gave it to him. He received it with a stately inclination of the head and stuck it in the twist of his sarong, with punctilious care to give his weapon a pacific position. Then he looked up at us with an austere smile. We were abashed and reproved. Hollis sat sideways on the table and, holding his chin in his hand, scrutinized him in pensive silence. I said—

"You must abide with your people. They need you. And there is forgetfulness in life. Even the dead cease to speak in time."

"Am I a woman, to forget long years before an eyelid has had the time to beat twice?" he exclaimed, with bitter resentment. He startled me. It was amazing. To him his life—that cruel mirage of love and peace—seemed as real, as undeniable, as theirs would be to any saint, philosopher, or fool of us all. Hollis muttered—

"You won't soothe him with your platitudes."

Karain spoke to me.

"You know us. You have lived with us. Why?—we cannot know; but you understand our sorrows and our thoughts. You have lived with my people, and you understand our desires and our fears. With you I will go. To your land—to your people. To your people, who live in unbelief; to whom day is day, and night is night—nothing more, because you understand all things seen, and despise all else! To your land of unbelief, where the dead do not speak, where every man is wise, and alone—and at peace!"

"Capital description," murmured Hollis, with the flicker of a smile.

Karain hung his head.

"I can toil, and fight—and be faithful," he whispered, in a weary tone, "but I cannot go back to him who waits for me on the shore. No! Take me with you . . . Or else give me some of your strength—of your unbelief . . . A charm . . . !"

He seemed utterly exhausted.

"Yes, take him home," said Hollis, very low, as if debating with himself. "That would be one way. The ghosts there are in society, and talk affably to ladies and gentlemen, but would scorn a naked human being—like our princely friend . . . Naked . . . Flayed! I should say. I am sorry for him. Impossible—of course. The end of all this shall be," he went on, looking up at us—"the end of this shall be, that some day he will run amuck amongst his faithful subjects and send *ad patres* ever so many of them before they make up their minds to the disloyalty of knocking him on the head."

I nodded. I thought it more than probable that such would be the end of Karain. It was evident that he had been hunted by his thought along the very limit of human endurance, and very little more pressing was needed to make him swerve over into the form of madness peculiar to his race. The respite he had during the old man's life made the return of the torment unbearable. That much was clear.

He lifted his head suddenly; we had imagined for a moment that he had been dozing.

"Give me your protection—or your strength!" he cried. "A charm . . . a weapon!"

Again his chin fell on his breast. We looked at him, then looked at one another with suspicious awe in our eyes, like men who come unexpectedly upon the scene of some mysterious disaster. He had given himself up to us; he had thrust into our hands his errors and his torment, his life and his peace; and we did not know what to do with that problem from the outer darkness. We three white men, looking at the Malay, could not find one word to the purpose amongst us—if indeed there existed a word that could solve that problem. We pondered, and our hearts sank. We felt as though we three had been called to the very gate of Infernal Regions to judge, to decide the fate of a wanderer coming suddenly from a world of sunshine and illusions.

"By Jove, he seems to have a great idea of our power," whispered Hollis, hopelessly. And then again there was a silence, the feeble plash of water, the steady tick of chronometers. Jackson, with bare arms crossed, leaned his shoulders against the bulkhead of the cabin. He was bending his head under the deck beam; his fair beard spread out magnificently over his chest; he looked colossal, ineffectual, and mild. There was something lugubrious in the aspect of the cabin; the air in it seemed to become slowly charged with the cruel chill of helplessness, with the pitiless anger of egoism against the incomprehensible form of an intruding pain. We had no idea what to do; we began to resent bitterly the hard necessity to get rid of him.

Hollis mused, muttered suddenly with a short laugh, "Strength . . . Protection . . . Charm." He slipped off the table and left the cuddy without a look at us. It seemed a base desertion. Jackson and I exchanged indignant glances. We could hear him rummaging in his pigeon-hole of a cabin. Was the fellow actually going to bed? Karain sighed. It was intolerable!

Then Hollis reappeared, holding in both hands a small leather box. He put it down gently on the table and looked at us with a queer gasp, we thought, as though he had from some cause become speechless for a moment, or were ethically uncertain about producing that box. But in an instant the insolent and unerring wisdom of his youth gave him the needed courage. He said, as he unlocked the box with a very small key, "Look as solemn as you can, you fellows."

Probably we looked only surprised and stupid, for he glanced over his shoulder, and said angrily—

"This is no play; I am going to do something for him. Look serious. Confound it! . . . Can't you lie a little . . . for a friend!"

Karain seemed to take no notice of us, but when Hollis threw open the lid of the box his eyes flew to it—and so did ours. The quilted crimson satin of the inside put a violent patch of colour into the sombre atmosphere; it was something positive to look at—it was fascinating.

VI

Hollis looked smiling into the box. He had lately made a dash home through the Canal. He had been away six months, and only joined us again just in time for this last trip. We had never seen the box before. His hands hovered above it; and he talked to us ironically, but his face became as grave as though he were pronouncing a powerful incantation over the things inside.

"Every one of us," he said, with pauses that somehow were more offensive than his words—"every one of us, you'll admit, has been haunted by some woman . . . And . . . as to fiends . . . dropped by the way . . . Well! . . . ask yourselves . . ."

He paused. Karain stared. A deep rumble was heard high up under the deck. Jackson spoke seriously—

"Don't be so beastly cynical."

"Ah! You are without guile," said Hollis, sadly. "You will learn . . . Meantime this Malay has been our friend . . ."

He repeated several times thoughtfully, "Friend . . . Malay. Friend, Malay," as though weighing the words against one another, then went on more briskly—

"A good fellow—a gentleman in his way. We can't, so to speak, turn our backs on his confidence and belief in us. Those Malays are easily impressed—all nerves, you know—therefore . . ."

He turned to me sharply.

"You know him best," he said, in a practical tone. "Do you think he is fanatical—I mean very strict in his faith?"

I stammered in profound amazement that "I did not think so."

"It's on account of its being a likeness—an engraved image," muttered Hollis, enigmatically, turning to the box. He plunged his fingers into it. Karain's lips were parted and his eyes shone. We looked into the box.

There were there a couple of reels of cotton, a packet of needles, a bit of silk ribbon, dark blue; a cabinet photograph, at which Hollis stole a glance before laying it on the table face downwards. A girl's portrait, I could see. There were, amongst a lot of various small objects, a bunch of flowers, a narrow white glove with many buttons, a slim packet of letters carefully tied up. Amulets of white men! Charms and talismans! Charms that keep them straight, that drive them crooked, that have the power to make a young man sigh, an old man smile. Potent things that procure dreams of joy, thoughts of regret; that soften hard hearts, and can temper a soft one to the hardness of steel. Gifts of heaven—things of earth . . .

Hollis rummaged in the box.

And it seemed to me, during that moment of waiting, that the cabin of the schooner was becoming filled with a stir invisible and living as of subtle breaths. All the ghosts driven out of the unbelieving West by men who pretend to be wise and alone and at peace—all the homeless ghosts of an unbelieving world—appeared suddenly round the figure of Hollis bending over the box; all the exiled and charming shades of loved women; all the beautiful and tender ghosts of ideals, remembered, forgotten, cherished, execrated; all the cast-out and reproachful ghosts of friends admired, trusted, traduced, betrayed, left dead by the way—they all seemed to come from the inhospitable regions of the earth to crowd into the gloomy cabin, as though it had been a refuge and, in all the unbelieving world, the only place of avenging belief . . . It lasted a second—all disappeared. Hollis was facing us alone with something small that glittered between his fingers. It looked like a coin.

"Ah! here it is," he said.

He held it up. It was a sixpence—a Jubilee sixpence. It was gilt; it had a hole punched near the rim. Hollis looked towards Karain.

"A charm for our friend," he said to us. "The thing itself is of great power—money, you know—and his imagination is struck. A loyal vagabond; if only his puritanism doesn't shy at a likeness . . ."

We said nothing. We did not know whether to be scandalized, amused, or relieved. Hollis advanced towards Karain, who stood up as if startled, and then, holding the coin up, spoke in Malay.

"This is the image of the Great Queen, and the most powerful thing the white men know," he said, solemnly.

Karain covered the handle of his kriss in sign of respect, and stared at the crowned head.

"The Invincible, the Pious," he muttered.

"She is more powerful than Suleiman the Wise, who commanded the genii, as you know," said Hollis, gravely. "I shall give this to you."

He held the sixpence in the palm of his hand, and looking at it thoughtfully, spoke to us in English.

"She commands a spirit, too—the spirit of her nation; a masterful, conscientious, unscrupulous, unconquerable devil . . . that does a lot of good—incidentally . . . a lot of good . . . at times—and wouldn't stand any fuss from the best ghost out for such a little thing as our friend's shot. Don't look thunderstruck, you fellows. Help me to make him believe—everything's in that."

"His people will be shocked," I murmured.

Hollis looked fixedly at Karain, who was the incarnation of the very essence of still excitement. He stood rigid, with head thrown back; his eyes rolled wildly, flashing; the dilated nostrils quivered.

"Hang it all!" said Hollis at last, "he is a good fellow. I'll give him something that I shall really miss."

He took the ribbon out of the box, smiled at it scornfully, then with a pair of scissors cut out a piece from the palm of the glove.

"I shall make him a thing like those Italian peasants wear, you know."

He sewed the coin in the delicate leather, sewed the leather to the ribbon, tied the ends together. He worked with haste. Karain watched his fingers all the time.

"Now then," he said—then stepped up to Karain. They looked close into one another's eyes. Those of Karain stared in a lost glance, but Hollis's seemed to grow darker and looked out masterful and compelling. They were in violent contrast together—one motionless and the colour of bronze, the other dazzling white and lifting his arms, where the powerful muscles rolled slightly under a skin that gleamed like satin. Jackson moved near with the air of a man closing up to a chum in a tight place. I said impressively, pointing to Hollis—

"He is young, but he is wise. Believe him!"

Karain bent his head: Hollis threw lightly over it the dark-blue ribbon and stepped back.

"Forget, and be at peace!" I cried.

Karain seemed to wake up from a dream. He said, "Ha!" shook himself as if throwing off a burden. He looked round with assurance. Someone on deck dragged off the skylight cover, and a flood of light fell into the cabin. It was morning already.

"Time to go on deck," said Jackson.

Hollis put on a coat, and we went up. Karain leading.

The sun had risen beyond the hills, and their long shadows stretched far over the bay in the pearly light. The air was clear, stainless, and cool. I pointed at the curved line of yellow sands.

"He is not there," I said, emphatically, to Karain. "He waits no more. He has departed forever."

A shaft of bright hot rays darted into the bay between the summits of two hills, and the water all round broke out as if by magic into a dazzling sparkle.

"No! He is not there waiting," said Karain, after a long look over the beach. "I do not hear him," he went on, slowly. "No!"

He turned to us.

"He has departed again—forever!" he cried.

We assented vigorously, repeatedly, and without compunction. The great thing was to impress him powerfully; to suggest absolute safety—the end of all trouble. We did our best; and I hope we affirmed our faith in the power of Hollis's charm efficiently enough to put the matter beyond the shadow of a doubt. Our voices rang around him joyously in the still air, and above his head the sky, pellucid, pure, stainless, arched its tender blue from shore to shore and over the bay, as if to envelop the water, the earth, and the man in the caress of its light.

The anchor was up, the sails hung still, and half-a-dozen big boats were seen sweeping over the bay to give us a tow out. The paddlers in the first one that came alongside lifted their heads and saw their ruler standing amongst us. A low murmur of surprise arose—then a shout of greeting.

He left us, and seemed straightway to step into the glorious splendour of his stage, to wrap himself in the illusion of unavoidable success. For a moment he stood erect, one foot over the gangway, one hand on the hilt of his kriss, in a martial pose; and, relieved from the fear of outer darkness, he held his head high, he swept a serene look over his conquered foothold on the earth. The boats far off took up the cry of greeting; a great clamour rolled on the water; the hills echoed it, and seemed to toss back at him the words invoking long life and victories.

He descended into a canoe, and as soon as he was clear of the side we gave him three cheers. They sounded faint and orderly after the wild tumult of his loyal subjects, but it was the best we could do. He stood up in the boat, lifted up both his arms, then pointed to the infallible charm. We cheered again; and the Malays in the boats stared—very much puzzled and impressed. I wondered what they thought; what he thought; . . . what the reader thinks?

We towed out slowly. We saw him land and watch us from the beach. A figure approached him humbly but openly—not at all like a ghost with a grievance. We could see other men running towards him. Perhaps he had been missed? At any rate there was a great stir. A group formed itself rapidly near him, and he walked along the sands, followed by a growing *cortège* and kept nearly abreast of the schooner. With our glasses we could see the blue ribbon on his neck and a patch of white on his brown chest. The bay was waking up. The smokes of morning fires stood in faint spirals higher than the heads of palms; people moved between the houses; a herd of buffaloes galloped clumsily across a green slope; the slender figures of boys brandishing sticks appeared black and leaping in the long grass; a coloured line of women, with water bamboos on their heads, moved swaying through a thin grove of fruit-trees. Karain stopped in the midst of his men and waved his hand; then, detaching himself from the splendid group, walked alone to the water's edge and waved his hand again. The schooner passed out to sea between the steep headlands that shut in the bay, and at the same instant Karain passed out of our life forever.

But the memory remains. Some years afterwards I met Jackson, in the Strand. He was magnificent as ever. His head was high above the crowd. His beard was gold, his face red, his eyes blue; he had a wide-brimmed gray hat and no collar or waistcoat; he was inspiring; he had just come home—had landed that very day! Our meeting caused an eddy in the current of humanity. Hurried people would run against us, then walk round us, and turn back to look at that giant. We tried to compress seven years of life into seven exclamations; then, suddenly appeased, walked sedately along, giving one another the news of yesterday. Jackson gazed about him, like a man who looks for landmarks, then stopped before Bland's window. He always had a passion for firearms; so he stopped short and contemplated the row of weapons, perfect and severe, drawn up in a line behind the black-framed panes. I stood by his side. Suddenly he said—

"Do you remember Karain?"

I nodded.

"The sight of all this made me think of him," he went on, with his face near the glass . . . and I could see another man, powerful and bearded, peering at him intently from amongst the dark and polished tubes that can cure so many illusions. "Yes; it made me think of him," he continued, slowly. "I saw a paper this morning; they are fighting over there again. He's sure to be in it. He will make it hot for the caballeros. Well, good luck to him, poor devil! He was perfectly stunning."

We walked on.

"I wonder whether the charm worked—you remember Hollis's charm, of course. If it did . . . never was a sixpence wasted to better advantage! Poor devil! I wonder whether he got rid of that friend of his. Hope so. . . . Do you know, I sometimes think that—"

I stood still and looked at him.

"Yes . . . I mean, whether the thing was so, you know . . . whether it really happened to him. . . . What do you think?"

"My dear chap," I cried, "you have been too long away from home. What a question to ask! Only look at all this."

A watery gleam of sunshine flashed from the west and went out between two long lines of walls; and then the broken confusion of roofs, the chimney-stacks, the gold letters sprawling over the fronts of houses, the sombre polish of windows, stood resigned and sullen under the falling gloom. The whole length of the street, deep as a well and narrow like a corridor, was full of a sombre and ceaseless stir. Our ears were filled by a headlong shuffle and beat of rapid footsteps and an underlying rumour—a rumour vast, faint, pulsating, as of panting breaths, of beating hearts, of gasping voices. Innumerable eyes stared straight in front, feet moved hurriedly, blank faces flowed, arms swung. Over all, a narrow ragged strip of smoky sky wound about between the high roofs, extended and motionless, like a soiled streamer flying above the rout of a mob.

"Ye-e-e-s," said Jackson, meditatively.

The big wheels of hansoms turned slowly along the edge of sidewalks; a pale-faced youth strolled, overcome by weariness, by the side of his stick and with the tails of his overcoat flapping gently near his heels; horses stepped gingerly on the greasy pavement, tossing their heads; two young girls passed by, talking vivaciously and with shining eyes; a fine old fellow strutted, red-faced, stroking a white moustache; and a line of yellow boards with blue letters on them approached us slowly, tossing on high behind one another like some queer wreckage adrift upon a river of hats.

"Ye-e-es," repeated Jackson. His clear blue eyes looked about, contemptuous, amused and hard, like the eyes of a boy. A clumsy string of red, yellow, and green omnibuses rolled swaying, monstrous and gaudy; two shabby children ran across the road; a knot of dirty men with red neckerchiefs round their bare throats lurched along, discussing filthily; a ragged old man with a face of despair yelled horribly in the mud the name of a paper; while far off, amongst the tossing heads of horses, the dull flash of harnesses, the jumble of lustrous panels and roofs of carriages, we could see a policeman, helmeted and dark, stretching out a rigid arm at the crossing of the streets.

"Yes; I see it," said Jackson, slowly. "It is there; it pants, it runs, it rolls; it is strong and alive; it would smash you if you didn't look out; but I'll be hanged if it is yet as real to me as . . . as the other thing . . . say, Karain's story."

I think that, decidedly, he had been too long away from home.

AMY FOSTER

Kennedy is a country doctor, and lives in Colebrook, on the shores of Eastbay. The high ground rising abruptly behind the red roofs of the little town crowds the quaint High Street against the wall which defends it from the sea. Beyond the sea-wall there curves for miles in a vast and regular sweep the barren beach of shingle, with the village of Brenzett standing out darkly across the water, a spire in a clump of trees; and still further out the perpendicular column of a lighthouse, looking in the distance no bigger than a lead-pencil, marks the vanishing-point of land. The country at the back of Brenzett is low and flat; but the bay is fairly well sheltered from the seas, and occasionally a big ship, wind-bound or through stress of weather, makes use of the anchoring ground a mile and a half due north from you as you stand at the back door of the Ship Inn in Brenzett. A dilapidated windmill near by, lifting its shattered arms from a mound no loftier than a rubbish-heap, and a Martello tower squatting at the water's edge half a mile to the south of the Coastguard cottages, are familiar to the skippers of small craft. These are the official seamarks for the patch of trustworthy bottom represented on the Admirality charts by an irregular oval of dots enclosing several figures six, with a tiny anchor engraved among them, and the legend "mud and shells" over all.

The brow of the upland overtops the square tower of the Colebrook Church. The slope is green and looped by a white road. Ascending along this road, you open a valley broad and shallow, a wide green trough of pastures and hedges merging inland into a vista of purple tints and flowing lines closing the view.

In this valley down to Brenzett and Colebrook and up to Darnford, the market town fourteen miles away, lies the practice of my friend Kennedy. He had begun life as surgeon in the Navy, and afterwards had been the companion of a famous traveller, in the days when there were continents with unexplored interiors. His papers on the fauna and flora made him known to scientific societies. And now he had come to a country practice—from choice. The penetrating power of his mind, acting like a corrosive fluid, had destroyed his ambition, I fancy. His intelligence is of a scientific order, of an investigating habit, and of that unappeasable curiosity which believes that there is a particle of a general truth in every mystery.

A good many years ago now, on my return from abroad, he invited me to stay with him. I came readily enough, and as he could not neglect his patients to keep me company, he took me on his rounds—thirty miles or so of an afternoon, sometimes. I waited for him on the roads; the horse reached after the leafy twigs, and, sitting high in the dogcart, I could hear Kennedy's laugh through the half-open door of some cottage. He had a big, hearty laugh that would have fitted a man twice his size, a brisk manner, a bronzed face, and a pair of grey, profoundly attentive eyes. He had the talent of making people talk to him freely, and an inexhaustible patience in listening to their tales.

One day, as we trotted out of a large village into a shady bit of road, I saw on our left hand a low, brick cottage, with diamond panes in the windows, a creeper on the end wall, a roof of shingle, and some roses climbing on the rickety trellis-work of the tiny porch. Kennedy pulled up to a walk. A woman, in full sunlight, was throwing a dripping blanket over a line stretched between two old apple-trees. And as the bobtailed, long-necked chestnut, trying to get his head, jerked the left hand, covered by a thick dogskin glove, the doctor raised his voice over the hedge: "How's your child, Amy?"

I had the time to see her dull face, red, not with a mantling blush, but as if her flat cheeks had been vigorously slapped, and to take in the squat figure, the scanty, dusty brown hair drawn into a tight knot at the back of the head. She looked quite young. With a distinct catch in her breath, her voice sounded low and timid.

"He's well, thank you."

We trotted again. "A young patient of yours," I said; and the doctor, flicking the chestnut absently, muttered, "Her husband used to be."

"She seems a dull creature," I remarked listlessly.

"Precisely," said Kennedy. "She is very passive. It's enough to look at the red hands hanging at the end of those short arms, at those slow, prominent brown eyes, to know the inertness of her mind—an inertness that one would think made it everlastingly safe from all the surprises of imagination. And yet which of us is safe? At any rate, such as you see her, she had enough imagination to fall in love. She's the daughter of one Isaac Foster, who from a small farmer has sunk into a shepherd, the beginning of his misfortunes dating from his runaway marriage with the cook of his widowed father—a well-to-do, apoplectic grazier, who passionately struck his name off his will, and had been heard to utter threats against his life. But this old affair, scandalous enough to serve as a motive for a Greek tragedy, arose from the similarity of their characters. There are other tragedies, less scandalous and of a subtler poignancy, arising from irreconcilable differences and from that fear of the Incomprehensible that hangs over all our heads—over all our heads. . . ."

The tired chestnut dropped into a walk; and the rim of the sun, all red in a speckless sky, touched familiarly the smooth top of a ploughed rise near the road as I had seen it times innumerable touch the distant horizon of the sea. The uniform brownness of the harrowed field glowed with a rosy tinge, as though the powdered clods had sweated out in minute pearls of blood the toil of uncounted ploughmen. From the edge of a copse a waggon with two horses was rolling gently along the ridge. Raised above our heads upon the sky-line, it loomed up against the red sun, triumphantly big, enormous, like a chariot of giants drawn by two slow-stepping steeds of legendary proportions. And the clumsy figure of the man plodding at the head of the leading horse projected itself on the background of the Infinite with a heroic uncouthness. The end of his carter's whip quivered high up in the blue. Kennedy discoursed.

"She's the eldest of a large family. At the age of fifteen they put her out to service at the New Barns Farm. I attended Mrs. Smith, the tenant's wife, and saw that girl there for the first time. Mrs. Smith, a genteel person with a sharp nose, made her put on a black dress every afternoon. I don't know what induced me to notice her at all. There are faces that call your attention by a curious want of definiteness in their whole aspect, as, walking in a mist, you peer attentively at a vague shape which, after all, may be nothing more curious or strange than a signpost. The only peculiarity I perceived in her was a slight hesitation in her utterance: a sort of preliminary stammer which passes away with the first word. When sharply spoken to, she was apt to lose her head at once, but her heart was of the kindest. She had never been heard to express a dislike for a single human being, and she was tender to every living creature. She was devoted to Mrs. Smith, to Mr. Smith, to their dogs, cats, canaries; and as to Mrs. Smith's grey parrot, its peculiarities exercised upon her a positive fascination. Nevertheless, when that outlandish bird, attacked by the cat, shrieked for help in human accents, she ran out into the yard stopping her ears, and did not prevent the crime. For Mrs. Smith this was another evidence of her stupidity; on the other hand, her want of charm, in view of Smith's well-known frivolousness, was a great recommendation. Her short-sighted eyes would swim with pity for a poor mouse in a trap, and she had been seen once by some boys on her knees in the wet grass helping a toad in difficulties. If it's true, as some German fellow has said, that without phosphorous there is no thought, it is still more true that there is no kindness of heart without a certain amount of imagination. She had some. She had even more than is necessary to understand suffering and to be moved by pity. She fell in love under circumstances that leave no room for doubt in the matter; for you need imagination to form a notion of beauty at all, and still more to discover your ideal in an unfamiliar shape.

"How this aptitude came to her, what it did feed upon, is an inscrutable mystery. She was born in the village, and had never been further away from it than Colebrook or perhaps Darnford. She lived for four years with the Smiths. New Barns is an isolated farmhouse a mile away from the road, and she was content to look day after day at the same fields, hollows, rises; at the trees and the hedgerows; at the faces of the four men about the farm, always the same—day after day, month after month, year after year. She never showed a desire for conversation, and, as it seemed to me, she did not know how to smile. Sometimes of a fine Sunday afternoon she would put on her best dress, a pair of stout boots, a large grey hat trimmed with a black feather (I've seen her in that finery), seize an absurdly slender parasol, climb over two stiles, tramp over three fields and along two hundred yards of road—never further. There stood Foster's cottage. She would help her mother to give their tea to the younger children, wash up the crockery, kiss the little ones, and go back to the farm. That was all. All the rest, all the change, all the relaxation. She never seemed to wish for anything more. And then she fell in love. She fell in love silently, obstinately—perhaps helplessly. It came slowly, but when it came it worked like a powerful spell; it was love as the Ancients understood it: an irresistible and fateful impulse—a possession! Yes, it was in her to become haunted and possessed by a face, by a presence, fatally, as though she had been a pagan worshipper of form under a joyous sky—and to be awakened at last from that mysterious forgetfulness of self, from that enchantment, from that transport, by a fear resembling the unaccountable terror of a brute. . . ."

With the sun hanging low on its western limit, the expanse of the grass-lands framed in the counterscarps of the rising ground took on a gorgeous and sombre aspect. A sense of penetrating sadness, like that inspired by a grave strain of music, disengaged itself from the silence of the fields. The men we met walked past, slow, unsmiling, with downcast eyes, as if the melancholy of an overburdened earth had weighted their feet, bowed their shoulders, borne down their glances.

"Yes," said the doctor to my remark, "one would think the earth is under a curse, since of all her children these that cling to her the closest are uncouth in body and as leaden of gait as if their very hearts were loaded with chains. But here on this same road you might have seen amongst these heavy men a being lithe, supple and long-limbed, straight like a pine, with something striving upwards in his appearance as though the heart within him had been buoyant. Perhaps it was only the force of the contrast, but when he was passing one of these villagers here, the soles of his feet did not seem to me to touch the dust of the road. He vaulted over the stiles, paced these slopes with a long elastic stride that made him noticeable at a great distance, and had lustrous black eyes. He was so different from the mankind around that, with his freedom of movement, his soft—a little startled—glance, his olive complexion and graceful bearing, his humanity suggested to me the nature of a woodland creature. He came from there."

The doctor pointed with his whip, and from the summit of the descent seen over the rolling tops of the trees in a park by the side of the road, appeared the level sea far below us, like the floor of an immense edifice inlaid with bands of dark ripple, with still trails of glitter, ending in a belt of glassy water at the foot of the sky. The light blur of smoke, from an invisible steamer, faded on the great clearness of the horizon like the mist of a breath on a mirror; and, inshore, the white sails of a coaster, with the appearance of disentangling themselves slowly from under the branches, floated clear of the foliage of the trees.

"Shipwrecked in the bay?" I said.

"Yes; he was a castaway. A poor emigrant from Central Europe bound to America and washed ashore here in a storm. And for him, who knew nothing of the earth, England was an undiscovered country. It was some time before he learned its name; and for all I know he might have expected to find wild beasts or wild men here, when, crawling in the dark over the sea-wall, he rolled down the other side into a dyke, where it was another miracle he didn't get drowned. But he struggled instinctively like an animal under a net, and this blind struggle threw him out into a field. He must have been, indeed, of a tougher fibre than he looked to withstand without expiring such buffetings, the violence of his exertions, and so much fear. Later on, in his broken English that resembled curiously the speech of a young child, he told me himself that he put his trust in God, believing he was no longer in this world. And truly—he would add—how was he to know? He fought his way against the rain and the gale on all fours, and crawled at last among some sheep huddled close under the lee of a hedge. They ran off in all directions, bleating in the darkness, and he welcomed the first familiar sound he heard on these shores. It must have been two in the morning then. And this is all we know of the manner of his landing, though he did not arrive unattended by any means. Only his grisly company did not begin to come ashore till much later in the day. . . ."

The doctor gathered the reins, clicked his tongue; we trotted down the hill. Then turning, almost directly, a sharp corner into the High Street, we rattled over the stones and were home.

Late in the evening Kennedy, breaking a spell of moodiness that had come over him, returned to the story. Smoking his pipe, he paced the long room from end to end. A reading-lamp concentrated all its light upon the papers on his desk; and, sitting by the open window, I saw, after the windless, scorching day, the frigid splendour of a hazy sea lying motionless under the moon. Not a whisper, not a splash, not a stir of the shingle, not a footstep, not a sigh came up from the earth below—never a sign of life but the scent of climbing jasmine: and Kennedy's voice, speaking behind me, passed through the wide casement, to vanish outside in a chill and sumptuous stillness.

". . . The relations of shipwrecks in the olden time tell us of much suffering. Often the castaways were only saved from drowning to die miserably from starvation on a barren coast; others suffered violent death or else slavery, passing through years of precarious existence with people to whom their strangeness was an object of suspicion, dislike or fear. We read about these things, and they are very pitiful. It is indeed hard upon a man to find himself a lost stranger, helpless, incomprehensible, and of a mysterious origin, in some obscure corner of the earth. Yet amongst all the adventurers shipwrecked in all the wild parts of the world, there is not one, it seems to me, that ever had to suffer a fate so simply tragic as the man I am speaking of, the most innocent of adventurers cast out by the sea in the bight of this bay, almost within sight from this very window.

"He did not know the name of his ship. Indeed, in the course of time we discovered he did not even know that ships had names—'like Christian people'; and when, one day, from the top of the Talfourd Hill, he beheld the sea lying open to his view, his eyes roamed afar, lost in an air of wild surprise, as though he had never seen such a sight before. And probably he had not. As far as I could make out, he had been hustled together with many others on board an emigrant ship lying at the mouth of the Elbe, too bewildered to take note of his surroundings, too weary to see anything, too anxious to care. They were driven below into the 'tween-deck and battened down from the very start. It was a low timber dwelling—he would say—with wooden beams overhead, like the houses in his country, but you went into it down a ladder. It was very large, very cold, damp and sombre, with places in the manner of wooden boxes where people had to sleep one above another, and it kept on rocking all ways at once all the time. He crept into one of these boxes and lay down there in the clothes in which he had left his home many days before, keeping his bundle and his stick by his side. People groaned, children cried, water dripped, the lights went out, the walls of the place creaked, and everything was being shaken so that in one's little box one dared not lift one's head. He had lost touch with his only companion (a young man from the same valley, he said), and all the time a great noise of wind went on outside and heavy blows fell—boom! boom! An awful sickness overcame him, even to the point of making him neglect his prayers. Besides, one could not tell whether it was morning or evening. It seemed always to be night in that place.

"Before that he had been travelling a long, long time on the iron track. He looked out of the window, which had a wonderfully clear glass in it, and the trees, the houses, the fields, and the long roads seemed to fly round and round about him till his head swam. He gave me to understand that he had on his passage beheld uncounted multitudes of people—whole nations—all dressed in such clothes as the rich wear. Once he was made to get out of the carriage, and slept through a night on a bench in a house of bricks with his bundle under his head; and once for many hours he had to sit on a floor of flat stones dozing, with his knees up and with his bundle between his feet. There was a roof over him, which seemed made of glass, and was so high that the tallest mountain-pine he had ever seen would have had room to grow under it. Steam-machines rolled in at one end and out at the other. People swarmed more than you can see on a feast-day round the miraculous Holy Image in the yard of the Carmelite Convent down in the plains where, before he left his home, he drove his mother in a wooden cart—a pious old woman who wanted to offer prayers and make a vow for his safety. He could not give me an idea of how large and lofty and full of noise and smoke and gloom, and clang of iron, the place was, but some one had told him it was called Berlin. Then they rang a bell, and another steam-machine came in, and again he was taken on and on through a land that wearied his eyes by its flatness without a single bit of a hill to be seen anywhere. One more night he spent shut up in a building like a good stable with a litter of straw on the floor, guarding his bundle amongst a lot of men, of whom not one could understand a single word he said. In the morning they were all led down to the stony shores of an extremely broad muddy river, flowing not between hills but between houses that seemed immense. There was a steam-machine that went on the water, and they all stood upon it packed tight, only now there were with them many women and children who made much noise. A cold rain fell, the wind blew in his face; he was wet through, and his teeth chattered. He and the young man from the same valley took each other by the hand.

"They thought they were being taken to America straight away, but suddenly the steam-machine bumped against the side of a thing like a great house on the water. The walls were smooth and black, and there uprose, growing from the roof as it were, bare trees in the shape of crosses, extremely high. That's how it appeared to him then, for he had never seen a ship before. This was the ship that was going to swim all the way to America. Voices shouted, everything swayed; there was a ladder dipping up and down. He went up on his hands and knees in mortal fear of falling into the water below, which made a great splashing. He got separated from his companion, and when he descended into the bottom of that ship his heart seemed to melt suddenly within him.

"It was then also, as he told me, that he lost contact for good and all with one of those three men who the summer before had been going about through all the little towns in the foothills of his country. They would arrive on market-days driving in a peasant's cart, and would set up an office in an inn or some other Jew's house. There were three of them, of whom one with a long beard looked venerable; and they had red cloth collars round their necks and gold lace on their sleeves like Government officials. They sat proudly behind a long table; and in the next room, so that the common people shouldn't hear, they kept a cunning telegraph machine, through which they could talk to the Emperor of America. The fathers hung about the door, but the young men of the mountains would crowd up to the table asking many questions, for there was work to be got all the year round at three dollars a day in America, and no military service to do.

"But the American Kaiser would not take everybody. Oh no! He himself had a great difficulty in getting accepted, and the venerable man in uniform had to go out of the room several times to work the telegraph on his behalf. The American Kaiser engaged him at last at three dollars, he being young and strong. However, many able young men backed out, afraid of the great distance; besides, those only who had some money could be taken. There were some who sold their huts and their land because it cost a lot of money to get to America; but then, once there, you had three dollars a day, and if you were clever you could find places where true gold could be picked up on the ground. His father's house was getting over-full. Two of his brothers were married and had children. He promised to send money home from America by post twice a year. His father sold an old cow, a pair of piebald mountain ponies of his own raising, and a cleared plot of fair pasture land on the sunny slope of a pine-clad pass to a Jew inn-keeper, in order to pay the people of the ship that took men to America to get rich in a short time.

"He must have been a real adventurer at heart, for how many of the greatest enterprises in the conquest of the earth had for their beginning just such a bargaining away of the paternal cow for the mirage of true gold far away! I have been telling you more or less in my own words what I learned fragmentarily in the course of two or three years, during which I seldom missed an opportunity of a friendly chat with him. He told me this story of his adventure with many flashes of white teeth and lively glances of black eyes, at first in a sort of anxious baby-talk, then, as he acquired the language, with great fluency, but always with that singing, soft, and at the same time vibrating intonation that instilled a strangely penetrating power into the sound of the most familiar English words, as if they had been the words of an unearthly language. And he always would come to an end, with many emphatic shakes of his head, upon that awful sensation of his heart melting within him directly he set foot on board that ship. Afterwards there seemed to come for him a period of blank ignorance, at any rate as to facts. No doubt he must have been abominably seasick and abominably unhappy—this soft and passionate adventurer, taken thus out of his knowledge, and feeling bitterly as he lay in his emigrant bunk his utter loneliness; for his was a highly sensitive nature. The next thing we know of him for certain is that he had been hiding in Hammond's pig-pound by the side of the road to Norton, six miles, as the crow flies, from the sea. Of these experiences he was unwilling to speak: they seemed to have seared into his soul a sombre sort of wonder and indignation. Through the rumours of the countryside, which lasted for a good many days after his arrival, we know that the fishermen of West Colebrook had been disturbed and startled by heavy knocks against the walls of weatherboard cottages, and by a voice crying piercingly strange words in the night. Several of them turned out even, but, no doubt, he had fled in sudden alarm at their rough angry tones hailing each other in the darkness. A sort of frenzy must have helped him up the steep Norton hill. It was he, no doubt, who early the following morning had been seen lying (in a swoon, I should say) on the roadside grass by the Brenzett carrier, who actually got down to have a nearer look, but drew back, intimidated by the perfect immobility, and by something queer in the aspect of that tramp, sleeping so still under the showers. As the day advanced, some children came dashing into school at Norton in such a fright that the schoolmistress went out and spoke indignantly to a 'horrid-looking man' on the road. He edged away, hanging his head, for a few steps, and then suddenly ran off with extraordinary fleetness. The driver of Mr. Bradley's milk-cart made no secret of it that he had lashed with his whip at a hairy sort of gipsy fellow who, jumping up at a turn of the road by the Vents, made a snatch at the pony's bridle. And he caught him a good one too, right over the face, he said, that made him drop down in the mud a jolly sight quicker than he had jumped up; but it was a good half mile before he could stop the pony. Maybe that in his desperate endeavours to get help, and in his need to get in touch with some one, the poor devil had tried to stop the cart. Also three boys confessed afterwards to throwing stones at a funny tramp, knocking about all wet and muddy, and, it seemed, very drunk, in the narrow deep lane by the limekilns. All this was the talk of three villages for days; but we have Mrs. Finn's (the wife of Smith's waggoner) unimpeachable testimony that she saw him get over the low wall of Hammond's pig-pound and lurch straight at her, babbling aloud in a voice that was enough to make one die of fright. Having the baby with her in a perambulator, Mrs. Finn called out to him to go away, and as he persisted in coming nearer, she hit him courageously with her umbrella over the head, and, without once looking back, ran like the wind with the perambulator as far as the first house in the village. She stopped then, out of breath, and spoke to old Lewis, hammering there at a heap of stones; and the old chap, taking off his immense black wire goggles, got up on his shaky legs to look where she pointed. Together they followed with their eyes the figure of the man running over a field; they saw him fall down, pick himself up, and run on again, staggering and waving his long arms above his head, in the direction of the New Barns Farm. From that moment he is plainly in the toils of his obscure and touching destiny. There is no doubt after this of what happened to him. All is certain now: Mrs. Smith's intense terror; Amy Foster's stolid conviction held against the other's nervous attack, that the man 'meant no harm'; Smith's exasperation (on his return from Darnford Market) at finding the dog barking himself into a fit, the back door locked, his wife in hysterics; and all for an unfortunate dirty tramp, supposed to be even then lurking in his stackyard. Was he? He would teach him to frighten women.

"Smith is notoriously hot-tempered, but the sight of some nondescript and miry creature sitting cross-legged amongst a lot of loose straw, and swinging itself to and fro like a bear in a cage, made him pause. Then this tramp stood up silently before him, one mass of mud and filth from head to foot. Smith, alone amongst his stacks with this apparition, in the stormy twilight ringing with the infuriated barking of the dog, felt the dread of an inexplicable strangeness. But when that being, parting with his black hands the long matted locks that hung before his face, as you part the two halves of a curtain, looked out at him with glistening, wild, black-and-white eyes, the weirdness of this silent encounter fairly staggered him. He has admitted since (for the story has been a legitimate subject of conversation about here for years) that he made more than one step backwards. Then a sudden burst of rapid, senseless speech persuaded him at once that he had to do with an escaped lunatic. In fact, that impression never wore off completely. Smith has not in his heart given up his secret conviction of the man's essential insanity to this very day.

"As the creature approached him, jabbering in a most discomposing manner, Smith (unaware that he was being addressed as 'gracious lord,' and adjured in God's name to afford food and shelter) kept on speaking firmly but gently to it, and retreating all the time into the other yard. At last, watching his chance, by a sudden charge he bundled him headlong into the wood-lodge, and instantly shot the bolt. Thereupon he wiped his brow, though the day was cold. He had done his duty to the community by shutting up a wandering and probably dangerous maniac. Smith isn't a hard man at all, but he had room in his brain only for that one idea of lunacy. He was not imaginative enough to ask himself whether the man might not be perishing with cold and hunger. Meantime, at first, the maniac made a great deal of noise in the lodge. Mrs. Smith was screaming upstairs, where she had locked herself in her bedroom; but Amy Foster sobbed piteously at the kitchen-door, wringing her hands and muttering 'Don't! don't!' I daresay Smith had a rough time of it that evening with one noise and another, and this insane, disturbing voice crying obstinately through the door only added to his irritation. He couldn't possibly have connected this troublesome lunatic with the sinking of a ship in Eastbay, of which there had been a rumour in the Darnford market-place. And I daresay the man inside had been very near to insanity on that night. Before his excitement collapsed and he became unconscious he was throwing himself violently about in the dark, rolling on some dirty sacks, and biting his fists with rage, cold, hunger, amazement, and despair.

"He was a mountaineer of the eastern range of the Carpathians, and the vessel sunk the night before in Eastbay was the Hamburg emigrant ship *Herzogin Sophia-Dorothea,* of appalling memory.

"A few months later we could read in the papers the accounts of the bogus 'Emigration Agencies' among the Sclavonian peasantry in the more remote provinces of Austria. The object of these scoundrels was to get hold of the poor ignorant people's homesteads, and they were in league with the local usurers. They exported their victims through Hamburg mostly. As to the ship, I had watched her out of this very window, reaching close-hauled under short canvas into the bay on a dark, threatening afternoon. She came to an anchor, correctly by the chart, off the Brenzett Coastguard station. I remember before the night fell looking out again at the outlines of her spars and rigging that stood out dark and pointed on a background of ragged, slaty clouds like another and a slighter spire to the left of the Brenzett church-tower. In the evening the wind rose. At midnight I could hear in my bed the terrific gusts and the sounds of a driving deluge.

"About that time the Coastguardmen thought they saw the lights of a steamer over the anchoring-ground. In a moment they vanished; but it is clear that another vessel of some sort had tried for shelter in the bay on that awful, blind night, had rammed the German ship amidships (a breach—as one of the divers told me afterwards—'that you could sail a Thames barge through'), and then had gone out either scathless or damaged, who shall say; but had gone out, unknown, unseen, and fatal, to perish mysteriously at sea. Of her nothing ever came to light, and yet the hue and cry that was raised all over the world would have found her out if she had been in existence anywhere on the face of the waters.

"A completeness without a clue, and a stealthy silence as of a neatly executed crime, characterise this murderous disaster, which, as you may remember, had its gruesome celebrity. The wind would have prevented the loudest outcries from reaching the shore; there had been evidently no time for signals of distress. It was death without any sort of fuss. The Hamburg ship, filling all at once, capsized as she sank, and at daylight there was not even the end of a spar to be seen above water. She was missed, of course, and at first the Coastguardmen surmised that she had either dragged her anchor or parted her cable some time during the night, and had been blown out to sea. Then, after the tide turned, the wreck must have shifted a little and released some of the bodies, because a child—a little fair-haired child in a red frock—came ashore abreast of the Martello tower. By the afternoon you could see along three miles of beach dark figures with bare legs dashing in and out of the tumbling foam, and rough-looking men, women with hard faces, children, mostly fair-haired, were being carried, stiff and dripping, on stretchers, on wattles, on ladders, in a long procession past the door of the Ship Inn, to be laid out in a row under the north wall of the Brenzett Church.

"Officially, the body of the little girl in the red frock is the first thing that came ashore from that ship. But I have patients amongst the seafaring population of West Colebrook, and, unofficially, I am informed that very early that morning two brothers, who went down to look after their cobble hauled up on the beach, found, a good way from Brenzett, an ordinary ship's hencoop lying high and dry on the shore, with eleven drowned ducks inside. Their families ate the birds, and the hencoop was split into firewood with a hatchet. It is possible that a man (supposing he happened to be on deck at the time of the accident) might have floated ashore on that hencoop. He might. I admit it is improbable, but there was the man—and for days, nay, for weeks—it didn't enter our heads that we had amongst us the only living soul that had escaped from that disaster. The man himself, even when he learned to speak intelligibly, could tell us very little. He remembered he had felt better (after the ship had anchored, I suppose), and that the darkness, the wind, and the rain took his breath away. This looks as if he had been on deck some time during that night. But we mustn't forget he had been taken out of his knowledge, that he had been seasick and battened down below for four days, that he had no general notion of a ship or of the sea, and therefore could have no definite idea of what was happening to him. The rain, the wind, the darkness he knew; he understood the bleating of the sheep, and he remembered the pain of his wretchedness and misery, his heartbroken astonishment that it was neither seen nor understood, his dismay at finding all the men angry and all the women fierce. He had approached them as a beggar, it is true, he said; but in his country, even if they gave nothing, they spoke gently to beggars. The children in his country were not taught to throw stones at those who asked for compassion. Smith's strategy overcame him completely. The wood-lodge presented the horrible aspect of a dungeon. What would be done to him next? . . . No wonder that Amy Foster appeared to his eyes with the aureole of an angel of light. The girl had not been able to sleep for thinking of the poor man, and in the morning, before the Smiths were up, she slipped out across the back yard. Holding the door of the wood-lodge ajar, she looked in and extended to him half a loaf of white bread—'such bread as the rich eat in my country,' he used to say.

"At this he got up slowly from amongst all sorts of rubbish, stiff, hungry, trembling, miserable, and doubtful. 'Can you eat this?' she asked in her soft and timid voice. He must have taken her for a 'gracious lady.' He devoured ferociously, and tears were falling on the crust. Suddenly he dropped the bread, seized her wrist, and imprinted a kiss on her hand. She was not frightened. Through his forlorn condition she had observed that he was good-looking. She shut the door and walked back slowly to the kitchen. Much later on, she told Mrs. Smith, who shuddered at the bare idea of being touched by that creature.

"Through this act of impulsive pity he was brought back again within the pale of human relations with his new surroundings. He never forgot it—never.

"That very same morning old Mr. Swaffer (Smith's nearest neighbour) came over to give his advice, and ended by carrying him off. He stood, unsteady on his legs, meek, and caked over in half-dried mud, while the two men talked around him in an incomprehensible tongue. Mrs. Smith had refused to come downstairs till the madman was off the premises; Amy Foster, far from within the dark kitchen, watched through the open back door; and he obeyed the signs that were made to him to the best of his ability. But Smith was full of mistrust. 'Mind, sir! It may be all his cunning,' he cried repeatedly in a tone of warning. When Mr. Swaffer started the mare, the deplorable being sitting humbly by his side, through weakness, nearly fell out over the back of the high two-wheeled cart. Swaffer took him straight home. And it is then that I come upon the scene.

"I was called in by the simple process of the old man beckoning to me with his forefinger over the gate of his house as I happened to be driving past. I got down, of course.

"'I've got something here,' he mumbled, leading the way to an outhouse at a little distance from his other farm-buildings.

"It was there that I saw him first, in a long low room taken upon the space of that sort of coach-house. It was bare and whitewashed, with a small square aperture glazed with one cracked, dusty pane at its further end. He was lying on his back upon a straw pallet; they had given him a couple of horse-blankets, and he seemed to have spent the remainder of his strength in the exertion of cleaning himself. He was almost speechless; his quick breathing under the blankets pulled up to his chin, his glittering, restless black eyes reminded me of a wild bird caught in a snare. While I was examining him, old Swaffer stood silently by the door, passing the tips of his fingers along his shaven upper lip. I gave some directions, promised to send a bottle of medicine, and naturally made some inquiries.

"'Smith caught him in the stackyard at New Barns,' said the old chap in his deliberate, unmoved manner, and as if the other had been indeed a sort of wild animal, 'That's how I came by him. Quite a curiosity, isn't he? Now tell me, doctor—you've been all over the world—don't you think that's a bit of a Hindoo we've got hold of here?'

"I was greatly surprised. His long black hair scattered over the straw bolster contrasted with the olive pallor of his face. It occurred to me he might be a Basque. It didn't necessarily follow that he should understand Spanish; but I tried him with a few words I know, and also with some French. The whispered sounds I caught by bending my ear to his lips puzzled me utterly. That afternoon the young ladies from the Rectory (one of them read Goethe with a dictionary, and the other had struggled with Dante for years), coming to see Miss Swaffer, tried their German and Italian on him from the doorway. They retreated, just the least bit scared by the flood of passionate speech which, turning on his pallet, he let out at them. They admitted that the sound was pleasant, soft, musical—but, in conjunction with his looks perhaps, it was startling—so excitable, so utterly unlike anything one had ever heard. The village boys climbed up the bank to have a peep through the little square aperture. Everybody was wondering what Mr. Swaffer would do with him.

"He simply kept him.

"Swaffer would be called eccentric were he not so much respected. They will tell you that Mr. Swaffer sits up as late as ten o'clock at night to read books, and they will tell you also that he can write a cheque for two hundred pounds without thinking twice about it. He himself would tell you that the Swaffers had owned land between this and Darnford for these three hundred years. He must be eighty-five to-day, but he does not look a bit older than when I first came here. He is a great breeder of sheep, and deals extensively in cattle. He attends market days for miles around in every sort of weather, and drives sitting bowed low over the reins, his lank grey hair curling over the collar of his warm coat, and with a green plaid rug round his legs. The calmness of advanced age gives a solemnity to his manner. He is clean-shaved; his lips are thin and sensitive; something rigid and monachal in the set of his features lends a certain elevation to the character of his face. He has been known to drive miles in the rain to see a new kind of rose in somebody's garden, or a monstrous cabbage grown by a cottager. He loves to hear tell of or to be shown something what he calls 'outlandish.' Perhaps it was just that outlandishness of the man which influenced old Swaffer. Perhaps it was only an inexplicable caprice. All I know is that at the end of three weeks I caught sight of Smith's lunatic digging in Swaffer's kitchen garden. They had found out he could use a spade. He dug barefooted.

"His black hair flowed over his shoulders. I suppose it was Swaffer who had given him the striped old cotton shirt; but he wore still the national brown cloth trousers (in which he had been washed ashore) fitting to the leg almost like tights; was belted with a broad leathern belt studded with brass discs; and had never yet ventured into the village. The land he looked upon seemed to him kept neatly, like the grounds round a landowner's house; the size of the cart-horses struck him with astonishment; the roads resembled garden walks, and the aspect of the people, especially on Sundays, spoke of opulence. He wondered what made them so hard-hearted and their children so bold. He got his food at the back door, carried it in both hands, carefully, to his outhouse, and, sitting alone on his pallet, would make the sign of the cross before he began. Beside the same pallet, kneeling in the early darkness of the short days, he recited aloud the Lord's Prayer before he slept. Whenever he saw old Swaffer he would bow with veneration from the waist, and stand erect while the old man, with his fingers over his upper lip, surveyed him silently. He bowed also to Miss Swaffer, who kept house frugally for her father—a broad-shouldered, big-boned woman of forty-five, with the pocket of her dress full of keys, and a grey, steady eye. She was Church—as people said (while her father was one of the trustees of the Baptist Chapel)—and wore a little steel cross at her waist. She dressed severely in black, in memory of one of the innumerable Bradleys of the neighbourhood, to whom she had been engaged some twenty-five years ago—a young farmer who broke his neck out hunting on the eve of the wedding-day. She had the unmoved countenance of the deaf, spoke very seldom, and her lips, thin like her father's, astonished one sometimes by a mysteriously ironic curl.

"These were the people to whom he owed allegiance, and an overwhelming loneliness seemed to fall from the leaden sky of that winter without sunshine. All the faces were sad. He could talk to no one, and had no hope of ever understanding anybody. It was as if these had been the faces of people from the other world—dead people—he used to tell me years afterwards. Upon my word, I wonder he did not go mad. He didn't know where he was. Somewhere very far from his mountains—somewhere over the water. Was this America, he wondered?

"If it hadn't been for the steel cross at Miss Swaffer's belt he would not, he confessed, have known whether he was in a Christian country at all. He used to cast stealthy glances at it, and feel comforted. There was nothing here the same as in his country! The earth and the water were different; there were no images of the Redeemer by the roadside. The very grass was different, and the trees. All the trees but the three old Norway pines on the bit of lawn before Swaffer's house, and these reminded him of his country. He had been detected once, after dusk, with his forehead against the trunk of one of them, sobbing, and talking to himself. They had been like brothers to him at that time, he affirmed. Everything else was strange. Conceive you the kind of an existence overshadowed, oppressed, by the everyday material appearances, as if by the visions of a nightmare. At night, when he could not sleep, he kept on thinking of the girl who gave him the first piece of bread he had eaten in this foreign land. She had been neither fierce nor angry, nor frightened. Her face he remembered as the only comprehensible face amongst all these faces that were as closed, as mysterious, and as mute as the faces of the dead who are possessed of a knowledge beyond the comprehension of the living. I wonder whether the memory of her compassion prevented him from cutting his throat. But there! I suppose I am an old sentimentalist, and forget the instinctive love of life which it takes all the strength of an uncommon despair to overcome.

"He did the work which was given him with an intelligence which surprised old Swaffer. By-and-by it was discovered that he could help at the ploughing, could milk the cows, feed the bullocks in the cattle-yard, and was of some use with the sheep. He began to pick up words, too, very fast; and suddenly, one fine morning in spring, he rescued from an untimely death a grandchild of old Swaffer.

"Swaffer's younger daughter is married to Wilcox, a solicitor and the Town Clerk of Colebrook. Regularly twice a year they come to stay with the old man for a few days. Their only child, a little girl not three years old at the time, ran out of the house alone in her little white pinafore, and, toddling across the grass of a terraced garden, pitched herself over a low wall head first into the horse-pond in the yard below.

"Our man was out with the waggoner and the plough in the field nearest to the house, and as he was leading the team round to begin a fresh furrow, he saw, through the gap of a gate, what for anybody else would have been a mere flutter of something white. But he had straight-glancing, quick, far-reaching eyes, that only seemed to flinch and lose their amazing power before the immensity of the sea. He was barefooted, and looking as outlandish as the heart of Swaffer could desire. Leaving the horses on the turn, to the inexpressible disgust of the waggoner he bounded off, going over the ploughed ground in long leaps, and suddenly appeared before the mother, thrust the child into her arms, and strode away.

"The pond was not very deep; but still, if he had not had such good eyes, the child would have perished—miserably suffocated in the foot or so of sticky mud at the bottom. Old Swaffer walked out slowly into the field, waited till the plough came over to his side, had a good look at him, and without saying a word went back to the house. But from that time they laid out his meals on the kitchen table; and at first, Miss Swaffer, all in black and with an inscrutable face, would come and stand in the doorway of the living-room to see him make a big sign of the cross before he fell to. I believe that from that day, too, Swaffer began to pay him regular wages.

"I can't follow step by step his development. He cut his hair short, was seen in the village and along the road going to and fro to his work like any other man. Children ceased to shout after him. He became aware of social differences, but remained for a long time surprised at the bare poverty of the churches among so much wealth. He couldn't understand either why they were kept shut up on week-days. There was nothing to steal in them. Was it to keep people from praying too often? The rectory took much notice of him about that time, and I believe the young ladies attempted to prepare the ground for his conversion. They could not, however, break him of his habit of crossing himself, but he went so far as to take off the string with a couple of brass medals the size of a sixpence, a tiny metal cross, and a square sort of scapulary which he wore round his neck. He hung them on the wall by the side of his bed, and he was still to be heard every evening reciting the Lord's Prayer, in incomprehensible words and in a slow, fervent tone, as he had heard his old father do at the head of all the kneeling family, big and little, on every evening of his life. And though he wore corduroys at work, and a slop-made pepper-and-salt suit on Sundays, strangers would turn round to look after him on the road. His foreignness had a peculiar and indelible stamp. At last people became used to seeing him. But they never became used to him. His rapid, skimming walk; his swarthy complexion; his hat cocked on the left ear; his habit, on warm evenings, of wearing his coat over one shoulder, like a hussar's dolman; his manner of leaping over the stiles, not as a feat of agility, but in the ordinary course of progression—all these peculiarities were, as one may say, so many causes of scorn and offense to the inhabitants of the village. *They* wouldn't in their dinner hour lie flat on their backs on the grass to stare at the sky. Neither did they go about the fields screaming dismal tunes. Many times have I heard his high-pitched voice from behind the ridge of some sloping sheep-walk, a voice light and soaring, like a lark's, but with a melancholy human note, over our fields that hear only the song of birds. And I would be startled myself. Ah! He was different: innocent of heart, and full of good will, which nobody wanted, this castaway, that, like a man transplanted into another planet, was separated by an immense space from his past and by an immense ignorance from his future. His quick, fervent utterance positively shocked everybody. 'An excitable devil' they called him. One evening, in the tap-room of the Coach and Horses, (having drunk some whisky), he upset them all by singing a love-song of his country. They hooted him down, and he was pained; but Preble, the lame wheelwright, and Vincent, the fat blacksmith, and the other notables too, wanted to drink their evening beer in peace. On another occasion he tried to show them how to dance. The dust rose in clouds from the sanded floor; he leaped straight up amongst the deal tables, struck his heels together, squatted on one heel in front of old Preble, shooting out the other leg, uttered wild and exulting cries, jumped up to whirl on one foot, snapping his fingers above his head—and a strange carter who was having a drink in there began to swear, and cleared out with his half-pint in his hand into the bar. But when suddenly he sprang upon a table and continued to dance among the glasses, the landlord interfered. He didn't want any 'acrobat tricks in the tap-room.' They laid their hands on him. Having had a glass or two, Mr. Swaffer's foreigner tired to expostulate; was ejected forcibly; got a black eye.

"I believe he felt the hostility of his human surroundings. But he was tough—tough in spirit, too, as well as in body. Only the memory of the sea frightened him, with that vague terror that is left by a bad dream. His home was far away; and he did not want now to go to America. I had often explained to him that there is no place on earth where true gold can be found lying ready and to be got for the trouble of the picking up. How then, he asked, could he ever return home with empty hands when there had been sold a cow, two ponies, and a bit of land to pay for his going? His eyes would fill with tears, and, averting them from the immense shimmer of the sea, he would throw himself face down on the grass. But sometimes, cocking his hat with the little conquering air, he would defy my wisdom. He had found his bit of true gold. That was Amy Foster's heart, which was 'a golden heart, and soft to people's misery,' he would say in the accents of overwhelming conviction.

"He was called Yanko. He had explained that this meant Little John; but as he would also repeat very often that he was a mountaineer (some word sounding in the dialect of his country like Goorall) he got it for his surname. And this is the only trace of him that the succeeding ages may find in the marriage register of the parish. There it stands—Yanko Goorall—in the rector's handwriting. The crooked cross made by the castaway, a cross whose tracing no doubt seemed to him the most solemn part of the whole ceremony, is all that remains now to perpetuate the memory of his name.

"His courtship had lasted some time—ever since he got his precarious footing in the community. It began by his buying for Amy Foster a green satin ribbon in Darnford. This was what you did in his country. You bought a ribbon at a Jew's stall on a fair-day. I don't suppose the girl knew what to do with it, but he seemed to think that his honourable intentions could not be mistaken.

"It was only when he declared his purpose to get married that I fully understood how, for a hundred futile and inappreciable reasons, how—shall I say odious?—he was to all the countryside. Every old woman in the village was up in arms. Smith, coming upon him near the farm, promised to break his head for him if he found him about again. But he twisted his little black moustache with such a bellicose air and rolled such big, black fierce eyes at Smith that this promise came to nothing. Smith, however, told the girl that she must be mad to take up with a man who was surely wrong in his head. All the same, when she heard him in the gloaming whistle from beyond the orchard a couple of bars of a weird and mournful tune, she would drop whatever she had in her hand—she would leave Mrs. Smith in the middle of a sentence—and she would run out to his call. Mrs. Smith called her a shameless hussy. She answered nothing. She said nothing at all to anybody, and went on her way as if she had been deaf. She and I alone in all the land, I fancy, could see his very real beauty. He was very good-looking, and most graceful in his bearing, with that something wild as of a woodland creature in his aspect. Her mother moaned over her dismally whenever the girl came to see her on her day out. The father was surly, but pretended not to know; and Mrs. Finn once told her plainly that 'this man, my dear, will do you some harm some day yet.' And so it went on. They could be seen on the roads, she tramping stolidly in her finery—grey dress, black feather, stout boots, prominent white cotton gloves that caught your eye a hundred yards away; and he, his coat slung picturesquely over one shoulder, pacing by her side, gallant of bearing and casting tender glances upon the girl with the golden heart. I wonder whether he saw how plain she was. Perhaps among types so different from what he had ever seen, he had not the power to judge; or perhaps he was seduced by the divine quality of her pity.

"Yanko was in great trouble meantime. In his country you get an old man for an ambassador in marriage affairs. He did not know how to proceed. However, one day in the midst of sheep in a field (he was now Swaffer's under-shepherd with Foster) he took off his hat to the father and declared himself humbly. 'I daresay she's fool enough to marry you,' was all Foster said. 'And then,' he used to relate, 'he puts his hat on his head, looks black at me as if he wanted to cut my throat, whistles the dog, and off he goes, leaving me to do the work.' The Fosters, of course, didn't like to lose the wages the girl earned: Amy used to give all her money to her mother. But there was in Foster a very genuine aversion to that match. He contended that the fellow was very good with sheep, but was not fit for any girl to marry. For one thing, he used to go along the hedges muttering to himself like a dam' fool; and then, these foreigners behave very queerly to women sometimes. And perhaps he would want to carry her off somewhere—or run off himself. It was not safe. He preached it to his daughter that the fellow might ill-use her in some way. She made no answer. It was, they said in the village, as if the man had done something to her. People discussed the matter. It was quite an excitement, and the two went on 'walking out' together in the face of opposition. Then something unexpected happened.

"I don't know whether old Swaffer ever understood how much he was regarded in the light of a father by his foreign retainer. Anyway the relation was curiously feudal. So when Yanko asked formally for an interview—'and the Miss too' (he called the severe, deaf Miss Swaffer simply *Miss*)—it was to obtain their permission to marry. Swaffer heard him unmoved, dismissed him by a nod, and then shouted the intelligence into Miss Swaffer's best ear. She showed no surprise, and only remarked grimly, in a veiled blank voice, 'He certainly won't get any other girl to marry him.'

"It is Miss Swaffer who has all the credit of the munificence: but in a very few days it came out that Mr. Swaffer had presented Yanko with a cottage (the cottage you've seen this morning) and something like an acre of ground—had made it over to him in absolute property. Willcox expedited the deed, and I remember him telling me he had a great pleasure in making it ready. It recited: 'In consideration of saving the life of my beloved grandchild, Bertha Willcox.'

"Of course, after that no power on earth could prevent them from getting married.

"Her infatuation endured. People saw her going out to meet him in the evening. She stared with unblinking, fascinated eyes up the road where he was expected to appear, walking freely, with a swing from the hip, and humming one of the love-tunes of his country. When the boy was born, he got elevated at the Coach and Horses, essayed again a song and a dance, and was again ejected. People expressed their commiseration for a woman married to that Jack-in-the-box. He didn't care. There was a man now (he told me boastfully) to whom he could sing and talk in the language of his country, and show how to dance by-and-by.

"But I don't know. To me he appeared to have grown less springy of step, heavier in body, less keen of eye. Imagination, no doubt; but it seems to me now as if the net of fate had been drawn closer round him already.

"One day I met him on the footpath over the Talfourd Hill. He told me that 'women were funny.' I had heard already of domestic differences. People were saying that Amy Foster was beginning to find out what sort of man she had married. He looked upon the sea with indifferent, unseeing eyes. His wife had snatched the child out of his arms one day as he sat on the doorstep crooning to it a song such as the mothers sing to babies in his mountains. She seemed to think he was doing it some harm. Women are funny. And she had objected to him praying aloud in the evening. Why? He expected the boy to repeat the prayer aloud after him by-and-by, as he used to do after his old father when he was a child—in his own country. And I discovered he longed for their boy to grow up so that he could have a man to talk with in that language that to our ears sounded so disturbing, so passionate, and so bizarre. Why his wife should dislike the idea he couldn't tell. But that would pass, he said. And tilting his head knowingly, he tapped his breastbone to indicate that she had a good heart: not hard, not fierce, open to compassion, charitable to the poor!

"I walked away thoughtfully; I wondered whether his difference, his strangeness, were not penetrating with repulsion that dull nature they had begun by irresistibly attracting. I wondered. . . ."

The Doctor came to the window and looked out at the frigid splendour of the sea, immense in the haze, as if enclosing all the earth with all the hearts lost among the passions of love and fear.

"Physiologically, now," he said, turning away abruptly, "it was possible. It was possible."

He remained silent. Then went on—

"At all events, the next time I saw him he was ill—lung trouble.

He was tough, but I daresay he was not acclimatised as well as I had supposed. It was a bad winter, and, of course, these mountaineers do get fits of homesickness; and a state of depression would make him vulnerable. He was lying half-dressed on a couch downstairs.

"A table covered with a dark oilcloth took up all the middle of the little room. There was a wicker cradle on the floor, a kettle spouting steam on the hob, and some child's linen lay drying on the fender. The room was warm, but the door opens right into the garden, as you noticed perhaps.

"He was very feverish, and kept on muttering to himself. She sat on a chair and looked at him fixedly across the table with her brown, blurred eyes. 'Why don't you have him upstairs?' I asked. With a start and a confused stammer she said, 'Oh! ah! I couldn't sit with him upstairs, sir.'

"I gave her certain directions; and going outside, I said again that he ought to be in bed upstairs. She wrung her hands. 'I couldn't. I couldn't. He keeps on saying something—I don't know what.' With the memory of all the talk against the man that had been dinned into her ears, I looked at her narrowly. I looked into her short-sighted eyes, at her dumb eyes that once in her life had seen an enticing shape, but seemed, staring at me, to see nothing at all now. But I saw she was uneasy.

"'What's the matter with him?' she asked in a sort of vacant trepidation. 'He doesn't look very ill. I never did see anybody look like this before. . . .'

"'Do you think,' I asked indignantly, 'he is shamming?'

"'I can't help it, sir,' she said stolidly. And suddenly she clapped her hands and looked right and left. 'And there's the baby. I am so frightened. He wanted me just now to give him the baby. I can't understand what he says to it.'

"'Can't you ask a neighbour to come in to-night?' I asked.

"'Please, sir, nobody seems to care to come,' she muttered, dully resigned all at once.

"I impressed upon her the necessity of the greatest care, and then had to go. There was a good deal of sickness that winter. 'Oh, I hope he won't talk!' she exclaimed softly just as I was going away.

"I don't know how it is I did not see—but I didn't. And yet, turning in my trap, I saw her lingering before the door, very still, and as if meditating a flight up the miry road.

"Towards the night his fever increased.

"He tossed, moaned, and now and then muttered a complaint. And she sat with the table between her and the couch, watching every movement and every sound, with the terror, the unreasonable terror, of that man she could not understand creeping over her. She had drawn the wicker cradle close to her feet. There was nothing in her now but the maternal instinct and that unaccountable fear.

"Suddenly coming to himself, parched, he demanded a drink of water. She did not move. She had not understood, though he may have thought he was speaking in English. He waited, looking at her, burning with fever, amazed at her silence and immobility, and then he shouted impatiently. 'Water! Give me water!'

"She jumped to her feet, snatched up the child, and stood still. He spoke to her, and his passionate remonstrances only increased her fear of that strange man. I believe he spoke to her for a long time, entreating, wondering, pleading, ordering, I suppose. She says she bore it as long as she could. And then a gust of rage came over him.

"He sat up and called out terribly one word—some word. Then he got up as though he hadn't been ill at all, she says. And as in fevered dismay, indignation, and wonder, he tried to get to her round the table, she simply opened the door and ran out with the child in her arms. She heard him call twice after her down the road in a terrible voice—and fled. . . . Ah! but you should have seen stirring behind the dull, blurred glance of those eyes the spectre of the fear which had hunted her on that night three miles and a half to the door of Foster's cottage! I did the next day.

"And it was I who found him lying face down and his body in a puddle, just outside the little wicket-gate.

"I had been called out that night to an urgent case in the village, and on my way home at daybreak passed by the cottage. The door stood open. My man helped me to carry him in. We laid him on the couch. The lamp smoked, the fire was out, the chill of the stormy night oozed from the cheerless yellow paper on the wall. 'Amy!' I called aloud, and my voice seemed to lose itself in the emptiness of this tiny house as if I had cried in a desert. He opened his eyes. 'Gone!' he said distinctly. 'I had only asked for water—only for a little water. . . .'

"He was muddy. I covered him up and stood waiting in silence, catching a painfully gasped word now and then. They were no longer in his own language. The fever had left him, taking with it the heat of life. And with his panting breast and lustrous eyes he reminded me again of a wild creature under the net; of a bird caught in a snare. She had left him. She had left him—sick—helpless—thirsty. The spear of the hunter had entered his very soul. 'Why?' he cried in the penetrating and indignant voice of a man calling to a responsible Maker. A gust of wind and a swish of rain answered.

"And as I turned away to shut the door he pronounced the word 'Merciful!' and expired.

"Eventually I certified heart-failure as the immediate cause of death. His heart must have indeed failed him, or else he might have stood this night of storm and exposure, too. I closed his eyes and drove away. Not very far from the cottage I met Foster walking sturdily between the dripping hedges with his collie at his heels.

" 'Do you know where your daughter is?' I asked.

" 'Don't I!' he cried. 'I am going to talk to him a bit. Frightening a poor woman like this.'

" 'He won't frighten her any more,' I said. 'He is dead.'

"He struck with his stick at the mud.

" 'And there's the child.'

"Then, after thinking deeply for a while—

" 'I don't know that it isn't for the best.'

"That's what he said. And she says nothing at all now. Not a word of him. Never. Is his image as utterly gone from her mind as his lithe and striding figure, his carolling voice are gone from our fields? He is no longer before her eyes to excite her imagination into a passion of love or fear; and his memory seems to have vanished from her dull brain as a shadow passes away upon a white screen. She lives in the cottage and works for Miss Swaffer. She is Amy Foster for everybody, and the child is 'Amy Foster's boy.' She calls him Johnny—which means Little John.

"It is impossible to say whether this name recalls anything to her. Does she ever think of the past? I have seen her hanging over the boy's cot in a very passion of maternal tenderness. The little fellow was lying on his back, a little frightened at me, but very still, with his big black eyes, with his fluttered air of a bird in a snare. And looking at him I seemed to see again the other one—the father, cast out mysteriously by the sea to perish in the supreme disaster of loneliness and despair."

THE WARRIOR'S SOUL

The old officer with long white moustaches gave rein to his indignation.

"It is possible that you youngsters should have no more sense than that! Some of you had better wipe the milk off your upper lip before you start to pass judgment on the few poor stragglers of a generation which has done and suffered not a little in its time."

His hearers having expressed much compunction the ancient warrior became appeased. But he was not silenced.

"I am one of them—one of the stragglers, I mean," he went on patiently. "And what did we do? What have we achieved? He—the great Napoleon—started upon us to emulate the Macedonian Alexander, with a ruck of nations at his back. We opposed empty spaces to French impetuosity, then we offered them an interminable battle so that their army went at last to sleep in its positions lying down on the heaps of its own dead. Then came the wall of fire in Moscow. It toppled down on them.

"Then began the long rout of the Grand Army. I have seen it stream on, like the doomed flight of haggard, spectral sinners across the innermost frozen circle of Dante's Inferno, ever widening before their despairing eyes.

"They who escaped must have had their souls doubly riveted inside their bodies to carry them out of Russia through that frost fit to split rocks. But to say that it was our fault that a single one of them got away is mere ignorance. Why! Our own men suffered nearly to the limit of their strength. Their Russian strength!

"Of course our spirit was not broken; and then our cause was good—it was holy. But that did not temper the wind much to men and horses.

"The flesh is weak. Good or evil purpose, Humanity has to pay the price. Why! In that very fight for that little village of which I have been telling you we were fighting for the shelter of those old houses as much as victory. And with the French it was the same.

"It wasn't for the sake of glory, or for the sake of strategy. The French knew that they would have to retreat before morning and we knew perfectly well that they would go. As far as the war was concerned there was nothing to fight about. Yet our infantry and theirs fought like wild cats, or like heroes if you like that better, amongst the houses—hot work enough—while the supports out in the open stood freezing in a tempestuous north wind which drove the snow on earth and the great masses of clouds in the sky at a terrific pace. The very air was inexpressibly sombre by contrast with the white earth. I have never seen God's creation look more sinister than on that day.

"We, the cavalry (we were only a handful), had not much to do except turn our backs to the wind and receive some stray French round shot. This, I may tell you, was the last of the French guns and it was the last time they had their artillery in position. Those guns never went away from there either. We found them abandoned next morning. But that afternoon they were keeping up an infernal fire on our attacking column; the furious wind carried away the smoke and even the noise but we could see the constant flicker of the tongues of fire along the French front. Then a driving flurry of snow would hide everything except the dark red flashes in the white swirl.

"At intervals when the line cleared we could see away across the plain to the right a sombre column moving endlessly; the great rout of the Grand Army creeping on and on all the time while the fight on our left went on with a great din and fury. The cruel whirlwind of snow swept over that scene of death and desolation. And then the wind fell as suddenly as it had arisen in the morning.

"Presently we got orders to charge the retreating column; I don't know why unless they wanted to prevent us from getting frozen in our saddles by giving us something to do. We changed front half right and got into motion at a walk to take that distant dark line in flank. It might have been half-past two in the afternoon.

"You must know that so far in this campaign my regiment had never been on the main line of Napoleon's advance. All these months since the invasion the army we belonged to had been wrestling with Oudinot in the north. We had only come down lately, driving him before us to the Beresina.

"This was the first occasion, then, that I and my comrades had a close view of Napoleon's Grand Army. It was an amazing and terrible sight. I had heard of it from others; I had seen the stragglers from it: small bands of marauders, parties of prisoners in the distance. But this was the very column itself! A crawling, stumbling, starved, half-demented mob. It issued from the forest a mile away and its head was lost in the murk of the fields. We rode into it at a trot, which was the most we could get out of our horses, and we stuck in that human mass as if in a moving bog. There was no resistance. I heard a few shots, half a dozen perhaps. Their very senses seemed frozen within them. I had time for a good look while riding at the head of my squadron. Well, I assure you, there were men walking on the outer edge so lost to everything but their misery that they never turned their heads to look at our charge. Soldiers!

"My horse pushed over one of them with his chest. The poor wretch had a dragoon's blue cloak, all torn and scorched, hanging from his shoulders and he didn't even put his hand out to snatch at my bridle and save himself. He just went down. Our troopers were pointing and slashing; well, and of course at first I myself . . . What would you have! An enemy is an enemy. Yet a sort of sickening awe crept into my heart. There was no tumult—only a low deep murmur dwelt over them interspersed with louder cries and groans while that mob kept on pushing and surging past us, sightless and without feeling. A smell of scorched rags and festering wounds hung in the air. My horse staggered in the eddies of swaying men. But it was like cutting down galvanized corpses that didn't care. Invaders! Yes . . . God was already dealing with them.

"I touched my horse with the spurs to get clear. There was a sudden rush and a sort of angry moan when our second squadron got into them on our right. My horse plunged and somebody got hold of my leg. As I had no mind to get pulled out of the saddle I gave a backhanded slash without looking. I heard a cry and my leg was let go suddenly.

"Just then I caught sight of the subaltern of my troop at some little distance from me. His name was Tomassov. That multitude of resurrected bodies with glassy eyes was seething round his horse as if blind, growling crazily. He was sitting erect in his saddle, not looking down at them and sheathing his sword deliberately.

"This Tomassov, well, he had a beard. Of course we all had beards then. Circumstances, lack of leisure, want of razors, too. No, seriously, we were a wild-looking lot in those unforgotten days which so many, so very many of us did not survive. You know our losses were awful, too. Yes, we looked wild. *Des Russes sauvages*—what!

"So he had a beard—this Tomassov I mean; but he did not look *sauvage*. He was the youngest of us all. And that meant real youth. At a distance he passed muster fairly well, what with the grime and the particular stamp of that campaign on our faces. But directly you were near enough to have a good look into his eyes, that was where his lack of age showed, though he was not exactly a boy.

"Those same eyes were blue, something like the blue of autumn skies, dreamy and gay, too—innocent, believing eyes. A topknot of fair hair decorated his brow like a gold diadem in what one would call normal times.

"You may think I am talking of him as if he were the hero of a novel. Why, that's nothing to what the adjutant discovered about him. He discovered that he had a 'lover's lips'—whatever that may be. If the adjutant meant a nice mouth, why, it was nice enough, but of course it was intended for a sneer. That adjutant of ours was not a very delicate fellow. 'Look at those lover's lips,' he would exclaim in a loud tone while Tomassov was talking.

"Tomassov didn't quite like that sort of thing. But to a certain extent he had laid himself open to banter by the lasting character of his impressions which were connected with the passion of love and, perhaps, were not of such a rare kind as he seemed to think them. What made his comrades tolerant of his rhapsodies was the fact that they were connected with France, with Paris!

"You of the present generation, you cannot conceive how much prestige there was then in those names for the whole world. Paris was the centre of wonder for all human beings gifted with imagination. There we were, the majority of us young and well connected, but not long out of our hereditary nests in the provinces; simple servants of God; mere rustics, if I may say so. So we were only too ready to listen to the tales of France from our comrade

Tomassov. He had been attached to our mission in Paris the year before the war. High protections very likely—or maybe sheer luck.

"I don't think he could have been a very useful member of the mission because of his youth and complete inexperience. And apparently all his time in Paris was his own. The use he made of it was to fall in love, to remain in that state, to cultivate it, to exist only for it in a manner of speaking.

"Thus it was something more than a mere memory that he had brought with him from France. Memory is a fugitive thing. It can be falsified, it can be effaced, it can be even doubted. Why! I myself come to doubt sometimes that I, too, have been in Paris in my turn. And the long road there with battles for its stages would appear still more incredible if it were not for a certain musket ball which I have been carrying about my person ever since a little cavalry affair which happened in Silesia at the very beginning of the Leipsic campaign.

"Passages of love, however, are more impressive perhaps than passages of danger. You don't go affronting love in troops as it were. They are rarer, more personal and more intimate. And remember that with Tomassov all that was very fresh yet. He had not been home from France three months when the war began.

"His heart, his mind were full of that experience. He was really awed by it, and he was simple enough to let it appear in his speeches. He considered himself a sort of privileged person, not because a woman had looked at him with favour, but simply because, how shall I say it, he had had the wonderful illumination of his worship for her, as if it were heaven itself that had done this for him.

"Oh yes, he was very simple. A nice youngster, yet no fool; and with that, utterly inexperienced, unsuspicious, and unthinking. You will find one like that here and there in the provinces. He had some poetry in him too. It could only be natural, something quite his own, not acquired. I suppose Father Adam had some poetry in him of that natural sort. For the rest *un Russe sauvage* as the French sometimes call us, but not of that kind which, they maintain, eats tallow candle for a delicacy. As to the woman, the French woman, well, though I have also been in France with a hundred thousand Russians, I have never seen her. Very likely she was not in Paris then. And in any case hers were not the doors that would fly open before simple fellows of my sort, you understand. Gilded salons were never in my way. I could not tell you how she looked, which is strange considering that I was, if I may say so, Tomassov's special confidant.

"He very soon got shy of talking before the others. I suppose the usual camp-fire comments jarred his fine feelings. But I was left to him and truly I had to submit. You can't very well expect a youngster in Tomassov's state to hold his tongue altogether; and I—I suppose you will hardly believe me—I am by nature a rather silent sort of person.

"Very likely my silence appeared to him sympathetic. All the month of September our regiment, quartered in villages, had come in for an easy time. It was then that I heard most of that—you can't call it a story. The story I have in my mind is not in that. Outpourings, let us call them.

"I would sit quite content to hold my peace, a whole hour perhaps, while Tomassov talked with exaltation. And when he was done I would still hold my peace. And then there would be produced a solemn effect of silence which, I imagine, pleased Tomassov in a way.

"She was of course not a woman in her first youth. A widow, maybe. At any rate I never heard Tomassov mention her husband. She had a salon, something very distinguished; a social centre in which she queened it with great splendour.

"Somehow, I fancy her court was composed mostly of men. But Tomassov, I must say, kept such details out of his discourses wonderfully well. Upon my word I don't know whether her hair was dark or fair, her eyes brown or blue; what was her stature, her features, or her complexion. His love soared above mere physical impressions. He never described her to me in set terms; but he was ready to swear that in her presence everybody's thoughts and feelings were bound to circle round her. She was that sort of woman. Most wonderful conversations on all sorts of subjects went on in her salon: but through them all there flowed unheard like a mysterious strain of music the assertion, the power, the tyranny of sheer beauty. So apparently the woman was beautiful. She detached all these talking people from their life interests, and even from their vanities. She was a secret delight and a secret trouble. All the men when they looked at her fell to brooding as if struck by the thought that their lives had been wasted. She was the very joy and shudder of felicity and she brought only sadness and torment to the hearts of men.

"In short, she must have been an extraordinary woman, or else Tomassov was an extraordinary young fellow to feel in that way and to talk like this about her. I told you the fellow had a lot of poetry in him and observed that all this sounded true enough. It would be just about the sorcery a woman very much out of the common would exercise, you know. Poets do get close to truth somehow—there is no denying that.

"There is no poetry in my composition, I know, but I have my share of common shrewdness, and I have no doubt that the lady was kind to the youngster, once he did find his way inside her salon. His getting in is the real marvel. However, he did get in, the innocent, and he found himself in distinguished company there, amongst men of considerable position. And you know what that means: thick waists, bald heads, teeth that are not—as some satirist puts it. Imagine amongst them a nice boy, fresh and simple, like an apple just off the tree; a modest, good-looking, impressionable, adoring young barbarian. My word! What a change! What a relief for jaded feelings! And with that, having in his nature that dose of poetry which saves even a simpleton from being a fool.

"He became an artlessly, unconditionally devoted slave. He was rewarded by being smiled on and in time admitted to the intimacy of the house. It may be that the unsophisticated young barbarian amused the exquisite lady. Perhaps—since he didn't feed on tallow candles—he satisfied some need of tenderness in the woman. You know, there are many kinds of tenderness highly civilized women are capable of. Women with heads and imagination, I mean, and no temperament to speak of, you understand. But who is going to fathom their needs or their fancies? Most of the time they themselves don't know much about their innermost moods, and blunder out of one into another, sometimes with catastrophic results. And then who is more surprised than they? However, Tomassov's case was in its nature quite idyllic. The fashionable world was amused. His devotion made for him a kind of social success. But he didn't care. There was his one divinity, and there was the shrine where he was permitted to go in and out without regard for official reception hours.

"He took advantage of that privilege freely. Well, he had no official duties, you know. The Military Mission was supposed to be more complimentary than anything else, the head of it being a personal friend of our Emperor Alexander; and he, too, was laying himself out for successes in fashionable life exclusively—as it seemed. As it seemed.

"One afternoon Tomassov called on the mistress of his thoughts earlier than usual. She was not alone. There was a man with her, not one of the thick-waisted, bald-headed personages, but a somebody all the same, a man over thirty, a French officer who to some extent was also a privileged intimate. Tomassov was not jealous of him. Such a sentiment would have appeared presumptuous to the simple fellow.

"On the contrary he admired that officer. You have no idea of the French military men's prestige in those days, even with us Russian soldiers who had managed to face them perhaps better than the rest. Victory had marked them on the forehead—it seemed for ever. They would have been more than human if they had not been conscious of it; but they were good comrades and had a sort of brotherly feeling for all who bore arms, even if it was against them.

"And this was quite a superior example, an officer of the major-general's staff, and a man of the best society besides. He was powerfully built, and thoroughly masculine, though he was as carefully groomed as a woman. He had the courteous self-possession of a man of the world. His forehead, white as alabaster, contrasted impressively with the healthy colour of his face.

"I don't know whether he was jealous of Tomassov, but I suspect that he might have been a little annoyed at him as at a sort of walking absurdity of the sentimental order. But these men of the world are impenetrable, and outwardly he condescended to recognize Tomassov's existence even more distinctly than was strictly necessary. Once or twice he had offered him some useful worldly advice with perfect tact and delicacy. Tomassov was completely conquered by that evidence of kindness under the cold polish of the best society.

"Tomassov, introduced into the *petit salon,* found these two exquisite people sitting on a sofa together and had the feeling of having interrupted some special conversation. They looked at him strangely, he thought; but he was not given to understand that he had intruded. After a time the lady said to the officer—his name was De Castel—'I wish you would take the trouble to ascertain the exact truth as to that rumour.'

"'It's much more than a mere rumour,' remarked the officer. But he got up submissively and went out. The lady turned to Tomassov and said: 'You may stay with me.'

"This express command made him supremely happy, though as a matter of fact he had had no idea of going.

"She regarded him with her kindly glances, which made something glow and expand within his chest. It was a delicious feeling, even though it did cut one's breath short now and then. Ecstatically he drank in the sound of her tranquil, seductive talk full of innocent gaiety and of spiritual quietude. His passion appeared to him to flame up and envelop her in blue fiery tongues from head to foot and over her head, while her soul reposed in the centre like a big white rose. . . .

"H'm, good this. He told me many other things like that. But this is the one I remember. He himself remembered everything because these were the last memories of that woman. He was seeing her for the last time though he did not know it then.

"M. De Castel returned, breaking into that atmosphere of enchantment Tomassov had been drinking in even to complete unconsciousness of the external world. Tomassov could not help being struck by the distinction of his movements, the ease of his manner, his superiority to all the other men he knew, and he suffered from it. It occurred to him that these two brilliant beings on the sofa were made for each other.

"De Castel sitting down by the side of the lady murmured to her discreetly, 'There is not the slightest doubt that it's true,' and they both turned their eyes to Tomassov. Roused thoroughly from his enchantment he became self-conscious; a feeling of shyness came over him. He sat smiling faintly at them.

"The lady without taking her eyes off the blushing Tomassov said with a dreamy gravity quite unusual to her:

"'I should like to know that your generosity can be supreme—without a flaw. Love at its highest should be the origin of every perfection.'

"Tomassov opened his eyes wide with admiration at this, as though her lips had been dropping real pearls. The sentiment, however, was not uttered for the primitive Russian youth but for the exquisitely accomplished man of the world, De Castel.

"Tomassov could not see the effect it produced because the French officer lowered his head and sat there contemplating his admirably polished boots. The lady whispered in a sympathetic tone:

"'You have scruples?'

"De Castel, without looking up, murmured: 'It could be turned into a nice point of honour.'

"She said vivaciously: 'That surely is artificial. I am all for natural feelings. I believe in nothing else. But perhaps your conscience . . .'

"He interrupted her: 'Not at all. My conscience is not childish. The fate of those people is of no military importance to us. What can it matter? The fortune of France is invincible.'

"'Well then . . .' she uttered, meaningly, and rose from the couch. The French officer stood up, too. Tomassov hastened to follow their example. He was pained by his state of utter mental darkness. While he was raising the lady's white hand to his lips he heard the French officer say with marked emphasis:

"'If he has the soul of a warrior (at that time, you know, people really talked in that way), if he has the soul of a warrior he ought to fall at your feet in gratitude.'

"Tomassov felt himself plunged into even denser darkness than before. He followed the French officer out of the room and out of the house; for he had a notion that this was expected of him.

"It was getting dusk, the weather was very bad, and the street was quite deserted. The Frenchman lingered in it strangely. And Tomassov lingered, too, without impatience. He was never in a hurry to get away from the house in which she lived. And besides, something wonderful had happened to him. The hand he had reverently raised by the tips of its fingers had been pressed against his lips. He had received a secret favour! He was almost frightened. The world had reeled—and it had hardly steadied itself yet. De Castel stopped short at the corner of the quiet street.

"'I don't care to be seen too much with you in the lighted thoroughfares, M. Tomassov,' he said in a strangely grim tone.

"'Why?' asked the young man, too startled to be offended.

"'From prudence,' answered the other curtly. 'So we will have to part here; but before we part I'll disclose to you something of which you will see at once the importance.'

"This, please note, was an evening in late March of the year 1812. For a long time already there had been talk of a growing coolness between Russia and France. The word war was being whispered in drawing rooms louder and louder, and at last was heard in official circles. Thereupon the Parisian police discovered that our military envoy had corrupted some clerks at the Ministry of War and had obtained from them some very important confidential documents. The wretched men (there were two of them) had confessed their crime and were to be shot that night. To-morrow all the town would be talking of the affair. But the worst was that the Emperor Napoleon was furiously angry at the discovery, and had made up his mind to have the Russian envoy arrested.

"Such was De Castel's disclosure; and though he had spoken in low tones Tomassov was stunned as by a great crash.

"'Arrested,' he murmured, desolately.

"'Yes, and kept as a state prisoner—with everybody belonging to him. . . .'

"The French officer seized Tomassov's arm above the elbow and pressed it hard.

"'And kept in France,' he repeated into Tomassov's very ear, and then letting him go stepped back a space and remained silent.

"'And it's you, you, who are telling me this!' cried Tomassov in an extremity of gratitude that was hardly greater than his admiration for the generosity of his future foe. Could a brother have done for him more! He sought to seize the hand of the French officer, but the latter remained wrapped up closely in his cloak. Possibly in the dark he had not noticed the attempt. He moved back a bit and in his self-possessed voice of a man of the world, as though he were speaking across a card table or something of the sort, he called Tomassov's attention to the fact that if he meant to make use of the warning the moments were precious.

"'Indeed they are,' agreed the awed Tomassov. 'Good-bye then. I have no word of thanks to equal your generosity; but if ever I have an opportunity, I swear it, you may command my life. . . .'

"But the Frenchman retreated, had already vanished in the dark lonely street. Tomassov was alone, and then he did not waste any of the precious minutes of that night.

"See how people's mere gossip and idle talk pass into history. In all the memoirs of the time if you read them you will find it stated that our envoy had a warning from some highly placed woman who was in love with him. Of course it's known that he had successes with women, and in the highest spheres, too, but the truth is that the person who warned him was no other than our simple Tomassov—an altogether different sort of lover from himself.

"This then is the secret of our Emperor's representative's escape from arrest. He and all his official household got out of France all right—as history records.

"And amongst that household there was our Tomassov of course. He had, in the words of the French officer, the soul of a warrior. And what more desolate prospect for a man with such a soul than to be imprisoned on the eve of war; to be cut off from his country in danger, from his military family, from his duty, from honour, and—well—from glory, too.

"Tomassov used to shudder at the mere thought of the moral torture he had escaped; and he nursed in his heart a boundless gratitude to the two people who had saved him from that cruel ordeal. They were wonderful! For him love and friendship were but two aspects of exalted perfection. He had found these fine examples of it and he vowed them indeed a sort of cult. It affected his attitude towards Frenchmen in general, great patriot as he was. He was naturally indignant at the invasion of his country, but this indignation had no personal animosity in it. His was fundamentally a fine nature. He grieved at the appalling amount of human suffering he saw around him. Yes, he was full of compassion for all forms of mankind's misery in a manly way.

"Less fine natures than his own did not understand this very well. In the regiment they had nicknamed him the Humane Tomassov.

"He didn't take offence at it. There is nothing incompatible between humanity and a warrior's soul. People without compassion are the civilians, government officials, merchants and such like. As to the ferocious talk one hears from a lot of decent people in war time—well, the tongue is an unruly member at best, and when there is some excitement going on there is no curbing its furious activity.

"So I had not been very surprised to see our Tomassov sheathe deliberately his sword right in the middle of that charge, you may say. As we rode away after it he was very silent. He was not a chatterer as a rule, but it was evident that this close view of the Grand Army had affected him deeply, like some sight not of this earth. I had always been a pretty tough individual myself—well, even I . . . and there was that fellow with a lot of poetry in his nature! You may imagine what he made of it to himself. We rode side by side without opening our lips. It was simply beyond words.

"We established our bivouac along the edge of the forest so as to get some shelter for our horses. However, the boisterous north wind had dropped as quickly as it had sprung up, and the great winter stillness lay on the land from the Baltic to the Black Sea. One could almost feel its cold, lifeless immensity reaching up to the stars.

"Our men had lighted several fires for their officers and had cleared the snow around them. We had big logs of wood for seats; it was a very tolerable bivouac upon the whole, even without the exultation of victory. We were to feel that later, but at present we were oppressed by our stern and arduous task.

"There were three of us round my fire. The third one was that adjutant. He was perhaps a well-meaning chap but not so nice as he might have been had he been less rough in manner and less crude in his perceptions. He would reason about people's conduct as though a man were as simple a figure as, say, two sticks laid across each other; whereas a man is much more like the sea whose movements are too complicated to explain, and whose depths may bring up God only knows what at any moment.

"We talked a little about that charge. Not much. That sort of thing does not lend itself to conversation. Tomassov muttered a few words about a mere butchery. I had nothing to say. As I told you I had very soon let my sword hang idle at my wrist. That starving mob had not even *tried* to defend itself. Just a few shots. We had two men wounded. Two! . . . and we had charged the main column of Napoleon's Grand Army.

"Tomassov muttered wearily: 'What was the good of it?' I did not wish to argue, so I only just mumbled: 'Ah, well!' But the adjutant struck in unpleasantly:

"'Why, it warmed the men a bit. It has made me warm. That's a good enough reason. But our Tomassov is so humane! And besides he has been in love with a French woman, and thick as thieves with a lot of Frenchmen, so he is sorry for them. Never mind, my boy, we are on the Paris road now and you shall soon see her!' This was one of his usual, as we believed them, foolish speeches. None of us but believed that the getting to Paris would be a matter of years—of years. And lo! less than eighteen months afterwards I was rooked of a lot of money in a gambling hell in the Palais Royal.

"Truth, being often the most senseless thing in the world, is sometimes revealed to fools. I don't think that adjutant of ours believed in his own words. He just wanted to tease Tomassov from habit. Purely from habit. We of course said nothing, and so he took his head in his hands and fell into a doze as he sat on a log in front of the fire.

"Our cavalry was on the extreme right wing of the army, and I must confess that we guarded it very badly. We had lost all sense of insecurity by this time; but still we did keep up a pretence of doing it in a way. Presently a trooper rode up leading a horse and Tomassov mounted stiffly and went off on a round of the outposts. Of the perfectly useless outposts.

"The night was still, except for the crackling of the fires. The raging wind had lifted far above the earth and not the faintest breath of it could be heard. Only the full moon swam out with a rush into the sky and suddenly hung high and motionless overhead. I remember raising my hairy face to it for a moment. Then, I verily believe, I dozed off, too, bent double on my log with my head towards the fierce blaze.

"You know what an impermanent thing such slumber is. One moment you drop into an abyss and the next you are back in the world that you would think too deep for any noise but the trumpet of the Last Judgment. And then off you go again. Your very soul seems to slip down into a bottomless black pit. Then up once more into a startled consciousness. A mere plaything of cruel sleep one is, then. Tormented both ways.

"However, when my orderly appeared before me, repeating: 'Won't your Honour be pleased to eat? . . . Won't your Honor be pleased to eat? . . .' I managed to keep my hold of it—I mean that gaping consciousness. He was offering me a sooty pot containing some grain boiled in water with a pinch of salt. A wooden spoon was stuck in it.

"At that time these were the only rations we were getting regularly. Mere chicken food, confound it! But the Russian soldier is wonderful. Well, my fellow waited till I had feasted and then went away carrying off the empty pot.

"I was no longer sleepy. Indeed, I had become awake with an exaggerated mental consciousness of existence extending beyond my immediate surroundings. Those are but exceptional moments with mankind, I am glad to say. I had the intimate sensation of the earth in all its enormous expanse wrapped in snow, with nothing showing on it but trees with their straight stalk-like trunks and their funeral verdure; and in this aspect of general mourning I seemed to hear the sighs of mankind falling to die in the midst of a nature without life. They were Frenchmen. We didn't hate them; they did not hate us; we had existed far apart—and suddenly they had come rolling in with arms in their hands, without fear of God, carrying with them other nations, and all to perish together in a long, long trail of frozen corpses. I had an actual vision of that trail: a pathetic multitude of small dark mounds stretching away under the moonlight in a clear, still, and pitiless atmosphere—a sort of horrible peace.

"But what other peace could there be for them? What else did they deserve? I don't know by what connection of emotions there came into my head the thought that the earth was a pagan planet and not a fit abode for Christian virtues.

"You may be surprised that I should remember all this so well. What is a passing emotion or half-formed thought to last in so many years of a man's changing, inconsequential life? But what has fixed the emotion of that evening in my recollection so that the slightest shadows remain indelible was an event of strange finality, an event not likely to be forgotten in a life-time—as you shall see.

"I don't suppose I had been entertaining those thoughts more than five minutes when something induced me to look over my shoulder. I can't think it was a noise; the snow deadened all the sounds. Something it must have been, some sort of signal reaching my consciousness. Anyway, I turned my head, and there was the event approaching me, not that I knew it or had the slightest premonition. All I saw in the distance were two figures approaching in the moonlight. One of them was our Tomassov. The dark mass behind him which moved across my sight were the horses which his orderly was leading away. Tomassov was a very familiar appearance, in long boots, a tall figure ending in a pointed hood. But by his side advanced another figure. I mistrusted my eyes at first. It was amazing! It had a shining crested helmet on its head and was muffled up in a white cloak. The cloak was not as white as snow. Nothing in the world is. It was white more like mist, with an aspect that was ghostly and martial to an extraordinary degree. I could see at once that he was leading this resplendent vision by the arm. Then I saw that he was holding it up. While I stared and stared, they crept on—for indeed they were creeping—and at last they crept into the light of our bivouac fire and passed beyond the log I was sitting on. The blaze played on the helmet. It was extremely battered and the frost-bitten face, full of sores, under it was framed in bits of mangy fur. No God of War this, but a French officer. The great white cuirassier's cloak was torn, burnt full of holes. His feet were wrapped up in old sheepskins over remnants of boots. They looked monstrous and he tottered on them, sustained by Tomassov who lowered him most carefully on to the log on which I sat.

"My amazement knew no bounds.

"'You have brought in a prisoner,' I said to Tomassov, as if I could not believe my eyes.

"You must understand that unless they surrendered in large bodies we made no prisoners. What would have been the good? Our Cossacks either killed the stragglers or else let them alone, just as it happened. It came really to the same thing in the end.

"Tomassov turned to me with a very troubled look.

"'He sprang up from the ground somewhere as I was leaving the outpost,' he said. 'I believe he was making for it, for he walked blindly into my horse. He got hold of my leg and of course none of our chaps dared touch him then.'

"'He had a narrow escape,' I said.

"'He didn't appreciate it,' said Tomassov, looking even more troubled than before. 'He came along holding to my stirrup leather. That's what made me so late. He told me he was a staff officer; and then talking in a voice such, I suppose, as the damned alone use, a croaking of rage and pain, he said he had a favour to beg of me. A supreme favour. Did I understand him, he asked in a sort of fiendish whisper.

"'Of course I told him that I did. I said: *oui, je vous comprends.*

"'Then,' he said, 'do it. Now! At once—in the pity of your heart.'

"Tomassov ceased and stared queerly at me above the head of the prisoner.

"I said, 'What did he mean?'

"'That's what I asked him,' answered Tomassov in a dazed tone, 'and he said that he wanted me to do him the favour to blow his brains out. As a fellow soldier,' he said. 'As a man of feeling—as—as a humane man.'

"The prisoner sat between us like an awful gashed mummy as to the face, a martial scarecrow, a grotesque horror of rags and dirt, with awful living eyes, full of vitality, full of unquenchable fire, in a body of horrible affliction, a skeleton at the feast of glory. And suddenly those shining unextinguishable eyes of his became fixed upon Tomassov. He, poor fellow, fascinated, returned the ghastly stare of a suffering soul in that mere husk of a man. The prisoner croaked at him in French.

"'I recognize, you know. You are her Russian youngster. You were very grateful. I call on you to pay the debt. Pay it, I say, with one liberating shot. You are a man of honour. I have not even a broken sabre. All my being recoils from my own degradation. You know me.'

"Tomassov said nothing.

"'Haven't you got the soul of a warrior?' the Frenchman asked in an angry whisper, but with something of a mocking intention in it.

"'I don't know,' said poor Tomassov.

"What a look of contempt that scarecrow gave him out of his unquenchable eyes. He seemed to live only by the force of infuriated and impotent despair. Suddenly he gave a gasp and fell forward writhing in the agony of cramp in all his limbs; a not unusual effect of the heat of a camp-fire. It resembled the application of some horrible torture. But he tried to fight against the pain at first. He only moaned low while we bent over him so as to prevent him rolling into the fire, and muttered feverishly at intervals: '*Tuez moi, tuez moi* . . .' till, vanquished by the pain, he screamed in agony, time after time, each cry bursting out through his compressed lips.

"The adjutant woke up on the other side of the fire and started swearing awfully at the beastly row that Frenchman was making.

"'What's this? More of your infernal humanity, Tomassov,' he yelled at us. 'Why don't you have him thrown out of this to the devil on the snow?'

"As we paid no attention to his shouts, he got up, cursing shockingly, and went away to another fire. Presently the French officer became easier. We propped him up against the log and sat silent on each side of him till the bugles started their call at the first break of day. The big flame, kept up all through the night, paled on the livid sheet of snow, while the frozen air all round rang with the brazen notes of cavalry trumpets. The Frenchman's eyes, fixed in a glassy stare, which for a moment made us hope that he had died quietly sitting there between us two, stirred slowly to right and left, looking at each of our faces in turn. Tomassov and I exchanged glances of dismay. Then De Castel's voice, unexpected in its renewed strength and ghastly self-possession, made us shudder inwardly.

"'*Bonjour, Messieurs.*'

"His chin dropped on his breast. Tomassov addressed me in Russian.

"'It is he, the man himself . . .' I nodded and Tomassov went on in a tone of anguish: 'Yes, he! Brilliant, accomplished, envied by men, loved by that woman—this horror—this miserable thing that cannot die. Look at his eyes. It's terrible.'

"I did not look, but I understood what Tomassov meant. We could do nothing for him. This avenging winter of fate held both the fugitives and the pursuers in its iron grip. Compassion was but a vain word before that unrelenting destiny. I tried to say something about a convoy being no doubt collected in the village—but I faltered at the mute glance Tomassov gave me. We knew what those convoys were like: appalling mobs of hopeless wretches driven on by the butts of Cossacks' lances, back to the frozen inferno, with their faces set away from their homes.

"Our two squadrons had been formed along the edge of the forest. The minutes of anguish were passing. The Frenchman suddenly struggled to his feet. We helped him almost without knowing what we were doing.

"'Come,' he said, in measured tones. 'This is the moment.' He paused for a long time, then with the same distinctness went on: 'On my word of honour, all faith is dead in me.'

"His voice lost suddenly its self-possession. After waiting a little while he added in a murmur: 'And even my courage. . . . Upon my honour.'

"Another long pause ensued before, with a great effort, he whispered hoarsely: 'Isn't this enough to move a heart of stone? Am I to go on my knees to you?'

"Again a deep silence fell upon the three of us. Then the French officer flung his last word of anger at Tomassov.

"'Milksop!'

"Not a feature of the poor fellow moved. I made up my mind to go and fetch a couple of our troopers to lead that miserable prisoner away to the village. There was nothing else for it. I had not moved six paces towards the group of horses and orderlies in front of our squadron when . . . but you have guessed it. Of course. And I, too, I guessed it, for I give you my word that the report of Tomassov's pistol was the most insignificant thing imaginable. The snow certainly does absorb sound. It was a mere feeble pop. Of the orderlies holding our horses I don't think one turned his head round.

"Yes. Tomassov had done it. Destiny had led that De Castel to the man who could understand him perfectly. But it was poor Tomassov's lot to be the predestined victim. You know what the world's justice and mankind's judgment are like. They fell heavily on him with a sort of inverted hypocrisy. Why! That brute of an adjutant, himself, was the first to set going horrified allusions to the shooting of a prisoner in cold blood! Tomassov was not dismissed from the service of course. But after the siege of Dantzig he asked for permission to resign from the army, and went away to bury himself in the depths of his province, where a vague story of some dark deed clung to him for years.

"Yes. He had done it. And what was it? One warrior's soul paying its debt a hundredfold to another warrior's soul by releasing it from a fate worse than death—the loss of all faith and courage. You may look on it in that way. I don't know. And perhaps poor Tomassov did not know himself. But I was the first to approach that appalling dark group on the snow: the Frenchman extended rigidly on his back, Tomassov kneeling on one knee rather nearer to the feet than to the Frenchman's head. He had taken his cap off and his hair shone like gold in the light drift of flakes that had begun to fall. He was stooping over the dead in a tenderly contemplative attitude. And his young, ingenuous face, with lowered eyelids, expressed no grief, no sternness, no horror—but was set in the repose of a profound, as if endless and endlessly silent, meditation."

III

Heart of Darkness

Conrad surrendered his command of the *Otago* in Australia at the end of March 1889. He then took passage for England, and once ashore began to look for a ship. Most of his experience had come under sail at a time when the balance was tipping to steam, while economies of scale meant that the British Merchant Service itself was shrinking. Tonnage increased, as ever, but there were fewer ships afloat, fewer commands to be had, and Conrad's ensuing period of unemployment proved decisive. He began to plan a trip back to Poland, his first since his 1874 departure, and he began something else as well: the opening chapters of *Almayer's Folly* were written in London that fall. Yet he still needed a job, and late in the year he started to think of the Congo, a place where, as he would later write, "I had no sort of business."

Leopold II of Belgium had been building trading stations along that river for a decade, and in 1884 the Berlin Conference recognized what was called the Congo Free State as his own private property. No European incursion into Africa did a more persuasive job in selling itself as a humanitarian venture. And none was operated more brutally. Leopold ran the state for profit, with ivory and rubber its chief products, and his administration relied on a recipe of forced labor with a leavening of atrocity. His soldiers were required, for example, to turn in a human hand for each bullet they used, as evidence that they had not shot astray. They often missed—and took the hand from the living. When in the early years of the twentieth century the knowledge of such practices became current, the other European governments forced the Belgian monarch to relinquish his personal control. A full account of this history can be readily found in Adam Hochschild's *King Leopold's Ghost* (1998).

In *A Personal Record* Conrad describes how, as a boy, he had looked at a map of Africa, put his finger on the "blank space then representing the unsolved mystery of that continent," and told himself that "When I grow up I shall go *there*." He gives Marlow the same desire, and the physical progress of his narrator's journey closely tracks his own. A complex of family and business connections helped Conrad get a three-year contract as a riverboat captain for the Société Anonyme Belge pour le Commerce du Haut-Congo, and he left for Africa in May 1890, arriving on the coast in mid-June. First came a short trip upriver to Matadi, where he met Roger Casement, whose 1903 report on the Congo would do so much to expose Leopold's atrocities. Then there was a month of walking through the forest to Kinshasa, the "Central Station" of the tale, where Conrad expected to take charge of a steamer. But the boat was in need of repair, and rather than worry like Marlow over "rivets," Conrad started upstream on another one, the *Roi des Belges*: a thousand-mile training voyage to Stanley Falls, Kurtz's "Inner Station," during which he was taught to navigate the river's difficult snags and currents. Conrad's Kurtz cannot be fully identified with Georges Klein, the agent in charge of the station at Stanley Falls; still, the desperately sick man was, like Kurtz, brought on board for the trip downriver, and died en route. The boat's captain got sick too, leaving Conrad in command for a part of the return journey. Then he too became ill, suffering from a cocktail of dysentery and malaria. His health had never been strong, but from this point on we must begin to call it weak. He decided to break his contract and got back to London in January 1891. Years later Conrad would tell Edward Garnett that before he went to Africa he had "not a thought in [my] head . . . I was a perfect animal."

He began the tale in December 1898, describing it in a letter to his publisher, William Blackwood, as "a narrative after the manner of *youth* [*sic*] told by the same man," and assuring him that despite its title the tale "is not gloomy." It was his second use of "the man Marlow" and the second, and last, time he drew upon his African experience, following on his 1897 "An Outpost of Progress." In a 1917 author's note, Conrad suggested that in "Heart of Darkness" he had presented "a record of experience . . . pushed a little (and only a very little) beyond the actual facts of the case." That statement pushes things a bit itself. The Congo that Conrad visited had a larger river traffic, more fully developed trading stations, and many more Europeans than the one he makes Marlow describe. Those changes serve to heighten the book's primitivist sense of isolation, of "travelling back to the earlier beginnings of the world," to a time when the "waterway ran on, deserted, into the gloom of overshadowed distances." Yet they also lay Conrad open to Chinua Achebe's charge that he has emptied the continent out, denuding that river of the peoples and the histories that have grown up beside it.

Conrad planned a work of some twenty thousand words, but though he doubled its length in the writing, he nevertheless worked quickly and finished in less than three months. It was immediately published in *Blackwood's* as "The Heart of Darkness," where it ran from February to April 1899; book publication waited until 1902, when it was bound with "The End of the Tether" and the title story in *Youth*. Over the years almost every conceivable aspect of the tale has been discussed, debated, argued over, and belabored, including Conrad's decision to drop the definite article from its title. The most recent movement in the scholarly literature has been a series of powerful feminist readings. Some of the best of them can be found, along with such historical documents as Casement's report on the Congo and Conrad's own journal of his voyage, in Paul B. Armstrong's superb fourth edition of the Norton Critical *Heart of Darkness*. But the story has also inspired something more, or other, than scholarship. Orson Welles dramatized it for radio and then tried to film it; when the project was cancelled, he made *Citizen Kane* instead. In his 1979 film, *Apocalypse Now,* Francis Ford Coppola changed the setting from the Congo to Vietnam, and the fact that it was possible to make that shift suggests both the relevance of Achebe's criticism and the degree to which the tale now serves as a modern myth. The story has supplied T. S. Eliot with an epigraph, and at least two important works of postcolonial fiction stand as direct replies to it, Tayib Salih's *Season of Migration to the North* (1969), and V. S. Naipaul's *A Bend in the River* (1979).

The text of "Heart of Darkness" used here is that of the 1902 Blackwood first British edition of *Youth: A Narrative; and Two Other Stories,* as prepared by Robert Hampson for his 1995 Penguin edition of the tale. Most of the differences between Hampson's text and that of the 1902 edition concern questions of punctuation; interested readers should see that volume for details.

HEART OF DARKNESS

I

The *Nellie,* a cruising yawl, swung to her anchor without a flutter of the sails, and was at rest. The flood had made, the wind was nearly calm, and being bound down the river, the only thing for it was to come to and wait for the turn of the tide.

The sea-reach of the Thames stretched before us like the beginning of an interminable waterway. In the offing the sea and the sky were welded together without a joint, and in the luminous space the tanned sails of the barges drifting up with the tide seemed to stand still in red clusters of canvas sharply peaked, with gleams of varnished sprits. A haze rested on the low shores that ran out to sea in vanishing flatness. The air was dark above Gravesend, and farther back still seemed condensed into a mournful gloom, brooding motionless over the biggest, and the greatest, town on earth.

The Director of Companies was our captain and our host. We four affectionately watched his back as he stood in the bows looking to seaward. On the whole river there was nothing that looked half so nautical. He resembled a pilot, which to a seaman is trustworthiness personified. It was difficult to realise his work was not out there in the luminous estuary, but behind him, within the brooding gloom.

Between us there was, as I have already said somewhere, the bond of the sea. Besides holding our hearts together through long periods of separation, it had the effect of making us tolerant of each other's yarns—and even convictions. The Lawyer—the best of old fellows—had, because of his many years and many virtues, the only cushion on deck, and was lying on the only rug. The Accountant had brought out already a box of dominoes, and was toying architecturally with the bones. Marlow sat cross-legged right aft, leaning against the mizzen-mast. He had sunken cheeks, a yellow complexion, a straight back, an ascetic aspect, and, with his arms dropped, the palms of hands outwards, resembled an idol. The Director, satisfied the anchor had good hold, made his way aft and sat down amongst us. We exchanged a few words lazily. Afterwards there was silence on board the yacht. For some reason or other we did not begin that game of dominoes. We felt meditative, and fit for nothing but placid staring. The day was ending in a serenity of still and exquisite brilliance. The water shone pacifically; the sky, without a speck, was a benign immensity of unstained light; the very mist on the Essex marshes was like a gauzy and radiant fabric, hung from the wooded rises inland, and draping the low shores in diaphanous folds. Only the gloom to the west, brooding over the upper reaches, became more sombre every minute, as if angered by the approach of the sun.

And at last, in its curved and imperceptible fall, the sun sank low, and from glowing white changed to a dull red without rays and without heat, as if about to go out suddenly, stricken to death by the touch of that gloom brooding over a crowd of men.

Forthwith a change came over the waters, and the serenity became less brilliant but more profound. The old river in its broad reach rested unruffled at the decline of day, after ages of good service done to the race that peopled its banks, spread out in the tranquil dignity of a waterway leading to the uttermost ends of the earth. We looked at the venerable stream not in the vivid flush of a short day that comes and departs for ever, but in the august light of abiding memories. And indeed nothing is easier for a man who has, as the phrase goes, "followed the sea" with reverence and affection, than to evoke the great spirit of the past upon the lower reaches of the Thames. The tidal current runs to and fro in its unceasing service, crowded with memories of men and ships it had borne to the rest of home or to the battles of the sea. It had known and served all the men of whom the nation is proud, from Sir Francis Drake to Sir John Franklin, knights all, titled and untitled—the great knights-errant of the sea. It had borne all the ships whose names are like jewels flashing in the night of time, from the *Golden Hind* returning with her round flanks full of treasure, to be visited by the Queen's Highness and thus pass out of the gigantic tale, to the *Erebus* and *Terror,* bound on other conquests—and that never returned. It had known the ships and the men. They had sailed from Deptford, from Greenwich, from Erith—the adventurers and the settlers; kings' ships and the ships of men on 'Change; captains, admirals, the dark "interlopers" of the Eastern trade, and the commissioned "generals" of East India fleets. Hunters for gold or pursuers of fame, they all had gone out on that stream, bearing the sword, and often the torch, messengers of the might within the land, bearers of a spark from the sacred fire. What greatness had not floated on the ebb of that river into the mystery of an unknown earth! . . . The dreams of men, the seed of commonwealths, the germs of empires.

The sun set; the dusk fell on the stream, and lights began to appear along the shore. The Chapman lighthouse, a three-legged thing erect on a mudflat, shone strongly. Lights of ships moved in the fairway—a great stir of lights going up and going down. And farther west on the upper reaches the place of the monstrous town was still marked ominously on the sky, a brooding gloom in sunshine, a lurid glare under the stars.

"And this also," said Marlow suddenly, "has been one of the dark places of the earth."

He was the only man of us who still "followed the sea." The worst that could be said of him was that he did not represent his class. He was a seaman, but he was a wanderer too, while most seamen lead, if one may so express it, a sedentary life. Their minds are of the stay-at-home order, and their home is always with them—the ship; and so is their country—the sea. One ship is very much like another, and the sea is always the same. In the immutability of their surroundings the foreign shores, the foreign faces, the changing immensity of life, glide past, veiled not by a sense of mystery but by a slightly disdainful ignorance; for there is nothing mysterious to a seaman unless it be the sea itself, which is the mistress of his existence and as inscrutable as Destiny. For the rest, after his hours of work, a casual stroll or a casual spree on shore suffices to unfold for him the secret of a whole continent, and generally he finds the secret not worth knowing. The yarns of seamen have a direct simplicity, the whole meaning of which lies within the shell of a cracked nut. But Marlow was not typical (if his propensity to spin yarns be excepted), and to him the meaning of an episode was not inside like a kernel but outside, enveloping the tale which brought it out only as a glow brings out a haze, in the likeness of one of these misty halos that sometimes are made visible by the spectral illumination of moonshine.

His remark did not seem at all surprising. It was just like Marlow. It was accepted in silence. No one took the trouble to grunt even; and presently he said, very slow,—

"I was thinking of very old times, when the Romans first came here, nineteen hundred years ago—the other day. . . . Light came out of this river since—you say Knights? Yes; but it is like a running blaze on a plain, like a flash of lightning in the clouds. We live in the flicker—may it last as long as the old earth keeps rolling! But darkness was here yesterday. Imagine the feelings of a commander of a fine—what d'ye call 'em?—trireme in the Mediterranean, ordered suddenly to the north; run overland across the Gauls in a hurry; put in charge of one of these craft the legionaries,—a wonderful lot of handy men they must have been too—used to build, apparently by the hundred, in a month or two, if we may believe what we read. Imagine him here—the very end of the world, a sea the colour of lead, a sky the colour of smoke, a kind of ship about as rigid as a concertina—and going up this river with stores, or orders, or what you like. Sandbanks, marshes, forests, savages,—precious little to eat fit for a civilised man, nothing but Thames water to drink. No Falernian wine here, no going ashore. Here and there a military camp lost in a wilderness, like a needle in a bundle of hay—cold, fog, tempests, disease, exile, and death,—death skulking in the air, in the water, in the bush. They must have been dying like flies here. Oh yes—he did it. Did it very well, too, no doubt, and without thinking much about it either, except afterwards to brag of what he had gone through in his time, perhaps. They were men enough to face the darkness. And perhaps he was cheered by keeping his eye on a chance of promotion to the fleet at Ravenna by-and-by, if he had good friends in Rome and survived the awful climate. Or think of a decent young citizen in a toga—perhaps too much dice, you know—coming out here in the train of some prefect, or tax-gatherer, or trader even, to mend his fortunes. Land in a swamp, march through the woods, and in some inland post feel the savagery, the utter savagery, had closed round him,—all that mysterious life of the wilderness that stirs in the forest, in the jungles, in the hearts of wild men. There's no initiation either into such mysteries. He has to live in the midst of the incomprehensible, which is also detestable. And it has a fascination, too, that goes to work upon him. The fascination of the abomination—you know. Imagine the growing regrets, the longing to escape, the powerless disgust, the surrender, the hate."

He paused.

"Mind," he began again, lifting one arm from the elbow, the palm of the hand outwards, so that, with his legs folded before him, he had the pose of a Buddha preaching in European clothes and without a lotus-flower—"Mind, none of us would feel exactly like this. What saves us is efficiency—the devotion to efficiency. But these chaps were not much account, really. They were no colonists; their administration was merely a squeeze, and nothing more, I suspect. They were conquerors, and for that you want only brute force—nothing to boast of, when you have it, since your strength is just an accident arising from the weakness of others. They grabbed what they could get for the sake of what was to be got. It was just robbery with violence, aggravated murder on a great scale, and men going at it blind—as is very proper for those who tackle a darkness. The conquest of the earth, which mostly means the taking it away from, those who have a different complexion or slightly flatter noses than ourselves, is not a pretty thing when you look into it too much. What redeems it is the idea only. An idea at the back of it; not a sentimental pretence but an idea; and an unselfish belief in the idea—something you can set up, and bow down before, and offer a sacrifice to. . . ."

He broke off. Flames glided in the river, small green flames, red flames, white flames, pursuing, overtaking, joining, crossing each other—then separating slowly or hastily. The traffic of the great city went on in the deepening night upon the sleepless river. We looked on, waiting patiently—there was nothing else to do till the end of the flood; but it was only after a long silence, when he said, in a hesitating voice, "I suppose you fellows remember I did once turn fresh-water sailor for a bit," that we knew we were fated, before the ebb began to run, to hear about one of Marlow's inconclusive experiences.

"I don't want to bother you much with what happened to me personally," he began, showing in this remark the weakness of many tellers of tales who seem so often unaware of what their audience would best like to hear; "yet to understand the effect of it on me you ought to know how I got out there, what I saw, how I went up that river to the place where I first met the poor chap. It was the farthest point of navigation and the culminating point of my experience. It seemed somehow to throw a kind of light on everything about me—and into my thoughts. It was sombre enough too—and pitiful—not extraordinary in any way—not very clear either. No, not very clear. And yet it seemed to throw a kind of light.

"I had then, as you remember, just returned to London after a lot of Indian Ocean, Pacific, China Seas—a regular dose of the East—six years or so, and I was loafing about, hindering you fellows in your work and invading your homes, just as though I had got a heavenly mission to civilise you. It was very fine for a time, but after a bit I did get tired of resting. Then I began to look for a ship—I should think the hardest work on earth. But the ships wouldn't even look at me. And I got tired of that game too.

"Now when I was a little chap I had a passion for maps. I would look for hours at South America, or Africa, or Australia, and lose myself in all the glories of exploration. At that time there were many blank spaces on the earth, and when I saw one that looked particularly inviting on a map (but they all look that) I would put my finger on it and say, When I grow up I will go there. The North Pole was one of these places, I remember. Well, I haven't been there yet, and shall not try now. The glamour's off. Other places were scattered about the Equator, and in every sort of latitude all over the two hemispheres. I have been in some of them, and . . . well, we won't talk about that. But there was one yet—the biggest, the most blank, so to speak—that I had a hankering after.

"True, by this time it was not a blank space any more. It had got filled since my boyhood with rivers and lakes and names. It had ceased to be a blank space of delightful mystery—a white patch for a boy to dream gloriously over. It had become a place of darkness. But there was in it one river especially, a mighty big river, that you could see on the map, resembling an immense snake uncoiled, with its head in the sea, its body at rest curving afar over a vast country, and its tail lost in the depths of the land. And as I looked at the map of it in a shop-window, it fascinated me as a snake would a bird—a silly little bird. Then I remembered there was a big concern, a Company for trade on that river. Dash it all! I thought to myself, they can't trade without using some kind of craft on that lot of fresh water—steamboats! Why shouldn't I try to get charge of one. I went on along Fleet Street, but could not shake off the idea. The snake had charmed me.

"You understand it was a Continental concern, that Trading society; but I have a lot of relations living on the Continent, because it's cheap and not so nasty as it looks, they say.

"I am sorry to own I began to worry them. This was already a fresh departure for me. I was not used to get things that way, you know. I always went my own road and on my own legs where I had a mind to go. I wouldn't have believed it of myself; but, then—you see—I felt somehow I must get there by hook or by crook. So I worried them. The men said 'My dear fellow,' and did nothing. Then—would you believe it?—I tried the women. I, Charlie Marlow, set the women to work—to get a job. Heavens! Well, you see, the notion drove me. I had an aunt, a dear enthusiastic soul. She wrote: 'It will be delightful. I am ready to do anything, anything for you. It is a glorious idea. I know the wife of a very high personage in the Administration, and also a man who has lots of influence with,' etc., etc. She was determined to make no end of fuss to get me appointed skipper of a river steamboat, if such was my fancy.

"I got my appointment—of course; and I got it very quick. It appears the Company had received news that one of their captains had been killed in a scuffle with the natives. This was my chance, and it made me the more anxious to go. It was only months and months afterwards, when I made the attempt to recover what was left of the body, that I heard the original quarrel arose from a misunderstanding about some hens. Yes, two black hens. Fresleven—that was the fellow's name, a Dane—thought himself wronged somehow in the bargain, so he went ashore and started to hammer the chief of the village with a stick. Oh, it didn't surprise me in the least to hear this, and at the same time to be told that Fresleven was the gentlest, quietest creature that ever walked on two legs. No doubt he was; but he had been a couple of years already out there engaged in the noble cause, you know, and he probably felt the need at last of asserting his self-respect in some way. Therefore he whacked the old nigger mercilessly, while a big crowd of his people watched him, thunderstruck, till some man,—I was told the chief's son—in desperation at hearing the old chap yell, made a tentative jab with a spear at the white man—and of course it went quite easy between the shoulder-blades. Then the whole population cleared into the forest, expecting all kinds of calamities to happen, while on the other hand, the steamer Fresleven commanded left also in a bad panic, in charge of the engineer, I believe. Afterwards nobody seemed to trouble much about Fresleven's remains, till I got out and stepped into his shoes. I couldn't let it rest, though; but when an opportunity offered at last to meet my predecessor, the grass growing through his ribs was tall enough to hide his bones. They were all there. The supernatural being had not been touched after he fell. And the village was deserted, the huts gaped black, rotting, all askew within the fallen enclosures. A calamity had come to it, sure enough. The people had vanished. Mad terror had scattered them, men, women, and children, through the bush, and they had never returned. What became of the hens I don't know either. I should think the cause of progress got them, anyhow. However, through this glorious affair I got my appointment, before I had fairly begun to hope for it.

"I flew around like mad to get ready, and before forty-eight hours I was crossing the Channel to show myself to my employers, and sign the contract. In a very few hours I arrived in a city that always makes me think of a whited sepulchre. Prejudice no doubt. I had no difficulty in finding the Company's offices. It was the biggest thing in the town, and everybody I met was full of it. They were going to run an over-sea empire, and make no end of coin by trade.

"A narrow and deserted street in deep shadow, high houses, innumerable windows with venetian blinds, a dead silence, grass sprouting between the stones, imposing carriage archways right and left, immense double doors standing ponderously ajar. I slipped through one of these cracks, went up a swept and ungarnished staircase, as arid as a desert, and opened the first door I came to.

Two women, one fat and the other slim, sat on straw-bottomed chairs, knitting black wool. The slim one got up and walked straight at me—still knitting with downcast eyes—and only just as I began to think of getting out of her way, as you would for a somnambulist, stood still, and looked up. Her dress was as plain as an umbrella-cover, and she turned round without a word and preceded me into a waiting-room. I gave my name, and looked about. Deal table in the middle, plain chairs all round the walls, on one end a large shining map, marked with all the colours of a rainbow. There was a vast amount of red—good to see at any time, because one knows that some real work is done in there, a deuce of a lot of blue, a little green, smears of orange, and, on the East Coast, a purple patch, to show where the jolly pioneers of progress drink the jolly lager-beer. However, I wasn't going into any of these. I was going into the yellow. Dead in the centre. And the river was there—fascinating—deadly—like a snake. Ough! A door opened, a white-haired secretarial head, but wearing a compassionate expression, appeared, and a skinny forefinger beckoned me into the sanctuary. Its light was dim, and a heavy writing-desk squatted in the middle. From behind that structure came out an impression of pale plumpness in a frock-coat. The great man himself. He was five feet six, I should judge, and had his grip on the handle-end of ever so many millions. He shook hands, I fancy, murmured vaguely, was satisfied with my French. *Bon voyage.*

"In about forty-five seconds I found myself again in the waiting-room with the compassionate secretary, who, full of desolation and sympathy, made me sign some document. I believe I undertook amongst other things not to disclose any trade secrets. Well, I am not going to.

"I began to feel slightly uneasy. You know I am not used to such ceremonies, and there was something ominous in the atmosphere. It was just as though I had been let into some conspiracy—I don't know—something not quite right; and I was glad to get out. In the outer room the two women knitted black wool feverishly. People were arriving, and the younger one was walking back and forth introducing them. The old one sat on her chair. Her fat cloth slippers were propped up on a foot-warmer, and a cat reposed on her lap. She wore a starched white affair on her head, had a wart on one cheek, and silver-rimmed spectacles hung on the tip of her nose. She glanced at me above the glasses. The swift and indifferent placidity of that look troubled me. Two youths with foolish and cheery countenances were being piloted over, and she threw at them the same quick glance of unconcerned wisdom. She seemed to know all about them and about me too. An eerie feeling came over me. She seemed uncanny and fateful. Often far away there I thought of these two, guarding the door of Darkness, knitting black wool as for a warm pall, one introducing, introducing continuously to the unknown, the other scrutinising the cheery and foolish faces with unconcerned old eyes. *Ave!* Old knitter of black wool. *Morituri te salutant.* Not many of those she looked at ever saw her again—not half, by a long way.

"There was yet a visit to the doctor. 'A simple formality,' assured me the secretary, with an air of taking an immense part in all my sorrows. Accordingly a young chap wearing his hat over the left eyebrow, some clerk I suppose,—there must have been clerks in the business, though the house was as still as a house in a city of the dead,—came from somewhere up-stairs, and led me forth. He was shabby and careless, with ink-stains on the sleeves of his jacket, and his cravat was large and billowy, under a chin shaped like the toe of an old boot. It was a little too early for the doctor, so I proposed a drink, and thereupon he developed a vein of joviality. As we sat over our vermuths he glorified the Company's business, and by-and-by I expressed casually my surprise at him not going out there. He became very cool and collected all at once. 'I am not such a fool as I look, quoth Plato to his disciples,' he said sententiously, emptied his glass with great resolution, and we rose.

"The old doctor felt my pulse, evidently thinking of something else the while. 'Good, good for there,' he mumbled, and then with a certain eagerness asked me whether I would let him measure my head. Rather surprised, I said Yes, when he produced a thing like calipers and got the dimensions back and front and every way, taking notes carefully. He was an unshaven little man in a threadbare coat like a gaberdine, with his feet in slippers, and I thought him a harmless fool. 'I always ask leave, in the interests of science, to measure the crania of those going out there,' he said. 'And when they come back too?' I asked. 'Oh, I never see them,' he remarked;

'and, moreover, the changes take place inside, you know.' He smiled, as if at some quiet joke. 'So you are going out there. Famous. Interesting too.' He gave me a searching glance, and made another note. 'Ever any madness in your family?' he asked, in a matter-of-fact tone. I felt very annoyed. 'Is that question in the interests of science too?' 'It would be,' he said, without taking notice of my irritation, 'interesting for science to watch the mental changes of individuals, on the spot, but . . .' 'Are you an alienist?' I interrupted. 'Every doctor should be—a little,' answered that original, imperturbably. 'I have a little theory which you Messieurs who go out there must help me to prove. This is my share in the advantages my country shall reap from the possession of such a magnificent dependency. The mere wealth I leave to others. Pardon my questions, but you are the first Englishman coming under my observation . . .' I hastened to assure him I was not in the least typical. 'If I were,' said I, 'I wouldn't be talking like this with you.' 'What you say is rather profound, and probably erroneous,' he said, with a laugh. 'Avoid irritation more than exposure to the sun. Adieu. How do you English say, eh? Good-bye. Ah! Good-bye. Adieu. In the tropics one must before everything keep calm.' . . . He lifted a warning forefinger. . . . *'Du calme, du calme. Adieu.'*

"One thing more remained to do—say good-bye to my excellent aunt. I found her triumphant. I had a cup of tea—the last decent cup of tea for many days—and in a room that most soothingly looked just as you would expect a lady's drawing-room to look, we had a long quiet chat by the fireside. In the course of these confidences it became quite plain to me I had been represented to the wife of the high dignitary, and goodness knows to how many more people besides, as an exceptional and gifted creature—a piece of good fortune for the Company—a man you don't get hold of every day. Good heavens! and I was going to take charge of a twopenny-halfpenny river-steamboat with a penny whistle attached! It appeared, however, I was also one of the Workers, with a capital—you know. Something like an emissary of light, something like a lower sort of apostle. There had been a lot of such rot let loose in print and talk just about that time, and the excellent woman, living right in the rush of all that humbug, got carried off her feet. She talked about 'weaning those ignorant millions from their horrid ways,' till, upon my word, she made me quite uncomfortable. I ventured to hint that the Company was run for profit.

"'You forget, dear Charlie, that the labourer is worthy of his hire,' she said, brightly. It's queer how out of touch with truth women are. They live in a world of their own, and there had never been anything like it, and never can be. It is too beautiful altogether, and if they were to set it up it would go to pieces before the first sunset. Some confounded fact we men have been living contentedly with ever since the day of creation would start up and knock the whole thing over.

"After this I got embraced, told to wear flannel, be sure to write often, and so on—and I left. In the street—I don't know why—a queer feeling came to me that I was an impostor. Odd thing that I, who used to clear out for any part of the world at twenty-four hours' notice, with less thought than most men give to the crossing of a street, had a moment—I won't say of hesitation, but of startled pause, before this commonplace affair. The best way I can explain it to you is by saying that, for a second or two, I felt as though, instead of going to the centre of a continent, I were about to set off for the centre of the earth.

"I left in a French steamer, and she called in every blamed port they have out there, for, as far as I could see, the sole purpose of landing soldiers and custom-house officers. I watched the coast. Watching a coast as it slips by the ship is like thinking about an enigma. There it is before you—smiling, frowning, inviting, grand, mean, insipid, or savage, and always mute with an air of whispering, Come and find out. This one was almost featureless, as if still in the making, with an aspect of monotonous grimness. The edge of a colossal jungle, so dark-green as to be almost black, fringed with white surf, ran straight, like a ruled line, far, far away along a blue sea whose glitter was blurred by a creeping mist. The sun was fierce, the land seemed to glisten and drip with steam. Here and there greyish-whitish specks showed up, clustered inside the white surf, with a flag flying above them perhaps. Settlements some centuries old, and still no bigger than pin-heads on the untouched expanse of their background. We pounded along, stopped, landed soldiers; went on, landed custom-house clerks to levy toll in what looked like a God-forsaken wilderness, with a tin shed and a flagpole lost in it; landed more soldiers—to take care of the custom-house clerks, presumably. Some, I heard, got drowned in the surf; but whether they did or not, nobody seemed particularly to care. They were just flung out there, and on we went. Every day the coast looked the same, as though we had not moved; but we passed various places—trading places—with names like Gran' Bassam, Little Popo, names that seemed to belong to some sordid farce acted in front of a sinister backcloth. The idleness of a passenger, my isolation amongst all these men with whom I had no point of contact, the oily and languid sea, the uniform sombreness of the coast, seemed to keep me away from the truth of things, within the toil of a mournful and senseless delusion. The voice of the surf heard now and then was a positive pleasure, like the speech of a brother. It was something natural, that had its reason, that had a meaning. Now and then a boat from the shore gave one a momentary contact with reality. It was paddled by black fellows. You could see from afar the white of their eyeballs glistening. They shouted, sang; their bodies streamed with perspiration; they had faces like grotesque masks—these chaps; but they had bone, muscle, a wild vitality, an intense energy of movement, that was as natural and true as the surf along their coast. They wanted no excuse for being there. They were a great comfort to look at. For a time I would feel I belonged still to a world of straightforward facts; but the feeling would not last long. Something would turn up to scare it away. Once, I remember, we came upon a man-of-war anchored off the coast. There wasn't even a shed there, and she was shelling the bush. It appears the French had one of their wars going on thereabouts. Her ensign dropped limp like a rag; the muzzles of the long eight-inch guns stuck out all over the low hull; the greasy, slimy swell swung her up lazily and let her down, swaying her thin masts. In the empty immensity of earth, sky, and water, there she was, incomprehensible, firing into a continent. Pop, would go one of the eight-inch guns; a small flame would dart and vanish, a little white smoke would disappear, a tiny projectile would give a feeble screech—and nothing happened. Nothing could happen. There was a touch of insanity in the proceeding, a sense of lugubrious drollery in the sight; and it was not dissipated by somebody on board assuring me earnestly there was a camp of natives—he called them enemies!—hidden out of sight somewhere.

"We gave her her letters (I heard the men in that lonely ship were dying of fever at the rate of three a-day) and went on. We called at some more places with farcical names, where the merry dance of death and trade goes on in a still and earthy atmosphere as of an overheated catacomb; all along the formless coast bordered by dangerous surf, as if Nature herself had tried to ward off intruders; in and out of rivers, streams of death in life, whose banks were rotting into mud, whose waters, thickened into slime, invaded the contorted mangroves, that seemed to writhe at us in the extremity of an impotent despair. Nowhere did we stop long enough to get a particularised impression, but the general sense of vague and oppressive wonder grew upon me. It was like a weary pilgrimage amongst hints for nightmares.

"It was upward of thirty days before I saw the mouth of the big river. We anchored off the seat of the government. But my work would not begin till some two hundred miles farther on. So as soon as I could I made a start for a place thirty miles higher up.

"I had my passage on a little sea-going steamer. Her captain was a Swede, and knowing me for a seaman, invited me on the bridge. He was a young man, lean, fair, and morose, with lanky hair and a shuffling gait. As we left the miserable little wharf, he tossed his head contemptuously at the shore. 'Been living there?' he asked. I said, 'Yes.' 'Fine lot these government chaps—are they not?' he went on, speaking English with great precision and considerable bitterness. 'It is funny what some people will do for a few francs a-month. I wonder what becomes of that kind when it goes up country?' I said to him I expected to see that soon. 'So-o-o!' he exclaimed. He shuffled athwart, keeping one eye ahead vigilantly. 'Don't be too sure,' he continued. 'The other day I took up a man who hanged himself on the road. He was a Swede, too.' 'Hanged himself! Why, in God's name?' I cried. He kept on looking out watchfully. 'Who knows? The sun too much for him, or the country perhaps.'

"At last we opened a reach. A rocky cliff appeared, mounds of turned-up earth by the shore, houses on a hill, others, with iron roofs, amongst a waste of excavations, or hanging to the declivity. A continuous noise of the rapids above hovered over this scene of inhabited devastation. A lot of people, mostly black and naked, moved about like ants. A jetty projected into the river. A blinding sunlight drowned all this at times in a sudden recrudescence of glare. 'There's your Company's station,' said the Swede, pointing to three wooden barrack-like structures on the rocky slope. 'I will send your things up. Four boxes did you say? So. Farewell.'

"I came upon a boiler wallowing in the grass, then found a path leading up the hill. It turned aside for the boulders, and also for an undersized railway-truck lying there on its back with its wheels in the air. One was off. The thing looked as dead as the carcass of some animal. I came upon more pieces of decaying machinery, a stack of rusty rails. To the left a clump of trees made a shady spot, where dark things seemed to stir feebly. I blinked, the path was steep. A horn tooted to the right, and I saw the black people run. A heavy and dull detonation shook the ground, a puff of smoke came out of the cliff, and that was all. No change appeared on the face of the rock. They were building a railway. The cliff was not in the way or anything; but this objectless blasting was all the work going on.

"A slight clinking behind me made me turn my head. Six black men advanced in a file, toiling up the path. They walked erect and slow, balancing small baskets full of earth on their heads, and the clink kept time with their footsteps. Black rags were wound round their loins, and the short ends behind wagged to and fro like tails. I could see every rib, the joints of their limbs were like knots in a rope; each had an iron collar on his neck, and all were connected together with a chain whose bights swung between them, rhythmically clinking. Another report from the cliff made me think suddenly of that ship of war I had seen firing into a continent. It was the same kind of ominous voice; but these men could by no stretch of imagination be called enemies. They were called criminals, and the outraged law, like the bursting shells, had come to them, an insoluble mystery from over the sea. All their meagre breasts panted together, the violently dilated nostrils quivered, the eyes stared stonily uphill. They passed me within six inches, without a glance, with that complete, deathlike indifference of unhappy savages. Behind this raw matter one of the reclaimed, the product of the new forces at work, strolled despondently, carrying a rifle by its middle. He had a uniform jacket with one button off, and seeing a white man on the path, hoisted his weapon to his shoulder with alacrity. This was simple prudence, white men being so much alike at a distance that he could not tell who I might be. He was speedily reassured, and with a large, white, rascally grin, and a glance at his charge, seemed to take me into partnership in his exalted trust. After all, I also was a part of the great cause of these high and just proceedings.

"Instead of going up, I turned and descended to the left. My idea was to let that chain-gang get out of sight before I climbed the hill. You know I am not particularly tender; I've had to strike and to fend off. I've had to resist and to attack sometimes—that's only one way of resisting—without counting the exact cost, according to the demands of such sort of life as I had blundered into. I've seen the devil of violence, and the devil of greed, and the devil of hot desire; but, by all the stars! these were strong, lusty, red-eyed devils, that swayed and drove men—men, I tell you. But as I stood on this hillside, I foresaw that in the blinding sunshine of that land I would become acquainted with a flabby, pretending, weak-eyed devil of a rapacious and pitiless folly. How insidious he could be, too, I was only to find out several months later and a thousand miles farther. For a moment I stood appalled, as though by a warning. Finally I descended the hill, obliquely, towards the trees I had seen.

"I avoided a vast artificial hole somebody had been digging on the slope, the purpose of which I found it impossible to divine. It wasn't a quarry or a sandpit, anyhow. It was just a hole. It might have been connected with the philanthropic desire of giving the criminals something to do. I don't know. Then I nearly fell into a very narrow ravine, almost no more than a scar in the hillside. I discovered that a lot of imported drainage-pipes for the settlement had been tumbled in there. There wasn't one that was not broken. It was a wanton smash-up. At last I got under the trees. My purpose was to stroll into the shade for a moment; but no sooner within that it seemed to me I had stepped into the gloomy circle of some Inferno. The rapids were near, and an uninterrupted, uniform, headlong, rushing noise filled the mournful stillness of the grove, where not a breath stirred, not a leaf moved, with a mysterious sound—as though the tearing pace of the launched earth had suddenly become audible.

"Black shapes crouched, lay, sat between the trees, leaning against the trunks, clinging to the earth, half coming out, half effaced within the dim light, in all the attitudes of pain, abandonment, and despair. Another mine on the cliff went off, followed by a slight shudder of the soil under my feet. The work was going on. The work! And this was the place where some of the helpers had withdrawn to die.

"They were dying slowly—it was very clear. They were not enemies, they were not criminals, they were nothing earthly now,—nothing but black shadows of disease and starvation, lying confusedly in the greenish gloom. Brought from all the recesses of the coast in all the legality of time contracts, lost in uncongenial surroundings, fed on unfamiliar food, they sickened, became inefficient, and were then allowed to crawl away and rest. These moribund shapes were free as air—and nearly as thin. I began to distinguish the gleam of eyes under the trees. Then, glancing down, I saw a face near my hand. The black bones reclined at full length with one shoulder against the tree, and slowly the eyelids rose and the sunken eyes looked up at me, enormous and vacant, a kind of blind, white flicker in the depths of the orbs, which died out slowly. The man seemed young—almost a boy—but you know with them it's hard to tell. I found nothing else to do but to offer him one of my good Swede's ship biscuits I had in my pocket. The fingers closed slowly on it and held—there was no other movement and no other glance. He had tied a bit of white worsted round his neck—Why? Where did he get it? Was it a badge—an ornament—a charm—a propitiatory act? Was there any idea at all connected with it? It looked startling round his black neck, this bit of white thread from beyond the seas.

"Near the same tree two more bundles of acute angles sat with their legs drawn up. One, with his chin propped on his knees, stared at nothing, in an intolerable and appalling manner: his brother phantom rested its forehead, as if overcome with a great weariness; and all about others were scattered in every pose of contorted collapse, as in some picture of a massacre or a pestilence. While I stood horrorstruck, one of these creatures rose to his hands and knees, and went off on all-fours towards the river to drink. He lapped out of his hand, then sat up in the sunlight, crossing his shins in front of him, and after a time let his woolly head fall on his breastbone.

"I didn't want any more loitering in the shade, and I made haste towards the station. When near the buildings I met a white man, in such an unexpected elegance of get-up that in the first moment I took him for a sort of vision. I saw a high starched collar, white cuffs, a light alpaca jacket, snowy trousers, a clear necktie, and varnished boots. No hat. Hair parted, brushed, oiled, under a green-lined parasol held in a big white hand. He was amazing, and had a penholder behind his ear.

"I shook hands with this miracle, and I learned he was the Company's chief accountant, and that all the book-keeping was done at this station. He had come out for a moment, he said, 'to get a breath of fresh air.' The expression sounded wonderfully odd, with its suggestion of sedentary desk-life. I wouldn't have mentioned the fellow to you at all, only it was from his lips that I first heard the name of the man who is so indissolubly connected with the memories of that time. Moreover, I respected the fellow. Yes; I respected his collars, his vast cuffs, his brushed hair. His appearance was certainly that of a hairdresser's dummy; but in the great demoralisation of the land he kept up his appearance. That's backbone. His starched collars and got-up shirt-fronts were achievements of character. He had been out nearly three years; and, later on, I could not help asking him how he managed to sport such linen. He had just the faintest blush, and said modestly, 'I've been teaching one of the native women about the station. It was difficult. She had a distaste for the work.' Thus this man had verily accomplished something. And he was devoted to his books, which were in apple-pie order.

"Everything else in the station was in a muddle,—heads, things, buildings. Strings of dusty niggers with splay feet arrived and departed; a stream of manufactured goods, rubbishy cottons, beads, and brass wire set into the depths of darkness, and in return came a precious trickle of ivory.

"I had to wait in the station for ten days—an eternity. I lived in a hut in the yard, but to be out of the chaos I would sometimes get into the accountant's office. It was built of horizontal planks, and so badly put together that, as he bent over his high desk, he was barred from neck to heels with narrow strips of sunlight. There was no need to open the big shutter to see. It was hot there too; big flies buzzed fiendishly, and did not sting, but stabbed. I sat generally on the floor, while, of faultless appearance (and even slightly scented), perching on a high stool, he wrote, he wrote. Sometimes he stood up for exercise. When a truckle-bed with a sick man (some invalided agent from up-country) was put in there, he exhibited a gentle annoyance. 'The groans of this sick person,' he said, 'distract my attention. And without that it is extremely difficult to guard against clerical errors in this climate.'

"One day he remarked, without lifting his head, 'In the interior you will no doubt meet Mr Kurtz.' On my asking who Mr Kurtz was, he said he was a first-class agent; and seeing my disappointment at this information, he added slowly, laying down his pen, 'He is a very remarkable person.' Further questions elicited from him that Mr Kurtz was at present in charge of a trading post, a very important one, in the true ivory-country, at 'the very bottom of there. Sends in as much ivory as all the others put together . . .' He began to write again. The sick man was too ill to groan. The flies buzzed in a great peace.

"Suddenly there was a growing murmur of voices and a great tramping of feet. A caravan had come in. A violent babble of uncouth sounds burst out on the other side of the planks. All the carriers were speaking together, and in the midst of the uproar the lamentable voice of the chief agent was heard 'giving it up' tearfully for the twentieth time that day. . . . He rose slowly. 'What a frightful row,' he said. He crossed the room gently to look at the sick man, and returning, said to me, 'He does not hear.' 'What! Dead?' I asked, startled. 'No, not yet,' he answered, with great composure. Then, alluding with a toss of the head to the tumult in the station yard, 'When one has got to make correct entries, one comes to hate those savages—hate them to the death.' He remained thoughtful for a moment. 'When you see Mr Kurtz,' he went on, 'tell him from me that everything here'—he glanced at the desk—'is very satisfactory. I don't like to write to him—with those messengers of ours you never know who may get hold of your letter—at that Central Station.' He stared at me for a moment with his mild, bulging eyes. 'Oh, he will go far, very far,' he began again. 'He will be a somebody in the Administration before long. They, above—the Council in Europe, you know—mean him to be.'

"He turned to his work. The noise outside had ceased, and presently in going out I stopped at the door. In the steady buzz of flies the homeward-bound agent was lying flushed and insensible;

the other, bent over his books, was making correct entries of perfectly correct transactions; and fifty feet below the doorstep I could see the still tree-tops of the grove of death.

"Next day I left that station at last, with a caravan of sixty men, for a two-hundred-mile tramp.

"No use telling you much about that. Paths, paths, everywhere; a stamped-in network of paths spreading over the empty land, through long grass, through burnt grass, through thickets, down and up chilly ravines, up and down stony hills ablaze with heat; and a solitude, a solitude, nobody, not a hut. The population had cleared out a long time ago. Well, if a lot of mysterious niggers armed with all kinds of fearful weapons suddenly took to travelling on the road between Deal and Gravesend, catching the yokels right and left to carry heavy loads for them, I fancy every farm and cottage thereabouts would get empty very soon. Only here the dwellings were gone too. Still I passed through several abandoned villages. There's something pathetically childish in the ruins of grass walls. Day after day, with the stamp and shuffle of sixty pair of bare feet behind me, each pair under a 60-lb load. Camp, cook, sleep, strike camp, march. Now and then a carrier dead in harness at rest in the long grass near the path, with an empty water-gourd and his long staff lying by his side. A great silence around and above. Perhaps on some quiet night the tremor of far-off drums, sinking, swelling, a tremor vast, faint; a sound weird, appealing, suggestive, and wild—and perhaps with as profound a meaning as the sound of bells in a Christian country. Once a white man in an unbuttoned uniform, camping on the path with an armed escort of lank Zanzibaris, very hospitable and festive—not to say drunk. Was looking after the upkeep of the road, he declared. Can't say I saw any road or any upkeep, unless the body of a middle-aged negro, with a bullet-hole in the forehead, upon which I absolutely stumbled three miles farther on, may be considered as a permanent improvement. I had a white companion too, not a bad chap, but rather too fleshy and with the exasperating habit of fainting on the hot hillsides, miles away from the least bit of shade and water. Annoying, you know, to hold your own coat like a parasol over a man's head while he is coming-to. I couldn't help asking him once what he meant by coming there at all. 'To make money, of course. What do you think?' he said, scornfully. Then he got fever, and had to be carried in a hammock slung under a pole. As he weighed sixteen stone I had no end of rows with the carriers. They jibbed, ran away, sneaked off with their loads in the night—quite a mutiny. So, one evening, I made a speech in English with gestures, not one of which was lost to the sixty pairs of eyes before me, and the next morning I started the hammock off in front all right. An hour afterwards I came upon the whole concern wrecked in a bush—man, hammock, groans, blankets, horrors. The heavy pole had skinned his poor nose. He was very anxious for me to kill somebody, but there wasn't the shadow of a carrier near. I remembered the old doctor,—'It would be interesting for science to watch the mental changes of individuals, on the spot.' I felt I was becoming scientifically interesting. However, all that is to no purpose. On the fifteenth day I came in sight of the big river again, and hobbled into the Central Station. It was on a back water surrounded by scrub and forest, with a pretty border of smelly mud on one side, and on the three others enclosed by a crazy fence of rushes. A neglected gap was all the gate it had, and the first glance at the place was enough to let you see the flabby devil was running that show. White men with long staves in their hands appeared languidly from amongst the buildings, strolling up to take a look at me, and then retired out of sight somewhere. One of them, a stout, excitable chap with black moustaches, informed me with great volubility and many digressions, as soon as I told him who I was, that my steamer was at the bottom of the river. I was thunderstruck. What, how, why? Oh, it was 'all right.' The 'manager himself' was there. All quite correct. 'Everybody had behaved splendidly! splendidly!'—'you must,' he said in agitation, 'go and see the general manager at once. He is waiting!'

"I did not see the real significance of that wreck at once. I fancy I see it now, but I am not sure—not at all. Certainly the affair was too stupid—when I think of it—to be altogether natural. Still. . . . But at the moment it presented itself simply as a confounded nuisance. The steamer was sunk. They had started two days before in a sudden hurry up the river with the manager on board, in charge of some volunteer skipper, and before they had been out three hours they tore the bottom out of her on stones, and she sank near the south bank. I asked myself what I was to do there, now my boat was lost. As a matter of fact, I had plenty to do in fishing my command out of the river. I had to set about it the very next day. That, and the repairs when I brought the pieces to the station, took some months.

"My first interview with the manager was curious. He did not ask me to sit down after my twenty-mile walk that morning. He was commonplace in complexion, in feature, in manners, and in voice. He was of middle size and of ordinary build. His eyes, of the usual blue, were perhaps remarkably cold, and he certainly could make his glance fall on one as trenchant and heavy as an axe. But even at these times the rest of his person seemed to disclaim the intention. Otherwise there was only an indefinable, faint expression of his lips, something stealthy—a smile—not a smile—I remember it, but I can't explain. It was unconscious, this smile was, though just after he had said something it got intensified for an instant. It came at the end of his speeches like a seal applied on the words to make the meaning of the commonest phrase appear absolutely inscrutable. He was a common trader, from his youth up employed in these parts—nothing more. He was obeyed, yet he inspired neither love nor fear, nor even respect. He inspired uneasiness. That was it! Uneasiness. Not a definite mistrust—just uneasiness—nothing more. You have no idea how effective such a . . . a . . . faculty can be. He had no genius for organising, for initiative, or for order even. That was evident in such things as the deplorable state of the station. He had no learning, and no intelligence. His position had come to him—why? Perhaps because he was never ill . . . He had served three terms of three years out there . . . Because triumphant health in the general rout of constitutions is a kind of power in itself. When he went home on leave he rioted on a large scale—pompously. Jack ashore—with a difference—in externals only. This one could gather from his casual talk. He originated nothing, he could keep the routine going—that's all. But he was great. He was great by this little thing that it was impossible to tell what could control such a man. He never gave that secret away. Perhaps there was nothing within him. Such a suspicion made one pause—for out there there were no external checks. Once when various tropical diseases had laid low almost every 'agent' in the station, he was heard to say, 'Men who come out here should have no entrails.' He sealed the utterance with that smile of his, as though it had been a door opening into a darkness he had in his keeping. You fancied you had seen things—but the seal was on. When annoyed at meal-times by the constant quarrels of the white men about precedence, he ordered an immense round table to be made, for which a special house had to be built. This was the station's mess-room. Where he sat was the first place—the rest were nowhere. One felt this to be his unalterable conviction. He was neither civil nor uncivil. He was quiet. He allowed his 'boy'—an overfed young negro from the coast—to treat the white men, under his very eyes, with provoking insolence.

"He began to speak as soon as he saw me. I had been very long on the road. He could not wait. Had to start without me. The up-river stations had to be relieved. There had been so many delays already that he did not know who was dead and who was alive, and how they got on—and so on, and so on. He paid no attention to my explanations, and, playing with a stick of sealing-wax, repeated several times that the situation was 'very grave, very grave.' There were rumours that a very important station was in jeopardy, and its chief, Mr Kurtz, was ill. Hoped it was not true. Mr Kurtz was . . . I felt weary and irritable. Hang Kurtz, I thought. I interrupted him by saying I had heard of Mr Kurtz on the coast. 'Ah! So they talk of him down there,' he murmured to himself. Then he began again, assuring me Mr Kurtz was the best agent he had, an exceptional man, of the greatest importance to the Company; therefore I could understand his anxiety. He was, he said, 'very, very uneasy.' Certainly he fidgeted on his chair a good deal, exclaimed, 'Ah, Mr Kurtz!' broke the stick of sealing-wax and seemed dumfounded by the accident. Next thing he wanted to know 'how long it would take to' . . . I interrupted him again. Being hungry, you know, and kept on my feet too, I was getting savage. 'How could I tell,' I said. 'I hadn't even seen the wreck yet—some months, no doubt.' All this talk seemed to me so futile. 'Some months,' he said. 'Well, let us say three months before we can make a start. Yes. That ought to do the affair.' I flung out of his hut (he lived all alone in a clay hut with a sort of verandah) muttering to myself my opinion of him. He was a chattering idiot. Afterwards I took it back when it was borne in upon me startlingly with what extreme nicety he had estimated the time requisite for the 'affair.'

"I went to work the next day, turning, so to speak, my back on that station. In that way only it seemed to me I could keep my hold on the redeeming facts of life. Still, one must look about sometimes; and then I saw this station, these men strolling aimlessly about in the sunshine of the yard. I asked myself sometimes what it all meant. They wandered here and there with their absurd long staves in their hands, like a lot of faithless pilgrims bewitched inside a rotten fence. The word 'ivory' rang in the air, was whispered, was sighed. You would think they were praying to it. A taint of imbecile rapacity blew through it all, like a whiff from some corpse. By Jove! I've never seen anything so unreal in my life. And outside, the silent wilderness surrounding this cleared speck on the earth struck me as something great and invincible, like evil or truth, waiting patiently for the passing away of this fantastic invasion.

"Oh, these months! Well, never mind. Various things happened. One evening a grass shed full of calico, cotton prints, beads, and I don't know what else, burst into a blaze so suddenly that you would have thought the earth had opened to let an avenging fire consume all that trash. I was smoking my pipe quietly by my dismantled steamer, and saw them all cutting capers in the light, with their arms lifted high, when the stout man with moustaches came tearing down to the river, a tin pail in his hand, assured me that everybody was 'behaving splendidly, splendidly,' dipped about a quart of water and tore back again. I noticed there was a hole in the bottom of his pail.

"I strolled up. There was no hurry. You see the thing had gone off like a box of matches. It had been hopeless from the very first. The flame had leaped high, driven everybody back, lighted up everything—and collapsed. The shed was already a heap of embers glowing fiercely. A nigger was being beaten near by. They said he had caused the fire in some way; be that as it may, he was screeching most horribly. I saw him, later on, for several days, sitting in a bit of shade looking very sick and trying to recover himself: afterwards he arose and went out—and the wilderness without a sound took him into its bosom again. As I approached the glow from the dark I found myself at the back of two men, talking. I heard the name of Kurtz pronounced, then the words, 'take advantage of this unfortunate accident.' One of the men was the manager. I wished him a good evening. 'Did you ever see anything like it—eh? it is incredible,' he said, and walked off. The other man remained. He was a first-class agent, young, gentlemanly, a bit reserved, with a forked little beard and a hooked nose. He was stand-offish with the other agents, and they on their side said he was the manager's spy upon them. As to me, I had hardly ever spoken to him before. We got into talk, and by-and-by we strolled away from the hissing ruins. Then he asked me to his room, which was in the main building of the station. He struck a match, and I perceived that this young aristocrat had not only a silver-mounted dressing-case but also a whole candle all to himself. Just at that time the manager was the only man supposed to have any right to candles. Native mats covered the clay walls; a collection of spears, assegais, shields, knives was hung up in trophies. The business intrusted to this fellow was the making of bricks—so I had been informed; but there wasn't a fragment of a brick anywhere in the station, and he had been there more than a year—waiting. It seems he could not make bricks without something, I don't know what—straw maybe. Anyways, it could not be found there, and as it was not likely to be sent from Europe, it did not appear clear to me what he was waiting for. An act of special creation perhaps. However, they were all waiting—all the sixteen or twenty pilgrims of them—for something; and upon my word it did not seem an uncongenial occupation, from the way they took it, though the only thing that ever came to them was disease—as far as I could see. They beguiled the time by backbiting and intriguing against each other in a foolish kind of way. There was an air of plotting about that station, but nothing came of it, of course. It was as unreal as everything else—as the philanthropic pretence of the whole concern, as their talk, as their government, as their show of work. The only real feeling was a desire to get appointed to a trading-post where ivory was to be had, so that they could earn percentages. They intrigued and slandered and hated each other only on that account,—but as to effectually lifting a little finger—oh, no. By heavens! there is something after all in the world allowing one man to steal a horse while another must not look at a halter. Steal a horse straight out. Very well. He has done it. Perhaps he can ride. But there is a way of looking at a halter that would provoke the most charitable of saints into a kick.

"I had no idea why he wanted to be sociable, but as we chatted in there it suddenly occurred to me the fellow was trying to get at something—in fact, pumping me. He alluded constantly to Europe, to the people I was supposed to know there—putting leading questions as to my acquaintances in the sepulchral city, and so on. His little eyes glittered like mica discs—with curiosity,—though he tried to keep up a bit of superciliousness. At first I was astonished, but very soon I became awfully curious to see what he would find out from me. I couldn't possibly imagine what I had in me to make it worth his while. It was very pretty to see how he baffled himself, for in truth my body was full of chills, and my head had nothing in it but that wretched steamboat business. It was evident he took me for a perfectly shameless prevaricator. At last he got angry, and, to conceal a movement of furious annoyance, he yawned. I rose. Then I noticed a small sketch in oils, on a panel, representing a woman, draped and blindfolded, carrying a lighted torch. The background was sombre—almost black. The movement of the woman was stately, and the effect of the torchlight on the face was sinister.

"It arrested me, and he stood by civilly, holding a half-pint champagne bottle (medical comforts) with the candle stuck in it. To my question he said Mr Kurtz had painted this—in this very station more than a year ago—while waiting for means to go to his trading-post. 'Tell me, pray,' said I, 'who is this Mr Kurtz?'

"'The chief of the Inner Station,' he answered in a short tone, looking away. 'Much obliged,' I said, laughing. 'And you are the brickmaker of the Central Station. Every one knows that.' He was silent for a while. 'He is a prodigy,' he said at last. 'He is an emissary of pity, and science, and progress, and devil knows what else. We want,' he began to declaim suddenly, 'for the guidance of the cause intrusted to us by Europe, so to speak, higher intelligence, wide sympathies, a singleness of purpose.' 'Who says that?' I asked. 'Lots of them,' he replied. 'Some even write that; and so *he* comes here, a special being, as you ought to know.' 'Why ought I to know?' I interrupted, really surprised. He paid no attention. 'Yes. To-day he is chief of the best station, next year he will be assistant-manager, two years more and . . . but I daresay you know what he will be in two years' time. You are of the new gang—the gang of virtue. The same people who sent him specially also recommended you. Oh, don't say no. I've my own eyes to trust.' Light dawned upon me. My dear aunt's influential acquaintances were producing an unexpected effect upon that young man. I nearly burst into a laugh. 'Do you read the Company's confidential correspondence?' I asked. He hadn't a word to say. It was great fun. 'When Mr Kurtz,' I continued severely, 'is General Manager, you won't have the opportunity.'

"He blew the candle out suddenly, and we went outside. The moon had risen. Black figures strolled about listlessly, pouring water on the glow, whence proceeded a sound of hissing; steam ascended in the moonlight, the beaten nigger groaned somewhere. 'What a row the brute makes!' said the indefatigable man with the moustaches, appearing near us. 'Serve him right. Transgression—punishment—bang! Pitiless, pitiless. That's the only way. This will prevent all conflagrations for the future. I was just telling the manager . . .' He noticed my companion, and became crestfallen all at once. 'Not in bed yet,' he said, with a kind of servile heartiness; 'it's so natural. Ha! Danger—agitation.' He vanished. I went on to the river-side, and the other followed me. I heard a scathing murmur at my ear, 'Heap of muffs—go to.' The pilgrims could be seen in knots gesticulating, discussing. Several had still their staves in their hands. I verily believe they took these sticks to bed with them. Beyond the fence the forest stood up spectrally in the moonlight, and through the dim stir, through the faint sounds of that lamentable courtyard, the silence of the land went home to one's very heart,—its mystery, its greatness, the amazing reality of its concealed life. The hurt nigger moaned feebly somewhere near by, and then fetched a deep sigh that made me mend my pace away from there. I felt a hand introducing itself under my arm. 'My dear sir,' said the fellow, 'I don't want to be misunderstood, and especially by you, who will see Mr Kurtz long before I can have that pleasure. I wouldn't like him to get a false idea of my disposition. . . .'

"I let him run on, this papier-maché Mephistopheles, and it seemed to me that if I tried I could poke my forefinger through him, and would find nothing inside but a little loose dirt, maybe. He, don't you see, had been planning to be assistant-manager by-and-by under the present man, and I could see that the coming of that Kurtz had upset them both not a little. He talked precipitately, and I did not try to stop him. I had my shoulders against the wreck of my steamer, hauled up on the slope like a carcass of some big river animal. The smell of mud, of primeval mud, by Jove! was in my nostrils, the high stillness of primeval forest was before my eyes; there were shiny patches on the black creek. The moon had spread over everything a thin layer of silver—over the rank grass, over the mud, upon the wall of matted vegetation standing higher than the wall of a temple, over the great river I could see through a sombre gap glittering, glittering, as it flowed broadly by without a murmur. All this was great, expectant, mute, while the man jabbered about himself. I wondered whether the stillness on the face of the immensity looking at us two were meant as an appeal or as a menace. What were we who had strayed in here? Could we handle that dumb thing, or would it handle us? I felt how big, how confoundedly big, was that thing that couldn't talk, and perhaps was deaf as well. What was in there? I could see a little ivory coming out from there, and I had heard Mr Kurtz was in there. I had heard enough about it too—God knows! Yet somehow it didn't bring any image with it—no more than if I had been told an angel or a fiend was in there. I believed it in the same way one of you might believe there are inhabitants in the planet Mars. I knew once a Scotch sailmaker who was certain, dead sure, there were people in Mars. If you asked him for some idea how they looked and behaved, he would get shy and mutter something about 'walking on all-fours.' If you as much as smiled, he would—though a man of sixty—offer to fight you. I would not have gone so far as to fight for Kurtz, but I went for him near enough to a lie. You know I hate, detest, and can't bear a lie, not because I am straighter than the rest of us, but simply because it appals me. There is a taint of death, a flavour of mortality in lies,—which is exactly what I hate and detest in the world—what I want to forget. It makes me miserable and sick, like biting something rotten would do. Temperament, I suppose. Well, I went near enough to it by letting the young fool there believe anything he liked to imagine as to my influence in Europe. I became in an instant as much of a pretence as the rest of the bewitched pilgrims. This simply because I had a notion it somehow would be of help to that Kurtz whom at the time I did not see—you understand. He was just a word for me. I did not see the man in the name any more than you do. Do you see him? Do you see the story? Do you see anything? It seems to me I am trying to tell you a dream—making a vain attempt, because no relation of a dream can convey the dream-sensation, that commingling of absurdity, surprise, and bewilderment in a tremor of struggling revolt, that notion of being captured by the incredible which is of the very essence of dreams. . . ."

He was silent for a while.

". . . No, it is impossible; it is impossible to convey the life-sensation of any given epoch of one's existence,—that which makes its truth, its meaning—its subtle and penetrating essence. It is impossible. We live, as we dream—alone. . . ."

He paused again as if reflecting, then added—

"Of course in this you fellows see more than I could then. You see me, whom you know. . . ."

It had become so pitch dark that we listeners could hardly see one another. For a long time already he, sitting apart, had been no more to us than a voice. There was not a word from anybody. The others might have been asleep, but I was awake. I listened, I listened on the watch for the sentence, for the word, that would give me the clue to the faint uneasiness inspired by this narrative that seemed to shape itself without human lips in the heavy night-air of the river.

". . . Yes—I let him run on," Marlow began again, "and think what he pleased about the powers that were behind me. I did! And there was nothing behind me! There was nothing but that wretched, old, mangled steamboat I was leaning against, while he talked fluently about 'the necessity for every man to get on.' 'And when one comes out here, you conceive, it is not to gaze at the moon.' Mr Kurtz was a 'universal genius,' but even a genius would find it easier to work with 'adequate tools—intelligent men.' He did not make bricks—why, there was a physical impossibility in the way—as I was well aware; and if he did secretarial work for the manager, it was because 'no sensible man rejects wantonly the confidence of his superiors.' Did I see it? I saw it. What more did I want? What I really wanted was rivets, by heaven! Rivets. To get on with the work—to stop the hole. Rivets I wanted. There were cases of them down at the coast—cases—piled up—burst—split! You kicked a loose rivet at every second step in that station yard on the hillside. Rivets had rolled into the grove of death. You could fill your pockets with rivets for the trouble of stooping down—and there wasn't one rivet to be found where it was wanted. We had plates that would do, but nothing to fasten them with. And every week the messenger, a lone negro, letter-bag on shoulder and staff in hand, left our station for the coast. And several times a week a coast caravan came in with trade goods,—ghastly glazed calico that made you shudder only to look at it, glass beads value about a penny a quart, confounded spotted cotton handkerchiefs. And no rivets. Three carriers could have brought all that was wanted to set that steamboat afloat.

"He was becoming confidential now, but I fancy my unresponsive attitude must have exasperated him at last, for he judged it necessary to inform me he feared neither God nor devil, let alone any mere man. I said I could see that very well, but what I wanted was a certain quantity of rivets—and rivets were what really Mr Kurtz wanted, if he had only known it. Now letters went to the coast every week. . . . 'My dear sir,' he cried, 'I write from dictation.' I demanded rivets. There was a way—for an intelligent man. He changed his manner; became very cold, and suddenly began to talk about a hippopotamus; wondered whether sleeping on board the steamer (I stuck to my salvage night and day) I wasn't disturbed. There was an old hippo that had the bad habit of getting out on the bank and roaming at night over the station grounds. The pilgrims used to turn out in a body and empty every rifle they could lay hands on at him. Some even had sat up o' nights for him. All this energy was wasted, though. 'That animal has a charmed life,' he said; 'but you can say this only of brutes in this country. No man—you apprehend me?—no man here bears a charmed life.' He stood there for a moment in the moonlight with his delicate hooked nose set a little askew, and his mica eyes glittering without a wink, then, with a curt Good night, he strode off. I could see he was disturbed and considerably puzzled, which made me feel more hopeful than I had been for days. It was a great comfort to turn from that chap to my influential friend, the battered, twisted, ruined, tin-pot steamboat. I clambered on board. She rang under my feet like an empty Huntley & Palmer biscuit-tin kicked along a gutter; she was nothing so solid in make, and rather less pretty in shape, but I had expended enough hard work on her to make me love her. No influential friend would have served me better. She had given me a chance to come out a bit—to find out what I could do. No, I don't like work. I had rather laze about and think of all the fine things that can be done. I don't like work—no man does—but I like what is in the work,—the chance to find yourself. Your own reality—for yourself, not for others—what no other man can ever know. They can only see the mere show, and never can tell what it really means.

"I was not surprised to see somebody sitting aft, on the deck, with his legs dangling over the mud. You see I rather chummed with the few mechanics there were in that station, whom the other pilgrims naturally despised—on account of their imperfect manners, I suppose. This was the foreman—a boiler-maker by trade—a good worker. He was a lank, bony, yellow-faced man, with big intense eyes. His aspect was worried, and his head was as bald as the palm of my hand; but his hair in falling seemed to have stuck to his chin, and had prospered in the new locality, for his beard hung down to his waist. He was a widower with six young children (he had left them in charge of a sister of his to come out there), and the passion of his life was pigeon-flying. He was an enthusiast and a connoisseur. He would rave about pigeons. After work hours he used sometimes to come over from his hut for a talk about his children and his pigeons; at work, when he had to crawl in the mud under the bottom of the steamboat, he would tie up that beard of his in a kind of white serviette he brought for the purpose. It had loops to go over his ears. In the evening he could be seen squatted on the bank rinsing that wrapper in the creek with great care, then spreading it solemnly on a bush to dry.

"I slapped him on the back and shouted 'We shall have rivets!' He scrambled to his feet exclaiming 'No! Rivets!' as though he couldn't believe his ears. Then in a low voice, 'You . . . eh?' I don't know why we behaved like lunatics. I put my finger to the side of my nose and nodded mysteriously. 'Good for you!' he cried, snapped his fingers above his head, lifting one foot. I tried a jig. We capered on the iron deck. A frightful clatter came out of that hulk, and the virgin forest on the other bank of the creek sent it back in a thundering roll upon the sleeping station. It must have made some of the pilgrims sit up in their hovels. A dark figure obscured the lighted doorway of the manager's hut, vanished, then, a second or so after, the doorway itself vanished too. We stopped, and the silence driven away by the stamping of our feet flowed back again from the recesses of the land. The great wall of vegetation, an exuberant and entangled mass of trunks, branches, leaves, boughs, festoons, motionless in the moonlight, was like a rioting invasion of soundless life, a rolling wave of plants, piled up, crested, ready to topple over the creek, to sweep every little man of us out of his little existence. And it moved not. A deadened burst of mighty splashes and snorts reached us from afar, as though an ichthyosaurus had been taking a bath of glitter in the great river. 'After all,' said the boiler-maker in a reasonable tone, 'why shouldn't we get the rivets?' Why not, indeed! I did not know of any reason why we shouldn't. 'They'll come in three weeks,' I said, confidently.

"But they didn't. Instead of rivets there came an invasion, an infliction, a visitation. It came in sections during the next three weeks, each section headed by a donkey carrying a white man in new clothes and tan shoes, bowing from that elevation right and left to the impressed pilgrims. A quarrelsome band of footsore sulky niggers trod on the heels of the donkey; a lot of tents, camp-stools, tin boxes, white cases, brown bales would be shot down in the courtyard, and the air of mystery would deepen a little over the muddle of the station. Five such instalments came, with their absurd air of disorderly flight with the loot of innumerable outfit shops and provision stores, that, one would think, they were lugging, after a raid, into the wilderness for equitable division. It was an inextricable mess of things decent in themselves but that human folly made look like the spoils of thieving.

"This devoted band called itself the Eldorado Exploring Expedition, and I believe they were sworn to secrecy. Their talk, however, was the talk of sordid buccaneers: it was reckless without hardihood, greedy without audacity, and cruel without courage; there was not an atom of foresight or of serious intention in the whole batch of them, and they did not seem aware these things are wanted for the work of the world. To tear treasure out of the bowels of the land was their desire, with no more moral purpose at the back of it than there is in burglars breaking into a safe. Who paid the expenses of the noble enterprise I don't know; but the uncle of our manager was leader of that lot.

"In exterior he resembled a butcher in a poor neighbourhood, and his eyes had a look of sleepy cunning. He carried his fat paunch with ostentation on his short legs, and during the time his gang infested the station spoke to no one but his nephew. You could see these two roaming about all day long with their heads close together in an everlasting confab.

"I had given up worrying myself about the rivets. One's capacity for that kind of folly is more limited than you would suppose. I said Hang!—and let things slide. I had plenty of time for meditation, and now and then I would give some thought to Kurtz. I wasn't very interested in him. No. Still, I was curious to see whether this man, who had come out equipped with moral ideas of some sort, would climb to the top after all, and how he would set about his work when there."

II

"One evening as I was lying flat on the deck of my steamboat, I heard voices approaching—and there were the nephew and the uncle strolling along the bank. I laid my head on my arm again, and had nearly lost myself in a doze, when somebody said in my ear, as it were: 'I am as harmless as a little child, but I don't like to be dictated to. Am I the manager—or am I not? I was ordered to send him there. It's incredible.' . . . I became aware that the two were standing on the shore alongside the forepart of the steamboat, just below my head. I did not move; it did not occur to me to move: I was sleepy. 'It *is* unpleasant,' grunted the uncle. 'He has asked the Administration to be sent there,' said the other, 'with the idea of showing what he could do; and I was instructed accordingly. Look at the influence that man must have. Is it not frightful?' They both agreed it was frightful, then made several bizarre remarks: 'Make rain and fine weather—one man—the Council—by the nose'—bits of absurd sentences that got the better of my drowsiness, so that I had pretty near the whole of my wits about me when the uncle said, 'The climate may do away with this difficulty for you. Is he alone there?' 'Yes,' answered the manager; 'he sent his assistant down the river with a note to me in these terms: "Clear this poor devil out of the country, and don't bother sending more of that sort. I had rather be alone than have the kind of men you can dispose of with me." It was more than a year ago. Can you imagine such impudence!' 'Anything since then?' asked the other, hoarsely. 'Ivory,' jerked the nephew; 'lots of it—prime sort—lots—most annoying, from him.' 'And with that?' questioned the heavy rumble, 'Invoice,' was the reply fired out, so to speak. Then silence. They had been talking about Kurtz.

"I was broad awake by this time, but, lying perfectly at ease, remained still, having no inducement to change my position. 'How did that ivory come all this way?' growled the elder man, who seemed very vexed. The other explained that it had come with a fleet of canoes in charge of an English half-caste clerk Kurtz had with him; that Kurtz had apparently intended to return himself, the station being by that time bare of goods and stores, but after coming three hundred miles, had suddenly decided to go back, which he started to do alone in a small dug-out with four paddlers, leaving the half-caste to continue down the river with the ivory. The two fellows there seemed astounded at anybody attempting such a thing. They were at a loss for an adequate motive. As to me, I seemed to see Kurtz for the first time. It was a distinct glimpse: the dug-out, four paddling savages, and the lone white man turning his back suddenly on the headquarters, on relief, on thoughts of home—perhaps; setting his face towards the depths of the wilderness, towards his empty and desolate station. I did not know the motive. Perhaps he was just simply a fine fellow who stuck to his work for its own sake. His name, you understand, had not been pronounced once. He was 'that man.' The half-caste, who, as far as I could see, had conducted a difficult trip with great prudence and pluck, was invariably alluded to as 'that scoundrel.' The 'scoundrel' had reported that the 'man' had been very ill—had recovered imperfectly. . . . The two below me moved away then a few paces, and strolled back and forth at some little distance. I heard: 'Military post—doctor—two hundred miles—quite alone now—unavoidable delays—nine months—no news—strange rumours.' They approached again, just as the manager was saying, 'No one, as far as I know, unless a species of wandering trader—a pestilential fellow, snapping ivory from the natives.' Who was it they were talking about now? I gathered in snatches that this was some man supposed to be in Kurtz's district, and of whom the manager did not approve. 'We will not be free from unfair competition till one of these fellows is hanged for an example,' he said. 'Certainly,' grunted the other; 'get him hanged! Why not? Anything—anything can be done in this country. That's what I say; nobody here, you understand, *here,* can endanger your position. And why? You stand the climate—you outlast them all. The danger is in Europe; but there before I left I took care to——' They moved off and whispered, then their voices rose again. 'The extraordinary series of delays is not my fault. I did my possible.' The fat man sighed, 'Very sad.' 'And the pestiferous absurdity of his talk,' continued the other, 'he bothered me enough when he was here. "Each station should be like a beacon on the road towards better things, a centre for trade of course, but also for humanising, improving, instructing." Conceive you—that ass! And he wants to be manager! No, it's——' Here he got choked by excessive indignation, and I lifted my head the least bit. I was surprised to see how near they were—right under me. I could have spat upon their hats. They were looking on the ground, absorbed in thought. The manager was switching his leg with a slender twig: his sagacious relative lifted his head. 'You have been well since you came out this time?' he asked. The other gave a start. 'Who? I? Oh! Like a charm—like a charm. But the rest—oh, my goodness! All sick. They die so quick, too, that I haven't the time to send them out of the country—it's incredible!' 'H'm. Just so,' grunted the uncle. 'Ah! my body, trust to this—I say, trust to this.' I saw him extend his short flipper of an arm for a gesture that took in the forest, the creek, the mud, the river,—seemed to beckon with a dishonouring flourish before the sunlit face of the land a treacherous appeal to the lurking death, to the hidden evil, to the profound darkness of its heart. It was so startling that I leaped to my feet and looked back at the edge of the forest, as though I had expected an answer of some sort to that black display of confidence. You know the foolish notions that come to one sometimes. The high stillness confronted these two figures with its ominous patience, waiting for the passing away of a fantastic invasion.

"They swore aloud together—out of sheer fright, I believe—then pretending not to know anything of my existence, turned back to the station. The sun was low; and leaning forward side by side, they seemed to be tugging painfully uphill their two ridiculous shadows of unequal length, that trailed behind them slowly over the tall grass without bending a single blade.

"In a few days the Eldorado Expedition went into the patient wilderness, that closed upon it as the sea closes over a diver. Long afterwards the news came that all the donkeys were dead. I know nothing as to the fate of the less valuable animals. They, no doubt, like the rest of us, found what they deserved. I did not inquire. I was then rather excited at the prospect of meeting Kurtz very soon. When I say very soon I mean it comparatively. It was just two months from the day we left the creek when we came to the bank below Kurtz's station.

"Going up that river was like travelling back to the earliest beginnings of the world, when vegetation rioted on the earth and the big trees were kings. An empty stream, a great silence, an impenetrable forest. The air was warm, thick, heavy, sluggish. There was no joy in the brilliance of sunshine. The long stretches of the waterway ran on, deserted, into the gloom of overshadowed distances. On silvery sandbanks hippos and alligators sunned themselves side by side. The broadening waters flowed through a mob of wooded islands; you lost your way on that river as you would in a desert, and butted all day long against shoals, trying to find the channel, till you thought yourself bewitched and cut off for ever from everything you had known once—somewhere—far away—in another existence perhaps. There were moments when one's past came back to one, as it will sometimes when you have not a moment to spare to yourself; but it came in the shape of an unrestful and noisy dream, remembered with wonder amongst the overwhelming realities of this strange world of plants, and water, and silence. And this stillness of life did not in the least resemble a peace. It was the stillness of an implacable force brooding over an inscrutable intention. It looked at you with a vengeful aspect. I got used to it afterwards; I did not see it any more; I had no time. I had to keep guessing at the channel; I had to discern, mostly by inspiration, the signs of hidden banks; I watched for sunken stones; I was learning to clap my teeth smartly before my heart flew out, when I shaved by a fluke some infernal sly old snag that would have ripped the life out of the tin-pot steamboat and drowned all the pilgrims; I had to keep a look-out for the signs of dead wood we could cut up in the night for next day's steaming. When you have to attend to things of that sort, to the mere incidents of the surface, the reality—the reality, I tell you—fades. The inner truth is hidden—luckily, luckily. But I felt it all the same; I felt often its mysterious stillness watching me at my monkey tricks, just as it watches you fellows performing on your respective tight-ropes for—what is it? half-a-crown a tumble——"

"Try to be civil, Marlow," growled a voice, and I knew there was at least one listener awake besides myself.

"I beg your pardon. I forgot the heartache which makes up the rest of the price. And indeed what does the price matter, if the trick be well done? You do your tricks very well. And I didn't do badly either, since I managed not to sink that steamboat on my first trip. It's a wonder to me yet. Imagine a blindfolded man set to drive a van over a bad road. I sweated and shivered over that business considerably, I can tell you. After all, for a seaman, to scrape the bottom of the thing that's supposed to float all the time under his care is the unpardonable sin. No one may know of it, but you never forget the thump—eh? A blow on the very heart. You remember it, you dream of it, you wake up at night and think of it—years after—and go hot and cold all over. I don't pretend to say that steamboat floated all the time. More than once she had to wade for a bit, with twenty cannibals splashing around and pushing. We had enlisted some of these chaps on the way for a crew. Fine fellows—cannibals—in their place. They were men one could work with, and I am grateful to them. And, after all, they did not eat each other before my face: they had brought along a provision of hippo-meat which went rotten, and made the mystery of the wilderness stink in my nostrils. Phoo! I can sniff it now. I had the manager on board and three or four pilgrims with their staves—all complete. Sometimes we came upon a station close by the bank, clinging to the skirts of the unknown, and the white men rushing out of a tumble-down hovel, with great gestures of joy and surprise and welcome, seemed very strange,—had the appearances of being held there captive by a spell. The word ivory would ring in the air for a while—and on we went again into the silence, along empty reaches, round the still bends, between the high walls of our winding way, reverberating in hollow claps the ponderous beat of the stern-wheel. Trees, trees, millions of trees, massive, immense, running up high; and at their foot, hugging the bank against the stream, crept the little begrimed steamboat, like a sluggish beetle crawling on the floor of a lofty portico. It made you feel very small, very lost, and yet it was not altogether depressing that feeling. After all, if you were small, the grimy beetle crawled on—which was just what you wanted it to do. Where the pilgrims imagined it crawled to I don't know. To some place where they expected to get something, I bet! For me it crawled towards Kurtz—exclusively; but when the steam-pipes started leaking we crawled very slow. The reaches opened before us and closed behind, as if the forest had stepped leisurely across the water to bar the way for our return. We penetrated deeper and deeper into the heart of darkness. It was very quiet there. At night sometimes the roll of drums behind the curtain of trees would run up the river and remain sustained faintly, as if hovering in the air high over our heads, till the first break of day. Whether it meant war, peace, or prayer we could not tell. The dawns were heralded by the descent of a chill stillness; the wood-cutters slept, their fires burned low; the snapping of a twig would make you start. We were wanderers on a prehistoric earth, on an earth that wore the aspect of an unknown planet. We could have fancied ourselves the first of men taking possession of an accursed inheritance, to be subdued at the cost of profound anguish and of excessive toil. But suddenly, as we struggled round a bend, there would be a glimpse of rush walls, of peaked grass-roofs, a burst of yells, a whirl of black limbs, a mass of hands clapping, of feet stamping, of bodies swaying, of eyes rolling, under the droop of heavy and motionless foliage. The steamer toiled along slowly on the edge of a black and incomprehensible frenzy. The prehistoric man was cursing us, praying to us, welcoming us—who could tell? We were cut off from the comprehension of our surroundings; we glided past like phantoms, wondering and secretly appalled, as sane men would be before an enthusiastic outbreak in a madhouse. We could not understand, because we were too far and could not remember, because we were travelling in the night of first ages, of those ages that are gone, leaving hardly a sign—and no memories.

"The earth seemed unearthly. We are accustomed to look upon the shackled form of a conquered monster, but there—there you could look at a thing monstrous and free. It was unearthly, and the men were—— No, they were not inhuman. Well, you know, that was the worst of it—this suspicion of their not being inhuman. It would come slowly to one. They howled, and leaped, and spun, and made horrid faces; but what thrilled you was just the thought of their humanity—like yours—the thought of your remote kinship with this wild and passionate uproar. Ugly. Yes, it was ugly enough; but if you were man enough you would admit to yourself that there was in you just the faintest trace of a response to the terrible frankness of that noise, a dim suspicion of there being a meaning in it which you—you so remote from the night of first ages—could comprehend. And why not? The mind of man is capable of anything—because everything is in it, all the past as well as all the future. What was there after all? Joy, fear, sorrow, devotion, valour, rage—who can tell?—but truth—truth stripped of its cloak of time. Let the fool gape and shudder—the man knows, and can look on without a wink. But he must at least be as much of a man as these on the shore. He must meet that truth with his own true stuff—with his own inborn strength. Principles? Principles won't do. Acquisitions, clothes, pretty rags—rags that would fly off at the first good shake. No; you want a deliberate belief. An appeal to me in this fiendish row—is there? Very well; I hear; I admit, but I have a voice too, and for good or evil mine is the speech that cannot be silenced. Of course, a fool, what with sheer fright and fine sentiments, is always safe. Who's that grunting? You wonder I didn't go ashore for a howl and a dance? Well, no—I didn't. Fine sentiments, you say? Fine sentiments, be hanged! I had no time. I had to mess about with white-lead and strips of woollen blanket helping to put bandages on those leaky steam-pipes—I tell you. I had to watch the steering, and circumvent those snags, and get the tin-pot along by hook or by crook. There was surface-truth enough in these things to save a wiser man. And between whiles I had to look after the savage who was fireman. He was an improved specimen; he could fire up a vertical boiler. He was there below me, and, upon my word, to look at him was as edifying as seeing a dog in a parody of breeches and a feather hat, walking on his hind-legs. A few months of training had done for that really fine chap. He squinted at the steam-gauge and at the water-gauge with an evident effort of intrepidity—and he had filed teeth too, the poor devil, and the wool of his pate shaved into queer patterns, and three ornamental scars on each of his cheeks. He ought to have been clapping his hands and stamping his feet on the bank, instead of which he was hard at work, a thrall to strange witchcraft, full of improving knowledge. He was useful because he had been instructed; and what he knew was this—that should the water in that transparent thing disappear, the evil spirit inside the boiler would get angry through the greatness of his thirst, and take a terrible vengeance. So he sweated and fired up and watched the glass fearfully (with an impromptu charm, made of rags, tied to his arm, and a piece of polished bone, as big as a watch, stuck flatways through his lower lip), while the wooded banks slipped past us slowly, the short noise was left behind, the interminable miles of silence—and we crept on, towards Kurtz. But the snags were thick, the water was treacherous and shallow, the boiler seemed indeed to have a sulky devil in it, and thus neither that fireman nor I had any time to peer into our creepy thoughts.

"Some fifty miles below the Inner Station we came upon a hut of reeds, an inclined and melancholy pole, with the unrecognisable tatters of what had been a flag of some sort flying from it, and a neatly stacked wood-pile. This was unexpected. We came to the bank, and on the stack of firewood found a flat piece of board with some faded pencil-writing on it. When deciphered it said: 'Wood for you. Hurry up. Approach cautiously.' There was a signature, but it was illegible—not Kurtz—a much longer word. Hurry up. Where? Up the river? 'Approach cautiously.' We had not done so. But the warning could not have been meant for the place where it could be only found after approach. Something was wrong above. But what—and how much? That was the question. We commented adversely upon the imbecility of that telegraphic style. The bush around said nothing, and would not let us look very far, either. A torn curtain of red twill hung in the doorway of the hut, and flapped sadly in our faces. The dwelling was dismantled; but we could see a white man had lived there not very long ago. There remained a rude table—a plank on two posts; a heap of rubbish reposed in a dark corner, and by the door I picked up a book. It had lost its covers, and the pages had been thumbed into a state of extremely dirty softness, but the back had been lovingly stitched afresh with white cotton thread, which looked clean yet. It was an extraordinary find. Its title was, 'An Inquiry into some Points of Seamanship,' by a man Towser, Towson—some such name—Master in his Majesty's Navy. The matter looked dreary reading enough, with illustrative diagrams and repulsive tables of figures, and the copy was sixty years old. I handled this amazing antiquity with the greatest possible tenderness, lest it should dissolve in my hands. Within, Towson or Towser was inquiring earnestly into the breaking strain of ships' chains and tackle, and other such matter. Not a very enthralling book; but at the first glance you could see there a singleness of intention, an honest concern for the right way of going to work, which made these humble pages, thought out so many years ago, luminous with another than a professional light. The simple old sailor, with his talk of chains and purchases, made me forget the jungle and the pilgrims in a delicious sensation of having come upon something unmistakably real. Such a book being there was wonderful enough; but still more astounding were the notes pencilled in the margin, and plainly referring to the text. I couldn't believe my eyes! They were in cipher! Yes, it looked like cipher. Fancy a man lugging with him a book of that description into this nowhere and studying it—and making notes—in cipher at that! It was an extravagant mystery.

"I had been dimly aware for some time of a worrying noise, and when I lifted my eyes I saw the wood-pile was gone, and the manager, aided by all the pilgrims, was shouting at me from the riverside. I slipped the book into my pocket. I assure you to leave off reading was like tearing myself away from the shelter of an old and solid friendship.

"I started the lame engine ahead. 'It must be this miserable trader—this intruder,' exclaimed the manager, looking back malevolently at the place we had left. 'He must be English,' I said. 'It will not save him from getting into trouble if he is not careful,' muttered the manager darkly. I observed with assumed innocence that no man was safe from trouble in this world.

"The current was more rapid now, the steamer seemed at her last gasp, the stern-wheel flopped languidly, and I caught myself listening on tiptoe for the next beat of the float, for in sober truth I expected the wretched thing to give up every moment. It was like watching the last flickers of a life. But still we crawled. Sometimes

I would pick out a tree a little way ahead to measure our progress towards Kurtz by, but I lost it invariably before we got abreast. To keep the eyes so long on one thing was too much for human patience. The manager displayed a beautiful resignation. I fretted and fumed and took to arguing with myself whether or no I would talk openly with Kurtz; but before I could come to any conclusion it occurred to me that my speech or my silence, indeed any action of mine, would be a mere futility. What did it matter what any one knew or ignored? What did it matter who was manager? One gets sometimes such a flash of insight. The essentials of this affair lay deep under the surface, beyond my reach, and beyond my power of meddling.

"Towards the evening of the second day we judged ourselves about eight miles from Kurtz's station. I wanted to push on; but the manager looked grave, and told me the navigation up there was so dangerous that it would be advisable, the sun being very low already, to wait where we were till next morning. Moreover, he pointed out that if the warning to approach cautiously were to be followed, we must approach in daylight—not at dusk, or in the dark. This was sensible enough. Eight miles meant nearly three hours' steaming for us, and I could also see suspicious ripples at the upper end of the reach. Nevertheless, I was annoyed beyond expression at the delay, and most unreasonably too, since one night more could not matter much after so many months. As we had plenty of wood, and caution was the word, I brought up in the middle of the stream. The reach was narrow, straight, with high sides like a railway cutting. The dusk came gliding into it long before the sun had set. The current ran smooth and swift, but a dumb immobility sat on the banks. The living trees, lashed together by the creepers and every living bush of the undergrowth, might have been changed into stone, even to the slenderest twig, to the lightest leaf. It was not sleep—it seemed unnatural, like a state of trance. Not the faintest sound of any kind could be heard. You looked on amazed, and began to suspect yourself of being deaf—then the night came suddenly, and struck you blind as well. About three in the morning some large fish leaped, and the loud splash made me jump as though a gun had been fired. When the sun rose there was a white fog, very warm and clammy, and more blinding than the night. It did not shift or drive; it was just there, standing all round you like something solid. At eight or nine, perhaps, it lifted as a shutter lifts. We had a glimpse of the towering multitude of trees, of the immense matted jungle, with the blazing little ball of the sun hanging over it—all perfectly still—and then the white shutter came down again, smoothly, as if sliding in greased grooves. I ordered the chain, which we had begun to heave in, to be paid out again. Before it stopped running with a muffled rattle, a cry, a very loud cry, as of infinite desolation, soared slowly in the opaque air. It ceased. A complaining clamour, modulated in savage discords, filled our ears. The sheer unexpectedness of it made my hair stir under my cap. I don't know how it struck the others: to me it seemed as though the mist itself had screamed, so suddenly, and apparently from all sides at once, did this tumultuous and mournful uproar arise. It culminated in a hurried outbreak of almost intolerably excessive shrieking, which stopped short, leaving us stiffened in a variety of silly attitudes, and obstinately listening to the nearly as appalling and excessive silence. 'Good God! What is the meaning——?' stammered at my elbow one of the pilgrims,—a little fat man, with sandy hair and red whiskers, who wore side-spring boots, and pink pyjamas tucked into his socks. Two others remained open-mouthed a whole minute, then dashed into the little cabin, to rush out incontinently and stand darting scared glances, with Winchesters at 'ready' in their hands. What we could see was just the steamer we were on, her outlines blurred as though she had been on the point of dissolving, and a misty strip of water, perhaps two feet broad, around her—and that was all. The rest of the world was nowhere, as far as our eyes and ears were concerned. Just nowhere. Gone, disappeared; swept off without leaving a whisper or a shadow behind.

"I went forward, and ordered the chain to be hauled in short, so as to be ready to trip the anchor and move the steamboat at once if necessary. 'Will they attack?' whispered an awed voice. 'We will be all butchered in this fog,' murmured another. The faces twitched with the strain, the hands trembled slightly, the eyes forgot to wink. It was very curious to see the contrast of expressions of the white men and of the black fellows of our crew, who were as much strangers to that part of the river as we, though their homes were only eight hundred miles away. The whites, of course greatly discomposed, had besides a curious look of being painfully shocked by such an outrageous row. The others had an alert, naturally interested expression; but their faces were essentially quiet, even those of the one or two who grinned as they hauled at the chain. Several exchanged short, grunting phrases, which seemed to settle the matter to their satisfaction. Their headman, a young, broad-chested black, severely draped in dark-blue fringed cloths, with fierce nostrils and his hair all done up artfully in oily ringlets, stood near me. 'Aha!' I said, just for good fellowship's sake. 'Catch 'im,' he snapped, with a bloodshot widening of his eyes and a flash of sharp teeth—'catch 'im. Give 'im to us.' 'To you, eh?' I asked; 'what would you do with them?' 'Eat 'im!' he said, curtly, and, leaning his elbow on the rail, looked out into the fog in a dignified and profoundly pensive attitude. I would no doubt have been properly horrified, had it not occurred to me that he and his chaps must be very hungry: that they must have been growing increasingly hungry for at least this month past. They had been engaged for six months (I don't think a single one of them had any clear idea of time, as we at the end of countless ages have. They still belonged to the beginnings of time—had no inherited experience to teach them as it were), and of course, as long as there was a piece of paper written over in accordance with some farcical law or other made down the river, it didn't enter anybody's head to trouble how they would live. Certainly they had brought with them some rotten hippo-meat, which couldn't have lasted very long, anyway, even if the pilgrims hadn't, in the midst of a shocking hullabaloo, thrown a considerable quantity of it overboard. It looked like a high-handed proceeding; but it was really a case of legitimate self-defence. You can't breathe dead hippo waking, sleeping, and eating, and at the same time keep your precarious grip on existence. Besides that, they had given them every week three pieces of brass wire, each about nine inches long; and the theory was they were to buy their provisions with that currency in river-side villages. You can see how *that* worked. There were either no villages, or the people were hostile, or the director, who like the rest of us fed out of tins, with an occasional old he-goat thrown in, didn't want to stop the steamer for some more or less recondite reason. So, unless they swallowed the wire itself, or made loops of it to snare the fishes with, I don't see what good their extravagant salary could be to them. I must say it was paid with a regularity worthy of a large and honourable trading company. For the rest, the only thing to eat—though it didn't look eatable in the least—I saw in their possession was a few lumps of some stuff like half-cooked dough, of a dirty lavender colour, they kept wrapped in leaves, and now and then swallowed a piece of, but so small that it seemed done more for the looks of the thing than for any serious purpose of sustenance. Why in the name of all the gnawing devils of hunger they didn't go for us—they were thirty to five—and have a good tuck in for once, amazes me now when I think of it. They were big powerful men, with not much capacity to weigh the consequences, with courage, with strength, even yet, though their skins were no longer glossy and their muscles no longer hard. And I saw that something restraining, one of those human secrets that baffle probability, had come into play there. I looked at them with a swift quickening of interest—not because it occurred to me I might be eaten by them before very long, though I own to you that just then I perceived—in a new light, as it were—how unwholesome the pilgrims looked, and I hoped, yes, I positively hoped, that my aspect was not so—what shall I say?—so—unappetising: a touch of fantastic vanity which fitted well with the dream-sensation that pervaded all my days at that time. Perhaps I had a little fever too. One can't live with one's finger everlastingly on one's pulse. I had often 'a little fever,' or a little touch of other things—the playful paw-strokes of the wilderness, the preliminary trifling before the more serious onslaught which came in due course. Yes; I looked at them as you would on any human being, with a curiosity of their impulses, motives, capacities, weaknesses, when brought to the test of an inexorable physical necessity. Restraint! What possible restraint? Was it superstition, disgust, patience, fear—or some kind of primitive honour? No fear can stand up to hunger, no patience can wear it out, disgust simply does not exist where hunger is; and as to superstition, beliefs, and what you may call principles, they are less than chaff in a breeze. Don't you know the devilry of lingering starvation, its exasperating torment, its black thoughts, its sombre and brooding ferocity? Well, I do. It takes a man all his inborn strength to fight hunger properly. It's really easier to face bereavement, dishonour, and the perdition of one's soul—than this kind of prolonged hunger. Sad, but true. And these chaps too had no earthly reason for any kind of scruple. Restraint! I would just as soon have expected restraint from a hyena prowling amongst the corpses of a battlefield. But there was the fact facing me—the fact dazzling, to be seen, like the foam on the depths of the sea, like a ripple on an unfathomable enigma, a mystery greater—when I thought of it—than the curious, inexplicable note of desperate grief in this savage clamour that had swept by us on the river-bank, behind the blind whiteness of the fog.

"Two pilgrims were quarrelling in hurried whispers as to which bank. 'Left.' 'No, no; how can you? Right, right, of course.' 'It is very serious,' said the manager's voice behind me; 'I would be desolated if anything should happen to Mr Kurtz before we came up.' I looked at him, and had not the slightest doubt he was sincere. He was just the kind of man who would wish to preserve appearances. This was his restraint. But when he muttered something about going on at once, I did not even take the trouble to answer him. I knew, and he knew, that it was impossible. Were we to let go our hold of the bottom, we would be absolutely in the air—in space. We wouldn't be able to tell where we were going to—whether up or down stream, or across—till we fetched against one bank or the other,—and then we wouldn't know at first which it was. Of course I made no move. I had no mind for a smash-up. You couldn't imagine a more deadly place for a shipwreck. Whether drowned at once or not, we were sure to perish speedily in one way or another. 'I authorise you to take all the risks,' he said, after a short silence. 'I refuse to take any,' I said shortly; which was just the answer he expected, though its tone might have surprised him. 'Well, I must defer to your judgment. You are captain,' he said, with marked civility. I turned my shoulder to him in sign of my appreciation, and looked into the fog. How long would it last? It was the most hopeless look-out. The approach to this Kurtz grubbing for ivory in the wretched bush was beset by as many dangers as though he had been an enchanted princess sleeping in a fabulous castle. 'Will they attack, do you think?' asked the manager, in a confidential tone.

"I did not think they would attack, for several obvious reasons. The thick fog was one. If they left the bank in their canoes they would get lost in it, as we would be if we attempted to move. Still,

I had also judged the jungle of both banks quite impenetrable—and yet eyes were in it, eyes that had seen us. The river-side bushes were certainly very thick, but the undergrowth behind was evidently penetrable. However, during the short lift I had seen no canoes anywhere in the reach—certainly not abreast of the steamer. But what made the idea of attack inconceivable to me was the nature of the noise—of the cries we had heard. They had not the fierce character boding of immediate hostile intention. Unexpected, wild, and violent as they had been, they had given me an irresistible impression of sorrow. The glimpse of the steamboat had for some reason filled those savages with unrestrained grief. The danger, if any, I expounded, was from our proximity to a great human passion let loose. Even extreme grief may ultimately vent itself in violence—but more generally takes the form of apathy. . . .

"You should have seen the pilgrims stare! They had no heart to grin, or even to revile me; but I believe they thought me gone mad—with fright, maybe. I delivered a regular lecture. My dear boys, it was no good bothering. Keep a look-out? Well, you may guess I watched the fog for the signs of lifting as a cat watches a mouse; but for anything else our eyes were of no more use to us than if we had been buried miles deep in a heap of cotton-wool. It felt like it too—choking, warm, stifling. Besides, all I said, though it sounded extravagant, was absolutely true to fact. What we afterwards alluded to as an attack was really an attempt at repulse. The action was very far from being aggressive—it was not even defensive, in the usual sense: it was undertaken under the stress of desperation, and in its essence was purely protective.

"It developed itself, I should say, two hours after the fog lifted, and its commencement was at a spot, roughly speaking, about a mile and a half below Kurtz's station. We had just floundered and flopped round a bend, when I saw an islet, a mere grassy hummock of bright green, in the middle of the stream. It was the only thing of the kind; but as we opened the reach more, I perceived it was the head of a long sandbank, or rather of a chain of shallow patches stretching down the middle of the river. They were discoloured, just awash, and the whole lot was seen just under the water, exactly as a man's backbone is seen running down the middle of his back under the skin. Now, as far as I did see, I could go to the right or to the left of this. I didn't know either channel, of course. The banks looked pretty well alike, the depth appeared the same; but as I had been informed the station was on the west side, I naturally headed for the western passage.

"No sooner had we fairly entered it than I became aware it was much narrower than I had supposed. To the left of us there was the long uninterrupted shoal, and to the right a high, steep bank heavily overgrown with bushes. Above the bush the trees stood in serried ranks. The twigs overhung the current thickly, and from distance to distance a large limb of some tree projected rigidly over the stream. It was then well on in the afternoon, the face of the forest was gloomy, and a broad strip of shadow had already fallen on the water. In this shadow we steamed up—very slowly, as you may imagine. I sheered her well inshore—the water being deepest near the bank, as the sounding-pole informed me.

"One of my hungry and forbearing friends was sounding in the bows just below me. This steamboat was exactly like a decked scow. On the deck there were two little teak-wood houses, with doors and windows. The boiler was in the fore-end, and the machinery right astern. Over the whole there was a light roof, supported on stanchions. The funnel projected through that roof, and in front of the funnel a small cabin built of light planks served for a pilot-house. It contained a couch, two camp-stools, a loaded Martini-Henry leaning in one corner, a tiny table, and the steering-wheel. It had a wide door in front and a broad shutter at each side. All these were always thrown open, of course. I spent my days perched up there on the extreme fore-end of that roof, before the door. At night I slept, or tried to, on the couch. An athletic black belonging to some coast tribe, and educated by my poor predecessor, was the helmsman. He sported a pair of brass earrings, wore a blue cloth wrapper from the waist to the ankles, and thought all the world of himself. He was the most unstable kind of fool I had ever seen. He steered with no end of a swagger while you were by; but if he lost sight of you, he became instantly the prey of an abject funk, and would let that cripple of a steamboat get the upper hand of him in a minute.

"I was looking down at the sounding-pole, and feeling much annoyed to see at each try a little more of it stick out of that river, when I saw my poleman give up the business suddenly, and stretch himself flat on the deck, without even taking the trouble to haul his pole in. He kept hold on it though, and it trailed in the water. At the same time the fireman, whom I could also see below me, sat down abruptly before his furnace and ducked his head. I was amazed. Then I had to look at the river mighty quick, because there was a snag in the fairway. Sticks, little sticks, were flying about—thick: they were whizzing before my nose, dropping below me, striking behind me against my pilot-house. All this time the river, the shore, the woods, were very quiet—perfectly quiet. I could only hear the heavy splashing thump of the stern-wheel and the patter of these things. We cleared the snag clumsily. Arrows, by Jove! We were being shot at! I stepped in quickly to close the shutter on the landside. That fool-helmsman, his hands on the spokes, was lifting his knees high, stamping his feet, champing his mouth, like a reined-in horse. Confound him! And we were staggering within ten feet of the bank. I had to lean right out to swing the heavy shutter, and I saw a face amongst the leaves on the level with my own, looking at me very fierce and steady; and then suddenly, as though a veil had been removed from my eyes, I made out, deep in the tangled gloom, naked breasts, arms, legs, glaring eyes,—the bush was swarming with human limbs in movement, glistening, of bronze colour. The twigs shook, swayed, and rustled, the arrows flew out of them, and then the shutter came to. 'Steer her straight,' I said to the helmsman. He held his head rigid, face forward; but his eyes rolled, he kept on lifting and setting down his feet gently, his mouth foamed a little. 'Keep quiet!' I said in a fury. I might just as well have ordered a tree not to sway in the wind. I darted out. Below me there was a great scuffle of feet on the iron deck; confused exclamations; a voice screamed, 'Can you turn back?' I caught sight of a V-shaped ripple on the water ahead. What? Another snag! A fusillade burst out under my feet. The pilgrims had opened with their Winchesters, and were simply squirting lead into that bush. A deuce of a lot of smoke came up and drove slowly forward. I swore at it. Now I couldn't see the ripple or the snag either. I stood in the doorway, peering, and the arrows came in swarms. They might have been poisoned, but they looked as though they wouldn't kill a cat. The bush began to howl. Our wood-cutters raised a warlike whoop; the report of a rifle just at my back deafened me. I glanced over my shoulder, and the pilot-house was yet full of noise and smoke when I made a dash at the wheel. The fool-nigger had dropped everything, to throw the shutter open and let off that Martini-Henry. He stood before the wide opening, glaring, and I yelled at him to come back, while I straightened the sudden twist out of that steamboat. There was no room to turn even if I had wanted to, the snag was somewhere very near ahead in that confounded smoke, there was no time to lose, so I just crowded her into the bank—right into the bank, where I knew the water was deep.

"We tore slowly along the overhanging bushes in a whirl of broken twigs and flying leaves. The fusillade below stopped short, as I had foreseen it would when the squirts got empty. I threw my head back to a glinting whizz that traversed the pilot-house, in at one shutter-hole and out at the other. Looking past that mad helmsman, who was shaking the empty rifle and yelling at the shore, I saw vague forms of men running bent double, leaping, gliding, distinct, incomplete, evanescent. Something big appeared in the air before the shutter, the rifle went overboard, and the man stepped back swiftly, looked at me over his shoulder in an extraordinary, profound, familiar manner, and fell upon my feet. The side of his head hit the wheel twice, and the end of what appeared a long cane clattered round and knocked over a little camp-stool. It looked as though after wrenching that thing from somebody ashore he had lost his balance in the effort. The thin smoke had blown away, we were clear of the snag, and looking ahead I could see that in another hundred yards or so I would be free to sheer off, away from the bank; but my feet felt so very warm and wet that I had to look down. The man had rolled on his back and stared straight up at me; both his hands clutched that cane. It was the shaft of a spear that, either thrown or lunged through the opening, had caught him in the side just below the ribs; the blade had gone in out of sight, after making a frightful gash; my shoes were full; a pool of blood lay very still, gleaming dark-red under the wheel; his eyes shone with an amazing lustre. The fusillade burst out again. He looked at me anxiously, gripping the spear like something precious, with an air of being afraid I would try to take it away from him. I had to make an effort to free my eyes from his gaze and attend to the steering. With one hand I felt above my head for the line of the steam-whistle, and jerked out screech after screech hurriedly. The tumult of angry and warlike yells was checked instantly, and then from the depths of the woods went out such a tremulous and prolonged wail of mournful fear and utter despair as may be imagined to follow the flight of the last hope from the earth. There was a great commotion in the bush; the shower of arrows stopped, a few dropping shots rang out sharply—then silence, in which the languid beat of the stern-wheel came plainly to my ears. I put the helm hard a-starboard at the moment when the pilgrim in pink pyjamas, very hot and agitated, appeared in the doorway. 'The manager sends me——' he began in an official tone, and stopped short. 'Good God!' he said, glaring at the wounded man.

"We two whites stood over him, and his lustrous and inquiring glance enveloped us both. I declare it looked as though he would presently put to us some question in an understandable language; but he died without uttering a sound, without moving a limb, without twitching a muscle. Only in the very last moment, as though in response to some sign we could not see, to some whisper we could not hear, he frowned heavily, and that frown gave to his black death-mask an inconceivably sombre, brooding, and menacing expression. The lustre of inquiring glance faded swiftly into vacant glassiness. 'Can you steer?' I asked the agent eagerly. He looked very dubious; but I made a grab at his arm, and he understood at once I meant him to steer whether or no. To tell you the truth, I was morbidly anxious to change my shoes and socks. 'He is dead,' murmured the fellow, immensely impressed. 'No doubt about it,' said I, tugging like mad at the shoe-laces. 'And, by the way, I suppose Mr Kurtz is dead as well by this time.'

"For the moment that was the dominant thought. There was a sense of extreme disappointment, as though I had found out I had been striving after something altogether without a substance. I couldn't have been more disgusted if I had travelled all this way for the sole purpose of talking with Mr Kurtz. Talking with. . . . I flung one shoe overboard, and became aware that that was exactly what I had been looking forward to—a talk with Kurtz. I made the strange discovery that I had never imagined him as doing, you know, but as discoursing. I didn't say to myself, 'Now I will never see him,' or 'Now I will never shake him by the hand,' but, 'Now I will never hear him.' The man presented himself as a voice. Not of course that I did not connect him with some sort of action. Hadn't I been told in all the tones of jealousy and admiration that he had collected, bartered, swindled, or stolen more ivory than all the other agents together. That was not the point. The point was in his being a gifted creature, and that of all his gifts the one that stood out pre-eminently, that carried with it a sense of real presence, was his ability to talk, his words—the gift of expression, the bewildering, the illuminating, the most exalted and the most contemptible, the pulsating stream of light, or the deceitful flow from the heart of an impenetrable darkness.

"The other shoe went flying unto the devil-god of that river. I thought, By Jove! it's all over. We are too late; he has vanished—the gift has vanished, by means of some spear, arrow, or club. I will never hear that chap speak after all,—and my sorrow had a startling extravagance of emotion, even such as I had noticed in the howling sorrow of these savages in the bush. I couldn't have felt more of lonely desolation somehow, had I been robbed of a belief or had missed my destiny in life. . . . Why do you sigh in this beastly way, somebody? Absurd? Well, absurd. Good Lord! mustn't a man ever—— Here, give me some tobacco." . . .

There was a pause of profound stillness, then a match flared, and Marlow's lean face appeared, worn, hollow, with downward folds and dropped eyelids, with an aspect of concentrated attention; and as he took vigorous draws at his pipe, it seemed to retreat and advance out of the night in the regular flicker of the tiny flame. The match went out.

"Absurd!" he cried. "This is the worst of trying to tell. . . . Here you all are, each moored with two good addresses, like a hulk with two anchors, a butcher round one corner, a policeman round another, excellent appetites, and temperature normal—you hear—normal from year's end to year's end. And you say, Absurd! Absurd be—exploded! Absurd! My dear boys, what can you expect from a man who out of sheer nervousness had just flung overboard a pair of new shoes. Now I think of it, it is amazing I did not shed tears. I am, upon the whole, proud of my fortitude. I was cut to the quick at the idea of having lost the inestimable privilege of listening to the gifted Kurtz. Of course I was wrong. The privilege was waiting for me. Oh yes, I heard more than enough. And I was right, too. A voice. He was very little more than a voice. And I heard—him—it—this voice—other voices—all of them were so little more than voices—and the memory of that time itself lingers around me, impalpable, like a dying vibration of one immense jabber, silly, atrocious, sordid, savage, or simply mean, without any kind of sense. Voices, voices—even the girl herself—now——"

He was silent for a long time.

"I laid the ghost of his gifts at last with a lie," he began suddenly. "Girl! What? Did I mention a girl? Oh, she is out of it—completely. They—the women I mean—are out of it—should be out of it. We must help them to stay in that beautiful world of their own, lest ours gets worse. Oh, she had to be out of it. You should have heard the disinterred body of Mr Kurtz saying, 'My Intended.' You would have perceived directly then how completely she was out of it. And the lofty frontal bone of Mr Kurtz! They say the hair goes on growing sometimes, but this—ah—specimen, was impressively bald. The wilderness had patted him on the head, and, behold, it was like a ball—an ivory ball; it had caressed him, and—lo!—he had withered; it had taken him, loved him, embraced him, got into his veins, consumed his flesh, and sealed his soul to its own by the inconceivable ceremonies of some devilish initiation. He was its spoiled and pampered favourite. Ivory? I should think so. Heaps of it, stacks of it. The old mud shanty was bursting with it. You would think there was not a single tusk left either above or below the ground in the whole country. 'Mostly fossil,' the manager had remarked disparagingly. It was no more fossil than I am; but they call it fossil when it is dug up. It appears these niggers do bury the tusks sometimes—but evidently they couldn't bury this parcel deep enough to save the gifted Mr Kurtz from his fate. We filled the steamboat with it, and had to pile a lot on the deck. Thus he could see and enjoy as long as he could see, because the appreciation of this favour had remained with him to the last. You should have heard him say, 'My ivory.' Oh yes, I heard him. 'My Intended, my ivory, my station, my river, my——' everything belonged to him. It made me hold my breath in expectation of hearing the wilderness burst into a prodigious peal of laughter that would shake the fixed stars in their places. Everything belonged to him—but that was a trifle. The thing was to know what he belonged to, how many powers of darkness claimed him for their own. That was the reflection that made you creepy all over. It was impossible—it was not good for one either—trying to imagine. He had taken a high seat amongst the devils of the land—I mean literally. You can't understand. How could you?—with solid pavement under your feet, surrounded by kind neighbours ready to cheer you or to fall on you, stepping delicately between the butcher and the policeman, in the holy terror of scandal and gallows and lunatic asylums—how can you imagine what particular region of the first ages a man's untrammelled feet may take him into by the way of solitude—utter solitude without a policeman—by the way of silence—utter silence, where no warning voice of a kind neighbour can be heard whispering of public opinion? These little things make all the great difference. When they are gone you must fall back upon your own innate strength, upon your own capacity for faithfulness. Of course you may be too much of a fool to go wrong—too dull even to know you are being assaulted by the powers of darkness. I take it, no fool ever made a bargain for his soul with the devil: the fool is too much of a fool, or the devil too much of a devil—I don't know which. Or you may be such a thunderingly exalted creature as to be altogether deaf and blind to anything but heavenly sights and sounds. Then the earth for you is only a standing place—and whether to be like this is your loss or your gain I won't pretend to say. But most of us are neither one nor the other. The earth for us is a place to live in, where we must put up with sights, with sounds, with smells too, by Jove!—breathe dead hippo, so to speak, and not be contaminated. And there, don't you see? your strength comes in, the faith in your ability for the digging of unostentatious holes to bury the stuff in—your power of devotion, not to yourself, but to an obscure, back-breaking business. And that's difficult enough. Mind, I am not trying to excuse or even explain—I am trying to account to myself for—for—Mr Kurtz—for the shade of Mr Kurtz. This initiated wraith from the back of Nowhere honoured me with its amazing confidence before it vanished altogether. This was because it could speak English to me. The original Kurtz had been educated partly in England, and—as he was good enough to say himself—his sympathies were in the right place. His mother was half-English, his father was half-French. All Europe contributed to the making of Kurtz; and by-and-by I learned that, most appropriately, the International Society for the Suppression of Savage Customs had intrusted him with the making of a report, for its future guidance. And he had written it too. I've seen it. I've read it. It was eloquent, vibrating with eloquence, but too high-strung, I think. Seventeen pages of close writing he had found time for! But this must have been before his—let us say—nerves, went wrong, and caused him to preside at certain midnight dances ending with unspeakable rites, which—as far as I reluctantly gathered from what I heard at various times—were offered up to him—do you understand?—to Mr Kurtz himself. But it was a beautiful piece of writing. The opening paragraph, however, in the light of later information, strikes me now as ominous. He began with the argument that we whites, from the point of development we had arrived at, 'must necessarily appear to them [savages] in the nature of supernatural beings—we approach them with the might as of a deity,' and so on, and so on. 'By the simple exercise of our will we can exert a power for good practically unbounded,' etc., etc. From that point he soared and took me with him. The peroration was magnificent, though difficult to remember, you know. It gave me the notion of an exotic Immensity ruled by an august Benevolence. It made me tingle with enthusiasm. This was the unbounded power of eloquence—of words—of burning noble words. There were no practical hints to interrupt the magic current of phrases, unless a kind of note at the foot of the last page, scrawled evidently much later, in an unsteady hand, may be regarded as the exposition of a method. It was very simple, and at the end of that moving appeal to every altruistic sentiment it blazed at you, luminous and terrifying, like a flash of lightning in a serene sky: 'Exterminate all the brutes!' The curious part was that he had apparently forgotten all about that valuable postscriptum, because, later on, when he in a sense came to himself, he repeatedly entreated me to take good care of 'my pamphlet' (he called it), as it was sure to have in the future a good influence upon his career. I had full information about all these things, and, besides, as it turned out, I was to have the care of his memory. I've done enough for it to give me the indisputable right to lay it, if I choose, for an everlasting rest in the dust-bin of progress, amongst all the sweepings and, figuratively speaking, all the dead cats of civilisation. But then, you see, I can't choose. He won't be forgotten. Whatever he was, he was not common. He had the power to charm or frighten rudimentary souls into an aggravated witch-dance in his honour; he could also fill the small souls of the pilgrims with bitter misgivings: he had one devoted friend at least, and he had conquered one soul in the world that was neither rudimentary nor tainted with self-seeking. No; I can't forget him, though I am not prepared to affirm the fellow was exactly worth the life we lost in getting to him. I missed my late helmsman awfully,—I missed him even while his body was still lying in the pilot-house. Perhaps you will think it passing strange this regret for a savage who was no more account than a grain of sand in a black Sahara. Well, don't you see, he had done something, he had steered; for months I had him at my back—a help—an instrument. It was a kind of partnership. He steered for me—I had to look after him, I worried about his deficiencies, and thus a subtle bond had been created, of which I only became aware when it was suddenly broken. And the intimate profundity of that look he gave me when he received his hurt remains to this day in my memory—like a claim of distant kinship affirmed in a supreme moment.

"Poor fool! If he had only left that shutter alone. He had no restraint, no restraint—just like Kurtz—a tree swayed by the wind. As soon as I had put on a dry pair of slippers, I dragged him out, after first jerking the spear out of his side, which operation I confess I performed with my eyes shut tight. His heels leaped together over the little doorstep; his shoulders were pressed to my breast; I hugged him from behind desperately. Oh! he was heavy, heavy; heavier than any man on earth, I should imagine. Then without more ado I tipped him overboard. The current snatched him as though he had been a wisp of grass, and I saw the body roll over twice before I lost sight of it for ever. All the pilgrims and the manager were then congregated on the awning-deck about the pilot-house, chattering at each other like a flock of excited magpies, and there was a scandalised murmur at my heartless promptitude. What they wanted to keep that body hanging about for I can't guess. Embalm it, maybe. But I had also heard another, and a very ominous, murmur on the deck below. My friends the wood-cutters were likewise scandalised, and with a better show of reason—though I admit that the reason itself was quite inadmissible. Oh, quite! I had made up my mind that if my late helmsman was to be eaten, the fishes alone should have him. He had been a very second-rate helmsman while alive, but now he was dead he might have become a first-class temptation, and possibly cause some startling trouble. Besides, I was anxious to take the wheel, the man in pink pyjamas showing himself a hopeless duffer at the business.

"This I did directly the simple funeral was over. We were going half-speed, keeping right in the middle of the stream, and I listened to the talk about me. They had given up Kurtz, they had given up the station; Kurtz was dead, and the station had been burnt—and so on—and so on. The red-haired pilgrim was beside himself with the thought that at least this poor Kurtz had been properly revenged. 'Say! We must have made a glorious slaughter of them in the bush. Eh? What do you think? Say?' He positively danced, the bloodthirsty little gingery beggar. And he had nearly fainted when he saw the wounded man! I could not help saying, 'You made a glorious lot of smoke, anyhow.' I had seen, from the way the tops of the bushes rustled and flew, that almost all the shots had gone too high. You can't hit anything unless you take aim and fire from the shoulder; but these chaps fired from the hip with their eyes shut. The retreat, I maintained—and I was right—was caused by the screeching of the steam-whistle. Upon this they forgot Kurtz, and began to howl at me with indignant protests.

"The manager stood by the wheel murmuring confidentially about the necessity of getting well away down the river before dark at all events, when I saw in the distance a clearing on the river-side and the outlines of some sort of building. 'What's this?' I asked. He clapped his hands in wonder. 'The station!' he cried. I edged in at once, still going half-speed.

"Through my glasses I saw the slope of a hill interspersed with rare trees and perfectly free from undergrowth. A long decaying building on the summit was half buried in the high grass; the large holes in the peaked roof gaped black from afar; the jungle and the woods made a background. There was no enclosure or fence of any kind; but there had been one apparently, for near the house half-a-dozen slim posts remained in a row, roughly trimmed, and with their upper ends ornamented with round carved balls. The rails, or whatever there had been between, had disappeared. Of course the forest surrounded all that. The river-bank was clear, and on the water-side I saw a white man under a hat like a cart-wheel beckoning persistently with his whole arm. Examining the edge of the forest above and below, I was almost certain I could see movements—human forms gliding here and there. I steamed past prudently, then stopped the engines and let her drift down. The man on the shore began to shout, urging us to land. 'We have been attacked,' screamed the manager. 'I know—I know. It's all right,' yelled back the other, as cheerful as you please. 'Come along. It's all right. I am glad.'

"His aspect reminded me of something I had seen—something funny I had seen somewhere. As I manœuvred to get alongside, I was asking myself, 'What does this fellow look like?' Suddenly I got it. He looked like a harlequin. His clothes had been made of some stuff that was brown holland probably, but it was covered with patches all over, with bright patches, blue, red, and yellow,—patches on the back, patches on front, patches on elbows, on knees; coloured binding round his jacket, scarlet edging at the bottom of his trousers; and the sunshine made him look extremely gay and wonderfully neat withal, because you could see how beautifully all this patching had been done. A beardless, boyish face, very fair, no features to speak of, nose peeling, little blue eyes, smiles and frowns chasing each other over that open countenance like sunshine and shadow on a wind-swept plain. 'Look out, captain!' he cried; 'there's a snag lodged in here last night.' What! Another snag? I confess I swore shamefully. I had nearly holed my cripple, to finish off that charming trip. The harlequin on the bank turned his little pug nose up to me. 'You English?' he asked, all smiles. 'Are you?' I shouted from the wheel. The smiles vanished, and he shook his head as if sorry for my disappointment. Then he brightened up. 'Never mind!' he cried encouragingly. 'Are we in time?' I asked. 'He is up there,' he replied, with a toss of the head up the hill, and becoming gloomy all of a sudden. His face was like the autumn sky, overcast one moment and bright the next.

"When the manager, escorted by the pilgrims, all of them armed to the teeth, had gone to the house, this chap came on board. 'I say, I don't like this. These natives are in the bush,' I said. He assured me earnestly it was all right. 'They are simple people,' he added; 'well, I am glad you came. It took me all my time to keep them off.' 'But you said it was all right,' I cried. 'Oh, they meant no harm,' he said; and as I stared he corrected himself, 'Not exactly.' Then vivaciously, 'My faith, your pilot-house wants a clean up!' In the next breath he advised me to keep enough steam on the boiler to blow the whistle in case of any trouble. 'One good screech will do more for you than all your rifles. They are simple people,' he repeated. He rattled away at such a rate he quite overwhelmed me. He seemed to be trying to make up for lots of silence, and actually hinted, laughing, that such was the case. 'Don't you talk with Mr Kurtz?' I said. 'You don't talk with that man—you listen to him,' he exclaimed with severe exaltation. 'But now——' He waved his arm, and in the twinkling of an eye was in the uttermost depths of despondency. In a moment he came up again with a jump, possessed himself of both my hands, shook them continuously, while he gabbled: 'Brother sailor . . . honour . . . pleasure . . . delight . . . introduce myself . . . Russian . . . son of an arch-priest . . . Government of Tambov . . . What? Tobacco? English tobacco; the excellent English tobacco! Now, that's brotherly. Smoke? Where's a sailor that does not smoke?'

"The pipe soothed him, and gradually I made out he had run away from school, had gone to sea in a Russian ship; ran away again; served some time in English ships; was now reconciled with the arch-priest. He made a point of that. 'But when one is young one must see things, gather experience, ideas; enlarge the mind.' 'Here!' I interrupted. 'You can never tell! Here I have met Mr Kurtz,' he said, youthfully solemn and reproachful. I held my tongue after that. It appears he had persuaded a Dutch trading-house on the coast to fit him out with stores and goods, and had started for the interior with a light heart, and no more idea of what would happen to him than a baby. He had been wandering about that river for nearly two years alone, cut off from everybody and everything. 'I am not so young as I look. I am twenty-five,' he said. 'At first old Van Shuyten would tell me to go to the devil,' he narrated with keen enjoyment; 'but I stuck to him, and talked and talked, till at last he got afraid I would talk the hind-leg off his favourite dog, so he gave me some cheap things and a few guns, and told me he hoped he would never see my face again. Good old Dutchman, Van Shuyten. I've sent him one small lot of ivory a year ago, so that he can't call me a little thief when I get back. I hope he got it. And for the rest I don't care. I had some wood stacked for you. That was my old house. Did you see?'

"I gave him Towson's book. He made as though he would kiss me, but restrained himself. 'The only book I had left, and I thought I had lost it,' he said, looking at it ecstatically. 'So many accidents happen to a man going about alone, you know. Canoes get upset sometimes—and sometimes you've got to clear out so quick when the people get angry.' He thumbed the pages. 'You made notes in Russian?' I asked. He nodded. 'I thought they were written in cipher,' I said. He laughed, then became serious. 'I had lots of trouble to keep these people off,' he said. 'Did they want to kill you?' I asked. 'Oh no!' he cried, and checked himself. 'Why did they attack us?' I pursued. He hesitated, then said shamefacedly, 'they don't want him to go.' 'Don't they?' I said, curiously. He nodded a nod full of mystery and wisdom. 'I tell you,' he cried, 'this man has enlarged my mind.' He opened his arms wide, staring at me with his little blue eyes that were perfectly round."

III

"I looked at him, lost in astonishment. There he was before me, in motley, as though he had absconded from a troupe of mimes, enthusiastic, fabulous. His very existence was improbable, inexplicable, and altogether bewildering. He was an insoluble problem. It was inconceivable how he had existed, how he had succeeded in getting so far, how he had managed to remain—why he did not instantly disappear. 'I went a little farther,' he said, 'then still a little farther—till I had gone so far that I don't know how I'll ever get back. Never mind. Plenty time. I can manage. You take Kurtz away quick—quick—I tell you.' The glamour of youth enveloped his particoloured rags, his destitution, his loneliness, the essential desolation of his futile wanderings. For months—for years—his life hadn't been worth a day's purchase; and there he was gallantly, thoughtlessly alive, to all appearance indestructible solely by the virtue of his few years and of his unreflecting audacity. I was seduced into something like admiration—like envy. Glamour urged him on, glamour kept him unscathed. He surely wanted nothing from the wilderness but space to breathe in and to push on through. His need was to exist, and to move onwards at the greatest possible risk, and with a maximum of privation. If the absolutely pure, uncalculating, unpractical spirit of adventure had ever ruled a human being, it ruled this be-patched youth. I almost envied him the possession of this modest and clear flame. It seemed to have consumed all thought of self so completely, that, even while he was talking to you, you forgot that it was he—the man before your eyes—who had gone through these things. I did not envy him his devotion to Kurtz, though. He had not meditated over it. It came to him, and he accepted it with a sort of eager fatalism. I must say that to me it appeared about the most dangerous thing in every way he had come upon so far.

"They had come together unavoidably, like two ships becalmed near each other, and lay rubbing sides at last. I suppose Kurtz wanted an audience, because on a certain occasion, when encamped in the forest, they had talked all night, or more probably Kurtz had talked. 'We talked of everything,' he said, quite transported at the recollection. 'I forgot there was such a thing as sleep. The night did not seem to last an hour. Everything! Everything! . . . Of love too.' 'Ah, he talked to you of love!' I said, much amused. 'It isn't what you think,' he cried, almost passionately. 'It was in general. He made me see things—things.'

"He threw his arms up. We were on deck at the time, and the headman of my wood-cutters, lounging near by, turned upon him his heavy and glittering eyes. I looked around, and I don't know why, but I assure you that never, never before, did this land, this river, this jungle, the very arch of this blazing sky, appear to me so hopeless and so dark, so impenetrable to human thought, so pitiless to human weakness. 'And, ever since, you have been with him, of course?' I said.

"On the contrary. It appears their intercourse had been very much broken by various causes. He had, as he informed me proudly, managed to nurse Kurtz through two illnesses (he alluded to it as you would to some risky feat), but as a rule Kurtz wandered alone, far in the depths of the forest. 'Very often coming to this station, I had to wait days and days before he would turn up,' he said. 'Ah, it was worth waiting for!—sometimes.' 'What was he doing? exploring or what?' I asked. 'Oh yes, of course'; he had discovered lots of villages, a lake too—he did not know exactly in what direction; it was dangerous to inquire too much—but mostly his expeditions had been for ivory. 'But he had no goods to trade with by that time,' I objected. 'There's a good lot of cartridges left even yet,' he answered, looking away. 'To speak plainly, he raided the country,' I said. He nodded. 'Not alone, surely!' He muttered something about the villages round that lake. 'Kurtz got the tribe to follow him did he?' I suggested. He fidgeted a little. 'They adored him,' he said. The tone of these words was so extraordinary that I looked at him searchingly. It was curious to see his mingled eagerness and reluctance to speak of Kurtz. The man filled his life, occupied his thoughts, swayed his emotions. 'What can you expect?' he burst out; 'he came to them with thunder and lightning, you know—and they had never seen anything like it—and very terrible. He could be very terrible. You can't judge Mr Kurtz as you would an ordinary man. No, no, no! Now—just to give you an idea—I don't mind telling you, he wanted to shoot me too one day—but I don't judge him.' 'Shoot you!' I cried. 'What for?' 'Well, I had a small lot of ivory the chief of that village near my house gave me. You see I used to shoot game for them. Well, he wanted it, and wouldn't hear reason. He declared he would shoot me unless I gave him the ivory and then cleared out of the country, because he could do so, and had a fancy for it, and there was nothing on earth to prevent him killing whom he jolly well pleased. And it was true too. I gave him the ivory. What did I care! But I didn't clear out. No, no. I couldn't leave him. I had to be careful, of course, till we got friendly again for a time. He had his second illness then. Afterwards I had to keep out of the way; but I didn't mind. He was living for the most part in those villages on the lake. When he came down to the river, sometimes he would take to me, and sometimes it was better for me to be careful. This man suffered too much. He hated all this, and somehow he couldn't get away. When I had a chance I begged him to try and leave while there was time; I offered to go back with him. And he would say yes, and then he would remain; go off on another ivory hunt; disappear for weeks; forget himself amongst these people—forget himself—you know.' 'Why! he's mad,' I said. He protested indignantly. Mr Kurtz couldn't be mad. If I had heard him talk, only two days ago, I wouldn't dare hint at such a thing. . . . I had taken up my binoculars while we talked, and was looking at the shore, sweeping the limit of the forest at each side and at the back of the house. The consciousness of there being people in that bush, so silent, so quiet—as silent and quiet as the ruined house on the hill—made me uneasy. There was no sign on the face of nature of this amazing tale that was not so much told as suggested to me in desolate exclamations, completed by shrugs, in interrupted phrases, in hints ending in deep sighs. The woods were unmoved, like a mask—heavy, like the closed door of a prison—they looked with their air of hidden knowledge, of patient expectation, of unapproachable silence. The Russian was explaining to me that it was only lately that Mr Kurtz had come down to the river, bringing along with him all the fighting men of that lake tribe. He had been absent for several months—getting himself adored, I suppose—and had come down unexpectedly, with the intention to all appearance of making a raid either across the river or down stream. Evidently the appetite for more ivory had got the better of the—what shall I say?—less material aspirations. However he had got much worse suddenly. 'I heard he was lying helpless, and so I came up—took my chance,' said the Russian. 'Oh, he is bad, very bad.' I directed my glass to the house. There were no signs of life, but there was the ruined roof, the long mud wall peeping above the grass, with three little square window-holes, no two of the same size; all this brought within reach of my hand, as it were. And then I made a brusque movement, and one of the remaining posts of that vanished fence leaped up in the field of my glass. You remember I told you I had been struck at the distance by certain attempts at ornamentation, rather remarkable in the ruinous aspect of the place. Now I had suddenly a nearer view, and its first result was to make me throw my head back as if before a blow. Then I went carefully from post to post with my glass, and I saw my mistake. These round knobs were not ornamental but symbolic; they were expressive and puzzling, striking and disturbing—food for thought and also for the vultures if there had been any looking down from the sky; but at all events for such ants as were industrious enough to ascend the pole. They would have been even more impressive, those heads on the stakes, if their faces had not been turned to the house. Only one, the first I had made out, was facing my way. I was not so shocked as you may think. The start back I had given was really nothing but a movement of surprise. I had expected to see a knob of wood there, you know. I returned deliberately to the first I had seen—and there it was, black, dried, sunken, with closed eyelids,—a head that seemed to sleep at the top of that pole, and, with the shrunken dry lips showing a narrow white line of the teeth, was smiling too, smiling continuously at some endless and jocose dream of that eternal slumber.

"I am not disclosing any trade secrets. In fact the manager said afterwards that Mr Kurtz's methods had ruined the district. I have no opinion on that point, but I want you clearly to understand that there was nothing exactly profitable in these heads being there. They only showed that Mr Kurtz lacked restraint in the gratification of his various lusts, that there was something wanting in him—some small matter which, when the pressing need arose, could not be found under his magnificent eloquence. Whether he knew of this deficiency himself I can't say. I think the knowledge came to him at last—only at the very last. But the wilderness had found him out early, and had taken on him a terrible vengeance for the fantastic invasion. I think it had whispered to him things about himself which he did not know, things of which he had no conception till he took counsel with this great solitude—and the whisper had proved irresistibly fascinating. It echoed loudly within him because he was hollow at the core. . . . I put down the glass, and the head that had appeared near enough to be spoken to seemed at once to have leaped away from me into inaccessible distance.

"The admirer of Mr Kurtz was a bit crestfallen. In a hurried, indistinct voice he began to assure me he had not dared to take these—say, symbols—down. He was not afraid of the natives; they would not stir till Mr Kurtz gave the word. His ascendancy was extraordinary. The camps of these people surrounded the place, and the chiefs came every day to see him. They would crawl. . . . 'I don't want to know anything of the ceremonies used when approaching Mr Kurtz,' I shouted. Curious, this feeling that came over me that such details would be more intolerable than those heads drying on the stakes under Mr Kurtz's windows. After all, that was only a savage sight, while I seemed at one bound to have been transported into some lightless region of subtle horrors, where pure, uncomplicated savagery was a positive relief, being something that had a right to exist—obviously—in the sunshine. The young man looked at me with surprise. I suppose it did not occur to him Mr Kurtz was no idol of mine. He forgot I hadn't heard any of these splendid monologues on, what was it? on love, justice, conduct of life—or what not. If it had come to crawling before Mr Kurtz, he crawled as much as the veriest savage of them all. I had no idea of the conditions, he said: these heads were the heads of rebels. I shocked him excessively by laughing. Rebels! What would be the next definition I was to hear? There had been enemies, criminals, workers—and these were rebels. Those rebellious heads looked very subdued to me on their sticks. 'You don't know how such a life tries a man like Kurtz,' cried Kurtz's last disciple. 'Well, and you?' I said. 'I! I! I am a simple man. I have no great thoughts. I want nothing from anybody. How can you compare me to . . . ?' His feelings were too much for speech, and suddenly he broke down. 'I don't understand,' he groaned. 'I've been doing my best to keep him alive, and that's enough. I had no hand in all this. I have no abilities. There hasn't been a drop of medicine or a mouthful of invalid food for months here. He was shamefully abandoned. A man like this, with such ideas. Shamefully! Shamefully! I—I—haven't slept for the last ten nights. . . .'

"His voice lost itself in the calm of the evening. The long shadows of the forest had slipped down-hill while we talked, had gone far beyond the ruined hovel, beyond the symbolic row of stakes. All this was in the gloom, while we down there were yet in the sunshine, and the stretch of the river abreast of the clearing glittered in a still and dazzling splendour, with a murky and overshadowed bend above and below. Not a living soul was seen on the shore. The bushes did not rustle.

"Suddenly round the corner of the house a group of men appeared, as though they had come up from the ground. They waded waist-deep in the grass, in a compact body, bearing an improvised stretcher in their midst. Instantly, in the emptiness of the landscape, a cry arose whose shrillness pierced the still air like a sharp arrow flying straight to the very heart of the land; and, as if by enchantment, streams of human beings—of naked human beings—with spears in their hands, with bows, with shields, with wild glances and savage movements, were poured into the clearing by the dark-faced and pensive forest. The bushes shook, the grass swayed for a time, and then everything stood still in attentive immobility.

"'Now, if he does not say the right thing to them we are all done for,' said the Russian at my elbow. The knot of men with the stretcher had stopped too, half-way to the steamer, as if petrified. I saw the man on the stretcher sit up, lank and with an uplifted arm, above the shoulders of the bearers. 'Let us hope that the man who can talk so well of love in general will find some particular reason to spare us this time,' I said. I resented bitterly the absurd danger of our situation, as if to be at the mercy of that atrocious phantom had been a dishonouring necessity. I could not hear a sound, but through my glasses I saw the thin arm extended commandingly, the lower jaw moving, the eyes of that apparition shining darkly far in its bony head that nodded with grotesque jerks. Kurtz—Kurtz—that means short in German—don't it? Well, the name was as true as everything else in his life—and death. He looked at least seven feet long. His covering had fallen off, and his body emerged from it pitiful and appalling as from a winding-sheet. I could see the cage of his ribs all astir, the bones of his arm waving. It was as though an animated image of death carved out of old ivory had been shaking its hand with menaces at a motionless crowd of men made of dark and glittering bronze. I saw him open his mouth wide—it gave him a weirdly voracious aspect, as though he had wanted to swallow all the air, all the earth, all the men before him. A deep voice reached me faintly. He must have been shouting. He fell back suddenly. The stretcher shook as the bearers staggered forward again, and almost at the same time I noticed that the crowd of savages was vanishing without any perceptible movement of retreat, as if the forest that had ejected these beings so suddenly had drawn them in again as the breath is drawn in a long aspiration.

"Some of the pilgrims behind the stretcher carried his arms—two shot-guns, a heavy rifle, and a light revolver-carbine—the thunderbolts of that pitiful Jupiter. The manager bent over him murmuring as he walked beside his head. They laid him down in one of the little cabins—just a room for a bed-place and a camp-stool or two, you know. We had brought his belated correspondence, and a lot of torn envelopes and open letters littered his bed.

His hand roamed feebly amongst these papers. I was struck by the fire of his eyes and the composed languor of his expression. It was not so much the exhaustion of disease. He did not seem in pain. This shadow looked satiated and calm, as though for the moment it had had its fill of all the emotions.

"He rustled one of the letters, and looking straight in my face said, 'I am glad.' Somebody had been writing to him about me. These special recommendations were turning up again. The volume of tone he emitted without effort, almost without the trouble of moving his lips, amazed me. A voice! a voice! It was grave, profound, vibrating, while the man did not seem capable of a whisper. However, he had enough strength in him—factitious no doubt—to very nearly make an end of us, as you shall hear directly.

"The manager appeared silently in the doorway; I stepped out at once and he drew the curtain after me. The Russian, eyed curiously by the pilgrims, was staring at the shore. I followed the direction of his glance.

"Dark human shapes could be made out in the distance, flitting indistinctly against the gloomy border of the forest, and near the river two bronze figures, leaning on tall spears, stood in the sunlight under fantastic head-dresses of spotted skins, warlike and still in statuesque repose. And from right to left along the lighted shore moved a wild and gorgeous apparition of a woman.

"She walked with measured steps, draped in striped and fringed cloths, treading the earth proudly, with a slight jingle and flash of barbarous ornaments. She carried her head high; her hair was done in the shape of a helmet; she had brass leggings to the knee, brass wire gauntlets to the elbow, a crimson spot on her tawny cheek, innumerable necklaces of glass beads on her neck; bizarre things, charms, gifts of witch-men, that hung about her, glittered and trembled at every step. She must have had the value of several elephant tusks upon her. She was savage and superb, wild-eyed and magnificent; there was something ominous and stately in her deliberate progress. And in the hush that had fallen suddenly upon the whole sorrowful land, the immense wilderness, the colossal body of the fecund and mysterious life seemed to look at her, pensive, as though it had been looking at the image of its own tenebrous and passionate soul.

"She came abreast of the steamer, stood still, and faced us. Her long shadow fell to the water's edge. Her face had a tragic and fierce aspect of wild sorrow and of dumb pain mingled with the fear of some struggling, half-shaped resolve. She stood looking at us without a stir, and like the wilderness itself, with an air of brooding over an inscrutable purpose. A whole minute passed, and then she made a step forward. There was a low jingle, a glint of yellow metal, a sway of fringed draperies, and she stopped as if her heart had failed her. The young fellow by my side growled. The pilgrims murmured at my back. She looked at us all as if her life had depended upon the unswerving steadiness of her glance. Suddenly she opened her bared arms and threw them up rigid above her head, as though in an uncontrollable desire to touch the sky, and at the same time the swift shadows darted out on the earth, swept around on the river, gathering the steamer into a shadowy embrace. A formidable silence hung over the scene.

"She turned away slowly, walked on, following the bank, and passed into the bushes to the left. Once only her eyes gleamed back at us in the dusk of the thickets before she disappeared.

"'If she had offered to come aboard I really think I would have tried to shoot her,' said the man of patches, nervously. 'I had been risking my life every day for the last fortnight to keep her out of the house. She got in one day and kicked up a row about those miserable rags I picked up in the storeroom to mend my clothes with. I wasn't decent. At least it must have been that, for she talked like a fury to Kurtz for an hour, pointing at me now and then. I don't understand the dialect of this tribe. Luckily for me, I fancy Kurtz felt too ill that day to care, or there would have been mischief. I don't understand. . . . No—it's too much for me. Ah, well, it's all over now.'

"At this moment I heard Kurtz's deep voice behind the curtain, 'Save me!—save the ivory, you mean. Don't tell me. Save *me*! Why, I've had to save you. You are interrupting my plans now. Sick! Sick! Not so sick as you would like to believe. Never mind. I'll carry my ideas out yet—I will return. I'll show you what can be done. You with your little peddling notions—you are interfering with me. I will return. I . . .'

"The manager came out. He did me the honour to take me under the arm and lead me aside. 'He is very low, very low,' he said. He considered it necessary to sigh, but neglected to be consistently sorrowful. 'We have done all we could for him—haven't we? But there is no disguising the fact, Mr Kurtz has done more harm than good to the Company. He did not see the time was not ripe for vigorous action. Cautiously, cautiously—that's my principle. We must be cautious yet. The district is closed to us for a time. Deplorable! Upon the whole, the trade will suffer. I don't deny there is a remarkable quantity of ivory—mostly fossil. We must save it, at all events—but look how precarious the position is—and why? Because the method is unsound.' 'Do you,' said I, looking at the shore, 'call it "unsound method"?' 'Without doubt,' he exclaimed, hotly. 'Don't you?' . . . 'No method at all,' I murmured after a while. 'Exactly,' he exulted. 'I anticipated this. Shows a complete want of judgment. It is my duty to point it out in the proper quarter.' 'Oh,' said I, 'that fellow—what's his name?—the brickmaker, will make a readable report for you.' He appeared confounded for a moment. It seemed to me I had never breathed an atmosphere so vile, and I turned mentally to Kurtz for relief—positively for relief. 'Nevertheless I think Mr Kurtz is a remarkable man,' I said with emphasis. He started, dropped on me a cold heavy glance, said very quietly, 'He *was,*' and turned his back on me. My hour of favour was over; I found myself lumped along with Kurtz as a partisan of methods for which the time was not ripe: I was unsound! Ah! but it was something to have at least a choice of nightmares.

"I had turned to the wilderness really, not to Mr Kurtz, who, I was ready to admit, was as good as buried. And for a moment it seemed to me as if I also were buried in a vast grave full of unspeakable secrets. I felt an intolerable weight oppressing my breast, the smell of the damp earth, the unseen presence of victorious corruption, the darkness of an impenetrable night. . . . The Russian tapped me on the shoulder. I heard him mumbling and stammering something about 'brother seaman—couldn't conceal—knowledge of matters that would affect Mr Kurtz's reputation.' I waited. For him evidently Mr Kurtz was not in his grave; I suspect that for him Mr Kurtz was one of the immortals. 'Well!' said I at last, 'speak out. As it happens, I am Mr Kurtz's friend—in a way.'

"He stated with a good deal of formality that had we not been 'of the same profession,' he would have kept the matter to himself without regard to consequences. 'He suspected there was an active ill-will towards him on the part of these white men that——' 'You are right,' I said, remembering a certain conversation I had overheard. 'The manager thinks you ought to be hanged.' He showed a concern at this intelligence which amused me at first. 'I had better get out of the way quietly,' he said, earnestly. 'I can do no more for Kurtz now, and they would soon find some excuse. What's to stop them? There's a military post three hundred miles from here.' 'Well, upon my word,' said I, 'perhaps you had better go if you have any friends amongst the savages near by.' 'Plenty,' he said. 'They are simple people—and I want nothing, you know.' He stood biting his lip, then: 'I don't want any harm to happen to these whites here, but of course I was thinking of Mr Kurtz's reputation—but you are a brother seaman and——' 'All right,' said I, after a time. 'Mr Kurtz's reputation is safe with me.' I did not know how truly I spoke.

"He informed me, lowering his voice, that it was Kurtz who had ordered the attack to be made on the steamer. 'He hated sometimes the idea of being taken away—and then again. . . . But I don't understand these matters. I am a simple man. He thought it would scare you away—that you would give it up, thinking him dead. I could not stop him. Oh, I had an awful time of it this last month.' 'Very well,' I said. 'He is all right now.' 'Ye-e-es,' he muttered, not very convinced apparently. 'Thanks,' said I; 'I shall keep my eyes open.' 'But quiet—eh?' he urged, anxiously. 'It would be awful for his reputation if anybody here——' I promised a complete discretion with great gravity. 'I have a canoe and three black fellows waiting not very far. I am off. Could you give me a few Martini-Henry cartridges?' I could, and did, with proper secrecy. He helped himself, with a wink at me, to a handful of my tobacco. 'Between sailors—you know—good English tobacco.' At the door of the pilot-house he turned round—'I say, haven't you a pair of shoes you could spare?' He raised one leg. 'Look.' The soles were tied with knotted strings sandal-wise under his bare feet. I rooted out an old pair, at which he looked with admiration before tucking it under his left arm. One of his pockets (bright red) was bulging with cartridges, from the other (dark blue) peeped 'Towson's Inquiry,' etc., etc. He seemed to think himself excellently well equipped for a renewed encounter with the wilderness. 'Ah! I'll never, never meet such a man again. You ought to have heard him recite poetry—his own too it was, he told me. Poetry!' He rolled his eyes at the recollection of these delights. 'Oh, he enlarged my mind!' 'Good-bye,' said I. He shook hands and vanished in the night. Sometimes I ask myself whether I had ever really seen him—whether it was possible to meet such a phenomenon! . . .

'When I woke up shortly after midnight his warning came to my mind with its hint of danger that seemed, in the starred darkness, real enough to make me get up for the purpose of having a look round. On the hill a big fire burned, illuminating fitfully a crooked corner of the station-house. One of the agents with a picket of a few of our blacks, armed for the purpose, was keeping guard over the ivory; but deep within the forest, red gleams that wavered, that seemed to sink and rise from the ground amongst confused columnar shapes of intense blackness, showed the exact position of the camp where Mr Kurtz's adorers were keeping their uneasy vigil. The monotonous beating of a big drum filled the air with muffled shocks and a lingering vibration. A steady droning sound of many men chanting each to himself some weird incantation came out from the black, flat wall of the woods as the humming of bees comes out of a hive, and had a strange narcotic effect upon my half-awake senses. I believed I dozed off leaning over the rail, till an abrupt burst of yells, an overwhelming outbreak of a pent-up and mysterious frenzy, woke me up in a bewildered wonder. It was cut short all at once, and the low droning went on with an effect of audible and soothing silence. I glanced casually into the little cabin. A light was burning within, but Mr Kurtz was not there.

"I think I would have raised an outcry if I had believed my eyes. But I didn't believe them at first—the thing seemed so impossible. The fact is I was completely unnerved by a sheer blank fright, pure abstract terror, unconnected with any distinct shape of physical danger. What made this emotion so overpowering was—how shall I define it?—the moral shock I received, as if something altogether monstrous, intolerable to thought and odious to the soul, had been thrust upon me unexpectedly. This lasted of course the merest fraction of a second, and then the usual sense of commonplace, deadly danger, the possibility of a sudden onslaught and massacre, or something of the kind, which I saw impending, was positively welcome and composing. It pacified me, in fact, so much, that I did not raise an alarm.

"There was an agent buttoned up inside an ulster and sleeping on a chair on deck within three feet of me. The yells had not awakened him; he snored very slightly; I left him to his slumbers and leaped ashore. I did not betray Mr Kurtz—it was ordered I should never betray him—it was written I should be loyal to the nightmare of my choice. I was anxious to deal with this shadow by myself alone,—and to this day I don't know why I was so jealous of sharing with any one the peculiar blackness of that experience.

"As soon as I got on the bank I saw a trail—a broad trail through the grass. I remember the exultation with which I said to myself, 'He can't walk—he is crawling on all-fours—I've got him.' The grass was wet with dew. I strode rapidly with clenched fists. I fancy I had some vague notion of falling upon him and giving him a drubbing. I don't know. I had some imbecile thoughts. The knitting old woman with the cat obtruded herself upon my memory as a most improper person to be sitting at the other end of such an affair. I saw a row of pilgrims squirting lead in the air out of Winchesters held to the hip. I thought I would never get back to the steamer, and imagined myself living alone and unarmed in the woods to an advanced age. Such silly things—you know. And I remember I confounded the beat of the drum with the beating of my heart, and was pleased at its calm regularity.

"I kept to the track though—then stopped to listen. The night was very clear: a dark blue space, sparkling with dew and starlight, in which black things stood very still. I thought I could see a kind of motion ahead of me. I was strangely cocksure of everything that night. I actually left the track and ran in a wide semicircle (I verily believe chuckling to myself) so as to get in front of that stir, of that motion I had seen—if indeed I had seen anything. I was circumventing Kurtz as though it had been a boyish game.

"I came upon him, and, if he had not heard me coming, I would have fallen over him too, but he got up in time. He rose, unsteady, long, pale, indistinct, like a vapour exhaled by the earth, and swayed slightly, misty and silent before me; while at my back the fires loomed between the trees, and the murmur of many voices issued from the forest. I had cut him off cleverly; but when actually confronting him I seemed to come to my senses, I saw the danger in its right proportion. It was by no means over yet. Suppose he began to shout? Though he could hardly stand, there was still plenty of vigour in his voice. 'Go away—hide yourself,' he said, in that profound tone. It was very awful. I glanced back. We were within thirty yards from the nearest fire. A black figure stood up, strode on long black legs, waving long black arms, across the glow. It had horns—antelope horns, I think—on its head. Some sorcerer, some witch-man, no doubt: it looked fiend-like enough. 'Do you know what you are doing?' I whispered. 'Perfectly,' he answered, raising his voice for that single word: it sounded to me far off and yet loud, like a hail through a speaking-trumpet. If he makes a row we are lost, I thought to myself. This clearly was not a case for fisticuffs, even apart from the very natural aversion I had to beat that Shadow—this wandering and tormented thing. 'You will be lost,' I said—'utterly lost.' One gets sometimes such a flash of inspiration, you know. I did say the right thing, though indeed he could not have been more irretrievably lost than he was at this very moment, when the foundations of our intimacy were being laid—to endure—to endure—even to the end—even beyond.

"'I had immense plans,' he muttered irresolutely. 'Yes,' said I; 'but if you try to shout I'll smash your head with——' there was not a stick or a stone near. 'I will throttle you for good,' I corrected myself. 'I was on the threshold of great things,' he pleaded, in a voice of longing, with a wistfulness of tone that made my blood run cold. 'And now for this stupid scoundrel——' 'Your success in Europe is assured in any case,' I affirmed, steadily. I did not want to have the throttling of him, you understand—and indeed it would have been very little use for any practical purpose. I tried to break the spell—the heavy, mute spell of the wilderness—that seemed to draw him to its pitiless breast by the awakening of forgotten and brutal instincts, by the memory of gratified and monstrous passions. This alone, I was convinced, had driven him out to the edge of the forest, to the bush, towards the gleam of fires, the throb of drums, the drone of weird incantations; this alone had beguiled his unlawful soul beyond the bounds of permitted aspirations. And, don't you see, the terror of the position was not in being knocked on the head—though I had a very lively sense of that danger too—but in this, that I had to deal with a being to whom I could not appeal in the name of anything high or low. I had, even like the niggers, to invoke him—himself—his own exalted and incredible degradation. There was nothing either above or below him, and I knew it. He had kicked himself loose of the earth. Confound the man! he had kicked the very earth to pieces. He was alone, and I before him did not know whether I stood on the ground or floated in the air. I've been telling you what we said—repeating the phrases we pronounced,—but what's the good? They were common everyday words,—the familiar, vague sounds exchanged on every waking day of life. But what of that? They had behind them, to my mind, the terrific suggestiveness of words heard in dreams, of phrases spoken in nightmares. Soul! If anybody had ever struggled with a soul, I am the man. And I wasn't arguing with a lunatic either. Believe me or not, his intelligence was perfectly clear—concentrated, it is true, upon himself with horrible intensity, yet clear; and therein was my only chance—barring of course, the killing him there and then, which wasn't so good, on account of unavoidable noise. But his soul was mad. Being alone in the wilderness, it had looked within itself, and, by heavens! I tell you, it had gone mad. I had—for my sins, I suppose—to go through the ordeal of looking into it myself. No eloquence could have been so withering to one's belief in mankind as his final burst of sincerity. He struggled with himself, too. I saw it,—I heard it. I saw the inconceivable mystery of a soul that knew no restraint, no faith, and no fear, yet struggling blindly with itself. I kept my head pretty well; but when I had him at last stretched on the couch, I wiped my forehead, while my legs shook under me as though I had carried half a ton on my back down that hill. And yet I had only supported him, his bony arm clasped round my neck—and he was not much heavier than a child.

"When next day we left at noon, the crowd, of whose presence behind the curtain of trees I had been acutely conscious all the time, flowed out of the woods again, filled the clearing, covered the slope with a mass of naked, breathing, quivering, bronze bodies. I steamed up a bit, then swung down-stream, and two thousand eyes followed the evolutions of the splashing, thumping, fierce river-demon beating the water with its terrible tail and breathing black smoke into the air. In front of the first rank, along the river, three men, plastered with bright red earth from head to foot, strutted to and fro restlessly. When we came abreast again, they faced the river, stamped their feet, nodded their horned heads, swayed their scarlet bodies; they shook towards the fierce river-demon a bunch of black feathers, a mangy skin with a pendent tail—something that looked like a dried gourd; they shouted periodically together strings of amazing words that resembled no sounds of human language; and the deep murmurs of the crowd, interrupted suddenly, were like the responses of some satanic litany.

"We had carried Kurtz into the pilot-house: there was more air there. Lying on the couch, he stared through the open shutter. There was an eddy in the mass of human bodies, and the woman with helmeted head and tawny cheeks rushed out to the very brink of the stream. She put out her hands, shouted something, and all that wild mob took up the shout in a roaring chorus of articulated, rapid, breathless utterance.

"'Do you understand this?' I asked.

"He kept on looking out past me with fiery, longing eyes, with a mingled expression of wistfulness and hate. He made no answer, but I saw a smile, a smile of indefinable meaning, appear on his colourless lips that a moment after twitched convulsively. 'Do I not?' he said slowly, gasping, as if the words had been torn out of him by a supernatural power.

"I pulled the string of the whistle, and I did this because I saw the pilgrims on deck getting out their rifles with an air of anticipating a jolly lark. At the sudden screech there was a movement of abject terror through that wedged mass of bodies. 'Don't! don't! you frighten them away,' cried some one on deck disconsolately. I pulled the string time after time. They broke and ran, they leaped, they crouched, they swerved, they dodged the flying terror of the sound. The three red chaps had fallen flat, face down on the shore, as though they had been shot dead. Only the barbarous and superb woman did not so much as flinch, and stretched tragically her bare arms after us over the sombre and glittering river.

"And then that imbecile crowd down on the deck started their little fun, and I could see nothing more for smoke.

"The brown current ran swiftly out of the heart of darkness, bearing us down towards the sea with twice the speed of our upward progress; and Kurtz's life was running swiftly too, ebbing, ebbing out of his heart into the sea of inexorable time. The manager was very placid, he had no vital anxieties now, he took us both in with a comprehensive and satisfied glance: the 'affair' had come off as well as could be wished. I saw the time approaching when I would be left alone of the party of 'unsound method.' The pilgrims looked upon me with disfavour. I was, so to speak, numbered with the dead. It is strange how I accepted this unforeseen partnership, this choice of nightmares forced upon me in the tenebrous land invaded by these mean and greedy phantoms.

"Kurtz discoursed. A voice! a voice! It rang deep to the very last. It survived his strength to hide in the magnificent folds of eloquence the barren darkness of his heart. Oh, he struggled! he struggled! The wastes of his weary brain were haunted by shadowy images now—images of wealth and fame revolving obsequiously round his unextinguishable gift of noble and lofty expression. My Intended, my station, my career, my ideas—these were the subjects for the occasional utterances of elevated sentiments. The shade of the original Kurtz frequented the bedside of the hollow sham, whose fate it was to be buried present in the mould of primeval earth. But both the diabolic love and the unearthly hate of the mysteries it had penetrated fought for the possession of that soul satiated with primitive emotions, avid of lying fame, of sham distinction, of all the appearances of success and power.

"Sometimes he was contemptibly childish. He desired to have kings meet him at railway-stations on his return from some ghastly Nowhere, where he intended to accomplish great things. 'You show them you have in you something that is really profitable, and then there will be no limits to the recognition of your ability,' he would say. 'Of course you must take care of the motives—right motives—always.' The long reaches that were like one and the same reach, monotonous bends that were exactly alike, slipped past the steamer with their multitude of secular trees looking patiently after this grimy fragment of another world, the forerunner of change, of conquest, of trade, of massacres, of blessings. I looked ahead—piloting. 'Close the shutter,' said Kurtz suddenly one day; 'I can't bear to look at this.' I did so. There was a silence. 'Oh, but I will wring your heart yet!' he cried at the invisible wilderness.

"We broke down—as I had expected—and had to lie up for repairs at the head of an island. This delay was the first thing that shook Kurtz's confidence. One morning he gave me a packet of papers and a photograph,—the lot tied together with a shoe-string. 'Keep this for me,' he said. 'This noxious fool' (meaning the manager) 'is capable of prying into my boxes when I am not looking.' In the afternoon I saw him. He was lying on his back with closed eyes, and I withdrew quietly, but I heard him mutter, 'Live rightly, die, die . . .' I listened. There was nothing more. Was he rehearsing some speech in his sleep, or was it a fragment of a phrase from some newspaper article? He had been writing for the papers and meant to do so again, 'for the furthering of my ideas. It's a duty.'

"His was an impenetrable darkness. I looked at him as you peer down at a man who is lying at the bottom of a precipice where the sun never shines. But I had not much time to give him, because I was helping the engine-driver to take to pieces the leaky cylinders, to straighten a bent connecting-rod, and in other such matters. I lived in an infernal mess of rust, filings, nuts, bolts, spanners, hammers, ratchet-drills—things I abominate, because I don't get on with them. I tended the little forge we fortunately had aboard; I toiled wearily in a wretched scrap-heap—unless I had the shakes too bad to stand.

"One evening coming in with a candle I was startled to hear him say a little tremulously, 'I am lying here in the dark waiting for death.' The light was within a foot of his eyes. I forced myself to murmur, 'Oh, nonsense!' and stood over him as if transfixed.

"Anything approaching the change that came over his features I have never seen before, and hope never to see again. Oh, I wasn't touched. I was fascinated. It was as though a veil had been rent. I saw on that ivory face the expression of sombre pride, of ruthless power, of craven terror—of an intense and hopeless despair. Did he live his life again in every detail of desire, temptation, and surrender during that supreme moment of complete knowledge? He cried in a whisper at some image, at some vision,—he cried out twice, a cry that was no more than a breath—

"'The horror! The horror!'

"I blew the candle out and left the cabin. The pilgrims were dining in the mess-room, and I took my place opposite the manager, who lifted his eyes to give me a questioning glance, which I successfully ignored. He leaned back, serene, with that peculiar smile of his sealing the unexpressed depths of his meanness. A continuous shower of small flies streamed upon the lamp, upon the cloth, upon our hands and faces. Suddenly the manager's boy put his insolent black head in the doorway, and said in a tone of scathing contempt—

"'Mistah Kurtz—he dead.'

"All the pilgrims rushed out to see. I remained, and went on with my dinner. I believe I was considered brutally callous. However, I did not eat much. There was a lamp in there—light, don't you know—and outside it was so beastly, beastly dark. I went no more near the remarkable man who had pronounced a judgment upon the adventures of his soul on this earth. The voice was gone. What else had been there? But I am of course aware that next day the pilgrims buried something in a muddy hole.

"And then they very nearly buried me.

"However, as you see, I did not go to join Kurtz there and then. I did not. I remained to dream the nightmare out to the end, and to show my loyalty to Kurtz once more. Destiny. My destiny! Droll thing life is—that mysterious arrangement of merciless logic for a futile purpose. The most you can hope from it is some knowledge of yourself—that comes too late—a crop of unextinguishable regrets. I have wrestled with death. It is the most unexciting contest you can imagine. It takes place in an impalpable greyness, with nothing underfoot, with nothing around, without spectators, without clamour, without glory, without the great desire of victory, without the great fear of defeat, in a sickly atmosphere of tepid scepticism, without much belief in your own right, and still less in that of your adversary. If such is the form of ultimate wisdom, then life is a greater riddle than some of us think it to be. I was within a hair's-breadth of the last opportunity for pronouncement, and I found with humiliation that probably I would have nothing to say. This is the reason why I affirm that Kurtz was a remarkable man. He had something to say. He said it. Since I had peeped over the edge myself, I understand better the meaning of his stare, that could not see the flame of the candle, but was wide enough to embrace the whole universe, piercing enough to penetrate all the hearts that beat in the darkness. He had summed up—he had judged. 'The horror!' He was a remarkable man. After all, this was the expression of some sort of belief; it had candour, it had conviction, it had a vibrating note of revolt in its whisper, it had the appalling face of a glimpsed truth—the strange commingling of desire and hate. And it is not my own extremity I remember best—a vision of greyness without form filled with physical pain, and a careless contempt for the evanescence of all things—even of this pain itself. No! It is his extremity that I seem to have lived through. True, he had made that last stride, he had stepped over the edge, while I had been permitted to draw back my hesitating foot. And perhaps in this is the whole difference; perhaps all the wisdom, and all truth, and all sincerity, are just compressed into that inappreciable moment of time in which we step over the threshold of the invisible. Perhaps! I like to think my summing-up would not have been a word of careless contempt. Better his cry—much better. It was an affirmation, a moral victory paid for by innumerable defeats, by abominable terrors, by abominable satisfactions. But it was a victory! That is why I have remained loyal to Kurtz to the last, and even beyond, when a long time after I heard once more, not his own voice, but the echo of his magnificent eloquence thrown to me from a soul as translucently pure as a cliff of crystal.

"No, they did not bury me, though there is a period of time which I remember mistily, with a shuddering wonder, like a passage through some inconceivable world that had no hope in it and no desire. I found myself back in the sepulchral city resenting the sight of people hurrying through the streets to filch a little money from each other, to devour their infamous cookery, to gulp their unwholesome beer, to dream their insignificant and silly dreams. They trespassed upon my thoughts. They were intruders whose knowledge of life was to me an irritating pretence, because I felt so sure they could not possibly know the things I knew. Their bearing, which was simply the bearing of commonplace individuals going about their business in the assurance of perfect safety, was offensive to me like the outrageous flauntings of folly in the face of a danger it is unable to comprehend. I had no particular desire to enlighten them, but I had some difficulty in restraining myself from laughing in their faces, so full of stupid importance. I daresay I was not very well at that time. I tottered about the streets—there were various affairs to settle—grinning bitterly at perfectly respectable persons. I admit my behaviour was inexcusable, but then my temperature was seldom normal in these days. My dear aunt's endeavours to 'nurse up my strength' seemed altogether beside the mark. It was not my strength that wanted nursing, it was my imagination that wanted soothing. I kept the bundle of papers given me by Kurtz, not knowing exactly what to do with it. His mother had died lately, watched over, as I was told, by his Intended. A clean-shaved man, with an official manner and wearing gold-rimmed spectacles, called on me one day and made inquiries, at first circuitous, afterwards suavely pressing, about what he was pleased to denominate certain 'documents.' I was not surprised, because I had had two rows with the manager on the subject out there. I had refused to give up the smallest scrap out of that package, and I took the same attitude with the spectacled man. He became darkly menacing at last, and with much heat argued that the Company had the right to every bit of information about its 'territories.' And, said he, 'Mr Kurtz's knowledge of unexplored regions must have been necessarily extensive and peculiar—owing to his great abilities and to the deplorable circumstances in which he had been placed: therefore——' I assured him Mr Kurtz's knowledge, however extensive, did not bear upon the problems of commerce or administration. He invoked then the name of science. 'It would be an incalculable loss if,' etc., etc. I offered him the report on the 'Suppression of Savage Customs,' with the postscriptum torn off. He took it up eagerly, but ended by sniffing at it with an air of contempt. 'This is not what we had a right to expect,' he remarked. 'Expect nothing else,' I said. 'There are only private letters.' He withdrew upon some threat of legal proceedings, and I saw him no more; but another fellow, calling himself Kurtz's cousin, appeared two days later, and was anxious to hear all the details about his dear relative's last moments. Incidentally he gave me to understand that Kurtz had been essentially a great musician. 'There was the making of an immense success,' said the man, who was an organist, I believe, with lank grey hair flowing over a greasy coat-collar. I had no reason to doubt his statement; and to this day I am unable to say what was Kurtz's profession, whether he ever had any—which was the greatest of his talents. I had taken him for a painter who wrote for the papers, or else for a journalist who could paint—but even the cousin (who took snuff during the interview) could not tell me what he had been—exactly. He was a universal genius—on that point I agreed with the old chap, who thereupon blew his nose nosily into a large cotton handkerchief and withdrew in senile agitation, bearing off some family letters and memoranda without importance. Ultimately a journalist anxious to know something of the fate of his 'dear colleague' turned up. This visitor informed me Kurtz's proper sphere ought to have been politics 'on the popular side.' He had furry straight eyebrows, bristly hair cropped short, an eye-glass on a broad ribbon, and, becoming expansive, confessed his opinion that Kurtz really couldn't write a bit—'but heavens! how that man could talk! He electrified large meetings. He had faith—don't you see?—he had the faith. He could get himself to believe anything—anything. He would have been a splendid leader of an extreme party.' 'What party?' I asked. 'Any party,' answered the other. 'He was an—an—extremist.' Did I not think so? I assented. Did I know, he asked, with a sudden flash of curiosity, 'what it was that had induced him to go out there?' 'Yes,' said I, and forthwith handed him the famous Report for publication, if he thought fit. He glanced through it hurriedly, mumbling all the time, judged 'it would do,' and took himself off with this plunder.

"Thus I was left at last with a slim packet of letters and the girl's portrait. She struck me as beautiful—I mean she had a beautiful expression. I know that the sunlight can be made to lie too, yet one felt that no manipulation of light and pose could have conveyed the delicate shade of truthfulness upon those features. She seemed ready to listen without mental reservation, without suspicion, without a thought for herself. I concluded I would go and give her back her portrait and those letters myself. Curiosity? Yes; and also some other feeling perhaps. All that had been Kurtz's had passed out of my hands: his soul, his body, his station, his plans, his ivory, his career. There remained only his memory and his Intended—and I wanted to give that up too to the past, in a way,—to surrender personally all that remained of him with me to that oblivion which is the last word of our common fate. I don't defend myself. I had no clear perception of what it was I really wanted. Perhaps it was an impulse of unconscious loyalty, or the fulfilment of one of these ironic necessities that lurk in the facts of human existence. I don't know. I can't tell. But I went.

"I thought his memory was like the other memories of the dead that accumulate in every man's life,—a vague impress on the brain of shadows that had fallen on it in their swift and final passage; but before the high and ponderous door, between the tall houses of a street as still and decorous as a well-kept alley in a cemetery, I had a vision of him on the stretcher, opening his mouth voraciously, as if to devour all the earth with all its mankind. He lived then before me; he lived as much as he had ever lived—a shadow insatiable of splendid appearances, of frightful realities; a shadow darker than the shadow of the night, and draped nobly in the folds of a gorgeous eloquence. The vision seemed to enter the house with me—the stretcher, the phantom-bearers, the wild crowd of obedient worshippers, the gloom of the forests, the glitter of the reach between the murky bends, the beat of the drum, regular and muffled like the beating of a heart—the heart of a conquering darkness. It was a moment of triumph for the wilderness, an invading and vengeful rush which, it seemed to me, I would have to keep back alone for the salvation of another soul. And the memory of what I had heard him say afar there, with the horned shapes stirring at my back, in the glow of fires, within the patient woods, those broken phrases came back to me, were heard again in their ominous and terrifying simplicity. I remembered his abject pleading, his abject threats, the colossal scale of his vile desires, the meanness, the torment, the tempestuous anguish of his soul. And later on I seemed to see his collected languid manner, when he said one day, 'This lot of ivory now is really mine. The Company did not pay for it. I collected it myself at a very great personal risk. I am afraid they will try to claim it as theirs though. H'm. It is a difficult case. What do you think I ought to do—resist? Eh? I want no more than justice.' . . . He wanted no more than justice—no more than justice. I rang the bell before a mahogany door on the first floor, and while I waited he seemed to stare at me out of the glassy panel—stare with that wide and immense stare embracing, condemning, loathing all the universe. I seemed to hear the whispered cry, 'The horror! The horror!'

"The dusk was falling. I had to wait in a lofty drawing-room with three long windows from floor to ceiling that were like three luminous and bedraped columns. The bent gilt legs and backs of the furniture shone in indistinct curves. The tall marble fireplace had a cold and monumental whiteness. A grand piano stood massively in a corner, with dark gleams on the flat surfaces like a sombre and polished sarcophagus. A high door opened—closed. I rose.

"She came forward, all in black, with a pale head, floating towards me in the dusk. She was in mourning. It was more than a year since his death, more than a year since the news came; she seemed as though she would remember and mourn for ever. She took both my hands in hers and murmured, 'I had heard you were coming.' I noticed she was not very young—I mean not girlish. She had a mature capacity for fidelity, for belief, for suffering. The room seemed to have grown darker, as if all the sad light of the cloudy evening had taken refuge on her forehead. This fair hair, this pale visage, this pure brow, seemed surrounded by an ashy halo from which the dark eyes looked out at me. Their glance was guileless, profound, confident, and trustful. She carried her sorrowful head as though she were proud of that sorrow, as though she would say, I—I alone know how to mourn for him as he deserves. But while we were still shaking hands, such a look of awful desolation came upon her face that I perceived she was one of those creatures that are not the playthings of Time. For her he had died only yesterday. And, by Jove! the impression was so powerful that for me too he seemed to have died only yesterday—nay, this very minute. I saw her and him in the same instant of time—his death and her sorrow—I saw her sorrow in the very moment of his death. Do you understand? I saw them together—I heard them together. She had said, with a deep catch of the breath, 'I have survived'; while my strained ears seemed to hear distinctly, mingled with her tone of despairing regret, the summing-up whisper of his eternal condemnation. I asked myself what I was doing there, with a sensation of panic in my heart as though I had blundered into a place of cruel and absurd mysteries not fit for a human being to behold. She motioned me to a chair. We sat down. I laid the packet gently on the little table, and she put her hand over it. . . . 'You knew him well,' she murmured, after a moment of mourning silence.

"'Intimacy grows quickly out there,' I said. 'I knew him as well as it is possible for one man to know another.'

"'And you admired him,' she said. 'It was impossible to know him and not to admire him. Was it?'

"'He was a remarkable man,' I said, unsteadily. Then before the appealing fixity of her gaze, that seemed to watch for more words on my lips, I went on, 'It was impossible not to——'

"'Love him,' she finished eagerly, silencing me into an appalled dumbness. 'How true! how true! But when you think that no one knew him so well as I! I had all his noble confidence. I knew him best.'

"'You knew him best,' I repeated. And perhaps she did. But with every word spoken the room was growing darker, and only her forehead, smooth and white, remained illumined by the unextinguishable light of belief and love.

"'You were his friend,' she went on. 'His friend,' she repeated, a little louder. 'You must have been, if he had given you this, and sent you to me. I feel I can speak to you—and oh! I must speak. I want you—you who have heard his last words—to know I have been worthy of him. . . . It is not pride. . . . Yes! I am proud to know I understood him better than any one on earth—he told me so himself. And since his mother died I have had no one—no one—to—to——'

"I listened. The darkness deepened. I was not even sure whether he had given me the right bundle. I rather suspect he wanted me to take care of another batch of his papers which, after his death, I saw the manager examining under the lamp. And the girl talked, easing her pain in the certitude of my sympathy; she talked as thirsty men drink. I had heard that her engagement with Kurtz had been disapproved by her people. He wasn't rich enough or something. And indeed I don't know whether he had not been a pauper all his life. He had given me some reason to infer that it was his impatience of comparative poverty that drove him out there.

"'. . . Who was not his friend who had heard him speak once?' she was saying. 'He drew men towards him by what was best in them.' She looked at me with intensity. 'It is the gift of the great,' she went on, and the sound of her low voice seemed to have the accompaniment of all the other sounds, full of mystery, desolation, and sorrow, I had ever heard—the ripple of the river, the soughing of the trees swayed by the wind, the murmurs of wild crowds, the faint ring of incomprehensible words cried from afar, the whisper of a voice speaking from beyond the threshold of an eternal darkness. 'But you have heard him! You know!' she cried.

"'Yes, I know,' I said with something like despair in my heart, but bowing my head before the faith that was in her, before that great and saving illusion that shone with an unearthly glow in the darkness, in the triumphant darkness from which I could not have defended her—from which I could not even defend myself.

"'What a loss to me—to us!' she corrected herself with beautiful generosity; then added in a murmur, 'To the world.' By the last gleams of twilight I could see the glitter of her eyes, full of tears—of tears that would not fall.

"'I have been very happy—very fortunate—very proud,' she went on. 'Too fortunate. Too happy for a little while. And now I am unhappy for—for life.'

"She stood up; her fair hair seemed to catch all the remaining light in a glimmer of gold. I rose too.

"'And of all this,' she went on, mournfully, 'of all his promise, and of all his greatness, of his generous mind, of his noble heart, nothing remains—nothing but a memory. You and I——'

"'We shall always remember him,' I said, hastily.

"'No!' she cried. 'It is impossible that all this should be lost—that such a life should be sacrificed to leave nothing—but sorrow. You know what vast plans he had. I knew of them too—I could not perhaps understand,—but others knew of them. Something must remain. His words, at least, have not died.'

"'His words will remain,' I said.

"'And his example,' she whispered to herself. 'Men looked up to him,—his goodness shone in every act. His example——'

"'True,' I said; 'his example too. Yes, his example. I forgot that.'

"'But I do not. I cannot—I cannot believe—not yet. I cannot believe that I shall never see him again, that nobody will see him again, never, never, never.'

"She put out her arms as if after a retreating figure, stretching them black and with clasped pale hands across the fading and narrow sheen of the window. Never see him! I saw him clearly enough then. I shall see this eloquent phantom as long as I live, and I shall see her too, a tragic and familiar Shade, resembling in this gesture another one, tragic also, and bedecked with powerless charms, stretching bare brown arms over the glitter of the infernal stream, the stream of darkness. She said suddenly very low, 'He died as he lived.'

"'His end,' said I, with dull anger stirring in me, 'was in every way worthy of his life.'

"'And I was not with him,' she murmured. My anger subsided before a feeling of infinite pity.

"'Everything that could be done——' I mumbled.

"'Ah, but I believed in him more than any one on earth—more than his own mother, more than—himself. He needed me! Me! I would have treasured every sigh, every word, every sign, every glance.'

"I felt like a chill grip on my chest. 'Don't,' I said, in a muffled voice.

"'Forgive me. I—I—have mourned so long in silence—in silence. . . . You were with him—to the last? I think of his loneliness. Nobody near to understand him as I would have understood. Perhaps no one to hear . . .'

"'To the very end,' I said, shakily. 'I heard his very last words. . . .' I stopped in a fright.

"'Repeat them,' she said in a heart-broken tone. 'I want—I want—something—something—to—to live with.'

"I was on the point of crying at her, 'Don't you hear them?' The dusk was repeating them in a persistent whisper all around us, in a whisper that seemed to swell menacingly like the first whisper of a rising wind. 'The horror! the horror!'

"'His last word—to live with,' she murmured. 'Don't you understand I loved him—I loved him—I loved him!'

"I pulled myself together and spoke slowly.

"'The last word he pronounced was—your name.'

"I heard a light sigh, and then my heart stood still, stopped dead short by an exulting and terrible cry, by the cry of inconceivable triumph and of unspeakable pain. 'I knew it—I was sure!' . . . She knew. She was sure. I heard her weeping; she had hidden her face in her hands. It seemed to me that the house would collapse before I could escape, that the heavens would fall upon my head. But nothing happened. The heavens do not fall for such a trifle. Would they have fallen, I wonder, if I had rendered Kurtz that justice which was his due? Hadn't he said he wanted only justice? But I couldn't. I could not tell her. It would have been too dark—too dark altogether . . ."

Marlow ceased, and sat apart, indistinct and silent, in the pose of a meditating Buddha. Nobody moved for a time. "We have lost the first of the ebb," said the Director, suddenly. I raised my head. The offing was barred by a black bank of clouds, and the tranquil waterway leading to the uttermost ends of the earth flowed sombre under an overcast sky—seemed to lead into the heart of an immense darkness.

IV

The Secret Agent

Here are the facts on which Conrad built this most perfectly formed of his novels. In February 1894 a bomb exploded in Greenwich Park, killing the young man who had been carrying it. His name was Martial Bourdin, and he was linked to an anarchist association called the Autonomie Club, while his brother-in-law, H. B. Samuels, was both the editor of an anarchist newspaper and a police spy to boot. The bomb appears to have gone off accidentally, and some aspects of what the newspapers called an "outrage" remain obscure. Samuels had certainly supplied the explosives, but to what end? At the inquest the government argued that Bourdin had planned to blow up the Royal Greenwich Observatory, and that remains the generally accepted explanation. The anarchist press suggested, in contrast, that Bourdin was meant only to be discovered and arrested in possession of a bomb. In either case, however, Samuels had been acting as an agent provocateur and hoping to spark a police crackdown.

The plot of *The Secret Agent* draws directly on the Greenwich explosion. Conrad got much of his background information from Ford Madox Ford, the "omniscient" friend of his author's note; Ford had cousins in anarchist circles and had already given Conrad the material he used in writing "The Informer" (1906). But there had been bombings in London before, a series of explosions throughout the 1880s that were planned and executed by such Irish secret societies as the Clan-na-Gael. Conrad drew on those as well, and who knows what he might have recalled from childhood of the atmosphere in which plots and politics are made? A full account of his sources and research, along with some informed speculation about the originals of his characters, will be found in Norman Sherry's invaluable *Conrad's Western World* (1971).

Some readers have always questioned Conrad's picture of the European revolutionary movements, wondering just how deep his knowledge went, and quizzing the fairness and accuracy of his portrait. He himself wrote to R. B. Cunninghame Graham that this novel's collection of incompetents "are not revolutionaries—they are shams," though he exempted the Professor, who is "incorruptible . . . a megalomaniac of an extreme type. And every extremist is respectable." The rest of his cast hardly seems capable of producing a revolution, and in fact they did not; the real dangers were elsewhere, the Geneva of *Under Western Eyes* included. Still, such questions would not arise without the pressure of those later events that have made Conrad seem so prescient, without the central role played by violent underground movements in the history of the century that followed. To speak only of recent years, most of the analogies so frequently suggested between *The Secret Agent* and the destruction of the World Trade Center appear to me overdrawn. They do justice neither to the mendaciousness of Conrad's world nor to the seriousness of the al-Qaeda attack. But they do make sense in terms of the "frail" and apparently "insignificant" Professor, a one-man sleeper cell, "unsuspected and deadly." Conrad's portrait of London does, however, find an echo in the city that has known both the Irish Republican Army and the 2005 Islamist bombings, while newspaper headlines of that year characterizing London as a switching yard for terrorists cannot help but evoke Mr. Vladimir's complaints about English liberty. Theodore Kaczynski, the Unabomber, employed the name Conrad as an alias, and the exploding letters that he used before his 1996 arrest recall the Professor's search for a "perfect detonator." The most appropriate comparison, however, is perhaps to the Bologna train-station massacre of 1980, when a bomb planted by a neofascist group that enjoyed some protection from the authorities was at first blamed upon, and intended to discredit, the Red Brigades on the left.

None of Conrad's other novels has the same terse unity of tone; it makes me wish he had written more often in this mordant and aloof third person. And none of them can match *The Secret Agent* in its range of memorable characters, some of whom exist for but a few pages only, such as Winnie's mother, the widow whom Conrad presents as "heroic" and absurd at once. My own favorite is that "Hyperborean swine" Mr. Vladimir, the First Secretary of an unnamed but identifiably Russian embassy, and the figure from whom the title character, Adolf Verloc, receives his instructions. Captivating, mad, and almost entirely persuasive, Mr. Vladimir rejects the idea of an assault on a chief of state as "almost conventional," while an "outrage" against a church might well assume "the character of a religious manifestation." So why not have "a go at astronomy" instead? He is the provocateur's provocateur, a comic—indeed almost camp—version of the great tempters of nineteenth-century fiction, such as Balzac's Vautrin or Dostoevsky's Svidrigailov. His speeches remind us of how little, in contrast, we actually get to hear of Kurtz's own voice in "Heart of Darkness." On the page that famous orator hardly ever speaks, and while that absence, that hole at the center of the story, is doubtless a part of Conrad's purpose, it also allows him to evade the difficulty of dramatizing Kurtz's allegedly seductive power. By the time he wrote *The Secret Agent* Conrad could trust himself just a little bit more.

He began the novel in February 1906 and characteristically saw it first as a short story. A month later it had become a long one, and a month after that Conrad knew he was writing a novel. An early form of the book ran that autumn in a short-lived American magazine called *Ridgway's: A Militant Weekly for God and Country.* Conrad had to scramble to meet their deadlines, and the serial's concluding chapters are but a sketch of what he wanted to do. He returned to the book in May 1907, adding a chapter and fixing the faults of his earlier haste, and it was published that September by Methuen. He himself made the first adaptation of the novel, writing a version for the London stage that closed after ten performances in November 1922. Conrad doesn't seem to have expected more, and did not make a single curtain. There have been a number of film and video versions; the most notable remains the first, Alfred Hitchcock's *Sabotage* (1936). Conrad added the author's note in 1920 for his collected edition. The text given here of both the note and the novel itself is that of the Doubleday Sun-Dial edition of 1921, whose plates were leased by Dent for its Uniform Edition of 1924 and subsequently licensed by Penguin.

AUTHOR'S NOTE

The origin of *The Secret Agent:* subject, treatment, artistic purpose, and every other motive that may induce an author to take up his pen, can, I believe, be traced to a period of mental and emotional reaction.

The actual facts are that I began this book impulsively and wrote it continuously. When in due course it was bound and delivered to the public gaze I found myself reproved for having produced it at all. Some of the admonitions were severe, others had a sorrowful note. I have not got them textually before me but I remember perfectly the general argument, which was very simple; and also my surprise at its nature. All this sounds a very old story now! And yet it is not such a long time ago. I must conclude that I had still preserved much of my pristine innocence in the year 1907. It seems to me now that even an artless person might have foreseen that some criticisms would be based on the ground of sordid surroundings and the moral squalor of the tale.

That of course is a serious objection. It was not universal. In fact it seems ungracious to remember so little reproof amongst so much intelligent and sympathetic appreciation; and I trust that the readers of this Preface will not hasten to put it down to wounded vanity or a natural disposition to ingratitude. I suggest that a charitable heart could very well ascribe my choice to natural modesty. Yet it isn't exactly modesty that makes me select reproof for the illustration of my case. No, it isn't exactly modesty. I am not at all certain that I am modest; but those who have read so far through my work will credit me with enough decency, tact, *savoir-faire,* what you will, to prevent me from making a song for my own glory out of the words of other people. No! The true motive of my selection lies in quite a different trait. I have always had a propensity to justify my action. Not to defend. To justify. Not to insist that I was right but simply to explain that there was no perverse intention, no secret scorn for the natural sensibilities of mankind at the bottom of my impulses.

That kind of weakness is dangerous only so far that it exposes one to the risk of becoming a bore; for the world generally is not interested in the motives of any overt act but in its consequences. Man may smile and smile but he is not an investigating animal. He loves the obvious. He shrinks from explanations. Yet I will go on with mine. It's obvious that I need not have written that book. I was under no necessity to deal with that subject; using the word subject both in the sense of the tale itself and in the larger one of a special manifestation in the life of mankind. This I fully admit. But the thought of elaborating mere ugliness in order to shock, or even simply to surprise my readers by a change of front, has never entered my head. In making this statement I expect to be believed, not only on the evidence of my general character but also for the reason, which anybody can see, that the whole treatment of the tale, its inspiring indignation and underlying pity and contempt, prove my detachment from the squalor and sordidness which lie simply in the outward circumstances of the setting.

The inception of *The Secret Agent* followed immediately on a two years' period of intense absorption in the task of writing that remote novel, *Nostromo,* with its far-off Latin-American atmosphere; and the profoundly personal *Mirror of the Sea.* The first an intense creative effort on what I suppose will always remain my largest canvas, the second an unreserved attempt to unveil for a moment the profounder intimacies of the sea and the formative influences of nearly half my lifetime. It was a period, too, in which my sense of the truth of things was attended by a very intense imaginative and emotional readiness which, all genuine and faithful to facts as it was, yet made me feel (the task once done) as if I were left behind, aimless amongst mere husks of sensations and lost in a world of other, of inferior, values.

I don't know whether I really felt that I wanted a change, change in my imagination, in my vision, and in my mental attitude. I rather think that a change in the fundamental mood had already stolen over me unawares. I don't remember anything definite happening. With *The Mirror of the Sea* finished in the full consciousness that I had dealt honestly with myself and my readers in every line of that book, I gave myself up to a not unhappy pause. Then, while I was yet standing still, as it were, and certainly not thinking of going out of my way to look for anything ugly, the subject of *The Secret Agent*—I mean the tale—came to me in the shape of a few words uttered by a friend in a casual conversation about anarchists or rather anarchist activities; how brought about I don't remember now.

I remember, however, remarking on the criminal futility of the whole thing, doctrine, action, mentality; and on the contemptible aspect of the half-crazy pose as of a brazen cheat exploiting the poignant miseries and passionate credulities of a mankind always so tragically eager for self-destruction. That was what made for me its philosophical pretences so unpardonable. Presently, passing to particular instances, we recalled the already old story of the attempt to blow up the Greenwich Observatory; a blood-stained inanity of so fatuous a kind that it was impossible to fathom its origin by any reasonable or even unreasonable process of thought. For perverse unreason has its own logical processes. But that outrage could not be laid hold of mentally in any sort of way, so that one remained faced by the fact of a man blown to bits for nothing even most remotely resembling an idea, anarchistic or other. As to the outer wall of the Observatory it did not show as much as the faintest crack.

I pointed all this out to my friend who remained silent for a while and then remarked in his characteristically casual and omniscient manner: "Oh, that fellow was half an idiot. His sister committed suicide afterwards." These were absolutely the only words that passed between us; for extreme surprise at this unexpected piece of information kept me dumb for a moment and he began at once to talk of something else. It never occurred to me later to ask how he arrived at his knowledge. I am sure that if he had seen once in his life the back of an anarchist that must have been the whole extent of his connection with the underworld. He was, however, a man who liked to talk with all sorts of people, and he may have gathered those illuminating facts at second or third hand, from a crossing-sweeper, from a retired police officer, from some vague man in his club, or even perhaps from a Minister of State met at some public or private reception.

Of the illuminating quality there could be no doubt whatever. One felt like walking out of a forest on to a plain—there was not much to see but one had plenty of light. No, there was not much to see and, frankly, for a considerable time I didn't even attempt to perceive anything. It was only the illuminating impression that remained. It remained satisfactory but in a passive way. Then, about a week later, I came upon a book which as far as I know had never attained any prominence, the rather summary recollections of an Assistant Commissioner of Police, an obviously able man with a strong religious strain in his character who was appointed to his post at the time of the dynamite outrages in London, away back in the eighties. The book was fairly interesting, very discreet of course; and I have by now forgotten the bulk of its contents. It contained no revelations, it ran over the surface agreeably, and that was all. I won't even try to explain why I should have been arrested by a little passage of about seven lines, in which the author (I believe his name was Anderson) reproduced a short dialogue held in the Lobby of the House of Commons after some unexpected anarchist outrage, with the Home Secretary. I think it was Sir William Harcourt then. He was very much irritated and the official was very apologetic. The phrase, amongst the three which passed between them, that struck me most was Sir W. Harcourt's angry sally: "All that's very well. But your idea of secrecy over there seems to consist of keeping the Home Secretary in the dark." Characteristic enough of Sir W. Harcourt's temper but not much in itself. There must have been, however, some sort of atmosphere in the whole incident because all of a sudden I felt myself stimulated. And then ensued in my mind what a student of chemistry would best understand from the analogy of the addition of the tiniest little drop of the right kind, precipitating the process of crystallization in a test tube containing some colourless solution.

It was at first for me a mental change, disturbing a quieted-down imagination, in which strange forms, sharp in outline but imperfectly apprehended, appeared and claimed attention as crystals will do by their bizarre and unexpected shapes. One fell to musing before the phenomenon—even of the past: of South America, a continent of crude sunshine and brutal revolutions, of the sea, the vast expanse of salt waters, the mirror of heaven's frowns and smiles, the reflector of the world's light. Then the vision of an enormous town presented itself, of a monstrous town more populous than some continents and in its man-made might as if indifferent to heaven's frowns and smiles; a cruel devourer of the world's light. There was room enough there to place any story, depth enough for any passion, variety enough there for any setting, darkness enough to bury five millions of lives.

Irresistibly the town became the background for the ensuing period of deep and tentative meditations. Endless vistas opened before me in various directions. It would take years to find the right way! It seemed to take years! . . . Slowly the dawning conviction of Mrs Verloc's maternal passion grew up to a flame between me and that background, tingeing it with its secret ardour and receiving from it in exchange some of its own sombre colouring. At last the story of Winnie Verloc stood out complete from the days of her childhood to the end, unproportioned as yet, with everything still on the first plan, as it were; but ready now to be dealt with. It was a matter of about three days.

This book is *that* story, reduced to manageable proportions, its whole course suggested and centred round the absurd cruelty of the Greenwich Park explosion. I had there a task I will not say arduous but of the most absorbing difficulty. But it had to be done. It was a necessity. The figures grouped about Mrs Verloc and related directly or indirectly to her tragic suspicion that "life doesn't stand much looking into," are the outcome of that very necessity. Personally I have never had any doubt of the reality of Mrs Verloc's story; but it had to be disengaged from its obscurity in that immense town, it had to be made credible, I don't mean so much as to her soul but as to her surroundings, not so much as to her psychology but as to her humanity. For the surroundings hints were not lacking. I had to fight hard to keep at arm's length the memories of my solitary and nocturnal walks all over London in my early days, lest they should rush in and overwhelm each page of the story as these emerged one after another from a mood as serious in feeling and thought as any in which I ever wrote a line. In that respect I really think that *The Secret Agent* is a perfectly genuine piece of work. Even the purely artistic purpose, that of applying an ironic method to a subject of that kind, was formulated with deliberation and in the earnest belief that ironic treatment alone would enable me to say all I felt I would have to say in scorn as well as in pity. It is one of the minor satisfactions of my writing life that having taken that resolve I did manage, it seems to me, to carry it right through to the end. As to the personages whom the absolute necessity of the case—Mrs Verloc's case—brings out in front of the London background, from them, too, I obtained those little satisfactions which really count for so much against the mass of oppressive doubts that haunt so persistently every attempt at creative work. For instance, of Mr Vladimir himself (who was fair game for a caricatural presentation) I was gratified to hear that an experienced man of the world had said "that Conrad must have been in touch with that sphere or else has an excellent intuition of things," because Mr Vladimir was "not only possible in detail but quite right in essentials." Then a visitor from America informed me that all sorts of revolutionary refugees in New York would have it that the book was written by somebody who knew a lot about them. This seemed to me a very high compliment, considering that, as a matter of hard fact, I had seen even less of their kind than the omniscient friend who gave me the first suggestion for the novel. I have no doubt, however, that there had been moments during the writing of the book when I was an extreme revolutionist, I won't say more convinced than they but certainly cherishing a more concentrated purpose than any of them had ever done in the whole course of his life. I don't say this to boast. I was simply attending to my business. In the matter of all my books I have always attended to my business. I have attended to it with complete self-surrender. And this statement, too, is not a boast. I could not have done otherwise. It would have bored me too much to make-believe.

The suggestions for certain personages of the tale, both law-abiding and lawless, came from various sources which, perhaps, here and there, some reader may have recognized. They are not very recondite. But I am not concerned here to legitimize any of those people, and even as to my general view of the moral reactions as between the criminal and the police all I will venture to say is that it seems to me to be at least arguable.

The twelve years that have elapsed since the publication of the book have not changed my attitude. I do not regret having written it. Lately, circumstances, which have nothing to do with the general tenor of this Preface, have compelled me to strip this tale of the literary robe of indignant scorn it has cost me so much to fit on it decently, years ago. I have been forced, so to speak, to look upon its bare bones. I confess that it makes a grisly skeleton. But still I will submit that telling Winnie Verloc's story to its anarchistic end of utter desolation, madness, and despair, and telling it as I have told it here, I have not intended to commit a gratuitous outrage on the feelings of mankind.

1920
J.C.

THE SECRET AGENT

A Simple Tale

CHAPTER 1

Mr Verloc, going out in the morning, left his shop nominally in charge of his brother-in-law. It could be done, because there was very little business at any time, and practically none at all before the evening. Mr Verloc cared but little about his ostensible business. And moreover, his wife was in charge of his brother-in-law.

The shop was small, and so was the house. It was one of those grimy brick houses which existed in large quantities before the era of reconstruction dawned upon London. The shop was a square box of a place, with the front glazed in small panes. In the daytime the door remained closed; in the evening it stood discreetly but suspiciously ajar.

The window contained photographs of more or less undressed dancing girls; nondescript packages in wrappers like patent medicines; closed yellow paper envelopes, very flimsy, and marked two and six in heavy black figures; a few numbers of ancient French comic publications hung across a string as if to dry; a dingy blue china bowl, a casket of black wood, bottles of marking ink, and rubber stamps; a few books with titles hinting at impropriety; a few apparently old copies of obscure newspapers, badly printed, with titles like the *Torch,* the *Gong*—rousing titles. And the two gas-jets inside the panes were always turned low, either for economy's sake or for the sake of the customers.

These customers were either very young men, who hung about the window for a time before slipping in suddenly; or men of a more mature age, but looking generally as if they were not in funds. Some of that last kind had the collars of their overcoats turned right up to their moustaches, and traces of mud on the bottom of their nether garments, which had the appearance of being much worn and not very valuable. And the legs inside them did not, as a general rule, seem of much account either. With their hands plunged deep in the side pockets of their coats, they dodged in sideways, one shoulder first, as if afraid to start the bell going.

The bell, hung on the door by means of a curved ribbon of steel, was difficult to circumvent. It was hopelessly cracked; but of an evening, at the slightest provocation, it clattered behind the customer with impudent virulence.

It clattered; and at that signal, through the dusty glass door behind the painted deal counter, Mr Verloc would issue hastily from the parlour at the back. His eyes were naturally heavy; he had an air of having wallowed, fully dressed, all day on an unmade bed. Another man would have felt such an appearance a distinct disadvantage. In a commercial transaction of the retail order much depends on the seller's engaging and amiable aspect. But Mr Verloc knew his business, and remained undisturbed by any sort of aesthetic doubt about his appearance. With a firm, steady-eyed impudence, which seemed to hold back the threat of some abominable menace, he would proceed to sell over the counter some object looking obviously and scandalously not worth the money which passed in the transaction: a small cardboard box with apparently nothing inside, for instance, or one of those carefully closed yellow flimsy envelopes, or a soiled volume in paper covers with a promising title. Now and then it happened that one of the faded, yellow dancing girls would get sold to an amateur, as though she had been alive and young.

Sometimes it was Mrs Verloc who would appear at the call of the cracked bell. Winnie Verloc was a young woman with a full bust, in a tight bodice, and with broad hips. Her hair was very tidy. Steady-eyed like her husband, she preserved an air of unfathomable indifference behind the rampart of the counter. Then the customer of comparatively tender years would get suddenly disconcerted at having to deal with a woman, and with rage in his heart would proffer a request for a bottle of marking ink, retail value sixpence (price in Verloc's shop one and sixpence), which, once outside, he would drop stealthily into the gutter.

The evening visitors—the men with collars turned up and soft hats rammed down—nodded familiarly to Mrs Verloc, and with a muttered greeting, lifted up the flap at the end of the counter in order to pass into the back parlour, which gave access to a passage and to a steep flight of stairs. The door of the shop was the only means of entrance to the house in which Mr Verloc carried on his business of a seller of shady wares, exercised his vocation of a protector of society, and cultivated his domestic virtues. These last were pronounced. He was thoroughly domesticated. Neither his spiritual, nor his mental, nor his physical needs were of the kind to take him much abroad. He found at home the ease of his body and the peace of his conscience, together with Mrs Verloc's wifely attentions and Mrs Verloc's mother's deferential regard.

Winnie's mother was a stout, wheezy woman, with a large brown face. She wore a black wig under a white cap. Her swollen legs rendered her inactive. She considered herself to be of French descent, which might have been true; and after a good many years of married life with a licensed victualler of the more common sort, she provided for the years of widowhood by letting furnished apartments for gentlemen near Vauxhall Bridge Road in a square once of some splendour and still included in the district of Belgravia. This topographical fact was of some advantage in advertising her rooms; but the patrons of the worthy widow were not exactly of the fashionable kind. Such as they were, her daughter Winnie helped to look after them. Traces of the French descent which the widow boasted of were apparent in Winnie, too. They were apparent in the extremely neat and artistic arrangement of her glossy dark hair. Winnie had also other charms: her youth; her full, rounded form; her clear complexion; the provocation of her unfathomable reserve, which never went so far as to prevent conversation, carried on on the lodger's part with animation, and on hers with an equable amiability. It must be that Mr Verloc was susceptible to these fascinations. Mr Verloc was an intermittent patron. He came and went without any very apparent reason. He generally arrived in London (like the influenza) from the Continent, only he arrived unheralded by the press; and his visitations set in with great severity. He breakfasted in bed, and remained wallowing there with an air of quiet enjoyment till noon every day—and sometimes even to a later hour. But when he went out he seemed to experience a great difficulty in finding his way back to his temporary home in the Belgravian square. He left it late, and returned to it early—as early as three or four in the morning; and on waking up at ten addressed Winnie, bringing in the breakfast tray, with jocular, exhausted civility, in the hoarse, failing tones of a man who had been talking vehemently for many hours together. His prominent, heavy-lidded eyes rolled sideways amorously and languidly, the bedclothes were pulled up to his chin, and his dark smooth moustache covered his thick lips capable of much honeyed banter.

In Winnie's mother's opinion Mr Verloc was a very nice gentleman. From her life's experience gathered in various "business houses" the good woman had taken into her retirement an ideal of gentlemanliness as exhibited by the patrons of private-saloon bars. Mr. Verloc approached that ideal; he attained it, in fact.

"Of course, we'll take over your furniture, mother," Winnie had remarked.

The lodging-house was to be given up. It seems it would not answer to carry it on. It would have been too much trouble for Mr Verloc. It would not have been convenient for his other business. What his business was he did not say; but after his engagement to Winnie he took the trouble to get up before noon, and descending the basement stairs, make himself pleasant to Winnie's mother in the breakfast-room downstairs where she had her motionless being. He stroked the cat, poked the fire, had his lunch served to him there. He left its slightly stuffy cosiness with evident reluctance, but, all the same, remained out till the night was far advanced. He never offered to take Winnie to theatres, as such a nice gentleman ought to have done. His evenings were occupied. His work was in a way political, he told Winnie once. She would have, he warned her, to be very nice to his political friends. And with her straight, unfathomable glance she answered that she would be so, of course.

How much more he told her as to his occupation it was impossible for Winnie's mother to discover. The married couple took her over with the furniture. The mean aspect of the shop surprised her. The change from the Belgravian square to the narrow street in Soho affected her legs adversely. They became of an enormous size. On the other hand, she experienced a complete relief from material cares. Her son-in-law's heavy good nature inspired her with a sense of absolute safety. Her daughter's future was obviously assured, and even as to her son Stevie she need have no anxiety. She had not been able to conceal from herself that he was a terrible encumbrance, that poor Stevie. But in view of Winnie's fondness for her delicate brother, and of Mr Verloc's kind and generous disposition, she felt that the poor boy was pretty safe in this rough world. And in her heart of hearts she was not perhaps displeased that the Verlocs had no children. As that circumstance seemed perfectly indifferent to Mr Verloc, and as Winnie found an object of quasi-maternal affection in her brother, perhaps this was just as well for poor Stevie.

For he was difficult to dispose of, that boy. He was delicate and, in a frail way, good-looking, too, except for the vacant droop of his lower lip. Under our excellent system of compulsory education he had learned to read and write, notwithstanding the unfavourable aspect of the lower lip. But as errand-boy he did not turn out a great success. He forgot his messages; he was easily diverted from the straight path of duty by the attractions of stray cats and dogs, which he followed down narrow alleys into unsavory courts; by the comedies of the streets, which he contemplated open-mouthed, to the detriment of his employer's interests; or by the dramas of fallen horses, whose pathos and violence induced him sometimes to shriek piercingly in a crowd, which disliked to be disturbed by sounds of distress in its quiet enjoyment of the national spectacle. When led away by a grave and protecting policeman, it would often become apparent that poor Stevie had forgotten his address—at least for a time. A brusque question caused him to stutter to the point of suffocation. When startled by anything perplexing he used to squint horribly. However, he never had any fits (which was encouraging); and before the natural outbursts of impatience on the part of his father he could always, in his childhood's days, run for protection behind the short skirts of his sister Winnie. On the other hand, he might have been suspected of hiding a fund of reckless naughtiness. When he had reached the age of fourteen a friend of his late father, an agent for a foreign preserved milk firm, having given him an opening as office-boy, he was discovered one foggy afternoon, in his chief's absence, busy letting off fireworks on the staircase. He touched off in quick succession a set of fierce rockets, angry catherine wheels, loudly exploding squibs—and the matter might have turned out very serious. An awful panic spread through the whole building. Wild-eyed, choking clerks stampeded through the passages full of smoke; silk hats and elderly businessmen could be seen rolling independently down the stairs. Stevie did not seem to derive any personal gratification from what he had done. His motives for this stroke of originality were difficult to discover. It was only later on that Winnie obtained from him a misty and confused confession. It seems that two other office-boys in the building had worked upon his feelings by tales of injustice and oppression till they had wrought his compassion to the pitch of that frenzy. But his father's friend, of course, dismissed him summarily as likely to ruin his business. After that altruistic exploit Stevie was put to help wash the dishes in the basement kitchen, and to black the boots of the gentlemen patronizing the Belgravian mansion. There was obviously no future in such work. The gentlemen tipped him a shilling now and then. Mr Verloc showed himself the most generous of lodgers. But altogether all that did not amount to much either in the way of gain or prospects; so that when Winnie announced her engagement to Mr Verloc her mother could not help wondering, with a sigh and a glance towards the scullery, what would become of poor Stephen now.

It appeared that Mr Verloc was ready to take him over together with his wife's mother and with the furniture, which was the whole visible fortune of the family. Mr Verloc gathered everything as it came to his broad, good-natured breast. The furniture was disposed to the best advantage all over the house, but Mrs Verloc's mother was confined to two back rooms on the first floor. The luckless Stevie slept in one of them. By this time a growth of thin fluffy hair had come to blur, like a golden mist, the sharp line of his small lower jaw. He helped his sister with blind love and docility in her household duties. Mr Verloc thought that some occupation would be good for him. His spare time he occupied by drawing circles with compass and pencil on a piece of paper. He applied himself to that pastime with great industry, with his elbows spread out and bowed low over the kitchen table. Through the open door of the parlour at the back of the shop Winnie, his sister, glanced at him from time to time with maternal vigilance.

CHAPTER 2

Such was the house, the household, and the business Mr Verloc left behind him on his way westward at the hour of half past ten in the morning. It was unusually early for him; his whole person exhaled the charm of almost dewy freshness; he wore his blue cloth overcoat unbuttoned; his boots were shiny; his cheeks, freshly shaven, had a sort of gloss; and even his heavy-lidded eyes, refreshed by a night of peaceful slumber, sent out glances of comparative alertness. Through the park railings these glances beheld men and women riding in the Row, couples cantering past harmoniously, others advancing sedately at a walk, loitering groups of three or four, solitary horsemen looking unsociable, and solitary women followed at a long distance by a groom with a cockade to his hat and a leather belt over his tight-fitting coat. Carriages went bowling by, mostly two-horse broughams, with here and there a victoria with the skin of some wild beast inside and a woman's face and hat emerging above the folded hood. And a peculiarly London sun—against which nothing could be said except that it looked bloodshot—glorified all this by its stare. It hung at a moderate elevation above Hyde Park Corner with an air of punctual and benign vigilance. The very pavement under Mr Verloc's feet had an old-gold tinge in that diffused light, in which neither wall, nor tree, nor beast, nor man cast a shadow. Mr Verloc was going westward through a town without shadows in an atmosphere of powdered old gold. There were red, coppery gleams on the roofs of houses, on the corners of walls, on the panels of carriages, on the very coats of the horses, and on the broad back of Mr Verloc's overcoat, where they produced a dull effect of rustiness. But Mr Verloc was not in the least conscious of having got rusty. He surveyed through the park railings the evidences of the town's opulence and luxury with an approving eye. All these people had to be protected. Protection is the first necessity of opulence and luxury. They had to be protected; and their horses, carriages, houses, servants had to be protected; and the source of their wealth had to be protected in the heart of the city and the heart of the country; the whole social order favourable to their hygienic idleness had to be protected against the shallow enviousness of unhygienic labour. It had to—

and Mr Verloc would have rubbed his hands with satisfaction had he not been constitutionally averse from every superfluous exertion. His idleness was not hygienic, but it suited him very well. He was in a manner devoted to it with a sort of inert fanaticism, or perhaps rather with a fanatical inertness. Born of industrious parents for a life of toil, he had embraced indolence from an impulse as profound, as inexplicable and as imperious as the impulse which directs a man's preference for one particular woman in a given thousand. He was too lazy even for a mere demagogue, for a workman orator, for a leader of labour. It was too much trouble. He required a more perfect form of ease; or it might have been that he was the victim of a philosophical unbelief in the effectiveness of every human effort. Such a form of indolence requires, implies, a certain amount of intelligence. Mr Verloc was not devoid of intelligence—and at the notion of a menaced social order he would perhaps have winked to himself if there had not been an effort to make in that sign of scepticism. His big, prominent eyes were not well adapted to winking. They were rather of the sort that closes solemnly in slumber with majestic effect.

Undemonstrative and burly in a fat-pig style, Mr Verloc, without either rubbing his hands with satisfaction or winking sceptically at his thoughts, proceeded on his way. He trod the pavement heavily with his shiny boots, and his general get-up was that of a well-to-do mechanic in business for himself. He might have been anything from a picture-frame maker to a locksmith; an employer of labour in a small way. But there was also about him an indescribable air which no mechanic could have acquired in the practice of his handicraft however dishonestly exercised: the air common to men who live on the vices, the follies, or the baser fears of mankind; the air of moral nihilism common to keepers of gambling hells and disorderly houses; to private detectives and inquiry agents; to drink sellers and, I should say, to the sellers of invigorating electric belts and to the inventors of patent medicines. But of that last I am not sure, not having carried my investigations so far into the depths. For all I know, the expression of these last may be perfectly diabolic. I shouldn't be surprised. What I want to affirm is that Mr Verloc's expression was by no means diabolic.

Before reaching Knightsbridge, Mr Verloc took a turn to the left out of the busy main thoroughfare, uproarious with the traffic of swaying omnibuses and trotting vans, in the almost silent, swift flow of hansoms. Under his hat, worn with a slight backward tilt, his hair had been carefully brushed into respectful sleekness; for his business was with an embassy. And Mr Verloc, steady like a rock—a soft kind of rock—marched now along a street which could with every propriety be described as private. In its breadth, emptiness, and extent it had the majesty of inorganic nature, of matter that never dies. The only reminder of mortality was a doctor's brougham arrested in august solitude close to the kerbstone. The polished knockers of the doors gleamed as far as the eye could reach, the clean windows shone with a dark opaque lustre. And all was still. But a milk cart rattled noisily across the distant perspective; a butcher boy, driving with the noble recklessness of a charioteer at Olympic Games, dashed round the corner sitting high above a pair of red wheels. A guilty-looking cat issuing from under the stones ran for a while in front of Mr Verloc, then dived into another basement; and a thick police constable, looking a stranger to every emotion, as if he, too, were part of inorganic nature, surging apparently out of a lamp-post, took not the slightest notice of Mr Verloc. With a turn to the left Mr Verloc pursued his way along a narrow street by the side of a yellow wall which, for some inscrutable reason, had No. 1 Chesham Square written on it in black letters. Chesham Square was at least sixty yards away, and Mr Verloc, cosmopolitan enough not to be deceived by London's topographical mysteries, held on steadily, without a sign of surprise or indignation. At last, with business-like persistency, he reached the Square, and made diagonally for the number 10. This belonged to an imposing carriage gate in a high, clean wall between two houses, of which one rationally enough bore the number 9 and the other was numbered 37; but the fact that this last belonged to Porthill Street, a street well known in the neighbourhood, was proclaimed by an inscription placed above the ground-floor windows by whatever highly efficient authority is charged with the duty of keeping track of London's strayed houses. Why powers are not asked of Parliament (a short Act would do) for compelling those edifices to return where they belong is one of the mysteries of municipal administration. Mr Verloc did not trouble his head about it, his mission in life being the protection of the social mechanism, not its perfectionment or even its criticism.

It was so early that the porter of the Embassy issued hurriedly out of his lodge still struggling with the left sleeve of his livery coat. His waistcoat was red, and he wore knee-breeches, but his aspect was flustered. Mr Verloc, aware of the rush on his flank, drove it off by simply holding out an envelope stamped with the arms of the Embassy, and passed on. He produced the same talisman also to the footman who opened the door, and stood back to let him enter the hall.

A clear fire burned in a tall fireplace, and an elderly man standing with his back to it, in evening dress and with a chain round his neck, glanced up from the newspaper he was holding spread out in both hands before his calm and severe face. He didn't move; but another lackey, in brown trousers and clawhammer coat edged with thin yellow cord, approaching Mr Verloc listened to the murmur of his name, and turning round on his heel in silence, began to walk, without looking back once. Mr Verloc, thus led along a ground-floor passage to the left of the great carpeted staircase, was suddenly motioned to enter a quite small room furnished with a heavy writing-table and a few chairs. The servant shut the door, and Mr Verloc remained alone. He did not take a seat. With his hat and stick held in one hand he glanced about, passing his other podgy hand over his uncovered sleek head.

Another door opened noiselessly, and Mr Verloc immobilizing his glance in that direction saw at first only black clothes. The bald top of a head, and a drooping dark grey whisker on each side of a pair of wrinkled hands. The person who had entered was holding a batch of papers before his eyes and walked up to the table with a rather mincing step, turning the papers over the while. Privy Councillor Wurmt, Chancelier d'Ambassade, was rather shortsighted. This meritorious official, laying the papers on the table, disclosed a face of pasty complexion and of melancholy ugliness surrounded by a lot of fine, long, dark grey hairs, barred heavily by thick and bushy eyebrows. He put on a black-framed pince-nez upon a blunt and shapeless nose, and seemed struck by Mr Verloc's appearance. Under the enormous eyebrows his weak eyes blinked pathetically through the glasses.

He made no sign of greeting; neither did Mr Verloc who certainly knew his place; but a subtle change about the general outlines of his shoulders and back suggested a slight bending of Mr

Verloc's spine under the vast surface of his overcoat. The effect was of unobtrusive deference.

"I have here some of your reports," said the bureaucrat in an unexpectedly soft and weary voice, and pressing the tip of his forefinger on the papers with force. He paused; and Mr Verloc, who had recognized his own handwriting very well, waited in an almost breathless silence. "We are not very satisfied with the attitude of the police here," the other continued, with every appearance of mental fatigue.

The shoulders of Mr Verloc, without actually moving, suggested a shrug. And for the first time since he left his home that morning his lips opened.

"Every country has its police," he said, philosophically. But as the official of the Embassy went on blinking at him steadily he felt constrained to add: "Allow me to observe that I have no means of action upon the police here."

"What is desired," said the man of papers, "is the occurrence of something definite which should stimulate their vigilance. That is within your province—is it not so?"

Mr Verloc made no answer except by a sigh, which escaped him involuntarily, for instantly he tried to give his face a cheerful expression. The official blinked doubtfully, as if affected by the dim light of the room. He repeated vaguely:

"The vigilance of the police—and the severity of the magistrates. The general leniency of the judicial procedure here, and the utter absence of all repressive measures, are a scandal to Europe. What is wished for just now is the accentuation of the unrest—of the fermentation which undoubtedly exists—"

"Undoubtedly, undoubtedly," broke in Mr Verloc in a deep, deferential bass of an oratorical quality, so utterly different from the tone in which he had spoken before that his interlocutor remained profoundly surprised. "It exists to a dangerous degree. My reports for the last twelve months make it sufficiently clear."

"Your reports for the last twelve months," State Councillor Wurmt began in his gentle and dispassionate tone, "have been read by me. I failed to discover why you wrote them at all."

A sad silence reigned for a time. Mr Verloc seemed to have swallowed his tongue, and the other gazed at the papers on the table fixedly. At last he gave them a slight push.

"The state of affairs you expose there is assumed to exist as the first condition of your employment. What is required at present is not writing, but the bringing to light of a distinct, significant fact—I would almost say of an alarming fact."

"I need not say that all my endeavours shall be directed to that end," Mr Verloc said, with convinced modulations in his conversational husky tone. But the sense of being blinked at watchfully behind the blind glitter of these eyeglasses on the other side of the table disconcerted him. He stopped short with a gesture of absolute devotion. The useful hard-working, if obscure member of the Embassy had an air of being impressed by some newly born thought.

"You are very corpulent," he said.

This observation, really of a psychological nature, and advanced with the modest hesitation of an officeman more familiar with ink and paper than with the requirements of active life, stung Mr Verloc in the manner of a rude personal remark. He stepped back a pace.

"Eh? What were you pleased to say?" he exclaimed, with husky resentment.

The Chancelier d'Ambassade, entrusted with the conduct of this interview, seemed to find it too much for him.

"I think," he said, "that you had better see Mr Vladimir. Yes, decidedly I think you ought to see Mr Vladimir. Be good enough to wait here," he added, and went out with mincing steps.

At once Mr Verloc passed his hand over his hair. A slight perspiration had broken out of his forehead. He let the air escape from his pursed-up lips like a man blowing at a spoonful of hot soup. But when the servant in brown appeared at the door silently, Mr Verloc had not moved an inch from the place he had occupied throughout the interview. He had remained motionless, as if feeling himself surrounded by pitfalls.

He walked along a passage lighted by a lonely gas-jet, then up a flight of winding stairs, and through a glazed and cheerful corridor on the first floor. The footman threw open a door, and stood aside. The feet of Mr Verloc felt a thick carpet. The room was large, with three windows; and a young man with a shaven, big face, sitting in a roomy armchair before a vast mahogany writing-table, said in French to the Chancelier d'Ambassade, who was going out with the papers in his hand:

"You are quite right, *mon cher.* He's fat—the animal."

Mr Vladimir, First Secretary, had a drawing-room reputation as an agreeable and entertaining man. He was something of a favourite in society. His wit consisted in discovering droll connections between incongruous ideas; and when talking in that strain he sat well forward on his seat, with his left hand raised, as if exhibiting his funny demonstrations between the thumb and forefinger, while his round and clean-shaven face wore an expression of merry perplexity.

But there was no trace of merriment or perplexity in the way he looked at Mr Verloc. Lying far back in the deep armchair, with squarely spread elbows, and throwing one leg over a thick knee, he had with his smooth and rosy countenance the air of a preternaturally thriving baby that will not stand nonsense from anybody.

"You understand French, I suppose?" he said.

Mr Verloc stated huskily that he did. His whole vast bulk had a forward inclination. He stood on the carpet in the middle of the room, clutching his hat and stick in one hand; the other hung lifelessly by his side. He muttered unobtrusively somewhere deep down in his throat something about having done his military service in the French artillery. At once, with contemptuous perversity, Mr Vladimir changed the language, and began to speak idiomatic English without the slightest trace of a foreign accent.

"Ah! Yes. Of course. Let's see. How much did you get for obtaining the design of the improved breech-block of their new field-gun?"

"Five years' rigorous confinement in a fortress," Mr Verloc answered, unexpectedly, but without any sign of feeling.

"You got off easily," was Mr Vladimir's comment. "And, anyhow, it served you right for letting yourself get caught. What made you go in for that sort of thing—eh?"

Mr Verloc's husky conversational voice was heard speaking of youth, of a fatal infatuation for an unworthy—

"Aha! *Cherchez la femme,*" Mr Vladimir deigned to interrupt, unbending, but without affability; there was, on the contrary, a touch of grimness in his condescension. "How long have you been employed by the Embassy here?" he asked.

"Ever since the time of the late Baron Stott-Wartenheim," Mr Verloc answered in subdued tones, and protruding his lips sadly, in sign of sorrow for the deceased diplomat. The First Secretary observed this play of physiognomy steadily.

"Ah! ever since . . . Well! What have you got to say for yourself?" he asked, sharply.

Mr Verloc answered with some surprise that he was not aware of having anything special to say. He had been summoned by a letter—And he plunged his hand busily into the side pocket of his overcoat, but before the mocking, cynical watchfulness of Mr Vladimir, concluded to leave it there.

"Bah!" said the latter. "What do you mean by getting out of condition like this? You haven't got even the physique of your profession. You—a member of a starving proletariat—never! You—a desperate socialist or anarchist—which is it?"

"Anarchist," stated Mr Verloc in a deadened tone.

"Bosh!" went on Mr Vladimir, without raising his voice. "You startled old Wurmt himself. You wouldn't deceive an idiot. They all are that by-the-by, but you seem to me simply impossible. So you began your connection with us by stealing the French gun designs. And you got yourself caught. That must have been very disagreeable to our Government. You don't seem to be very smart."

Mr Verloc tried to exculpate himself huskily.

"As I've had occasion to observe before, a fatal infatuation for an unworthy—"

Mr Vladimir raised a large, white, plump hand.

"Ah, yes. The unlucky attachment—of your youth. She got hold of the money, and then sold you to the police—eh?"

The doleful change in Mr Verloc's physiognomy, the momentary drooping of his whole person, confessed that such was the regrettable case. Mr Vladimir's hand clasped the ankle reposing on his knee. The sock was of dark blue silk.

"You see, that was not very clever of you. Perhaps you are too susceptible."

Mr Verloc intimated in a throaty, veiled murmur that he was no longer young.

"Oh! That's a failing which age does not cure," Mr Vladimir remarked, with sinister familiarity. "But no! You are too fat for that. You could not have come to look like this if you had been at all susceptible. I'll tell you what I think is the matter: you are a lazy fellow. How long have you been drawing pay from this Embassy?"

"Eleven years," was the answer, after a moment of sulky hesitation. "I've been charged with several missions to London while His Excellency Baron Stott-Wartenheim was still Ambassador in Paris. Then by his Excellency's instructions I settled down in London. I am English."

"You are! Are you? Eh?"

"A natural-born British subject," Mr Verloc said, stolidly. "But my father was French, and so—"

"Never mind explaining," interrupted the other. "I daresay you could have been legally a Marshal of France and a Member of Parliament in England—and then, indeed, you would have been of some use to our Embassy."

This flight of fancy provoked something like a faint smile on Mr Verloc's face. Mr Vladimir retained an imperturbable gravity.

"But, as I've said, you are a lazy fellow; you don't use your opportunities. In the time of Baron Stott-Wartenheim we had a lot of soft-headed people running this Embassy. They caused fellows of your sort to form a false conception of the nature of a secret service fund. It is my business to correct this misapprehension by telling you what the secret service is not. It is not a philanthropic institution. I've had you called here on purpose to tell you this."

Mr Vladimir observed the forced expression of bewilderment on Verloc's face, and smiled sarcastically.

"I see that you understand me perfectly. I daresay you are intelligent enough for your work. What we want now is activity—activity."

On repeating this last word Mr Vladimir laid a long white forefinger on the edge of the desk. Every trace of huskiness disappeared from Verloc's voice. The nape of his gross neck became crimson above the velvet collar of his overcoat. His lips quivered before they came widely open.

"If you'll only be good enough to look up my record," he boomed out in his great, clear, oratorical bass, "you'll see I gave a warning only three months ago on the occasion of the Grand Duke Romuald's visit to Paris, which was telegraphed from here to the French police, and—"

"Tut, tut!" broke out Mr Vladimir, with a frowning grimace. "The French police had no use for your warning. Don't roar like this. What the devil do you mean?"

With a note of proud humility Mr Verloc apologized for forgetting himself. His voice, famous for years at open-air meetings and at workmen's assemblies in large halls, had contributed, he said, to his reputation of a good and trustworthy comrade. It was, therefore, a part of his usefulness. It had inspired confidence in his principles. "I was always put up to speak by the leaders at a critical moment," Mr Verloc declared, with obvious satisfaction. There was no uproar above which he could not make himself heard, he added; and suddenly he made a demonstration.

"Allow me," he said. With lowered forehead, without looking up, swiftly and ponderously, he crossed the room to one of the french windows. As if giving way to an uncontrollable impulse, he opened it a little. Mr Vladimir, jumping up amazed from the depths of the armchair, looked over his shoulder; and below, across the courtyard of the Embassy, well beyond the open gate, could be seen the broad back of a policeman watching idly the gorgeous perambulator of a wealthy baby being wheeled in state across the Square.

"Constable!" said Mr Verloc, with no more effort than if he were whispering; and Mr Vladimir burst into a laugh on seeing the policeman spin round as if prodded by a sharp instrument. Mr Verloc shut the window quietly, and returned to the middle of the room.

"With a voice like that," he said, putting on the husky conversational pedal, "I was naturally trusted. And I knew what to say, too."

Mr Vladimir, arranging his cravat, observed him in the glass over the mantelpiece.

"I daresay you have the social revolutionary jargon by heart well enough," he said, contemptuously. "*Vox et* . . . You haven't ever studied Latin—have you?"

"No," growled Mr Verloc. "You did not expect me to know it. I belong to the million. Who knows Latin? Only a few hundred imbeciles who aren't fit to take care of themselves."

For some thirty seconds longer Mr Vladimir studied in the mirror the fleshy profile, the gross bulk, of the man behind him. And at the same time he had the advantage of seeing his own face, clean-shaved and round, rosy about the gills, and with the thin, sensitive lips formed exactly for the utterance of those delicate witticisms which had made him such a favourite in the very highest society. Then he turned, and advanced into the room with such determination that the very ends of his quaintly old-fashioned bow necktie seemed to bristle with unspeakable menaces. The movement was so swift and fierce that Mr Verloc, casting an oblique glance, quailed inwardly.

"Aha! You dare be impudent," Mr Vladimir began, with an amazingly guttural intonation not only utterly un-English, but absolutely un-European, and startling even to Mr Verloc's experience of cosmopolitan slums. "You dare! Well, I am going to speak English to you. Voice won't do. We have no use for your voice. We don't want a voice. We want facts—startling facts—damn you," he added, with a sort of ferocious discretion, right into Mr Verloc's face.

"Don't you try to come over me with your Hyperborean manners." Mr Verloc defended himself, huskily, looking at the carpet. At this his interlocutor, smiling mockingly above the bristling bow of his necktie, switched the conversation into French.

"You give yourself for an *agent provocateur.* The proper business of an *agent provocateur* is to provoke. As far as I can judge from your record kept here, you have done nothing to earn your money for the last three years."

"Nothing!" exclaimed Verloc, stirring not a limb, and not raising his eyes, but with the note of sincere feeling in his tone. "I have several times prevented what might have been—"

"There is a proverb in this country which says prevention is better than cure," interrupted Mr Vladimir, throwing himself into the armchair. "It is stupid in a general way. There is no end to prevention. But it is characteristic. They dislike finality in this country. Don't you be too English. And in this particular instance, don't be absurd. The evil is already here. We don't want prevention—we want cure."

He paused, turned to the desk, and turning over some papers lying there, spoke in a changed, business-like tone, without looking at Mr Verloc.

"You know, of course, of the International Conference assembled in Milan?"

Mr Verloc intimated hoarsely that he was in the habit of reading the daily papers. To a further question his answer was that, of course, he understood what he read. At this Mr Vladimir, smiling faintly at the documents he was still scanning one after another, murmured "As long as it is not written in Latin, I suppose."

"Or Chinese," added Mr Verloc, stolidly.

"H'm. Some of your revolutionary friends' effusions are written in a *charabia* every bit as incomprehensible as Chinese—" Mr Vladimir let fall disdainfully a grey sheet of printed matter. "What are all these leaflets headed F.P. with a hammer, pen, and torch crossed? What does it mean, the F.P.?" Mr Verloc approached the imposing writing-table.

"The Future of the Proletariat. It's a society," he explained, standing ponderously by the side of the armchair, "not anarchist in principle, but open to all shades of revolutionary opinion."

"Are you in it?"

"One of the Vice-Presidents," Mr Verloc breathed out heavily; and the First Secretary of the Embassy raised his head to look at him.

"Then you ought to be ashamed of yourself," he said, incisively. "Isn't your society capable of anything else but printing this prophetic bosh in blunt type on this filthy paper—eh? Why don't you do something? Look here. I've this matter in hand now, and I tell you plainly that you will have to earn your money. The good old Stott-Wartenheim times are over. No work, no pay."

Mr Verloc felt a queer sensation of faintness in his stout legs. He stepped back one pace, and blew his nose loudly.

He was, in truth, startled and alarmed. The rusty London sunshine struggling clear of the London mist shed a lukewarm brightness into the First Secretary's private room: and in the silence Mr Verloc heard against a window-pane the faint buzzing of a fly—his first fly of the year—heralding better than any number of swallows the approach of spring. The useless fussing of that tiny, energetic organism affected unpleasantly this big man threatened in his indolence.

In the pause Mr Vladimir formulated in his mind a series of disparaging remarks concerning Mr Verloc's face and figure. The fellow was unexpectedly vulgar, heavy, and impudently unintelligent. He looked uncommonly like a master plumber come to present his bill. The First Secretary of the Embassy, from his occasional excursions into the field of American humour, had formed a special notion of that class of mechanic as the embodiment of fraudulent laziness and incompetency.

This was then the famous and trusty secret agent, so secret that he was never designated otherwise but by the symbol Δ in the late Baron Stott-Wartenheim's official, semi-official, and confidential correspondence; the celebrated agent Δ whose warnings had the power to change the schemes and the dates of royal, imperial, grand-ducal journeys, and sometimes cause them to be put off altogether! This fellow! And Mr Vladimir indulged mentally in an enormous and derisive fit of merriment, partly at his own astonishment, which he judged naïve, but mostly at the expense of the universally regretted Baron Stott-Wartenheim. His late Excellency, whom the august favour of his Imperial master had imposed as Ambassador upon several reluctant Ministers of Foreign Affairs, had enjoyed in his lifetime a fame for an owlish, pessimistic gullibility. His Excellency had the social revolution on the brain. He imagined himself to be a diplomatist set apart by a special dispensation to watch the end of diplomacy, and pretty nearly the end of the world, in a horrid, democratic upheaval. His prophetic and doleful dispatches had been for years the joke of Foreign Offices. He was said to have exclaimed on his death-bed (visited by his Imperial friend and master): "Unhappy Europe! Thou shalt perish by the moral insanity of thy children!" He was fated to be the victim of the first humbugging rascal that came along, thought Mr Vladimir, smiling vaguely at Mr Verloc.

"You ought to venerate the memory of Baron Stott-Wartenheim," he exclaimed, suddenly.

The lowered physiognomy of Mr Verloc expressed a sombre and weary annoyance.

"Permit me to observe to you," he said, "that I came here because I was summoned by a peremptory letter. I have been here only twice before in the last eleven years, and certainly never at eleven in the morning. It isn't very wise to call me up like this. There is just a chance of being seen. And that would be no joke for me."

Mr Vladimir shrugged his shoulders.

"It would destroy my usefulness," continued the other hotly.

"That's your affair," murmured Mr Vladimir, with soft brutality. "When you cease to be useful you shall cease to be employed. Yes. Right off. Cut short. You shall—" Mr Vladimir, frowning, paused, at a loss for a sufficiently idiomatic expression, and instantly brightened up, with a grin of beautifully white teeth. "You shall be chucked," he brought out, ferociously.

Once more Mr Verloc had to react with all the force of his will against the sensation of faintness running down one's legs which once upon a time had inspired some poor devil with the felicitous expression: "My heart went down into my boots." Mr Verloc, aware of the sensation, raised his head bravely.

Mr Vladimir bore the look of heavy inquiry with perfect serenity.

"What we want is to administer a tonic to the Conference in Milan," he said, airily. "Its deliberations upon international action for the suppression of political crime don't seem to get anywhere. England lags. This country is absurd with its sentimental regard for individual liberty. It's intolerable to think that all your friends have got only to come over to—"

"In that way I have them all under my eye," Mr Verloc interrupted, huskily.

"It would be much more to the point to have them all under lock and key. England must be brought into line. The imbecile bourgeoisie of this country make themselves the accomplices of the very people whose aim is to drive them out of their houses to starve in ditches. And they have the political power still, if they only had the sense to use it for their preservation. I suppose you agree that the middle classes are stupid?"

Mr Verloc agreed hoarsely.

"They are."

"They have no imagination. They are blinded by an idiotic vanity. What they want just now is a jolly good scare. This is the psychological moment to set your friends to work. I have had you called here to develop to you my idea."

And Mr Vladimir developed his idea from on high, with scorn and condescension, displaying at the same time an amount of ignorance as to the real aims, thoughts, and methods of the revolutionary world which filled the silent Mr Verloc with inward consternation. He confounded causes with effects more than was excusable, the most distinguished propagandists with impulsive bomb throwers; assumed organizations where in the nature of things it could not exist; spoke of the social revolutionary party one moment as of a perfectly disciplined army, where the word of chiefs was supreme, and at another as if it had been the loosest association of desperate brigands that ever camped in a mountain gorge. Once Mr Verloc had opened his mouth for a protest, but the raising of a shapely, large white hand arrested him. Very soon he became too appalled to even try to protest. He listened in a stillness of dread which resembled the immobility of profound attention.

"A series of outrages," Mr Vladimir continued, calmly, "executed here in this country; not only *planned* here—that would not do—they would not mind. Your friends could set half the Continent on fire without influencing the public opinion here in favour of a universal repressive legislation. They will not look outside their backyard here."

Mr Verloc cleared his throat, but his heart failed him, and he said nothing.

"These outrages need not be especially sanguinary," Mr Vladimir went on, as if delivering a scientific lecture, "but they must be sufficiently startling—effective. Let them be directed against buildings, for instance. What is the fetish of the hour that all the bourgeoisie recognize—eh, Mr Verloc?"

Mr Verloc opened his hands and shrugged his shoulders slightly.

"You are too lazy to think," was Mr Vladimir's comment upon that gesture. "Pay attention to what I say. The fetish of today is neither royalty nor religion. Therefore the palace and the church should be left alone. You understand what I mean, Mr Verloc?"

The dismay and the scorn of Mr Verloc found vent in an attempt at levity.

"Perfectly. But what of the Embassies? A series of attacks on the various Embassies," he began; but he could not withstand the cold, watchful stare of the First Secretary.

"You can be facetious, I see," the latter observed, carelessly. "That's all right. It may enliven your oratory at socialistic congresses. But this room is no place for it. It would be infinitely safer for you to follow carefully what I am saying. As you are being called upon to furnish facts instead of cock-and-bull stories, you had better try to make your profit off what I am taking the trouble to explain to you. The sacrosanct fetish of today is science. Why don't you get some of your friends to go for that wooden-faced panjandrum—eh? Is it not part of these institutions which must be swept away before the F.P. comes along?"

Mr Verloc said nothing. He was afraid to open his lips lest a groan should escape him.

"This is what you should try for. An attempt upon a crowned head or on a president is sensational enough in a way, but not so much as it used to be. It has entered into the general conception of the existence of all chiefs of state. It's almost conventional—especially since so many presidents have been assassinated. Now let us take an outrage upon—say, a church. Horrible enough at first sight, no doubt, and yet not so effective as a person of an ordinary mind might think. No matter how revolutionary and anarchist in inception, there would be fools enough to give such an outrage the character of a religious manifestation. And that would detract from the especial alarming significance we wish to give to the act. A murderous attempt on a restaurant or a theatre would suffer in the same way from the suggestion of non-political passion; the exasperation of a hungry man, an act of social revenge. All this is used up; it is no longer instructive as an object lesson in revolutionary anarchism. Every newspaper has ready-made phrases to explain such manifestations away. I am about to give you the philosophy of bomb throwing from my point of view; from the point of view you pretend to have been serving for the last eleven years. I will try not to talk above your head. The sensibilities of the class you are attacking are soon blunted. Property seems to them an indestructible thing. You can't count upon their emotions either of pity or fear for very long. A bomb outrage to have any influence on public opinion now must go beyond the intention of vengeance or terrorism. It must be purely destructive. It must be that, and only that, beyond the faintest suspicion of any other object. You anarchists should make it clear that you are perfectly determined to make a clean sweep of the whole social creation. But how to get that appallingly absurd notion into the heads of the middle classes so that there should be no mistake? That's the question. By directing your blows at something outside the ordinary passions of humanity is the answer. Of course, there is art. A bomb in the National Gallery would make some noise. But it would not be serious enough. Art has never been their fetish. It's like breaking a few back windows in a man's house; whereas, if you want to make him really sit up, you must try at least to raise the roof. There would be some screaming of course, but from whom? Artists—art critics and such like—people of no account. Nobody minds what they say. But there is learning—science. Any imbecile that has got an income believes in that. He does not know why, but he believes it matters somehow. It is the sacrosanct fetish. All the damned professors are radicals at heart. Let them know that their great panjandrum has got to go, too, to make room for the Future of the Proletariat. A howl from all these intellectual idiots is bound to help forward the labours of the Milan Conference. They will be writing to the papers. Their indignation would be above suspicion, no material interests being openly at stake, and it will alarm every selfishness of the class which should be impressed. They believe that in some mysterious way science is at the source of their material prosperity. They do. And the absurd ferocity of such a demonstration will affect them more profoundly than the mangling of a whole street—or theatre—full of their own kind. To that last they can always say: 'Oh! It's mere class hate.' But what is one to say to an act of destructive ferocity so absurd as to be incomprehensible, inexplicable, almost unthinkable; in fact, mad? Madness alone is truly terrifying, inasmuch as you cannot placate it either by threats, persuasion, or bribes. Moreover, I am a civilized man. I would never dream of directing you to organize a mere butchery, even if I expected the best results from it. But I wouldn't expect from a butchery the result I want. Murder is always with us. It is almost an institution. The demonstration must be against learning—science. But not every science will do. The attack must have all the shocking senselessness of gratuitous blasphemy. Since bombs are your means of expression, it would be really telling if one could throw a bomb into pure mathematics. But that is impossible. I have been trying to educate you; I have expounded to you the higher philosophy of your usefulness, and suggested to you some serviceable arguments. The practical application of my teaching interests *you* mostly. But from the moment I have undertaken to interview you I have also given some attention to the practical aspect of the question. What do you think of having a go at astronomy?"

For some time already Mr Verloc's immobility by the side of the armchair resembled a state of collapsed coma—a sort of passive insensibility interrupted by slight convulsive starts, such as may be observed in a domestic dog having a nightmare on the hearth-rug. And it was in an uneasy, doglike growl that he repeated the word:

"Astronomy."

He had not recovered thoroughly as yet from the state of bewilderment brought about by the effort to follow Mr Vladimir's rapid, incisive utterance. It had overcome his power of assimilation. It had made him angry. This anger was complicated by incredulity. And suddenly it dawned upon him that all this was an elaborate joke. Mr Vladimir exhibited his white teeth in a smile, with dimples on his round, full face posed with a complacent inclination above the bristling bow of his necktie. The favourite of intelligent society women had assumed his drawing-room attitude accompanying the delivery of delicate witticisms. Sitting well forward, his white hand upraised, he seemed to hold delicately between his thumb and forefinger the subtlety of his suggestion.

"There could be nothing better. Such an outrage combines the greatest possible regard for humanity with the most alarming display of ferocious imbecility. I defy the ingenuity of journalists to persuade their public that any given member of the proletariat can have a personal grievance against astronomy. Starvation itself could hardly be dragged in there—eh? And there are other advantages. The whole civilized world has heard of Greenwich. The very bootblacks in the basement of Charing Cross Station know something of it. See?"

The features of Mr Vladimir, so well known in the best society by their humorous urbanity, beamed with cynical self-satisfaction, which would have astonished the intelligent women his wit entertained so exquisitely. "Yes," he continued, with a contemptuous smile, "the blowing up of the first meridian is bound to raise a howl of execration."

"A difficult business," Mr Verloc mumbled, feeling that this was the only safe thing to say.

"What is the matter? Haven't you the whole gang under your hand? The very pick of the basket? That old terrorist Yundt is here. I see him walking about Piccadilly in his green havelock almost every day. And Michaelis, the ticket-of-leave apostle—you don't mean to say you don't know where he is? Because if you don't, I can tell you," Mr Vladimir went on menacingly. "If you imagine that you are the only one in the secret fund list, you are mistaken."

This perfectly gratuitous suggestion caused Mr Verloc to shuffle his feet slightly.

"And the whole Lausanne lot—eh? Haven't they been flocking over here at the first hint of the Milan Conference? This is an absurd country."

"It will cost money," Mr Verloc said, by a sort of instinct.

"That cock won't fight," Mr Vladimir retorted, with an amazingly genuine English accent. "You'll get your screw every month, and no more till something happens. And if nothing happens very soon you won't get even that. What's your ostensible occupation? What are you supposed to live by?"

"I keep a shop," answered Mr Verloc.

"A shop! What sort of shop?"

"Stationery, newspapers. My wife—"

"Your what?" interrupted Mr Vladimir in his guttural Central Asian tones.

"My wife." Mr Verloc raised his husky voice slightly. "I am married."

"That be damned for a yarn!" exclaimed the other in unfeigned astonishment. "Married! And you a professional anarchist, too! What is this confounded nonsense? But I suppose it's merely a manner of speaking. Anarchists don't marry. It's well known. They can't. It would be apostasy."

"My wife isn't one," Mr Verloc mumbled, sulkily. "Moreover, it's no concern of yours."

"Oh, yes, it is," snapped Mr Vladimir. "I am beginning to be convinced that you are not at all the man for the work you've been employed on. Why, you must have discredited yourself completely in your own world by your marriage. Couldn't you have managed without? This is your virtuous attachment—eh? What with one sort of attachment and another you are doing away with your usefulness."

Mr Verloc, puffing out his cheeks, let the air escape violently, and that was all. He had armed himself with patience. It was not to be tried much longer. The First Secretary became suddenly very curt, detached, final.

"You may go now," he said. "A dynamite outrage must be provoked. I give you a month. The sittings of the Conference are suspended. Before it reassembles again something must have happened here, or your connection with us ceases."

He changed the note once more with an unprincipled versatility. "Think over my philosophy, Mr—Mr—Verloc," he said, with a sort of chaffing condescension, waving his hand towards the door. "Go for the first meridian. You don't know the middle classes as well as I do. Their sensibilities are jaded. The first meridian. Nothing better, and nothing easier, I should think."

He had got up, and with his thin sensitive lips twitching humorously, watched in the glass over the mantelpiece Mr Verloc backing out of the room heavily, hat and stick in hand. The door closed.

The footman in trousers, appearing suddenly in the corridor, led Mr Verloc another way out and through a small door in the corner of the courtyard. The porter standing at the gate ignored his exit completely; and Mr Verloc retraced the path of his morning's pilgrimage as if in a dream—an angry dream. This detachment from the material world was so complete that, though the mortal envelope of Mr Verloc had not hastened unduly along the streets, that part of him to which it would be unwarrantably rude to refuse immortality, found itself at the shop door all at once, as borne from west to east on the wings of a great wind. He walked straight behind the counter, and sat down on a wooden chair that stood there. No one appeared to disturb his solitude. Stevie, put into a green baize apron, was now sweeping and dusting upstairs, intent and conscientious, as though he were playing at it; and Mrs Verloc, warned in the kitchen by the clatter of the cracked bell, had merely come to the glazed door of the parlour, and putting the curtain aside a little, had peered into the dim shop. Seeing her husband sitting there shadowy and bulky, with his hat tilted far back on his head, she had at once returned to her stove. An hour or more later she took the green baize apron off her brother Stevie, and instructed him to wash his hands and face in the peremptory tone she had used in that connection for fifteen years or so—ever since she had, in fact, ceased to attend to the boy's hands and face herself. She spared presently a glance away from her dishing-up for the inspection of that face and those hands which Stevie, approaching the kitchen table, offered for her approval with an air of self-assurance hiding a perpetual residue of anxiety. Formerly the anger of the father was the supremely effective sanction of these rites, but Mr Verloc's placidity in domestic life would have made all mention of anger incredible—even to poor Stevie's nervousness. The theory was that Mr Verloc would have been inexpressibly pained and shocked by any deficiency of cleanliness at meal times. Winnie after the death of her father found considerable consolation in the feeling that she need no longer tremble for poor Stevie. She could not bear to see the boy hurt. It maddened her. As a little girl she had often faced with blazing eyes the irascible licensed victualler in defence of her brother. Nothing now in Mrs Verloc's appearance could lead one to suppose that she was capable of a passionate demonstration.

She finished her dishing-up. The table was laid in the parlour. Going to the foot of the stairs she screamed out "Mother!" Then opening the glazed door leading to the shop, "Adolf!" Mr Verloc had not changed his position; he had not apparently stirred a limb for an hour and a half. He got up heavily, and came to his dinner in his overcoat and with his hat on, without uttering a word. His silence in itself had nothing startlingly unusual in this household, hidden in the shades of the sordid street seldom touched by the sun, behind the dim shop with its wares of disreputable rubbish. Only that day Mr Verloc's taciturnity was so obviously thoughtful that the two women were impressed by it. They sat silent themselves, keeping a watchful eye on poor Stevie, lest he should break out into one of his fits of loquacity. He faced Mr Verloc across the table, and remained very good and quiet, staring vacantly. The endeavour to keep him from making himself objectionable in any way to the master of the house put no inconsiderable anxiety into these two women's lives. "The boy," as they alluded to him softly between themselves, had been a source of that sort of anxiety almost from the very day of his birth. The late licensed victualler's humiliation at having such a very peculiar boy for a son manifested itself by a propensity to brutal treatment; for he was a person of fine sensibilities, and his sufferings as a man and a father were perfectly genuine. Afterwards Stevie had to be kept from making himself a nuisance to the single gentlemen lodgers, who are themselves a queer lot, and are easily aggrieved. And there was always the anxiety of his mere existence to face. Visions of a workhouse infirmary for her child had haunted the old woman in the basement breakfast-room of the decayed Belgravian house. "If you had not found such a good husband, my dear," she used to say to her daughter, "I don't know what would have become of that poor boy."

Mr Verloc extended as much recognition to Stevie as a man not particularly fond of animals may give to his wife's beloved cat; and this recognition, benevolent and perfunctory, was essentially of the same quality. Both women admitted to themselves that not much more could be reasonably expected. It was enough to earn for Mr Verloc the old woman's reverential gratitude. In the early days, made sceptical by the trials of friendless life, she used sometimes to ask anxiously: "You don't think, my dear, that Mr Verloc is getting tired of seeing Stevie about?" To this Winnie replied habitually by a slight toss of her head. Once, however, she retorted, with a rather grim pertness: "He'll have to get tired of me first." A long silence ensued. The mother, with her feet propped up on a stool, seemed to be trying to get to the bottom of that answer, whose feminine profundity had struck her all of a heap. She had never really understood why Winnie had married Mr Verloc. It was very sensible of her, and evidently had turned out for the best, but the girl might have naturally hoped to find somebody of a more suitable age. There had been a steady young fellow, only son of a butcher in the next street, helping his father in business, with whom Winnie had been walking out with obvious gusto. He was dependent on his father, it is true; but the business was good, and his prospects excellent. He took her girl to the theatre on several evenings. Then just as she began to dread to hear of their engagement (for what could she have done with that big house alone, with Stevie on her hands), that romance came to an abrupt end, and Winnie went about looking very dull. But Mr Verloc, turning up providentially to occupy the first-floor front bedroom, there had been no more question of the young butcher. It was clearly providential.

CHAPTER 3

". . . All idealization makes life poorer. To beautify it is to take away its character of complexity—it is to destroy it. Leave that to the moralists, my boy. History is made by men, but they do not make it in their heads. The ideas that are born in their consciousness play an insignificant part in the march of events. History is dominated and determined by the tool and the production—by the force of economic conditions. Capitalism has made socialism, and the laws made by the capitalist for the protection of property are responsible for anarchism. No one can tell what form the social organization may take in the future. Then why indulge in prophetic phantasies? At best they can only interpret the mind of the prophet, and can have no objective value. Leave that pastime to the moralists, my boy."

Michaelis, the ticket-of-leave apostle, was speaking in an even voice, a voice that wheezed as if deadened and oppressed by the layer of fat on his chest. He had come out of a highly hygienic prison round like a tub, with an enormous stomach and distended cheeks of a pale, semi-transparent complexion, as though for fifteen years the servants of an outraged society had made a point of stuffing him with fattening foods in a damp and lightless cellar. And ever since he had never managed to get his weight down as much as an ounce.

It was said that for three seasons running a very wealthy old lady had sent him for a cure to Marienbad—where he was about to share the public curiosity once with a crowned head—but the police on that occasion ordered him to leave within twelve hours. His martyrdom was continued by forbidding him all access to the healing waters. But he was resigned now.

With his elbow presenting no appearance of a joint, but more like a bend in a dummy's limb, thrown over the back of a chair, he leaned forward slightly over his short and enormous thighs to spit into the grate.

"Yes! I had the time to think things out a little," he added without emphasis. "Society has given me plenty of time for meditation."

On the other side of the fireplace, in the horse-hair armchair where Mrs Verloc's mother was generally privileged to sit, Karl Yundt giggled grimly, with a faint black grimace of a toothless mouth. The terrorist, as he called himself, was old and bald, with a narrow, snow-white wisp of a goatee hanging limply from his chin. An extraordinary expression of underhand malevolence survived in his extinguished eyes. When he rose painfully the thrusting forward of a skinny groping hand deformed by gouty swellings suggested the effort of a moribund murderer summoning all his remaining strength for a last stab. He leaned on a thick stick, which trembled under his other hand. "I have always dreamed," he mouthed, fiercely, "of a band of men absolute in their resolve to discard all scruples in the choice of means, strong enough to give themselves frankly the name of destroyers, and free from the taint of that resigned pessimism which rots the world. No pity for anything on earth, including themselves, and death enlisted for good and all in the service of humanity—that's what I would have liked to see."

His little bald head quivered, imparting a comical vibration to the wisp of white goatee. His enunciation would have been almost totally unintelligible to a stranger. His worn-out passion, resembling in its impotent fierceness the excitement of a senile sensualist, was badly served by a dried throat and toothless gums which seemed to catch the tip of his tongue. Mr Verloc, established in the corner of the sofa at the other end of the room, emitted two hearty grunts of assent.

The old terrorist turned slowly his head on his skinny neck from side to side.

"And I could never get as many as three such men together. So much for your rotten pessimism," he snarled at Michaelis, who uncrossed his thick legs similar to bolsters, and slid his feet abruptly under his chair in sign of exasperation.

He a pessimist! Preposterous! He cried out that the charge was outrageous. He was so far from pessimism that he saw already the end of all private property coming along logically, unavoidably, by the mere development of its inherent viciousness. The possessors of property had not only to face the awakened proletariat, but they had also to fight amongst themselves. Yes. Struggle, warfare, was the condition of private ownership. It was fatal. Ah! he did not depend upon emotional excitement to keep up his belief, no declamations, no anger, no visions of blood-red flags waving, or metaphorical lurid suns of vengeance rising above the horizon of a doomed society. Not he! Cold reason, he boasted, was the basis of his optimism. Yes optimism—

His laborious wheezing stopped, then, after a gasp or two, he added:

"Don't you think that, if I had not been the optimist I am, I could not have found in fifteen years some means to cut my throat? And, in the last instance, there were always the walls of my cell to dash my head against."

The shortness of breath took all fire, all animation out of his voice; his great, pale cheeks hung like filled pouches, motionless, without a quiver; but in his blue eyes, narrowed as if peering, there was the same look of confident shrewdness, a little crazy in its fixity, they must have had while the indomitable optimist sat thinking at night in his cell. Before him, Karl Yundt remained standing, one wing of his faded greenish havelock thrown back cavalierly over his shoulder. Seated in front of the fireplace, Comrade Ossipon, ex-medical student, the principal writer of the F.P. leaflets, stretched out his robust legs, keeping the soles of his boots turned up to the glow in the grate. A bush of crinkly yellow hair topped his red, freckled face, with a flattened nose and prominent mouth cast in the rough mould of the Negro type. His almond-shaped eyes leered languidly over the high cheek-bones. He wore a grey flannel shirt, the loose ends of a black silk tie hung down the buttoned breast of his serge coat; and his head resting on the back of his chair, his throat largely exposed, he raised to his lips a cigarette in a long wooden tube, puffing jets of smoke straight up at the ceiling.

Michaelis pursued his idea—*the* idea of his solitary reclusion—the thought vouchsafed to his captivity and growing like a faith revealed in visions. He talked to himself, indifferent to the sympathy or hostility of his hearers, indifferent indeed to their presence, from the habit he had acquired of thinking aloud hopefully in the solitude of the four whitewashed walls of his cell, in the sepulchral silence of the great blind pile of bricks near a river, sinister and ugly like a colossal mortuary for the socially drowned.

He was no good in discussion, not because any amount of argument could shake his faith, but because the mere fact of hearing another voice disconcerted him painfully, confusing his thoughts at once—these thoughts that for so many years, in a mental solitude more barren than a waterless desert, no living voice had ever combated, commented, or approved.

No one interrupted him now, and he made again the confession of his faith, mastering him irresistible and complete like an act of grace: the secret of fate discovered in the material side of life; the economic condition of the world responsible for the past and shaping the future; the source of all ideas, guiding the mental development of mankind and the very impulses of their passion—

A harsh laugh from Comrade Ossipon cut the tirade dead short in a sudden faltering of the tongue and a bewildered unsteadiness of the apostle's mildly exalted eyes. He closed them slowly for a moment, as if to collect his routed thoughts. A silence fell; but what with the two gas-jets over the table and the glowing grate the little parlour behind Mr Verloc's shop had become frightfully hot. Mr Verloc, getting off the sofa with ponderous reluctance, opened the door leading into the kitchen to get more air, and thus disclosed the innocent Stevie, seated very good and quiet at a deal table, drawing circles, circles; innumerable circles, concentric, eccentric; a coruscating whirl of circles that by their tangled multitude of repeated curves, uniformity of form, and confusion of interesting lines suggested a rendering of cosmic chaos, the symbolism of a mad art attempting the inconceivable. The artist never turned his head; and in all his soul's application to the task his back quivered, his thin neck, sunk into a deep hollow at the base of the skull, seemed ready to snap.

Mr Verloc, after a grunt of disapproving surprise, returned to the sofa. Alexander Ossipon got up, tall in his threadbare blue serge suit under the low ceiling, shook off the stiffness of long immobility, and strolled away into the kitchen (down two steps) to look over Stevie's shoulder. He came back, pronouncing oracularly: "Very good. Very characteristic, perfectly typical."

"What's very good?" grunted, inquiringly, Mr Verloc, settled again in the corner of the sofa. The other explained his meaning negligently, with a shade of condescension and a toss of his head towards the kitchen:

"Typical of this form of degeneracy—these drawings, I mean."

"You would call that lad a degenerate, would you?" mumbled Mr Verloc.

Comrade Alexander Ossipon—nicknamed the Doctor, ex-medical student without a degree; afterwards wandering lecturer to workingmen's associations upon the socialist aspects of hygiene; author of a popular quasi-medical study (in the form of a cheap pamphlet seized promptly by the police) entitled *The Corroding Vices of the Middle Classes;* special delegate of the more or less mysterious Red Committee, together with Karl Yundt and

Michaelis, for the work of literary propaganda—turned upon the obscure familiar of at least two Embassies that glance of insufferable, hopelessly dense sufficiency which nothing but the frequentation of science can give to the dullness of common morals.

"That's what he may be called scientifically. Very good type, too, altogether, of that sort of degenerate. It's good enough to glance at the lobes of his ears. If you read Lombroso—"

Mr Verloc, moody and spread largely on the sofa, continued to look down the row of his waistcoat buttons; but his cheeks became tinged by a faint blush. Of late even the merest derivative of the word science (a term in itself inoffensive and of indefinite meaning) had the curious power of evoking a definitely offensive mental vision of Mr Vladimir, in his body as he lived, with an almost supernatural clearness. And this phenomenon deserving justly to be classed amongst the marvels of science, induced in Mr Verloc an emotional state of dread and exasperation tending to express itself in violent swearing. But he said nothing. It was Karl Yundt who was heard, implacable to his last breath.

"Lombroso is an ass."

Comrade Ossipon met the shock of this blasphemy by an awful, vacant stare. And the other, his extinguished eyes without gleams blackening the deep shadows under the great, bony forehead, mumbled, catching the tip of his tongue between his lips at every second word as though he were chewing it angrily:

"Did you ever see such an idiot? For him the criminal is the prisoner. Simple, is it not? What about those who shut him up there—forced him in there? Exactly. Forced him in there. And what is crime? Does he know that, this imbecile who has made his way in this world of gorged fools by looking at the ears and teeth of a lot of poor, luckless devils? Teeth and ears mark the criminal? Do they? And what about the law that marks him still better—the pretty branding instrument invented by the overfed to protect themselves against the hungry? Red-hot applications on their vile skins—hey? Can't you smell and hear from here the thick hide of the people burn and sizzle? That's how criminals are made for your Lombrosos to write their silly stuff about."

The knob of his stick and his legs shook together with passion, whilst the trunk, draped in the wings of the havelock, preserved his historic attitude of defiance. He seemed to sniff the tainted air of social cruelty, to strain his ear for its atrocious sounds. There was an extraordinary force of suggestion in this posturing. The all but moribund veteran of dynamite wars had been a great actor in his time—actor on platforms, in secret assemblies, in private interviews. The famous terrorist had never in his life raised personally as much as his little finger against the social edifice. He was no man of action; he was not even an orator of torrential eloquence, sweeping the masses along in the rushing noise and foam of a great enthusiasm. With a more subtle intention, he took the part of an insolent and venomous evoker of sinister impulses which lurk in the blind envy and exasperated vanity of ignorance, in the suffering and misery of poverty, in all the hopeful and noble illusions of righteous anger, pity, and revolt. The shadow of his evil gift clung to him yet like the smell of a deadly drug in an old vial of poison, emptied now, useless, ready to be thrown away upon the rubbish-heap of things that had served their time.

Michaelis, the ticket-of-leave apostle, smiled vaguely with his glued lips; his pasty moon face drooped under the weight of melancholy assent. He had been a prisoner himself. His own skin had sizzled under the red-hot brand, he murmured softly. But Comrade Ossipon, nicknamed the Doctor, had got over the shock by that time.

"You don't understand," he began, disdainfully, but stopped short, intimidated by the dead blackness of the cavernous eyes in the face turned slowly towards him with a blind stare, as if guided only by the sound. He gave the discussion up, with a slight shrug of the shoulders.

Stevie, accustomed to move about disregarded, had got up from the kitchen table, carrying off his drawing to bed with him. He had reached the parlour door in time to receive in full the shock of Karl Yundt's eloquent imagery. The sheet of paper covered with circles dropped out of his fingers, and he remained staring at the old terrorist, as if rooted suddenly to the spot by his morbid horror and dread of physical pain. Stevie knew very well that hot iron applied to one's skin hurt very much. His scared eyes blazed with indignation: it would hurt terribly. His mouth dropped open.

Michaelis by staring unwinkingly at the fire had regained that sentiment of isolation necessary for the continuity of his thought. His optimism had begun to flow from his lips. He saw Capitalism doomed in its cradle, born with the poison of the principle of competition in its system. The great capitalists devouring the little capitalists, concentrating the power and the tools of production in great masses, perfecting industrial processes, and in the madness of self-aggrandizement only preparing, organizing, enriching, making ready the lawful inheritance of the suffering proletariat. Michaelis pronounced the great word "Patience"—and his clear blue glance, raised to the low ceiling of Mr Verloc's parlour, had a character of seraphic trustfulness. In the doorway Stevie, calmed, seemed sunk in hebetude.

Comrade Ossipon's face twitched with exasperation.

"Then it's no use doing anything—no use whatever."

"I don't say that," protested Michaelis, gently. His vision of truth had grown so intense that the sound of a strange voice failed to rout it this time. He continued to look down at the red coals. Preparation for the future was necessary, and he was willing to admit that the great change would perhaps come in the upheaval of a revolution. But he argued that revolutionary propaganda was a delicate work of high conscience. It was the education of the masters of the world. It should be as careful as the education given to kings. He would have it advance its tenets cautiously, even timidly, in our ignorance of the effect that may be produced by any given economic change upon the happiness, the morals, the intellect, the history of mankind. For history is made with tools, not with ideas; and everything is changed by economic conditions—art, philosophy, love, virtue—truth itself!

The coals in the grate settled down with a slight crash; and Michaelis, the hermit of visions in the desert of a penitentiary, got up impetuously. Round like a distended balloon, he opened his short, thick arms, as if in a pathetically hopeless attempt to embrace and hug to his breast a self-regenerated universe. He gasped with ardour.

"The future is as certain as the past—slavery, feudalism, individualism, collectivism. This is the statement of a law, not an empty prophecy."

The disdainful pout of Comrade Ossipon's thick lips accentuated the Negro type of his face.

"Nonsense," he said, calmly enough. "There is no law and no certainty. The teaching propaganda be hanged. What the people knows does not matter, were its knowledge ever so accurate. The only thing that matters to us is the emotional state of the masses. Without emotion there is no action."

He paused, then added with modest firmness:

"I am speaking now to you scientifically—scientifically—Eh? What did you say, Verloc?"

"Nothing," growled from the sofa Mr Verloc, who, provoked by the abhorrent sound, had merely muttered a "Damn."

The venomous spluttering of the old terrorist without teeth was heard.

"Do you know how I would call the nature of the present economic conditions? I would call it cannibalistic. That's what it is! They are nourishing their greed on the quivering flesh and the warm blood of the people—nothing else."

Stevie swallowed the terrifying statement with an audible gulp, and at once, as though it had been swift poison, sank limply in a sitting posture on the steps of the kitchen door.

Michaelis gave no signs of having heard anything. His lips seemed glued together for good; not a quiver passed over his heavy cheeks. With troubled eyes he looked for his round, hard hat, and put it on his round head. His round and obese body seemed to float low between the chairs under the sharp elbow of Karl Yundt. The old terrorist, raising an uncertain and clawlike hand, gave a swaggering tilt to a black felt sombrero shading the hollows and ridges of his wasted face. He got in motion slowly, striking the floor with his stick at every step. It was rather an affair to get him out of the house because, now and then, he would stop, as if to think, and did not offer to move again till impelled forward by Michaelis. The gentle apostle grasped his arm with brotherly care; and behind them, his hands in his pockets, the robust Ossipon yawned vaguely. A blue cap with a patent leather peak set well at the back of his yellow bush of hair gave him the aspect of a Norwegian sailor bored with the world after a thundering spree. Mr Verloc saw his guests off the premises, attending them bareheaded, his heavy overcoat hanging open, his eyes on the ground.

He closed the door behind their backs with restrained violence, turned the key, shot the bolt. He was not satisfied with his friends. In the light of Mr Vladimir's philosophy of bomb throwing they appeared hopelessly futile. The part of Mr Verloc in revolutionary politics having been to observe, he could not all at once, either in his own home or in larger assemblies, take the initiative of action. He had to be cautious. Moved by the just indignation of a man well over forty, menaced in what is dearest to him—his repose and his security—he asked himself scornfully what else could have been expected from such a lot, this Karl Yundt, this Michaelis—this Ossipon.

Pausing in his intention to turn off the gas burning in the middle of the shop, Mr Verloc descended into the abyss of moral reflections. With the insight of a kindred temperament he pronounced his verdict. A lazy lot—this Karl Yundt, nursed by a blear-eyed old woman, a woman he had years ago enticed away from a friend, and afterwards had tried more than once to shake off into the gutter. Jolly lucky for Yundt that she had persisted in coming up time after time, or else there would have been no one now to help him out of the bus by the Green Park railings, where that spectre took its constitutional crawl every fine morning. When that indomitable snarling old witch died the swaggering spectre would have to vanish, too—there would be an end to fiery Karl Yundt. And Mr Verloc's morality was offended also by the optimism of Michaelis, annexed by his wealthy old lady, who had taken lately to sending him to a cottage she had in the country. The ex-prisoner could moon about the shady lanes for days together in a delicious and humanitarian idleness. As to Ossipon, that beggar was sure to want for nothing as long as there were silly girls with savings-bank books in the world. And Mr Verloc, temperamentally identical with his associates, drew fine distinctions in his mind on the strength of insignificant differences. He drew them with a certain complacency, because the instinct of conventional respectability was strong within him, being only overcome by his dislike of all kinds of recognized labour—a temperamental defect which he shared with a large proportion of revolutionary reformers of a given social state. For obviously one does not revolt against the advantages and opportunities of that state, but against the price which must be paid for the same in the coin of accepted morality, self-restraint, and toil. The majority of revolutionists are the enemies of discipline and fatigue mostly. There are natures, too, to whose sense of justice the price exacted looms up monstrously enormous, odious, oppressive, worrying, humiliating, extortionate, intolerable. Those are the fanatics. The remaining portion of social rebels is accounted for by vanity, the mother of all noble and vile illusions, the companion of poets, reformers, charlatans, prophets, and incendiaries.

Lost for a whole minute in the abyss of meditation, Mr Verloc did not reach the depth of these abstract considerations. Perhaps he was not able. In any case, he had not the time. He was pulled up painfully by the sudden recollection of Mr Vladimir, another of his associates, whom in virtue of subtle moral affinities he was capable of judging correctly. He considered him as dangerous. A shade of envy crept into his thoughts. Loafing was all very well for these fellows, who knew not Mr Vladimir, and had women to fall back upon; whereas he had a woman to provide for—

At this point, by a simple association of ideas, Mr Verloc was brought face to face with the necessity of going to bed some time or other that evening. Then why not go now—at once? He sighed. The necessity was not so normally pleasurable as it ought to have been for a man of his age and temperament. He dreaded the demon of sleeplessness, which he felt had marked him for its own. He raised his arm, and turned off the flaring gas-jet above his head.

A bright band of light fell through the parlour door into the part of the shop behind the counter. It enabled Mr Verloc to ascertain at a glance the number of silver coins in the till. These were but few; and for the first time since he opened his shop he took a commercial survey of its value. This survey was unfavourable. He had gone into trade for no commercial reasons. He had been guided in the selection of this peculiar line of business by an instinctive leaning towards shady transactions, where money is picked up easily. Moreover, it did not take him out of his own sphere—the sphere which is watched by the police. On the contrary, it gave him a publicly confessed standing in that sphere, and as Mr Verloc had unconfessed relations which made him familiar with yet careless of the police, there was a distinct advantage in such a situation. But as a means of livelihood it was by itself insufficient.

He took the cash-box out of the drawer, and turning to leave the shop, became aware that Stevie was still downstairs.

What on earth is he doing there? Mr Verloc asked himself. What's the meaning of these antics? He looked dubiously at his brother-in-law, but did not ask him for information. Mr Verloc's intercourse with Stevie was limited to the casual mutter of a morning, after breakfast, "My boots," and even that was more a communication at large of a need than a direct order or request. Mr Verloc perceived with some surprise that he did not know really what to say to Stevie. He stood still in the middle of the parlour, and looked into the kitchen in silence. Nor yet did he know what would happen if he did say anything. And this appeared very queer to Mr Verloc in view of the fact, borne upon him suddenly, that he had to provide for this fellow, too. He had never given a moment's thought till then to that aspect of Stevie's existence.

Positively he did not know how to speak to the lad. He watched him gesticulating and murmuring in the kitchen. Stevie prowled round the table like an excited animal in a cage. A tentative "Hadn't you better go to bed now?" produced no effect whatever; and Mr Verloc, abandoning the stony contemplation of his brother-in-law's behaviour, crossed the parlour wearily, cash-box in hand. The cause of the general lassitude he felt while climbing the stairs being purely mental, he became alarmed by its inexplicable character. He hoped he was not sickening for anything. He stopped on the dark landing to examine his sensations. But a slight and continuous sound of snoring pervading the obscurity interfered with their clearness. The sound came from his mother-in-law's room. Another one to provide for, he thought—and on this thought walked into the bedroom.

Mrs Verloc had fallen asleep with the lamp (no gas was laid upstairs) turned up full on the table by the side of the bed. The light thrown down by the shade fell dazzingly on the white pillow sunk by the weight of her head reposing with closed eyes and dark hair done up in several plaits for the night. She woke up with the sound of her name in her ears, and saw her husband standing over her.

"Winnie! Winnie!"

At first she did not stir, lying very quiet and looking at the cash-box in Mr Verloc's hand. But when she understood that her brother was "capering all over the place downstairs" she swung out in one sudden movement on to the edge of the bed. Her bare feet, as if poked through the bottom of an unadorned, sleeved calico sack buttoned tightly at neck and wrists, felt over the rug for the slippers while she looked upward into her husband's face.

"I don't know how to manage him," Mr Verloc explained, peevishly. "Won't do to leave him downstairs alone with the lights."

She said nothing, glided across the room swiftly, and the door closed upon her white form.

Mr Verloc deposited the cash-box on the night table, and began the operation of undressing by flinging his overcoat on to a distant chair. His coat and waistcoat followed. He walked about the room in his stockinged feet, and his burly figure, with the hands worrying nervously at his throat, passed and repassed across the long strip of looking-glass in the door of his wife's wardrobe. Then after slipping his braces off his shoulders he pulled up violently the venetian blind, and leaned his forehead against the cold window-pane—a fragile film of glass stretched between him and the enormity of cold, black, wet, muddy, inhospitable accumulation of bricks, slates, and stones, things in themselves unlovely and unfriendly to man.

Mr Verloc felt the latent unfriendliness of all out of doors with a force approaching to positive bodily anguish. There is no occupation that fails a man more completely than that of a secret agent of police. It's like your horse suddenly falling dead under you in the midst of an uninhabited and thirsty plain. The comparison occurred to Mr Verloc because he had sat astride various army horses in his time, and had now the sensation of an incipient fall. The prospect was as black as the window-pane against which he was leaning his forehead. And suddenly the face of Mr Vladimir, clean-shaved and witty, appeared enhaloed in the glow of its rosy complexion like a sort of pink seal impressed on the fatal darkness.

This luminous and mutilated vision was so ghastly physically that Mr Verloc started away from the window, letting down the venetian blind with a great rattle. Discomposed and speechless with the apprehension of more such visions, he beheld his wife re-enter the room and get into bed in a calm, business-like manner which made him feel hopelessly lonely in the world. Mrs Verloc expressed her surprise at seeing him up yet.

"I don't feel very well," he muttered, passing his hands over his moist brow.

"Giddiness?"

"Yes. Not at all well."

Mrs Verloc, with all the placidity of an experienced wife, expressed a confident opinion as to the cause, and suggested the usual remedies; but her husband, rooted in the middle of the room, shook his lowered head sadly.

"You'll catch cold standing there," she observed.

Mr Verloc made an effort, finished undressing, and got into bed. Down below in the quiet, narrow street measured footsteps approached the house, then died away, unhurried and firm, as if the passer-by had started to pace out all eternity, from gas-lamp to gas-lamp in a night without end; and the drowsy ticking of the old clock on the landing became distinctly audible in the bedroom.

Mrs Verloc, on her back, and staring at the ceiling, made a remark.

"Takings very small today."

Mr Verloc, in the same position, cleared his throat as if for an important statement, but merely inquired:

"Did you turn off the gas downstairs?"

"Yes; I did," answered Mrs Verloc, conscientiously. "That poor boy is in a very excited state tonight," she murmured, after a pause which lasted for three ticks of the clock.

Mr Verloc cared nothing for Stevie's excitement, but he felt horribly wakeful, and dreaded facing the darkness and silence that would follow the extinguishing of the lamp. This dread led him to make the remark that Stevie had disregarded his suggestion to go to bed. Mrs Verloc, falling into the trap, started to demonstrate at length to her husband that this was not "impudence" of any sort, but simply "excitement." There was no young man of his age in London more willing and docile than Stephen, she affirmed; none more affectionate and ready to please, and even useful, as long as people did not upset his poor head. Mrs Verloc, turning towards her recumbent husband, raised herself on her elbow, and hung over him in her anxiety that he should believe Stevie to be a useful member of the family. That ardour of protecting compassion exalted morbidly in her childhood by the misery of another child tinged her sallow cheeks with a faint dusky blush, made her big eyes gleam under the dark lids. Mrs Verloc then looked younger; she looked as young as Winnie used to look, and much more animated than the Winnie of the Belgravian mansion days had ever allowed herself to appear to gentlemen lodgers. Mr Verloc's anxieties had prevented him from attaching any sense to what his wife was saying. It was as if her voice was talking on the other side of a very thick wall. It was her aspect that recalled him to himself.

He appreciated this woman, and the sentiment of this appreciation, stirred by a display of something resembling emotion, only added another pang to his mental anguish. When her voice ceased he moved uneasily, and said:

"I haven't been feeling well for the last few days."

He might have meant this as an opening to a complete confidence; but Mrs Verloc laid her head on the pillow again, and staring upward, went on:

"That boy hears too much of what is talked about here. If I had known they were coming tonight I would have seen to it that he went to bed at the same time I did. He was out of his mind with something he overheard about eating people's flesh and drinking blood. What's the good of talking like that?"

There was a note of indignant scorn in her voice. Mr Verloc was fully responsive now.

"Ask Karl Yundt," he growled, savagely.

Mrs Verloc, with great decision, pronounced Karl Yundt "a disgusting old man." She declared openly her affection for Michaelis. Of the robust Ossipon, in whose presence she always felt uneasy behind an attitude of stony reserve, she said nothing whatever. And continuing to talk of that brother, who had been for so many years an object of care and fears:

"He isn't fit to hear what's said here. He believes it's all true. He knows no better. He gets into his passions over it."

Mr Verloc made no comment.

"He glared at me, as if he didn't know who I was, when I went downstairs. His heart was going like a hammer. He can't help being excitable. I woke mother up, and asked her to sit with him till he went to sleep. It isn't his fault. He's no trouble when he's left alone."

Mr Verloc made no comment.

"I wish he had never been to school," Mrs Verloc began again, brusquely. "He's always taking away those newspapers from the window to read. He gets a red face poring over them. We don't get rid of a dozen numbers in a month. They only take up room in the front window. And Mr Ossipon brings every week a pile of these

F.P. tracts to sell at a halfpenny each. I wouldn't give a halfpenny for the whole lot. It's silly reading—that's what it is. There's no sale for it. The other day Stevie got hold of one, and there was a story in it of a German soldier officer tearing half-off the ear of a recruit, and nothing was done to him for it. The brute! I couldn't do anything with Stevie that afternoon. The story was enough, too, to make one's blood boil. But what's the use of printing things like that? We aren't German slaves here, thank God. It's not our business—is it?"

Mr Verloc made no reply.

"I had to take the carving knife from the boy," Mrs Verloc continued, a little sleepily now. "He was shouting and stamping and sobbing. He can't stand the notion of any cruelty. He would have stuck that officer like a pig if he had seen him then. It's true, too! Some people don't deserve much mercy." Mrs Verloc's voice ceased, and the expression of her motionless eyes became more and more contemplative and veiled during the long pause. "Comfortable, dear?" she asked in a faint, far-away voice. "Shall I put out the light now?"

The dreary conviction that there was no sleep for him held Mr Verloc mute and hopelessly inert in his fear of darkness. He made a great effort.

"Yes. Put it out," he said at last in a hollow tone.

CHAPTER 4

Most of the thirty or so little tables covered by red cloths with a white design stood ranged at right angles to the deep brown wainscoting of the underground hall. Bronze chandeliers with many globes depended from the low, slightly vaulted ceiling, and the fresco paintings ran flat and dull all round the walls without windows, representing scenes of the chase and of outdoor revelry in medieval costumes. Varlets in green jerkins brandished hunting knives and raised on high tankards of foaming beer.

"Unless I am very much mistaken, you are the man who would know the inside of this confounded affair," said the robust Ossipon, leaning over, his elbows far out on the table and his feet tucked back completely under his chair. His eyes stared with wild eagerness.

An upright semi-grand piano near the door, flanked by two palms in pots, executed suddenly all by itself a valse tune with aggressive virtuosity. The din it raised was deafening. When it ceased, as abruptly as it had started, the bespectacled, dingy little man who faced Ossipon behind a heavy glass mug full of beer emitted calmly what had the sound of a general proposition.

"In principle what one of us may or may not know as to any given fact can't be a matter for inquiry to the others."

"Certainly not," Comrade Ossipon agreed in a quiet undertone. "In principle."

With his big florid face held between his hands he continued to stare hard, while the dingy little man in spectacles coolly took a drink of beer and stood the glass mug back on the table. His flat, large ears departed widely from the sides of his skull, which looked frail enough for Ossipon to crush between thumb and forefinger; the dome of the forehead seemed to rest on the rim of the spectacles; the flat cheeks, of a greasy, unhealthy complexion, were merely smudged by the miserable poverty of a thin dark whisker. The lamentable inferiority of the whole physique was made ludicrous by the supremely self-confident bearing of the individual. His speech was curt, and he had a particularly impressive manner of keeping silent.

Ossipon spoke again from between his hands in a mutter.

"Have you been out much today?"

"No. I stayed in bed all the morning," answered the other. "Why?"

"Oh! Nothing," said Ossipon, gazing earnestly and quivering inwardly with the desire to find out something, but obviously intimidated by the little man's overwhelming air of unconcern. When talking with this comrade—which happened but rarely—the big Ossipon suffered from a sense of moral and even physical insignificance. However, he ventured another question. "Did you walk down here?"

"No; omnibus," the little man answered, readily enough. He lived far away in Islington, in a small house down a shabby street, littered with straw and dirty paper, where out of school hours a troop of assorted children ran and squabbled with a shrill, joyless, rowdy clamour. His single back room, remarkable for having an extremely large cupboard, he rented furnished from two elderly spinsters, dressmakers in a humble way with a clientele of servant girls mostly. He had a heavy padlock put on the cupboard, but otherwise he was a model lodger, giving no trouble, and requiring practically no attendance. His oddities were that he insisted on being present when his room was being swept, and that when he went out he locked his door, and took the key away with him.

Ossipon had a vision of these round black-rimmed spectacles progressing along the streets on the top of an omnibus, their self-confident glitter falling here and there on the walls of houses or lowered upon the heads of the unconscious stream of people on the pavements. The ghost of a sickly smile altered the set of Ossipon's thick lips at the thought of the walls nodding, of people running for life at the sight of those spectacles. If they had only known! What a panic! He murmured interrogatively: "Been sitting long here?"

"An hour or more," answered the other, negligently, and took a pull at the dark beer. All his movements—the way he grasped the mug, the act of drinking, the way he set the heavy glass down and folded his arms—had a firmness, an assured precision which made the big and muscular Ossipon, leaning forward with staring eyes and protruding lips, look the picture of eager indecision.

"An hour," he said. "Then it may be you haven't heard yet the news I've heard just now—in the street. Have you?"

The little man shook his head negatively the least bit. But as he gave no indication of curiosity Ossipon ventured to add that he had heard it just outside the place. A newspaper boy had yelled the thing under his very nose, and not being prepared for anything of that sort, he was very much startled and upset. He had to come in there with a dry mouth. "I never thought of finding you here," he added, murmuring steadily, with his elbows planted on the table.

"I come here sometimes," said the other, preserving his provoking coolness of demeanour.

"It's wonderful that you of all people should have heard nothing of it," the big Ossipon continued. His eyelids snapped nervously upon the shining eyes. "You of all people," he repeated, tentatively. This obvious restraint argued an incredible and inexplicable timidity of the big fellow before the calm little man, who again lifted the glass mug, drank, and put it down with brusque and assured movements. And that was all. Ossipon, after waiting for something, word or sign, that did not come, made an effort to assume a sort of indifference.

"Do you," he said, deadening his voice still more, "give your stuff to anybody who's up to asking you for it?"

"My absolute rule is never to refuse anybody—as long as I have a pinch by me," answered the little man with decision.

"That's a principle?" commented Ossipon.

"It's a principle."

"And you think it's sound?"

The large round spectacles, which gave a look of staring self-confidence to the sallow face, confronted Ossipon like sleepless, unwinking orbs flashing a cold fire.

"Perfectly. Always. Under every circumstance. What could stop me? Why should I not? Why should I think twice about it?"

Ossipon gasped, as it were, discreetly.

"Do you mean to say you would hand it over to a tec if one came to ask you for your wares?"

The other smiled faintly.

"Let them come and try it on, and you will see," he said. "They know me, but I know also every one of them. They won't come near me—not they."

His thin, livid lips snapped together firmly. Ossipon began to argue.

"But they could send someone—rig a plant on you. Don't you see? Get the stuff from you in that way, and then arrest you with the proof in their hands."

"Proof of what? Dealing in explosives without a licence perhaps." This was meant for a contemptuous jeer, though the expression of the thin, sickly man remained unchanged, and the utterance was negligent. "I don't think there's one of them anxious to make that arrest. I don't think they could get one of them to apply for a warrant. I mean one of the best. Not one."

"Why?" Ossipon asked.

"Because they know very well I take care never to part with the last handful of my wares. I've it always by me." He touched the breast of his coat lightly. "In a thick glass flask," he added.

"So I have been told," said Ossipon, with a shade of wonder in his voice. "But I didn't know if—"

"They know," interrupted the little man, crisply, leaning against the straight chair back, which rose higher than his fragile head. "I shall never be arrested. The game isn't good enough for any policeman of them all. To deal with a man like me you require sheer, naked, inglorious heroism."

Again his lips closed with a self-confident snap. Ossipon repressed a movement of impatience.

"Or recklessness—or simply ignorance," he retorted. "They've only to get somebody for the job who does not know you carry enough stuff in your pocket to blow yourself and everything within sixty yards of you to pieces."

"I never affirmed I could not be eliminated," rejoined the other. "But that wouldn't be an arrest. Moreover, it's not so easy as it looks."

"Bah!" Ossipon contradicted. "Don't be too sure of that. What's to prevent half a dozen of them jumping upon you from behind in the street? With your arms pinned to your sides you could do nothing—could you?"

"Yes; I could. I am seldom out in the streets after dark," said the little man, impassively, "and never very late. I walk always with my right hand closed round the indiarubber ball which I have in my trouser pocket. The pressing of this ball actuates a detonator inside the flask I carry in my pocket. It's the principle of the pneumatic instantaneous shutter for a camera lens. The tube leads up—"

With a swift, disclosing gesture he gave Ossipon a glimpse of an indiarubber tube, resembling a slender brown worm, issuing from the armhole of his waistcoat and plunging into the inner breast pocket of his jacket. His clothes, of a nondescript brown mixture, were threadbare and marked with stains, dusty in the folds, with ragged button-holes. "The detonator is partly mechanical, partly chemical," he explained, with casual condescension.

"It is instantaneous, of course?" murmured Ossipon, with a slight shudder.

"Far from it," confessed the other, with a reluctance which seemed to twist his mouth dolorously. "A full twenty seconds must elapse from the moment I press the ball till the explosion takes place."

"Phew!" whistled Ossipon, completely appalled. "Twenty seconds! Horrors! You mean to say that you could face that? I should go crazy—"

"Wouldn't matter if you did. Of course, it's the weak point of this special system, which is only for my own use. The worst is that the manner of exploding is always the weak point with us. I am trying to invent a detonator that would adjust itself to all conditions of action, and even to unexpected changes of conditions. A variable and yet perfectly precise mechanism. A really intelligent detonator."

"Twenty seconds," muttered Ossipon again. "Ough! And then—"

With a slight turn of the head the glitter of the spectacles seemed to gauge the size of the beer saloon in the basement of the renowned Silenus Restaurant.

"Nobody in this room could hope to escape," was the verdict of that survey. "Nor yet this couple going up the stairs now."

The piano at the foot of the staircase clanged through a mazurka with brazen impetuosity, as though a vulgar and impudent ghost were showing off. The keys sank and rose mysteriously. Then it all became still. For a moment Ossipon imagined the overlighted place changed into a dreadful black hole belching horrible fumes, choked with ghastly rubbish of smashed brickwork and mutilated corpses. He had such a distinct perception of ruin and death that he shuddered again. The other observed, with an air of calm sufficiency:

"In the last instance it is character alone that makes for one's safety. There are very few people in the world whose character is as well established as mine."

"I wonder how you managed it," growled Ossipon.

"Force of personality," said the other, without raising his voice; and coming from the mouth of that obviously miserable organism the assertion caused the robust Ossipon to bite his lower lip. "Force of personality," he repeated, with ostentatious calm.

"I have the means to make myself deadly, but that by itself, you understand, is absolutely nothing in the way of protection. What is effective is the belief those people have in my will to use the means. That's their impression. It is absolute. Therefore I am deadly."

"There are individuals of character amongst that lot, too," muttered Ossipon ominously.

"Possibly. But it is a matter of degree obviously, since, for instance, I am not impressed by them. Therefore they are inferior. They cannot be otherwise. Their character is built upon conventional morality. It leans on the social order. Mine stands free from everything artificial. They are bound in all sorts of conventions. They depend on life, which, in this connection, is a historical fact surrounded by all sorts of restraints and considerations, a complex, organized fact open to attack at every point; whereas I depend on death, which knows no restraint and cannot be attacked. My superiority is evident."

"This is a transcendental way of putting it," said Ossipon, watching the cold glitter of the round spectacles. "I've heard Karl Yundt say much the same thing not very long ago."

"Karl Yundt," mumbled the other, contemptuously, "the delegate of the International Red Committee, has been a posturing shadow all his life. There are three of you delegates, aren't there? I won't define the other two, as you are one of them. But what you say means nothing. You are the worthy delegates for revolutionary propaganda, but the trouble is not only that you are as unable to think independently as any respectable grocer or journalist of them all, but that you have no character whatever."

Ossipon could not restrain a start of indignation.

"But what do you want from us?" he exclaimed in a deadened voice. "What is it you are after yourself?"

"A perfect detonator," was the peremptory answer. "What are you making that face for? You see, you can't even bear the mention of something conclusive."

"I am not making a face," growled the annoyed Ossipon bearishly.

"You revolutionists," the other continued, with leisurely self-confidence, "are the slaves of the social convention, which is afraid of you; slaves of it as much as the very police that stand up in the defence of that convention. Clearly you are, since you want to revolutionize it. It governs your thought, of course, and your action, too, and thus neither your thought nor your action can ever be conclusive." He paused, tranquil, with that air of close, endless silence, then almost immediately went on: "You are not a bit better than the forces arrayed against you—than the police, for instance. The other day I came suddenly upon Chief Inspector Heat at the corner of Tottenham Court Road. He looked at me very steadily. But I did not look at him. Why should I give him more than a glance? He was thinking of many things—of his superiors, of his reputation, of the law courts, of his salary, of newspapers—of a hundred things. But I was thinking of my perfect detonator only. He meant nothing to me. He was as insignificant as—I can't call to mind anything insignificant enough to compare him with—except Karl Yundt perhaps. Like to like. The terrorist and the policeman both come from the same basket. Revolution, legality—counter moves in the same game; forms of idleness at bottom identical. He plays his little game—so do you propagandists. But I don't play; I work fourteen hours a day, and go hungry sometimes. My experiments cost money now and again, and then I must do without food for a day or two. You're looking at my beer. Yes. I have had two glasses already, and shall have another presently. This is a little holiday, and I celebrate it alone. Why not? I've the grit to work alone, quite alone, absolutely alone. I've worked alone for years."

Ossipon's face had turned dusky red.

"At the perfect detonator—eh?" he sneered, very low.

"Yes," retorted the other. "It is a good definition. You couldn't find anything half so precise to define the nature of your activity with all your committees and delegations. It is I who am the true propagandist."

"We won't discuss that point," said Ossipon, with an air of rising above personal considerations. "I am afraid I'll have to spoil your holiday for you, though. There's a man blown up in Greenwich Park this morning."

"How do you know?"

"They have been yelling the news in the streets since two o'clock. I bought the paper, and just ran in here. Then I saw you sitting at this table. I've got it in my pocket now."

He pulled the newspaper out. It was a good-sized, rosy sheet, as if flushed by the warmth of its own convictions which were optimistic. He scanned the pages rapidly.

"Ah! Here it is. Bomb in Greenwich Park. There isn't much so far. Half past eleven. Foggy morning. Effects of explosion felt as far as Romney Road and Park Place. Enormous hole in the ground under a tree filled with smashed roots and broken branches. All round fragments of a man's body blown to pieces. That's all. The rest's mere newspaper gup. No doubt a wicked attempt to blow up the Observatory, they say. H'm. That's hardly credible."

He looked at the paper for a while longer in silence then passed it to the other, who, after gazing abstractedly at the print, laid it down without comment.

It was Ossipon who spoke first—still resentful.

"The fragments of only *one* man, you note. *Ergo:* blew *himself* up. That spoils your day off for you—don't it? Were you expecting that sort of move? I hadn't the slightest idea—not the ghost of a notion of anything of the sort being planned to come off here—in this country. Under the present circumstances it's nothing short of criminal."

The little man lifted his thin black eyebrows with dispassionate scorn.

"Criminal! What is that? What *is* crime? What can be the meaning of such an assertion?"

"How am I to express myself? One must use the current words," said Ossipon, impatiently. "The meaning of this assertion is that this business may affect our position very adversely in this country. Isn't that crime enough for you? I am convinced you have been giving away some of your stuff lately."

Ossipon stared hard. The other, without flinching, lowered and raised his head slowly.

"You have!" burst out the editor of the F.P. leaflets in an intense whisper. "No! And are you really handing it over at large like this, for the asking, to the first fool that comes along?"

"Just so! The condemned social order has not been built up on paper and ink, and I don't fancy that a combination of paper and ink will ever put an end to it, whatever you may think. Yes, I would give the stuff with both hands to every man, woman, or fool that likes to come along. I know what you are thinking about. But I am not taking my cue from the Red Committee. I would see you all hounded out of here, or arrested—or beheaded for that matter—without turning a hair. What happens to us as individuals is not of the least consequence."

He spoke carelessly, without heat, almost without feeling, and Ossipon, secretly much affected, tried to copy this detachment.

"If the police here knew their business they would shoot you full of holes with revolvers, or else try to sand-bag you from behind in broad daylight."

The little man seemed already to have considered that point of view in his dispassionate, self-confident manner.

"Yes," he assented with the utmost readiness. "But for that they would have to face their own institutions. Do you see? That requires uncommon grit. Grit of a special kind."

Ossipon blinked.

"I fancy that's exactly what would happen to you if you were to set up your laboratory in the States. They don't stand on ceremony with their institutions there."

"I am not likely to go and see. Otherwise your remark is just," admitted the other. "They have more character over there, and their character is essentially anarchistic. Fertile ground for us, the States—very good ground. The great Republic has the root of the destructive matter in her. The collective temperament is lawless. Excellent. They may shoot us down, but—"

"You are too transcendental for me," growled Ossipon, with moody concern.

"Logical," protested the other. "There are several kinds of logic. This is the enlightened kind. America is all right. It is this country that is dangerous, with her idealistic conception of legality. The social spirit of this people is wrapped up in scrupulous prejudices, and that is fatal to our work. You talk of England being our only refuge! So much the worse. Capua! What do we want with refuges? Here you talk, print, plot, and do nothing. I daresay it's very convenient for such Karl Yundts."

He shrugged his shoulders slightly, then added with the same leisurely assurance: "To break up the superstition and worship of legality should be our aim. Nothing would please me more than to see Inspector Heat and his likes take to shooting us down in broad daylight with the approval of the public. Half our battle would be won then: the disintegration of the old morality would have set in in its very temple. That is what you ought to aim at. But you revolutionists will never understand that. You plan the future, you lose yourselves in reveries of economical systems derived from what is; whereas what's wanted is a clean sweep and a clear start for a new conception of life. That sort of future will take care of itself if you will only make room for it. Therefore I would shovel my stuff in heaps at the corners of the streets if I had enough for that; and as I haven't, I do my best by perfecting a really dependable detonator."

Ossipon, who had been mentally swimming in deep waters, seized upon the last word as if it were a saving plank.

"Yes. Your detonators. I shouldn't wonder if it weren't one of your detonators that made a clean sweep of the man in the park."

A shade of vexation darkened the determined, sallow face confronting Ossipon.

"My difficulty consists precisely in experimenting practically with the various kinds. They must be tried, after all. Besides—"

Ossipon interrupted.

"Who could that fellow be? I assure you that we in London had no knowledge—Couldn't you describe the person you gave the stuff to?"

The other turned his spectacles upon Ossipon like a pair of searchlights.

"Describe him," he repeated, slowly. "I don't think there can be the slightest objection now. I will describe him to you in one word—Verloc."

Ossipon, whom curiosity had lifted a few inches off his seat, dropped back, as if hit in the face.

"Verloc! Impossible."

The self-possessed little man nodded slightly once.

"Yes. He's the person. You can't say that in this case I was giving my stuff to the first fool that came along. He was a prominent member of the group as far as I understand."

"Yes," said Ossipon. "Prominent. No, not exactly. He was the centre for general intelligence, and usually received comrades coming over here. More useful than important. Man of no ideas. Years ago he used to speak at meetings—in France, I believe. Not very well, though. He was trusted by such men as Latorre, Moser, and all that old lot. The only talent he showed really was his ability to elude the attentions of the police somehow. Here, for instance, he did not seem to be looked after very closely. He was regularly married, you know. I suppose it's with her money that he started that shop. Seemed to make it pay, too."

Ossipon paused abruptly, muttered to himself "I wonder what that woman will do now?" and fell into thought.

The other waited with ostentatious indifference. His parentage was obscure, and he was generally known only by his nickname of Professor. His title to that designation consisted in his having been once assistant demonstrator in chemistry at some technical institute. He quarrelled with the authorities upon a question of unfair treatment. Afterwards he obtained a post in the laboratory of a manufactory of dyes. There, too, he had been treated with revolting injustice. His struggles, his privations, his hard work to raise himself in the social scale, had filled him with such an exalted conviction of his merits that it was extremely difficult for the world to treat him with justice—the standard of that notion depending so much upon the patience of the individual. The Professor had genius, but lacked the great social virtue of resignation.

"Intellectually a nonentity," Ossipon pronounced aloud, abandoning suddenly the inward contemplation of Mrs Verloc's bereaved person and business. "Quite an ordinary personality. You are wrong in not keeping more in touch with the comrades, Professor," he added in a reproving tone. "Did he say anything to you—give you some idea of his intentions? I hadn't seen him for a month. It seems impossible that he should be gone."

"He told me it was going to be a demonstration against a building," said the Professor. "I had to know that much to prepare the missile. I pointed out to him that I had hardly a sufficient quantity for a completely destructive result, but he pressed me very earnestly to do my best. As he wanted something that could be carried openly in the hand, I proposed to make use of an old one-gallon copal varnish can I happened to have by me. He was pleased at the idea. It gave me some trouble, because I had to cut out the bottom first and solder it on again afterwards. When prepared for use, the can enclosed a wide-mouthed, well-corked jar of thick glass packed around with some wet clay and containing sixteen ounces of X2 green powder. The detonator was connected with the screw top of the can. It was ingenious—a combination of time and shock. I explained the system to him. It was a thin tube of tin enclosing—"

Ossipon's attention had wandered.

"What do you think has happened?" he interrupted.

"Can't tell. Screwed the top on tight, which would make the connection, and then forgot the time. It was set for twenty minutes. On the other hand, the time contact being made, a sharp shock would bring about the explosion at once. He either ran the time too close, or simply let the thing fall. The contact was made all right—that's clear to me at any rate. The system's worked perfectly. And yet you would think that a common fool in a hurry would be much more likely to forget to make the contact altogether. I was worrying myself about that sort of failure mostly. But there are more kinds of fools than one can guard against. You can't expect a detonator to be absolutely foolproof."

He beckoned to a waiter. Ossipon sat rigid, with the abstracted gaze of mental travail. After the man had gone away with the money he roused himself, with an air of profound dissatisfaction.

"It's extremely unpleasant for me," he mused. "Karl has been in bed with bronchitis for a week. There's an even chance that he will never get up again. Michaelis is luxuriating in the country somewhere. A fashionable publisher has offered him five hundred pounds for a book. It will be a ghastly failure. He has lost the habit of consecutive thinking in prison, you know."

The Professor on his feet, now buttoning his coat, looked about him with perfect indifference.

"What are you going to do?" asked Ossipon, wearily. He dreaded the blame of the Central Red Committee, a body which had no permanent place of abode, and of whose membership he was not exactly informed. If this affair eventuated in the stoppage of the modest subsidy allotted to the publication of the F.P. pamphlets, then indeed he would have to regret Verloc's inexplicable folly.

"Solidarity with the extremist form of action is one thing, and silly recklessness is another," he said, with a sort of moody brutality. "I don't know what came to Verloc. There's some mystery there. However, he's gone. You may take it as you like, but under the circumstances the only policy for the militant revolutionary group is to disclaim all connection with this damned freak of yours. How to make the disclaimer convincing enough is what bothers me."

The little man on his feet, buttoned up and ready to go, was no taller than the seated Ossipon. He levelled his spectacles at the latter's face point-blank.

"You might ask the police for a testimonial of good conduct. They know where every one of you slept last night. Perhaps if you asked them they would consent to publish some sort of official statement."

"No doubt they are aware well enough that we had nothing to do with this," mumbled Ossipon, bitterly. "What they will say is another thing." He remained thoughtful, disregarding the short, owlish, shabby figure standing by his side. "I must lay hands on

Michaelis at once, and get him to speak from his heart at one of our gatherings. The public has a sort of sentimental regard for that fellow. His name is known. And I am in touch with a few reporters on the big dailies. What he would say would be utter bosh, but he has a turn of talk that makes it go down all the same."

"Like treacle," interjected the Professor, rather low, keeping an impassive expression.

The perplexed Ossipon went on communing with himself half audibly, after the manner of a man reflecting in perfect solitude.

"Confounded ass! To leave such an imbecile business on my hands. And I don't even know if—"

He sat with compressed lips. The idea of going for news straight to the shop lacked charm. His notion was that Verloc's shop might have been turned already into a police trap. They will be bound to make some arrests, he thought, with something resembling virtuous indignation, for the even tenor of his revolutionary life was menaced by no fault of his. And yet unless he went there he ran the risk of remaining in ignorance of what perhaps it would be very material for him to know. Then he reflected that, if the man in the park had been so very much blown to pieces as the evening papers said, he could not have been identified. And if so, the police could have no special reason for watching Verloc's shop more closely than any other place known to be frequented by marked anarchists—no more reason, in fact, than for watching the doors of the Silenus. There would be a lot of watching all round, no matter where he went. Still—

"I wonder what I had better do now?" he muttered, taking counsel with himself.

A rasping voice at his elbow said, with sedate scorn:

"Fasten yourself upon the woman for all she's worth."

After uttering these words the Professor walked away from the table. Ossipon, whom that piece of insight had taken unawares, gave one ineffectual start, and remained still, with a helpless gaze, as though nailed fast to the seat of his chair. The lonely piano, without as much as a music stool to help it, struck a few chords courageously, and beginning a selection of national airs, played him out at last to the tune of "The Blue Bells of Scotland." The painfully detached notes grew faint behind his back while he went slowly upstairs, across the hall, and into the street.

In front of the great doorway a dismal row of newspaper sellers standing clear of the pavement dealt with their wares from the gutter. It was a raw, gloomy day of the early spring; and the grimy sky, the mud of the street, the rags of the dirty men harmonized excellently with the eruption of the damp, rubbishy sheets of paper soiled with printers' ink. The posters, maculated with filth, garnished like tapestry the sweep of the kerbstone. The trade in afternoon papers was brisk, yet, in comparison with the swift, constant march of foot traffic, the effect was of indifference, of a disregarded distribution. Ossipon looked hurriedly both ways before stepping out into the cross-currents, but the Professor was already out of sight.

CHAPTER 5

The Professor had turned into a street to the left, and walked along, with his head carried rigidly erect, in a crowd whose every individual almost overtopped his stunted stature. It was vain to pretend to himself that he was not disappointed. But that was mere feeling; the stoicism of his thought could not be disturbed by this or any other failure. Next time, or the time after next, a telling stroke would be delivered—something really startling—a blow fit to open the first crack in the imposing front of the great edifice of legal conceptions sheltering the atrocious injustice of society. Of humble origin, and with an appearance really so mean as to stand in the way of his considerable natural abilities, his imagination had been fired early by the tales of men rising from the depths of poverty to positions of authority and affluence. The extreme, almost ascetic purity of his thought, combined with an astounding ignorance of worldly conditions, had set before him a goal of power and prestige to be attained without the medium of arts, graces, tact, wealth—by sheer weight of merit alone. On that view he considered himself entitled to undisputed success. His father, a delicate dark enthusiast with a sloping forehead, had been an itinerant and rousing preacher of some obscure but rigid Christian sect—a man supremely confident in the privileges of his righteousness. In the son, individualist by temperament, once the science of colleges had replaced thoroughly the faith of conventicles, this moral attitude translated itself into a frenzied puritanism of ambition. He nursed it as something secularly holy. To see it thwarted opened his eyes to the true nature of the world, whose morality was artificial, corrupt and blasphemous. The way of even the most justifiable revolutions is prepared by personal impulses disguised into creeds. The Professor's indignation found in itself a final cause that absolved him from the sin of turning to destruction as the agent of his ambition. To destroy public faith in legality was the imperfect formula of his pedantic fanaticism; but the subconscious conviction that the framework of an established social order cannot be effectually shattered except by some form of collective or individual violence was precise and correct. He was a moral agent—that was settled in his mind. By exercising his agency with ruthless defiance he procured for himself the appearances of power and personal prestige. That was undeniable to his vengeful bitterness. It pacified its unrest; and in their own way the most ardent of revolutionaries are perhaps doing no more but seeking for peace in common with the rest of mankind—the peace of soothed vanity, of satisfied appetites, or perhaps of appeased conscience.

Lost in the crowd, miserable and undersized, he meditated confidently on his power, keeping his hand in the left pocket of his trousers, grasping lightly the indiarubber ball, the supreme guarantee of his sinister freedom: but after a while he became disagreeably affected by the sight of the roadway thronged with vehicles and of the pavement crowded with men and women. He was in a long, straight street, peopled by a mere fraction of an immense multitude; but all round him, on and on, even to the limits of the horizon hidden by the enormous piles of bricks, he felt the mass of mankind mighty in its numbers. They swarmed numerous like locusts, industrious like ants, thoughtless like a natural force, pushing on blind and orderly and absorbed, impervious to sentiment, to logic, to terror, too, perhaps.

That was the form of doubt he feared most. Impervious to fear! Often while walking abroad, when he happened also to come out of himself, he had such moments of dreadful and sane mistrust of mankind. What if nothing could move them? Such moments come to all men whose ambition aims at a direct grasp upon humanity—to artists, politicians, thinkers, reformers, or saints. A despicable emotional state this, against which solitude fortifies a superior character; and with severe exultation the Professor thought of the refuge of his room, with its padlocked cupboard, lost in a wilderness of poor houses, the hermitage of the perfect anarchist. In order to reach sooner the point where he could take his omnibus, he turned brusquely out of the populous street into a narrow and dusky alley paved with flagstones. On one side the low brick houses had in their dusty windows the sightless, moribund look of incurable decay—empty shells awaiting demolition. From the other side life had not departed wholly as yet. Facing the only gas-lamp yawned the cavern of a second-hand-furniture dealer, where, deep in the gloom of a sort of narrow avenue winding through a bizarre forest of wardrobes, with an undergrowth tangle of table legs, a tall pier-glass glimmered like a pool of water in a wood. An unhappy, homeless couch, accompanied by two unrelated chairs, stood in the open. The only human being making use of the alley besides the Professor, coming stalwart and erect from the opposite direction, checked his swinging pace suddenly.

"Hallo!" he said, and stood a little on one side watchfully.

The Professor had already stopped, with a ready half turn which brought his shoulders very near the other wall. His right hand fell lightly on the back of the outcast couch, the left remained purposefully plunged deep in the trouser pocket, and the roundness of the heavy rimmed spectacles imparted an owlish character to his moody, unperturbed face.

It was like a meeting in a side corridor of a mansion full of life. The stalwart man was buttoned up in a dark overcoat, and carried an umbrella. His hat, tilted back, uncovered a good deal of forehead, which appeared very white in the dusk. In the dark patches of the orbits the eyeballs glimmered piercingly. Long, drooping moustaches, the colour of ripe corn, framed with their points the square block of his shaved chin.

"I am not looking for you," he said, curtly.

The Professor did not stir an inch. The blended noises of the enormous town sank down to an inarticulate low murmur. Chief Inspector Heat of the Special Crime Department changed his tone.

"Not in a hurry to get home?" he asked, with mocking simplicity.

The unwholesome-looking little moral agent of destruction exulted silently in the possession of personal prestige, keeping in check this man armed with the defensive mandate of a menaced society. More fortunate than Caligula, who wished that the Roman Senate had only one head for the better satisfaction of his cruel lust, he beheld in that one man all the forces he had set at defiance: the force of law, property, oppression, and injustice. He beheld all his enemies and fearlessly confronted them all in a supreme satisfaction of his vanity. They stood perplexed before him, as if before a dreadful portent. He gloated inwardly over the chance of this meeting affirming his superiority over all the multitude of mankind.

It was in reality a chance meeting. Chief Inspector Heat had had a disagreeably busy day since his department received the first telegram from Greenwich a little before eleven in the morning. First of all, the fact of the outrage being attempted less than a week after he had assured a high official that no outbreak of anarchist activity was to be apprehended was sufficiently annoying. If he ever thought himself safe in making a statement, it was then. He had made that statement with infinite satisfaction to himself, because it was clear that the high official desired greatly to hear that very thing. He had affirmed that nothing of the sort could even be thought of without the department being aware of it within twenty-four hours; and he had spoken thus in his consciousness of being the great expert of his department. He had gone even so far as to utter words which true wisdom would have kept back. But Chief Inspector Heat was not very wise—at least not truly so. True wisdom, which is not certain of anything in this world of contradictions, would have prevented him from attaining his present position. It would have alarmed his superiors, and done away with his chances of promotion. His promotion had been very rapid.

"There isn't one of them, sir, that we couldn't lay our hands on at any time of night or day. We know what each of them is doing hour by hour," he had declared. And the high official had deigned to smile. This was so obviously the right thing to say for an officer of Chief Inspector Heat's reputation that it was perfectly delightful. The high official believed the declaration, which chimed in with his idea of the fitness of things. His wisdom was of an official kind, or else he might have reflected upon a matter not of theory but of experience that in the close-woven stuff of relations between the conspirator and police there occur unexpected solutions of continuity, sudden holes in space and time. A given anarchist may be watched inch by inch and minute by minute, but a moment always comes when somehow all sight and touch of him are lost for a few hours, during which something (generally an explosion) more or less deplorable does happen. But the high official, carried away by his sense of fitness of things, had smiled, and now the recollection of that smile was very annoying to Chief Inspector Heat, principal expert in anarchist procedure.

This was not the only circumstance whose recollection depressed the usual serenity of the eminent specialist. There was another dating back only to that very morning. The thought that when called urgently to his Assistant Commissioner's private room he had been unable to conceal his astonishment was distinctly vexing. His instinct of a successful man had taught him long ago that, as a general rule, a reputation is built on manner as much as on achievement. And he felt that his manner when confronted with the telegram had not been impressive. He had opened his eyes widely, and had exclaimed "Impossible!" exposing himself thereby to the unanswerable retort of a finger-tip laid forcibly on the telegram which the Assistant Commissioner, after reading it aloud, had flung on the desk. To be crushed, as it were, under the tip of a forefinger was an unpleasant experience. Very damaging, too! Furthermore, Chief Inspector Heat was conscious of not having mended matters by allowing himself to express a conviction.

"One thing I can tell you at once: none of our lot had anything to do with this."

He was strong in his integrity of a good detective, but he saw now that an impenetrably attentive reserve towards this incident would have served his reputation better. On the other hand, he admitted to himself that it was difficult to preserve one's reputation if rank outsiders were going to take a hand in the business. Outsiders are the bane of the police as of other professions. The tone of the Assistant Commissioner's remarks had been sour enough to set one's teeth on edge.

And since breakfast Chief Inspector Heat had not managed to get anything to eat.

Starting immediately to begin his investigation on the spot, he had swallowed a good deal of raw, unwholesome fog in the park. Then he had walked over to the hospital; and when the investigation in Greenwich was concluded at last he had lost his inclination for food. Not accustomed, as the doctors are, to examine closely the mangled remains of human beings, he had been shocked by the sight disclosed to his view when a waterproof sheet had been lifted off a table in a certain apartment of the hospital.

Another waterproof sheet was spread over that table in the manner of a tablecloth with the corners turned up over a sort of mound—a heap of rags, scorched and bloodstained, half concealing what might have been an accumulation of raw material for a cannibal feast. It required considerable firmness of mind not to recoil before that sight. Chief Inspector Heat, an efficient officer of his department, stood his ground, but for a whole minute he did not advance. A local constable in uniform cast a sidelong glance, and said with stolid simplicity:

"He's all there. Every bit of him. It was a job."

He had been the first man on the spot after the explosion. He mentioned the fact again. He had seen something like a heavy flash of lightning in the fog. At that time he was standing at the door of the King William Street Lodge talking to the keeper. The concussion made him tingle all over. He ran between the trees towards the Observatory. "As fast as my legs would carry me," he repeated twice.

Chief Inspector Heat, bending forward over the table in a gingerly and horrified manner, let him run on. The hospital porter and another man turned down the corners of the cloth, and stepped aside. The Chief Inspector's eyes searched the gruesome detail of that heap of mixed things, which seemed to have been collected in shambles and rag shops.

"You used a shovel," he remarked, observing a sprinkling of small gravel, tiny brown bits of bark, and particles of splintered wood as fine as needles.

"Had to in one place," said the stolid constable. "I sent a keeper to fetch a spade. When he heard me scraping the ground with it he leaned his forehead against a tree, and was as sick as a dog."

The Chief Inspector, stooping guardedly over the table, fought down the unpleasant sensation in his throat. The shattering violence of destruction which had made of that body a heap of nameless fragments affected his feelings with a sense of ruthless cruelty, though his reason told him the effect must have been as swift as a flash of lightning. The man, whoever he was, had died instantaneously; and yet it seemed impossible to believe that a human body could have reached that state of disintegration without passing through the pangs of inconceivable agony. No physiologist, and still less of a metaphysician, Chief Inspector Heat rose by the force of sympathy, which is a form of fear, above the vulgar conception of time. Instantaneous! He remembered all he had ever read in popular publications of long and terrifying dreams dreamed in the instant of waking; of the whole past life lived with frightful intensity by a drowning man as his doomed head bobs up, screaming, for the last time. The inexplicable mysteries of conscious existence beset Chief Inspector Heat till he evolved a horrible notion that ages of atrocious pain and mental torture could be contained between two successive winks of an eye. And meantime the Chief Inspector went on peering at the table with a calm face and the slightly anxious attention of an indigent customer bending over what may be called the by-products of a butcher's shop with a view to an inexpensive Sunday dinner. All the time his trained faculties of an excellent investigator, who scorns no chance of information, followed the self-satisfied, disjointed loquacity of the constable.

"A fair-haired fellow," the last observed in a placid tone, and paused. "The old woman who spoke to the sergeant noticed a fair-haired fellow coming out of Maze Hill Station." He paused. "And he was a fair-haired fellow. She noticed two men coming out of the station after the uptrain had gone on," he continued, slowly. "She couldn't tell if they were together. She took no particular notice of the big one, but the other was a fair, slight chap, carrying a tin varnish can in one hand." The constable ceased.

"Know the woman?" muttered the Chief Inspector, with his eyes fixed on the table, and a vague notion in his mind of an inquest to be held presently upon a person likely to remain for ever unknown.

"Yes. She's housekeeper to a retired publican, and attends the chapel in Park Place sometimes," the constable uttered weightily, and paused, with another oblique glance at the table. Then suddenly: "Well, here he is—all of him I could see. Fair. Slight—slight enough. Look at that foot there. I picked up the legs first, one after another. He was that scattered you didn't know where to begin."

The constable paused; the least flicker of an innocent, self-laudatory smile invested his round face with an infantile expression.

"Stumbled," he announced, positively. "I stumbled once myself, and pitched on my head, too, while running up. Them roots do stick out all about the place. Stumbled against the root of a tree and fell, and the thing he was carrying must have gone off right under his chest, I expect."

The echo of the words "Persons unknown" repeating itself in his inner consciousness bothered the Chief Inspector considerably. He would have liked to trace this affair back to its mysterious origin for his own information. He was professionally curious. Before the public he would have liked to vindicate the efficiency of his department by establishing the identity of that man. He was a loyal servant. That, however, appeared impossible. The first term of the problem was unreadable—lacked all suggestion but that of atrocious cruelty.

Overcoming his physical repugnance, Chief Inspector Heat stretched out his hand without conviction for the salving of his conscience, and took up the least soiled of the rags. It was a narrow strip of velvet with a larger triangular piece of dark blue cloth hanging from it. He held it up to his eyes; and the police constable spoke.

"Velvet collar. Funny the old woman should have noticed the velvet collar. Dark blue overcoat with a velvet collar, she has told us. He was the chap she saw, and no mistake. And here he is all complete, velvet collar and all. I don't think I missed a single piece as big as a postage stamp."

At this point the trained faculties of the Chief Inspector ceased to hear the voice of the constable. He moved to one of the windows for better light. His face, averted from the room, expressed a startled, intense interest while he examined closely the triangular piece of broadcloth. By a sudden jerk he detached it, and only after stuffing it into his pocket turned round to the room, and flung the velvet collar back on the table.

"Cover up," he directed the attendants, curtly, without another look, and, saluted by the constable, carried off his spoil hastily.

A convenient train whirled him up to town, alone and pondering deeply, in a third-class compartment. That singed piece of cloth was incredibly valuable, and he could not defend himself from astonishment at the casual manner it had come into his possession. It was as if Fate had thrust that clue into his hands. And after the manner of the average man, whose ambition is to command events, he began to mistrust such a gratuitous and accidental success—just because it seemed forced upon him. The practical value of success depends not a little on the way you look at it. But Fate looks at nothing. It has no discretion. He no longer considered it eminently desirable all round to establish publicly the identity of the man who had blown himself up that morning with such horrible completeness. But he was not certain of the view his department would take. A department is to those it employs a complex personality with ideas and even fads of its own. It depends on the loyal devotion of its servants, and the devoted loyalty of trusted servants is associated with a certain amount of affectionate contempt, which keeps it sweet, as it were. By a benevolent provision of Nature no man is a hero to his valet, or else the heroes would have to brush their own clothes. Likewise no department appears perfectly wise to the intimacy of its workers. A department does not know so much as some of its servants. Being a dispassionate organism, it can never be perfectly informed. It would not be good for its efficiency to know too much. Chief Inspector Heat got out of the train in a state of thoughtfulness entirely untainted with disloyalty, but not quite free of that jealous mistrust which so often springs on the ground of perfect devotion, whether to women or to institutions.

It was in this mental disposition, physically very empty, but still nauseated by what he had seen, that he had come upon the Professor. Under these conditions which make for irascibility in a sound, normal man, this meeting was specially unwelcome to Chief Inspector Heat. He had not been thinking of the Professor; he had not been thinking of any individual anarchist at all. The complexion of that case had somehow forced upon him the general idea of the absurdity of things human, which in the abstract is sufficiently annoying to an unphilosophical temperament, and in concrete instances becomes exasperating beyond endurance. At the beginning of his career Chief Inspector Heat had been concerned with the more energetic forms of thieving. He had gained his spurs in that sphere, and naturally enough had kept for it, after his promotion to another department, a feeling not very far removed from affection. Thieving was not a sheer absurdity. It was a form of human industry, perverse indeed, but still an industry exercised in an industrious world; it was work undertaken for the same reason as the work in potteries, in coal mines, in fields, in tool-grinding shops. It was labour, whose practical difference from the other forms of labour consisted in the nature of its risk, which did not lie in ankylosis, or lead poisoning, or fire-damp, or gritty dust, but in what may be briefly defined in its own special phraseology as "Seven years' hard." Chief Inspector Heat was, of course, not insensible to the gravity of moral differences. But neither were the thieves he had been looking after. They submitted to the severe sanction of a morality familiar to Chief Inspector Heat with a certain resignation. They were his fellow citizens gone wrong because of imperfect education, Chief Inspector Heat believed; but allowing for that difference, he could understand the mind of a burglar, because, as a matter of fact, the mind and the instincts of a burglar are of the same kind as the mind and the instincts of a police officer. Both recognize the same conventions, and have a working knowledge of each other's methods and of the routine of their respective trades. They understand each other, which is advantageous to both, and establishes a sort of amenity in their relations. Products of the same machine, one classed as useful and the other as noxious, they take the machine for granted in different ways, but with a seriousness essentially the same. The mind of Chief Inspector Heat was inaccessible to ideas of revolt. But his thieves were not rebels. His bodily vigour, his cool, inflexible manner, his courage, and his fairness, had secured for him much respect and some adulation in the sphere of his early successes. He had felt himself revered and admired. And Chief Inspector Heat, arrested within six paces of the anarchist nicknamed the Professor, gave a thought of regret to the world of thieves—sane, without morbid ideals, working by routine, respectful of constituted authorities, free from all taint of hate and despair.

After paying this tribute to what is normal in the constitution of society (for the idea of thieving appeared to his instinct as normal as the idea of property), Chief Inspector Heat felt very angry with himself for having stopped, for having spoken, for having taken that way at all on the ground of it being a short cut from the station to the headquarters. And he spoke again in his big, authoritative voice, which, being moderated, had a threatening character.

"You are not wanted, I tell you," he repeated.

The anarchist did not stir. An inward laugh of derision uncovered not only his teeth but his gums as well, shook him all over, without the slightest sound. Chief Inspector Heat was led to add, against his better judgment:

"Not yet. When I want you I will know where to find you."

Those were perfectly proper words, within the tradition and suitable to his character of a police officer addressing one of his special flock. But the reception they got departed from tradition and propriety. It was outrageous. The stunted, weakly figure before him spoke at last.

"I've no doubt the papers would give you an obituary notice then. You know best what that would be worth to you. I should think you can imagine easily the sort of stuff that would be printed. But you may be exposed to the unpleasantness of being buried together with me, though I suppose your friends would make an effort to sort us out as much as possible."

With all his healthy contempt for the spirit dictating such speeches, the atrocious allusiveness of the words had its effect on Chief Inspector Heat. He had too much insight, and too much exact information as well, to dismiss them as rot. The dusk of this narrow lane took on a sinister tint from the dark, frail little figure, its back to the wall, and speaking with a weak, self-confident voice. To the vigorous, tenacious vitality of the Chief Inspector, the physical wretchedness of that being, so obviously not fit to live, was ominous; for it seemed to him that if he had the misfortune to be such a miserable object he would not have cared how soon he died. Life had such a strong hold upon him that a fresh wave of nausea broke out in slight perspiration upon his brow. The murmur of town life, the subdued rumble of wheels in the two invisible streets to the right and left, came through the curve of the sordid lane to his ears with a precious familiarity and an appealing sweetness. He was human. But Chief Inspector Heat was also a man, and he could not let such words pass.

"All this is good to frighten children with," he said. "I'll have you yet."

It was very well said, without scorn, with an almost austere quietness.

"Doubtless," was the answer; "but there's no time like the present, believe me. For a man of real convictions this is a fine opportunity of self-sacrifice. You may not find another so favourable, so humane. There isn't even a cat near us, and these condemned old houses would make a good heap of bricks where you stand. You'll never get me at so little cost to life and property, which you are paid to protect."

"You don't know who you're speaking to," said Chief Inspector Heat, firmly. "If I were to lay my hands on you now I would be no better than yourself."

"Ah! The game!"

"You may be sure our side will win in the end. It may yet be necessary to make people believe that some of you ought to be shot at sight like mad dogs. Then that will be the game. But I'll be damned if I know what yours is. I don't believe you know yourselves. You'll never get anything by it."

"Meantime, it's you who get something from it—so far. And you get it easily, too. I won't speak of your salary, but haven't you made your name simply by not understanding what we are after?"

"What are you after, then?" asked Chief Inspector Heat, with scornful haste, like a man in a hurry who perceives he is wasting his time.

The perfect anarchist answered by a smile which did not part his thin, colourless lips; and the celebrated Chief Inspector felt a sense of superiority which induced him to raise a warning finger.

"Give it up—whatever it is," he said in an admonishing tone, but not so kindly as if he were condescending to give good advice to a cracksman of repute. "Give it up. You'll find we are too many for you."

The fixed smile on the Professor's lips wavered, as if the mocking spirit within had lost its assurance. Chief Inspector Heat went on:

"Don't you believe me—eh? Well, you've only got to look about you. We are. And anyway, you're not doing it well. You're always making a mess of it. Why, if the thieves didn't know their work better they would starve."

The hint of an invincible multitude behind that man's back roused a sombre indignation in the breast of the Professor. He smiled no longer his enigmatic and mocking smile. The resisting power of numbers, the unattackable stolidity of a great multitude, was the haunting fear of his sinister loneliness. His lips trembled for some time before he managed to say in a strangled voice:

"I am doing my work better than you're doing yours."

"That'll do now," interrupted Chief Inspector Heat, hurriedly; and the Professor laughed right out this time. While still laughing he moved on; but he did not laugh long. It was a sad-faced, miserable little man who emerged from the narrow passage into the bustle of the broad thoroughfare. He walked with the nerveless gait of a tramp going on, still going on, indifferent to rain or sun in a sinister detachment from the aspects of sky and earth. Chief Inspector Heat, on the other hand, after watching him for a while, stepped out with the purposeful briskness of a man disregarding indeed the inclemencies of the weather, but conscious of having an authorized mission on this earth and the moral support of his kind. All the inhabitants of the immense town, the population of the whole country, and even the teeming millions struggling upon the planet, were with him—down to the very thieves and mendicants. Yes, the thieves themselves were sure to be with him in his present work. The consciousness of universal support in his general activity heartened him to grapple with the particular problem.

The problem immediately before the Chief Inspector was that of managing the Assistant Commissioner of his department, his immediate superior. This is the perennial problem of trusty and loyal servants; anarchism gave it its particular complexion, but nothing more. Truth to say, Chief Inspector Heat thought but little of anarchism. He did not attach undue importance to it, and could never bring himself to consider it seriously. It had more the character of disorderly conduct; disorderly without the human excuse of drunkenness, which at any rate implies good feeling and an amiable leaning towards festivity. As criminals, anarchists were distinctly no class—no class at all. And recalling the Professor, Chief Inspector Heat, without checking his swinging pace, muttered through his teeth:

"Lunatic."

Catching thieves was another matter altogether. It had that quality of seriousness belonging to every form of open sport where the best man wins under perfectly comprehensible rules.

There were no rules for dealing with anarchists. And that was distasteful to the Chief Inspector. It was all foolishness, but that foolishness excited the public mind, affected persons in high places, and touched upon international relations. A hard, merciless contempt settled rigidly on the Chief Inspector's face as he walked on. His mind ran over all the anarchists of his flock. Not one of them had half the spunk of this or that burglar he had known. Not half—not one tenth.

At headquarters the Chief Inspector was admitted at once to the Assistant Commissioner's private room. He found him pen in hand, bent over a great table bestrewn with papers, as if worshipping an enormous double inkstand of bronze and crystal. Speaking-tubes resembling snakes were tied by the heads to the back of the Assistant Commissioner's wooden armchair, and their gaping mouths seemed ready to bite his elbows. And in this attitude he raised only his eyes, whose lids were darker than his face and very much creased. The reports had come in: every anarchist had been exactly accounted for.

After saying this he lowered his eyes, signed rapidly two single sheets of paper, and only then laid down his pen, and sat well back, directing an inquiring gaze at his renowned subordinate. The Chief Inspector stood it well, deferential but inscrutable.

"I daresay you were right," said the Assistant Commissioner, "in telling me at first that the London anarchists had nothing to do with this. I quite appreciate the excellent watch kept on them by your men. On the other hand, this, for the public, does not amount to more than a confession of ignorance."

The Assistant Commissioner's delivery was leisurely, as it were cautious. His thought seemed to rest poised on a word before passing to another, as though words had been the stepping-stones for his intellect picking its way across the waters of error. "Unless you have brought something useful from Greenwich," he added.

The Chief Inspector began at once the account of his investigation in a clear, matter-of-fact manner. His superior, turning his chair a little, and crossing his thin legs, leaned sideways on his elbow, with one hand shading his eyes. His listening attitude had a sort of angular and sorrowful grace. Gleams as of highly burnished silver played on the sides of his ebony-black head when he inclined it slowly at the end.

Chief Inspector Heat waited with the appearance of turning

over in his mind all he had just said, but, as a matter of fact, considering the advisability of saying something more. The Assistant Commissioner cut his hesitation short.

"You believe there were two men?" he asked, without uncovering his eyes.

The Chief Inspector thought it more than probable. In his opinion, the two men had parted from each other within a hundred yards from the Observatory walls. He explained also how the other man could have got out of the park speedily without being observed. The fog, though not very dense, was in his favour. He seemed to have escorted the other to the spot, and then to have left him there to do the job single-handed. Taking the time those two were seen coming out of Maze Hill Station by the old woman, and the time when the explosion was heard, the Chief Inspector thought that the other man might have been actually at the Greenwich Park Station, ready to catch the next train up, at the moment his comrade was destroying himself so thoroughly.

"Very thoroughly—eh?" murmured the Assistant Commissioner from under the shadow of his hand.

The Chief Inspector in a few vigorous words described the aspects of the remains. "The coroner's jury will have a treat," he added, grimly.

The Assistant Commissioner uncovered his eyes.

"We shall have nothing to tell them," he remarked, languidly.

He looked up, and for a time watched the markedly noncommittal attitude of his Chief Inspector. His nature was one that is not easily accessible to illusions. He knew that a department is at the mercy of its subordinate officers, who have their own conceptions of loyalty. His career had begun in a tropical colony. He had liked his work there. It was police work. He had been very successful in tracking and breaking up certain nefarious secret societies amongst the natives. Then he took his long leave, and got married rather impulsively. It was a good match from a worldly point of view, but his wife formed an unfavourable opinion of the colonial climate on hearsay evidence. On the other hand, she had influential connections. It was an excellent match. But he did not like the work he had to do now. He felt himself dependent on too many subordinates and too many masters. The near presence of that strange emotional phenomenon called public opinion weighed upon his spirits, and alarmed him by its irrational nature. No doubt that from ignorance he exaggerated to himself its power for good and evil—especially for evil; and the rough east winds of the English spring (which agreed with his wife) augmented his general mistrust of men's motives and of the efficiency of their organization. The futility of office work especially appalled him on those days so trying to his sensitive liver.

He got up, unfolding himself to his full height, and with a heaviness of step remarkable in so slender a man, moved across the room to the window. The panes streamed with rain, and the short street he looked down into lay wet and empty, as if swept clear suddenly by a great flood. It was a very trying day, choked in raw fog to begin with, and now drowned in cold rain. The flickering, blurred flames of gas-lamps seemed to be dissolving in a watery atmosphere. And the lofty pretensions of a mankind oppressed by the miserable indignities of the weather appeared as a colossal and hopeless vanity deserving of scorn, wonder, and compassion.

"Horrible, horrible!" thought the Assistant Commissioner to himself, with his face near the window-pane. "We have been having this sort of thing now for ten days; no, a fortnight—a fortnight." He ceased to think completely for a time. That utter stillness of his brain lasted about three seconds. Then he said, perfunctorily: "You have set inquiries on foot for tracing that other man up and down the line?"

He had no doubt that everything needful had been done. Chief Inspector Heat knew, of course, thoroughly the business of man-hunting. And these were the routine steps, too, that would be taken as a matter of course by the merest beginner. A few inquiries amongst the ticket collectors and the porters of the two small railway stations would give additional details as to the appearance of the two men; the inspection of the collected tickets would show at once where they came from that morning. It was elementary, and could not have been neglected. Accordingly, the Chief Inspector answered that all this had been done directly the old woman had come forward with her deposition. And he mentioned the name of a station. "That's where they came from, sir," he went on. "The porter who took the tickets at Maze Hill remembers two chaps answering to the description passing the barrier. They seemed to him two respectable working-men of a superior sort—sign painters or house decorators. The big man got out of a third-class compartment backward, with a bright tin can in his hand. On the platform he gave it to carry to the fair young fellow who followed him. All this agrees exactly with what the old woman told the police sergeant in Greenwich."

The Assistant Commissioner, still with his face turned to the window, expressed his doubt as to these two men having had anything to do with the outrage. All this theory rested upon the utterances of an old charwoman who had been nearly knocked down by a man in a hurry. Not a very substantial authority indeed, unless on the ground of sudden inspiration, which was hardly tenable.

"Frankly now, could she have been really inspired?" he queried, with grave irony, keeping his back to the room, as if entranced by the contemplation of the town's colossal forms half lost in the night. He did not even look round when he heard the mutter of the word "Providential" from the principal subordinate of his department, whose name, printed sometimes in the papers, was familiar to the great public as that of one of its zealous and hard-working protectors. Chief Inspector Heat raised his voice a little.

"Strips and bits of bright tin were quite visible to me," he said. "That's a pretty good corroboration."

"And these men came from that little country station," the Assistant Commissioner mused aloud, wondering. He was told that such was the name on two tickets out of three given up out of that train at Maze Hill. The third person who got out was a hawker from Gravesend well known to the porters. The Chief Inspector imparted that information in a tone of finality with some ill humour, as loyal servants will do in the consciousness of their fidelity and with the sense of the value of their loyal exertions. And still the Assistant Commissioner did not turn away from the darkness outside, as vast as a sea.

"Two foreign anarchists coming from that place," he said, apparently to the window-pane. "It's rather unaccountable."

"Yes, sir. But it would be still more unaccountable if that Michaelis weren't staying in a cottage in the neighbourhood."

At the sound of that name, falling unexpectedly into this annoying affair, the Assistant Commissioner dismissed brusquely the vague remembrance of his daily whist party at his club. It was the most comforting habit of his life, in a mainly successful display of his skill without the assistance of any subordinate. He entered his club to play from five to seven, before going home to dinner, forgetting for those two hours whatever was distasteful in his life, as though the game were a beneficent drug for allaying the pangs of moral discontent. His partners were the gloomily humorous editor of a celebrated magazine; a silent, elderly barrister with malicious little eyes; and a highly martial, simple-minded old Colonel with nervous brown hands. They were his club acquaintances merely. He never met them elsewhere except at the card-table. But they all seemed to approach the game in the spirit of co-sufferers, as if it were indeed a drug against the secret ills of existence; and every day as the sun declined over the countless roofs of the town, a mellow, pleasurable impatience, resembling the impulse of a sure and profound friendship, lightened his professional labours. And now this pleasurable sensation went out of him with something resembling a physical shock and was replaced by a special kind of interest in his work of social protection—an improper sort of interest, which may be defined best as a sudden and alert mistrust of the weapon in his hand.

CHAPTER 6

The lady patroness of Michaelis, the ticket-of-leave apostle of humanitarian hopes, was one of the most influential and distinguished connections of the Assistant Commissioner's wife, whom she called Annie, and treated still rather as a not very wise and utterly inexperienced young girl. But she had consented to accept him on a friendly footing, which was by no means the case with all of his wife's influential connections. Married young and splendidly at some remote epoch of the past, she had had for a time a close view of great affairs, and even of some great men. She herself was a great lady. Old now in the number of her years, she had that sort of exceptional temperament which defies time with scornful disregard, as if it were a rather vulgar convention submitted to by the mass of inferior mankind. Many other conventions easier to set aside, alas! failed to obtain her recognition, also on temperamental grounds—either because they bored her, or else because they stood in the way of her scorns and sympathies. Admiration was a sentiment unknown to her (it was one of the secret griefs of her most noble husband against her)—first, as always more or less tainted with mediocrity, and next as being in a way an admission of inferiority. And both were frankly inconceivable to her nature. To be fearlessly outspoken in her opinions came easily to her, since she judged solely from the standpoint of her social position. She was equally untrammelled in her actions; and as her tactfulness proceeded from genuine humanity, her bodily vigour remained remarkable and her superiority was serene and cordial, three generations had admired her infinitely, and the last she was likely to see had pronounced her a wonderful woman. Meantime, intelligent, with a sort of lofty simplicity, and curious at heart, but not like many women merely of social gossip, she amused her age by attracting within her ken through the power of her great, almost historical, social prestige everything that rose above the dead level of mankind, lawfully or unlawfully, by position, wit, audacity, fortune or misfortune. Royal Highnesses, artists, men of science, young statesmen, and charlatans of all ages and conditions, who, unsubstantial and light, bobbing up like corks, show best the direction of the surface currents, had been welcomed in that house, listened to, penetrated, understood, appraised, for her own edification. In her own words, she liked to watch what the world was coming to. And as she had a practical mind her judgement of men and things, though based on special prejudices, was seldom totally wrong, and almost never wrongheaded. Her drawing-room was probably the only place in the wide world where an Assistant Commissioner of Police could meet a convict liberated on a ticket-of-leave on other than professional and official ground. Who had brought Michaelis there one afternoon the Assistant Commissioner did not remember very well. He had a notion it must have been a certain Member of Parliament of illustrious parentage and unconventional sympathies, which were the standing joke of the comic papers. The notabilities and even the simple notorieties of the day brought each other freely to that temple of an old woman's not ignoble curiosity. You never could guess whom you were likely to come upon being received in semi-privacy within the faded blue silk and gilt frame screen, making a cosy nook for a couch and a few armchairs in the great drawing-room, with its hum of voices and the groups of people seated or standing in the light of six tall windows.

Michaelis had been the object of a revulsion of popular sentiment, the same sentiment which years ago had applauded the ferocity of the life sentence passed upon him for complicity in a rather mad attempt to rescue some prisoners from a police van. The plan of the conspirators had been to shoot down the horses and overpower the escort. Unfortunately, one of the police constables got shot, too. He left a wife and three small children, and the death of that man aroused through the length and breadth of a realm for whose defence, welfare, and glory men die every day as matter of duty, an outburst of furious indignation, of a raging, implacable pity for the victim. Three ringleaders got hanged. Michaelis, young and slim, locksmith by trade, and great frequenter of evening schools, did not even know that anybody had been killed, his part with a few others being to force open the door at the back of the special conveyance. When arrested he had a bunch of skeleton keys in one pocket, a heavy chisel in another, and a short crowbar in his hand; neither more nor less than a burglar. But no burglar would have received such a heavy sentence. The death of the constable had made him miserable at heart, but the failure of the plot also. He did not conceal either of these sentiments from his empanelled countrymen, and that sort of compunction appeared shockingly imperfect to the crammed court. The judge on passing sentence commented feelingly upon the depravity and callousness of the young prisoner.

That made the groundless fame of his condemnation; the fame of his release was made for him on no better grounds by people who wished to exploit the sentimental aspect of his imprisonment either for purposes of their own or for no intelligible purpose. He let them do so in the innocence of his heart and the simplicity of his mind. Nothing that happened to him individually had any importance. He was like those saintly men whose personality is lost in the contemplation of their faith. His ideas were not in the nature of convictions. They were inaccessible to reasoning. They formed in all their contradictions and obscurities an invincible and humanitarian creed, which he confessed rather than preached, with an obstinate gentleness, a smile of pacific assurance on his lips, and his candid blue eyes cast down because the sight of faces troubled his inspiration developed in solitude. In that characteristic attitude, pathetic in his grotesque and incurable obesity which he had to drag like a galley slave's bullet to the end of his days, the Assistant Commissioner of Police beheld the ticket-of-leave apostle filling a privileged armchair within the screen. He sat there by the head of the old lady's couch, mild-voiced and quiet, with no more self-consciousness than a very small child, and with something of a child's charm—the appealing charm of trustfulness. Confident of the future, whose secret ways had been revealed to him within the four walls of a well-known penitentiary, he had no reason to look with suspicion upon anybody. If he could not give the great and curious lady a very definite idea as to what the world was coming to, he had managed without effort to impress her by his unembittered faith, by the sterling quality of his optimism.

A certain simplicity of thought is common to serene souls at both ends of the social scale. The great lady was simple in her own way. His views and beliefs had nothing in them to shock or startle her, since she judged them from the standpoint of her lofty position. Indeed, her sympathies were easily accessible to a man of that sort. She was not an exploiting capitalist herself; she was, as it were, above the play of economic conditions. And she had a great capacity of pity for the more obvious forms of common human miseries, precisely because she was such a complete stranger to them that she had to translate her conception into terms of mental suffering before she could grasp the notion of their cruelty. The Assistant Commissioner remembered very well the conversation between these two. He had listened in silence. It was something as exciting in a way, and even touching in its foredoomed futility, as the efforts at moral intercourse between the inhabitants of remote planets. But this grotesque incarnation of humanitarian passion appealed, somehow, to one's imagination. At last Michaelis rose, and taking the great lady's extended hand, shook it, retained it for a moment in his great cushioned palm with unembarrassed friendliness, and turned upon the semi-private nook of the drawing-room his back, vast and square, and as if distended under the short tweed jacket. Glancing about in serene benevolence, he waddled along to the distant door between the knots of other visitors. The murmur of conversations paused on his passage. He smiled innocently at a tall, brilliant girl, whose eyes met his accidentally, and went out unconscious of the glances following him across the room. Michaelis's first appearance in the world was a success—a success of esteem unmarred by a single murmur of derision. The interrupted conversations were resumed in their proper tone, grave or light. Only a well-set-up, long-limbed, active-looking man of forty talking with two ladies near a window remarked aloud, with an unexpected depth of feeling: "Eighteen stone, I should say, and not five foot six. Poor fellow! It's terrible—terrible."

The lady of the house gazing absently at the Assistant Commissioner, left alone with her on the private side of the screen, seemed to be rearranging her mental impressions behind her thoughtful immobility of a handsome old face. Men with grey moustaches and full, healthy, vaguely smiling countenances approached, circling round the screen; two mature women with a matronly air of gracious resolution; a clean-shaved individual with sunken cheeks, and dangling a gold-mounted eyeglass on a broad black ribbon with an old-world, dandified effect. A silence deferential, but full of reserves, reigned for a moment, and then the great lady exclaimed, not with resentment, but with a sort of protesting indignation:

"And that officially is supposed to be a revolutionist! What nonsense." She looked hard at the Assistant Commissioner, who murmured, apologetically:

"Not a dangerous one perhaps."

"Not dangerous—I should think not indeed. He is a mere believer. It's the temperament of a saint," declared the great lady in a firm tone. "And they kept him shut up for twenty years. One shudders at the stupidity of it. And now they have let him out everybody belonging to him is gone away somewhere or dead. His parents are dead; the girl he was to marry has died while he was in prison; he has lost the skill necessary for his manual occupation. He told me all this himself with the sweetest patience; but then, he said, he had had plenty of time to think out things for himself. A pretty compensation! If that's the stuff revolutionists are made of some of us may well go on their knees to them," she continued in a slightly bantering voice, while the banal society smiles hardened on the worldly faces turned towards her with conventional deference. "The poor creature is obviously no longer in a position to take care of himself. Somebody will have to look after him a little."

"He should be recommended to follow a treatment of some sort," the soldierly voice of the active-looking man was heard advising earnestly from a distance. He was in the pink of condition for his age, and even the texture of his long frock-coat had a character of elastic soundness, as if it were a living tissue. "The man is virtually a cripple," he added with unmistakable feeling.

Other voices, as if glad of the opening, murmured hasty compassion. "Quite startling," "Monstrous," "Most painful to see." The lank man, with the eyeglass on a broad ribbon, pronounced mincingly the word "Grotesque," whose justness was appreciated by those standing near him. They smiled at each other.

The Assistant Commissioner had expressed no opinion either then or later, his position making it impossible for him to ventilate any independent view of a ticket-of-leave convict. But, in truth, he shared the view of his wife's friend and patron that Michaelis was a humanitarian sentimentalist, a little mad, but upon the whole incapable of hurting a fly intentionally. So when that name cropped up suddenly in this vexing bomb affair he realized all the danger of it for the ticket-of-leave apostle, and his mind reverted at once to the old lady's well-established infatuation. Her arbitrary kindness would not brook patiently any interference with Michaelis's freedom. It was a deep, calm, convinced infatuation. She had not only felt him to be inoffensive, but she had said so, which last by a confusion of her absolutist mind became a sort of incontrovertible demonstration. It was as if the monstrosity of the man, with his candid infant's eyes and a fat angelic smile, had fascinated her. She had come to believe almost his theory of the future, since it was not repugnant to her prejudices. She disliked the new element of plutocracy in the social compound, and industrialism as a method of human development appeared to her singularly repulsive in its mechanical and unfeeling character. The humanitarian hopes of the mild Michaelis tended not towards utter destruction, but merely towards the complete economic ruin of the system. And she did not really see where was the moral harm of it. It would do away with all the multitude of the parvenus, whom she disliked and mistrusted, not because they had arrived anywhere (she denied that), but because of their profound unintelligence of the world, which was the primary cause of the crudity of their perceptions and the aridity of their hearts. With the annihilation of all capital they would vanish, too; but universal ruin (providing it was universal, as it was revealed to Michaelis) would leave the social values untouched. The disappearance of the last piece of money could not affect people of position. She could not conceive how it could affect her position, for instance. She had developed these discoveries to the Assistant Commissioner with all the serene fearlessness of an old woman who had escaped the blight of indifference. He had made for himself the rule to receive everything of that sort in a silence which he took care from policy and inclination not to make offensive. He had an affection for the aged disciple of Michaelis, a complex sentiment depending a little on her prestige, on her personality, but most of all on the instinct of flattered gratitude. He felt himself really liked in her house. She was kindness personified. And she was practically wise, too, after the manner of experienced women. She made his married life much easier than it would have been without her generously full recognition of his rights as Annie's husband. Her influence upon his wife, a woman devoured by all sorts of small selfishnesses, small envies, small jealousies, was excellent. Unfortunately, both her kindness and her wisdom were of unreasonable complexion, distinctly feminine, and difficult to deal with. She remained a perfect woman all along her full tale of years, and not as some of them do become—a sort of slippery, pestilential old man in petticoats. And it was as of a woman that he thought of her—the specially choice incarnation of the feminine, wherein is recruited the tender, ingenuous, and fierce bodyguard for all sorts of men who talk under the influence of an emotion, true or fraudulent; for preachers, seers, prophets, or reformers.

Appreciating the distinguished and good friend of his wife, and himself, in that way, the Assistant Commissioner became alarmed at the convict Michaelis's possible fate. Once arrested on suspicion of being in some way, however remote, a party to this outrage, the man could hardly escape being sent back to finish his sentence at least. And that would kill him; he would never come out alive. The Assistant Commissioner made a reflection extremely unbecoming his official position without being really creditable to his humanity.

"If the fellow is laid hold of again," he thought, "she will never forgive me."

The frankness of such a secretly outspoken thought could not go without some derisive self-criticism. No man engaged in a work he does not like can preserve many saving illusions about himself. The distaste, the absence of glamour, extend from the occupation to the personality. It is only when our appointed activities seem by a lucky accident to obey the particular earnestness of our temperament that we can taste the comfort of complete self-deception. The Assistant Commissioner did not like his work at home. The police work he had been engaged on in a distant part of the globe had the saving character of an irregular sort of warfare or at least the risk and excitement of open-air sport. His real abilities, which were mainly of an administrative order, were combined with an adventurous disposition. Chained to a desk in the thick of four millions of men, he considered himself the victim of an ironic fate—the same, no doubt, which had brought about his marriage with a woman exceptionally sensitive in the matter of colonial climate, besides other limitations testifying to the delicacy of her nature—and her tastes. Though he judged his alarm sardonically he did not dismiss the improper thought from his mind. The instinct of self-preservation was strong within him. On the contrary, he repeated it mentally with profane emphasis and a fuller precision: "Damn it! If that infernal Heat has his way the fellow'll die in prison smothered in his fat, and she'll never forgive me."

His black, narrow figure, with the white band of the collar under the silvery gleams on the close-cropped hair at the back of the head, remained motionless. The silence had lasted such a long time that Chief Inspector Heat ventured to clear his throat. This noise produced its effect. The zealous and intelligent officer was asked by his superior, whose back remained turned to him immovably:

"You connect Michaelis with this affair?"

Chief Inspector Heat was very positive, but cautious.

"Well sir," he said, "we have enough to go upon. A man like that has no business to be at large, anyhow."

"You will want some conclusive evidence," came the observation in a murmur.

Chief Inspector Heat raised his eyebrows at the black, narrow back, which remained obstinately presented to his intelligence and his zeal.

"There will be no difficulty in getting up sufficient evidence against *him,*" he said, with virtuous complacency. "You may trust me for that, sir," he added, quite unnecessarily, out of the fullness of his heart; for it seemed to him an excellent thing to have that man in hand to be thrown down to the public should it think fit to roar with any special indignation in this case. It was impossible to say yet whether it would roar or not. That in the last instance depended, of course, on the newspaper press. But in any case, Chief Inspector Heat, purveyor of prisons by trade, and a man of legal instincts, did logically believe that incarceration was the proper fate for every declared enemy of the law. In the strength of that conviction he committed a fault of tact. He allowed himself a little conceited laugh, and repeated:

"Trust me for that, sir."

This was too much for the forced calmness under which the Assistant Commissioner had for upwards of eighteen months concealed his irritation with the system and the subordinates of his office. A square peg forced into a round hole, he had felt like a daily outrage that long-established smooth roundness into which a man of less sharply angular shape would have fitted himself, with voluptuous acquiescence, after a shrug or two. What he resented most was just the necessity of taking so much on trust. At the little laugh of Chief Inspector Heat's he spun swiftly on his heels, as if whirled away from the window-pane by an electric shock. He caught on the latter's face not only the complacency proper to the occasion lurking under the moustache, but the vestiges of experimental watchfulness in the round eyes, which had been, no doubt, fastened on his back, and now met his glance for a second before the intent character of their stare had the time to change to a merely startled appearance.

The Assistant Commissioner of Police had really some qualifications for his post. Suddenly his suspicion was awakened. It is but fair to say that his suspicions of the police methods (unless the police happened to be a semi-military body organized by himself) was not difficult to arouse. If it ever slumbered from sheer weariness, it was but lightly: and his appreciation of Chief Inspector Heat's zeal and ability, moderate in itself, excluded all notion of moral confidence. "He's up to something," he exclaimed, mentally, and at once became angry. Crossing over to his desk with headlong strides, he sat down violently. "Here I am stuck in a litter of paper," he reflected, with unreasonable resentment, "supposed to hold all the threads in my hands and yet I can but hold what is put in my hand, and nothing else. And they can fasten the other ends of the threads where they please."

He raised his head, and turned towards his subordinate a long, meagre face with the accentuated features of an energetic Don Quixote.

"Now what is it you've got up your sleeve?"

The other stared. He stared without winking in a perfect immobility of his round eyes, as he was used to stare at the various members of the criminal class when, after being duly cautioned, they made their statements in the tones of injured innocence, or false simplicity, or sullen resignation. But behind that professional and stony fixity there was some surprise, too, for in such a tone, combining nicely the note of contempt and impatience, Chief Inspector Heat, the right-hand man of the department, was not used to be addressed. He began in a procrastinating manner, like a man taken unawares by a new and unexpected experience.

"What I've got against that man Michaelis you mean, sir?"

The Assistant Commissioner watched the bullet head; the points of that Norse rover's moustache, falling below the line of the heavy jaw; the whole full and pale physiognomy, whose determined character was marred by too much flesh; at the cunning wrinkles radiating from the outer corners of the eyes—and in that purposeful contemplation of the valuable and trusted officer he drew a conviction so sudden that it moved him like an inspiration.

"I have reason to think what when you came into this room," he said in measured tones, "it was not Michaelis who was in your mind; not principally—perhaps not at all."

"You have reason to think, sir?" muttered Chief Inspector Heat with every appearance of astonishment, which up to a certain point was genuine enough. He had discovered in this affair a delicate and perplexing side, forcing upon the discoverer a certain amount of insincerity—that sort of insincerity which, under the names of skill, prudence, discretion, turns up at one point or another in most human affairs. He felt at the moment like a tightrope artist might feel if suddenly, in the middle of the performance, the manager of the Music Hall were to rush out of the proper managerial seclusion and begin to shake the rope. Indignation, the sense of moral insecurity engendered by such a treacherous proceeding joined to the immediate apprehension of a broken neck, would, in the colloquial phrase, put him in a state. And there would be also some scandalized concern for his art, too, since a man must identify himself with something more tangible than his own personality, and establish his pride somewhere, either in his social position, or in the quality of the work he is obliged to do, or simply in the superiority of the idleness he may be fortunate enough to enjoy.

"Yes," said the Assistant Commissioner; "I have. I do not mean to say that you have not thought of Michaelis at all. But you are giving the fact you've mentioned a prominence which strikes me as not quite candid, Inspector Heat. If that is really the track of discovery, why haven't you followed it up at once, either personally or by sending one of your men to that village?"

"Do you think, sir, I have failed in my duty there?" the Chief Inspector asked, in a tone which he sought to make simply reflective. Forced unexpectedly to concentrate his faculties upon the task of preserving his balance, he had seized upon that point, and exposed himself to a rebuke; for the Assistant Commissioner, frowning slightly, observed that this was a very improper remark to make.

"But since you've made it," he continued, coldly, "I'll tell you that this is not my meaning."

He paused, with a straight glance of his sunken eyes which was a full equivalent of the unspoken termination "and you know it." The head of the so-called Special Crimes Department, debarred by his position from going out of doors personally in quest of secrets locked up in guilty breasts, had a propensity to exercise his considerable gifts for the detection of incriminating truth upon his own subordinates. That peculiar instinct could hardly be called a weakness. It was natural. He was a born detective. It had unconsciously governed his choice of a career, and if it ever failed him in life it was perhaps in the one exceptional circumstance of his marriage—which was also natural. It fed, since it could not roam abroad, upon the human material which was brought to it in its official seclusion. We can never cease to be ourselves.

His elbow on the desk, his thin legs crossed and nursing his cheek in the palm of his meagre hand, the Assistant Commissioner in charge of the Special Crimes branch was getting hold of the case with growing interest. His Chief Inspector, if not an absolutely worthy foeman of his penetration, was at any rate the most worthy of all within his reach. A mistrust of established reputations was strictly in character with the Assistant Commissioner's ability as detector. His memory evoked a certain old, fat and wealthy native chief in the distant colony whom it was a tradition for the successive Colonial Governors to trust and make much of as a firm friend and supporter of the order and legality established by white men; whereas, when examined sceptically, he was found out to be principally his own good friend, and nobody else's. Not precisely a traitor, but still a man of many dangerous reservations in his fidelity, caused by a due regard for his own advantage, comfort, and safety. A fellow of some innocence in his naïve duplicity, but none the less dangerous. He took some finding out. He was physically a big man, too, and (allowing for the difference of colour, of course) Chief Inspector Heat's appearance recalled him to the memory of his superior. It was not the eyes nor yet the lips exactly. It was bizarre. But does not Alfred Wallace relate in his famous book on the Malay Archipelago how, amongst the Aru Islanders, he discovered in an old and naked savage with a sooty skin a peculiar resemblance to a dear friend at home?

For the first time since he took up his appointment the Assistant Commissioner felt as if he were going to do some real work for his salary. And that was a pleasurable sensation. "I'll turn him inside out like an old glove," thought the Assistant Commissioner, with his eyes resting pensively upon Chief Inspector Heat.

"No, that was not my thought," he began again. "There is no doubt about you knowing your business—no doubt at all; and that's precisely why I—" He stopped short, and changing his tone: "What could you bring up against Michaelis of a definite nature? I mean apart from the fact that the two men under suspicion—you're certain there were two of them—came last from a railway station within three miles of the village where Michaelis is living now."

"This by itself is enough for us to go upon, sir, with that sort of man," said the Chief Inspector, with returning composure. The slight, approving movement of the Assistant Commissioner's head went far to pacify the resentful astonishment of the renowned officer. For Chief Inspector Heat was a kind man, an excellent husband, a devoted father; and the public and departmental confidence he enjoyed, acting favourably upon an amiable nature, disposed him to feel friendly towards the successive Assistant Commissioners he had seen pass through that very room. There had been three in his time. The first one, a soldierly, abrupt, red-faced person, with white eyebrows and an explosive temper, could be managed with a silken thread. He left on reaching the age limit. The second, a perfect gentleman, knowing his own and everybody else's place to a nicety, on resigning to take up a higher appointment out of England got decorated for (really) Inspector Heat's services. To work with him had been a pride and a pleasure. The third, a bit of a dark horse from the first, was at the end of eighteen months something of a dark horse still to the department. Upon the whole Chief Inspector Heat believed him to be in the main harmless—odd-looking, but harmless. He was speaking now, and the Chief Inspector listened with outward deference (which means nothing, being a matter of duty) and inwardly with benevolent toleration.

"Michaelis reported himself before leaving London for the country?"

"Yes, sir. He did."

"And what may he be doing there?" continued the Assistant Commissioner, who was perfectly informed on that point. Fitted with painful tightness into an old wooden armchair, before a worm-eaten oak table in an upstairs room of a four-roomed cottage with a roof of moss-grown tiles, Michaelis was writing night and day in a shaky, slanting hand that *Autobiography of a Prisoner* which was to be like a book of Revelation in the history of mankind. The conditions of confined space, seclusion, and solitude in a small four-roomed cottage were favourable to his inspiration. It was like being in prison, except that one was never disturbed for the odious purpose of taking exercise according to the tyrannical regulations of his old home in the penitentiary. He could not tell whether the sun still shone on the earth or not. The perspiration of the literary labour dropped from his brow. A delightful enthusiasm urged him on. It was the liberation of his inner life, the letting out of his soul into the wide world. And the zeal of his guileless vanity (first awakened by the offer of five hundred pounds from a publisher) seemed something predestined and holy.

"It would be, of course, most desirable to be informed exactly," insisted the Assistant Commissioner, uncandidly.

Chief Inspector Heat, conscious of renewed irritation at this display of scrupulousness, said that the county police had been notified from the first of Michaelis's arrival, and that a full report could be obtained in a few hours. A wire to the superintendent—

Thus he spoke, rather slowly, while his mind seemed already to be weighing the consequences. A slight knitting of the brow was the outward sign of this. But he was interrupted by a question.

"You've sent that wire already?"

"No sir," he answered, as if surprised.

The Assistant Commissioner uncrossed his legs suddenly. The briskness of that movement contrasted with the casual way in which he threw out a suggestion.

"Would you think that Michaelis had anything to do with the preparation of that bomb, for instance?"

The Chief Inspector assumed a reflective manner.

"I wouldn't say so. There's no necessity to say anything at present. He associates with men who are classed as dangerous. He was made a delegate of the Red Committee less than a year after his release on licence. A sort of compliment, I suppose."

And the Chief Inspector laughed a little angrily, a little scornfully. With a man of that sort scrupulousness was a misplaced and even an illegal sentiment. The celebrity bestowed upon Michaelis on his release two years ago by some emotional journalists in want of special copy had rankled ever since in his breast. It was perfectly legal to arrest that man on the barest suspicion. It was legal and expedient on the face of it. His two former chiefs would have seen the point, at once; whereas this one, without saying either yes or no, sat there, as if lost in a dream. Moreover, besides being legal and expedient, the arrest of Michaelis solved a little personal difficulty which worried Chief Inspector Heat somewhat. This difficulty had its bearing upon his reputation, upon his comfort, and even upon the efficient performance of his duties. For, if Michaelis no doubt knew something about this outrage, the Chief Inspector was fairly certain that he did not know too much. This was just as well. He knew much less—the Chief Inspector was positive—than certain other individuals he had in his mind, but whose arrest seemed to him inexpedient, besides being a more complicated matter, on account of the rules of the game. The rules of the game did not protect so much Michaelis, who was an ex-convict. It would be stupid not to take advantage of legal facilities, and the journalists who had written him up with emotional gush would be ready to write him down with emotional indignation.

This prospect, viewed with confidence, had the attraction of a personal triumph for Chief Inspector Heat. And deep down in his blameless bosom of an average married citizen, almost unconscious but potent nevertheless, the dislike of being compelled by events to meddle with the desperate ferocity of the Professor had its say. This dislike had been strengthened by the chance meeting in the lane. The encounter did not leave behind with Chief Inspector Heat that satisfactory sense of superiority the members of the police force get from the unofficial but intimate side of their intercourse with the criminal classes, by which the vanity of power is soothed, and the vulgar love of domination over our fellow creatures is flattered as worthily as it deserves.

The perfect anarchist was not recognized as a fellow creature by Chief Inspector Heat. He was impossible—a mad dog to be left alone. Not that the Chief Inspector was afraid of him; on the contrary, he meant to have him some day. But not yet: he meant to get hold of him in his own time, properly and effectively, according to the rules of the game. The present was not the right time for attempting that feat, not the right time for many reasons, personal and of public service. This being the strong feeling of Inspector Heat, it appeared to him just and proper that this affair should be shunted off its obscure and inconvenient track, leading goodness knows where, into a quiet (and lawful) siding called Michaelis. And he repeated, as if reconsidering the suggestion conscientiously:

"The bomb. No, I would not say that exactly. We may never find that out. But it's clear that he is connected with this in some way, which we can find out without much trouble."

His countenance had that look of grave, overbearing indifference once well known and much dreaded by the better sort of thieves. Chief Inspector Heat, though what is called a man, was not a smiling animal. But his inward state was that of satisfaction at the passively receptive attitude of the Assistant Commissioner, who murmured gently:

"And you really think that the investigation should be made in that direction?"

"I do, sir."

"Quite convinced?"

"I am, sir. That's the true line for us to take."

The Assistant Commissioner withdrew the support of his hand from his reclining head with a suddenness that, considering his languid attitude, seemed to menace his whole person with collapse. But, on the contrary, he sat up, extremely alert, behind the great writing-table on which his hand had fallen with the sound of a sharp blow.

"What I want to know is what put it out of your head till now."

"Put it out of my head," repeated the Chief Inspector very slowly.

"Yes. Till you were called into this room—you know."

The Chief Inspector felt as if the air between his clothing and his skin had become unpleasantly hot. It was the sensation of an unprecedented and incredible experience.

"Of course," he said, exaggerating the deliberation of his utterance to the utmost limits of possibility, "if there is a reason, of which I know nothing, for not interfering with the convict Michaelis, perhaps it's just as well I didn't start the county police after him."

This took such a long time to say that the unflagging attention of the Assistant Commissioner seemed a wonderful feat of endurance. His retort came without delay.

"No reason whatever that I know of. Come, Chief Inspector, this finessing with me is highly improper on your part—highly improper. And it's also unfair, you know. You shouldn't leave me to puzzle things out for myself like this. Really, I am surprised."

He paused, then added smoothly: "I need scarcely tell you that this conversation is altogether unofficial."

These words were far from pacifying the Chief Inspector. The indignation of a betrayed tight-rope performer was strong within him. In his pride of a trusted servant he was affected by the assurance that the rope was not shaken for the purpose of breaking his neck, as by an exhibition of impudence. As if anybody were afraid! Assistant Commissioners come and go, but a valuable Chief Inspector is not an ephemeral office phenomenon. He was not afraid of getting a broken neck. To have his performance spoiled was more than enough to account for the glow of honest indignation. And as thought is no respecter of persons, the thought of Chief Inspector Heat took a threatening and prophetic shape. "You, my boy," he said to himself, keeping his round and habitually roving eyes fastened upon the Assistant Commissioner's face—"you, my boy, you don't know your place, and your place won't know you very long either, I bet."

As if in provoking answer to that thought, something like the ghost of an amiable smile passed on the lips of the Assistant Commissioner. His manner was easy and businesslike while he persisted in administering another shake to the tight-rope.

"Let us come now to what you have discovered on the spot, Chief Inspector," he said.

"A fool and his job are soon parted," went on the train of prophetic thought in Chief Inspector Heat's head. But it was immediately followed by the reflection that a higher official, even when "fired out" (this was the precise image), has still the time as he flies through the door to launch a nasty kick at the shin-bones of a subordinate. Without softening very much the basilisk nature of his stare, he said, impassively:

"We are coming to that part of my investigation, sir."

"That's right. Well, what have you brought away from it?"

The Chief Inspector, who had made up his mind to jump off the rope, came to the ground with gloomy frankness.

"I've brought away an address," he said, pulling out of his pocket without haste a singed rag of dark blue cloth. "This belongs to the overcoat the fellow who got himself blown to pieces was wearing. Of course, the overcoat may not have been his, and may even have been stolen. But that's not at all probable if you look at this."

The Chief Inspector, stepping up to the table, smoothed out carefully the rag of blue cloth. He had picked it up from the repulsive heap in the mortuary, because a tailor's name is found sometimes under the collar. It is not often of much use, but still— He only half expected to find anything useful, but certainly he did not expect to find—not under the collar at all, but stitched carefully on the under-side of the lapel—a square piece of calico with an address written on it in marking ink.

The Chief Inspector removed his smoothing hand.

"I carried it off with me without anybody taking notice," he said. "I thought it best. It can always be produced if required."

The Assistant Commissioner, rising a little in his chair, pulled the cloth over to his side of the table. He sat looking at it in silence. Only the number 32 and the name of Brett Street were written in marking ink on a piece of calico slightly larger than an ordinary cigarette paper. He was genuinely surprised.

"Can't understand why he should have gone about labelled like this," he said, looking up at Chief Inspector Heat. "It's a most extraordinary thing."

"I met once in the smoking-room of a hotel an old gentleman who went about with his name and address sewn on in all his coats in case of an accident or sudden illness," said the Chief Inspector. "He professed to be eighty-four years old, but he didn't look his age. He told me he was also afraid of losing his memory suddenly, like those people he had been reading of in the papers."

A question from the Assistant Commissioner, who wanted to know what was No. 32 Brett Street, interrupted that reminiscence abruptly. The Chief Inspector, driven down to the ground by unfair artifices, had elected to walk the path of unreserved openness. If he believed firmly that to know too much was not good for the department, the judicious holding back of knowledge was as far as his loyalty dared to go for the good of the service. If the Assistant Commissioner wanted to mismanage this affair nothing, of course, could prevent him. But, on his own part, he now saw no reason for a display of alacrity. So he answered concisely:

"It's a shop, sir."

The Assistant Commissioner, with his eyes lowered on the rag of blue cloth, waited for more information. As that did not come he proceeded to obtain it by a series of questions propounded with gentle patience. Thus he acquired an idea of the nature of Mr Verloc's commerce, of his personal appearance, and heard at last his name. In a pause the Assistant Commissioner raised his eyes, and discovered some animation on the Chief Inspector's face. They looked at each other in silence.

"Of course," said the latter, "the department has no record of that man."

"Did any of my predecessors have any knowledge of what you have told me now?" asked the Assistant Commissioner, putting his elbows on the table and raising his joined hands before his face, as if about to offer prayer, only that his eyes had not a pious expression.

"No, sir; certainly not. What would have been the object? That sort of man could never be produced publicly to any good purpose. It was sufficient for me to know who he was, and to make use of him in a way that could be used publicly."

"And do you think that sort of private knowledge consistent with the official position you occupy?"

"Perfectly, sir. I think it's quite proper. I will take the liberty to tell you, sir, that it makes me what I am—and I am looked upon as a man who knows his work. It's a private affair of my own. A personal friend of mine in the French police gave me the hint that the fellow was an Embassy spy. Private friendship, private information, private use of it—that's how I look upon it."

The Assistant Commissioner, after remarking to himself that the mental state of the renowned Chief Inspector seemed to affect the outline of his lower jaw, as if the lively sense of his high professional distinction had been located in that part of his anatomy, dismissed the point for the moment with a calm "I see." Then leaning his cheek on his joined hands:

"Well, then—speaking privately if you like—how long have you been in private touch with this Embassy spy?"

To this inquiry the private answer of the Chief Inspector, so private that it was never shaped into audible words, was:

"Long before you were even thought of for your place here."

The so-to-speak public utterance was much more precise.

"I saw him for the first time in my life a little more than seven years ago, when two Imperial Highnesses and the Imperial Chancellor were on a visit here. I was put in charge of all the arrangements for looking after them. Baron Stott-Wartenheim was Ambassador then. He was a very nervous old gentleman. One evening, three days before the Guildhall Banquet, he sent word that he wanted to see me for a moment. I was downstairs, and the carriages were at the door to take the Imperial Highnesses and the Chancellor to the opera. I went up at once. I found the Baron walking up and down his bedroom in a pitiable state of distress, squeezing his hands together. He assured me he had the fullest confidence in our police and in my abilities, but he had there a man just come over from Paris whose information could be trusted implicitly. He wanted me to hear what that man had to say. He took me at once into a dressing-room next door, where I saw a big fellow in a heavy overcoat sitting all alone on a chair, and holding his hat and stick in one hand. The Baron said to him in French 'Speak, my friend.' The light in that room was not very good. I talked with him for some five minutes perhaps. He certainly gave me a piece of very startling news. Then the Baron took me aside nervously to praise him up to me, and when I turned round again I discovered that the fellow had vanished like a ghost. Got up and sneaked out down some back stairs, I suppose. There was no time to run after him, as I had to hurry off after the Ambassador down the great staircase, and see the party started safe for the opera. However, I acted upon the information that very night. Whether it was perfectly correct or not, it did look serious enough. Very likely it saved us from an ugly trouble on the day of the Imperial visit to the City.

"Some time later, a month or so after my promotion to Chief Inspector, my attention was attracted to a big burly man, I thought I had seen somewhere before, coming out in a hurry from a jeweller's shop in the Strand. I went after him, as it was on my way towards Charing Cross, and there seeing one of our detectives across the road, I beckoned him over, and pointed out the fellow to him, with instructions to watch his movements for a couple of days and then report to me. No later than next afternoon my man turned up to tell me that the fellow had married his landlady's daughter at a registrar's office that very day at 11:30 a.m., and had gone off with her to Margate for a week. Our man had seen the luggage being put on the cab. There were some old Paris labels on one of the bags. Somehow I couldn't get the fellow out of my head, and the very next time I had to go to Paris on service I spoke about him to that friend of mine in the Paris police. My friend said: 'From what you tell me I think you must mean a rather well-known hanger-on and emissary of the Revolutionary Red Committee. He says he is an Englishman by birth. We have an idea that he has been for a good few years now a secret agent of one of the foreign Embassies in London.' This woke up my memory completely. He was the vanishing fellow I saw sitting on a chair in Baron Stott-Wartenheim's bathroom. I told my friend that he was quite right. The fellow was a secret agent to my certain knowledge. Afterwards my friend took the trouble to ferret out the complete record of that man for me. I thought I had better know all there was to know; but I don't suppose you want to hear his history now, sir?"

The Assistant Commissioner shook his supported head. "The history of your relations with that useful personage is the only thing that matters just now," he said, closing slowly his weary, deep-set eyes, and then opening them swiftly with a greatly refreshed glance.

"There's nothing official about them," said the Chief Inspector, bitterly. "I went into his shop one evening, told him who I was, and reminded him of our first meeting. He didn't as much as twitch an eyebrow. He said that he was married and settled now, and that all he wanted was not to be interfered with in his little business. I took it upon myself to promise him that, as long as he didn't go in for anything obviously outrageous, he would be left alone by the police. That was worth something to him, because a word from us to the Custom-House people would have been enough to get some of these packages he gets from Paris and Brussels opened in Dover, with confiscation to follow for certain, and perhaps a prosecution as well at the end of it."

"That's a very precarious trade," murmured the Assistant Commissioner. "Why did he go in for that?"

The Chief Inspector raised scornful eyebrows dispassionately.

"Most likely got a connection—friends on the Continent—amongst people who deal in such wares. They would be just the sort he would consort with. He's a lazy dog, too—like the rest of them."

"What do you get from him in exchange for your protection?"

The Chief Inspector was not inclined to enlarge on the value of Mr Verloc's services.

"He would not be much good to anybody but myself. One has got to know a good deal beforehand to make use of a man like that. I can understand the sort of hint he can give. And when I want a hint he can generally furnish it to me."

The Chief Inspector lost himself suddenly in a discreet reflective mood; and the Assistant Commissioner repressed a smile at the fleeting thought that the reputation of Chief Inspector Heat might possibly have been made in a great part by the Secret Agent Verloc.

"In a more general way of being of use, all our men of the Special Crimes section on duty at Charing Cross and Victoria have orders to take careful notice of anybody they may see with him. He meets the new arrivals frequently, and afterwards keeps track of them. He seems to have been told off for that sort of duty. When I want an address in a hurry, I can always get it from him. Of course, I know how to manage our relations. I haven't seen him to speak to three times in the last two years. I drop him a line, unsigned, and he answers me in the same way at my private address."

From time to time the Assistant Commissioner gave an almost imperceptible nod. The Chief Inspector added that he did not suppose Mr Verloc to be deep in the confidence of the prominent members of the Revolutionary International Council, but that he was generally trusted of that there could be no doubt. "Whenever I've had reason to think there was something in the wind," he concluded, "I've always found he could tell me something worth knowing."

The Assistant Commissioner made a significant remark.

"He failed you this time."

"Neither had I wind of anything in any other way," reported Chief Inspector Heat. "I asked him nothing so he could tell me nothing. He isn't one of our men. It isn't as if he were in our pay."

"No," muttered the Assistant Commissioner. "He's a spy in the pay of a foreign government. We could never confess to him."

"I must do my work in my own way," declared the Chief Inspector. "When it comes to that I would deal with the devil himself, and take the consequences. There are things not fit for everybody to know."

"Your idea of secrecy seems to consist in keeping the chief of your department in the dark. That's stretching it perhaps a little too far, isn't it? He lives over his shop?"

"Who—Verloc? Oh, yes. He lives over his shop. The wife's mother, I fancy, lives with them."

"Is the house watched?"

"Oh, dear, no. It wouldn't do. Certain people who come there are watched. My opinion is that he knows nothing of this affair."

"How do you account for this?" The Assistant Commissioner nodded at the cloth rag lying before him on the table.

"I don't account for it at all, sir. It's simply unaccountable. It can't be explained by what I know." The Chief Inspector made those admissions with the frankness of a man whose reputation is established as if on a rock. "At any rate not at this present moment. I think that the man who had most to do with it will turn out to be Michaelis."

"You do?"

"Yes, sir; because I can answer for all the others."

"What about that other man supposed to have escaped from the park?"

"I should think he's far away by this time," opined the Chief Inspector.

The Assistant Commissioner looked hard at him, and rose suddenly, as though having made up his mind to some course of action. As a matter of fact, he had that very moment succumbed to a fascinating temptation. The Chief Inspector heard himself dismissed with instructions to meet his superior early next morning for further consultation upon the case. He listened with an impenetrable face, and walked out of the room with measured steps.

Whatever might have been the plans of the Assistant Commissioner they had nothing to do with that desk work, which was the bane of his existence because of its confined nature and apparent lack of reality. It could not have had, or else the general air of alacrity that came upon the Assistant Commissioner would have been inexplicable. As soon as he was left alone he looked for his hat impulsively, and put it on his head. Having done that, he sat down again to reconsider the whole matter. But as his mind was already made up, this did not take long. And before Chief Inspector Heat had gone very far on the way home, he also left the building.

CHAPTER 7

The Assistant Commissioner walked along a short and narrow street like a wet, muddy trench, then crossing a very broad thoroughfare entered a public edifice, and sought speech with a young private secretary (unpaid) of a great personage.

This fair, smooth-faced young man, whose symmetrically arranged hair gave him the air of a large and neat schoolboy, met the Assistant Commissioner's request with a doubtful look, and spoke with bated breath.

"Would he see you? I don't know about that. He has walked

over from the House an hour ago to talk with the Permanent Under-Secretary, and now he's ready to walk back again. He might have sent for him; but he does it for the sake of a little exercise, I suppose. It's all the exercise he can find time for while this session lasts. I don't complain; I rather enjoy these little strolls. He leans on my arm, and doesn't open his lips. But, I say, he's very tired, and—well—not in the sweetest of tempers just now."

"It's in connection with that Greenwich affair."

"Oh! I say! He's very bitter against you people. But I will go and see, if you insist."

"Do. That's a good fellow," said the Assistant Commissioner.

The unpaid secretary admired this pluck. Composing for himself an innocent face, he opened a door, and went in with the assurance of a nice and privileged child. And presently he reappeared, with a nod to the Assistant Commissioner, who passing through the same door left open for him, found himself with the great personage in a large room.

Vast in bulk and stature, with a long white face, which, broadened at the base by a big double chin, appeared egg-shaped in the fringe of greyish whisker, the great personage seemed an expanding man. Unfortunate from a tailoring point of view, the crossfolds in the middle of a buttoned black coat added to the impression, as if the fastenings of the garment were tried to the utmost. From the head, set upward on a thick neck, the eyes, with puffy lower lids, stared with a haughty droop on each side of a hooked, aggressive nose, nobly salient in the vast pale circumference of the face. A shiny silk hat and a pair of worn gloves lying ready at the end of a long table looked expanded, too, enormous.

He stood on the hearthrug in big, roomy boots, and uttered no word of greeting.

"I would like to know if this is the beginning of another dynamite campaign," he asked at once in a deep, very smooth voice. "Don't go into details. I have no time for that."

The Assistant Commissioner's figure before this big and rustic Presence had the frail slenderness of a reed addressing an oak. And indeed the unbroken record of that man's descent surpassed in the number of centuries the age of the oldest oak in the country.

"No. As far as one can be positive about anything I can assure you that it is not."

"Yes. But your idea of assurances over there," said the great man, with a contemptuous wave of his hand towards a window giving on the broad thoroughfare, "seem to consist mainly in making the Secretary of State look a fool. I have been told positively in this very room less than a month ago that nothing of the sort was even possible."

The Assistant Commissioner glanced in the direction of the window calmly.

"You will allow me to remark, Sir Ethelred, that so far I have had no opportunity to give you assurances of any kind."

The haughty droop of the eyes was focused now upon the Assistant Commissioner.

"True," confessed the deep, smooth voice. "I sent for Heat. You are still rather a novice in your new berth. And how are you getting on over there?"

"I believe I am learning something every day."

"Of course, of course. I hope you will get on."

"Thank you, Sir Ethelred. I've learned something today, and even within the last hour or so. There is much in this affair of a kind that does not meet the eye in a usual anarchist outrage, even if one looked into it as deep as can be. That's why I am here."

The great man put his arms akimbo, the backs of his big hands resting on his hips.

"Very well. Go on. Only no details, pray. Spare me the details."

"You shall not be troubled with them, Sir Ethelred," the Assistant Commissioner began, with a calm and untroubled assurance. While he was speaking the hands on the face of the clock behind the great man's back—a heavy, glistening affair of massive scrolls in the same dark marble as the mantelpiece, and with a ghostly, evanescent tick—had moved through the space of seven minutes. He spoke with a studious fidelity to a parenthetical manner, into which every little fact—that is, every detail—fitted with delightful ease. Not a murmur nor even a movement hinted at interruption. The great Personage might have been the statue of one of his own princely ancestors stripped of a Crusader's war harness, and put into an ill-fitting frock-coat. The Assistant Commissioner felt as though he were at liberty to talk for an hour. But he kept his head, and at the end of the time mentioned above he broke off with a sudden conclusion, which, reproducing the opening statement, pleasantly surprised Sir Ethelred by its apparent swiftness and force.

"The kind of thing which meets us under the surface of this affair, otherwise without gravity, is unusual—in this precise form at least—and requires special treatment."

The tone of Sir Ethelred was deepened, full of conviction.

"I should think so—involving the Ambassador of a foreign power!"

"Oh! The Ambassador!" protested the other, erect and slender, allowing himself a mere half smile, "It would be stupid of me to advance anything of the kind. And it is absolutely unnecessary, because if I am right in my surmises, whether ambassador or hall porter it's a mere detail."

Sir Ethelred opened a wide mouth, like a cavern, into which the hooked nose seemed anxious to peer; there came from it a subdued rolling sound, as from a distant organ with the scornful indignation stop.

"No! These people are too impossible. What do they mean by importing their methods of Crim-Tartary here? A Turk would have more decency."

"You forget, Sir Ethelred, that strictly speaking we know nothing positively—as yet."

"No! But how would you define it? Shortly?"

"Barefaced audacity amounting to childishness of a peculiar sort."

"We can't put up with the innocence of nasty little children," said the great and expanded personage, expanding a little more as it were. The haughty, drooping glance struck crushingly the carpet at the Assistant Commissioner's feet. "They'll have to get a hard rap on the knuckles over this affair. We must be in a position to—What is your general idea, stated shortly? No need to go into details."

"No, Sir Ethelred. In principle. I should lay it down that the existence of secret agents should not be tolerated, as tending to augment the positive dangers of the evil against which they are used. That the spy will fabricate his information is a mere commonplace. But in the sphere of political and revolutionary action, relying partly on violence, the professional spy has every facility to fabricate the very facts themselves, and will spread the double evil of emulation in one direction, and of panic, hasty legislation, unreflecting hate, in the other. However, this is an imperfect world—"

The deep-voiced Presence on the hearthrug, motionless, with big elbows stuck out, said hastily:

"Be lucid, please."

"Yes, Sir Ethelred—An imperfect world. Therefore directly the character of this affair suggested itself to me, I thought it should be dealt with with special secrecy, and ventured to come over here."

"That's right," approved the great Personage, glancing down complacently over his double chin. "I am glad there's somebody over at your shop who thinks that the Secretary of State may be trusted now and then."

The Assistant Commissioner had an amused smile. "I was really thinking that it might be better at this stage for Heat to be replaced by—"

"What! Heat? An ass—eh?" exclaimed the great man with distinct animosity.

"Not at all. Pray, Sir Ethelred, don't put that unjust interpretation on my remarks."

"Then what? Too clever by half?"

"Neither—at least not as a rule. All the grounds of my surmises I have from him. The only thing I've discovered by myself is that he has been making use of that man privately. Who could blame him? He's an old police hand. He told me virtually that he must have tools to work with. It occurred to me that this tool should be surrendered to the Special Crimes division as a whole, instead of remaining the private property of Chief Inspector Heat. I extended my conception of our departmental duties to the suppression of the secret agent. But Chief Inspector Heat is an old departmental hand. He would accuse me of perverting its morality and attacking its efficiency. He would define it bitterly as protection extended to the criminal class of revolutionists. It would mean just that to him."

"Yes. But what do you mean?"

"I mean to say, first, that there's but poor comfort in being able to declare that any given act of violence—damaging property or destroying life—is not the work of anarchism at all, but of something else altogether—some species of authorized scoundrelism. This, I fancy, is much more frequent than we suppose. Next, it's obvious that the existence of these people in the pay of foreign governments destroys in a measure the efficiency of our supervision. A spy of that sort can afford to be more reckless than the most reckless of conspirators. His occupation is free from all restraint. He's without as much faith as is necessary for complete negation, and without that much law as is implied in lawlessness. Thirdly, the existence of these spies amongst the revolutionary groups, which we are reproached for harbouring here, does away with all certitude. You have received a reassuring statement from Chief Inspector Heat some time ago. It was by no means groundless—and yet this episode happens. I call it an episode, because this affair, I make bold to say, is episodic; it is no part of any general scheme, however wild. The very peculiarities which surprise and perplex Chief Inspector Heat establish its character in my eyes. I am keeping clear of details, Sir Ethelred."

The Personage on the hearthrug had been listening with profound attention.

"Just so. Be as concise as you can."

The Assistant Commissioner intimated by an earnest, deferential gesture that he was anxious to be concise.

"There is a peculiar stupidity and feebleness in the conduct of this affair which gives me excellent hopes of getting behind it and finding there something else than an individual freak of fanaticism. For it is a planned thing, undoubtedly. The actual perpetrator seems to have been led by the hand to the spot, and then abandoned hurriedly to his own devices. The inference is that he was imported from abroad for the purpose of committing this outrage. At the same time one is forced to the conclusion that he did not know enough English to ask his way, unless one were to accept the fantastic theory that he was a deaf mute. I wonder now—But this is idle. He has destroyed himself by an accident, obviously. Not an extraordinary accident. But an extraordinary little fact remains: the address on his clothing discovered by the merest accident, too. It is an incredible little fact, so incredible that the explanation which will account for it is bound to touch the bottom of this affair. Instead of instructing Heat to go on with this case, my intention is to seek this explanation personally—by myself, I mean—where it may be picked up. That is in a certain shop in Brett Street, and on the lips of a certain secret agent once upon a time the confidential and trusted spy of the late Baron Stott-Wartenheim, Ambassador of a Great Power to the Court of St James's."

The Assistant Commissioner paused, then added: "Those fellows are a perfect pest." In order to raise his drooping glance to the speaker's face, the Personage on the hearthrug had gradually tilted his head farther back, which gave him an aspect of extraordinary haughtiness.

"Why not leave it to Heat?"

"Because he is an old departmental hand. They have their own morality. My line of inquiry would appear to him an awful perversion of duty. For him the plain duty is to fasten the guilt upon as many prominent anarchists as he can on some slight indications he had picked up in the course of his investigation on the spot; whereas I, he would say, am bent upon vindicating their innocence. I am trying to be as lucid as I can in presenting this obscure matter to you without details."

"He would, would he?" muttered the proud head of Sir Ethelred from its lofty elevation.

"I am afraid so—with an indignation and disgust of which you or I can have no idea. He's an excellent servant. We must not put an undue strain on his loyalty. That's always a mistake. Besides, I want a free hand—a freer hand than it would be perhaps advisable to give Chief Inspector Heat. I haven't the slightest wish to spare this man Verloc. He will, I imagine, be extremely startled to find his connection with this affair, whatever it may be, brought home to him so quickly. Frightening him will not be very difficult. But our true objective lies behind him somewhere. I want your authority to give him such assurances of personal safety as I may think proper."

"Certainly," said the Personage on the hearthrug. "Find out as much as you can; find it out in your own way."

"I must set about it without loss of time, this very evening," said the Assistant Commissioner.

Sir Ethelred shifted one hand under his coat tails, and tilting back his head looked at him steadily.

"We'll have a late sitting tonight," he said. "Come to the House with your discoveries if we are not gone home. I'll warn Toodles to look out for you. He'll take you into my room."

The numerous family and the wide connections of the youthful-looking Private Secretary cherished for him the hope of an austere and exalted destiny. Meantime, the social sphere he adorned in his hours of idleness chose to pet him under the above nickname.

And Sir Ethelred, hearing it on the lips of his wife and girls every day (mostly at breakfast-time), had conferred upon it the dignity of unsmiling adoption.

The Assistant Commissioner was surprised and gratified extremely.

"I shall certainly bring my discoveries to the House on the chance of you having the time to—"

"I won't have the time," interrupted the great Personage. "But I will see you. I haven't the time now—And you are going yourself?"

"Yes, Sir Ethelred. I think it the best way."

The Personage had tilted his head so far back that, in order to keep the Assistant Commissioner under his observation, he had to nearly close his eyes.

"H'm. Ha! And how do you propose—Will you assume a disguise?"

"Hardly a disguise! I'll change my clothes, of course."

"Of course," repeated the great man, with a sort of absent-minded loftiness. He turned his big head slowly, and over his shoulder gave a haughty, oblique stare to the ponderous marble timepiece with the sly, feeble tick. The gilt hands had taken the opportunity to steal through no less than five and twenty minutes behind his back.

The Assistant Commissioner, who could not see them, grew a little nervous in the interval. But the great man presented to him a calm and undismayed face.

"Very well," he said, and paused, as if in deliberate contempt of the official clock. "But what first put you in motion in this direction?"

"I have been always of opinion," began the Assistant Commissioner.

"Ah. Yes! Opinion. That's of course. But the immediate motive?"

"What shall I say, Sir Ethelred? A new man's antagonism to old methods. A desire to know something at first hand. Some impatience. It's my old work, but the harness is different. It has been chafing me a little in one or two tender places."

"I hope you'll get on over there," said the great man, kindly, extending his hand, soft to the touch, but broad and powerful like the hand of a glorified farmer. The Assistant Commissioner shook it, and withdrew.

In the outer room Toodles, who had been waiting perched on

the edge of a table, advanced to meet him, subduing his natural buoyancy.

"Well? Satisfactory?" he asked, with airy importance.

"Perfectly. You've earned my undying gratitude," answered the Assistant Commissioner, whose long face looked wooden in contrast with the peculiar character of the other's gravity, which seemed perpetually ready to break into ripples and chuckles.

"That's all right. But, seriously, you can't imagine how irritated he is by the attacks on his Bill for the Nationalization of Fisheries. They call it the beginning of social revolution. Of course, it is a revolutionary measure. But these fellows have no decency. The personal attacks—"

"I read the papers," remarked the Assistant Commissioner.

"Odious? Eh? And you have no notion what a mass of work he has got to get through every day. He does it all himself. Seems unable to trust any one with these Fisheries."

"And yet he's given a whole half hour to the consideration of my very small sprat," interjected the Assistant Commissioner.

"Small! Is it? I'm glad to hear that. But it's a pity you didn't keep away, then. This fight takes it out of him frightfully. The man's getting exhausted. I feel it by the way he leans on my arm as we walk over. And, I say, is he safe in the streets? Mullins has been marching his men up here this afternoon. There's a constable stuck by every lamp-post, and every second person we meet between this and Palace Yard is an obvious tec. It will get on his nerves presently. I say, these foreign scoundrels aren't likely to throw something at him—are they? It would be a national calamity. The country can't spare him."

"Not to mention yourself. He leans on your arm," suggested the Assistant Commissioner, soberly. "You would both go."

"It would be an easy way for a young man to go down into history. Not so many British Ministers have been assassinated as to make it a minor incident. But seriously now—"

"I am afraid that if you want to go down into history you'll have to do something for it. Seriously, there's no danger whatever for both of you but from overwork."

The sympathetic Toodles welcomed this opening for a chuckle.

"The Fisheries won't kill me. I am used to late hours," he declared, with ingenuous levity. But, feeling an instant compunction, he began to assume an air of statesmanlike moodiness, as one draws on a glove. "His massive intellect will stand any amount of work. It's his nerves that I am afraid of. The reactionary gang, with that abusive brute Cheeseman at their head, insult him every night."

"If he will insist on beginning a revolution!" murmured the Assistant Commissioner.

"The time has come, and he is the only man great enough for the work," protested the revolutionary Toodles, flaring up under the calm, speculative gaze of the Assistant Commissioner. Somewhere in a corridor a distant bell tinkled urgently, and with devoted vigilance the young man pricked up his ears at the sound. "He's ready to go now," he exclaimed in a whisper, snatched up his hat, and vanished from the room.

The Assistant Commissioner went out by another door in a less elastic manner. Again he crossed the wide thoroughfare, walked along a narrow street, and re-entered hastily his own departmental buildings. He kept up this accelerated pace to the door of his private room. Before he had closed it fairly his eyes sought his desk. He stood still for a moment, then walked up, looked all round on the floor, sat down in his chair, rang a bell, and waited.

"Chief Inspector Heat gone yet?"

"Yes, sir. Went away half an hour ago."

He nodded. "That will do." And sitting still, with his hat pushed off his forehead, he thought that it was just like Heat's confounded cheek to carry off quietly the only piece of material evidence. But he thought this without animosity. Old and valued servants will take liberties. The piece of overcoat with the address sewn on was certainly not a thing to leave about. Dismissing from his mind this manifestation of Chief Inspector Heat's mistrust, he wrote and dispatched a note to his wife, charging her to make his apologies to Michaelis's great lady, with whom they were engaged to dine that evening.

The short jacket and the low, round hat he assumed in a sort of curtained alcove containing a washstand, a row of wooden pegs and a shelf, brought out wonderfully the length of his grave, brown face. He stepped back into the full light of the room, looking like the vision of a cool, reflective Don Quixote, with the sunken eyes of a dark enthusiast and a very deliberate manner. He left the scene of his daily labours quickly like an unobtrusive shadow. His descent into the street was like the descent into a slimy aquarium from which the water had been run off. A murky, gloomy dampness enveloped him. The walls of the houses were wet, the mud of the roadway glistened with an effect of phosphorescence, and when he emerged into the Strand out of a narrow street by the side of Charing Cross Station the genius of the locality assimilated him. He might have been but one more of the queer foreign fish that can be seen of an evening about there flitting round the dark corners.

He came to a stand on the very edge of the pavement, and waited. His exercised eyes had made out in the confused movement of lights and shows thronging the roadway the crawling approach of a hansom. He gave no sign; but when the low step gliding along the kerbstone came to his feet he dodged in skilfully in front of the big turning wheel, and spoke up through the little trap door almost before the man gazing supinely ahead from his perch was aware of having been boarded by a fare.

It was not a long drive. It ended by signal abruptly, nowhere in particular, between two lamp-posts before a large drapery establishment—a long range of shops already lapped up in sheets of corrugated iron for the night. Tendering a coin through the trap door the fare slipped out and away, leaving an effect of uncanny, eccentric ghostliness upon the driver's mind. But the size of the coin was satisfactory to his touch, and his education not being literary, he remained untroubled by the fear of finding it presently turned to a dead leaf in his pocket. Raised above the world of fares by the nature of his calling, he contemplated their action with a limited interest. The sharp pulling of his horse right round expressed his philosophy.

Meantime, the Assistant Commissioner was already giving his order to a waiter in a little Italian restaurant round the corner—one of those traps for the hungry, long and narrow, baited with a perspective of mirrors and white napery; without air, but with an atmosphere of their own—an atmosphere of fraudulent cookery mocking an abject mankind in the most pressing of its miserable necessities. In this immoral atmosphere the Assistant Commissioner, reflecting upon his enterprise, seemed to lose some more of his identity. He had a sense of loneliness, of evil freedom. It was rather pleasant. When, after paying for his short meal, he stood up and waited for his change, he saw himself in the sheet of glass, and was struck by his foreign appearance. He contemplated his own image with a melancholy and inquisitive gaze, then by sudden inspiration raised the collar of his jacket. This arrangement appeared to him commendable, and he completed it by giving an upward twist to the ends of his black moustache. He was satisfied by the subtle modification of his personal aspect caused by these small changes. "That'll do very well," he thought. "I'll get a little wet, a little splashed—"

He became aware of the waiter at his elbow and of a small pile of silver coins on the edge of the table before him. The waiter kept one eye on it, while his other eye followed the long back of a tall, not very young girl, who passed up to a distant table looking perfectly sightless and altogether unapproachable. She seemed to be an habitual customer.

On going out the Assistant Commissioner made to himself the observation that the patrons of the place had lost in the frequentation of fraudulent cookery all their national and private characteristics. And this was strange, since the Italian restaurant is such a peculiarly British institution. But these people were as denationalized as the dishes set before them with every circumstance of unstamped respectability. Neither was their personality stamped in any way, professionally, socially or racially. They seemed created for the Italian restaurant, unless the Italian restaurant had been perchance created for them. But that last hypothesis was unthinkable, since one could not place them anywhere outside those special establishments. One never met these enigmatical persons elsewhere. It was impossible to form a precise idea what occupations they followed by day and where they went to bed at night. And he himself had become unplaced. It would have been impossible for anybody to guess his occupation. As to going to bed, there was a doubt even in his own mind. Not indeed in regard to his domicile itself, but very much so in respect of the time when he would be able to return there. A pleasurable feeling of independence possessed him when he heard the glass doors swing to behind his back with a sort of imperfect baffled thud. He advanced at once into an immensity of greasy slime and damp plaster interspersed with lamps, and enveloped, oppressed, penetrated, choked, and suffocated by the blackness of a wet London night, which is composed of soot and drops of water.

Brett Street was not very far away. It branches off, narrow, from the side of an open triangular space surrounded by dark and mysterious houses, temples of petty commerce emptied of traders for the night. Only a fruiterer's stall at the corner made a violent blaze of light and colour. Beyond all was black, and the few people passing in that direction vanished at one stride beyond the glowing heaps of oranges and lemons. No footsteps echoed. They would never be heard of again. The adventurous head of the Special Crimes Department watched these disappearances from a distance with an interested eye. He felt light-hearted, as though he had been ambushed all alone in a jungle many thousands of miles away from departmental desks and official inkstands. This joyousness and dispersion of thought before a task of some importance seems to prove that this world of ours is not such a very serious affair after all. For the Assistant Commissioner was not constitutionally inclined to levity.

The policeman on the beat projected his sombre and moving form against the luminous glory of oranges and lemons, and entered Brett Street without haste. The Assistant Commissioner, as though he were a member of the criminal classes, lingered out of sight, awaiting his return. But this constable seemed to be lost for ever to the force. He never returned: must have gone out at the other end of Brett Street.

The Assistant Commissioner, reaching this conclusion, entered the street in his turn, and came upon a large van arrested in front of the dimly lit window-panes of a carter's eating-house. The man was refreshing himself inside, and the horses, their big heads lowered to the ground, fed out of nose-bags steadily. Farther on, on the opposite side of the street, another suspect patch of dim light issued from Mr Verloc's shop front, hung with papers, heaving with vague piles of cardboard boxes and the shapes of books. The Assistant Commissioner stood observing it across the roadway. There could be no mistake. By the side of the front window, encumbered by the shadows of nondescript things, the door, standing ajar, let escape on the pavement a narrow, clear streak of gas-light within.

Behind the Assistant Commissioner the van and horses, merged into one mass, seemed something alive—a square-backed black monster blocking half the street, with sudden iron-shod stampings, fierce jingles, and heavy, blowing sighs. The harshly festive, ill-omened glare of a large and prosperous public-house faced the other end of Brett Street across a wide road. This barrier of blazing lights, opposing the shadows gathered about the humble abode of Mr Verloc's domestic happiness, seemed to drive the obscurity of the street back upon itself, make it more sullen, brooding, and sinister.

CHAPTER 8

Having infused by persistent importunities some sort of heat into the chilly interest of several licensed victuallers (the acquaintances once upon a time of her late unlucky husband), Mrs Verloc's mother had at last secured her admission to certain almshouses founded by a wealthy innkeeper for the destitute widows of the trade.

This end, conceived in the astuteness of her uneasy heart, the old woman had pursued with secrecy and determination. That was the time when her daughter Winnie could not help passing a remark to Mr Verloc that "mother has been spending half-crowns and five shillings almost every day this last week in cab fares." But the remark was not made grudgingly. Winnie respected her mother's infirmities. She was only a little surprised at this sudden mania for locomotion. Mr Verloc, who was sufficiently magnificent in his way, had grunted the remark impatiently aside as interfering with his meditations. These were frequent, deep, and prolonged; they bore upon a matter more important than five shillings. Distinctly more important, and beyond all comparison more difficult to consider in all its aspects with philosophical serenity.

Her object attained in astute secrecy, the heroic old woman had made a clean breast of it to Mrs Verloc. Her soul was triumphant and her heart tremulous. Inwardly, she quaked, because she dreaded and admired the calm, self-contained character of her daughter Winnie, whose displeasure was made redoubtable by a diversity of dreadful silences. But she did not allow her inward apprehensions to rob her of the advantage of venerable placidity conferred upon her outward person by her triple chin, the floating ampleness of her ancient form, and the impotent condition of her legs.

The shock of the information was so unexpected that Mrs Verloc, against her usual practice when addressed, interrupted the domestic occupation she was engaged upon. It was the dusting of the furniture in the parlour behind the shop. She turned her head towards her mother.

"Whatever did you want to do that for?" she exclaimed, in scandalized astonishment.

The shock must have been severe to make her depart from that distant and uninquiring acceptance of facts which was her force and her safeguard in life.

"Weren't you made comfortable enough here?"

She had lapsed into these inquiries, but next moment she saved the consistency of her conduct by resuming her dusting, while the old woman sat scared and dumb under her dingy white cap and lustreless dark wig.

Winnie finished the chair, and ran the duster along the mahogany at the back of the horsehair sofa on which Mr Verloc loved to take his ease in hat and overcoat. She was intent on her work, but presently she permitted herself another question.

"How in the world did you manage it, mother?"

As not affecting the inwardness of things, which it was Mrs Verloc's principle to ignore, this curiosity was excusable. It bore merely on the methods. The old woman welcomed it eagerly as bringing forward something that could be talked about with much sincerity.

She favoured her daughter by an exhaustive answer full of names and enriched by side-comments upon the ravages of time as observed in the alteration of human countenances. The names were principally the names of licensed victuallers—"poor daddy's friends, my dear." She enlarged with special appreciation on the kindness and condescension of a large brewer, a Baronet and an M.P., the Chairman of the Governors of the Charity. She expressed herself thus warmly because she had been allowed to interview by appointment his Private Secretary—"a very polite gentleman, all in black, with a gentle, sad voice, but so very, very thin and quiet. He was like a shadow, my dear."

Winnie, prolonging her dusting operations till the tale was told to the end, walked out of the parlour into the kitchen (down two steps) in her usual manner, without the slightest comment.

Shedding a few tears in sign of rejoicing at her daughter's mansuetude in this terrible affair, Mrs Verloc's mother gave play to her astuteness in the direction of her furniture, because it was her own; and sometimes she wished it hadn't been. Heroism is all very well, but there are circumstances when the disposal of a few tables and chairs, brass bedsteads, and so on, may be big with remote and disastrous consequences. She required a few pieces herself, the Foundation which, after many importunities, had gathered her to its charitable breast, giving nothing but bare planks and cheaply papered bricks to the objects of its solicitude. The delicacy guiding her choice to the least valuable and most dilapidated articles passed unacknowledged, because Winnie's philosophy consisted in not taking notice of the inside of facts; she assumed that mother took what suited her best. As to Mr Verloc, his intense meditation, like a sort of Chinese wall, isolated him completely from the phenomena of this world of vain effort and illusory appearances.

Her selection made, the disposal of the rest became a perplexing question in a particular way. She was leaving it in Brett Street, of course. But she had two children. Winnie was provided for by her sensible union with that excellent husband, Mr Verloc. Stevie was destitute—and a little peculiar. His position had to be considered before the claims of legal justice and even the promptings of partiality. The possession of the furniture would not be in any sense a provision. He ought to have it—the poor boy. But to give it to him would be like tampering with his position of complete dependence. It was a sort of claim which she feared to weaken. Moreover, the susceptibilities of Mr Verloc would perhaps not brook being beholden to his brother-in-law for the chairs he sat on. In a long experience of gentlemen lodgers, Mrs Verloc's mother had acquired a dismal but resigned notion of the fantastic side of human nature. What if Mr Verloc suddenly took it into his head to tell Stevie to take his blessed sticks somewhere out of that? A division, on the other hand, however carefully made, might give some cause of offence to Winnie. No. Stevie must remain destitute and dependent. And at the moment of leaving Brett Street she had said to her daughter: "No use waiting till I am dead, is there? Everything I leave here is altogether your own now, my dear."

Winnie, with her hat on, silent behind her mother's back, went on arranging the collar of the old woman's cloak. She got her handbag, an umbrella, with an impassive face. The time had come for the expenditure of the sum of three and sixpence on what might well be supposed the last cab-drive of Mrs Verloc's mother's life. They went out at the shop door.

The conveyance awaiting them would have illustrated the proverb that "truth can be more cruel than caricature," if such a proverb existed. Crawling behind an infirm horse, a metropolitan hackney drew up on wobbly wheels and with a maimed driver on the box. This last peculiarity caused some embarrassment. Catching sight of a hooked iron contrivance protruding from the left sleeve of the man's coat, Mrs Verloc's mother lost suddenly the heroic courage of these days. She really couldn't trust herself. "What do you think, Winnie?" She hung back. The passionate expostulations of the big-faced cabman seemed to be squeezed out of a blocked throat. Leaning over from his box, he whispered with mysterious indignation. What was the matter now? Was it possible to treat a man so? His enormous and unwashed countenance flamed red in the muddy stretch of the street. Was it likely they would have given him a licence, he inquired desperately, if—

The police constable of the locality quieted him by a friendly glance; then addressing himself to the two women without marked consideration, said:

"He's been driving a cab for twenty years. I never knew him to have an accident."

"Accident!" shouted the driver in a scornful whisper.

The policeman's testimony settled it. The modest assemblage of seven people, mostly under age, dispersed. Winnie followed her mother into the cab. Stevie climbed on the box. His vacant mouth and distressed eyes depicted the state of his mind in regard to the transactions which were taking place. In the narrow streets the progress of the journey was made sensible to those within by the near fronts of the houses gliding past slowly and shakily, with a great rattle and jingling of glass, as if about to collapse behind the cab; and the infirm horse, with the harness hung over his sharp backbone flapping very loose about his thighs, appearing to be dancing mincingly on his toes with infinite patience. Later on, in the wider space of Whitehall, all visual evidences of motion became imperceptible. The rattle and jingle of glass went on indefinitely in front of the long Treasury building—and time itself seemed to stand still.

At last Winnie observed: "This isn't a very good horse."

Her eyes gleamed in the shadow of the cab straight ahead, immovable. On the box, Stevie shut his vacant mouth first, in order to ejaculate earnestly: "Don't."

The driver, holding high the reins twisted around the hook, took no notice. Perhaps he had not heard. Stevie's breast heaved.

"Don't whip."

The man turned slowly his bloated and sodden face of many colours bristling with white hairs. His little red eyes glistened with moisture. His big lips had a violet tint. They remained closed. With the dirty back of his whip-hand he rubbed the stubble sprouting on his enormous chin.

"You mustn't," stammered out Stevie, violently, "it hurts."

"Mustn't whip," queried the other in a thoughtful whisper, and immediately whipped. He did this, not because his soul was cruel and his heart evil, but because he had to earn his fare. And for a time the walls of St Stephen's, with its towers and pinnacles, contemplated in immobility and silence a cab that jingled. It rolled, too, however. But on the bridge there was a commotion. Stevie suddenly proceeded to get down from the box. There were shouts on the pavement, people ran forward, the driver pulled up, whispering curses of indignation and astonishment. Winnie lowered the window, and put her head out, white as a ghost. In the depths of the cab, her mother was exclaiming, in tones of anguish: "Is that boy hurt? Is that boy hurt?"

Stevie was not hurt, he had not even fallen, but excitement as usual had robbed him of the power of connected speech. He could do no more than stammer at the window: "Too heavy. Too heavy." Winnie put out her hand on to his shoulder.

"Stevie! Get up on the box directly, and don't try to get down again."

"No. No. Walk. Must walk."

In trying to state the nature of that necessity he stammered himself into utter incoherence. No physical impossibility stood in the way of his whim. Stevie could have managed easily to keep pace with the infirm, dancing horse without getting out of breath. But his sister withheld her consent decisively. "The idea! Whoever heard of such a thing! Run after a cab!" Her mother, frightened and helpless in the depth of the conveyance, entreated:

"Oh, don't let him, Winnie. He'll get lost. Don't let him."

"Certainly not. What next! Mr Verloc will be sorry to hear of this nonsense, Stevie—I can tell you. He won't be happy at all."

The idea of Mr Verloc's grief and unhappiness acting as usual powerfully upon Stevie's fundamentally docile disposition, he abandoned all resistance and climbed up again on the box, with a face of despair.

The cabby turned at him his enormous and inflamed countenance truculently. "Don't you go for trying this silly game again, young fellow."

After delivering himself thus in a stern whisper, strained almost to extinction, he drove on, ruminating solemnly. To his mind the incident remained somewhat obscure. But his intellect, though it had lost its pristine vivacity in the benumbing years of sedentary exposure to the weather, lacked not independence or sanity. Gravely he dismissed the hypothesis of Stevie being a drunken young nipper.

Inside the cab the spell of silence, in which the two women had endured shoulder to shoulder the jolting, rattling, and jingling of the journey, had been broken by Stevie's outbreak. Winnie raised her voice.

"You've done what you wanted, mother. You have only yourself to thank for it if you aren't happy afterwards. And I don't think you'll be. That I don't. Weren't you comfortable enough in the house? Whatever people'll think of us—you throwing yourself like this on a Charity?"

"My dear," screamed the old woman earnestly above the noise, "you've been the best of daughters to me. As to Mr Verloc—there—"

Words failing her on the subject of Mr Verloc's excellence, she turned her old tearful eyes to the roof of the cab. Then she averted her head on the pretence of looking out of the window, as if to judge of their progress. It was insignificant, and went on close to the kerbstone. Night, the early dirty night, the sinister, noisy, hopeless, and rowdy night of South London, had overtaken her on her last cab drive. In the gas-light of the low-fronted shops her big cheeks glowed with an orange hue under a black and mauve bonnet.

Mrs Verloc's mother's complexion had become yellow by the effect of age and from a natural predisposition to biliousness, favoured by the trials of a difficult and worried existence, first as wife, then as widow. It was a complexion that under the influence of a blush would take on an orange tint. And this woman, modest indeed but hardened in the fires of adversity, of an age, moreover, when blushes are not expected, had positively blushed before her daughter. In the privacy of a four-wheeler, on her way to a charity cottage (one of a row) which by the exiguity of its dimensions and the simplicity of its accommodation, might well have been devised in kindness as a place of training for the still more straitened circumstances of the grave, she was forced to hide from her own child a blush of remorse and shame.

Whatever people will think? She knew very well what they did think, the people Winnie had in her mind—the old friends of her husband, and others too, whose interests she had solicited with such flattering success. She had not known before what a good beggar she could be. But she guessed very well what inference was drawn from her application. On account of that shrinking delicacy, which exists side by side with aggressive brutality in masculine nature, the inquiries into her circumstances had not been pushed very far. She had checked them by a visible compression of the lips and some display of an emotion determined to be eloquently silent. And the men would become suddenly incurious, after the manner of their kind. She congratulated herself more than once on having nothing to do with women, who being naturally more callous and avid of details, would have been anxious to be exactly informed by what sort of unkind conduct her daughter and son-in-law had driven her to that sad extremity. It was only before the Secretary of the great brewer M.P. and Chairman of the Charity, who, acting for his principal, felt bound to be conscientiously inquisitive as to the real circumstances of the applicant, that she had burst into tears outright and aloud, as a cornered woman will weep. The thin and polite gentleman, after contemplating her with an air of being "struck all of a heap," abandoned his position under the cover of soothing remarks. She must not distress herself.

The deed of the Charity did not absolutely specify "childless widows." In fact, it did not by any means disqualify her. But the discretion of the Committee must be an informed discretion. One could understand very well her unwillingness to be a burden, etc., etc. Thereupon, to his profound disappointment, Mrs Verloc's mother wept some more with an augmented vehemence.

The tears of that large female in a dark, dusty wig, and ancient silk dress festooned with dingy white cotton lace, were the tears of genuine distress. She had wept because she was heroic and unscrupulous and full of love for both her children. Girls frequently get sacrificed to the welfare of the boys. In this case she was sacrificing Winnie. By the suppression of truth she was slandering her. Of course, Winnie was independent, and need not care for the opinion of people that she would never see and who would never see her; whereas poor Stevie had nothing in the world he could call his own except his mother's heroism and unscrupulousness.

The first sense of security following on Winnie's marriage wore off in time (for nothing lasts), and Mrs Verloc's mother, in the seclusion of the back bedroom, had recalled the teaching of that experience which the world impresses upon a widowed woman. But she had recalled it without vain bitterness; her store of resignation amounted almost to dignity. She reflected stoically that everything decays, wears out, in this world; that the way of kindness should be made easy to the well disposed; that her daughter Winnie was a most devoted sister, and a very self-confident wife indeed. As regards Winnie's sisterly devotion, her stoicism flinched. She excepted that sentiment from the rule of decay affecting all things human and some things divine. She could not help it; not to do so would have frightened her too much. But in considering the conditions of her daughter's married state, she rejected firmly all flattering illusions. She took the cold and reasonable view that the less strain put on Mr Verloc's kindness the longer its effects were likely to last. That excellent man loved his wife, of course, but he would, no doubt, prefer to keep as few of her relations as was consistent with the proper display of that sentiment. It would be better if its whole effect were concentrated on poor Stevie. And the heroic old woman resolved on going away from her children as an act of devotion and as a move of deep policy.

The "virtue" of this policy consisted in this (Mrs Verloc's mother was subtle in her way), that Stevie's moral claim would be strengthened. The poor boy—a good, useful boy, if a little peculiar—had not a sufficient standing. He had been taken over with his mother, somewhat in the same way as the furniture of the Belgravian mansion had been taken over, as if on the ground of belonging to her exclusively. What will happen, she asked herself (for Mrs Verloc's mother was in a measure imaginative), when I die? And when she asked herself that question it was with dread. It was also terrible to think that she would not then have the means of knowing what happened to the poor boy. But by making him over to his sister, by going thus away, she gave him the advantage of a directly dependent position. This was the more subtle sanction of Mrs Verloc's mother's heroism and unscrupulousness. Her act of abandonment was really an arrangement for settling her son permanently in life. Other people made material sacrifices for such an object, she in that way. It was the only way. Moreover, she would be able to see how it worked. Ill or well she would avoid the horrible incertitude on the death-bed. But it was hard, hard, cruelly hard.

The cab rattled, jingled, jolted; in fact, the last was quite extraordinary. By its disproportionate violence and magnitude it obliterated every sensation of onward movement; and the effect was of being shaken in a stationary apparatus like a medieval device for the punishment of crime, or some very new-fangled invention for the cure of a sluggish liver. It was extremely distressing; and the raising of Mrs Verloc's mother's voice sounded like a wail of pain.

"I know, my dear, you'll come to see me as often as you can spare the time. Won't you?"

"Of course," answered Winnie, shortly, staring straight before her.

And the cab jolted in front of a steamy, greasy shop in a blaze of gas and in the smell of fried fish.

The old woman raised a wail again.

"And, my dear, I must see that poor boy every Sunday. He won't mind spending the day with his old mother—"

Winnie screamed out stolidly:

"Mind! I should think not. That poor boy will miss you something cruel. I wish you had thought a little of that, mother."

Not think of it! The heroic woman swallowed a playful and inconvenient object like a billiard ball, which had tried to jump out of her throat. Winnie sat mute for a while, pouting at the front of the cab, then snapped out, which was an unusual tone with her:

"I expect I'll have a job with him at first, he'll be that restless—"

"Whatever you do, don't let him worry your husband, my dear."

Thus they discussed on familiar lines the bearings of a new situation. And the cab jolted. Mrs Verloc's mother expressed some misgivings. Could Stevie be trusted to come all that way alone? Winnie maintained that he was much less "absent-minded" now. They agreed as to that. It could not be denied. Much less—hardly at all. They shouted at each other in the jingle with comparative cheerfulness. But suddenly the maternal anxiety broke out afresh. There were two omnibuses to take, and a short walk between. It was too difficult! The old woman gave way to grief and consternation.

Winnie stared forward.

"Don't you upset yourself like this, mother. You must see him, of course."

"No, my dear. I'll try not to."

She mopped her streaming eyes.

"But you can't spare the time to come with him, and if he should forget himself and lose his way and somebody spoke to him sharply, his name and address may slip his memory, and he'll remain lost for days and days—"

The vision of a workhouse infirmary for poor Stevie—if only during inquiries—wrung her heart. For she was a proud woman. Winnie's stare had grown hard, intent, inventive.

"I can't bring him to you myself every week," she cried. "But don't you worry, mother. I'll see to it that he don't get lost for long."

They felt a peculiar bump; a vision of brick pillars lingered before the rattling windows of the cab; a sudden cessation of atrocious jolting and uproarious jingling dazed the two women. What had happened? They sat motionless and scared in the profound stillness, till the door came open, and a rough, strained whispering was heard:

" 'Ere you are!"

A range of gabled little houses, each with one dim yellow window, on the ground floor, surrounded the dark open space of a grass plot planted with shrubs and railed off from the patchwork of lights and shadows in the wide road, resounding with the dull rumble of traffic. Before the door of one of these tiny houses—one without a light in the little downstairs window—the cab had come to a standstill. Mrs Verloc's mother got out first, backwards, with a key in her hand. Winnie lingered on the flagstone path to pay the cabman. Stevie, after helping to carry inside a lot of small parcels, came out and stood under the light of a gas-lamp belonging to the Charity. The cabman looked at the pieces of silver, which, appearing very minute in his big, grimy palm, symbolized the insignificant results which reward the ambitious courage and toil of a mankind whose day is short on this earth of evil.

He had been paid decently—four one-shilling pieces—and he contemplated them in perfect stillness, as if they had been the surprising terms of a melancholy problem. The slow transfer of that treasure to an inner pocket demanded much laborious groping in the depths of decayed clothing. His form was squat and without flexibility. Stevie, slender, his shoulders a little up, and his hands thrust deep in the side pockets of his warm overcoat, stood at the edge of the path, pouting.

The cabman, pausing in his deliberate movements, seemed struck by some misty recollection.

"Oh! 'Ere you are, young fellow," he whispered. "You'll know him again—won't you?"

Stevie was staring at the horse, whose hind quarters appeared unduly elevated by the effect of emancipation. The little stiff tail seemed to have been fitted in for a heartless joke; and at the other end the thin, flat neck, like a plank covered with old horse-hide, drooped to the ground under the weight of an enormous bony head. The ears hung at different angles, negligently; and the macabre figure of that mute dweller on the earth steamed straight up from ribs and backbone in the muggy stillness of the air.

The cabman struck lightly Stevie's breast with the iron hook protruding from a ragged, greasy sleeve.

"Look 'ere young feller. 'Owd *you* like to sit behind this 'oss up to two o'clock in the morning p'raps?"

Stevie looked vacantly into the fierce little eyes with red-edged lids.

"He ain't lame," pursued the other, whispering with energy. "He ain't got no sore places on 'im. 'Ere he is. 'Ow would *you* like—"

His strained, extinct voice invested his utterance with a character of vehement secrecy. Stevie's vacant gaze was changing slowly into dread.

"You may well look! Till three and four o'clock in the morning. Cold and 'ungry. Looking for fares. Drunks."

His jovial purple cheeks bristled with white hairs; and like Virgil's Silenus, who, his face smeared with the juice of berries, discoursed of Olympian Gods to the innocent shepherds of Sicily, he talked to Stevie of domestic matters and the affairs of men whose sufferings are great and immortality by no means assured.

"I am a night cabby, I am," he whispered, with a sort of boastful exasperation. "I've got to take out what they will blooming well give me at the yard. I've got my missus and four kids at 'ome."

The monstrous nature of that declaration of paternity seemed to strike the world dumb. A silence reigned, during which the flanks of the old horse, the steed of apocalyptic misery, smoked upwards in the light of the charitable gas-lamp.

The cabman grunted, then added in his mysterious whisper:

"This ain't an easy world."

Stevie's face had been twitching for some time and at last his feelings burst out in their usual concise form.

"Bad! Bad!"

His gaze remained fixed on the ribs of the horse, self-conscious and sombre, as though he were afraid to look about him at the badness of the world. And his slenderness, his rosy lips and pale, clear complexion, gave him the aspect of a delicate boy, notwithstanding the fluffy growth of golden hair on his cheeks. He pouted in a scared way like a child. The cabman, short and broad, eyed him with his fierce little eyes that seemed to smart in a clear and corroding liquid.

"'Ard on 'osses, but dam' sight 'arder on poor chaps like me," he wheezed just audibly.

"Poor! Poor!" stammered out Stevie, pushing his hands deeper into his pockets with convulsive sympathy. He could say nothing; for the tenderness to all pain and all misery, the desire to make the horse happy and the cabman happy, had reached the point of a bizarre longing to take them to bed with him. And that, he knew, was impossible. For Stevie was not mad. It was, as it were, a symbolic longing; and at the same time it was very distinct, because springing from experience, the mother of wisdom. Thus when as a child he cowered in a dark corner scared, wretched, sore, and miserable with the black, black misery of the soul, his sister Winnie used to come along and carry him off to bed with her, as into a heaven of consoling peace. Stevie, though apt to forget mere facts, such as his name and address for instance, had a faithful memory of sensations. To be taken into a bed of compassion was the supreme remedy, with the only one disadvantage of being difficult of application on a large scale. And looking at the cabman, Stevie perceived this clearly, because he was reasonable.

The cabman went on with his leisurely preparations as if Stevie had not existed. He made as if to hoist himself on the box, but at the last moment, from some obscure motive, perhaps merely from disgust with carriage exercise, desisted. He approached instead the motionless partner of his labours, and stooping to seize the bridle, lifted up the big, weary head to the height of his shoulder with one effort of his right arm, like a feat of strength.

"Come on," he whispered, secretly.

Limping, he led the cab away. There was an air of austerity in this departure, the scrunched gravel of the drive crying out under the slowly turning wheels, the horse's lean thighs moving with ascetic deliberation away from the light into the obscurity of the open space bordered dimly by the pointed roofs and the feebly shining windows of the little almshouses. The plaint of the gravel travelled slowly all round the drive. Between the lamps of the charitable gateway the slow cortège reappeared, lighted up for a moment, the short, thick man limping busily, with the horse's head held aloft in his fist, the lank animal walking in stiff and forlorn dignity, the dark, low box on wheels rolling behind comically with an air of waddling. They turned to the left. There was a pub down the street, within fifty yards of the gate.

Stevie, left alone beside the private lamp-post of the Charity, his hands thrust deep into his pockets, glared with vacant sulkiness. At the bottom of his pockets his incapable, weak hands were clenched hard into a pair of angry fists. In the face of anything which affected directly or indirectly his morbid dread of pain, Stevie ended by turning vicious. A magnanimous indignation swelled his frail chest to bursting, and caused his candid eyes to squint. Supremely wise in knowing his own powerlessness, Stevie was not wise enough to restrain his passions. The tenderness of his universal charity had two phases as indissolubly joined and connected as the reverse and obverse sides of a medal. The anguish of immoderate compassion was succeeded by the pain of an innocent but pitiless rage. Those two states expressing themselves outwardly by the same signs of futile bodily agitation, his sister Winnie soothed his excitement without ever fathoming its twofold character. Mrs Verloc wasted no portion of this transient life in seeking for fundamental information. This is a sort of economy having all the appearances and some of the advantages of prudence. Obviously it may be good for one not to know too much. And such a view accords very well with constitutional indolence.

On that evening on which it may be said that Mrs Verloc's mother having parted for good from her children had also departed this life, Winnie Verloc did not investigate her brother's psychology. The poor boy was excited, of course. After once more assuring the old woman on the threshold that she would know how to guard against the risk of Stevie losing himself for very long on his pilgrimages of filial piety, she took her brother's arm to walk away. Stevie did not even mutter to himself, but with the special sense of sisterly devotion developed in her earliest infancy, she felt that the boy was very much excited indeed. Holding tight to his arm, under the appearance of leaning on it, she thought of some words suitable to the occasion.

"Now, Stevie, you must look well after me at the crossings, and get first into the bus, like a good brother."

This appeal to manly protection was received by Stevie with his usual docility. It flattered him. He raised his head and threw out his chest.

"Don't be nervous, Winnie. Mustn't be nervous! Bus all right," he answered in a brusque, slurring stammer partaking of the timorousness of a child and the resolution of a man. He advanced fearlessly with the woman on his arm, but his lower lip drooped. Nevertheless, on the pavement of the squalid and wide thoroughfare, whose poverty in all the amenities of life stood foolishly exposed by a mad profusion of gas-lights, their resemblance to each other was so pronounced as to strike the casual passers-by.

Before the doors of the public-house at the corner, where the profusion of gas-light reached the height of positive wickedness, a four-wheeled cab standing by the kerbstone, with no one on the box, seemed cast out into the gutter on account of irremediable decay. Mrs Verloc recognized the conveyance. Its aspect was so profoundly lamentable, with such a perfection of grotesque misery and weirdness of macabre detail, as if it were the Cab of Death itself that Mrs Verloc, with that ready compassion of a woman for a horse (when she is not sitting behind him), exclaimed vaguely!

"Poor brute."

Hanging back suddenly, Stevie inflicted an arresting jerk upon his sister.

"Poor! Poor!" he ejaculated appreciatively. "Cabman poor, too. He told me himself."

The contemplation of the infirm and lonely steed overcame him. Jostled, but obstinate, he would remain there, trying to express the view newly opened to his sympathies of the human and equine misery in close association. But it was very difficult. "Poor brute, poor people!" was all he could repeat. It did not seem forcible enough, and he came to a stop with an angry splutter: "Shame!" Stevie was no master of phrases, and perhaps for that very reason his thoughts lacked clearness and precision. But he felt with great completeness and some profundity. That little word contained all his sense of indignation and horror at one sort of wretchedness having to feed upon the anguish of the other—as the poor cabman beating the poor horse in the name, as it were, of his poor kids at home. And Stevie knew what it was to be beaten. He knew it from experience. It was a bad world. Bad! Bad!

Mrs Verloc, his only sister, guardian, and protector, could not pretend to such depths of insight. Moreover, she had not experienced the magic of the cabman's eloquence. She was in the dark as to the inwardness of the word "Shame." And she said placidly:

"Come along, Stevie. You can't help that."

The docile Stevie went along; but now he went along without pride, shamblingly, and muttering half words, and even words that would have been whole if they had not been made up of halves that did not belong to each other. It was as though he had been trying to fit all the words he could remember to his sentiments in order to get some sort of corresponding idea. And, as a matter of fact, he got it at last. He hung back to utter it at once.

"Bad world for poor people."

Directly he had expressed that thought he became aware that it was familiar to him already in all its consequences. This circumstance strengthened his conviction immensely, but also augmented his indignation. Somebody, he felt, ought to be punished for it—punished with great severity. Being no sceptic, but a moral creature, he was in a manner at the mercy of his righteous passions.

"Beastly!" he added, concisely.

It was clear to Mrs Verloc that he was greatly excited.

"Nobody can help that," she said. "Do come along. Is that the way you're taking care of me?"

Stevie mended his pace obediently. He prided himself on being a good brother. His morality, which was very complete, demanded that from him. Yet he was pained at the information imparted by his sister Winnie—who was good. Nobody could help that! He came along gloomily, but presently he brightened up. Like the rest of mankind, perplexed by the mystery of the universe, he had his moments of consoling trust in the organized powers of the earth.

"Police," he suggested, confidently.

"The police aren't for that," observed Mrs Verloc, cursorily, hurrying on her way.

Stevie's face lengthened considerably. He was thinking. The more intense his thinking, the slacker was the droop of his lower jaw. And it was with an aspect of hopeless vacancy that he gave up his intellectual enterprise.

"Not for that?" he mumbled, resigned but surprised. "Not for that?" He had formed for himself an ideal conception for the metropolitan police as a sort of benevolent institution for the suppression of evil. The notion of benevolence especially was very closely associated with his sense of the power of the men in blue. He had liked all police constables tenderly, with a guileless trustfulness. And he was pained. He was irritated, too, by a suspicion of duplicity in the members of the force. For Stevie was frank and as open as the day himself. What did they mean by pretending then? Unlike his sister, who put her trust in face values, he wished to go to the bottom of the matter. He carried on his inquiry by means of an angry challenge.

"What are they for then, Winn? What are they for? Tell me."

Winnie disliked controversy. But fearing most a fit of black depression consequent on Stevie missing his mother very much at first, she did not altogether decline the discussion. Guiltless of all irony, she answered yet in a form which was not perhaps unnatural in the wife of Mr Verloc, Delegate of the Central Red Committee, personal friend of certain anarchists, and a votary of social revolution.

"Don't you know what the police are for, Stevie? They are there so that them as have nothing shouldn't take anything away from them who have."

She avoided using the verb "to steal," because it always made her brother uncomfortable. For Stevie was delicately honest. Certain simple principles had been instilled into him so anxiously (on account of his "queerness") that the mere names of certain transgressions filled him with horror. He had been always easily impressed by speeches. He was impressed and startled now, and his intelligence was very alert.

"What?" he asked at once, anxiously. "Not even if they were hungry? Mustn't they?"

The two had paused in their walk.

"Not if they were ever so," said Mrs Verloc, with the equanimity of a person untroubled by the problem of the distribution of wealth and exploring the perspective of the roadway for an omnibus of the right colour. "Certainly not. But what's the use of talking about all that? You aren't ever hungry."

She cast a swift glance at the boy, like a young man, by her side. She saw him amiable, attractive, affectionate and only a little, a very little peculiar. And she could not see him otherwise, for he was connected with what there was of the salt of passion in her tasteless life—the passion of indignation, of courage, of pity, and even of self-sacrifice. She did not add: "And you aren't likely ever to be as long as I live." But she might very well have done so, since she had taken effectual steps to that end. Mr Verloc was a very good husband. It was her honest impression that nobody could help liking the boy. She cried out suddenly:

"Quick, Stevie. Stop that green bus."

And Stevie, tremulous and important with his sister Winnie on his arm, flung up the other high above his head at the approaching bus, with complete success.

An hour afterwards Mr Verloc raised his eyes from a newspaper he was reading, or at any rate looking at, behind the counter, and in the expiring clatter of the door-bell beheld Winnie, his wife, enter and cross the shop on her way upstairs, followed by Stevie, his brother-in-law. The sight of his wife was agreeable to Mr Verloc. It was his idiosyncrasy. The figure of his brother-in-law remained imperceptible to him because of the morose thoughtfulness that lately had fallen like a veil between Mr Verloc and the appearances of the world of senses. He looked after his wife fixedly, without a word, as though she had been a phantom. His voice for home use was husky and placid, but now it was heard not at all. It was not heard at supper, to which he was called by his wife in the usual brief manner: "Adolf." He sat down to consume it without conviction, wearing his hat pushed far back on his head. It was not devotion to an outdoor life, but the frequentation of foreign cafés which was responsible for that habit, investing with a character of unceremonious impermanency Mr Verloc's steady fidelity to his own fireside. Twice at the clatter of the cracked bell he arose without a word, disappeared into the shop, and came back silently. During these absences Mrs Verloc, becoming acutely aware of the vacant place at her right hand, missed her mother very much and stared stonily; while Stevie, from the same reason, kept on shuffling his feet, as though the floor under the table were uncomfortably hot. When Mr Verloc returned to it in his place, like the very embodiment of silence, the character of Mrs Verloc's stare underwent a subtle change, and Stevie ceased to fidget with his feet, because of his great and awed regard for his sister's husband. He directed at him glances of respectful compassion. Mr Verloc was sorry. His sister Winnie had impressed upon him (in the omnibus) that Mr Verloc would be found at home in a state of sorrow, and must not be worried. His father's anger, the irritability of gentlemen lodgers, and Mr Verloc's predisposition to immoderate grief, had been the main sanctions of Stevie's self-restraint. Of these sentiments, all easily provoked, but not always easy to understand, the last had the greatest moral efficiency—because Mr Verloc was *good*. His mother and his sister had established that ethical fact on an unshakable foundation. They had established, erected, consecrated it behind Mr Verloc's back, for reasons that had nothing to do with abstract morality. And

Mr Verloc was not aware of it. It is but bare justice to him to say that he had no notion of appearing good to Stevie. Yet so it was. He was even the only man so qualified in Stevie's knowledge, because the gentlemen lodgers had been too transient and too remote to have anything very distinct about them but perhaps their boots; and as regards the disciplinary measures of his father, the desolation of his mother and sister shrank from setting up a theory of goodness before the victim. It would have been too cruel. And it was even possible that Stevie would not have believed them. As far as Mr Verloc was concerned, nothing could stand in the way of Stevie's belief. Mr Verloc was obviously yet mysteriously *good*. And the grief of a good man is august.

Stevie gave glances of reverential compassion to his brother-in-law. Mr Verloc was sorry. The brother of Winnie had never before felt himself in such close communion with the mystery of that man's goodness. It was an understandable sorrow. And Stevie himself was sorry. He was very sorry. The same sort of sorrow. And his attention being drawn to this unpleasant state, Stevie shuffled his feet. His feelings were habitually manifested by the agitation of his limbs.

"Keep your feet quiet, dear," said Mrs Verloc, with authority and tenderness; then turning towards her husband in an indifferent voice, the masterly achievement of instinctive tact: "Are you going out tonight?" she asked.

The mere suggestion seemed repugnant to Mr Verloc. He shook his head moodily, and then sat still with downcast eyes, looking at the piece of cheese on his plate for a whole minute. At the end of that time he got up, and went out—went right out in the clatter of the shop-door bell. He acted thus inconsistently, not from any desire to make himself unpleasant, but because of an unconquerable restlessness. It was no earthly good going out. He could not find anywhere in London what he wanted. But he went out. He led a cortège of dismal thoughts along dark streets, through lighted streets, in and out of two flash bars, as if in a half-hearted attempt to make a night of it, and finally back again to his menaced home, where he sat down fatigued behind the counter, and they crowded urgently round him, like a pack of hungry black hounds. After locking up the house and putting out the gas he took them upstairs with him—a dreadful escort for a man going to bed. His wife had preceded him some time before, and with her ample form defined vaguely under the counterpane, her head on the pillow, and a hand under the cheek, offered to his distraction the view of early drowsiness arguing the possession of an equable soul. Her big eyes stared wide open, inert and dark against the snowy whiteness of the linen. She did not move.

She had an equable soul. She felt profoundly that things do not stand much looking into. She made her force and her wisdom of that instinct. But the taciturnity of Mr Verloc had been lying heavily upon her for a good many days. It was, as a matter of fact, affecting her nerves. Recumbent and motionless, she said placidly:

"You'll catch cold walking about in your socks like this."

This speech, becoming the solicitude of the wife and the prudence of the woman, took Mr Verloc unawares. He had left his boots downstairs, but he had forgotten to put on his slippers, and he had been turning about the bedroom on noiseless pads like a bear in a cage. At the sound of his wife's voice he stopped and stared at her with a somnambulistic, expressionless gaze so long that Mrs Verloc moved her limbs slightly under the bedclothes. But she did not move her black head sunk in the white pillow, one hand under her cheek and the big, dark, unwinking eyes.

Under her husband's expressionless stare, and remembering her mother's empty room across the landing, she felt an acute pang of loneliness. She had never been parted from her mother before. They had stood by each other. She felt that they had, and she said to herself that now mother was gone—gone for good. Mrs Verloc had no illusions. Stevie remained, however. And she said:

"Mother's done what she wanted to do. There's no sense in it that I can see. I'm sure she couldn't have thought you had enough of her. It's perfectly wicked, leaving us like that."

Mr Verloc was not a well-read person; his range of allusive phrases was limited, but there was a peculiar aptness in circumstances which made him think of rats leaving a doomed ship. He very nearly said so. He had grown suspicious and embittered. Could it be that the old woman had such an excellent nose? But the unreasonableness of such a suspicion was patent, and Mr Verloc held his tongue. Not altogether, however. He muttered, heavily:

"Perhaps it's just as well."

He began to undress. Mrs Verloc kept very still, perfectly still, with her eyes fixed in a dreamy, quiet stare. And her heart for the fraction of a second seemed to stand still, too. That night she was "not quite herself," as the saying is, and it was borne upon her with some force that a simple sentence may hold several diverse meanings—mostly disagreeable. *How* was it just as well? And why? But she did not allow herself to fall into the idleness of barren speculation. She was rather confirmed in her belief that things did not stand being looked into. Practical and subtle in her way, she brought Stevie to the front without loss of time, because in her the singleness of purpose had the unerring nature and the force of an instinct.

"What I am going to do to cheer up that boy for the first few days I'm sure I don't know. He'll be worrying himself from morning till night before he gets used to mother being away. And he's such a good boy. I couldn't do without him."

Mr Verloc went on divesting himself of his clothing with the unnoticing inward concentration of a man undressing in the solitude of a vast and hopeless desert. For thus inhospitably did this fair earth, our common inheritance, present itself to the mental vision of Mr Verloc. All was so still without and within that the lonely ticking of the clock on the landing stole into the room as if for the sake of company.

Mr Verloc, getting into bed on his own side, remained prone and mute behind Mrs Verloc's back. His thick arms rested abandoned on the outside of the counterpane like dropped weapons, like discarded tools. At that moment he was within a hair's breadth of making a clean breast of it all to his wife. The moment seemed propitious. Looking out of the corners of his eyes, he saw her ample shoulders draped in white, the back of her head, with the hair done for the night in three plaits tied up with black tapes at the ends. And he forbore. Mr Verloc loved his wife as a wife should be loved—that is, maritally, with the regard one has for one's chief possession. This head arranged for the night, those ample shoulders, had an aspect of familiar sacredness—the sacredness of domestic peace. She moved not, massive and shapeless like a recumbent statue in the rough; he remembered her wide-open eyes looking into the empty room. She was mysterious, with the mysteriousness of living beings. The far-famed secret agent D of the late Baron Stott-Wartenheim's alarmist dispatches was not the man to break into such mysteries. He was easily intimidated. And he was also indolent, with the indolence which is so often the secret of good nature. He forbore touching that mystery out of love, timidity, and indolence. There would be always time enough. For several minutes he bore his sufferings silently in the drowsy silence of the room. And then he disturbed it by a resolute declaration.

"I am going on the Continent tomorrow."

His wife might have fallen asleep already. He could not tell. As a matter of fact, Mrs Verloc had heard him. Her eyes remained very wide open, and she lay very still, confirmed in her instinctive conviction that things don't bear looking into very much. And yet it was nothing very unusual for Mr Verloc to take such a trip. He renewed his stock from Paris and Brussels. Often he went over to make his purchases personally. A little select connection of amateurs was forming around the shop in Brett Street, a secret connection eminently proper for any business undertaken by Mr Verloc, who, by a mystic accord of temperament and necessity, had been set apart to be a secret agent all his life.

He waited for a while, then added: "I'll be away a week or perhaps a fortnight. Get Mrs Neale to come for the day."

Mrs Neale was the charwoman of Brett Street. Victim of her marriage with a debauched joiner, she was oppressed by the needs of many infant children. Red-armed, and aproned in coarse sacking up to the armpits, she exhaled the anguish of the poor in a breath of soap-suds and rum, in the uproar of scrubbing, in the clatter of tin pails.

Mrs Verloc, full of deep purpose, spoke in the tone of the shallowest indifference.

"There is no need to have the woman here all day. I shall do very well with Stevie."

She let the lonely clock on the landing count off fifteen ticks into the abyss of eternity, and asked:

"Shall I put the light out?"

Mr Verloc snapped at his wife huskily.

"Put it out."

CHAPTER 9

Mr Verloc, returning from the Continent at the end of ten days, brought back a mind evidently unrefreshed by the wonders of foreign travel and a countenance unlighted by the joys of homecoming. He entered in the clatter of the shop-bell with an air of sombre and vexed exhaustion. His bag in hand, his head lowered, he strode straight behind the counter, and let himself fall into the chair, as though he had tramped all the way from Dover. It was early morning. Stevie, dusting various objects displayed in the front windows, turned to gape at him with reverence and awe.

"Here!" said Mr Verloc, giving a slight kick to the gladstone bag on the floor; and Stevie flung himself upon it, seized it, bore it off with triumphant devotion. He was so prompt that Mr Verloc was distinctly surprised.

Already at the clatter of the shop-bell Mrs Neale, blackleading the parlour grate, had looked through the door, and rising from her knees had gone, aproned, and grimy with everlasting toil, to tell Mrs Verloc in the kitchen that "there was the master come back."

Winnie came no farther than the inner shop door.

"You'll want some breakfast," she said from a distance.

Mr Verloc moved his hands slightly, as if overcome by an impossible suggestion. But once enticed into the parlour he did not reject the food set before him. He ate as if in a public place, his hat pushed off his forehead, the skirts of his heavy overcoat hanging in a triangle on each side of the chair. And across the length of the table covered with brown oilcloth Winnie, his wife, talked evenly at him the wifely talk, as artfully adapted, no doubt, to the circumstances of this return as the talk of Penelope to the return of the wandering Odysseus. Mrs Verloc, however, had done no weaving during her husband's absence. But she had had all the upstairs rooms cleaned thoroughly, had sold some wares, had seen Mr Michaelis several times. He had told her the last time that he was going away to live in a cottage in the country, somewhere on the London, Chatham, and Dover line. Karl Yundt had come, too, once led under the arm by that "wicked old house-keeper of his." He was a "disgusting old man." Of Comrade Ossipon, whom she had received curtly, entrenched behind the counter with a stony face and a far-away gaze, she said nothing, her mental reference to the robust anarchist being marked by a short pause, with the faintest possible blush. And bringing in her brother Stevie as soon as she could into the current of domestic events, she mentioned that the boy had moped a good deal.

"It's all along of mother leaving us like this."

Mr Verloc neither said "Damn!" nor yet "Stevie be hanged!" And Mrs Verloc, not let into the secret of his thoughts, failed to appreciate the generosity of this restraint.

"It isn't that he doesn't work as well as ever," she continued. "He's been making himself very useful. You'd think he couldn't do enough for us."

Mr Verloc directed a casual and somnolent glance at Stevie, who sat on his right, delicate, pale-faced, his rosy mouth open vacantly. It was not a critical glance. It had no intention. And if Mr Verloc thought for a moment that his wife's brother looked uncommonly useless, it was only a dull and fleeting thought, devoid of that force and durability which enables sometimes a thought to move the world. Leaning back, Mr Verloc uncovered his head. Before his extended arm could put down the hat Stevie pounced upon it, and bore it off reverently into the kitchen. And again Mr Verloc was surprised.

"You could do anything with that boy, Adolf," Mrs Verloc said, with her best air of inflexible calmness. "He would go through fire for you. He—"

She paused attentive, her ear turned towards the door of the kitchen.

There Mrs Neale was scrubbing the floor. At Stevie's appearance she groaned lamentably, having observed that he could be induced easily to bestow for the benefit of her infant children the shilling his sister Winnie presented him with from time to time. On all fours amongst the puddles, wet and begrimed, like a sort of amphibious and domestic animal living in ashbins and dirty water, she uttered the usual exordium; "It's all very well for you, kept doing nothing, like a gentleman." And she followed it with the everlasting plaint of the poor, pathetically mendacious, miserably authenticated by the horrible breath of cheap rum and soap-suds. She scrubbed hard, snuffling all the time, and talking volubly. And she was sincere. And on each side of her thin red nose her bleared, misty eyes swam in tears, because she felt really the want of some sort of stimulant in the morning.

In the parlour Mrs Verloc observed, with knowledge:

"There's Mrs Neale at it again with her harrowing tales about her little children. They can't be all so little as she makes them out. Some of them must be big enough by now to try to do something for themselves. It only makes Stevie angry."

These words were confirmed by a thud as of a fist striking the kitchen table. In the normal evolution of his sympathy Stevie had become angry on discovering that he had no shilling in his pocket. In his inability to relieve at once Mrs Neale's "little 'uns'" privations, he felt that somebody should be made to suffer for it. Mrs Verloc rose and went into the kitchen to "stop that nonsense." And she did it firmly but gently. She was well aware that directly Mrs Neale received her money she went round the corner to drink ardent spirits in a mean and musty public-house—the unavoidable station on the *via dolorosa* of her life. Mrs Verloc's comment upon this practice had an expected profundity, as coming from a person disinclined to look under the surface of things. "Of course, what is she to do to keep up? If I were like Mrs Neale I expect I wouldn't act any different."

In the afternoon of the same day, as Mr Verloc, coming with a start out of the last of a long series of dozes before the parlour fire, declared his intention of going out for a walk, Winnie said from the ship:

"I wish you would take that boy out with you, Adolf."

For the third time that day Mr Verloc was surprised. He stared stupidly at his wife. She continued in her steady manner. The boy, whenever he was not doing anything, moped in the house. It made her uneasy; it made her nervous, she confessed. And that from the calm Winnie sounded like exaggeration. But in truth, Stevie moped in the striking fashion of an unhappy domestic animal. He would go up on the dark landing, to sit on the floor at the foot of the tall clock, with his knees drawn up and his head in his hands. To come upon his pallid face, with its big eyes gleaming in the dusk, was discomposing; to think of him up there was uncomfortable.

Mr Verloc got used to the startling novelty of the idea. He was fond of his wife as a man should be—that is, generously. But a weighty objection presented itself to his mind, and he formulated it.

"He'll lose sight of me perhaps, and get lost in the street," he said.

Mrs Verloc shook her head competently.

"He won't. You don't know him. That boy just worships you. But if you should miss him—"

Mrs Verloc paused for a moment, but only for a moment.

"You just go on, and have your walk out. Don't worry. He'll be all right. He's sure to turn up safe here before very long."

This optimism procured for Mr Verloc his fourth surprise of the day.

"Is he?" he grunted doubtfully. But perhaps his brother-in-law was not such an idiot as he looked. His wife would know best. He turned away his heavy eyes, saying huskily: "Well, let him come along, then," and relapsed into the clutches of black care, that perhaps prefers to sit behind a horseman, but knows also how to tread close on the heels of people not sufficiently well off to keep horses—like Mr Verloc, for instance.

Winnie, at the shop door, did not see this fatal attendant upon Mr Verloc's walks. She watched the two figures down the squalid street, one tall and burly, the other slight and short, with a thin neck, and the peaked shoulders raised slightly under the large semi-transparent ears. The material of their overcoats was the same, their hats were black and round in shape. Inspired by the similarity of wearing apparel, Mrs Verloc gave rein to her fancy.

"Might be father and son," she said to herself. She thought also that Mr Verloc was as much of a father as poor Stevie ever had in his life. She was aware also that it was her work. And with peaceful pride she congratulated herself on a certain resolution she had taken a few years before. It had cost her some effort, and even a few tears.

She congratulated herself still more on observing in the course of days that Mr Verloc seemed to be taking kindly to Stevie's companionship. Now, when ready to go out for his walk, Mr Verloc called aloud to the boy, in the spirit, no doubt, in which a man invites the attendance of the household dog, though, of course, in a different manner. In the house Mr Verloc could be detected staring curiously at Stevie a good deal. His own demeanour had changed. Taciturn still, he was not so listless. Mrs Verloc thought that he was rather jumpy at times. It might have been regarded as an improvement. As to Stevie, he moped no longer at the foot of the clock, but muttered to himself in corners instead in a threatening tone. When asked "What is it you're saying, Stevie?" he merely opened his mouth, and squinted at his sister. At odd times he clenched his fists without apparent cause, and when discovered in solitude would be scowling at the wall, with the sheet of paper and the pencil given him for drawing circles lying blank and idle on the kitchen table. This was a change, but it was no improvement. Mrs Verloc, including all these vagaries under the general definition of excitement, began to fear that Stevie was hearing more than was good for him of her husband's conversations with his friends. During his "walks" Mr Verloc, of course, met and conversed with various persons. It could hardly be otherwise. His walks were an integral part of his outdoor activities, which his wife had never looked deeply into. Mrs Verloc felt that the position was delicate, but she faced it with the same impenetrable calmness which impressed and even astonished the customers of the shop and made the other visitors keep their distance a little wonderingly. No! She feared that there were things not good for Stevie to hear of, she told her husband. It only excited the poor boy, because he could not help them being so. Nobody could.

It was in the shop. Mr Verloc made no comment. He made no retort, and yet the retort was obvious. But he refrained from pointing out to his wife that the idea of making Stevie the companion of his walks was her own, and nobody else's. At that moment, to an impartial observer, Mr Verloc would have appeared more than human in his magnanimity. He took down a small cardboard box from a shelf, peeped in to see that the contents were all right, and put it down gently on the counter. Not till that was done did he break the silence, to the effect that most likely Stevie would profit greatly by being sent out of town for a while; only he supposed his wife could not get on without him.

"Could not get on without him!" repeated Mrs Verloc, slowly. "I couldn't get on without him if it were for his good! The idea! Of course, I can get on without him. But there's nowhere for him to go."

Mr Verloc got out some brown paper and a ball of string; and meanwhile he muttered that Michaelis was living in a little cottage in the country. Michaelis wouldn't mind giving Stevie a room to sleep in. There were no visitors and no talk there. Michaelis was writing a book.

Mrs Verloc declared her affection for Michaelis; mentioned her abhorrence of Karl Yundt, "nasty old man"; and of Ossipon she said nothing. As to Stevie, he could be no other than very pleased. Mr Michaelis was always so nice and kind to him. He seemed to like the boy. Well, the boy was a good boy.

"You, too, seem to have grown quite fond of him of late," she added, after a pause, with her inflexible assurance.

Mr Verloc, tying up the cardboard box into a parcel for the post, broke the string by an injudicious jerk, and muttered several swearwords confidentially to himself. Then raising his tone to the usual husky mutter, he announced his willingness to take Stevie into the country himself, and leave him safe with Michaelis.

He carried out this scheme on the very next day. Stevie offered no objection. He seemed rather eager, in a bewildered sort of way. He turned his candid gaze inquisitively to Mr Verloc's heavy countenance at frequent intervals, especially when his sister was not looking at him. His expression was proud, apprehensive, and concentrated, like that of a small child entrusted for the first time with a box of matches and the permission to strike a light. But Mrs Verloc, gratified by her brother's docility, recommended him not to dirty his clothes unduly in the country. At this Stevie gave his sister, guardian, and protector a look, which for the first time in his life seemed to lack the quality of perfect childlike trustfulness. It was haughtily gloomy. Mrs Verloc smiled.

"Goodness me! You needn't be offended. You know you do get yourself very untidy when you get a chance, Stevie."

Mr Verloc was already gone some way down the street.

Thus in consequence of her mother's heroic proceedings, and of her brother's absence on this villegiature, Mrs Verloc found herself oftener than usual all alone not only in the shop, but in the house. For Mr Verloc had to take his walks. She was alone longer than usual on the day of the attempted bomb outrage in Greenwich Park, because Mr Verloc went out very early that morning and did not come back till nearly dusk. She did not mind being alone. She had no desire to go out. The weather was too bad, and the shop was cosier than the streets. Sitting behind the counter with some sewing, she did not raise her eyes from her work when Mr Verloc entered in the aggressive clatter of the bell. She had recognized his step on the pavement outside.

She did not raise her eyes, but as Mr Verloc, silent, and with his hat rammed down upon his forehead, made straight for the parlour door, she said, serenely:

"What a wretched day. You've been perhaps to see Stevie?"

"No! I haven't," said Mr Verloc, softly, and slammed the glazed parlour door behind him with unexpected energy.

For some time Mrs Verloc remained quiescent, with her work dropped in her lap, before she put it away under the counter and got up to light the gas. This done, she went into the parlour on her way to the kitchen. Mr Verloc would want his tea presently. Confident of the power of her charms, Winnie did not expect from her husband in the daily intercourse of their married life a ceremonious amenity of address and courtliness of manner; vain and antiquated forms at best, probably never very exactly observed, discarded nowadays even in the highest spheres, and always foreign to the standards of her class. She did not look for courtesies from him. But he was a good husband, and she had a loyal respect for his rights.

Mrs Verloc would have gone through the parlour and on to her domestic duties in the kitchen with the perfect serenity of a woman sure of the power of her charms. But a slight, very slight, and rapid rattling sound grew upon her hearing. Bizarre and incomprehensible, it arrested Mrs Verloc's attention. Then as its character became plain to the ear she stopped short, amazed and concerned. Striking a match on the box she held in her hand, she turned on and lighted, above the parlour table, one of the two gas-burners, which, being defective, first whistled as if astonished, and then went on purring comfortably like a cat.

Mr Verloc, against his usual practice, had thrown off his overcoat. It was lying on the sofa. His hat, which he must also have thrown off, rested overturned under the edge of the sofa. He had dragged a chair in front of the fireplace, and his feet planted inside the fender, his head held between his hands, he was hanging low over the glowing grate. His teeth rattled with an ungovernable violence, causing his whole enormous back to tremble at the same rate. Mrs Verloc was startled.

"You've been getting wet," she said.

"Not very," Mr Verloc managed to falter out, in a profound shudder. By a great effort he suppressed the rattling of his teeth.

"I'll have you laid up on my hands," she said, with genuine uneasiness.

"I don't think so," remarked Mr Verloc, snuffling huskily.

He had certainly contrived somehow to catch an abominable cold between seven in the morning and five in the afternoon. Mrs Verloc looked at his bowed back.

"Where have you been today?" she asked.

"Nowhere," answered Mr Verloc in a low, choked nasal tone. His attitude suggested aggrieved sulks or a severe headache. The unsufficiency and uncandidness of his answer became painfully apparent in the dead silence of the room. He snuffled apologetically, and added: "I've been to the bank."

Mrs Verloc became attentive.

"You have!" she said, dispassionately. "What for?"

Mr Verloc mumbled, with his nose over the grate, and with marked unwillingness:

"Draw the money out!"

"What do you mean? All of it?"

"Yes. All of it."

Mrs Verloc spread out with care the scanty tablecloth, got two knives and two forks out of the table drawer, and suddenly stopped in her methodical proceedings.

"What did you do that for?"

"May want it soon," snuffled vaguely Mr Verloc, who was coming to the end of his calculated indiscretions.

"I don't know what you mean," remarked his wife in a tone perfectly casual, but standing stock-still between the table and the cupboard.

"You know you can trust me," Mr Verloc remarked to the grate, with hoarse feeling.

Mrs Verloc turned slowly towards the cupboard, saying with deliberation:

"Oh, yes. I can trust you."

And she went on with her methodical proceedings. She laid two plates, got the bread, the butter, going to and fro quietly between the table and the cupboard in the peace and silence of her home. On the point of taking out the jam, she reflected practically: "He will be feeling hungry, having been away all day," and she returned to the cupboard once more to get the cold beef. She set it under the purring gas-jet, and with a passing glance at her motionless husband hugging the fire, she went (down two steps) into the kitchen. It was only when coming back, carving knife and fork in hand, that she spoke again.

"If I hadn't trusted you I wouldn't have married you."

Bowed under the overmantel, Mr Verloc, holding his head in both hands, seemed to have gone to sleep. Winnie made the tea, and called out in an undertone:

"Adolf."

Mr Verloc got up at once, and staggered a little before he sat down at the table. His wife, examining the sharp edge of the carving knife, placed it on the dish, and called his attention to the cold beef. He remained insensible to the suggestion, with his chin on his breast.

"You should feed your cold," Mrs Verloc said, dogmatically.

He looked up, and shook his head. His eyes were bloodshot and his face red. His fingers had ruffled his hair into a dissipated untidiness. Altogether he had a disreputable aspect, expressive of the discomfort, the irritation, and the gloom following a heavy debauch. But Mr Verloc was not a debauched man. In his conduct he was respectable. His appearance might have been the effect of a feverish cold. He drank three cups of tea, but abstained from food entirely. He recoiled from it with sombre aversion when urged by Mrs Verloc, who said at last:

"Aren't your feet wet? You had better put on your slippers. You aren't going out any more this evening."

Mr Verloc intimated by morose grunts and signs that his feet were not wet, and that anyhow he did not care. The proposal as to slippers was disregarded as beneath his notice. But the question of going out in the evening received an unexpected development. It was not of going out in the evening that Mr Verloc was thinking. His thoughts embraced a vaster scheme. From moody and incomplete phrases it became apparent that Mr Verloc had been considering the expediency of emigrating. It was not very clear whether he had in his mind France or California.

The utter unexpectedness, improbability, and inconceivableness of such an event robbed this vague declaration of all its effect. Mrs Verloc, as placidly as if her husband had been threatening her with the end of the world, said:

"The idea!"

Mr Verloc declared himself sick and tired of everything, and besides—She interrupted him.

"You've a bad cold."

It was indeed obvious that Mr Verloc was not in his usual state, physically or even mentally. A sombre irresolution held him silent for a while. Then he murmured a few ominous generalities on the theme of necessity.

"Will have to," repeated Winnie, sitting calmly back, with folded arms, opposite her husband. "I should like to know who's to make you. You ain't a slave. No one need be a slave in this country—and don't you make yourself one." She paused, and with invincible and steady candour: "The business isn't so bad," she went on. "You've a comfortable home."

She glanced all round the parlour, from the corner cupboard to the good fire in the grate. Ensconced cosily behind the shop of doubtful wares, with the mysteriously dim window, and its door suspiciously ajar in the obscure and narrow street, it was in all essentials of domestic propriety and domestic comfort a respectable home. Her devoted affection missed out of it her brother Stevie, now enjoying a damp villegiature in the Kentish lanes under the care of Mr Michaelis. She missed him poignantly, with all the force of her protecting passion. This was the boy's home, too—the roof, the cupboard, the stoked grate. On this thought Mrs Verloc rose, and walking to the other end of the table, said in the fullness of her heart:

"And you are not tired of me."

Mr Verloc made no sound. Winnie leaned on his shoulder from behind, and pressed her lips to his forehead. Thus she lingered. Not a whisper reached them from the outside world. The sound of footsteps on the pavement died out in the discreet dimness of the shop. Only the gas-jet above the table went on purring equably in the brooding silence of the parlour.

During the contact of that unexpected and lingering kiss Mr Verloc, gripping with both hands the edges of his chair, preserved a hieratic immobility. When the pressure was removed he let go the chair, rose, and went to stand before the fireplace. He turned no longer his back to the room. With his features swollen and an air of being drugged, he followed his wife's movements with his eyes.

Mrs Verloc went about serenely, clearing up the table. Her tranquil voice commented on the idea thrown out in a reasonable and domestic tone. It wouldn't stand examination. She condemned it from every point of view. But her only real concern was Stevie's welfare. He appeared to her thought in that connection as sufficiently "peculiar" not to be taken rashly abroad. And that was all. But talking round that vital point, she approached absolute vehemence in her delivery. Meanwhile, with brusque movements, she arrayed herself in an apron for the washing up of cups. And as if excited by the sound of her uncontradicted voice, she went so far as to say in a tone almost tart:

"If you go abroad you'll have to go without me."

"You know I wouldn't," said Mr Verloc, huskily, and the unresonant voice of his private life trembled with an enigmatical emotion.

Already Mrs Verloc was regretting her words. They had sounded more unkind than she meant them to be. They had also the unwisdom of unnecessary things. In fact, she had not meant them at all. It was a sort of phrase that is suggested by the demon of perverse inspiration. But she knew a way to make it as if it had not been.

She turned her head over her shoulder and gave that man planted heavily in front of the fireplace a glance, half arch, half cruel, out of her large eyes—a glance of which the Winnie of the Belgravian mansion days would have been incapable, because of her respectability and her ignorance. But the man was her husband now, and she was no longer ignorant. She kept it on him for a whole second, with her grave face motionless like a mask, while she said playfully:

"You couldn't. You would miss me too much."

Mr Verloc started forward.

"Exactly," he said in a louder tone, throwing his arms out and making a step towards her. Something wild and doubtful in his expression made it appear uncertain whether he meant to strangle or to embrace his wife. But Mrs Verloc's attention was called away from that manifestation by the clatter of the shop-bell.

"Shop, Adolf. You go."

He stopped, his arms came down slowly.

"You go," repeated Mrs Verloc. "I've got my apron on."

Mr Verloc obeyed woodenly, stony-eyed, and like an automaton whose face had been painted red. And this resemblance to a mechanical figure went so far that he had an automaton's absurd air of being aware of the machinery inside of him.

He closed the parlour door, and Mrs Verloc, moving briskly, carried the tray into the kitchen. She washed the cups and some other things before she stopped in her work to listen. No sound reached her. The customer was a long time in the shop. It was a customer, because if he had not been Mr Verloc would have taken him inside. Undoing the strings of her apron with a jerk, she threw it on a chair, and walked back to the parlour slowly.

At that precise moment Mr Verloc entered from the shop.

He had gone in red. He came out a strange papery white. His face, losing its drugged, feverish stupor, had in that short time acquired a bewildered and harassed expression. He walked straight to the sofa, and stood looking down at his overcoat lying there, as though he were afraid to touch it.

"What's the matter?" asked Mrs Verloc in a subdued voice. Through the door left ajar she could see that the customer was not gone yet.

"I find I'll have to go out this evening," said Mr Verloc. He did not attempt to pick up his outer garment.

Without a word Winnie made for the shop, and shutting the door after her, walked in behind the counter. She did not look overtly at the customer till she had established herself comfortably on the chair. But by that time she had noted that he was tall and thin, and wore his moustaches twisted up. In fact, he gave the sharp points a twist just then. His long, bony face rose out of a turned-up collar. He was a little splashed, a little wet. A dark man, with the ridge of the cheek-bone well defined under the slightly hollow temple. A complete stranger. Not a customer either.

Mrs Verloc looked at him placidly.

"You came over from the Continent?" she said after a time.

The long, thin stranger, without exactly looking at Mrs Verloc, answered only by a faint and peculiar smile.

Mrs Verloc's steady, incurious gaze rested on him.

"You understand English, don't you?"

"Oh yes. I understand English."

There was nothing foreign in his accent, except that he seemed in his slow enunciation to be taking pains with it. And Mrs Verloc, in her varied experience, had come to the conclusion that some foreigners could speak better English than the natives. She said, looking at the door of the parlour fixedly:

"You don't think perhaps of staying in England for good?"

The stranger gave her again a silent smile. He had a kindly mouth and probing eyes. And he shook his head a little sadly, it seemed.

"My husband will see you through all right. Meantime, for a few days you couldn't do better than taking lodgings with Mr Guigliani. Continental Hotel it's called. Private. It's quiet. My husband will take you there."

"A good idea," said the thin, dark man, whose glance had hardened suddenly.

"You knew Mr Verloc before—didn't you? Perhaps in France?"

"I have heard of him," admitted the visitor in his slow, painstaking tone, which yet had a certain curtness of intention.

There was a pause. Then he spoke again, in a far less elaborate manner.

"Your husband has not gone out to wait for me in the street by chance?"

"In the street!" repeated Mrs Verloc, surprised. "He couldn't. There's no other door to the house."

For a moment she sat impassive, then left her seat to go and peep through the glazed door. Suddenly she opened it, and disappeared into the parlour.

Mr Verloc had done no more than put on his overcoat. But why he should remain afterwards leaning over the table propped up on his two arms as though he were feeling giddy or sick, she could not understand. "Adolf," she called out half aloud; and when he had raised himself:

"Do you know that man?" she asked, rapidly.

"I've heard of him," whispered uneasily Mr Verloc, darting a wild glance at the door.

Mrs Verloc's fine, incurious eyes lighted up with a flash of abhorrence.

"One of Karl Yundt's friends—beastly old man."

"No! No!" protested Mr Verloc, busy fishing for his hat. But when he got it from under the sofa he held it as if he did not know the use of a hat.

"Well—he's waiting for you," said Mrs Verloc at last. "I say, Adolf, he ain't one of them Embassy people you have been bothered with of late?"

"Bothered with Embassy people," repeated Mr Verloc, with a heavy start of surprise and fear. "Who's been talking to you of the Embassy people?"

"Yourself."

"I! I! Talked of the Embassy to you!"

Mr Verloc seemed scared and bewildered beyond measure. His wife explained:

"You've been talking a little in your sleep of late, Adolf."

"What—what did I say? What do you know?"

"Nothing much. It seemed mostly nonsense. Enough to let me guess that something worried you."

Mr Verloc rammed his hat on his head. A crimson flood of anger ran over his face.

"Nonsense—eh? The Embassy people! I would cut their hearts out one after another. But let them look out. I've got a tongue in my head."

He fumed, pacing up and down between the table and the sofa, his open overcoat catching against the angles. The red flood of anger ebbed out, and left his face all white, with quivering nostrils. Mrs Verloc, for the purposes of practical existence, put down these appearances to the cold.

"Well," she said, "get rid of the man whoever he is, as soon as you can, and come back home to me. You want looking after for a day or two."

Mr Verloc calmed down, and, with resolution imprinted on his pale face, had already opened the door, when his wife called him back in a whisper:

"Adolf! Adolf!" He came back, startled. "What about that money you drew out?" she asked. "You've got it in your pocket? Hadn't you better—"

Mr Verloc gazed stupidly into the palm of his wife's extended hand for some time before he slapped his brow.

"Money! Yes! Yes! I didn't know what you meant."

He drew out of his breast-pocket a new pigskin pocket-book. Mrs Verloc received it without another word, and stood still till the bell, clattering after Mr Verloc and Mr Verloc's visitor, had quietened down. Only then she peeped in at the amount, drawing the notes out for the purpose. After this inspection she looked round thoughtfully, with an air of mistrust in the silence and solitude of the house. This abode of her married life appeared to her as lonely and unsafe as though it had been situated in the midst of a forest. No receptacle she could think of amongst the solid, heavy furniture seemed other but flimsy and particularly tempting to her conception of a housebreaker. It was an ideal conception, endowed with sublime faculties and a miraculous insight. The till was not to be thought of. It was the first spot a thief would make for. Mrs Verloc, unfastening hastily a couple of hooks, slipped the pocket-book under the bodice of her dress. Having thus disposed of her husband's capital, she was rather glad to hear the clatter of the door-bell, announcing an arrival. Assuming the fixed, unabashed stare and the stony expression reserved for the casual customer, she walked in behind the counter.

A man standing in the middle of the shop was inspecting it with a swift, cool, all-round glance. His eyes ran over the walls, took in the ceiling, noted the floor—all in a moment. The points of a long fair moustache fell below the line of the jaw. He smiled the smile of an old if distant acquaintance, and Mrs Verloc remembered having seen him before. Not a customer. She softened her "customer stare" to mere indifference, and faced him across the counter.

He approached, on his side, confidentially, but not too markedly so.

"Husband at home, Mrs Verloc?" he asked in an easy, full tone.

"No. He's gone out."

"I am sorry for that. I've called to get from him a little private information."

This was the exact truth. Chief Inspector Heat had been all the way home and had even gone so far as to think of getting into his slippers, since practically he was, he told himself, chucked out of that case. He indulged in some scornful and in a few angry thoughts, and found the occupation so unsatisfactory that he resolved to seek relief out of doors. Nothing prevented him paying a friendly call on Mr Verloc, casually as it were. It was in the character of a private citizen that walking out privately he made use of his customary conveyances. Their general direction was towards Mr Verloc's home. Chief Inspector Heat respected his own private character so consistently that he took especial pains to avoid all the police constables on point and patrol duty in the vicinity of Brett Street.

This precaution was much more necessary for a man of his standing than for an obscure Assistant Commissioner. Private Citizen Heat entered the street, manœuvring in a way which in a member of the criminal classes would have been stigmatized as slinking. The piece of cloth picked up in Greenwich was in his pocket. Not that he had the slightest intention of producing it in his private capacity. On the contrary, he wanted to know just what Mr Verloc would be disposed to say voluntarily. He hoped Mr Verloc's talk would be of a nature to incriminate Michaelis. It was a conscientiously professional hope in the main, but not without its moral value. For Chief Inspector Heat was a servant of justice. Finding Mr Verloc from home, he felt disappointed.

"I would wait for him a little if I were sure he wouldn't be long," he said.

Mrs Verloc volunteered no assurance of any kind.

"The information I need is quite private," he repeated. "You understand what I mean? I wonder if you could give me a notion where he's gone to?"

Mrs Verloc shook her head.

"Can't say."

She turned away to range some boxes on the shelves behind the counter. Chief Inspector Heat looked at her thoughtfully for a time.

"I suppose you know who I am?" he said.

Mrs Verloc glanced over her shoulder. Chief Inspector Heat was amazed at her coolness.

"Come! You know I am in the police," he said, sharply.

"I don't trouble my head much about it," Mrs Verloc remarked, returning to the ranging of her boxes.

"My name is Heat. Chief Inspector Heat of the Special Crimes section."

Mrs Verloc adjusted nicely in its place a small cardboard box, and turning round, faced him again, heavy-eyed, with idle hands hanging down. A silence reigned for a time.

"So your husband went out a quarter of an hour ago! And he didn't say when he would be back?"

"He didn't go out alone," Mrs Verloc let fall negligently.

"A friend?"

Mrs Verloc touched the back of her hair. It was in perfect order.

"A stranger who called."

"I see. What sort of man was that stranger? Would you mind telling me?"

Mrs Verloc did not mind. And when Chief Inspector Heat heard of a man dark, thin, with a long face and turned-up moustaches, he gave signs of perturbation, and exclaimed:

"Dash me if I didn't think so! He hasn't lost any time."

He was intensely disgusted in the secrecy of his heart at the unofficial conduct of his immediate chief. But he was not quixotic. He lost all desire to await Mr Verloc's return. What they had gone out for he did not know, but he imagined it possible that they would return together. The case is not followed properly, it's being tampered with, he thought, bitterly.

"I am afraid I haven't time to wait for your husband," he said.

Mrs Verloc received this declaration listlessly. Her detachment had impressed Chief Inspector Heat all along. At this precise moment it whetted his curiosity. Chief Inspector Heat hung in the wind, swayed by his passions like the most private of citizens.

"I think," he said, looking at her steadily, "that you could give me a pretty good notion of what's going on if you liked."

Forcing her fine, inert eyes to return his gaze, Mrs Verloc murmured:

"Going on! What *is* going on?"

"Why, the affair I came to talk about a little with your husband."

That day Mrs Verloc had glanced at a morning paper as usual. But she had not stirred out of doors. The newsboys never invaded Brett Street. It was not a street for their business. And the echo of their cries, drifting along the populous thoroughfares, expired between the dirty brick walls without reaching the threshold of the shop. Her husband had not brought an evening paper home. At any rate she had not seen it. Mrs Verloc knew nothing whatever of any affair. And she said so, with a genuine note of wonder in her quiet voice.

Chief Inspector Heat did not believe for a moment in so much ignorance. Curtly, without amiability, he stated the bare fact.

Mrs Verloc turned away her eyes.

"I call it silly," she pronounced, slowly. She paused. "We ain't downtrodden slaves here."

The Chief Inspector waited watchfully. Nothing more came.

"And your husband didn't mention anything to you when he came home?"

Mrs Verloc simply turned her face from right to left in sign of negation. A languid, baffling silence reigned in the shop. Chief Inspector Heat felt provoked beyond endurance.

"There was another small matter," he began in a detached tone, "which I wanted to speak to your husband about. There came into our hands a—a—what we believe is—a stolen overcoat."

Mrs Verloc, with her mind specially aware of thieves that evening, touched lightly the bosom of her dress.

"We have lost no overcoat," she said, calmly.

"That's funny," continued Private Citizen Heat. "I see you keep a lot of marking ink here—"

He took up a small bottle, and looked at it against the gas-jet in the middle of the shop.

"Purple—isn't it?" he remarked, setting it down again. "As I said, it's strange. Because the overcoat has got a label sewn on the inside with your address written in marking ink."

Mrs Verloc leaned over the counter with a low exclamation.

"That's my brother's, then."

"Where's your brother? Can I see him?" asked the Chief Inspector, briskly. Mrs Verloc leaned a little more over the counter.

"No. He isn't here. I wrote that label myself."

"Where's your brother now?"

"He's been away living with—a friend—in the country."

"The overcoat comes from the country. And what's the name of the friend?"

"Michaelis," confessed Mrs Verloc in an awed whisper.

The Chief Inspector let out a whistle. His eyes snapped.

"Just so. Capital. And your brother now, what's he like—a sturdy, darkish chap—eh?"

"Oh, no," exclaimed Mrs Verloc, fervently. "That must be the thief. Stevie's slight and fair."

"Good," said the Chief Inspector in an approving tone. And while Mrs Verloc, wavering between alarm and wonder, stared at him, he sought for information. Why have the address sewn like this inside the coat? And he heard that the mangled remains he had inspected that morning with extreme repugnance were those of a youth, nervous, absent-minded, peculiar, and also that the woman who was speaking to him had had the charge of that boy since he was a baby.

"Easily excitable?" he suggested.

"Oh, yes. He is. But how did he come to lose his coat—"

Chief Inspector Heat suddenly pulled out a pink newspaper he had bought less than half an hour ago. He was interested in horses. Forced by his calling into an attitude of doubt and suspicion towards his fellow citizens, Chief Inspector Heat relieved the instinct of credulity implanted in the human breast by putting unbounded faith in the sporting prophets of that particular evening publication. Dropping the extra special on to the counter, he plunged his hand again into his pocket, and pulling out the piece of cloth fate had presented him with out of a heap of things that seemed to have been collected in shambles and rag shops, he offered it to Mrs Verloc for inspection.

"I suppose you recognize this?"

She took it mechanically in both her hands. Her eyes seemed to grow bigger as she looked.

"Yes," she whispered, then raised her head, and staggered backward a little.

"Whatever for is it torn out like this?"

The Chief Inspector snatched across the counter the cloth out of her hands, and she sat heavily on the chair. He thought: identification's perfect. And in that moment he had a glimpse into the whole amazing truth. Verloc was the "other man."

"Mrs Verloc," he said, "it strikes me that you know more of this bomb affair than even you yourself are aware of."

Mrs Verloc sat still, amazed, lost in boundless astonishment. What was the connection? And she became so rigid all over that she was not able to turn her head at the clatter of the bell, which caused the private investigator Heat to spin round on his heel. Mr Verloc had shut the door, and for a moment the two men looked at each other.

Mr Verloc, without looking at his wife, walked up to the Chief Inspector, who was relieved to see him return alone.

"You here!" muttered Mr Verloc, heavily. "Who are you after?"

"No one," said Chief Inspector Heat in a low tone. "Look here, I would like a word or two with you."

Mr Verloc, still pale, had brought an air of resolution with him. Still he didn't look at his wife. He said:

"Come in here, then." And he led the way into the parlour.

The door was hardly shut when Mrs Verloc, jumping up from the chair, ran to it as if to fling it open, but instead of doing so fell on her knees, with her ear to the keyhole. The two men must have stopped directly they were through, because she heard plainly the Chief Inspector's voice, though she could not see his finger pressed against her husband's breast emphatically.

"You are the other man, Verloc. Two men were seen entering the park."

And the voice of Mr Verloc said:

"Well, take me now. What's to prevent you? You have the right."

"Oh, no! I know too well who you have been giving yourself away to. He'll have to manage this little affair all by himself. But don't you make a mistake, it's I who found you out."

Then she heard only muttering. Inspector Heat must have been showing to Mr Verloc the piece of Stevie's overcoat, because Stevie's sister, guardian, and protector heard her husband a little louder.

"I never noticed that she had hit upon that dodge."

Again for a time Mrs Verloc heard nothing but murmurs, whose mysteriousness was less nightmarish to her brain than the horrible suggestions of shaped words. Then Chief Inspector Heat, on the other side of the door, raised his voice:

"You must have been mad."

And Mr Verloc's voice answered, with a sort of gloomy fury:

"I have been mad for a month or more, but I am not mad now. It's all over. It shall all come out of my head, and hang the consequences."

There was a silence, and then Private Citizen Heat murmured:

"What's coming out?"

"Everything," exclaimed the voice of Mr Verloc, and than sank very low.

After a while it rose again.

"You have known me for several years now, and you've found me useful, too. You know I was a straight man. Yes, straight."

This appeal to old acquaintance must have been extremely distasteful to the Chief Inspector.

His voice took on a warning note.

"Don't you trust so much to what you have been promised. If I were you I would clear out. I don't think we will run after you."

Mr Verloc was heard to laugh a little.

"Oh, yes; you hope the others will get rid of me for you—don't you? No, no; you don't shake me off now. I have been a straight man to those people too long, and now everything must come out."

"Let it come out, then," the indifferent voice of Chief Inspector Heat assented. "But tell me now how did you get away?"

"I was making for Chesterfield Walk," Mrs Verloc heard her husband's voice, "when I heard the bang. I started running then. Fog. I saw no one till I was past the end of George Street. Don't think I met anyone till then."

"So easy as that!" marvelled the voice of Chief Inspector Heat. "The bang startled you, eh?"

"Yes; it came too soon," confessed the gloomy, husky voice of Mr Verloc.

Mrs Verloc pressed her ear to the keyhole; her lips were blue, her hands cold as ice, and her pale face, in which the two eyes seemed like two black holes, felt to her as if it were enveloped in flames.

On the other side of the door the voices sank very low. She caught words now and then sometimes in her husband's voice, sometimes in the smooth tones of the Chief Inspector. She heard this last say:

"We believe he stumbled against the root of a tree."

There was a husky, voluble murmur, which lasted for some time, and then the Chief Inspector, as if answering some inquiry, spoke emphatically:

"Of course. Blown to small bits: limbs, gravel, clothing, bones, splinters—all mixed up together. I tell you they had to fetch a shovel to gather him up with."

Mrs Verloc sprang suddenly from her crouching position, and stopping her ears, reeled to and fro between the counter and the shelves on the wall towards the chair. Her crazed eyes noted the sporting sheet left by the Chief Inspector, and as she knocked herself against the counter she snatched it up, fell into the chair, tore the optimistic, rosy sheet right across in trying to open it, then flung it on the floor. On the other side of the door, Chief Inspector Heat was saying to Mr Verloc, the secret agent:

"So your defence will be practically a full confession?"

"It will. I am going to tell the whole story."

"You won't be believed as much as you fancy you will."

And the Chief Inspector remained thoughtful. The turn this affair was taking meant the disclosure of many things—the laying waste of fields of knowledge, which, cultivated by a capable man, had a distinct value for the individual and for the society. It was sorry, sorry meddling. It would leave Michaelis unscathed; it would drag to light the Professor's home industry; disorganize the whole system of supervision; make no end of a row in the papers, which, from that point of view, appeared to him by a sudden illumination as invariably written by fools for the reading of imbeciles. Mentally he agreed with the words Mr Verloc let fall at last in answer to his last remark.

"Perhaps not. But it will upset many things. I have been a straight man, and I shall keep straight in this—"

"If they let you," said the Chief Inspector, cynically. "You will be preached to, no doubt, before they put you into the dock. And in the end you may yet get let in for a sentence that will surprise you. I wouldn't trust too much the gentleman who's been talking to you."

Mr Verloc listened, frowning.

"My advice to you is to clear out while you may. I have no instructions. There are some of them," continued Chief Inspector Heat, laying a peculiar stress on the word "them," "who think you are already out of the world."

"Indeed!" Mr Verloc was moved to say. Though since his return from Greenwich he had spent most of his time sitting in the tap-room of an obscure little public-house, he could hardly have hoped for such favourable news.

"That's the impression about you." The Chief Inspector nodded at him. "Vanish. Clear out."

"Where to?" snarled Mr Verloc. He raised his head, and gazing at the closed door of the parlour, muttered feelingly: "I only wish you would take me away tonight. I would go quietly."

"I daresay," assented sardonically the Chief Inspector, following the direction of his glance.

The brow of Mr Verloc broke into slight moisture. He lowered his husky voice confidentially before the unmoved Chief Inspector.

"The lad was half-witted, irresponsible. Any court would have seen that at once. Only fit for the asylum. And that was the worst that would've happened to him if—"

The Chief Inspector, his hand on the door handle, whispered into Mr Verloc's face:

"He may've been half-witted, but you must have been crazy. What drove you off your head like this?"

Mr Verloc, thinking of Mr Vladimir, did not hesitate in the choice of words.

"A Hyperborean swine," he hissed, forcibly. "A what you might call a—gentleman."

The Chief Inspector, steady-eyed, nodded briefly his comprehension, and opened the door. Mrs Verloc, behind the counter, might have heard but did not see his departure, pursued by the aggressive clatter of the bell. She sat at her post of duty behind the counter. She sat rigidly erect in the chair with two dirty pink pieces of paper lying spread out at her feet. The palms of her hands were pressed convulsively to her face, with the tips of the fingers contracted against the forehead, as though the skin had been a mask which she was ready to tear off violently. The perfect immobility of her pose expressed the agitation of rage and despair, all the potential violence of tragic passions, better than any shallow display of shrieks, with the beating of a distracted head against the walls, could have done. Chief Inspector Heat, crossing the shop at his busy, swinging pace, gave her only a cursory glance. And when the cracked bell ceased to tremble on its curved ribbon of steel nothing stirred near Mrs Verloc, as if her attitude had the locking power of a spell. Even the butterfly-shaped gas flames posed on the ends of the suspended T-bracket burned without a quiver. In that shop of shady wares fitted with deal shelves painted a dull brown, which seemed to devour the sheen of the light, the gold circlet of the wedding ring on Mrs Verloc's left hand glittered exceedingly with the untarnished glory of a piece from some splendid treasure of jewels, dropped in a dust-bin.

CHAPTER 10

The Assistant Commissioner, driven rapidly in a hansom from the neighbourhood of Soho in the direction of Westminster, got out at the very centre of the Empire on which the sun never sets. Some stalwart constables, who did not seem particularly impressed by the duty of watching the august spot, saluted him. Penetrating through a portal by no means lofty into the precincts of the House which is *the* House, *par excellence,* in the minds of many millions of men, he was met at last by the volatile and revolutionary Toodles.

That neat and nice young man concealed his astonishment at the early appearance of the Assistant Commissioner, whom he had been told to look out for some time about midnight. His turning up so early he concluded to be the sign that things, whatever they were, had gone wrong. With an extremely ready sympathy, which in nice youngsters goes often with a joyous temperament, he felt sorry for the great Presence he called "The Chief," and also for the Assistant Commissioner, whose face appeared to him more ominously wooden than ever before, and quite wonderfully long. "What a queer, foreign-looking chap he is," he thought to himself, smiling from a distance with friendly buoyancy. And directly they came together he began to talk with the kind intention of burying the awkwardness of failure under a heap of words. It looked as if the great assault threatened for that night were going to fizzle out. An inferior henchman of "that brute Cheeseman" was up boring mercilessly a very thin House with some shamelessly cooked statistics. He, Toodles, hoped he would bore them into a count out every minute. But then he might be only marking time to let that guzzling Cheeseman dine at his leisure. Anyway, the Chief could not be persuaded to go home.

"He will see you at once, I think. He's sitting all alone in his room thinking of all the fishes of the sea," concluded Toodles, airily. "Come along."

Notwithstanding the kindness of his disposition, the young Private Secretary (unpaid) was accessible to the common failings of humanity. He did not wish to harrow the feelings of the Assistant Commissioner, who looked to him uncommonly like a man who has made a mess of his job. But his curiosity was too strong to be restrained by mere compassion. He could not help, as they went along, to throw over his shoulder lightly:

"And your sprat?"

"Got him," answered the Assistant Commissioner with a concision which did not mean to be repellent in the least.

"Good. You've no idea how these great men dislike to be disappointed in small things."

After this profound observation the experienced Toodles seemed to reflect. At any rate he said nothing for quite two seconds. Then:

"I'm glad. But—I say—is it really such a very small thing as you make it out?"

"Do you know what may be done with a sprat?" the Assistant Commissioner asked in his turn.

"He's sometimes put into a sardine box," chuckled Toodles, whose erudition on the subject of the fishing industry was fresh and, in comparison with his ignorance of all other industrial matters, immense. "There are sardine canneries on the Spanish coast which—"

The Assistant Commissioner interrupted the apprentice statesman.

"Yes. Yes. But a sprat is also thrown away sometimes in order to catch a whale."

"A whale. Phew!" exclaimed Toodles, with bated breath. "You're after a whale, then?"

"Not exactly. What I am after is more like a dog-fish. You don't know perhaps what a dog-fish is like."

"Yes; I do. We're buried in special books up to our necks—whole shelves full of them—with plates . . . It's a noxious, rascally looking, altogether detestable beast, with a sort of smooth face and moustaches."

"Described to a T," commended the Assistant Commissioner. "Only mine is clean-shaven altogether. You've seen him. It's a witty fish."

"I have seen him!" said Toodles, incredulously. "I can't conceive where I could have seen him."

"At the Explorers', I should say," dropped the Assistant Commissioner, calmly. At the name of that extremely exclusive club Toodles looked scared, and stopped short.

"Nonsense," he protested, but in an awestruck tone. "What do you mean? A member?"

"Honorary," muttered the Assistant Commissioner through his teeth.

"Heavens!"

Toodles looked so thunderstruck that the Assistant Commissioner smiled faintly.

"That's between ourselves strictly," he said.

"That's the beastliest thing I've ever heard in my life," declared Toodles, feebly, as if astonishment had robbed him of all his buoyant strength in a second.

The Assistant Commissioner gave him an unsmiling glance. Till they came to the door of the great man's room, Toodles preserved a scandalized and solemn silence, as though he were offended with the Assistant Commissioner for exposing such an unsavoury and disturbing fact. It revolutionized his idea of the Explorers' Club's extreme selectness, of its social purity. Toodles was revolutionary only in politics; his social beliefs and personal feelings he wished to preserve unchanged through all the years allotted to him on this earth which, upon the whole, he believed to be a nice place to live on.

He stood aside.

"Go in without knocking," he said.

Shades of green silk fitted low over all the lights imparted to the room something of a forest's deep gloom. The haughty eyes were physically the great man's weak point. This point was wrapped up in secrecy. When an opportunity offered, he rested them conscientiously. The Assistant Commissioner entering saw at first only a big pale hand supporting a big head, and concealing the upper part of a big pale face. An open dispatch-box stood on the writing-table near a few oblong sheets of paper and a scattered handful of quill pens. There was absolutely nothing else on the flat surface except a little bronze statuette draped in a toga, mysteriously watchful in its shadowy immobility. The Assistant Commissioner, invited to take a chair, sat down. In the dim light, the salient points of his personality, the long face, the black hair, his lankiness, made him look more foreign than ever.

The great man manifested no surprise, no eagerness, no sentiment whatever. The attitude in which he rested his menaced eyes was profoundly meditative. He did not alter it the least bit. But his tone was not dreamy.

"Well! What is it that you've found out already? You came upon something unexpected on the first step."

"Not exactly unexpected, Sir Ethelred. What I mainly came upon was a psychological state."

The Great Presence made a slight movement.

"You must be lucid, please."

"Yes, Sir Ethelred. You know no doubt that most criminals at some time or other feel an irresistible need of confessing—of making a clean breast of it to somebody—to anybody. And they do it often to the police. In that Verloc whom Heat wished so much to screen I've found a man in that particular psychological state. The man, figuratively speaking, flung himself on my breast. It was enough on my part to whisper to him who I was and to add 'I know that you are at the bottom of this affair.' It must have seemed miraculous to him that we should know already, but he took it all in the stride. The wonderfulness of it never checked him for a moment. There remained for me only to put to him the two questions: Who put you up to it? and Who was the man who did it? He answered the first with remarkable emphasis. As to the second question, I gather that the fellow with the bomb was his brother-in-law—quite a lad—a weak-minded creature . . . It is rather a curious affair—too long perhaps to state fully just now."

"What then have you learned?" asked the great man.

"First, I've learned that the ex-convict Michaelis had nothing to do with it, though indeed the lad had been living with him temporarily in the country up to eight o'clock this morning. It is more than likely that Michaelis knows nothing of it to this moment."

"You are positive as to that?" asked the great man.

"Quite certain, Sir Ethelred. This fellow Verloc went there this morning, and took away the lad on the pretence of going out for a walk in the lanes. As it was not the first time that he did this, Michaelis could not have the slightest suspicion of anything unusual. For the rest, Sir Ethelred, the indignation of this man Verloc had left nothing in doubt—nothing whatever. He had been driven out of his mind almost by an extraordinary performance, which for you or me it would be difficult to take as seriously meant, but which produced a great impression obviously on him."

The Assistant Commissioner then imparted briefly to the great man, who sat still, resting his eyes under the screen of his hand, Mr Verloc's appreciation of Mr Vladimir's proceedings and character. The Assistant Commissioner did not seem to refuse it a certain amount of competency. But the great personage remarked:

"All this seems very fantastic."

"Doesn't it? One would think a ferocious joke. But our man took it seriously, it appears. He felt himself threatened. Formerly, you know, he was in direct communication with old Stott-Wartenheim himself, and had come to regard his services as indispensable. It was an extremely rude awakening. I imagine that he lost his head. He became angry and frightened. Upon my word, my impression is that he thought these Embassy people quite capable not only to throw him out but to give him away, too, in some manner or other—"

"How long were you with him?" interrupted the Presence from behind his big hand.

"Some forty minutes, Sir Ethelred, in a house of bad repute called Continental Hotel, closeted in a room which by-the-by I took for the night. I found him under the influence of that reaction which follows the effort of crime. The man cannot be defined as a hardened criminal. It is obvious that he did not plan the death of that wretched lad—his brother-in-law. That was a shock to him—I could see that. Perhaps he is a man of strong sensibilities. Perhaps he was even fond of the lad—who knows? He might have hoped that the fellow would get clear away; in which case it would have been almost impossible to bring this thing home to anyone. At any rate, he risked consciously nothing more but arrest for him."

The Assistant Commissioner paused in his speculations to reflect for a moment.

"Though how, in that last case, he could hope to have his own share in the business concealed is more than I can tell," he continued, in his ignorance of poor Stevie's devotion to Mr Verloc (who was *good*), and of his truly peculiar dumbness, which in the old affair of fireworks on the stairs had for many years resisted entreaties, coaxing, anger, and other means of investigation used by his beloved sister. For Stevie was loyal . . . "No, I can't imagine. It's possible that he never thought of that at all. It sounds an extravagant way of putting it, Sir Ethelred, but his state of dismay suggested to me an impulsive man who, after committing suicide with the notion that it would end all his troubles, had discovered that it did nothing of the kind."

The Assistant Commissioner gave this definition in an apologetic voice. But in truth there is a sort of lucidity proper to extravagant language, and the great man was not offended. A slight jerky movement of the big body half lost in the gloom of the green silk shades, of the big head leaning on the big hand, accompanied an intermittent stifled but powerful sound. The great man had laughed.

"What have you done with him?"

The Assistant Commissioner answered very readily:

"As he seemed very anxious to get back to his wife in the shop I let him go, Sir Ethelred."

"You did? But the fellow will disappear."

"Pardon me. I don't think so. Where could he go to? Moreover, you must remember that he has got to think of the danger from his comrades, too. He's there at his post. How could he explain leaving it? But even if there were no obstacles to his freedom of action he would do nothing. At present he hasn't enough moral energy to take a resolution of any sort. Permit me also to point out that if I had detained him we would have been committed to a course of action on which I wished to know your precise intentions first."

The great personage rose heavily, an imposing, shadowy form in the greenish gloom of the room.

"I'll see the Attorney-General tonight, and will send for you tomorrow morning. Is there anything more you'd wish to tell me now?"

The Assistant Commissioner had stood up also, slender and flexible.

"I think not, Sir Ethelred, unless I were to enter into details which—"

"No. No details, please."

The great shadowy form seemed to shrink away as if in physical dread of details; then came forward, expanded, enormous, and weighty, offering a large hand. "And you say that this man has got a wife?"

"Yes, Sir Ethelred," said the Assistant Commissioner, pressing deferentially the extended hand. "A genuine wife and a genuinely, respectably, marital relation. He told me that after his interview at the Embassy he would have thrown everything up, would have tried to sell his shop, and leave the country, only he felt certain that his wife would not even hear of going abroad. Nothing could be more characteristic of the respectable bond than that," went on, with a touch of grimness, the Assistant Commissioner, whose own wife, too, had refused to hear of going abroad. "Yes, a genuine wife. And the victim was a genuine brother-in-law. From a certain point of view we are here in the presence of a domestic drama."

The Assistant Commissioner laughed a little; but the great man's thoughts seemed to have wandered far away, perhaps to the questions of his country's domestic policy, the battleground of his crusading valour against the paynim Cheeseman. The Assistant Commissioner withdrew quietly, unnoticed, as if already forgotten.

He had his own crusading instincts. This affair, which, in one way or another, disgusted Chief Inspector Heat, seemed to him a providentially given starting-point for a crusade. He had it much at heart to begin. He walked slowly home, meditating that enterprise on the way, and thinking over Mr Verloc's psychology in a composite mood of repugnance and satisfaction. He walked all the way home. Finding the drawing-room dark, he went upstairs, and spent some time between the bedroom and the dressing-room, changing his clothes, going to and fro with the air of a thoughtful somnambulist. But he shook it off before going out again to join his wife at the house of the great lady patroness of Michaelis.

He knew he would be welcomed there. On entering the smaller of the two drawing-rooms he saw his wife in a small group near the piano. A youngish composer in pass of becoming famous was discoursing from a music stool to two thick men whose backs looked old, and three slender women whose backs looked young. Behind the screen the great lady had only two persons with her: a man and a woman, who sat side by side on armchairs at the foot of her couch. She extended her hand to the Assistant Commissioner.

"I never hoped to see you here tonight. Annie told me—"

"Yes. I had no idea myself that my work would be over so soon."

The Assistant Commissioner added in a low tone: "I am glad to tell you that Michaelis is altogether clear of this—"

The patroness of the ex-convict received this assurance indignantly.

"Why? Were your people stupid enough to connect him with—"

"Not stupid," interrupted the Assistant Commissioner, contradicting deferentially. "Clever enough—quite clever enough for that."

A silence fell. The man at the foot of the couch had stopped speaking to the lady, and looked on with a faint smile.

"I don't know whether you ever met before," said the great lady.

Mr Vladimir and the Assistant Commissioner, introduced, acknowledged each other's existence with punctilious and guarded courtesy.

"He's been frightening me," declared suddenly the lady who sat by the side of Mr Vladimir, with an inclination of the head towards that gentleman. The Assistant Commissioner knew the lady.

"You do not look frightened," he pronounced, after surveying her conscientiously with his tired and equable gaze. He was thinking meantime to himself that in this house one met everybody sooner or later. Mr Vladimir's rosy countenance was wreathed in smiles, because he was witty, but his eyes remained serious, like the eyes of convinced man.

"Well, he tried to at least," amended the lady.

"Force of habit perhaps," said the Assistant Commissioner, moved by an irresistible inspiration.

"He has been threatening society with all sorts of horrors," continued the lady, whose enunciation was caressing and slow, "apropos of this explosion in Greenwich Park. It appears we all ought to quake in our shoes at what's coming if those people are not suppressed all over the world. I had no idea this was such a grave affair."

Mr Vladimir, affecting not to listen, leaned towards the couch, talking amiably in subdued tones, but he heard the Assistant Commissioner say:

"I've no doubt that Mr Vladimir has a very precise notion of the true importance of this affair."

Mr Vladimir asked himself what that confounded and intrusive policeman was driving at. Descended from generations victimized by the instruments of an arbitrary power, he was racially, nationally, and individually afraid of the police. It was an inherited weakness, altogether independent of his judgement, of his reason, of his experience. He was born to it. But that sentiment, which resembled the irrational horror some people have of cats, did not stand in the way of his immense contempt for the English police. He finished the sentence addressed to the great lady, and turned slightly in his chair.

"You mean that we have a great experience of these people. Yes; indeed, we suffer greatly from their activity, while you"—Mr Vladimir hesitated for a moment, in smiling perplexity—"While you suffer their presence gladly in your midst," he finished, displaying a dimple in each clean-shaven cheek. Then he added more gravely: "I may even say—because you do."

When Mr Vladimir ceased speaking the Assistant Commissioner lowered his glance, and the conversation dropped. Almost immediately afterwards Mr Vladimir took leave. Directly his back was turned on the couch the Assistant Commissioner rose, too.

"I thought you were going to stay and take Annie home," said the lady patroness of Michaelis.

"I find that I've yet a little work to do tonight."

"In connection—"

"Well, yes—in a way."

"Tell me, what is it really—this horror?"

"It's difficult to say what it is, but it may yet be a *cause célèbre,*" said the Assistant Commissioner.

He left the drawing-room hurriedly, and found Mr Vladimir still in the hall, wrapping up his throat carefully in a large silk handkerchief. Behind him a footman waited, holding his overcoat. Another stood ready to open the door. The Assistant Commissioner was duly helped into his coat, and let out at once. After descending the front steps he stopped, as if to consider the way he should take. On seeing this through the door held open, Mr Vladimir lingered in the hall to get out a cigar and asked for a light. It was furnished to him by an elderly man out of livery with an air of calm solicitude. But the match went out; the footman then closed the door, and Mr Vladimir lighted his large Havana with leisurely care. When at last he got out of the house, he saw with disgust the "confounded policeman" still standing on the pavement.

"Can he be waiting for me," thought Mr Vladimir, looking up and down for some signs of a hansom. He saw none. A couple of carriages waited by the kerbstone, their lamps blazing steadily, the horses standing perfectly still, as if carved in stone, the coachmen sitting motionless under the big fur capes, without as much as a quiver stirring the white thongs of their big whips. Mr Vladimir walked on, and the "confounded policeman" fell into step at his elbow. He said nothing. At the end of the fourth stride Mr Vladimir felt infuriated and uneasy. This could not last.

"Rotten weather," he growled, savagely.

"Mild," said the Assistant Commissioner without passion. He remained silent for a little while. "We've got hold of a man called Verloc," he announced, casually.

Mr Vladimir did not stumble, did not stagger back, did not change his stride. But he could not prevent himself from exclaiming: "What?"

The Assistant Commissioner did not repeat his statement. "You know him," he went on in the same tone.

Mr Vladimir stopped, and became guttural.

"What makes you say that?"

"I don't. It's Verloc who says that."

"A lying dog of some sort," said Mr Vladimir in somewhat Oriental phraseology. But in his heart he was almost awed by the miraculous cleverness of the English police. The change of his opinion on the subject was so violent that it made him for a moment feel slightly sick. He threw away his cigar, and moved on.

"What pleased me most in this affair," the Assistant Commissioner went on, talking slowly, "is that it makes such an excellent starting-point for a piece of work which I've felt must be taken in hand—that is, the clearing out of this country of all the foreign political spies, police, and that sort of—of—dogs. In my opinion they are a ghastly nuisance; also an element of danger. But we can't very well seek them out individually. The only way is to make their employment unpleasant to their employers. The thing's becoming indecent. And dangerous, too, for us, here."

Mr Vladimir stopped again for a moment.

"What do you mean?"

"The prosecution of this Verloc will demonstrate to the public both the danger and the indecency."

"Nobody will believe what a man of that sort says," said Mr Vladimir, contemptuously.

"The wealth and precision of detail will carry conviction to the great mass of the public," advanced the Assistant Commissioner gently.

"So that is seriously what you mean to do."

"We've got the man; we have no choice."

"You will be only feeding up the lying spirit of these revolutionary scoundrels," Mr Vladimir protested. "What do you want to make a scandal for?—from morality—or what?"

Mr Vladimir's anxiety was obvious. The Assistant Commissioner, having ascertained in this way that there must be some truth in the summary statements of Mr Verloc, said indifferently:

"There's a practical side, too. We have really enough to do to look after the genuine article. You can't say we are not effective. But we don't intend to let ourselves be bothered by shams under any pretext whatever."

Mr Vladimir's tone became lofty.

"For my part, I can't share your view. It is selfish. My sentiments for my own country cannot be doubted; but I've always felt that we ought to be good Europeans besides—I mean governments and men."

"Yes," said the Assistant Commissioner simply. "Only you look at Europe from its other end. But," he went on in a good-natured tone, "the foreign governments cannot complain of the inefficiency of our police. Look at this outrage; a case specially difficult to trace inasmuch as it was a sham. In less than twelve hours we have established the identity of a man literally blown to shreds, have found the organizer of the attempt, and have had a glimpse of the inciter behind him. And we could have gone further; only we stopped at the limits of our territory."

"So this instructive crime was planned abroad," Mr Vladimir said, quickly. "You admit it was planned abroad?"

"Theoretically. Theoretically only, on foreign territory; abroad only by a fiction," said the Assistant Commissioner, alluding to the character of Embassies which are supposed to be part and parcel of the country to which they belong. "But that's a detail. I talked to you of this business because it's your government that grumbles most at our police. You see that we are not so bad. I wanted particularly to tell you of our success."

"I'm sure I'm very grateful," muttered Mr Vladimir through his teeth.

"We can put our finger on every anarchist here," went on the Assistant Commissioner, as though he were quoting Chief Inspector Heat. "All that's wanted now is to do away with the *agent provocateur* to make everything safe."

Mr Vladimir held up his hand to a passing hansom.

"You're not going in here," remarked the Assistant Commissioner, looking at a building of noble proportions and hospitable aspect, with the light of a great hall falling through its glass doors on a broad flight of steps.

But Mr Vladimir, sitting, stony-eyed, inside the hansom, drove off without a word.

The Assistant Commissioner himself did not turn into the noble building. It was the Explorers' Club. The thought passed through his mind that Mr Vladimir, honorary member, would not be seen very often there in the future. He looked at his watch. It was only half past ten. He had had a very full evening.

CHAPTER 11

After Chief Inspector Heat had left him Mr Verloc moved about the parlour. From time to time he eyed his wife through the open door. "She knows all about it now," he thought to himself with commiseration for her sorrow and with some satisfaction as regarded himself. Mr Verloc's soul, if lacking greatness perhaps, was capable of tender sentiments. The prospects of having to break the news to her had put him into a fever. Chief Inspector Heat had relieved him of the task. That was good as far as it went. It remained for him now to face her grief.

Mr Verloc had never expected to have to face it on account of death, whose catastrophic character cannot be argued away by sophisticated reasoning or persuasive eloquence. Mr Verloc never meant Stevie to perish with such abrupt violence. He did not mean him to perish at all. Stevie dead was a much greater nuisance than ever he had been when alive. Mr Verloc had augured a favourable issue to his enterprise, basing himself not on Stevie's intelligence, which sometimes plays queer tricks with a man, but on the blind docility and on the blind devotion of the boy. Though not much of a psychologist, Mr Verloc had gauged the depth of Stevie's fanaticism. He dared cherish the hope of Stevie walking away from the walls of the Observatory as he had been instructed to do, taking the way shown to him several times previously, and rejoining his brother-in-law, the wise and good Mr Verloc, outside the precincts of the park. Fifteen minutes ought to have been enough for the veriest fool to deposit the engine and walk away. And the Professor had guaranteed more than fifteen minutes. But Stevie had stumbled within five minutes of being left to himself. And Mr Verloc was shaken morally to pieces. He had foreseen everything but that. He had foreseen Stevie distracted and lost—sought for—found in some police station or provincial workhouse in the end. He had foreseen Stevie arrested, and was not afraid, because Mr Verloc had a great opinion of Stevie's loyalty, which had been carefully indoctrinated with the necessity of silence in the course of many walks. Like a peripatetic philosopher, Mr Verloc, strolling along the streets of London, had modified Stevie's view of the police by conversations full of subtle reasonings. Never had a sage a more attentive and admiring disciple. The submission and worship were so apparent that Mr Verloc had come to feel something like a liking for the boy. In any case, he had not foreseen the swift bringing home of his connection. That his wife should hit upon the precaution of sewing the boy's address inside his overcoat was the last thing Mr Verloc would have thought of. One can't think of everything. That was what she meant when she said that he need not worry if he lost Stevie during their walks. She had assured him that the boy would turn up all right. Well, he had turned up with a vengeance!

"Well, well," muttered Mr Verloc in his wonder. What did she mean by it? Spare him the trouble of keeping an anxious eye on Stevie? Most likely she had meant well. Only she ought to have told him of the precaution she had taken.

Mr Verloc walked behind the counter of the shop. His intention was not to overwhelm his wife with bitter reproaches. Mr Verloc felt no bitterness. The unexpected march of events had converted him to the doctrine of fatalism. Nothing could be helped now. He said:

"I didn't mean any harm to come to the boy."

Mrs Verloc shuddered at the sound of her husband's voice. She did not uncover her face. The trusted secret agent of the late Baron Stott-Wartenheim looked at her for a time with a heavy, persistent, undiscerning glance. The torn evening paper was lying at her feet. It could not have told her much. Mr Verloc felt the need of talking to his wife.

"It's that damned Heat—eh?" he said. "He upset you. He's a brute, blurting it out like this to a woman. I made myself ill thinking of how to break it to you. I sat for hours in the little parlour of the Cheshire Cheese thinking over the best way. You understand I never meant any harm to come to that boy."

Mr Verloc, the secret agent, was speaking the truth. It was his marital affection that had received the greatest shock from the premature explosion. He added:

"I didn't feel particularly gay sitting there and thinking of you."

He observed another slight shudder of his wife, which affected his sensibility. As she persisted in hiding her face in her hands, he thought he had better leave her alone for a while. On this delicate impulse Mr Verloc withdrew into the parlour again, where the gas-jet purred like a contented cat. Mrs Verloc's wifely forethought had left the cold beef on the table with carving knife and fork and half a loaf of bread for Mr Verloc's supper. He noticed all these things now for the first time, and cutting himself a piece of bread and meat, began to eat.

His appetite did not proceed from callousness. Mr Verloc had not eaten any breakfast that day. He had left his home fasting. Not being an energetic man, he found his resolution in nervous excitement, which seemed to hold him mainly by the throat. He could not have swallowed anything solid. Michaelis's cottage was as destitute of provisions as the cell of a prisoner. The ticket-of-leave apostle lived on a little milk and crusts of stale bread. Moreover, when Mr Verloc arrived he had already gone upstairs after his frugal meal. Absorbed in the toil and delight of literary composition, he had not even answered Mr Verloc's shout up the little staircase.

"I am taking this young fellow home for a day or two."

And, in truth, Mr Verloc did not wait for an answer, but had marched out of the cottage at once, followed by the obedient Stevie.

Now that all action was over and his fate taken out of his hands with unexpected swiftness, Mr Verloc felt terribly empty physically. He carved the meat, cut the bread, and devoured his supper standing by the table, and now and then casting a glance towards his wife. Her prolonged immobility disturbed the comfort of his reflection. He walked again into the shop, and came up very close to her. This sorrow with a veiled face made Mr Verloc uneasy. He expected, of course, his wife to be very much upset, but he wanted her to pull herself together. He needed all her assistance and all her loyalty in these new conjectures his fatalism had already accepted.

"Can't be helped," he said in a tone of gloomy sympathy. "Come, Winnie, we've got to think of tomorrow. You'll want all your wits about you after I am taken away."

He paused. Mrs Verloc's breast heaved convulsively. This was not reassuring to Mr Verloc, in whose view the newly created situation required from the two people most concerned in it calmness, decision, and other qualities incompatible with the mental disorder of passionate sorrow. Mr Verloc was a humane man; he had come home prepared to allow every latitude to his wife's affection for her brother. Only he did not understand either the nature or the whole extent of that sentiment. And in this he was excusable, since it was impossible for him to understand it without ceasing to be himself. He was startled and disappointed, and his speech conveyed it by a certain roughness of tone.

"You might look at a fellow," he observed after waiting a while.

As if forced through the hands covering Mrs Verloc's face the answer came, deadened, almost pitiful.

"I don't want to look at you as long as I live."

"Eh? What!" Mr Verloc was merely startled by the superficial and literal meaning of this declaration. It was obviously unreasonable, the mere cry of exaggerated grief. He threw over it the mantle of his marital indulgence. The mind of Mr Verloc lacked profundity. Under the mistaken impression that the value of individuals consists in what they are in themselves, he could not possibly comprehend the value of Stevie in the eyes of Mrs Verloc. She was taking it confoundedly hard, he thought to himself. It was all the fault of that damned Heat. What did he want to upset the woman for? But she mustn't be allowed, for her own good, to carry on so till she got quite beside herself.

"Look here! You can't sit like this in the shop," he said with affected severity, in which there was some real annoyance; for urgent practical matters must be talked over if they had to sit up all night. "Somebody might come in at any minute," he added, and waited again. No effect was produced, and the idea of the finality of death occurred to Mr Verloc during the pause. He changed his tone. "Come. This won't bring him back," he said, gently, feeling ready to take her in his arms and press her to his breast, where impatience and compassion dwelt side by side. But except for a short shudder Mrs Verloc remained apparently unaffected by the force of that terrible truism. It was Mr Verloc himself who was moved. He was moved in his simplicity to urge moderation by asserting the claims of his own personality.

"Do be reasonable, Winnie. What would it have been if you had lost me?"

He had vaguely expected to hear her cry out. But she did not budge. She leaned back a little, quieted down to a complete, unreadable stillness. Mr Verloc's heart began to beat faster with exasperation and something resembling alarm. He laid his hand on her shoulder, saying:

"Don't be a fool, Winnie."

She gave no sign. It was impossible to talk to any purpose with a woman whose face one cannot see. Mr Verloc caught hold of his wife's wrists. But her hands seemed glued fast. She swayed forward bodily to his tug, and nearly went off the chair. Startled to feel her so helplessly limp, he was trying to put her back on the chair when she stiffened suddenly all over, tore herself out of his hands, ran out of the shop, across the parlour and into the kitchen. This was very swift. He had just a glimpse of her face and that much of her eyes that he knew she had not looked at him.

It all had the appearance of a struggle for the possession of a chair, because Mr Verloc instantly took his wife's place in it. Mr Verloc did not cover his face with his hands, but a sombre thoughtfulness veiled his features. A term of imprisonment could not be avoided. He did not wish now to avoid it. A prison was a place as safe from certain unlawful vengeances as the grave, with this advantage, that in prison there is room for hope. What he saw before him was a term of imprisonment, an early release, and then life abroad somewhere, such as he had contemplated already, in case of failure. Well, it was a failure, if not exactly the sort of failure he had feared. It had been so near success that he could have positively terrified Mr Vladimir out of his ferocious scoffing with this proof of occult efficiency. So at least it seemed now to Mr Verloc. His prestige with the Embassy would have been immense if—if his wife had not had the unlucky notion of sewing on the address inside Stevie's overcoat. Mr Verloc, who was no fool, had soon perceived the extraordinary character of the influence he had over Stevie though he did not understand exactly its origin—the doctrine of his supreme wisdom and goodness inculcated by two anxious women. In all the eventualities he had foreseen Mr Verloc had calculated with correct insight on Stevie's instinctive loyalty and blind discretion. The eventuality he had not foreseen had appalled him as a humane man and a fond husband. From every other point of view it was rather advantageous. Nothing can equal the everlasting discretion of death. Mr Verloc, sitting perplexed and frightened in the small parlour of the Cheshire Cheese, could not help acknowledging that to himself, because his sensibility did not stand in the way of his judgement. Stevie's violent disintegration, however disturbing to think about, only assured the success; for, of course, the knocking down of a wall was not the aim of Mr Vladimir's menaces, but the production of a moral effect. With much trouble and distress on Mr Verloc's part the effect might be said to have been produced. When, however, most unexpectedly, it came home to roost in Brett Street, Mr Verloc, who had been struggling like a man in a nightmare for the preservation of his position, accepted the blow in the spirit of a convinced fatalist. The position was gone through no one's fault really. A small, tiny fact had done it. It was like slipping on a bit of orange peel in the dark and breaking your leg.

Mr Verloc drew a weary breath. He nourished no resentment against his wife. He thought: "She will have to look after the shop while they keep me locked up." And thinking also how cruelly she would miss Stevie at first, he felt greatly concerned about her health and spirits. How would she stand her solitude—absolutely alone in that house? It would not do for her to break down while he was locked up. What would become of the shop then? The shop was an asset. Though Mr Verloc's fatalism accepted his undoing as a secret agent, he had no mind to be utterly ruined, mostly, it must be owned, from regard for his wife.

Silent, and out of his line of sight in the kitchen, she frightened him. If only she had her mother with her. But that silly old woman—An angry dismay possessed Mr Verloc. He must talk with his wife. He could tell her certainly that a man does get desperate under certain circumstances. But he did not go incontinently to impart to her that information. First of all, it was clear to him that this evening was no time for business. He got up to close the street door and put the gas out in the shop.

Having thus assured a solitude around his hearth-stone Mr Verloc walked into the parlour, and glanced down into the kitchen. Mrs Verloc was sitting in the place where poor Stevie usually established himself of an evening with paper and pencil for the pastime of drawing those coruscations of innumerable circles suggesting chaos and eternity. Her arms were folded on the table, and her head was lying on her arms. Mr Verloc contemplated her back and the arrangement of her hair for a time, then walked away from the kitchen door. Mrs Verloc's philosophical, almost disdainful incuriosity, the foundation of their accord in domestic life, made it extremely difficult to get into contact with her, now this tragic necessity had arisen. Mr Verloc felt this difficulty acutely. He turned around the table in the parlour with his usual air of a large animal in a cage.

Curiosity being one of the forms of self-revelation, a systematically incurious person remains always partly mysterious. Every time he passed near the door Mr Verloc glanced at his wife uneasily. It was not that he was afraid of her. Mr Verloc imagined himself loved by that woman. But she had not accustomed him to make confidences. And the confidence he had to make was of a profound psychological order. How with his want of practice could he tell her what he himself felt but vaguely: that there are conspiracies of fatal destiny, that a notion grows in a mind sometimes till it acquires an outward existence, an independent power of its own, and even a suggestive voice? He could not inform her that a man may be haunted by a fat, witty, clean-shaved face till the wildest expedient to get rid of it appears a child of wisdom.

On this mental reference to a First Secretary of a great Embassy, Mr Verloc stopped in the doorway, and looking down into the kitchen with an angry face and clenched fists, addressed his wife.

"You don't know what a brute I had to deal with."

He started off to make another perambulation of the table, then when he had come to the door again he stopped, glaring in from the height of two steps.

"A silly, jeering, dangerous brute, with no more sense than— After all these years! A man like me! And I have been playing my head at that game. You didn't know. Quite right, too. What was the good of telling you that I stood the risk of having a knife stuck into me any time these seven years we've been married? I am not a chap to worry a woman that's fond of me. You had no business to know."

Mr Verloc took another turn round the parlour, fuming.

"A venomous beast," he began again from the doorway. "Drive me out into a ditch to starve for a joke. I could see he thought it was a damned good joke. A man like me! Look here! Some of the highest in the world got to thank me for walking on their two legs to this day. That's the man you've got married to, my girl!"

He perceived that his wife had sat up. Mrs Verloc's arms remained lying stretched on the table. Mr Verloc watched her back as if he could read there the effect of his words.

"There isn't a murdering plot for the last eleven years that I hadn't my finger in at the risk of my life. There's scores of these revolutionists I've sent off with their bombs in their blamed pockets, to get themselves caught on the frontier. The old Baron knew what I was worth to his country. And here suddenly a swine comes along—an ignorant, overbearing swine."

Mr Verloc, stepping slowly down two steps, entered the kitchen, took a tumbler off the dresser, and holding it in his hand, approached the sink, without looking at his wife.

"It wasn't the old Baron who would have had the wicked folly of getting me to call on him at eleven in the morning. There are two or three in this town that, if they had seen me going in, would have made no bones about knocking me on the head sooner or later. It was a silly, murderous trick to expose for nothing a man—like me."

Mr Verloc, turning on the tap above the sink, poured three glasses of water, one after another, down his throat to quench the fires of his indignation. Mr Vladimir's conduct was like a hot brand which set his internal economy in a blaze. He could not get over the disloyalty of it. This man, who would not work at the usual hard tasks which society sets to its humbler members, had exercised his secret industry with an indefatigable devotion. There was in Mr Verloc a fund of loyalty. He had been loyal to his employers, to the cause of social stability—and to his affections, too—as became apparent when, after standing the tumbler in the sink, he turned about, saying:

"If I hadn't thought of you I would have taken the bullying brute by the throat and rammed his head into the fireplace. I'd have been more than a match for that pink-faced, smooth-shaved—"

Mr Verloc neglected to finish the sentence, as if there could be no doubt of the terminal word. For the first time in his life he was taking that incurious woman into his confidence. The singularity of the event, the force and importance of the personal feelings aroused in the course of this confession, drove Stevie's fate clean out of Mr Verloc's mind. The boy's stuttering existence of fears and indignations, together with the violence of his end, had passed out of Mr Verloc's mental sight for a time. For that reason, when he looked up he was startled by the inappropriate character of his wife's stare. It was not a wild stare, and it was not inattentive, but its attention was peculiar and not satisfactory, inasmuch that it seemed concentrated upon some point beyond Mr Verloc's person. The impression was so strong that Mr Verloc glanced over his shoulder. There was nothing behind him: there was just the whitewashed wall. The excellent husband of Winnie Verloc saw no writing on the wall. He turned to his wife again, repeating, with some emphasis:

"I would have taken him by the throat. As true as I stand here, if I hadn't thought of you then I would have half choked the life out of the brute before I let him get up. And don't you think he would have been anxious to call the police—either. He wouldn't have dared. You understand why—don't you?"

He blinked at his wife knowingly.

"No," said Mrs Verloc in an unresonant voice, and without looking at him at all. "What are you talking about?"

A great discouragement, the result of fatigue, came upon Mr Verloc. He had had a very full day, and his nerves had been tried to the utmost. After a month of maddening worry, ending in an unexpected catastrophe, the storm-tossed spirit of Mr Verloc longed for repose. His career as a secret agent had come to an end in a way no one could have foreseen; only, now, perhaps he could manage to get a night's sleep at last. But looking at his wife, he doubted it. She was taking it very hard—not at all like herself, he thought. He made an effort to speak.

"You'll have to pull yourself together, my girl," he said, sympathetically. "What's done can't be undone."

Mrs Verloc gave a slight start, though not a muscle of her white face moved in the least. Mr Verloc, who was not looking at her, continued ponderously:

"You go to bed now. What you want is a good cry."

This opinion had nothing to recommend it but the general consent of mankind. It is universally understood that, as if it were nothing more substantial than vapour floating in the sky, every emotion of a woman is bound to end in a shower. And it is very probable that had Stevie died in his bed under her despairing gaze, in her protecting arms, Mrs Verloc's grief would have found relief in a flood of bitter and pure tears. Mrs Verloc, in common with other human beings, was provided with a fund of unconscious resignation sufficient to meet the normal manifestation of human destiny. Without "troubling her head about it," she was aware that it "did not stand looking into very much." But the lamentable circumstances of Stevie's end, which to Mr Verloc's mind had only an episodic character, as part of a greater disaster, dried her tears at their very source. It was the effect of a white-hot iron drawn across her eyes; at the same time her heart, hardened and chilled into a lump of ice, kept her body in an inward shudder, set her features into a frozen, contemplative immobility addressed to a whitewashed wall with no writing on it. The exigencies of Mrs Verloc's temperament, which, when stripped of its philosophical reserve, was maternal and violent, forced her to roll a series of thoughts in her motionless head. These thoughts were rather imagined than expressed. Mrs Verloc was a woman of singularly few words, either for public or private use. With the rage and dismay of a betrayed woman, she reviewed the tenor of her life in visions concerned mostly with Stevie's difficult existence from its earliest days. It was a life of single purpose and of a noble unity of inspiration, like those rare lives that have left their mark on the thoughts and feelings of mankind. But the visions of Mrs Verloc lacked nobility and magnificence. She saw herself putting the boy to bed by the light of a single candle on the deserted top floor of a "business house," dark under the roof and scintillating exceedingly with lights and cut glass at the level of the street like a fairy palace. That meretricious splendour was the only one to be met in Mrs Verloc's visions. She remembered brushing the boy's hair and tying his pinafores—herself in a pinafore still; the consolations administered to a small and badly scared creature by another creature nearly as small but not quite so badly scared; she had the vision of the blows intercepted (often with her own head), of a door held desperately shut against a man's rage (not for very long); of a poker flung once (not very far), which stilled that particular storm into the dumb and awful silence which follows a thunder-clap. And all these scenes of violence came and went accompanied by the unrefined noise of deep vociferations proceeding from a man wounded in his paternal pride, declaring himself obviously accursed since one of his kids was a "slobbering idjut and the other a wicked she-devil." It was of her that this had been said many years ago.

Mrs Verloc heard the words again in a ghostly fashion, and then the dreary shadow of the Belgravian mansion descended upon her shoulders. It was a crushing memory, an exhausting vision of countless breakfast trays carried up and down innumerable stairs, of endless haggling over pence, of the endless drudgery of sweeping, dusting, cleaning, from basement to attics; while the impotent mother, staggering on swollen legs, cooked in a grimy kitchen, and poor Stevie, the unconscious presiding genius of all their toil, blacked the gentlemen's boots in the scullery. But this vision had a breath of a hot London summer in it, and for a central figure a young man wearing his Sunday best, with a straw hat on his dark head and a wooden pipe in his mouth. Affectionate and jolly, he was a fascinating companion for a voyage down the sparkling stream of life; only his boat was very small. There was room in it for a girl-partner at the oar, but no accommodation for passengers. He was allowed to drift away from the threshold of the Belgravian mansion while Winnie averted her tearful eyes. He was not a lodger. The lodger was Mr Verloc, indolent and keeping late hours, sleepily jocular of a morning from under his bedclothes, but with gleams of infatuation in his heavy-lidded eyes, and always with some money in his pockets. There was no sparkle of any kind on the lazy stream of his life. It flowed through secret places. But his barque seemed a roomy craft, and his taciturn magnanimity accepted as a matter of course the presence of passengers.

Mrs Verloc pursued the visions of seven years' security for Stevie loyally paid for on her part; of security growing into confidence, into a domestic feeling, stagnant and deep like a placid pool, whose guarded surface hardly shuddered on the occasional passage of Comrade Ossipon, the robust anarchist with shamelessly inviting eyes, whose glance had a corrupt clearness sufficient to enlighten any woman not absolutely imbecile.

A few seconds only had elapsed since the last word had been uttered aloud in the kitchen, and Mrs Verloc was staring already at the vision of an episode not more than a fortnight old. With eyes whose pupils were extremely dilated she stared at the vision of her husband and poor Stevie walking up Brett Street side by side away from the shop. It was the last scene of an existence created by Mrs Verloc's genius; an existence foreign to all grace and charm, without beauty and almost without decency, but admirable in the continuity of feeling and tenacity of purpose. And this last vision had such plastic relief, such nearness of form, such a fidelity of suggestive detail, that it wrung from Mrs Verloc an anguished and faint murmur, reproducing the supreme illusion of her life, an appalled murmur that died out on her blanched lips.

"Might have been father and son."

Mr Verloc stopped, and raised a careworn face. "Eh? What did you say?" he asked. Receiving no reply, he resumed his sinister tramping. Then with a menacing flourish of a thick, fleshy fist, he burst out:

"Yes. The Embassy people. A pretty lot, ain't they! Before a week's out I'll make some of them wish themselves twenty feet under ground. Eh? What?"

He glanced sideways, with his head down. Mrs Verloc gazed at the whitewashed wall. A blank wall—perfectly blank. A blankness to run at and dash your head against. Mrs Verloc remained immovably seated. She kept still as the population of half the globe would keep still in astonishment and despair, were the sun suddenly put out in the summer sky by the perfidy of a trusted providence.

"The Embassy," Mr Verloc began again, after a preliminary grimace which bared his teeth wolfishly. "I wish I could get loose in there with a cudgel for half an hour. I would keep on hitting till there wasn't a single unbroken bone left amongst the whole lot. But never mind, I'll teach them yet what it means trying to throw out a man like me to rot in the streets. I've a tongue in my head.

All the world shall know what I've done for them. I am not afraid. I don't care. Everything'll come out. Every damned thing. Let them look out!"

In these terms did Mr Verloc declare his thirst for revenge. It was a very appropriate revenge. It was in harmony with the promptings of Mr Verloc's genius. It had also the advantage of being within the range of his powers and of adjusting itself easily to the practice of his life, which had consisted precisely in betraying the secret and unlawful proceedings of his fellow men. Anarchists or diplomats were all one to him. Mr Verloc was temperamentally no respecter of persons. His scorn was equally distributed over the whole field of his operations. But as a member of a revolutionary proletariat—which he undoubtedly was—he nourished a rather inimical sentiment against social distinction.

"Nothing on earth can stop me now," he added, and paused, looking fixedly at his wife, who was looking fixedly at a blank wall.

The silence in the kitchen was prolonged, and Mr Verloc felt disappointed. He had expected his wife to say something. But Mrs Verloc's lips, composed in their usual form, preserved a statuesque immobility like the rest of her face. And Mr Verloc was disappointed. Yet the occasion did not, he recognized, demand speech from her. She was a woman of very few words. For reasons involved in the very foundation of his psychology, Mr Verloc was inclined to put his trust in any woman who had given herself to him. Therefore he trusted his wife. Their accord was perfect, but it was not precise. It was a tacit accord, congenial to Mrs Verloc's incuriosity and to Mr Verloc's habits of mind, which were indolent and secret. They refrained from going to the bottom of facts and motives.

This reserve, expressing, in a way, their profound confidence in each other, introduced at the same time a certain element of vagueness into their intimacy. No system of conjugal relations is perfect. Mr Verloc presumed that his wife had understood him but he would have been glad to hear her say what she thought at the moment. It would have been a comfort.

There were several reasons why this comfort was denied him. There was a physical obstacle: Mrs Verloc had not sufficient command over her voice. She did not see any alternative between screaming and silence, and instinctively she chose the silence.

Winnie Verloc was temperamentally a silent person. And there was the paralysing atrocity of the thought which occupied her. Her cheeks were blanched, her lips ashy, her immobility amazing. And she thought without looking at Mr Verloc: "This man took the boy away to murder him. He took the boy from his home to murder him. He took the boy away from me to murder him!"

Mrs Verloc's whole being was racked by that inconclusive and maddening thought. It was in her veins, in her bones, in the roots of her hair. Mentally she assumed the biblical attitude of mourning—the covered face, the rent garments; the sound of wailing and lamentation filled her head. But her teeth were violently clenched, and her tearless eyes were hot with rage, because she was not a submissive creature. The protection she had extended over her brother had been in its origin of a fierce and indignant complexion. She had to love him with a militant love. She had battled for him—even against herself. His loss had the bitterness of defeat, with the anguish of a baffled passion. It was not an ordinary stroke of death. Moreover, it was not death that took Stevie from her. It was Mr Verloc who took him away. She had seen him. She had watched him, without raising a hand, take the boy away. And she had let him go, like—like a fool—a blind fool. Then after he had murdered the boy he came home to her. Just came home like any other man would come home to his wife . . .

Through her set teeth Mrs Verloc muttered at the wall:

"And I thought he had caught a cold."

Mr Verloc heard these words and appropriated them.

"It was nothing," he said, moodily. "I was upset. I was upset on your account."

Mrs Verloc, turning her head slowly, transferred her stare from the wall to her husband's person. Mr Verloc, with the tips of his fingers between his lips, was looking on the ground.

"Can't be helped," he mumbled, letting his hand fall. "You must pull yourself together. You'll want all your wits about you. It is you who brought the police about our ears. Never mind, I won't say anything more about it," continued Mr Verloc, magnanimously. "You couldn't know."

"I couldn't," breathed out Mrs Verloc. It was as if a corpse had spoken. Mr Verloc took up the thread of his discourse.

"I don't blame you. I'll make them sit up. Once under lock and key it will be safe enough for me to talk—you understand. You must reckon on me being two years away from you," he continued, in a tone of sincere concern. "It will be easier for you than for me. You'll have something to do, while I—Look here, Winnie, what you must do is to keep this business going for two years. You know enough for that. You've a good head on you. I'll send you word when it's time to go about trying to sell. You'll have to be extra careful. The comrades will be keeping an eye on you all the time. You'll have to be as artful as you know how, and as close as the grave. No one must know what you are going to do. I have no mind to get a knock on the head or a stab in the back directly I am let out."

Thus spoke Mr Verloc, applying his mind with ingenuity and forethought to the problems of the future. His voice was sombre, because he had a correct sentiment of the situation. Everything which he did not wish to pass had come to pass. The future had become precarious. His judgement, perhaps, had been momentarily obscured by his dread of Mr Vladimir's truculent folly. A man somewhat over forty may be excusably thrown into considerable disorder by the prospect of losing his employment, especially if the man is a secret agent of political police, dwelling secure in the consciousness of his high value and in the esteem of high personages. He was excusable.

Now the thing had ended in a crash. Mr Verloc was cool; but he was not cheerful. A secret agent who throws his secrecy to the winds from desire of vengeance, and flaunts his achievements before the public eye, becomes the mark for desperate and bloodthirsty indignations. Without unduly exaggerating the danger, Mr Verloc tried to bring it clearly before his wife's mind. He repeated that he had no intention of letting the revolutionists do away with him.

He looked straight into his wife's eyes. The enlarged pupils of the woman received his stare into their unfathomable depths.

"I am too fond of you for that," he said, with a little nervous laugh.

A faint flush coloured Mrs Verloc's ghastly and motionless face. Having done with the visions of the past, she had not only heard, but had also understood the words uttered by her husband. By their extreme disaccord with her mental condition these words produced on her a slightly suffocating effect. Mrs Verloc's mental condition had the merit of simplicity; but it was not sound. It was governed too much by a fixed idea. Every nook and cranny of her brain was filled with the thought that this man, with whom she had lived without distaste for seven years, had taken the "poor boy" away from her in order to kill him—the man to whom she had grown accustomed in body and mind; the man whom she had trusted, took the boy away to kill him! In its form, in its substance, in its effect, which was universal, altering even the aspect of inanimate things, it was a thought to sit still and marvel at for ever and ever. Mrs Verloc sat still. And across that thought (not across the kitchen) the form of Mr Verloc went to and fro, familiarly in hat and overcoat, stamping with his boots upon her brain. He was probably talking, too; but Mrs Verloc's thoughts for the most part covered the voice.

Now and then, however, the voice would make itself heard. Several connected words emerged at times. Their purport was generally hopeful. On each of these occasions Mrs Verloc's dilated pupils, losing their far-off fixity, followed her husband's movements with the effect of black care and impenetrable attention. Well informed upon all matters relating to his secret calling, Mr Verloc augured well for the success of his plans and combinations. He really believed that it would be upon the whole easy for him to escape the knife of infuriated revolutionists. He had exaggerated the strength of their fury and the length of their arm (for professional purposes) too often to have many illusions one way or the other. For to exaggerate with judgement one must begin by measuring with nicety. He knew also how much virtue and how much infamy is forgotten in two years—two long years. His first really confidential discourse to his wife was optimistic from conviction. He also thought it good policy to display all the assurance he could muster. It would put heart into the poor woman. On his liberation, which harmonizing with the whole tenor of his life, would be secret, of course, they would vanish together without loss of time. As to covering up the tracks, he begged his wife to trust him for that. He knew how it was to be done so that the devil himself—

He waved his hand. He seemed to boast. He wished only to put heart into her. It was a benevolent intention, but Mr Verloc had the misfortune not to be in accord with his audience.

The self-confident tone grew upon Mrs Verloc's ear which let most of the words go by; for what were words to her now? What could words do to her for good or evil in the face of her fixed idea? Her black glance followed that man who was asserting his impunity—the man who had taken poor Stevie from home to kill him somewhere. Mrs Verloc could not remember exactly where, but her heart began to beat very perceptibly.

Mr Verloc, in a soft and conjugal tone, was now expressing his firm belief that there were yet a good few years of quiet life before them both. He did not go into the question of means. A quiet life it must be and, as it were, nestling in the shade, concealed among men whose flesh is grass; modest, like the life of violets. The words used by Mr Verloc were: "Lie low for a bit." And far from England, of course. It was not clear whether Mr Verloc had in his mind Spain or South America; but at any rate somewhere abroad.

This last word, falling into Mrs Verloc's ear, produced a definite impression. This man was talking of going abroad. The impression was completely disconnected; and such is the force of mental habit that Mrs Verloc at once and automatically asked herself: "And what of Stevie?"

It was a sort of forgetfulness; but instantly she became aware that there was no longer any occasion for anxiety on that score. There would never be any occasion any more. The poor boy had been taken out and killed. The poor boy was dead.

This shaking piece of forgetfulness stimulated Mrs Verloc's intelligence. She began to perceive certain consequences which would have surprised Mr Verloc. There was no need for her now to stay there, in that kitchen, in that house, with that man—since the boy was gone for ever. No need whatever. And on that Mrs Verloc rose as if raised by a spring. But neither could she see what there was to keep her in the world at all. And this inability arrested her. Mr Verloc watched her with marital solicitude.

"You're looking more like yourself," he said, uneasily. Something peculiar in the blackness of his wife's eyes disturbed his optimism. At that precise moment Mrs Verloc began to look upon herself as released from all earthly ties. She had her freedom. Her contract with existence, as represented by that man standing over there, was at an end. She was a free woman. Had this view become in some way perceptible to Mr Verloc he would have been extremely shocked. In his affairs of the heart Mr Verloc had been always carelessly generous, yet always with no other idea than that of being loved for himself. Upon this matter, his ethical notions being in agreement with his vanity, he was completely incorrigible. That this should be so in the case of his virtuous and legal connection he was perfectly certain. He had grown older, fatter, heavier, in the belief that he lacked no fascination for being loved for his own sake. When he saw Mrs Verloc starting to walk out of the kitchen without a word he was disappointed.

"Where are you going to?" he called out rather sharply. "Upstairs?"

Mrs Verloc in the doorway turned at the voice. An instinct of prudence born of fear, the excessive fear of being approached and touched by that man, induced her to nod at him slightly (from the height of two steps), with a stir of the lips which the conjugal optimism of Mr Verloc took for a wan and uncertain smile.

"That's right," he encouraged her gruffly. "Rest and quiet's what you want. Go on. It won't be long before I am with you."

Mrs Verloc, the free woman who had had really no idea where she was going to, obeyed the suggestion with rigid steadiness.

Mr Verloc watched her. She disappeared up the stairs. He was disappointed. There was that within him which would have been more satisfied if she had been moved to throw herself upon his breast. But he was generous and indulgent. Winnie was always undemonstrative and silent. Neither was Mr Verloc himself prodigal of endearments and words as a rule. But this was not an ordinary evening. It was an occasion when a man wants to be fortified and strengthened by open proofs of sympathy and affection. Mr Verloc sighed, and put out the gas in the kitchen. Mr Verloc's sympathy with his wife was genuine and intense. It almost brought tears into his eyes as he stood in the parlour reflecting on the loneliness hanging over her head. In this mood Mr Verloc missed Stevie very much out of a difficult world. He thought mournfully of his end. If only that lad had not stupidly destroyed himself!

The sensation of unappeasable hunger, not unknown after the strain of a hazardous enterprise to adventurers of tougher fibre than Mr Verloc, overcame him again. The piece of roast beef, laid out in the likeness of funereal baked meats for Stevie's obsequies, offered itself largely to his notice. And Mr Verloc again partook.

He partook ravenously, without restraint and decency, cutting thick slices with the sharp carving knife, and swallowing them without bread. In the course of that reflection it occurred to Mr Verloc that he was not hearing his wife move about in the bedroom as he should have done. The thoughts of finding her perhaps sitting on the bed in the dark not only cut Mr Verloc's appetite, but also took from him the inclination to follow her upstairs just yet. Laying down the carving knife, Mr Verloc listened with careworn attention.

He was comforted by hearing her move at last. She walked suddenly across the room, and threw the window up. After a period of stillness up there, during which he figured her to himself with her head out, he heard the sash being lowered slowly. Then she made a few steps, and sat down. Every resonance of this house was familiar to Mr Verloc, who was thoroughly domesticated. When next he heard his wife's footsteps overhead he knew, as well as if he had seen her doing it, that she had been putting on her walking shoes. Mr Verloc wriggled his shoulders slightly at this ominous symptom, and moving away from the table, stood with his back to the fireplace, his head on one side, and gnawing perplexedly at the tips of his fingers. He kept track of her movements by the sound. She walked here and there violently, with abrupt stoppages, now before the chest of drawers, then in front of the wardrobe. An immense load of weariness, the harvest of a day of shocks and surprises, weighed Mr Verloc's energies to the ground.

He did not raise his eyes till he heard his wife descending the stairs. It was as he had guessed, she was dressed for going out.

Mrs Verloc was a free woman. She had thrown open the window of the bedroom either with the intention of screaming Murder! Help! or of throwing herself out. For she did not exactly know what use to make of her freedom. Her personality seemed to have been torn into two pieces, whose mental operations did not adjust themselves very well to each other. The street, silent and deserted from end to end, repelled her by taking sides with that man who was so certain of his impunity. She was afraid to shout lest no one should come. Obviously no one would come. Her instinct of self-preservation recoiled from the depth of the fall into that sort of slimy, deep trench. Mrs Verloc closed the window, and dressed herself to go out into the street by another way.

She was a free woman. She had dressed herself thoroughly, down to the tying of a black veil over her face. As she appeared before him in the light of the parlour, Mr Verloc observed that she had even her little handbag hanging from her left wrist . . . Flying off to her mother, of course.

The thought that women were wearisome creatures after all presented itself to his fatigued brain. But he was too generous to harbour it for more than an instant. This man, hurt cruelly in his vanity, remained magnanimous in his conduct, allowing himself no satisfaction of a bitter smile or of a contemptuous gesture. With true greatness of soul, he only glanced at the wooden clock on the wall, and said in a perfectly calm but forcible manner:

"Five and twenty minutes past eight, Winnie. There's no sense in going over there so late. You will never manage to get back tonight."

Before his extended hand Mrs Verloc had stopped short. He added, heavily: "Your mother will be gone to bed before you get there. This is the sort of news that can wait."

Nothing was further from Mrs Verloc's thoughts than going to her mother. She recoiled at the mere idea, and feeling a chair behind her, she obeyed the suggestion of the touch, and sat down. Her intention had been simply to get outside the door for ever. And if this feeling was correct, its mental form took an unrefined shape corresponding to her origin and station. "I would rather walk the streets all the days of my life," she thought. But this creature, whose moral nature had been subjected to a shock of which, in the physical order, the most violent earthquake of history could only be a faint and languid rendering, was at the mercy of mere trifles, of casual contacts. She sat down. With her hat and veil she had the air of a visitor, of having looked in on Mr Verloc for a moment. Her instant docility encouraged him, whilst her aspect of only temporary and silent acquiescence provoked him a little.

"Let me tell you, Winnie," he said with authority, "that your place is here this evening. Hang it all! you brought the damned police high and low about my ears. I don't blame you—but it's your doing all the same. You'd better take this confounded hat off. I can't let you go out, old girl," he added in a softened voice.

Mrs Verloc's mind got hold of that declaration with morbid tenacity. The man who had taken Stevie out from under her very eyes to murder him in a locality whose name was at the moment not present to her memory would not allow her to go out. Of course he wouldn't. Now he had murdered Stevie he would never let her go. He would want to keep her for nothing. And on this characteristic reasoning, having all the force of insane logic, Mrs Verloc's disconnected wits went to work practically. She could slip by him, open the door, run out. But he would dash out after her, seize her round the body, drag her back into the shop. She could scratch, kick, and bite—and stab, too; but for stabbing she wanted a knife. Mrs Verloc sat still under her black veil, in her own house, like a masked and mysterious visitor of impenetrable intentions.

Mr Verloc's magnanimity was not more than human. She had exasperated him at last.

"Can't you say something? You have your own dodges for vexing a man. Oh, yes! I know your deaf-and-dumb trick. I've seen you at it before today. But just now it won't do. And to begin with, take this damned thing off. One can't tell whether one is talking to a dummy or to a live woman."

He advanced, and stretching out his hand, dragged the veil off, unmasking a still unreadable face, against which his nervous exasperation was shattered like a glass bubble flung against a rock. "That's better," he said, to cover his momentary uneasiness, and retreated back to his old station by the mantelpiece. It never entered his head that his wife could give him up. He felt a little ashamed of himself, for he was fond and generous. What could he do? Everything had been said already. He protested vehemently.

"By heavens! You know that I hunted high and low. I ran the risk of giving myself away to find somebody for that accursed job. And I tell you again I couldn't find any one crazy enough or hungry enough. What do you take me for—a murderer, or what? The boy is gone. Do you think I wanted him to blow himself up? He's gone. His troubles are over. Ours are just going to begin, I tell you, precisely because he did blow himself up. I don't blame you. But just try to understand that it was a pure accident; as much an accident as if he had been run over by a bus while crossing the street."

His generosity was not infinite, because he was a human being—and not a monster, as Mrs Verloc believed him to be.

He paused, and a snarl lifting his moustaches above a gleam of white teeth gave him the expression of a reflective beast, not very dangerous—a slow beast with a sleek head, gloomier than a seal, and with a husky voice.

"And when it comes to that, it's as much your doing as mine. That's so. You may glare as much as you like. I know what you can do in that way. Strike me dead if I ever would have thought of the lad for that purpose. It was you who kept on shoving him in my way when I was half distracted with the worry of keeping the lot of us out of trouble. What the devil made you? One would think you were doing it on purpose. And I am damned if I know that you didn't. There's no saying how much of what's going on you have got hold of on the sly with your infernal don't-care-a-damn way of looking nowhere in particular, and saying nothing at all . . ."

His husky, domestic voice ceased for a while. Mrs Verloc made no reply. Before that silence he felt ashamed of what he had said. But as often happens to peaceful men in domestic tiffs, being ashamed he pushed another point.

"You have a devilish way of holding your tongue sometimes," he began again, without raising his voice. "Enough to make some men go mad. It's lucky for you that I am not so easily put out as some of them would be by your deaf-and-dumb sulks. I am fond of you. But don't you go too far. This isn't the time for it. We ought to be thinking of what we've got to do. And I can't let you go out tonight, galloping off to your mother with some crazy tale or other about me. I won't have it. Don't you make any mistake about it: if you will have it that I killed the boy, then you've killed him as much as I."

In sincerity of feeling and openness of statement, these words went far beyond anything that had ever been said in this home, kept up on the wages of a secret industry eked out by the sale of more or less secret wares: the poor expedients devised by a mediocre mankind for preserving an imperfect society from the dangers of moral and physical corruption, both secret, too, of their kind. They were spoken because Mr Verloc had felt himself really outraged; but the reticent decencies of this home life, nestling in a shady street behind a shop where the sun never shone, remained apparently undisturbed. Mrs Verloc heard him out with perfect propriety, and then rose from her chair in her hat and jacket like a visitor at the end of a call. She advanced towards her husband, one arm extended as if for a silent leave-taking. Her net veil dangling down by one end of the left side of her face gave an air of disorderly formality to her restrained movements. But when she arrived as far as the hearthrug, Mr Verloc was no longer standing there. He had moved off in the direction of the sofa, without raising his eyes to watch the effect of his tirade. He was tired, resigned in a truly marital spirit. But he felt hurt in the tender spot of his secret weakness. If she would go on sulking in that dreadful overcharged silence—why then she must. She was a master in that domestic art. Mr Verloc flung himself heavily upon the sofa, disregarding as usual the fate of his hat, which, as if accustomed to take care of itself, made for a safe shelter under the table.

He was tired. The last particle of his nervous force had been expended in the wonders and agonies of this day full of surprising failures coming at the end of a harassing month of scheming and insomnia. He was tired. A man isn't made of stone. Hang everything! Mr Verloc reposed characteristically, clad in his outdoor garments. One side of his open overcoat was lying partly on the ground. Mr Verloc wallowed on his back. But he longed for a more perfect rest—for sleep—for a few hours of delicious forgetfulness. That would come later. Provisionally he rested. And he thought: "I wish she would give over this damned nonsense. It's exasperating."

There must have been something imperfect in Mrs Verloc's sentiment of regained freedom. Instead of taking the way of the door she leaned back, with her shoulders against the tablet of the mantelpiece, as a wayfarer rests against a fence. A tinge of wildness in her aspect was derived from the black veil hanging like a rag against her cheek, and from the fixity of her black gaze where the light of the room was absorbed and lost without the trace of a single gleam. This woman, capable of a bargain the mere suspicion of which would have been infinitely shocking to Mr Verloc's idea of love, remained irresolute, as if scrupulously aware of something wanting on her part for the formal closing of the transaction.

On the sofa Mr Verloc wriggled his shoulders into perfect comfort, and from the fullness of his heart emitted a wish which was certainly as pious as anything likely to come from such a source.

"I wish to goodness," he growled, huskily, "I had never seen Greenwich Park or anything belonging to it."

The veiled sound filled the small room with its moderate volume, well adapted to the modest nature of the wish. The waves of air of the proper length, propagated in accordance with correct mathematical formulas, flowed around all the inanimate things in the room, lapped against Mrs Verloc's head as if it had been a head of stone. And incredible as it may appear, the eyes of Mrs Verloc seemed to grow still larger. The audible wish of Mr Verloc's overflowing heart flowed into an enemy place in his wife's memory. Greenwich Park. A park! That's where the boy was killed. A park—smashed branches, torn leaves, gravel, bits of brotherly flesh and bone, all spouting up together in the manner of a firework. She remembered now what she had heard, and she remembered it pictorially. They had to gather him up with the shovel. Trembling all over with irrepressible shudders, she saw before her the very implement with its ghastly load scraped up from the ground. Mrs Verloc closed her eyes desperately, throwing upon that vision the night of her eyelids, where after a rainlike fall of mangled limbs the decapitated head of Stevie lingered suspended alone, and fading out slowly like the last star of a pyrotechnic display. Mrs Verloc opened her eyes.

Her face was no longer stony. Anybody could have noted the subtle change on her features, in the stare of her eyes, giving her a new and startling expression; an expression seldom observed by competent persons under the conditions of leisure and security demanded for thorough analysis, but whose meaning could not be mistaken at a glance. Mrs Verloc's doubts as to the end of the bargain no longer existed; her wits no longer disconnected, were working under the control of her will. But Mr Verloc observed nothing. He was reposing in that pathetic condition of optimism induced by excess of fatigue. He did not want any more trouble—with his wife, too—of all people in the world. He had been unanswerable in his vindication. He was loved for himself. The present phase of her silence he interpreted favourably. This was the time to make it up with her. The silence had lasted long enough. He broke it by calling to her in an undertone:

"Winnie."

"Yes," answered obediently Mrs Verloc the free woman. She

commanded her wits now, her vocal organs; she felt herself to be in an almost preternaturally perfect control of every fibre of her body. It was all her own, because the bargain was at an end. She was clear sighted. She had become cunning. She chose to answer him so readily for a purpose. She did not wish that man to change his position on the sofa which was very suitable to the circumstances. She succeeded. The man did not stir. But after answering him she remained leaning negligently against the mantelpiece in the attitude of a resting wayfarer. She was unhurried. Her brow was smooth. The head and shoulders of Mr Verloc were hidden from her by the high side of the sofa. She kept her eyes fixed on his feet.

She remained thus mysteriously still and suddenly collected till Mr Verloc was heard with an accent of marital authority, and moving slightly to make room for her to sit on the edge of the sofa.

"Come here," he said in a peculiar tone, which might have been the tone of brutality, but was intimately known to Mrs Verloc as the note of wooing.

She started forward at once, as if she was still a loyal woman bound to that man by an unbroken contract. Her right hand skimmed slightly the end of the table, and when she had passed on towards the sofa the carving knife had vanished without the slightest sound from the side of the dish. Mr Verloc heard the creaky plank in the floor, and was content. He waited. Mrs Verloc was coming. As if the homeless soul of Stevie had flown for shelter straight to the breast of his sister, guardian and protector, the resemblance of her face with that of her brother grew at every step, even to the droop of the lower lip, even to the slight divergence of the eyes. But Mr Verloc did not see that. He was lying on his back and staring upwards. He saw partly on the ceiling a clenched hand holding a carving knife. It flickered up and down. Its movements were leisurely. They were leisurely enough for Mr Verloc to recognize the limb and the weapon.

They were leisurely enough for him to take in the full meaning of the portent, and to taste the flavour of death rising in his gorge. His wife had gone raving mad—murdering mad. They were leisurely enough for the first paralysing effect of this discovery to pass away before a resolute determination to come out victorious from the ghastly struggle with that armed lunatic. They were leisurely enough for Mr Verloc to elaborate a plan of defence, involving a dash behind the table, and the felling of the woman to the ground with a heavy wooden chair. But they were not leisurely enough to allow Mr Verloc the time to move either hand or foot. The knife was already planted in his breast. It met no resistance on its way. Hazard has such accuracies. Into that plunging blow, delivered over the side of the couch, Mrs Verloc had put all the inheritance of her immemorial and obscure descent, the simple ferocity of the age of caverns, and the unbalanced nervous fury of the age of bar-rooms. Mr Verloc, the secret agent, turning slightly on his side with the force of the blow, expired without stirring a limb, in the muttered sound of the word "Don't" by way of protest.

Mrs Verloc had let go the knife, and her extraordinary resemblance to her late brother had faded, had become very ordinary. She drew a deep breath, the first easy breath since Chief Inspector Heat had exhibited to her the labelled piece of Stevie's overcoat. She leaned forward on her folded arms over the side of the sofa. She adopted that easy attitude not in order to watch or gloat over the body of Mr Verloc, but because of the undulatory and swinging movements of the parlour, which for some time behaved as though it were at sea in a tempest. She was giddy but calm. She had become a free woman with a perfection of freedom which left her nothing to desire and absolutely nothing to do, since Stevie's urgent claim on her devotion no longer existed. Mrs Verloc, who thought in images, was not troubled now by visions, because she did not think at all. And she did not move. She was a woman enjoying her complete irresponsibility and endless leisure, almost in the manner of a corpse. She did not move, she did not think. Neither did the moral envelope of the late Mr Verloc reposing on the sofa. Except for the fact that Mrs Verloc breathed these two would have been perfectly in accord: that accord of prudent reserve without superfluous words, and sparing of signs, which had been the foundation of their respectable home life. For it had been respectable, covering by a decent reticence the problems that may arise in the practice of a secret profession and the commerce of shady wares. To the last its decorum had remained undisturbed by unseemly shrieks and other misplaced sincerities of conduct. And after the striking of the blow, this respectability was continued in immobility and silence.

Nothing moved in the parlour till Mrs Verloc raised her head slowly and looked at the clock with inquiring mistrust. She had become aware of a ticking sound in the room. It grew upon her ear, while she remembered clearly that the clock on the wall was silent, had no audible tick. What did it mean by beginning to tick so loudly all of a sudden? Its face indicated ten minutes to nine. Mrs Verloc cared nothing for time, and the ticking went on. She concluded it could not be the clock, and her sullen gaze moved along the walls, wavered, and became vague, while she strained her hearing to locate the sound. Tic, tic, tic.

After listening for some time Mrs Verloc lowered her gaze deliberately on her husband's body. Its attitude of repose was so homelike and familiar that she could do so without feeling embarrassed by any pronounced novelty in the phenomena of her home life. Mr Verloc was taking his habitual ease. He looked comfortable.

By the position of the body the face of Mr Verloc was not visible to Mrs Verloc, his widow. Her fine, sleepy eyes, travelling downward on the track of the sound, became contemplative on meeting a flat object of bone which protruded a little beyond the edge of the sofa. It was the handle of the domestic carving knife with nothing strange about it but its position at right angles to Mr Verloc's waistcoat and the fact that something dripped from it. Dark drops fell on the floorcloth one after another, with a sound of ticking growing fast and furious like the pulse of an insane clock. At its highest speed this ticking changed into a continuous sound of trickling. Mrs Verloc watched that transformation with shadows of anxiety coming and going on her face. It was a trickle, dark, swift, thin . . . Blood!

At this unforeseen circumstance Mrs Verloc abandoned her pose of idleness and irresponsibility.

With a sudden snatch at her skirts and a faint shriek she ran to the door, as if the trickle had been the first sign of a destroying flood. Finding the table in her way she gave it a push with both hands as though it had been alive, with such force that it went for some distance on its four legs, making a loud, scraping racket, whilst the big dish with the joint crashed heavily on the floor.

Then all became still. Mrs Verloc on reaching the door had stopped. A round hat disclosed in the middle of the floor by the moving of the table rocked slightly on its crown in the wind of her flight.

CHAPTER 12

Winnie Verloc, the widow of Mr Verloc, the sister of the late faithful Stevie (blown to fragments in a state of innocence and in the conviction of being engaged in a humanitarian enterprise), did not run beyond the door of the parlour. She had indeed run away so far from a mere trickle of blood, but that was a movement of instinctive repulsion. And there she had paused, with staring eyes and lowered head. As though she had run through long years in her flight across the small parlour, Mrs Verloc by the door was quite a different person from the woman who had been leaning over the sofa, a little swimmy in her head, but otherwise free to enjoy the profound calm of idleness and irresponsibility. Mrs Verloc was no longer giddy. Her head was steady. On the other hand, she was no longer calm. She was afraid.

If she avoided looking in the direction of her reposing husband it was not because she was afraid of him. Mr Verloc was not frightful to behold. He looked comfortable. Moreover, he was dead. Mrs Verloc entertained no vain delusions on the subject of the dead. Nothing brings them back, neither love nor hate. They can do nothing to you. They are as nothing. Her mental state was tinged by a sort of austere contempt for that man who had let himself be killed so easily. He had been the master of a house, the husband of a woman, and the murderer of her Stevie. And now he was of no account in every respect. He was of less practical account than the clothing on his body, than his overcoat, than his boots—than that hat lying on the floor. He was nothing. He was not worth looking at. He was even no longer the murderer of poor Stevie. The only murderer that would be found in the room when people came to look for Mr Verloc would be—herself!

Her hands shook so that she failed twice in the task of refastening her veil. Mrs Verloc was no longer a person of leisure and irresponsibility. She was afraid. The stabbing of Mr Verloc had been only a blow. It had relieved the pent-up agony of shrieks strangled in her throat, of tears dried up in her hot eyes, of the maddening and indignant rage at the atrocious part played by that man, who was less than nothing now, in robbing her of the boy. It had been an obscurely prompted blow. The blood trickling on the floor off the handle of the knife had turned it into an extremely plain case of murder. Mrs Verloc, who always refrained from looking deep into things, was compelled to look into the very bottom of this thing. She saw there no haunting face, no reproachful shade, no vision of remorse, no sort of ideal conception. She saw there an object. That object was the gallows. Mrs Verloc was afraid of the gallows.

She was terrified of them ideally. Having never set eyes on the last argument of men's justice except in illustrative woodcuts to a certain type of tales, she first saw them erect against a black and stormy background, festooned with chains and human bones, circled about by birds that peck at dead men's eyes. This was frightful enough, but Mrs Verloc, though not a well-informed woman, had a sufficient knowledge of the institutions of her country to know that gallows are no longer erected romantically on the banks of dismal rivers or on wind-swept headlands, but in the yards of jails. There within four high walls, as if into a pit, at dawn of day, the murderer was brought out to be executed, with a horrible quietness and, as the reports in the newspapers always said, "in the presence of the authorities." With her eyes staring on the floor, her nostrils quivering with anguish and shame, she imagined herself all alone amongst a lot of strange gentlemen in silk hats who were calmly proceeding about the business of hanging her by the neck. That—never! Never! And how was it done? The impossibility of imagining the details of such quiet execution added something maddening to her abstract terror. The newspapers never gave any details except one, but that one with some affection was always there at the end of a meagre report. Mrs Verloc remembered its nature. It came with a cruel burning pain into her head, as if the words "The drop given was fourteen feet" had been scratched on her brain with a hot needle. "The drop given was fourteen feet."

These words affected her physically, too. Her throat became convulsed in waves to resist strangulation; and the apprehension of the jerk was so vivid that she seized her head in both hands as if to save it from being torn off her shoulders. "The drop given was fourteen feet." No! that must never be. She could not stand *that*. The thought of it even was not bearable. She could not stand thinking of it. Therefore Mrs Verloc formed the resolution to go at once and throw herself into the river off one of the bridges.

This time she managed to refasten her veil. With her face as if masked, all black from head to foot except for some flowers in her hat, she looked up mechanically at the clock. She thought it must have stopped. She could not believe that only two minutes had passed since she had looked at it last. Of course not. It had been stopped all the time. As a matter of fact, only three minutes had elapsed from the moment she had drawn the first deep, easy breath after the blow, to this moment when Mrs Verloc formed the resolution to drown herself in the Thames. But Mrs Verloc could not believe that. She seemed to have heard or read that clocks and watches always stopped at the moment of murder for the undoing of the murderer. She did not care. "To the bridge—and over I go." . . . But her movements were slow.

She dragged herself painfully across the shop, and had to hold on to the handle of the door before she found the necessary fortitude to open it. The street frightened her, since it led either to the gallows or to the river. She floundered over the doorstep head forward, arms thrown out, like a person falling over the parapet of a bridge. This entrance into the open air had a foretaste of drowning; a slimy dampness enveloped her, entered her nostrils, clung to her hair. It was not actually raining, but each gas-lamp had a rusty little halo of mist. The van and horses were gone, and in the black street the curtained window of the carters' eating-house made a square patch of soiled blood-red light glowing faintly very near the level of the pavement. Mrs Verloc, dragging herself slowly towards it, thought that she was a very friendless woman. It was true. It was so true that, in a sudden longing to see some friendly face, she could think of no one else but of Mrs Neale, the charwoman. She had no acquaintances of her own. Nobody would miss her in a social way. It must not be imagined that the Widow Verloc had forgotten her mother. This was not so. Winnie had been a good daughter because she had been a devoted sister. Her mother had always leaned on her for support. No consolation or advice could be expected there. Now that Stevie was dead the bond seemed to be broken. She could not face the old woman with the horrible tale. Moreover, it was too far. The river was her present destination. Mrs Verloc tried to forget her mother.

Each step cost her an effort of will which seemed the last possible. Mrs Verloc had dragged herself past the red glow of the eating-house window. "To the bridge—and over I go," she repeated to herself with fierce obstinacy. She put out her hand just in time to steady herself against a lamp-post. "I'll never get there before morning," she thought. The fear of death paralysed her efforts to escape the gallows. It seemed to her she had been staggering in that street for hours. "I'll never get there," she thought. "They'll find me knocking about the streets. It's too far." She held on, panting under her black veil.

"The drop given was fourteen feet."

She pushed the lamp-post away from her violently, and found herself walking. But another wave of faintness overtook her like a great sea, washing away her heart clean out of the breast. "I will never get there," she muttered, suddenly arrested, swaying lightly where she stood. "Never."

And perceiving the utter impossibility of walking as far as the nearest bridge, Mrs Verloc thought of a flight abroad.

It came to her suddenly. Murderers escaped. They escaped abroad. Spain or California. Mere names. The vast world created for the glory of man was only a vast blank to Mrs Verloc. She did not know which way to turn. Murderers had friends, relations, helpers—they had knowledge. She had nothing. She was the most lonely of murderers that ever struck a mortal blow. She was alone in London: and the whole town of marvels and mud, with its maze of streets and its mass of lights, was sunk in a hopeless night, rested at the bottom of a black abyss from which no unaided woman could hope to scramble out.

She swayed forward, and made a fresh start blindly, with an awful dread of falling down; but at the end of a few steps, unexpectedly, she found a sensation of support, of security. Raising her head, she saw a man's face peering closely at her veil. Comrade Ossipon was not afraid of strange women, and no feeling of false delicacy could prevent him from striking an acquaintance with a woman apparently very much intoxicated. Comrade Ossipon was interested in women. He held up this one between his two large palms, peering at her in a business-like way till he heard her say faintly "Mr Ossipon!" and then he very nearly let her drop to the ground.

"Mrs Verloc!" he exclaimed. "You here!"

It seemed impossible to him that she should have been drinking. But one never knows. He did not go into that question, but attentive not to discourage kind fate surrendering to him the widow of Comrade Verloc, he tried to draw her to his breast. To his astonishment she came quite easily, and even rested on his arm for a moment before she attempted to disengage herself. Comrade Ossipon would not be brusque with kind fate. He withdrew his arm in a natural way.

"You recognized me," she faltered out, standing before him, fairly steady on her legs.

"Of course I did," said Ossipon with perfect readiness. "I was afraid you were going to fall. I've thought of you too often lately not to recognize you anywhere, at any time. I've always thought of you—ever since I first set eyes on you."

Mrs Verloc seemed not to hear. "You were coming to the shop?" she said, nervously.

"Yes; at once," answered Ossipon. "Directly I read the paper."

In fact, Comrade Ossipon had been skulking for a good two hours in the neighbourhood of Brett Street, unable to make up his mind for a bold move. The robust anarchist was not exactly a bold conqueror. He remembered that Mrs Verloc had never responded to his glances by the slightest sign of encouragement. Besides, he thought the shop might be watched by the police, and Comrade Ossipon did not wish the police to form an exaggerated notion of his revolutionary sympathies. Even now he did not know precisely what to do. In comparison with his usual amatory speculations this was a big and serious undertaking. He ignored how much there was in it and how far he would have to go in order to get hold of what there was to get—supposing there was a chance at all. These perplexities checking his elation imparted to his tone a soberness well in keeping with the circumstances.

"May I ask you where you were going?" he inquired in a subdued voice.

"Don't ask me!" cried Mrs Verloc with a shuddering, repressed violence. All her strong vitality recoiled from the idea of death. "Never mind where I was going . . ."

Ossipon concluded that she was very much excited but perfectly sober. She remained silent by his side for a moment, then all at once she did something which he did not expect. She slipped her hand under his arm. He was startled by the act itself certainly, and quite as much, too, by the palpably resolute character of this movement. But this being a delicate affair, Comrade Ossipon behaved with delicacy. He contented himself by pressing the hand slightly against his robust ribs. At the same time he felt himself being impelled forward, and yielded to the impulse. At the end of Brett Street he became aware of being directed to the left. He submitted.

The fruiterer at the corner had put out the blazing glory of his oranges and lemons, and Brett Place was all darkness, interspersed with the misty halos of the few lamps defining its triangular shape, with a cluster of three lights on one stand in the middle. The dark forms of the man and woman glided slowly arm in arm along the walls with a loverlike and homeless aspect in the miserable night.

"What would you say if I were to tell you that I was going to find you?" Mrs Verloc asked, gripping his arm with force.

"I would say that you couldn't find anyone more ready to help you in your trouble," answered Ossipon, with a notion of making tremendous headway. In fact, the progress of this delicate affair was almost taking his breath away.

"In my trouble!" Mrs Verloc repeated, slowly.

"Yes."

"And do you know what my trouble is?" she whispered with strange intensity.

"Ten minutes after seeing the evening paper," explained Ossipon with ardour, "I met a fellow whom you may have seen once or twice at the shop perhaps, and I had a talk with him which left no doubt whatever in my mind. Then I started for here, wondering whether you—I've been fond of you beyond words ever since I set eyes on your face," he cried, as if unable to command his feelings.

Comrade Ossipon assumed correctly that no woman was capable of wholly disbelieving such a statement. But he did not know that Mrs Verloc accepted it with all the fierceness the instinct of self-preservation imparts to the grip of a drowning person. To the widow of Mr Verloc the robust anarchist was like a radiant messenger of life.

They walked slowly, in step. "I thought so," Mrs Verloc murmured, faintly.

"You've read it in my eyes," suggested Ossipon with great assurance.

"Yes," she breathed out into his inclined ear.

"A love like mine could not be concealed from a woman like you," he went on, trying to detach his mind from material considerations, such as the business value of the shop, and the amount of money Mr Verloc might have left in the bank. He applied himself to the sentimental side of the affair. In his heart of hearts he was a little shocked at his success. Verloc had been a good fellow, and certainly a very decent husband as far as one could see. However, Comrade Ossipon was not going to quarrel with his luck for the sake of a dead man. Resolutely he suppressed his sympathy for the ghost of Comrade Verloc, and went on:

"I could not conceal it. I was too full of you. I daresay you could not help seeing it in my eyes. But I could not guess it. You were always so distant . . ."

"What else did you expect?" burst out Mrs Verloc. "I was a respectable woman—"

She paused, then added, as if speaking to herself, in sinister resentment: "Till he made me what I am."

Ossipon let that pass, and took up his running.

"He never did seem to me to be quite worthy of you," he began, throwing loyalty to the winds. "You were worthy of a better fate."

Mrs Verloc interrupted bitterly:

"Better fate! He cheated me out of seven years of life."

"You seemed to live so happily with him." Ossipon tried to exculpate the lukewarmness of his past conduct. "It's that what's made me timid. You seemed to love him. I was surprised—and jealous," he added.

"Love him!" Mrs Verloc cried out in a whisper full of scorn and rage. "Love him! I was a good wife to him. I am a respectable woman. You thought I loved him! You did! Look here, Tom—"

The sound of this name thrilled Comrade Ossipon with pride. For his name was Alexander, and he was called Tom by arrangement with the most familiar of his intimates. It was a name of friendship—of moments of expansion. He had no idea that she had ever heard it used by anybody. It was apparent that she had not only caught it, but had treasured it in her memory—perhaps in her heart.

"Look here, Tom! I was a young girl. I was done up. I was tired. I had two people depending on what I could do, and it did seem as if I couldn't do any more. Two people—mother and the boy. He was much more mine than mother's. I sat up nights and nights with him on my lap, all alone upstairs, when I wasn't more than eight years old myself. And then—He was mine, I tell you . . . You can't understand that. No man can understand it. What was I to do? There was a young fellow—"

The memory of the early romance with the young butcher survived, tenacious, like the image of a glimpsed ideal in that heart quailing before the fear of the gallows and full of revolt against death.

"That was the man I loved then," went on the widow of Mr Verloc. "I suppose he could see it in my eyes, too. Five and twenty shillings a week, and his father threatened to kick him out of the business if he made such a fool of himself as to marry a girl with a crippled mother and a crazy idiot of a boy on her hands. But he would hang about me, till one evening I found the courage to slam the door in his face. I had to do it. I loved him dearly. Five and twenty shillings a week! There was that other man—a good lodger. What is a girl to do? Could I've gone on the streets? He seemed kind. He wanted me, anyhow. What was I to do with mother and that poor boy? Eh? I said yes. He seemed good-natured, he was freehanded, he had money, he never said anything. Seven years—seven years a good wife to him, the kind, the good, the generous, the—And he loved me. Oh, yes. He loved me till I sometimes wished myself—Seven years. Seven years a wife to him. And do you know what he was, that dear friend of yours? Do you know what he was? . . . He was a devil!"

The superhuman vehemence of that whispered statement completely stunned Comrade Ossipon. Winnie Verloc turning about held him by both arms, facing him under the falling mist in the darkness and solitude of Brett Place, in which all sounds of life seemed lost as if in a triangular well of asphalt and bricks, of blind houses and unfeeling stones.

"No; I didn't know," he declared, with a sort of flabby stupidity, whose comical aspect was lost upon a woman haunted by the fear of the gallows. "But I do now. I—I understand," he floundered on, his mind speculating as to what sort of atrocities Verloc could have practised under the sleepy, placid appearances of his married estate. It was positively awful. "I understand," he repeated, and then by a sudden inspiration uttered an "Unhappy woman!" of lofty commiseration instead of the more familiar "Poor darling!" of his usual practice. This was no usual case. He felt conscious of something abnormal going on, while he never lost sight of the greatness of the stake. "Unhappy, brave woman!"

He was glad to have discovered that variation; but he could discover nothing else. "Ah, but he is dead now," was the best he could do. And he put a remarkable amount of animosity into his guarded exclamation. Mrs Verloc caught at his arm with a sort of frenzy. "You guessed then he was dead," she murmured, as if beside herself. "You! You guessed what I had to do. Had to!"

There were suggestions of triumph, relief, gratitude in the indefinable tone of these words. It engrossed the whole attention of Ossipon to the detriment of mere literal sense. He wondered what was up with her, why she had worked herself into this state of wild excitement. He even began to wonder whether the hidden causes of that Greenwich Park affair did not lie deep in the unhappy circumstances of the Verlocs' married life. He went so far as to suspect Mr Verloc of having selected that extraordinary manner of committing suicide. By Jove! that would account for the utter inanity and wrong-headedness of the thing. No anarchist manifestation was required by the circumstances. Quite the contrary: and Verloc was as well aware of that as any other revolutionist of his standing. What an immense joke if Verloc had simply made fools of the whole of Europe, of the revolutionary world, of the police, of the press, and of the cocksure Professor as well. Indeed, thought Ossipon in astonishment, it seemed almost certain that he did! Poor beggar! It struck him as very possible that of that household of two it wasn't precisely the man who was the devil.

Alexander Ossipon, nicknamed the Doctor, was naturally inclined to think indulgently of his men friends. He eyed Mrs Verloc hanging on his arm. Of his women friends he thought in a specially practical way. Why Mrs Verloc should exclaim at his knowledge of Mr Verloc's death, which was no guess at all, did not disturb him beyond measure. Women often talked like lunatics. But he was curious to know how she had been informed. The papers could tell her nothing beyond the mere fact: the man blown to pieces in Greenwich Park not having been identified. It was inconceivable on any theory that Verloc should have given her an inkling of his intention—whatever it was. This problem interested Comrade Ossipon immensely. He stopped short. They had gone then along the three sides of Brett Place, and were near the end of Brett Street again.

"How did you first come to hear of it?" he asked in a tone he tried to render appropriate to the character of the revelations which had been made to him by the woman at his side.

She shook violently for a while before she answered in a listless voice.

"From the police. A chief inspector came. Chief Inspector Heat he said he was. He showed me—"

Mrs Verloc choked. "Oh, Tom, they had to gather him up with a shovel."

Her breast heaved with dry sobs. In a moment Ossipon found his tongue.

"The police! Do you mean to say the police came already? That Chief Inspector Heat himself actually came to tell you?"

"Yes," she confirmed in the same listless tone. "He came. Just like this. He came. I didn't know. He showed me a piece of overcoat, and—Just like that. Do you know this? he says."

"Heat! Heat! And what did he do?"

Mrs Verloc's head dropped. "Nothing. He did nothing. He went away. The police were on that man's side," she murmured tragically. "Another one came, too."

"Another—another inspector, do you mean?" asked Ossipon, in great excitement, and very much in the tone of the scared child.

"I don't know. He came. He looked like a foreigner. He may have been one of them Embassy people."

Comrade Ossipon nearly collapsed under this new shock.

"Embassy! Are you aware what you are saying? What Embassy? What on earth do you mean by Embassy?"

"It's that place in Chesham Square. The people he cursed so. I don't know. What does it matter!"

"And that fellow, what did he do or say to you?"

"I don't remember . . . Nothing . . . I don't care. Don't ask me," she pleaded in a weary voice.

"All right. I won't," assented Ossipon, tenderly. And he meant it, too, not because he was touched by the pathos of the pleading voice, but because he felt himself losing his footing in the depths of this tenebrous affair. Police! Embassy! Phew! For fear of adventuring his intelligence into ways where its natural lights might fail to guide it safely he dismissed resolutely all suppositions, surmises, and theories out of his mind. He had the woman there, absolutely flinging herself at him, and that was the principal consideration. But after what he had heard nothing could astonish him any more. And when Mrs Verloc, as if startled suddenly out of a dream of safety, began to urge upon him wildly the necessity of an immediate flight on the Continent, he did not exclaim in the least. He simply said with unaffected regret that there was no train till the morning, and stood looking thoughtfully at her face, veiled in black net, in the light of a gas-lamp veiled in a gauze of mist.

Near him, her black form merged in the night, like a figure half chiselled out of a block of black stone. It was impossible to say what she knew, how deep she was involved with policemen and Embassies. But if she wanted to get away, it was not for him to object. He was anxious to be off himself. He felt that the business, the shop so strangely familiar to chief inspectors and members of foreign Embassies, was not the place for him. That must be dropped. But there was the rest. These savings. The money!

"You must hide me till the morning somewhere," she said in a dismayed voice.

"Fact is, my dear, I can't take you where I live. I share the room with a friend."

He was somewhat dismayed himself. In the morning the blessed tecs will be out in all the stations, no doubt. And if they once got hold of her, for one reason or another she would be lost to him indeed.

"But you must. Don't you care for me at all—at all? What are you thinking of?"

She said this violently, but she let her clapsed hands fall in discouragement. There was a silence, while the mist fell, and darkness reigned undisturbed over Brett Place. Not a soul, not even the vagabond, lawless, and amorous soul of a cat, came near the man and the woman facing each other.

"It would be possible perhaps to find a safe lodging somewhere," Ossipon spoke at last. "But the truth is, my dear, I have not enough money to go and try with—only a few pence. We revolutionists are not rich."

He had fifteen shillings in his pocket. He added:

"And there's the journey before us, too—first thing in the morning at that."

She did not move, made no sound, and Comrade Ossipon's heart sank a little. Apparently she had no suggestion to offer. Suddenly she clutched at her breast, as if she had felt a sharp pain there.

"But I have," she gasped. "I have the money. I have enough money. Tom! Let us go from here."

"How much have you got?" he inquired, without stirring to her tug; for he was a cautious man.

"I have the money, I tell you. All the money."

"What do you mean by it? All the money there was in the bank, or what?" he asked, incredulously, but ready not to be surprised at anything in the way of luck.

"Yes, yes!" she said nervously. "All there was. I've it all."

"How on earth did you manage to get hold of it already?" he marvelled.

"He gave it to me," she murmured, suddenly subdued and trembling. Comrade Ossipon put down his rising surprise with a firm hand.

"Why, then—we are saved," he uttered slowly.

She leaned forward, and sank against his breast. He welcomed her there. She had all the money. Her hat was in the way of very marked effusion; her veil, too. He was adequate in his manifestations, but no more. She received them without resistance and without abandonment, passively, as if only half-sensible. She freed herself from his lax embrace without difficulty.

"You will save me, Tom," she broke out, recoiling, but still keeping her hold on him by the two lapels of his damp coat. "Save me. Hide me. Don't let them have me. You must kill me first. I couldn't do it myself—I couldn't, I couldn't—not even for what I am afraid of."

She was confoundedly bizarre, he thought. She was beginning to inspire him with an indefinite uneasiness. He said surlily, for he was busy with important thoughts:

"What the devil *are* you afraid of?"

"Haven't you guessed what I was driven to do!" cried the woman. Distracted by the vividness of her dreadful apprehensions, her head ringing with forceful words, that kept the horror of her position before her mind, she had imagined her incoherence to be clearness itself. She had no conscience of how little she had audibly said in the disjointed phrases completed only in her thought. She had felt the relief of a full confession, and she gave a special meaning to every sentence spoken by Comrade Ossipon, whose knowledge did not in the least resemble her own. "Haven't you guessed what I was driven to do!" Her voice fell. "You needn't be long in guessing then what I am afraid of," she continued in a bitter and sombre murmur. "I won't have it. I won't. I won't. I won't. You must promise to kill me first!" She shook the lapels of his coat. "It must never be!"

He assured her curtly that no promises on his part were necessary, but he took good care not to contradict her in set terms, because he had had much to do with excited women, and he was inclined in general to let his experience guide his conduct in preference to applying his sagacity to each special case. His sagacity in this case was busy in other directions. Women's words fell into water, but the shortcomings of time-tables remained. The insular nature of Great Britain obtruded itself upon his notice in an odious form. "Might just as well be put under lock and key every night," he thought irritably, as nonplussed as though he had a wall to scale with the woman on his back. Suddenly he slapped his forehead. He had by dint of cudgelling his brains just thought of the Southampton–St Malo service. The boat left about midnight. There was a train at 10.30. He became cheery and ready to act.

"From Waterloo. Plenty of time. We are all right after all . . . What's the matter now? This isn't the way," he protested.

Mrs Verloc, having hooked her arm into his, was trying to drag him into Brett Street again.

"I've forgotten to shut the shop door as I went out," she whispered, terribly agitated.

The shop and all that was in it had ceased to interest Comrade

Ossipon. He knew how to limit his desires. He was on the point of saying "What of that? Let it be," but he refrained. He disliked argument about trifles. He even mended his pace considerably on the thought that she might have left the money in the drawer. But his willingness lagged behind her feverish impatience.

The shop seemed to be quite dark at first. The door stood ajar. Mrs Verloc, leaning against the front, grasped out:

"Nobody has been in. Look! The light—the light in the parlour."

Ossipon, stretching his head forward, saw a faint gleam in the darkness of the shop.

"There is," he said.

"I forgot it." Mrs Verloc's voice came from behind her veil faintly. And as he stood waiting for her to enter first, she said louder: 'Go in and put it out—or I'll go mad."

He made no immediate objection to this proposal, so strangely motived. "Where's all that money?" he asked.

"On me! Go, Tom. Quick! Put it out . . . Go in!" she cried, seizing him by both shoulders from behind.

Not prepared for a display of physical force, Comrade Ossipon stumbled far into the shop before her push. He was astonished at the strength of the woman and scandalized by her proceedings. But he did not retrace his steps in order to remonstrate with her severely in the street. He was beginning to be disagreeably impressed by her fantastic behaviour. Moreover, this or never was the time to humour the woman. Comrade Ossipon avoided easily the end of the counter, and approached calmly the glazed door of the parlour. The curtain over the panes being drawn back a little he, by a very natural impulse, looked in, just as he made ready to turn the handle. He looked in without a thought, without intention, without curiosity of any sort. He looked in because he could not help looking in. He looked in, and discovered Mr Verloc reposing quietly on the sofa.

A yell coming from the innermost depths of his chest died out unheard and transformed into a sort of greasy, sickly taste on his lips. At the same time the mental personality of Comrade Ossipon executed a frantic leap backwards. But his body, left thus without intellectual guidance, held on to the door handle with the unthinking force of an instinct. The robust anarchist did not even totter. And he stared, his face close to the glass, his eyes protruding out of his head. He would have given anything to get away, but his returning reason informed him that it would not do to let go the door handle. What was it—madness, a nightmare, or a trap into which he had been decoyed with fiendish artfulness? Why—what for? He did not know. Without any sense of guilt in his breast, in the full peace of his conscience as far as these people were concerned, the idea that he would be murdered for mysterious reasons by the couple Verloc passed not so much across his mind as across the pit of his stomach, and went out, leaving behind a trail of sickly faintness—an indisposition. Comrade Ossipon did not feel very well in a very special way for a moment—a long moment. And he stared. Mr Verloc lay very still meanwhile, simulating sleep for reasons of his own, while that savage woman of his was guarding the door—invisible and silent in the dark and deserted street. Was all this some sort of terrifying arrangement invented by the police for his especial benefit? His modesty shrank from that explanation.

But the true sense of the scene he was beholding came to Ossipon through the contemplation of the hat. It seemed an extraordinary thing, an ominous object, a sign. Black, and rim upward, it lay on the floor before the couch as if prepared to receive the contributions of pence from people who would come presently to behold Mr Verloc in the fullness of his domestic ease reposing on a sofa. From the hat the eyes of the robust anarchist wandered to the displaced table, gazed at the broken dish for a time, received a kind of optical shock from observing a white gleam under the imperfectly closed eyelids of the man on the couch. Mr Verloc did not seem so much asleep now as lying down with a bent head and looking insistently at his left breast. And when Comrade Ossipon had made out the handle of the knife he turned away from the glazed door, and retched violently.

The crash of the street door flung to made his very soul leap in a panic. This house with its harmless tenant could still be made a trap of—a trap of a terrible kind. Comrade Ossipon had no settled conception now of what was happening to him. Catching his thigh against the end of the counter, he spun round, staggered with a cry of pain, felt in the distracting clatter of the bell his arms pinned to his side by a convulsive hug, while the cold lips of a woman moved creepily on his very ear to form the words:

"Policeman! He has seen me!"

He ceased to struggle; she never let him go. Her hands had locked themselves with an inseparable twist of fingers on his robust back. While the footsteps approached, they breathed quickly, breast to breast, with hard, laboured breaths, as if theirs had been the attitude of a deadly struggle, while, in fact, it was the attitude of deadly fear. And the time was long.

The constable on the beat had in truth seen something of Mrs Verloc; only coming from the lighted thoroughfare at the other end of Brett Street, she had been no more to him than a flutter in the darkness. And he was not even quite sure that there had been a flutter. He had no reason to hurry up. On coming abreast of the shop he observed that it had been closed early. There was nothing very unusual in that. The man on duty had special instructions about that shop; what went on about there was not to be meddled with unless absolutely disorderly, but any observations made were to be reported. There were no observations to make; but from a sense of duty and for the peace of his conscience, owing also to that doubtful flutter of the darkness, the constable crossed the road, and tried the door. The spring latch, whose key was reposing for ever off duty in the late Mr Verloc's waistcoat pocket, held as well as usual. While the conscientious officer was shaking the handle, Ossipon felt the cold lips of the woman stirring again creepily against his very ear:

"If he comes in kill me—kill me, Tom."

The constable moved away, flashing as he passed the light of his dark lantern, merely for form's sake, at the shop window. For a moment longer the man and the woman inside stood motionless, panting, breast to breast; then her fingers came unlocked, her arms fell by her side slowly. Ossipon leaned against the counter. The robust anarchist wanted support badly. This was awful. He was almost too disgusted for speech. Yet he managed to utter a plaintive thought, showing at least that he realized his position.

"Only a couple of minutes later and you'd have made me blunder against the fellow poking about here with his damned dark lantern."

The widow of Mr Verloc, motionless in the middle of the shop, said insistently:

"Go in and put that light out, Tom. It will drive me crazy."

She saw vaguely his vehement gesture of refusal. Nothing in the world would have induced Ossipon to go into the parlour. He was not superstitious, but there was too much blood on the floor; a beastly pool of it all round the hat. He judged he had been already too near that corpse for his peace of mind—for the safety of his neck, perhaps!

"At the meter then! There. Look. In that corner."

The robust form of Comrade Ossipon, striding brusque and shadowy across the shop, squatted in a corner obediently; but this obedience was without grace. He fumbled nervously—and suddenly in the sound of a muttered curse the light behind the glazed door flicked out to a gasping, hysterical sigh of a woman. Night, the inevitable reward of men's faithful labours on this earth, night had fallen on Mr Verloc, the tried revolutionist—"one of the old lot"—the humble guardian of society; the invaluable secret agent D of Baron Stott-Wartenheim's dispatches; a servant of law and order, faithful, trusted, accurate, admirable, with perhaps one single amiable weakness: the idealistic belief in being loved for himself.

Ossipon groped his way back through the stuffy atmosphere, as black as ink now, to the counter. The voice of Mrs Verloc, standing in the middle of the shop, vibrated after him in that blackness with a desperate protest.

"I will not be hanged, Tom. I will not—"

She broke off. Ossipon from the counter issued a warning: "Don't shout like this," then seemed to reflect profoundly. "You did this thing quite by yourself?" he inquired in a hollow voice, but with an appearance of masterful calmness which filled Mrs Verloc's heart with grateful confidence in his protecting strength.

"Yes," she whispered, invisible.

"I wouldn't have believed it possible," he muttered. "Nobody would." She heard him move about and the snapping of a lock in the parlour door. Comrade Ossipon had turned the key on Mr Verloc's repose; and this he did not from reverence for its eternal nature or any other obscurely sentimental consideration, but for the precise reason that he was not at all sure that there was not someone else hiding somewhere in the house. He did not believe the woman, or rather he was incapable by now of judging what could be true, possible, or even probable in this astounding universe. He was terrified out of all capacity for belief or disbelief in regard to this extraordinary affair, which began with police inspectors and Embassies and would end goodness knows where—on the scaffold for someone. He was terrified at the thought that he could not prove the use he made of his time ever since seven o'clock, for he had been skulking about Brett Street. He was terrified at this savage woman who had brought him in there, and would probably saddle him with complicity, at least if he were not careful. He was terrified at the rapidity with which he had been involved in such danger—decoyed into it. It was some twenty minutes since he had met her—not more.

The voice of Mrs Verloc rose subdued, pleading piteously: "Don't let them hang me, Tom! Take me out of the country. I'll work for you. I'll slave for you. I'll love you. I've no one in the world . . . Who would look at me if you don't!" She ceased for a moment; then in the depths of the loneliness made round her by an insignificant thread of blood trickling off the handle of a knife, she found a dreadful inspiration to her—who had been the respectable girl of the Belgravian mansion, the loyal, respectable wife of Mr Verloc. "I won't ask you to marry me," she breathed out in shamefaced accents.

She moved a step forward in the darkness. He was terrified at her. He would not have been surprised if she had suddenly produced another knife destined for his breast. He certainly would have made no resistance. He had really not enough fortitude in him just then to tell her to keep back. But he inquired in a cavernous, strange tone: "Was he asleep?"

"No," she cried, and went on rapidly: "He wasn't. Not he. He had been telling me that nothing could touch him. After taking the boy away from under my very eyes to kill him—the loving, innocent, harmless lad. My own, I tell you. He was lying on the couch quite easy—after killing the boy—my boy. I would have gone on the streets to get out of his sight. And he says to me like this: 'Come here,' after telling me I had helped to kill the boy. You hear, Tom? He says like this: 'Come here,' after taking my very heart out of me along with the boy to smash in the dirt."

She ceased, then dreamily repeated twice: "Blood and dirt. Blood and dirt." A great light broke upon Comrade Ossipon. It was that half-witted lad then who had perished in the park. And the fooling of everybody all round appeared more complete than ever—colossal. He exclaimed scientifically, in the extremity of his astonishment: "The degenerate—by heavens!"

"Come here." The voice of Mrs Verloc rose again. "What did he think I was made of? Tell me, Tom. Come here! Me! Like this! I had been looking at the knife, and I thought I would come then if he wanted me so much. Oh, yes! I came—for the last time . . . With the knife."

He was excessively terrified at her—the sister of the degenerate—a degenerate herself of a murdering type . . . or else of the lying type. Comrade Ossipon might have been said to be terrified scientifically in addition to all other kinds of fear. It was an immeasurable and composite funk, which from its very excess gave him in the dark a false appearance of calm and thoughtful deliberation. For he moved and spoke with difficulty, being as if half frozen in his will and mind—and no one could see his ghastly face. He felt half dead.

He leaped a foot high. Unexpectedly Mrs Verloc had desecrated the unbroken, reserved decency of her home by a shrill and terrible shriek.

"Help, Tom! Save me. I won't be hanged!"

He rushed forward, groping for her mouth with a silencing hand, and the shriek died out. But in his rush he had knocked her over. He felt her now clinging round his legs, and his terror reached its culminating point, became a sort of intoxication, entertained delusions, acquired the characteristics of delirium tremens. He positively saw snakes now. He saw the woman twined round him like a snake, not to be shaken off. She was not deadly. She was death itself—the companion of life.

Mrs Verloc, as if relieved by the outburst, was very far from behaving noisily now. She was pitiful.

"Tom, you can't throw me off now," she murmured from the floor. "Not unless you crush my head under your heel. I won't leave you."

"Get up," said Ossipon.

His face was so pale as to be quite visible in the profound black darkness of the shop; while Mrs Verloc, veiled, had no face, almost no discernible form. The trembling of something small and white, a flower in her hat, marked her place, her movements.

It rose in the blackness. She had got up from the floor, and Ossipon regretted not having run out at once into the street. But he perceived easily that it would not do. It would not do. She would run after him. She would pursue him shrieking till she sent every policeman within hearing in chase. And then goodness only knew what she would say of him. He was so frightened that for a moment the insane notion of strangling her in the dark passed through his mind. And he became more frightened than ever! She had him. He saw himself living in abject terror in some obscure hamlet in Spain or Italy; till some fine morning they found him dead, too, with a knife in his breast—like Mr Verloc. He sighed deeply. He dared not move. And Mrs Verloc waited in silence the good pleasure of her saviour, deriving comfort from his reflective silence.

Suddenly he spoke up in an almost natural voice. His reflections had come to an end.

"Let's get out, or we will lose the train."

"Where are we going to, Tom?" she asked, timidly. Mrs Verloc was no longer a free woman.

"Let's get to Paris first, the best way we can . . . Go out first, and see if the way's clear."

She obeyed. Her voice came subdued through the cautiously opened door.

"It's all right."

Ossipon came out. Notwithstanding his endeavours to be gentle, the cracked bell clattered behind the closed door in the empty shop, as if trying in vain to warn the reposing Mr Verloc of the final departure of his wife—accompanied by his friend.

In the hansom they presently picked up, the robust anarchist became explanatory. He was still awfully pale, with eyes that seemed to have sunk a whole half-inch into his tense face. But he seemed to have thought of everything with extraordinary method.

"When we arrive," he discoursed in a queer, monotonous tone, "you must go into the station ahead of me, as if we did not know each other. I will take the tickets, and slip yours into your hand as I pass you. Then you will go into the first-class ladies' waiting-room, and sit there till ten minutes before the train starts. Then you come out. I will be outside. You go in first on the platform, as if you did not know me. There may be eyes watching there that know what's what. Alone you are only a woman going off by train. I am known. With me, you may be guessed at as Mrs Verloc running away. Do you understand, my dear?" he added with an effort.

"Yes," said Mrs Verloc, sitting there against him in the hansom all rigid with the dread of the gallows and the fear of death. "Yes, Tom." And she added to herself, like an awful refrain: "The drop given was fourteen feet."

Ossipon, not looking at her, and with a face like a fresh plaster cast of himself after a wasting illness, said: "By-the-by, I ought to have the money for the tickets now."

Mrs Verloc, undoing some hooks of her bodice, while she went on staring ahead beyond the splashboard, handed over to him the new pigskin pocket-book. He received it without a word, and seemed to plunge it deep somewhere into his very breast. Then he slapped his coat on the outside.

All this was done without the exchange of a single glance; they were like two people looking out for the first sight of a desired goal. It was not till the hansom swung round a corner and towards the bridge that Ossipon opened his lips again.

"Do you know how much money there is in that thing?" he asked, as if addressing slowly some hob-goblin sitting between the ears of the horse.

"No," said Mrs Verloc. "He gave it to me. I didn't count. I thought nothing of it at the time. Afterwards—"

She moved her right hand a little. It was so expressive that little movement of that right hand which had struck the deadly blow into a man's heart less than an hour before that Ossipon could not repress a shudder. He exaggerated it then purposely, and muttered:

"I am cold. I got chilled through."

Mrs Verloc looked straight ahead at the perspective of her escape. Now and then, like a sable streamer blown across a road, the words "The drop given was fourteen feet" got in the way of her tense stare. Through the black veil the whites of her big eyes gleamed lustrously like the eyes of a masked woman.

Ossipon's rigidity had something business-like, a queer official expression. He was heard again all of a sudden, as though he had released a catch in order to speak.

"Look here! Do you know whether your—whether he kept his account at the bank in his own name or in some other name."

Mrs Verloc turned upon him her masked face and the big white gleam of her eyes.

"Other name?" she said, thoughtfully.

"Be exact in what you say," Ossipon lectured in the swift motion of the hansom. "It's extremely important. I will explain to you. The bank has the numbers of these notes. If they were paid to him in his own name, then when his—his death becomes known, the notes may serve to track us since we have no other money. You have no other money on you?"

She shook her head negatively.

"None whatever?" he insisted.

"A few coppers."

"It would be dangerous in that case. The money would have then to be dealt specially with. Very specially. We'd have perhaps to lose more than half the amount in order to get these notes changed in a certain safe place I know of in Paris. In the other case—I mean if he had his account and got paid out under some other name—say Smith, for instance—the money is perfectly safe to use. You understand? The bank has no means of knowing that Mr Verloc and, say, Smith are one and the same person. Do you see how important it is that you should make no mistake in answering me? Can you answer that query at all? Perhaps not. Eh?"

She said composedly:

"I remember now! He didn't bank in his own name. He told me once that it was on deposit in the name of Prozor."

"You are sure?"

"Certain."

"You don't think the bank had any knowledge of his real name? Or anybody in the bank or—"

She shrugged her shoulders.

"How can I know? Is it likely, Tom?"

"No. I suppose it's not likely. It would have been more comfortable to know . . . Here we are. Get out first, and walk straight in. Move smartly."

He remained behind, and paid the cabman out of his own loose silver. The programme traced by his minute foresight was carried out. When Mrs Verloc, with her ticket for St Malo in her hand, entered the ladies' waiting-room, Comrade Ossipon walked into the bar, and in seven minutes absorbed three goes of hot brandy and water.

"Trying to drive out a cold," he explained to the barmaid, with a friendly nod and a grimacing smile. Then he came out, bringing out from that festive interlude the face of a man who had drunk at the very Fountain of Sorrow. He raised his eyes to the clock. It was time. He waited.

Punctual, Mrs Verloc came out, with her veil down, and all black—black as commonplace death itself, crowned with a few cheap and pale flowers. She passed close to a little group of men who were laughing, but whose laughter could have been struck dead by a single word. Her walk was indolent, but her back was straight, and Comrade Ossipon looked after it in terror before making a start himself.

The train was drawn up, with hardly anybody about its row of open doors. Owing to the time of the year and to the abominable weather there were but few passengers. Mrs Verloc walked slowly along the line of empty compartments till Ossipon touched her elbow from behind.

"In here."

She got in, and he remained on the platform looking about. She bent forward, and in a whisper:

"What is it, Tom? Is there any danger?"

"Wait a moment. There's the guard."

She saw him accost the man in uniform. They talked for a while. She heard the guard say "Very well, sir," and saw him touch his cap. Then Ossipon came back, saying: "I told him not to let anybody get into our compartment."

She was leaning forward on her seat. "You think of everything . . . You'll get me off, Tom?" she asked in a gust of anguish, lifting her veil brusquely to look at her saviour.

She had uncovered a face like adamant. And out of this face the eyes looked on, big, dry, enlarged, lightless, burnt out like two black holes in the white, shining globes.

"There is no danger," he said, gazing into them with an earnestness almost rapt, which to Mrs Verloc, flying from the gallows, seemed to be full of force and tenderness. This devotion deeply moved her—and the adamantine face lost the stern rigidity of its terror. Comrade Ossipon gazed at it as no lover ever gazed at his mistress's face. Alexander Ossipon, anarchist, nicknamed the Doctor, author of a medical (and improper) pamphlet, late lecturer on the social aspects of hygiene to working men's clubs, was free from the trammels of conventional morality—but he submitted to the rule of science. He was scientific, and he gazed scientifically at that woman, the sister of a degenerate, a degenerate herself—of a murdering type. He gazed at her, and invoked Lombroso, as an Italian peasant recommends himself to his favourite saint. He gazed scientifically. He gazed at her cheeks, at her nose, at her eyes, at her ears . . . Bad! . . . Fatal! Mrs Verloc's pale lips parting, slightly relaxed under his passionately attentive gaze, he gazed also at her teeth . . . Not a doubt remained . . . a murdering type . . . If Comrade Ossipon did not recommend his terrified soul to Lombroso, it was only because on scientific grounds he could not believe that he carried about him such a thing as a soul. But he had in him the scientific spirit, which moved him to testify on the platform of a railway station in nervous, jerky phrases.

"He was an extraordinary lad, that brother of yours. Most interesting to study. A perfect type in a way. Perfect!"

He spoke scientifically in his secret fear. And Mrs Verloc, hearing these words of commendation vouchsafed to her beloved dead, swayed forward with a flicker of light in her sombre eyes, like a ray of sunshine heralding a tempest of rain.

"He was that indeed," she whispered, softly, with quivering lips. "You took a lot of notice of him, Tom. I loved you for it."

"It's almost incredible the resemblance there was between you two," pursued Ossipon, giving a voice to his abiding dread, and trying to conceal his nervous, sickening impatience for the train to start. "Yes, he resembled you."

These words were not especially touching or sympathetic. But the fact of that resemblance insisted upon was enough in itself to act upon her emotions powerfully. With a little faint cry, and throwing her arms out, Mrs Verloc burst into tears at last.

Ossipon entered the carriage, hastily closed the door and looked out to see the time by the station clock. Eight minutes more. For the first three of these Mrs Verloc wept violently and helplessly without pause or interruption. Then she recovered somewhat, and sobbed gently in an abundant fall of tears. She tried to talk to her saviour, to the man who was the messenger of life.

"Oh, Tom! How could I fear to die after he was taken away from me so cruelly! How could I! How could I be such a coward!"

She lamented aloud her love of life, that life without grace or charm, and almost without decency, but of an exalted faithfulness of purpose, even unto murder. And, as often happens in the lament of poor humanity rich in suffering but indigent in words, the truth—the very cry of truth—was found in a worn and artificial shape picked up somewhere among the phrases of sham sentiment.

"How could I be so afraid of death! Tom, I tried. But I am afraid. I tried to do away with myself. And I couldn't. Am I hard? I suppose the cup of horrors was not full enough for such as me. Then when you came . . ."

She paused. Then in a gust of confidence and gratitude: "I will live all my days for you, Tom!" she sobbed out.

"Go over into the other corner of the carriage, away from the platform," said Ossipon, solicitously. She let her saviour settle her comfortably, and he watched the coming on of another crisis of weeping, still more violent than the first. He watched the symptoms with a sort of medical air, as if counting seconds. He heard the guard's whistle at last. An involuntary contraction of the upper lip bared his teeth with all the aspect of savage resolution as he felt the train beginning to move. Mrs Verloc heard and felt nothing, and Ossipon, her saviour, stood still. He felt the train roll quicker, rumbling heavily to the sound of the woman's loud sobs, and then crossing the carriage in two long strides he opened the door deliberately, and leaped out.

He had leaped out at the very end of the platform; and such was his determination in sticking to his desperate plan that he managed by a sort of miracle, performed almost in the air, to slam to the door of the carriage. Only then did he find himself rolling, head over heels like a shot rabbit. He was bruised, shaken, pale as death, and out of breath when he got up. But he was calm, and perfectly able to meet the excited crowd of railwaymen who had gathered round him in a moment. He explained, in gentle and convincing tones, that his wife had started at a moment's notice for Brittany to her dying mother; that, of course, she was greatly upset, and he considerably concerned at her state; that he was trying to cheer her up, and had absolutely failed to notice at first that the train was moving out. To the general exclamation "Why didn't you go on to Southampton, then sir?" he objected the inexperience of a young sister-in-law left alone in the house with three small children, and her alarm at his absence, the telegraph offices being closed. He had acted on impulse. "But I don't think I'll ever try that again," he concluded; smiled all round; distributed some small change, and marched without a limp out of the station.

Outside, Comrade Ossipon, flush of safe banknotes as never before in his life, refused the offer of a cab.

"I can walk," he said, with a little friendly laugh to the civil driver.

He could walk. He walked. He crossed the bridge. Later on the towers of the Abbey saw in their massive immobility the yellow bush of his hair passing under the lamps. The lights of Victoria saw him, too, and Sloane Square, and the railings of the park. And Comrade Ossipon once more found himself on a bridge. The river, a sinister marvel of still shadows and flowing gleams mingling below in a black silence, arrested his attention. He stood looking over the parapet for a long time. The clock tower boomed a brazen blast above his drooping head. He looked up at the dial . . . Half past twelve of a wild night in the Channel.

And again Comrade Ossipon walked. His robust form was seen that night in distant parts of the enormous town slumbering monstrously on a carpet of mud under a veil of raw mist. It was seen crossing the streets without life and sound, or diminishing in the interminable straight perspectives of shadowy houses bordering empty roadways lined by strings of gas-lamps. He walked through Squares, Places, Ovals, Commons, through monotonous streets with unknown names where the dust of humanity settles inert and hopeless out of the stream of life. He walked. And suddenly turning into a strip of a front garden with a mangy grass plot, he let himself into a small grimy house with a latchkey he took out of his pocket.

He threw himself down on his bed all dressed, and lay still for a whole quarter of an hour. Then he sat up suddenly, drawing up his knees, and clasping his legs. The first dawn found him open-eyed, in that same posture. This man who could walk so long, so far, so aimlessly, without showing a sign of fatigue, could also remain sitting still for hours without stirring a limb or an eyelid. But when the late sun sent its rays into the room he unclasped his hands, and fell back on the pillow. His eyes stared at the ceiling. And suddenly they closed. Comrade Ossipon slept in the sunlight.

CHAPTER 13

The enormous iron padlock on the doors of the wall cupboard was the only object in the room on which the eye could rest without becoming afflicted by the miserable unloveliness of forms and the poverty of material. Unsaleable in the ordinary course of business on account of its noble proportions, it had been ceded to the Professor for a few pence by a marine dealer in the east of London. The room was large, clean, respectable, and poor with that poverty suggesting the starvation of every human need except mere bread. There was nothing on the walls but the paper, an expanse of arsenical green, soiled with indelible smudges here and there, and with stains resembling faded maps of uninhabited continents.

At a deal table near a window sat Comrade Ossipon, holding his head between his fists. The Professor, dressed in only his suit of shoddy tweeds, but flapping to and fro on the bare boards a pair of incredibly dilapidated slippers, had thrust his hands deep into the over-strained pockets of his jacket. He was relating to his robust guest a visit he had lately been paying to the Apostle Michaelis. The Perfect Anarchist had even been unbending a little.

"The fellow didn't know anything of Verloc's death. Of course! He never looks at the newspapers. They make him too sad, he says. But never mind. I walked into his cottage. Not a soul anywhere. I had to shout half a dozen times before he answered me. I thought he was fast asleep yet, in bed. But not at all. He had been writing his book for four hours already. He sat in that tiny cage in a litter of manuscript. There was a half-eaten raw carrot on the table near him. His breakfast. He lives on a diet of raw carrots and a little milk now."

"How does he look on it?" asked Comrade Ossipon, listlessly.

"Angelic . . . I picked up a handful of his pages from the floor. The poverty of reasoning is astonishing. He has no logic. He can't think consecutively. But that's nothing. He has divided his biography into three parts, entitled 'Faith, Hope, Charity.' He is elaborating now the idea of a world planned out like an immense and nice hospital, with gardens and flowers, in which the strong are to devote themselves to the nursing of the weak."

The Professor paused.

"Conceive you this folly, Ossipon? The weak! The source of all evil on this earth!" he continued with his grim assurance. "I told him that I dreamt of a world like shambles, where the weak would be taken in hand for utter extermination.

"Do you understand, Ossipon? The source of all evil! They are our sinister masters—the weak, the flabby, the silly, the cowardly, the faint of heart, and the slavish of mind. They have power. They are the multitude. Theirs is the kingdom of the earth. Exterminate, exterminate! That is the only way of progress. It is! Follow me, Ossipon. First the great multitude of the weak must go, then the only relatively strong. You see? First the blind, then the deaf and the dumb, then the halt and the lame—and so on. Every taint, every vice, every prejudice, every convention must meet its doom."

"And what remains?" asked Ossipon in a stifled voice.

"I remain—if I am strong enough," asserted the sallow little Professor, whose large ears, thin like membranes, and standing far out from the sides of his frail skull, took on suddenly a deep red tint.

"Haven't I suffered enough from this oppression of the weak?" he continued forcibly. Then tapping the breast-pocket of his jacket: "And yet I *am* the force," he went on. "But the time! The time! Give me time! Ah! that multitude, too stupid to feel either pity or fear. Sometimes I think they have everything on their side. Everything—even death—my own weapon."

"Come and drink some beer with me at the Silenus," said the robust Ossipon after an interval of silence pervaded by the rapid flap, flap of the slippers on the feet of the Perfect Anarchist. This last accepted. He was jovial that day in his own peculiar way. He slapped Ossipon's shoulder.

"Beer! So be it! Let us drink and be merry, for we are strong, and tomorrow we die."

He busied himself with putting on his boots, and talked meanwhile in his curt, resolute tones.

"What's the matter with you, Ossipon? You look glum and seek even my company. I hear that you are seen constantly in places where men utter foolish things over glasses of liquor. Why? Have you abandoned your collection of women? They are the weak who feed the strong—eh?"

He stamped one foot, and picked up his other laced boot,

heavy, thick-soled, unblacked, mended many times. He smiled to himself grimly.

"Tell me, Ossipon, terrible man, has ever one of your victims killed herself for you—or are your triumphs so far incomplete—for blood alone puts a seal on greatness? Blood. Death. Look at history."

"You be damned," said Ossipon, without turning his head.

"Why? Let that be the hope of the weak, whose theology has invented hell for the strong. Ossipon, my feeling for you is amicable contempt. You couldn't kill a fly."

But rolling to the feast on the top of the omnibus the Professor lost his high spirits. The contemplation of the multitudes thronging the pavements extinguished his assurance under a load of doubt and uneasiness which he could shake off after a period of seclusion in the room with the large cupboard closed by an enormous padlock.

"And so," said over his shoulder Comrade Ossipon, who sat on the seat behind. "And so Michaelis dreams of a world like a beautiful and cheery hospital."

"Just so. An immense charity for the healing of the weak," assented the Professor, sardonically.

"That's silly," admitted Ossipon. "You can't heal weakness. But after all Michaelis may not be so far wrong. In two hundred years doctors will rule the world. Science reigns already. It reigns in the shade maybe—but it reigns. And all science must culminate at last in the science of healing—not the weak, but the strong. Mankind wants to live—to live."

"Mankind," asserted the Professor with a self-confident glitter of his iron-rimmed spectacles, "does not know what it wants."

"But you do," growled Ossipon. "Just now you've been crying for time—time. Well, the doctors will serve you out your time—if you are good. You profess yourself to be one of the strong—because you carry in your pocket enough stuff to send yourself and, say, twenty other people into eternity. But eternity is a damned hole. It's time that you need. You—if you met a man who could give you for certain ten years of time, you would call him your master."

"My device is: No God! No master," said the Professor, sententiously, as he rose to get off the bus.

Ossipon followed. "Wait till you are lying flat on your back at the end of your time," he retorted, jumping off the footboard after the other. "Your scurvy, shabby, mangy little bit of time," he continued across the street, and hopping on to the kerbstone.

"Ossipon, I think you are a humbug," the Professor said, opening masterfully the doors of the renowned Silenus. And when they had established themselves at a little table he developed further this gracious thought. "You are not even a doctor. But you are funny. Your notion of a humanity universally putting out the tongue and taking the pill from pole to pole at the bidding of a few solemn jokers is worthy of the prophet. Prophecy! What's the good of thinking of what will be!" He raised his glass. "To the destruction of what is," he said, calmly.

He drank and relapsed into his peculiarly close manner of silence. The thought of a mankind as numerous as the sands of the seashore, as indestructible, as difficult to handle, oppressed him. The sound of exploding bombs was lost in their immensity of passive grains without an echo. For instance, this Verloc affair. Who thought of it now?

Ossipon, as if suddenly compelled by some mysterious force, pulled a much-folded newspaper out of his pocket. The Professor raised his head at the rustle. "What's that paper? Anything in it?" he asked.

Ossipon started like a scared somnambulist.

"Nothing. Nothing whatever. The thing's ten days old. I forgot it in my pocket, I suppose."

But he did not throw the old thing away. Before returning it to his pocket he stole a glance at the last lines of a paragraph. They ran thus: *"An impenetrable mystery seems destined to hang for ever over this act of madness or despair."*

Such were the end words of an item of news headed:

"Suicide of Lady Passenger from a cross-Channel Boat." Comrade Ossipon was familiar with the beauties of its journalistic style. *"An impenetrable mystery seems destined to hang for ever . . ."* He knew every word by heart. *"An impenetrable mystery . . ."* And the robust anarchist, hanging his head on his breast, fell into a long reverie.

He was menaced by this thing in the very sources of his existence. He could not issue forth to meet his various conquests, those that he courted on benches in Kensington Gardens, and those he met near area railings, without the dread of beginning to talk to them of an impenetrable mystery destined . . . He was becoming scientifically afraid of insanity lying in wait for him amongst these lines. *"To hang for ever over."* It was an obsession, a torture. He had lately failed to keep several of these appointments, whose note used to be an unbounded trustfulness in the language of sentiment and manly tenderness. The confiding disposition of various classes of women satisfied the need of his self-love, and put some material means into his hand. He needed it to live. It was there. But if he could no longer make use of it, he ran the risk of starving his ideals and his body . . . *"This act of madness or despair."*

"An impenetrable mystery" was sure "to hang for ever" as far as all mankind was concerned. But what of that if he alone of all men could never get rid of the cursed knowledge? And Comrade Ossipon's knowledge was as precise as the newspaper man could make it—up to the very threshold of the *"mystery destined to hang for ever . . ."*

Comrade Ossipon was well informed. He knew what the gangway man of the steamer had seen: "A lady in the black dress and a black veil, wandering at midnight alongside on the quay. 'Are you going by the boat, ma'am,' he had asked her, encouragingly. 'This way.' She seemed not to know what to do. He helped her on board. She seemed weak."

And Ossipon knew also what the stewardess had seen: a lady in black with a white face standing in the middle of the empty ladies' cabin. The stewardess induced her to lie down there. The lady seemed quite unwilling to speak, and as if she were in some awful trouble. The next the stewardess knew she was gone from the ladies' cabin. The stewardess then went on deck to look for her, and Comrade Ossipon was informed that the good woman found the unhappy lady lying down in one of the hooded seats. Her eyes were open, but she would not answer anything that was said to her. She seemed very ill. The stewardess fetched the chief steward, and those two people stood by the side of the hooded seat consulting over their extraordinary and tragic passenger. They talked in audible whispers (for she seemed past hearing) of St Malo and the Consul there, of communicating with her people in England.

Then they went away to arrange for her removal down below, for indeed by what they could see of her face she seemed to them to be dying. But Comrade Ossipon knew that behind that white mask of despair there was struggling against terror and despair a vigour of vitality, a love of life that could resist the furious anguish which drives to murder and the fear, the blind, mad fear of the gallows. He knew. But the stewardess and the chief steward knew nothing, except that when they came back for her in less than five minutes the lady in black was no longer in the hooded seat. She was nowhere. She was gone. It was then five o'clock in the morning, and it was no accident either. An hour afterwards one of the steamer's hands found a wedding ring left lying on the seat. It had stuck to the wood in a bit of wet, and its glitter caught the man's eye. There was a date, 24 June 1879, engraved inside. "*An impenetrable mystery is destined to hang for ever . . .*"

And Comrade Ossipon raised his bowed head, beloved of various humble women of these isles, Apollo-like in the sunniness of its bush of hair.

The Professor had grown restless meantime. He rose.

"Stay," said Ossipon, hurriedly. "Here, what do you know of madness and despair?"

The Professor passed the tip of his tongue on his dry, thin lips, and said doctorally:

"There are no such things. All passion is lost now. The world is mediocre, limp, without force. And madness and despair are a force. And force is a crime in the eyes of the fools, the weak and the silly who rule the roost. You are mediocre. Verloc, whose affair the police has managed to smother so nicely, was mediocre. And the police murdered him. He was mediocre. Everybody is mediocre. Madness and despair! Give me that for a lever, and I'll move the world. Ossipon, you have my cordial scorn. You are incapable of conceiving even what the fat-fed citizen would call a crime. You have no force." He paused, smiling sardonically under the fierce glitter of his thick glasses.

"And let me tell you that this little legacy they say you've come into has not improved your intelligence. You sit at your beer like a dummy. Good-bye."

"Will you have it?" said Ossipon, looking up with an idiotic grin.

"Have what?"

"The legacy. All of it."

The incorruptible Professor only smiled. His clothes were all but falling off him, his boots, shapeless with repairs, heavy like lead, let water in at every step. He said:

"I will send you by-and-by a small bill for certain chemicals which I shall order tomorrow. I need them badly. Understood—eh?"

Ossipon lowered his head slowly. He was alone. *"An impenetrable mystery . . ."* It seemed to him that suspended in the air before him he saw his own brain pulsating to the rhythm of an impenetrable mystery. It was diseased clearly. *". . . This act of madness or despair."*

The mechanical piano near the door played through a valse cheekily, then felt silent all at once, as if gone grumpy.

Comrade Ossipon, nicknamed the Doctor, went out of the Silenus beer-hall. At the door he hesitated, blinking at a not too splendid sunlight—and the paper with the report of the suicide of a lady was in his pocket. His heart was beating against it. The suicide of a lady—*"this act of madness or despair."*

He walked along the streets without looking where he put his feet; and he walked in a direction which would not bring him to the place of appointment with another lady (an elderly nursery governess putting her trust in an Apollo-like ambrosial head). He was walking away from it. He could face no woman. It was ruin. He could neither think, work, sleep, nor eat. But he was beginning to drink with pleasure, with anticipation, with hope. It was ruin. His revolutionary career, sustained by the sentiment and trustfulness of many women, was menaced by an impenetrable mystery—the mystery of a human brain pulsating wrongfully to the rhythm of journalistic phrases. *". . . Will hang for ever over this act . . ."*—it was inclining towards the gutter—*". . . of madness or despair."*

"I am seriously ill," he muttered to himself with scientific insight. Already his robust form, with an Embassy's secret-service money (inherited from Mr Verloc) in his pockets, was marching in the gutter as if in training for the task of an inevitable future. Already he bowed his broad shoulders, his head of ambrosial locks, as if ready to receive the leather yoke of the sandwich board. As on that night, more than a week ago, Comrade Ossipon walked without looking where he put his feet, feeling no fatigue, feeling nothing, seeing nothing, hearing not a sound. *"An impenetrable mystery . . .*" He walked disregarded. "*. . . This act of madness or despair.*"

And the incorruptible Professor walked, too, averting his eyes from the odious multitude of mankind. He had no future. He disdained it. He was a force. His thoughts caressed the images of ruin and destruction. He walked frail, insignificant, shabby, miserable—and terrible in the simplicity of his idea calling madness and despair to the regeneration of the world. Nobody looked at him. He passed on unsuspected and deadly, like a pest in the street full of men.

V

Essays, Autobiography, and Letters

Conrad left no body of criticism or travel writing, of essays, autobiography, or journals to rival that of Henry James or Virginia Woolf in either size or quality. Almost all his important work is in his fiction. He never got in the habit of reviewing, and early on was pleased to note that he had avoided "the degradation of daily journalism." Not that many editors were asking—he didn't have the necessary style, the easy prolix fluency on which Edwardian magazine writing relied. He digressed more interestingly in Marlow's voice than in his own, and his nonfiction has the defects of his novelistic virtues: he cannot stick to the point and backs his way into the most elliptically defined of subjects. After the success of *Chance* he did produce the odd bit of high-priced prose for one paper or another, and his author's notes, though rarely reliable as fact, contain some of the most interesting work of his last years. But those free-standing essays that remain worth reading date from an earlier time. They include brief tributes to writers he admired, such as Guy de Maupassant or Stephen Crane, a set of travel notes on his 1914 visit to Poland, and the two essays reprinted here. Conrad wrote "Autocracy and War" early in 1905, taking the Russo-Japanese conflict as the opportunity for a meditation on European history. To someone without Conrad's biography the essay's definition of the problem might then have seemed surprising; it was a time of Russophilia in Britain, and Germany was the more usual worry. The other piece, "Some Reflections on the Loss of the *Titanic*," is the first of two he wrote on the topic. It's more strictly occasional than "Autocracy and War," and I've edited it slightly to eliminate a few references that might otherwise require footnotes. But all the anger remains.

Conrad produced two slender books of reminiscence, *The Mirror of the Sea* (1906) and *A Personal Record* (1912). The first patches together a series of quickly written essays that he began in the interstices of his work on *Nostromo*. Conrad dictated many of them to Ford Madox Ford, relying on their conversations to lubricate his memory, and they struck a deliberately popular note; a number of them first appeared in the *Daily Mail*. The chapter I've selected, "Initiation," is one of the later and longer of these pieces, an essay with some of the complexity, pace, and structure of a short story. Beyond that, *The Mirror of the Sea* seems most successful when most technical—when discussing the details of anchors and ballast, landfall and departure. The book did well, and yet Conrad also noted that its success provided his reviewers with "an occasion to kick poor *Nostromo* . . . Beneath this chorus of praise, I can hear in a murmur: 'Keep to the open sea. Do not land'!"

A Personal Record is an altogether larger achievement. It tells two stories, that of his becoming a writer and that of his going to sea, and its cunning structure manages to make them as one: the book begins with the writing of *Almayer's Folly* and ends with Conrad's first steps toward England itself, when the sound of a voice from a nearby ship meant that "for the very first time in my life, I heard myself addressed in English."

Conrad's letters stand as a major source of information about his life and opinions, his finances and periodic despair, his friendships and habits of work. He wrote better criticism in his letters than he did for publication; the selection below includes extended comments on James and Proust as well as a slap at Dostoevsky. He remained reticent about his marriage, which no one supposes to have been terribly rewarding. Still, he and Jessie were rarely apart, and he wrote her a few letters before his 1923 trip to America. He could be warm and confiding in writing letters to such friends as John Galsworthy or R. B. Cunninghame Graham, or even the American collector John Quinn, whom he never met. But his most frequent correspondent was his agent, J. B. Pinker, on whom he relied for the smallest details of practical living, at one point asking him, from Provence, "to buy for me and send out by parcel post a fountain pen of good repute." He trusted Pinker, and he fought with him, until in the last decade of both their lives their professional relationship matured into an abiding friendship.

"Autocracy and War" appeared in the *Fortnightly Review* for

1 July 1905 and was later collected in *Notes on Life and Letters* (Dent, 1921); the text given here has been edited by Paul Kirschner for inclusion in a 2002 Penguin edition of *Under Western Eyes.* "Some Reflections on the Loss of the *Titanic*" was published in the *English Review* for May 1912, and then in *Notes on Life and Letters;* I have taken my text from the Doubleday, Page Kent edition of 1925. "Initiation" first ran in *Blackwood's Magazine* for January 1906 before its appearance later that year in *A Mirror of the Sea;* the text here is that of the Kent edition as well. *A Personal Record* was produced for serialization in Ford Madox Ford's *English Review,* where it appeared from December 1908 to June 1909. Conrad's insistence on writing it provoked his worst quarrel with Pinker, to whom he was heavily in debt; the agent demanded that he press on with *Under Western Eyes* instead. Its first British book publication came as *Some Reminiscences* in 1912; the American edition of that year gave it the title that all subsequent editions have carried. Here too, the text comes from the Kent edition. The letters are all taken from the great Cambridge edition of *The Collected Letters of Joseph Conrad* (9 vols., Cambridge: Cambridge University Press, 1983–2007), edited by Frederick R. Karl and Laurence Davies, et al., and are reprinted here by permission.

AUTOCRACY AND WAR

1905

From the firing of the first shot on the banks of the Sha-ho, the fate of the great battle of the Russo-Japanese war hung in the balance for more than a fortnight. The famous three-day battles, for which history has reserved the recognition of special pages, sink into insignificance before the struggles in Manchuria engaging half a million men on fronts of sixty miles, struggles lasting for weeks, flaming up fiercely and dying away from sheer exhaustion, to flame up again in desperate persistence, and end—as we have seen them end more than once—not from the victor obtaining a crushing advantage, but through the mortal weariness of the combatants.

We have seen these things, though we have seen them only in the cold, silent, colourless print of books and newspapers. In stigmatising the printed word as cold, silent and colourless, I have no intention of putting a slight upon the fidelity and the talents of men who have provided us with words to read about the battles in Manchuria. I only wished to suggest that in the nature of things, the war in the Far East has been made known to us, so far, in a grey reflection of its terrible and monotonous phases of pain, death, sickness; a reflection seen in the perspective of thousands of miles, in the dim atmosphere of official reticence, through the veil of inadequate words. Inadequate, I say, because what had to be reproduced is beyond the common experience of war, and our imagination, luckily for our peace of mind, has remained a slumbering faculty, notwithstanding the din of humanitarian talk and the real progress of humanitarian ideas. Direct vision of the fact, or the stimulus of a great art, can alone make it turn and open its eyes heavy with blessed sleep; and even there, as against the testimony of the senses and the stirring up of emotion, that saving callousness which reconciles us to the conditions of our existence, will assert itself under the guise of assent to fatal necessity, or in the enthusiasm of a purely æsthetic admiration of the rendering. In this age of knowledge our sympathetic imagination, to which alone we can look for the ultimate triumph of concord and justice, remains strangely impervious to information, however correctly and even picturesquely conveyed. As to the vaunted eloquence of a serried array of figures, it has all the futility of precision without force. It is the exploded superstition of enthusiastic statisticians. An overworked horse falling in front of our windows, a man writhing under a cart-wheel in the street, awaken more genuine emotion, more horror, pity, and indignation than the stream of reports, appalling in their monotony, of tens of thousands of decaying bodies tainting the air of the Manchurian plains, of other tens of thousands of maimed bodies groaning in ditches, crawling on the frozen ground, filling the field hospitals; of the hundreds of thousands of survivors no less pathetic and even more tragic in being left alive by fate to the wretched exhaustion of their pitiful toil.

An early Victorian, or perhaps a pre-Victorian, sentimentalist, looking out of an upstairs window, I believe, at a street—perhaps Fleet Street itself—full of people, is reported, by an admiring friend, to have wept for joy at seeing so much life. These arcadian tears, this facile emotion worthy of the golden age, comes to us from the past, with solemn approval, after the close of the Napoleonic wars and before the series of sanguinary surprises held in reserve by the nineteenth century for our hopeful grandfathers. We may well envy them their optimism of which this anecdote of an amiable wit and sentimentalist presents an extreme instance, but still, a true instance, and worthy of regard in the spontaneous testimony to that trust in the life of the earth, triumphant at last in the felicity of her children. Moreover, the psychology of individuals, even in the most extreme instances, reflects the general effect of the fears and hopes of its time. Wept for joy! I should think that now, after eighty years, the emotion would be of a sterner sort. One could not imagine anybody shedding tears of joy at the sight of much life in a street, unless, perhaps, he were an enthusiastic officer of a general staff or a popular politician, with a career yet to make. And hardly even that. In the case of the first tears would be unprofessional, and a stern repression of all signs of joy at the provision of so much food for powder more in accord with the rules of prudence; the joy of the second would be checked before it found issue in weeping by anxious doubts as to the soundness of these electors' views upon the question of the hour, and the fear of missing the consensus of their votes.

No! It seems that such a tender joy would be misplaced now as much as ever during the last hundred years, to go no further back. The end of the eighteenth century was, too, a time of optimism and of dismal mediocrity in which the French Revolution exploded like a bomb-shell. In its lurid blaze the insufficiency of Europe, the inferiority of minds, of military and administrative systems, stood exposed with pitiless vividness. And there is but little courage in saying at this time of the day that the glorified French Revolution itself, except for its destructive force, was in essentials a mediocre phenomenon. The parentage of that great social and political upheaval was intellectual, the idea was elevated; but it is the bitter fate of any idea to lose its royal form and power, to lose its "virtue" the moment it descends from its solitary throne to work its will among the people. It is a king whose destiny is never to know the obedience of his subjects except at the cost of degradation. The degradation of the ideas of freedom and justice at the root of the French Revolution is made manifest in the person of its heir: a personality without law or faith, whom it has been the fashion to represent as an eagle, but who was, in truth, more like a sort of vulture preying upon the body of a Europe which did, indeed, for some dozen of years, very much resemble a corpse. The subtle and manifold influence for evil of the Napoleonic episode as a school of violence, as a sower of national hatreds, as the direct provocator of obscurantism and reaction, of political tyranny and injustice, cannot well be exaggerated.

The nineteenth century began with wars which were the issue of a corrupted revolution. It may be said that the twentieth begins with a war which is like the explosive ferment of a moral grave, whence may yet emerge a new political organism to take the place of a gigantic and dreaded phantom. For a hundred years the ghost of Russian might, overshadowing with its fantastic bulk the councils of Central and Western Europe, sat upon the gravestone of autocracy, cutting off from air, from light, from all knowledge of themselves and of the world, the buried millions of Russian people. Not the most determined cockney sentimentalist could have had the heart to weep for joy at the thought of its teeming numbers! And yet they were living, they are alive yet, since, through the mist of print, we have seen their blood freezing crimson upon the snow of the squares and streets of St. Petersburg; since their generations born in the grave are yet alive enough to fill the ditches and cover the fields of Manchuria with their torn limbs; to send up from the frozen ground of battlefields a chorus of groans calling for vengeance from Heaven; to kill and retreat, or kill and advance, without intermission or rest for twenty hours, for fifty hours, for whole weeks of fatigue, hunger, cold, and murder—till their ghastly labour, worthy of a place amongst the punishments of Dante's Inferno, passing through the stages of courage, of fury, of hopelessness, sinks into the night of crazy despair.

It seems that in both armies many men are driven beyond the bounds of sanity by the stress of moral and physical misery. Great numbers of soldiers and regimental officers go mad as if by way of protest against the peculiar sanity of a state of war: mostly among the Russians, of course. The Japanese have in their favour the tonic effect of success; and the innate gentleness of their character stands them in good stead. But the Japanese grand army has yet another advantage in this nerve-destroying contest, which for endless, arduous toil of killing surpasses all the wars of history. It has a base for its operations; a base of a nature beyond the concern of the many books written upon the so-called art of war, which, considered by itself, purely as an exercise of human ingenuity, is at best only a thing of well-worn, simple artifices. The Japanese army has for its base a reasoned conviction; it has behind it the profound belief in the right of a logical necessity to be appeased at the cost of so much blood and treasure. And in that belief, whether well or ill founded, that army stands on the high ground of conscious assent, shouldering deliberately the burden of a long-tried faithfulness. The other people (since each people is an army nowadays), torn out from miserable quietude resembling death itself, hurled across space, amazed, without starting-point of its own, or knowledge of the aim, can feel nothing but a horror-stricken consciousness of having mysteriously become the plaything of a black and merciless fate.

The profound, the instructive nature of this war is resumed by the memorable difference in the spiritual state of the two armies: the one forlorn and dazed on being driven out from an abyss of mental darkness into the red light of a conflagration, the other with a full knowledge of its past and its future, "finding itself" as it were at every step of the trying war before the eyes of an astonished world. The greatness of the lesson has been dwarfed for most of us by an often half-conscious prejudice of race-difference. The West, having managed to lodge its hasty foot on the neck of the East, is prone to forget that it is from the East that the wonders of patience and wisdom have come to a world of men who set the value of life in the power to act rather than in the faculty of meditation. It has been dwarfed by this, and it has been obscured by a cloud of considerations with whose shaping wisdom and meditation had little or nothing to do; by the weary platitudes on the military situation which (apart from geographical conditions) is the same everlasting situation that has prevailed since the times of Hannibal and Scipio, and further back yet, since the beginning of historical record—since pre-historic times, for that matter; by the conventional expressions of horror at the tale of maiming and killing; by the rumours of peace with guesses more or less plausible as to its conditions. All this is made legitimate by the consecrated custom of writers in such time as this—the time of a great war. More legitimate in view of the situation created in Europe are the speculations as to the course of events after the war. More legitimate, but hardly more wise than the irresponsible talk of strategy that never changes, and of terms of peace that do not matter.

And above it all—unaccountably persistent—the decrepit, old, hundred years old, spectre of Russia's might still faces Europe from across the teeming graves of Russian people. This dreaded and strange apparition, bristling with bayonets, armed with chains, hung over with holy images; that something not of this world, partaking of a ravenous ghoul, of a blind Djinn grown up from a cloud, and of the Old Man of the Sea, still faces us with its old stupidity, with its strange mystical arrogance, stamping its shadowy feet upon the gravestone of autocracy already cracked beyond repair by the torpedoes of Togo and the guns of Oyama, already heaving in the blood-soaked ground with the first stirrings of a resurrection.

Never before had the Western world the opportunity to look so deep into the black abyss which separates a soulless autocracy posing as, and even believing itself to be, the arbiter of Europe, from the benighted, starved souls of its people. This is the real object-lesson of this war, its unforgettable information. And this war's true mission, disengaged from the economic origins of that contest, from doors open or shut, from the fields of Korea for Russian wheat or Japanese rice, from the ownership of ice-free ports and the command of the waters of the East—its true mission was to lay a ghost. It has accomplished it. Whether Kuropatkin was incapable or unlucky, whether or not Russia, issuing next year, or the year after next, from behind a rampart of piled-up corpses, will win or lose a fresh campaign, are minor considerations. The task of Japan is done, the mission accomplished; the ghost of Russia's might is laid. Only Europe, accustomed so long to the presence of that portent, seems unable to comprehend that, as in the fables of our childhood, the twelve strokes of the hour have rung, the cock has crowed, the apparition has vanished—never to haunt again this world which has been used to gaze at it with vague dread and many misgivings.

It was a fascination. And the hallucination still lasts, as inexplicable in its persistence as in its duration. It seems so unaccountable, that the doubt arises as to the sincerity of all that talk as to what Russia will or will not do: whether it will raise or not another army, whether it will bury the Japanese in Manchuria under seventy millions of sacrificed peasants' caps (as her Press boasted little more than a year ago) or give up to Japan that jewel of her crown, Saghalien, together with some other things; whether, perchance, as an interesting alternative, it will make peace on the Amur in order to make war beyond the Oxus.

All these speculations (with many others) have appeared gravely in print; and if they have been gravely considered to only one reader out of each hundred, there must be something subtly noxious to the human brain in the composition of newspaper ink; or else it is that the large page, the columns of words, the leaded headings, exalt the mind into a stage of feverish credulity. The printed page of the Press makes a sort of still uproar, taking from men both the power to reflect and the faculty of genuine feeling, leaving them only the artificially created need of having something exciting to talk about.

The truth is that the Russia of our fathers, of our childhood, of our middle-age; the testamentary Russia of Peter the Great—who imagined that all the nations were delivered into the hand of Tsardom—can do nothing. It can do nothing because it does not exist. It has vanished for ever at last, and as yet there is no new Russia to take the place of that ill-omened creation, which, being a fantasy of a madman's brain, could in reality be nothing else than a figure out of a nightmare seated upon a monument of fear and oppression.

The true greatness of a State does not spring from such a contemptible source. It is a matter of logical growth, of faith and courage. Its inspiration springs from the constructive instinct of the people, governed by the strong hand of a collective conscience and voiced in the wisdom and counsel of men who seldom reap the reward of gratitude. Many States have been powerful, but, perhaps, none have been truly great—as yet. That the position of a State in reference to the moral methods of its development can be seen only historically, is true. Perhaps mankind has not lived long enough for a comprehensive view of any particular case. Perhaps no one will ever live long enough; and perhaps this earth shared out amongst our clashing ambitions by the anxious arrangements of statesmen will come to an end before we attain the felicity of greeting with unanimous applause the perfect fruition of a great State. It is even possible that we are destined for another sort of bliss altogether: that sort which consists in being perpetually duped by false appearances. But whatever political illusion the future may hold out to our fear or our admiration, there will be none, it is safe to say, which in the magnitude of antihumanitarian effect will equal that phantom now driven out of the world by the thunder of thousands of guns; none that in its retreat will cling with an equally shameless sincerity to more unworthy supports, to the moral corruption and mental darkness of slavery, to the mere brute force of numbers.

This very ignominy of infatuation should make clear to men's feelings and reason that the downfall of Russia's might is unavoidable. Spectral it lived and spectral it disappears without leaving a memory of a single generous deed, of a single service rendered—even involuntarily—to the polity of nations. Other despotisms there have been, but none whose origin was so grimly fantastic in its baseness, and the beginning of whose end was so gruesomely ignoble. What is amazing is the myth of its irresistible strength which is dying so hard.

Considered historically, Russia's influence in Europe seems the most baseless thing in the world; a sort of convention invented by diplomatists for some dark purpose of their own, one would suspect, if the lack of grasp upon the realities of any given situation were not the main characteristic of the management of international relations. A glance back at the last hundred years shows the invariable, one may say the logical, powerlessness of Russia. As a military power it has never achieved by itself a single great thing. It has been indeed able to repel an ill-considered invasion, but only by having recourse to the extreme methods of desperation. In its attacks upon its specially selected victim this giant always struck as if with a withered right hand. All the campaigns against Turkey prove this, from Potemkin's time to the last Eastern war in 1878, entered upon with every advantage of a well-nursed prestige and a carefully fostered fanaticism. Even the half-armed were always too much for the might of Russia, or, rather, of the Tsardom. It was victorious only against the practically disarmed, as, in regard to its ideal of territorial expansion, a glance at a map will prove sufficiently. As an ally, Russia has been always unprofitable, taking her share in the defeats rather than in the victories of her friends, but always pushing her own claims with the arrogance of an arbiter of military success. She has been unable to help to any purpose a single principle to hold its own, not even the principle of authority and legitimism which Nicholas the First had declared so haughtily to rest under his special protection; just as Nicholas the Second has tried to make the maintenance of peace on earth his own exclusive affair. And the first Nicholas was a good Russian; he held the belief in the sacredness of his realm with such an intensity of faith that he could not survive the first shock of doubt. Rightly envisaged, the Crimean war was the end of what remained of absolutism and legitimism in Europe. It threw the way open for the liberation of Italy. The war in Manchuria makes an end of absolutism in Russia, whoever has got to perish from the shock behind a rampart of dead ukases, manifestoes, and rescripts. In the space of fifty years the self-appointed Apostle of

Absolutism and the self-appointed Apostle of Peace, the Augustus and the Augustulus of the *régime* that was wont to speak contemptuously to European Foreign Offices in the beautiful French phrases of Prince Gorchakov, have fallen victims, each after his kind, to their shadowy and dreadful familiar, to the phantom, part ghoul, part Djinn, part Old Man of the Sea, with beak and claws and a double head, looking greedily both east and west on the confines of two continents.

That nobody through all that time penetrated the true nature of the monster it is impossible to believe. But of the many who must have seen, all were either too modest, too cautious, perhaps too discreet, to speak; or else were too insignificant to be heard or believed. Yet not all.

In the very early sixties, Prince Bismarck, then about to leave his post of Prussian Minister in St. Petersburg, called—so the story goes—upon another distinguished diplomatist. After some talk upon the general situation, the future Chancellor of the German Empire remarked that it was his practice to resume the impressions he had carried out of every country where he had made a long stay, in a short sentence, which he caused to be engraved upon some trinket. "I am leaving this country now, and this is what I bring away from it," he continued, taking off his finger a new ring to show to his colleague the inscription inside: "*La Russie, c'est le néant.*"

Prince Bismarck had the truth of the matter and was neither too modest nor too discreet to speak out. Certainly he was not afraid of not being believed. Yet he did not shout his knowledge from the house-tops. He meant to have the phantom as his accomplice in an enterprise which has set the clock of peace back for many a year.

He had his way. The German Empire has been an accomplished fact for more than a third of a century—a great and dreadful legacy left to the world by the ill-omened phantom of Russia's might.

It is that phantom which is disappearing now—unexpectedly, astonishingly, as if by a touch of that wonderful magic for which the East has always been famous. The pretence of belief in its existence will no longer answer anybody's purposes (now Prince Bismarck is dead) unless the purposes of the writers of sensational paragraphs as to this *Néant* making an armed descent upon the plains of India. That sort of folly would be beneath notice if it did not distract attention from the real problem created for Europe by a war in the Far East.

For good or evil in the working out of her destiny, Russia is bound to remain a *Néant* for many long years, in a more even than a Bismarckian sense. The very fear of this spectre being gone, it behoves us to consider its legacy—the fact (no phantom that) accomplished in Central Europe by its help and connivance.

The German Empire may feel at bottom the loss of an old accomplice always amenable to the confidential whispers of a bargain; but in the first instance it cannot but rejoice at the fundamental weakening of a possible obstacle to its instincts of territorial expansion. There is a removal of that latent feeling of restraint which the presence of a powerful neighbour, however implicated with you in a sense of common guilt, is bound to inspire. The common guilt of the two Empires is defined precisely by their frontier line running through the Polish provinces. Without indulging in excessive feelings of indignation at that country's partition, or going so far as to believe—with a late French politician—in the "*immanente justice des choses,*" it is clear that a material situation, based upon an essentially immoral transaction, contains the germ of fatal differences in the temperament of the two partners in iniquity—whatever the iniquity is. Germany has been the evil counsellor of Russia on all the questions of her Polish problem. Always urging the adoption of the most repressive measures with a perfectly logical duplicity, Prince Bismarck's Empire has taken care to couple the neighbourly offers of military assistance with merciless advice. The thought of the Polish provinces accepting a frank reconciliation with a humanised Russia and bringing the weight of homogeneous loyalty within a few miles of Berlin, has been always intensely distasteful to the arrogant Germanising tendencies of the other partner in iniquity. And, besides, the way to the Baltic provinces leads over the Niemen and over the Vistula.

And now, when there is a possibility of serious internal disturbances destroying the sort of order autocracy has kept in Russia, the road over these rivers is seen wearing a more inviting aspect. At any moment the pretext of armed intervention may be found in a revolutionary outbreak provoked by Socialists, perhaps—but at any rate by the political immaturity of the enlightened classes and by the political barbarism of the Russian people. The throes of Russian resurrection will be long and painful. This is not the place to speculate upon the nature of these convulsions, but there must be some violent break-up of the lamentable tradition, a shattering of the social, of the administrative—certainly of the territorial—unity.

Voices have been heard saying that the time for reforms in Russia is already past. This is the superficial view of the more profound truth that for Russia there has never been such a time within the memory of mankind. It is impossible to initiate a rational scheme of reform upon a phase of blind absolutism; and in Russia there has never been anything else to which the faintest tradition could, after ages of error, go back as to a parting of ways.

In Europe the old monarchical principle stands justified in its historical struggle with the growth of political liberty by the evolution of the idea of nationality as we see it concreted at the present time; by the inception of that wider solidarity grouping together around the standard of monarchical power these larger agglomerations of mankind. This service of unification, creating close-knit communities possessing the ability, the will, and the power to pursue a common ideal, has prepared the ground for the advent of a still larger understanding: for the solidarity of Europeanism, which must be the next step towards the advent of Concord and Justice; an advent that, however delayed by the fatal worship of force and the errors of national selfishness, has been, and remains, the only possible goal of our progress.

The conceptions of legality, of larger patriotism, of national duties and aspirations have grown under the shadow of the old monarchies of Europe, which were the creations of historical necessity. There were seeds of wisdom in their very mistakes and abuses. They had a past and a future; they were human. But under the shadow of Russian autocracy nothing could grow. Russian autocracy succeeded to nothing; it had no historical past, and it cannot hope for a historical future. It can only end. By no industry of investigation, by no fantastic stretch of benevolence, can it be presented as a phase of development through which a Society, a State, must pass on the way to the full consciousness of its destiny. It lies outside the stream of progress. This despotism has been utterly un-European. Neither has it been Asiatic in its nature. Oriental despotisms belong to the history of mankind; they have left their trace on our minds and our imagination by their splendour, by their culture, by their art, by the exploits of great conquerors. The record of their rise and decay has an intellectual value; they are in their origins and their course the manifestations of human needs, the instruments of racial temperament, of catastrophic force, of faith and fanaticism. The Russian autocracy as we see it now is a thing apart. It is impossible to assign to it any rational origin in the vices, the misfortunes, the necessities, or the aspirations of mankind. That despotism has neither an European nor an Oriental parentage; more, it seems to have no root either in the institutions or the follies of this earth. What strikes one with a sort of awe is just this something inhuman in its character. It is like a visitation, like a curse from Heaven falling in the darkness of ages upon the immense plains of forest and steppe lying dumbly on the confines of two continents: a true desert harbouring no Spirit either of the East or of the West.

This pitiful fate of a country held by an evil spell, suffering from an awful visitation for which the responsibility cannot be traced either to her sins or her follies, has made Russia as a nation so difficult to understand by Europe. From the very first ghastly dawn of her existence as a State she had to breathe the atmosphere of despotism; she found nothing but the arbitrary will of an obscure autocrat at the beginning and end of her organisation. Hence arises her impenetrability to whatever is true in Western thought. Western thought, when it crosses her frontier, falls under the spell of her autocracy and becomes a noxious parody of itself. Hence the contradictions, the riddles of her national life, which are looked upon with such curiosity by the rest of the world. The curse had entered her very soul; autocracy, and nothing else in the world, has moulded her institutions, and with the poison of slavery drugged the national temperament into the apathy of a hopeless fatalism. It seems to have gone into the blood, tainting every mental activity in its source by a half-mystical, insensate, fascinating assertion of purity and holiness. The Government of Holy Russia, arrogating to itself the supreme power to torment and slaughter the bodies of its subjects like a God-sent scourge, has been most cruel to those whom it allowed to live under the shadow of its dispensation. The worst crime against humanity of that system we behold now crouching at bay behind vast heaps of mangled corpses is the ruthless destruction of innumerable minds. The greatest horror of the world—madness—walked faithfully in its train. Some of the best intellects of Russia, after struggling in vain against the spell, ended by throwing themselves at the feet of that hopeless despotism as a giddy man leaps into an abyss. An attentive survey of Russia's literature, of her Church, of her administration and the crosscurrents of her thought, must end in the verdict that the Russia of to-day has not the right to give her voice on a single question touching the future of humanity, because from the very inception of her being the brutal destruction of dignity, of truth, of rectitude, of all that is faithful in human nature has been made the imperative condition of her existence. The great governmental secret of that imperium which Prince Bismarck had the insight and the courage to call *"le néant"* has been the extirpation of every intellectual hope. To pronounce in the face of such a past the word Evolution, which is precisely the expression of the highest intellectual hope, is a gruesome pleasantry. There can be no evolution out of a grave. Another word of less scientific sound has been very much pronounced of late in connection with Russia's future, a word of more vague import, a word of dread as much as of hope—Revolution.

In the face of the events of the last four months, this word has sprung instinctively, as it were, on grave lips, and has been heard with solemn forebodings. More or less consciously, Europe is preparing herself for a spectacle of much violence and perhaps of an inspiring nobility of greatness. And there will be nothing of what she expects. She will see neither the anticipated character of the violence, nor yet any signs of generous greatness. Her expectations, more or less vaguely expressed, give the measure of her ignorance of that *Néant* which for so many years had remained hidden behind this phantom of invincible armies.

Néant! In a way, yes! And yet perhaps Prince Bismarck has let himself be led away by the seduction of a good phrase into the use of an inexact form. The form of his judgment had to be pithy, striking, engraved within a ring. If he erred, then, no doubt he erred deliberately. The saying was near enough the truth to serve, and perhaps he did not want to destroy utterly by a more severe definition the prestige of the sham that could not deceive his genius. Prince Bismarck has been really complimentary to the useful phantom of the autocratic might. There is an awe-inspiring idea of infinity conveyed in the word *Néant*—and in Russia there is no idea. She is not a *Néant,* she is and has been simply the negation of everything worth living for. She is not an empty void, she is a yawning chasm open between East and West; a bottomless abyss that has swallowed up every hope of mercy, every aspiration towards personal dignity, towards freedom, towards knowledge, every ennobling desire of the heart, every redeeming whisper of conscience. Those that have peered into that abyss, where the dreams of Panslavism, of universal conquest, mingled with the hate and contempt for Western ideas, drift impotently like shapes of mist, know well that it is bottomless; that there is in it no ground for anything that could in the remotest degree serve even the lowest interests of mankind—and certainly no ground ready for a revolution. The sin of the old European monarchies was not the absolutism inherent in every form of government; it was the inability to alter the forms of their legality, grown narrow and oppressive with the march of time. Every form of legality is bound to degenerate into oppression, and the legality in the forms of monarchical institutions sooner, perhaps, than any other. It has not been the business of monarchies to be adaptive from within. With the mission of uniting and consolidating the particular ambitions and interests of feudalism in favour of a larger conception of a State, of giving self-consciousness, force and nationality to the scattered energies of thought and action, they were fated to lag behind the march of ideas they had themselves set in motion in a direction they could neither understand nor approve. Yet, for all that, the thrones still remain, and what is more significant, perhaps, some of the dynasties, too, have survived. The revolutions of European States have never been in the nature of absolute protests *en masse* against the monarchical principle; they were the uprising of the people against the oppressive degeneration of legality. But there never has been any legality in Russia; she is a negation of that as of everything else that has its root in reason or conscience. The ground of every revolution had to be intellectually prepared. A revolution is a short cut in the rational development of national needs in response to the growth of world-wide ideals. It is conceivably possible for a monarch of genius to put himself at the head of a revolution without ceasing to be the king of his people. For the autocracy of Holy Russia the only conceivable self-reform is—suicide.

The same relentless fate holds in its grip the all-powerful ruler and his helpless people. Wielders of a power purchased by an unspeakable baseness of subjection to the Khans of the Tartar horde, the Princes of Russia who, in their heart of hearts had come in time to regard themselves as superior to every monarch of Europe, have never risen to be the chiefs of a nation. Their authority has never been sanctioned by popular tradition, by ideas of intelligent loyalty, of devotion, of political necessity, of simple expediency, or even by the power of the sword. In whatever form of upheaval autocratic Russia is to find her end, it can never be a revolution fruitful of moral consequences to mankind. It cannot be anything else but a rising of slaves. It is a tragic circumstance that the only thing one can wish to that people who had never seen face to face either law, order, justice, right, truth about itself or the rest of the world; who had known nothing outside the capricious will of its irresponsible masters, is that it should find in the approaching hour of need, not an organiser or a law-giver, with the wisdom of a Lycurgus or a Solon for their service, but at least the force of energy and desperation in some as yet unknown Spartacus.

A brand of hopeless mental and moral inferiority is set upon Russian achievements; and the coming events of her internal changes, however appalling they may be in their magnitude, will be nothing more impressive than the convulsions of a colossal body. As her boasted military force that, corrupt in its origin, has ever struck no other but faltering blows, so her soul, kept benumbed by her temporal and spiritual master with the poison of tyranny and superstition, will find itself on awakening possessed of no language, a monstrous full-grown child having first to learn the ways of living thought and articulate speech. It is safe to say tyranny, assuming a thousand protean shapes, will remain clinging to her struggles for a long time before her blind multitudes succeed at last in trampling her out of existence under their millions of bare feet.

That would be the beginning. What is to come after? The conquest of freedom to call your soul your own is only the first step on the road to excellence. We, in Europe, have gone a step or two further, have had the time to forget how little that freedom means. To Russia it must seem everything. A prisoner shut up in a noisome dungeon concentrates all his hope and desire on the moment of stepping out beyond the gates. It appears to him pregnant with an immense and final importance; whereas what is important is the spirit in which he will draw the first breath of freedom, the counsels he will hear, the hands he may find extended, the endless days of toil that must follow, wherein he will have to build his future with no other material but what he can find within himself.

It would be vain for Russia to hope for the support and counsel of collective wisdom. Since 1870 (as a distinguished statesman of the old tradition disconsolately exclaimed) *"Il n'y a plus d'Europe!"* There is, indeed, no Europe. The idea of a Europe united in the solidarity of her dynasties, which for a moment seemed to dawn on the horizon of the Vienna Congress through the subsiding dust of Napoleonic alarums and excursions, has been extinguished by the larger glamour of less restraining ideals. Instead of the doctrines of solidarity it was the doctrine of nationalities, much more favourable to spoliations, that came to the front, and since its greatest triumphs at Sadowa and Sedan there is no Europe. Meanwhile till the time comes when there will be no frontiers, there are alliances so shamelessly based upon the exigencies of suspicion and mistrust that their cohesive force waxes and wanes with every year, almost with the event of every passing month. This is the atmosphere Russia will find when the last rampart of tyranny has been beaten down. But what hands, what voices will she find on coming out into the light of day? An ally she has yet who more than any other of Russia's allies has found that it had parted with lots of solid substance in exchange for a shadow. It is true that the shadow was indeed the mightiest, the darkest that the modern world had ever known—and the most overbearing. But it is fading now, and the tone of truest anxiety as to what is to take place will come, no doubt, from that and no other direction, and no doubt, also, it will have that note of generosity which even in the moments of greatest aberration is seldom wanting in the voice of the French people.

Two neighbours Russia will find at her door. Austria, traditionally unaggressive whenever her hand is not forced, ruled by a dynasty of uncertain future, weakened by her duality, can only speak to her in an uncertain, bilingual phrase. Prussia, grown in something like forty years from an almost pitiful dependant into a bullying friend and evil counsellor of Russia's masters, may, indeed, hasten to extend a strong hand to the weakness of her exhausted body, but if so it will be only with the intention of tearing away the long-coveted part of her substance.

Pan-Germanism is by no means a shape of mists, and Germany is anything but a *Néant* where thought and effort are likely to lose themselves without sound or trace. It is a powerful and voracious organisation, full of unscrupulous self-confidence, whose appetite for aggrandisement will only be limited by the power of helping itself to the severed members of its friends and neighbours. The era of wars so eloquently denounced by the old Republicans as the peculiar blood guilt of dynastic ambitions is by no means over yet. They will be fought out differently, with lesser frequency, with an increased bitterness and the savage tooth-and-claw obstinacy of a struggle for existence. They will make us regret the time of dynastic ambitions, with their human absurdity moderated by prudence and even by shame, by the fear of personal responsibility and the regard paid to certain forms of conventional decency. For, if the monarchs of Europe have been derided for addressing each other as "brother" in autograph communications, that relationship was at least as effective as any form of brotherhood likely to be established between the rival nations of this continent, which, we are assured on all hands, is the heritage of democracy. In the ceremonial brotherhood of monarchs the reality of blood-ties, for what little it is worth, acted often as a drag on unscrupulous desires of glory or greed. Besides, there was always the common danger of exasperated peoples, and some respect for each other's divine right. No leader of a democracy, without other ancestry but the sudden shout of a multitude, and debarred by the very condition of his power from even thinking of a direct heir, will have any interest in calling brother the leader of another democracy—a chief as fatherless and heirless as himself.

The war of 1870, brought about by the third Napoleon's half-generous, half-selfish adoption of the principle of nationalities, was the first war characterised by a special intensity of hate, by a new note in the tune of an old song for which we may thank the Teutonic thoroughness. Was it not that excellent bourgeoise, Princess Bismarck (to keep only to great examples), who was so righteously anxious to see men, women, and children—emphatically the children, too—of the abominable French nation massacred off the face of the earth? This illustration of the new war-temper is artlessly revealed in the prattle of the amiable Busch, the Chancellor's pet "reptile" of the Press. And this was supposed to be a war for an idea! Too much, however, should not be made of that good wife's and mother's sentiments any more than of the good First Emperor William's tears, shed so abundantly after every battle, by letter, telegram, and otherwise, during the course of the same war, before a dumb and shamefaced continent. These were merely the expressions of the simplicity of a nation which more than any other has a tendency to run into the grotesque. There is worse to come.

To-day, in the fierce grapple of two nations of different race, the short era of national wars seems about to close. No war will be waged for an idea. The "noxious idle aristocracies" of yesterday fought without malice for an occupation, for the honour, for the fun of the thing. The virtuous, industrious democratic States of to-morrow may yet be reduced to fighting for a crust of dry bread, with all the hate, ferocity, and fury that must attach to the vital importance of such an issue. The dreams sanguine humanitarians raised almost to ecstasy about the year fifty of the last century by the moving sight of the Crystal Palace—crammed full with that variegated rubbish which it seems to be the bizarre fate of humanity to produce for the benefit of a few employers of labour—have vanished as quickly as they had arisen. The golden hopes of peace have in a single night turned to dead leaves in every drawer of every benevolent theorist's writing table. A swift disenchantment overtook the incredible infatuation which could put its trust in the peaceful nature of industrial and commercial competition.

Industrialism and commercialism—wearing high-sounding names in many languages (*Weltpolitik* may serve for one instance), picking up coins behind the severe and disdainful figure of science whose giant strides have widened for us the horizon of the universe by some few inches—stand ready, almost eager, to appeal to the sword as soon as the globe of the earth has shrunk beneath our growing numbers by another ell or so. And democracy, which has elected to pin its faith to the supremacy of material interests, will have to fight their battles to the bitter end, on a mere pittance—unless, indeed, some statesman of exceptional ability and overwhelming prestige succeeds in carrying through an international understanding for the delimitation of spheres of trade all over the earth, on the model of the territorial spheres of influence marked in Africa to keep the competitors for the privilege of improving the nigger (as a buying machine) from flying prematurely at each other's throats.

This seems the only expedient at hand for the temporary maintenance of European peace, with its alliances based on mutual distrust, preparedness for war as its ideal, and the fear of wounds, luckily stronger, so far, than the pinch of hunger, its only guarantee. The true peace of the world will be a place of refuge much less like a beleaguered fortress and more, let us hope, in the nature of an Inviolable Temple. It will be built on less perishable foundations than those of material interests. But it must be confessed that the architectural aspect of the universal city remains as yet inconceivable—that the very ground for its erection has not been cleared of the jungle.

Never before in history has the right of war been more fully admitted in the rounded periods of public speeches, in books, in public prints, in all the public works of peace, culminating in the establishment of the Hague Tribunal—that solemnly official recognition of the Earth as a House of Strife. To him whose indignation is qualified by a measure of hope and affection, the efforts of mankind to work its own salvation present a sight of alarming comicality. After clinging for ages to the steps of the heavenly throne, they are now, without much modifying their attitude, trying with touching ingenuity to steal one by one the thunderbolts of their Jupiter. They have removed war from the list of Heaven-sent visitations that could only be prayed against; they have erased its name from the supplication against the wrath of war, pestilence, and famine, as it is found in the litanies of the Roman Catholic Church; they have dragged the scourge down from the skies and have made it into a calm and regulated institution. At first sight the change does not seem for the better. Jove's thunderbolt looks a most dangerous plaything in the hands of the people. But a solemnly established institution begins to grow old at once in the discussion, abuse, worship, and execration of men. It grows obsolete, odious, and intolerable; it stands fatally condemned to an unhonoured old age.

Therein lies the best hope of advanced thought, and the best way to help its prospects is to provide in the fullest, frankest way for the conditions of the present day. War is one of its conditions; it is its principal condition. It lies at the heart of every question agitating the fears and hopes of a humanity divided against itself. The succeeding ages have changed nothing except the watchwords of the armies. The intellectual stage of mankind being as yet in its infancy, and States, like most individuals, having but a feeble and imperfect consciousness of the worth and force of the inner life, the need of making their existence manifest to themselves is determined in the direction of physical activity. The idea of ceasing to grow in territory, in strength, in wealth, in influence—in anything but wisdom and self-knowledge—is odious to them as the omen of the end. Action, in which is to be found the illusion of a mastered destiny, can alone satisfy our uneasy vanity and lay to rest the haunting fear of the future—a sentiment concealed, indeed, but proving its existence by the force it has, when invoked, to stir the passions of a nation. It will be long before we have learned that in the great darkness before us there is nothing that we need fear. Let us act lest we perish—is the cry. And the only form of action open to a State can be of no other than aggressive nature.

There are many kinds of aggressions, though the sanction of them is one and the same—the magazine rifle of the latest pattern. In preparation for or against that form of action the States of Europe are spending now such moments of uneasy leisure as they can snatch from the labours of factory and counting-house.

Never before has war received so much homage at the lips of men, and reigned with less disputed sway in their minds. It has harnessed science to its gun-carriages; it has enriched a few respectable manufacturers, scattered doles of food and raiment amongst a few thousand skilled workmen, devoured the first youth of whole generations, and reaped its harvest of countless corpses. It has perverted the intelligence of men, women, and children, and has made the speeches of Emperors, Kings, Presidents, and Ministers monotonous with ardent protestations of fidelity to peace. Indeed, war has made peace altogether its own, it has modelled it on its own image: a martial, overbearing, war-lord sort of peace, with a mailed fist, and turned-up moustaches, ringing with the din of grand manœuvres, eloquent with allusions to glorious feats of arms; it has made peace so magnificent as to be almost as expensive to keep up as itself. It has sent out apostles of its own, who at one time went about (mostly in newspapers) preaching the gospel of the mystic sanctity of its sacrifices, and the regenerating power of spilt blood, to the poor in mind—whose name is legion.

It has been observed that in the course of earthly greatness a day of culminating triumph is often paid for by a morrow of sudden extinction. Let us hope it is so. Yet the dawn of that day of retribution may be a long time breaking above a dark horizon. War is with us now; and, whether this one ends soon or late, war will be with us again. And it is the way of true wisdom for men and States to take account of things as they are.

Civilisation has done its little best by our sensibilities for whose growth it is responsible. It has managed to remove the sights and sounds of battlefields away from our doorsteps. But it cannot be expected to achieve the feat always and under every variety of circumstance. Some day it must fail, and we shall have then a wealth of appallingly unpleasant sensations brought home to us with painful intimacy. It is not absurd to suppose that whatever war comes to us next it will *not* be a distant war waged by Russia either beyond the Amur or beyond the Oxus.

The Japanese armies have laid that ghost for ever, because the Russia of the future will not, for the reasons explained above, be the Russia of to-day. It will not have the same thoughts, resentments and aims. It is even a question whether it will preserve its gigantic frame unaltered and unbroken. All speculation loses itself in the magnitude of the events made possible by the defeat of an autocracy whose only shadow of a title to existence was the invincible power of military conquest. That autocratic Russia will have a miserable end in harmony with its base origin and inglorious life does not seem open to doubt. The problem of the immediate future is posed not by the eventual manner but by the approaching fact of its disappearance.

The Japanese armies, in laying the oppressive ghost, have not only accomplished what will be recognized historically as an important mission in the world's struggle against all forms of evil, but have also created a situation. They have created a situation in the East which they are competent to manage by themselves; and in doing this they have brought about a change in the condition of the West with which Europe is not well prepared to deal. The common ground of concord, good faith and justice is not sufficient to establish an action upon, since the conscience of but very few men amongst us, and of no single Western nation as yet, will brook the restraint of abstract ideas as against the fascination of a material advantage. And eagle-eyed wisdom alone cannot take the lead of human action, which in its nature must for ever remain short-sighted. The trouble of the civilised world is the want of a common conservative principle abstract enough to give the impulse, practical enough to form the rallying point of international action tending towards the restraint of particular ambitions. Peace tribunals instituted for the greater glory of war will not replace it. Whether such a principle exists—who can say? If it does not, then it ought to be invented. A sage with a sense of humour and a heart of compassion should set about it without loss of time, and a solemn prophet full of words and fire ought to be given the task of preparing the minds. So far there is no trace of such a principle anywhere in sight; even its plausible imitations (never very effective) have disappeared long ago before the doctrine of national aspirations. *Il n'y a plus d'Europe*—there is only an armed and trading continent, the home of slowly maturing economical contests for life and death, and of loudly proclaimed world-wide ambitions. There are also other ambitions not so loud, but deeply rooted in the envious acquisitive temperament of the last comer amongst the great Powers of the Continent, whose feet are not exactly in the ocean—not yet—and whose head is very high up—in Pomerania, the breeding place of such precious Grenadiers that Prince Bismarck (whom it is a pleasure to quote) would not have given the bones of one of them for the settlement of the old Eastern Question. But times have changed since, by way of keeping up, I suppose, some old barbaric German rite, the faithful servant of the Hohenzollerns was buried alive to celebrate the accession of a new Emperor.

Already the voice of surmises has been heard hinting tentatively at a possible re-grouping of European Powers. The alliance of the three Empires is supposed possible. And it may be possible. The myth of Russia's power is dying very hard—hard enough for that combination to take place—such is the fascination that a discredited show of numbers will still exercise upon the imagination of a people trained to the worship of force. Germany may be willing to lend its support to a tottering autocracy for the sake of an undisputed first place and of a prepondering voice in the settlement of every question in that south-east of Europe which merges into Asia. No principle being involved in such an alliance of mere expediency, it would never be allowed to stand in the way of Germany's other ambitions. The fall of autocracy would bring its restraint automatically to an end. Thus it may be believed that the support Russian despotism may get from its once humble friend and client will not be stamped by that thoroughness which is supposed to be the mark of German superiority. Russia weakened down to the second place, or Russia eclipsed altogether during the throes of her regeneration, will answer equally well the plans of German policy—which are many and various and often incredible, though the aim of them all is the same: aggrandisement of territory and influence, with no regard to right and justice, either in the East or in the West. For that and no other is the true note of your *Weltpolitik* which desires to live.

The German eagle with a Prussian head looks all round the horizon, not so much for something to do that would count for good in the records of the earth, as simply for something good to get. He gazes upon the land and upon the sea with the same covetous steadiness, for he has become of late a maritime eagle, and has learned to box the compass. He gazes north and south, and east and west, and is inclined to look intemperately upon the waters of the Mediterranean when they are blue. The disappearance of the Russian phantom has given a foreboding of unwonted freedom to the *Weltpolitik*. According to the national tendency this assumption of Imperial impulses would run into the grotesque were it not for the spikes of the *pickelhaubes* peeping out grimly from behind. Germany's attitude proves that no peace for the earth can be found in the expansion of material interests which she seems to have adopted exclusively as her only aim, ideal, and watchword. For the use of those who gaze half-unbelieving at the passing away of the Russian phantom, part Ghoul, part Djinn, part Old Man of the Sea, and wait half-doubting for the birth of a nation's soul in this age which knows no miracles, the once-famous saying of poor Gambetta, tribune of the people (who was simple and believed in the "immanent justice of things"), may be adapted in the shape of a warning that, so far as a future of liberty, concord, and justice is concerned: *"Le Prussianisme—voilà l'ennemi!"*

SOME REFLECTIONS ON THE LOSS OF THE *TITANIC*

1912

It is with a certain bitterness that one must admit to oneself that the late S. S. *Titanic* had a "good press." It is perhaps because I have no great practice of daily newspapers (I have never seen so many of them together lying about my room) that the white spaces and the big lettering of the headlines have an incongruous festive air to my eyes, a disagreeable effect of a feverish exploitation of a sensational God-send. And if ever a loss at sea fell under the definition in the terms of a bill of lading, of Act of God, this one does, in its magnitude, suddenness and severity; and in the chastening influence it should have on the self-confidence of mankind.

I say this with all the seriousness the occasion demands, though I have neither the competence nor the wish to take a theological view of this great misfortune, sending so many souls to their last account. It is but a natural *reflection*. Another one flowing also from the phraseology of bills of lading (a bill of lading is a shipping document limiting in certain of its clauses the liability of the carrier) is that the "King's Enemies" of a more or less overt sort are not altogether sorry that this fatal mishap should strike the prestige of the greatest merchant service of the world. I believe that not a thousand miles from these shores certain public prints have betrayed in gothic letters their satisfaction—to speak plainly—by rather ill-natured comments.

In what light one is to look at the action of the American Senate is more difficult to say. From a certain point of view the sight of the august senators of a great power rushing to New York [. . .] seems to furnish the Shakespearian touch of the comic to the real tragedy of the fatuous drowning of all these people who to the last moment put their trust in mere bigness, in the reckless affirmations of commercial men and mere technicians and in the irresponsible paragraphs of the newspapers booming these ships! Yes, a grim touch of comedy. One asks oneself what these men are after, with this very provincial display of authority. I beg my friends in the United States pardon for calling these zealous senators men. I don't wish to be disrespectful. They may be of the stature of demi-gods for all I know, but at that great distance from the shores of effete Europe and in the presence of so many guileless dead, their size seems diminished from this side. What are they after? What is there for them to find out? We know what had happened. The ship scraped her side against a piece of ice, and sank after floating for two hours and a half, taking a lot of people down with her. What more can they find out [. . .]?

[. . .] Is it indignation at the loss of so many lives which is at work here? Well, the American railroads kill very many people during one single year, I dare say. Then why don't these dignitaries come down on the presidents of their own railroads, of which one can't say whether they are mere means of transportation or a sort of gambling game for the use of American plutocrats. Is it only an ardent and, upon the whole, praiseworthy desire for information? But the reports of the inquiry tell us that the august senators, though raising a lot of questions testifying to the complete innocence and even blankness of their minds, are unable to understand what the second officer is saying to them. We are so informed by the press from the other side. Even such a simple expression as that one of the look-out men was stationed in the "eyes of the ship" was too much for the senators of the land of graphic expression. What it must have been in the more recondite matters I won't even try to think, because I have no mind for smiles just now. They were greatly exercised about the sound of explosions heard when half the ship was under water already. Was there one? Were there two? They seemed to be smelling a rat there! Has not some charitable soul told them (what even schoolboys who read sea stories know) that when a ship sinks from a leak like this, a deck or two is always blown up; and that when a steamship goes down by the head, the boilers may, and often do break adrift with a sound which resembles the sound of an explosion? And they may, indeed, explode, for all I know. In the only case I have seen of a steamship sinking there was such a sound, but I didn't dive down after her to investigate. She was not of 45,000 tons and declared unsinkable, but the sight was impressive enough. I shall never forget the muffled, mysterious detonation, the sudden agitation of the sea round the slowly raised stem, and to this day I have in my eye the propeller, seen perfectly still in its frame against a clear evening sky.

But perhaps the second officer has explained to them by this time this and a few other little facts. Though why an officer of the merchant service should answer the questions of any king, emperor, autocrat, or senator of any foreign power (as to an event in which a British ship done was concerned, and which did not even take place in the territorial waters of that power) passes my understanding. The only authority he is bound to answer is the Board of Trade. But with what face the Board of Trade, which, having made the regulations for ten-thousand ton ships, put its dear old bald head under its wing for ten years, took it out only to shelve an important report, and with a dreary murmur "Unsinkable" put it back again, in the hope of not being disturbed for another ten years, with what face it will be putting questions to that man who has done his duty, as to the facts of this disaster and as to his professional conduct in it—well, I don't know! I have the greatest respect for our established authorities. I am a disciplined man, and I have a natural indulgence for the weaknesses of human institutions; but I will own that at times I have regretted their—how shall I say it?—their imponderability. A Board of Trade—what is it? A Board of . . . I believe the Speaker of the Irish Parliament is one of the members of it. A ghost. Less than that; as yet a mere memory. An office with adequate and no doubt comfortable furniture and a lot of perfectly irresponsible gentlemen who exist packed in its equable atmosphere softly, as if in a lot of cotton-wool, and with no care in the world; for there can be no care without personal responsibility—such, for instance, as the seamen have—those seamen from whose mouths this irresponsible institution can take away the bread—as a disciplinary measure. Yes—it's all that. And what more? The name of a politician, a party man! Less than nothing; a mere void without as much as a shadow of responsibility cast into it from that light in which move the masses of men who work, who deal in things and face the realities—not the words—of this life.

Years ago I remember overhearing two genuine shellbacks of the old type commenting on a ship's officer, who, if not exactly incompetent, did not commend himself to their severe judgment of accomplished sailor-men. Said one, resuming and concluding the discussion in a funnily judicial tone:

"The Board of Trade must have been drunk when they gave him his certificate."

I confess that this notion of the Board of Trade as an entity having a brain which could be overcome by the fumes of strong liquor charmed me exceedingly. For then it would have been unlike the limited companies of which some exasperated wit has once said that they had no souls to be saved and no bodies to be kicked, and thus were free in this world and the next from all the effective sanctions of conscientious conduct. But, unfortunately, the picturesque pronouncement overheard by me was only a characteristic sally of an annoyed sailor. The Board of Trade is composed of bloodless departments. It has no limbs and no physiognomy, or else at the forthcoming inquiry it might have paid to the victims of the *Titanic* disaster the small tribute of a blush. I ask myself whether the Marine Department of the Board of Trade did really believe, when they decided to shelve the report on equipment for a time, that a ship of 45,000 tons, that *any* ship, could be made practically indestructible by means of watertight bulkheads? It seems incredible to anybody who had ever reflected upon the properties of material, such as wood or steel. You can't, let builders say what they like, make a ship of such dimensions as strong proportionately as a much smaller one. The shocks our old whalers had to stand amongst the heavy floes in Baffin's Bay were perfectly staggering, notwithstanding the most skilful handling, and yet they lasted for years. The *Titanic,* if one may believe the last reports, has only scraped against a piece of ice which, I suspect, was not an enormously bulky and comparatively easily seen berg, but the low edge of a floe—and sank. Leisurely enough, God knows—and here the advantage of bulkheads comes in—for time is a great friend, a good helper—though in this lamentable case these bulkheads served only to prolong the agony of the passengers who could not be saved. But she sank, causing, apart from the sorrow and the pity of the loss of so many lives, a sort of surprising consternation that such a thing should have happened at all. Why? You build a 45,000 ton hotel of thin steel plates to secure the patronage of, say, a couple of thousand rich people (for if it had been for the emigrant trade done, there would have been no such exaggeration of mere size), you decorate it in the style of the Pharaohs or in the Louis Quinze style—I don't know which—and to please the aforesaid fatuous handful of individuals, who have more money than they know what to do with, and to the applause of two continents, you launch that mass with 2,000 people on board at twenty-one knots across the sea—a perfect exhibition of the modern blind trust in mere material and appliances. And then this happens. General uproar. The blind trust in material and appliances has received a terrible shock. I will say nothing of the credulity which accepts any statement which specialists, technicians, and office-people, are pleased to make, whether for purposes of gain or glory. You stand there astonished and hurt in your profoundest sensibilities. But what else under the circumstances could you expect?

For my part I could much sooner believe in an unsinkable ship of 3,000 tons than in one of 40,000 tons. It is one of those things that stand to reason. You can't increase the thickness of scantling and plates indefinitely. And the mere weight of this bigness is an added disadvantage. In reading the reports, the first reflection which occurs to one is that, if that luckless ship had been a couple of hundred feet shorter, she would have probably gone clear of the danger. But then, perhaps, she could not have had a swimming bath and a French café. That, of course, is a serious consideration. I am well aware that those responsible for her short and fatal existence ask us in desolate accents to believe that if she had hit end-on she would have survived. Which, by a sort of coy implication, seems to mean that it was all the fault of the officer of the watch (he is dead now) for trying to avoid the obstacle. We shall have presently, in deference to commercial and industrial interests, a new kind of seamanship. A very new and "progressive" kind. If you see anything in the way, by no means try to avoid it; smash at it full tilt. And then—and then only, you shall see the triumph of material, of clever contrivances, of the whole box of engineering tricks, in fact, and cover with glory a commercial concern of the most unmitigated sort, a great Trust, and a great shipbuilding yard, justly famed for the super-excellence of its material and workmanship. Unsinkable! See? I told you she was unsinkable, if only handled in accordance with the new seamanship. Everything's in that. And, doubtless, the Board of Trade, if properly approached, would consent to give the needed instructions to its examiners of Masters and Mates. Behold the examination-room of the future. Enter to the grizzled examiner a young man of modest aspect: "Are you well up in modern seamanship?" "I hope so, sir." "H'm, let's see. You are at night on the bridge in charge of a 150,000 tons ship, with a motor track, organ-loft, etc., etc., with a full cargo of passengers, a full crew of 1,500 café waiters, two sailors and a boy, three collapsible boats as per Board of Trade regulations, and going at your three quarter speed of, say, about forty knots. You perceive suddenly right ahead, and close to, something that looks like a large ice floe. What would you do?" "Put the helm amidships." "Very well. Why?" "In order to hit end on." "On what grounds should you endeavour to hit end on?" "Because we are taught by our builders and masters that the heavier the smash, the smaller the damage, and because the requirements of material should be attended to."

And so on and so on. The new seamanship: when in doubt try to ram fairly—whatever's before you. Very simple. If only the *Titanic* had rammed that piece of ice (which was *not* a monstrous berg) fairly, every puffing paragraph would have been vindicated in the eyes of the credulous public which pays. But would it have been? Well, I doubt it. I am well aware that in the 'eighties the steamship *Arizona,* one of the "greyhounds of the ocean" in the jargon of that day, did run bows on against a very unmistakeable iceberg, and managed to get into port on her collision bulkhead. But the *Arizona* was not, if I remember rightly, 5,000 tons register, let alone 45,000, and she was not going at twenty knots per hour. I can't be perfectly certain at this distance of time, but her sea-speed could not have been more than fourteen at the outside. Both these facts made for safety. And, even if she had been engined to go twenty knots, there would not have been behind that speed the enormous mass, so difficult to check in its impetus, the terrific weight of which is bound to do damage to itself or others at the slightest contact.

I assure you it is not for the vain pleasure of talking about my own poor experiences, but only to illustrate my point, that I will relate here a very unsensational little incident I witnessed now rather more than twenty years ago in Sydney, N.S.W. Ships were beginning then to grow bigger year after year, though, of course, the present dimensions were not even dreamt of. I was standing on the Circular Quay with a Sydney pilot, watching a big mail steamship of one of our best-known companies being brought alongside. We admired her lines, her noble appearance, and were impressed by her size as well, though her length, I imagine, was hardly half that of the *Titanic*.

She came into the Cove (as that part of the harbour is called), of course very slowly, and at some hundred feet or so short of the quay she lost her way. That quay was then a wooden one, a fine structure of mighty piles and stringers bearing a roadway—a thing of great strength. The ship, as I have said before, stopped moving when some hundred feet from it. Then her engines were rung on slow ahead, and immediately rung off again. The propeller made just about five turns, I should say. She began to move, stealing on, so to speak, without a ripple; coming alongside with the utmost gentleness. I went on looking her over, very much interested, but the man with me, the pilot, muttered under his breath: "Too much, too much." His exercised judgment had warned him of what I did not even suspect. But I believe that neither of us was exactly prepared for what happened. There was a faint concussion of the ground under our feet, a groaning of piles, a snapping of great iron bolts, and with a sound of ripping and splintering, as when a tree is blown down by the wind, a great strong piece of wood, a baulk of squared timber, was displaced several feet as if by enchantment. I looked at my companion in amazement. "I could not have believed it," I declared. "No," he said. "You would not have thought she would have cracked an egg—eh?"

I certainly wouldn't have thought that. He shook his head, and added: "Ah! These great, big things, they want some handling."

Some months afterwards I was back in Sydney. The same pilot brought me in from sea. And I found the same steamship, or else another as like her as two peas, lying at anchor not far from us. The pilot told me she had arrived the day before, and that he was to take her alongside tomorrow. I reminded him jocularly of the damage to the quay. "Oh!" he said, "we are not allowed now to bring them in under their own steam. We are using tugs."

A very wise regulation. And this is my point—that size is to a certain extent an element of weakness. The bigger the ship, the more delicately she must be handled. Here is a contact which, in the pilot's own words, you wouldn't think could have cracked an egg; with the astonishing result of something like eighty feet of good strong wooden quay shaken loose, iron bolts snapped, a baulk of stout timber splintered. Now, suppose that quay had been of granite (as surely it is now)—or, instead of the quay, if there had been, say, a North Atlantic fog there, with a full-grown iceberg in it, awaiting the gentle contact of a ship groping its way along blindfold? Something would have been hurt, but it would not have been the iceberg.

Apparently, there is a point in development when it ceases to be a true progress—in trade, in games, in the marvellous handiwork of men, and even in their demands and desires and aspirations of the moral and mental kind. There is a point when progress, to remain a real advance, must change slightly the direction of its line. But this is a wide question. What I wanted to point out here is—that the old *Arizona,* the marvel of her day, was proportionately stronger, handier, better equipped, than this triumph of modern naval architecture, the loss of which, in common parlance, shall remain the sensation of this year. The clatter of the presses has been worthy of the tonnage, or the preliminary paeans of triumph round that vanished hull, of the reckless statements, and elaborate descriptions of its ornate splendour. A great babble of news (and what sort of news too, good heavens!) and eager comment has arisen around this catastrophe, though it seems to me that a less strident note would have been more becoming in the presence of so many victims left struggling on the sea, of lives miserably thrown away for nothing, or worse than nothing: for false standards of achievement, to satisfy a vulgar demand of a few moneyed people for a banal hotel luxury—the only one they can understand—and because the big ship pays, in one way or another: in money or in advertising value.

It is in more ways than one a very ugly business, and a mere scrape along the ship's side, so slight that, if reports are to be believed, it did not interrupt a card party in the gorgeously fitted (but in chaste style) smoking-room—or was it in the delightful French café—is enough to bring on the exposure. All the people on board existed under a sense of false security. How false, it has been sufficiently demonstrated. And the fact which seems undoubted, that some of them actually were reluctant to enter the boats, when told to do so, shows the strength of that falsehood. Incidentally, it shows also the sort of discipline on board these ships, the sort of hold kept on the passengers in the face of the unforgiving sea. These people seemed to imagine it an optional matter: whereas the order to leave the ship should be an order of the sternest character, to be obeyed unquestioningly and promptly by every one on board, with men to enforce it at once, and to carry it out methodically and swiftly. And it is no use to say it cannot be done, for it can. It has been done. The only requisite is manageableness of the ship herself and of the numbers she carries on board. That is the great thing which makes for safety. A commander should be able to hold his ship and everything on board of her in the hollow of his hand, as it were. But with the modern foolish trust in material, and with those floating hotels, this has become impossible. A man may do his best, but he cannot succeed in a task which from greed, or more likely from sheer stupidity, has been made too great for anybody's strength.

The readers of *The English Review,* who cast a friendly eye nearly six years ago on my Reminiscences, and know how much the Merchant Service, ships and men, has been to me, will understand my indignation that those men of whom (speaking in no sentimental phrase, but in the very truth of feeling) I can't even now think otherwise than as brothers, have been put by their commercial employers in the impossibility to perform efficiently their plain duty; and this from motives which I shall not enumerate here, but whose intrinsic unworthiness is plainly revealed by the greatness, the miserable greatness, of that disaster. Some of them have perished. To die for commerce is hard enough, but to go under that sea we have been trained to combat, with a sense of failure in the supreme duty of one's calling is indeed a bitter fate. Thus they are gone, and the responsibility remains with the living who will have no difficulty in replacing them by others, just as good, at the same wages. It was their bitter fate. But I, who can look at some arduous years when their duty was my duty too, and their feelings were my feelings, can remember some of us who once upon a time were more fortunate.

It is of them that I would talk a little, for my own comfort partly, and also because I am sticking all the time to my subject to illustrate my point, the point of manageableness which I have raised just now. Since the memory of the lucky *Arizona* has been evoked by others than myself, and made use of by me for my own purpose, let me call up the ghost of another ship of that distant day whose less lucky destiny inculcates another lesson making for my argument. The *Douro,* a ship belonging to the Royal Mail Steam Packet Company, was rather less than one-tenth the measurement of the *Titanic.* Yet, strange as it may appear to the ineffable hotel exquisites who form the bulk of the first-class Cross-Atlantic Passengers, people of position and wealth and refinement did not consider it an intolerable hardship to travel in her, even all the way from South America, this being the service she was engaged upon. Of her speed I know nothing, but it must have been the average of the period, and the decorations of her saloons were, I dare say, quite up to the mark; but I doubt if her birth had been boastfully paragraphed all round the Press, because that was not the fashion of the time. She was not a mass of material gorgeously furnished and upholstered. She was a ship. And she was not, in the apt words of an article by Commander C. Crutchley, R.N.R., which I have just read, "run by a sort of hotel syndicate composed of the Chief Engineer, the Purser, and the Captain," as these monstrous Atlantic ferries are. She was really commanded, manned, and equipped as a ship meant to keep the sea: a ship first and last in the fullest meaning of the term, as the fact I am going to relate will show.

She was off the Spanish coast, homeward bound, and fairly full, just about like the *Titanic*; and further, the proportion of her crew, to her passengers, I remember quite well, was very much the same. The exact number of souls on board I have forgotten. It might have been nearly three hundred, certainly not more. The night was moonlit, but hazy, the weather fine with a heavy swell running from the westward, which means that she must have been rolling a good deal, and in that respect the conditions for her were worse than in the case of the *Titanic.* Some time either just before or just after midnight, to the best of my recollection, she was run into amidships and at right angles by a large steamer which after the blow backed out, and, herself apparently damaged, remained motionless at some distance.

My recollection is that the *Douro* remained afloat after the collision for fifteen minutes or thereabouts. It might have been twenty, but certainly something under the half hour. In that time the boats were lowered, all the passengers put into them, and the lot shoved off. There was no time to do anything more. All the crew of the *Douro* went down with her, literally without a murmur. When she went she plunged bodily down like a stone. The only members of the ship's company who survived were the third officer, who was from the first ordered to take charge of the boats, and the seamen told off to man them, two in each. Nobody else was picked up. A quartermaster, one of the saved in the way of duty, with whom I talked a month or so afterwards, told me that they pulled up to the spot, but could neither see a head nor hear the faintest cry.

But I have forgotten. A passenger was drowned. She was a lady's maid who, frenzied with terror, refused to leave the ship. One of the boats waited near by till the chief officer, finding himself absolutely unable to tear the girl away from the rail to which she clung with a frantic grasp, ordered the boat away out of danger. My quartermaster told me that he spoke over to them in his ordinary voice, and this was the last sound heard before the ship sank.

The rest is silence. I dare say there was the usual official inquiry, but who cared for it? That sort of thing speaks for itself with no uncertain voice; though the papers, I remember, gave the event no space to speak of: no large headlines—no headlines at all. You see it was not the fashion at the time. A seaman-like piece of work, of which one cherishes the old memory at this juncture more than ever before. She was a ship commanded, manned, equipped—not a sort of marine Ritz, proclaimed unsinkable and sent adrift with its casual population upon the sea, without enough boats, without enough seamen (but with a Parisian café and four hundred of poor devils of waiters) to meet dangers which, let the engineers say what they like, lurk always amongst the waves, sent with a blind trust in mere material, light heartedly, to a most miserable, most fatuous disaster.

And there are, too, many ugly developments about this tragedy.

The rush of the senatorial inquiry before the poor wretches escaped from the jaws of death had time to draw breath; the vituperative abuse of a man no more guilty than others in this matter [. . .] Perhaps there may be an excellent and worthy reason for it; but I venture to suggest that to take advantage of so many pitiful corpses, is not pretty. And the exploiting of the mere sensation on the other side is not pretty in its wealth of heartless inventions. Neither is the welter of Marconi lies which has not been sent vibrating without some reason, for which it would be nauseous to inquire too closely. And the calumnious, baseless, gratuitous, circumstantial lie, charging poor Captain Smith with desertion of his post by means of suicide is the vilest and most ugly thing of all in this outburst of journalistic enterprise, without feeling, without honour, without decency.

But all this has its moral. And that other sinking which I have related here and to the memory of which a seaman turns with relief and thankfulness, has its moral too. Yes, material may fail, and men, too, may fail sometimes; but more often men, when they are given the chance, will prove themselves truer than steel, that wonderful thin steel from which the sides and the bulkheads of our modern sea-leviathans are made.

FROM *THE MIRROR OF THE SEA*

Initiation

CHAPTER 36

The love that is given to ships is profoundly different from the love men feel for every other work of their hands—the love they bear to their houses, for instance—because it is untainted by the pride of possession. The pride of skill, the pride of responsibility, the pride of endurance there may be, but otherwise it is a disinterested sentiment. No seaman ever cherished a ship, even if she belonged to him, merely because of the profit she put in his pocket. No one, I think, ever did; for a ship-owner, even of the best, has always been outside the pale of that sentiment embracing in a feeling of intimate, equal fellowship the ship and the man, backing each other against the implacable, if sometimes dissembled, hostility of their world of waters. The sea—this truth must be confessed—has no generosity. No display of manly qualities—courage, hardihood, endurance, faithfulness—has ever been known to touch its irresponsible consciousness of power. The ocean has the conscienceless temper of a savage autocrat spoiled by much adulation. He cannot brook the slightest appearance of defiance, and has remained the irreconcilable enemy of ships and men ever since ships and men had the unheard-of audacity to go afloat together in the face of his frown. From that day he has gone on swallowing up fleets and men without his resentment being glutted by the number of victims—by so many wrecked ships and wrecked lives. To-day, as ever, he is ready to beguile and betray, to smash and to drown the incorrigible optimism of men who, backed by the fidelity of ships, are trying to wrest from him the fortune of their house, the dominion of their world, or only a dole of food for their hunger. If not always in the hot mood to smash, he is always stealthily ready for a drowning. The most amazing wonder of the deep is its unfathomable cruelty.

I felt its dread for the first time in mid-Atlantic one day, many years ago, when we took off the crew of a Danish brig homeward bound from the West Indies. A thin, silvery mist softened the calm and majestic splendour of light without shadows—seemed to render the sky less remote and the ocean less immense. It was one of the days, when the might of the sea appears indeed lovable, like the nature of a strong man in moments of quiet intimacy. At sunrise we had made out a black speck to the westward, apparently suspended high up in the void behind a stirring, shimmering veil of silvery blue gauze that seemed at times to stir and float in the breeze which fanned us slowly along. The peace of that enchanting forenoon was so profound, so untroubled, that it seemed that every word pronounced loudly on our deck would penetrate to the very heart of that infinite mystery born from the conjunction of water and sky. We did not raise our voices. "A water-logged derelict, I think, sir," said the second officer, quietly, coming down from aloft with the binoculars in their case slung across his shoulders; and our captain, without a word, signed to the helmsman to steer for the black speck. Presently we made out a low, jagged stump sticking up forward—all that remained of her departed masts.

The captain was expatiating in a low conversational tone to the chief mate upon the danger of these derelicts, and upon his dread of coming upon them at night, when suddenly a man forward screamed out, "There's people on board of her, sir! I see them!" in a most extraordinary voice—a voice never heard before in our ship; the amazing voice of a stranger. It gave the signal for a sudden tumult of shouts. The watch below ran up the forecastle head in a body, the cook dashed out of the galley. Everybody saw the poor fellows now. They were there! And all at once our ship, which had the well-earned name of being without a rival for speed in light winds, seemed to us to have lost the power of motion, as if the sea, becoming viscous, had clung to her sides. And yet she moved. Immensity, the inseparable companion of a ship's life, chose that day to breathe upon her as gently as a sleeping child. The clamour of our excitement had died out, and our living ship, famous for never losing steerage way as long as there was air enough to float a feather, stole, without a ripple, silent and white as a ghost, towards her mutilated and wounded sister, come upon at the point of death in the sunlit haze of a calm day at sea.

With the binoculars glued to his eyes, the captain said in a quavering tone: "They are waving to us with something aft there." He put down the glasses on the skylight brusquely, and began to walk about the poop. "A shirt or a flag," he ejaculated, irritably. "Can't make it out. . . . Some damn rag or other!" He took a few more turns on the poop, glancing down over the rail now and then to see how fast we were moving. His nervous footsteps rang sharply in the quiet of the ship, where the other men, all looking the same way, had forgotten themselves in a staring immobility. "This will never do!" he cried out, suddenly. "Lower the boats at once! Down with them!"

Before I jumped into mine he took me aside, as being an inexperienced junior, for a word of warning:

"You look out as you come alongside that she doesn't take you down with her. You understand?"

He murmured this confidentially, so that none of the men at the falls should overhear, and I was shocked. "Heavens! as if in such an emergency one stopped to think of danger!" I exclaimed to myself mentally, in scorn of such cold-blooded caution.

It takes many lessons to make a real seaman, and I got my rebuke at once. My experienced commander seemed in one searching glance to read my thoughts on my ingenuous face.

"What you're going for is to save life, not to drown your boat's crew for nothing," he growled, severely, in my ear. But as we shoved off he leaned over and cried out: "It all rests on the power of your arms, men. Give way for life!"

We made a race of it, and I would never have believed that a common boat's crew of a merchantman could keep up so much determined fierceness in the regular swing of their stroke. What our captain had clearly perceived before we left had become plain to all of us since. The issue of our enterprise hung on a hair above that abyss of waters which will not give up its dead till the Day of Judgment. It was a race of two ship's boats matched against Death for a prize of nine men's lives, and Death had a long start. We saw the crew of the brig from afar working at the pumps—still pumping on that wreck, which already had settled so far down that the gentle, low swell, over which our boats rose and fell easily without a check to their speed, welling up almost level with her head-rails, plucked at the ends of broken gear swinging desolately under her naked bowsprit.

We could not, in all conscience, have picked out a better day for our regatta had we had the free choice of all the days that ever dawned upon the lonely struggles and solitary agonies of ships since the Norse rovers first steered to the westward against the run of Atlantic waves. It was a very good race. At the finish there was not an oar's length between the first and second boat, with Death coming in a good third on the top of the very next smooth swell, for all one knew to the contrary. The scuppers of the brig gurgled softly all together when the water rising against her sides subsided sleepily with a low wash, as if playing about an immovable rock. Her bulwarks were gone fore and aft, and one saw her bare deck low-lying like a raft and swept clean of boats, spars, houses—of everything except the ringbolts and the heads of the pumps. I had one dismal glimpse of it as I braced myself up to receive upon my breast the last man to leave her, the captain, who literally let himself fall into my arms.

It had been a weirdly silent rescue—a rescue without a hail, without a single uttered word, without a gesture or a sign, without a conscious exchange of glances. Up to the very last moment those on board stuck to their pumps, which spouted two clear streams of water upon their bare feet. Their brown skin showed through the rents of their shirts; and the two small bunches of half-naked, tattered men went on bowing from the waist to each other in their back-breaking labour, up and down, absorbed, with no time for a glance over the shoulder at the help that was coming to them. As we dashed, unregarded, alongside a voice let out one, only one hoarse howl of command, and then, just as they stood, without caps, with the salt drying grey in the wrinkles and folds of their hairy, haggard faces, blinking stupidly at us their red eyelids, they made a bolt away from the handles, tottering and jostling against each other, and positively flung themselves over upon our very heads. The clatter they made tumbling into the boats had an extraordinarily destructive effect upon the illusion of tragic dignity our self-esteem had thrown over the contests of mankind with the sea. On that exquisite day of gentle breathing peace and veiled sunshine perished my romantic love to what men's imagination had proclaimed the most august aspect of Nature. The cynical indifference of the sea to the merits of human suffering and courage, laid bare in this ridiculous, panic-tainted performance extorted from the dire extremity of nine good and honourable seamen, revolted me. I saw the duplicity of the sea's most tender mood. It was so because it could not help itself, but the awed respect of the early days was gone. I felt ready to smile bitterly at its enchanting charm and glare viciously at its furies. In a moment, before we shoved off, I had looked coolly at the life of my choice. Its illusions were gone, but its fascination remained. I had become a seaman at last.

We pulled hard for a quarter of an hour, then laid on our oars waiting for our ship. She was coming down on us with swelling sails, looking delicately tall and exquisitely noble through the mist. The captain of the brig, who sat in the stern sheets by my side with his face in his hands, raised his head and began to speak with a sort of sombre volubility. They had lost their masts and sprung a leak in a hurricane; drifted for weeks, always at the pumps, met more bad weather; the ships they sighted failed to make them out, the leak gained upon them slowly, and the seas had left them nothing to make a raft of. It was very hard to see ship after ship pass by at a distance, "as if everybody had agreed that we must be left to drown," he added. But they went on trying to keep the brig afloat as long as possible, and working the pumps constantly on insufficient food, mostly raw, till "yesterday evening," he continued, monotonously, "just as the sun went down, the men's hearts broke."

He made an almost imperceptible pause here, and went on again with exactly the same intonation:

"They told me the brig could not be saved, and they thought they had done enough for themselves. I said nothing to that. It was true. It was no mutiny. I had nothing to say to them. They lay about aft all night, as still as so many dead men. I did not lie down. I kept a look-out. When the first light came I saw your ship at once. I waited for more light; the breeze began to fail on my face. Then I shouted out as loud as I was able, 'Look at that ship!' but only two men got up very slowly and came to me. At first only we three stood alone, for a long time, watching you coming down to us, and feeling the breeze drop to a calm almost; but afterwards others, too, rose, one after another, and by and by I had all my crew behind me. I turned round and said to them that they could see the ship was coming our way, but in this small breeze she might come too late after all, unless we turned to and tried to keep the brig afloat long enough to give you time to save us all. I spoke like that to them, and then I gave the command to man the pumps."

He gave the command, and gave the example, too, by going himself to the handles, but it seems that these men did actually hang back for a moment, looking at each other dubiously before they followed him. "He! he! he!" He broke out into a most unexpected, imbecile, pathetic, nervous little giggle. "Their hearts were broken so! They had been played with too long," he explained, apologetically, lowering his eyes, and became silent.

Twenty-five years is a long time—a quarter of a century is a dim and distant past; but to this day I remember the dark-brown feet, hands, and faces of two of these men whose hearts had been broken by the sea. They were lying very still on their sides on the bottom boards between the thwarts, curled up like dogs. My boat's crew, leaning over the looms of their oars, stared and listened as if at the play. The master of the brig looked up suddenly to ask me what day it was.

They had lost the date. When I told him it was Sunday, the 22nd, he frowned, making some mental calculation, then nodded twice sadly to himself, staring at nothing.

His aspect was miserably unkempt and wildly sorrowful. Had it not been for the unquenchable candour of his blue eyes, whose unhappy, tired glance every moment sought his abandoned, sinking brig, as if it could find rest nowhere else, he would have appeared mad. But he was too simple to go mad, too simple with that manly simplicity which alone can bear men unscathed in mind and body through an encounter with the deadly playfulness of the sea or with its less abominable fury.

Neither angry, nor playful, nor smiling, it enveloped our distant ship growing bigger as she neared us, our boats with the rescued men and the dismantled hull of the brig we were leaving behind, in the large and placid embrace of its quietness, half lost in the fair haze, as if in a dream of infinite and tender clemency. There was no frown, no wrinkle on its face, not a ripple. And the run of the slight swell was so smooth that it resembled the graceful undulation of a piece of shimmering grey silk shot with gleams of green. We pulled an easy stroke; but when the master of the brig, after a glance over his shoulder, stood up with a low exclamation, my men feathered their oars instinctively, without an order, and the boat lost her way.

He was steadying himself on my shoulder with a strong grip, while his other arm, flung up rigidly, pointed a denunciatory finger at the immense tranquillity of the ocean. After his first exclamation, which stopped the swing of our oars, he made no sound, but his whole attitude seemed to cry out an indignant "Behold!" . . . I could not imagine what vision of evil had come to him. I was startled, and the amazing energy of his immobilized gesture made my heart beat faster with the anticipation of something monstrous and unsuspected. The stillness around us became crushing.

For a moment the succession of silky undulations ran on innocently. I saw each of them swell up the misty line of the horizon, far, far away beyond the derelict brig, and the next moment, with a slight friendly toss of our boat, it had passed under us and was gone. The lulling cadence of the rise and fall, the invariable gentleness of this irresistible force, the great charm of the deep waters, warmed my breast deliciously, like the subtle poison of a love-potion. But all this lasted only a few soothing seconds before I jumped up, too, making the boat roll like the veriest land-lubber.

Something startling, mysterious, hastily confused was taking place. I watched it with incredulous and fascinated awe, as one watches the confused, swift movements of some deed of violence done in the dark. As if at a given signal, the run of the smooth undulations seemed checked suddenly around the brig. By a strange optical delusion the whole sea appeared to rise upon her in one overwhelming heave of its silky surface where in one spot a smother of foam broke out ferociously. And then the effort subsided. It was all over, and the smooth swell ran on as before from the horizon in uninterrupted cadence of motion, passing under us with a slight friendly toss of our boat. Far away, where the brig had been, an angry white stain undulating on the surface of steely-grey waters, shot with gleams of green, diminished swiftly without a hiss, like a patch of pure snow melting in the sun. And the great stillness after this initiation into the sea's implacable hate seemed full of dread thoughts and shadows of disaster.

"Gone!" ejaculated from the depths of his chest my bowman in a final tone. He spat in his hands, and took a better grip on his oar. The captain of the brig lowered his rigid arm slowly, and looked at our faces in a solemnly conscious silence, which called upon us to share in his simple-minded, marvelling awe. All at once he sat down by my side, and leaned forward earnestly at my boat's crew, who, swinging together in a long, easy stroke, kept their eyes fixed upon him faithfully.

"No ship could have done so well," he addressed them, firmly, after a moment of strained silence, during which he seemed with trembling lips to seek for words fit to bear such high testimony. "She was small, but she was good. I had no anxiety. She was strong. Last voyage I had my wife and two children in her. No other ship could have stood so long the weather she had to live through for days and days before we got dismasted a fortnight ago. She was fairly worn out, and that's all. You may believe me. She lasted under us for days and days, but she could not last for ever. It was long enough. I am glad it is over. No better ship was ever left to sink at sea on such a day as this."

He was competent to pronounce the funereal oration of a ship, this son of ancient sea-folk, whose national existence, so little stained by the excesses of manly virtues, had demanded nothing but the merest foothold from the earth. By the merits of his sea-wise forefathers and by the artlessness of his heart, he was made fit to deliver this excellent discourse. There was nothing wanting in its orderly arrangement—neither piety nor faith, nor the tribute of praise due to the worthy dead, with the edifying recital of their achievement. She had lived, he had loved her; she had suffered, and he was glad she was at rest. It was an excellent discourse. And it was orthodox, too, in its fidelity to the cardinal article of a seaman's faith, of which it was a single-minded confession. "Ships are all right." They are. They who live with the sea have got to hold by that creed first and last; and it came to me, as I glanced at him sideways, that some men were not altogether unworthy in honour and conscience to pronounce the funereal eulogium of a ship's constancy in life and death.

After this, sitting by my side with his loosely clasped hands hanging between his knees, he uttered no word, made no movement till the shadow of our ship's sails fell on the boat, when, at the loud cheer greeting the return of the victors with their prize, he lifted up his troubled face with a faint smile of pathetic indulgence. This smile of the worthy descendant of the most ancient sea-folk whose audacity and hardihood had left no trace of greatness and glory upon the waters, completed the cycle of my initiation. There was an infinite depth of hereditary wisdom in its pitying sadness. It made the hearty bursts of cheering sound like a childish noise of triumph. Our crew shouted with immense confidence—honest souls! As if anybody could ever make sure of having prevailed against the sea, which has betrayed so many ships of great "name," so many proud men, so many towering ambitions of fame, power, wealth, greatness!

As I brought the boat under the falls my captain, in high good-humour, leaned over, spreading his red and freckled elbows on the rail, and called down to me sarcastically out of the depths of his cynic philosopher's beard:

"So you have brought the boat back after all, have you?"

Sarcasm was "his way," and the most that can be said for it is that it was natural. This did not make it lovable. But it is a decorous and expedient to fall in with one's commander's way. "Yes. I brought the boat back all right, sir," I answered. And the good man believed me. It was not for him to discern upon me the marks of my recent initiation. And yet I was not exactly the same youngster who had taken the boat away—all impatience for a race against Death, with the prize of nine men's lives at the end.

Already I looked with other eyes upon the sea. I knew it capable of betraying the generous ardour of youth as implacably as, indifferent to evil and good, it would have betrayed the basest greed or the noblest heroism. My conception of its magnanimous greatness was gone. And I looked upon the true sea—the sea that plays with men till their hearts are broken, and wears stout ships to death. Nothing can touch the brooding bitterness of its soul. Open to all and faithful to none, it exercises its fascination for the undoing of the best. To love it is not well. It knows no bond of plighted troth, no fidelity to misfortune, to long companionship, to long devotion. The promise it holds out perpetually is very great; but the only secret of its possession is strength, strength—the jealous, sleepless strength of a man guarding a coveted treasure within his gates.

FROM *A PERSONAL RECORD*

CHAPTER I

Books may be written in all sorts of places. Verbal inspiration may enter the berth of a mariner on board a ship frozen fast in a river in the middle of a town; and since saints are supposed to look benignantly on humble believers, I indulge in the pleasant fancy that the shade of old Flaubert—who imagined himself to be (amongst other things) a descendant of Vikings—might have hovered with amused interest over the decks of a 2,000-ton steamer called the *Adowa,* on board of which, gripped by the inclement winter alongside a quay in Rouen, the tenth chapter of "Almayer's Folly" was begun. With interest, I say, for was not the kind Norman giant with enormous moustaches and a thundering voice the last of the Romantics? Was he not, in his unworldly, almost ascetic, devotion to his art a sort of literary, saint-like hermit?

"*'It has set at last,' said Nina to her mother, pointing to the hills behind which the sun had sunk.*" . . . These words of Almayer's romantic daughter I remember tracing on the grey paper of a pad which rested on the blanket of my bed-place. They referred to a sunset in Malayan Isles, and shaped themselves in my mind, in a hallucinated vision of forests and rivers and seas, far removed from a commercial and yet romantic town of the northern hemisphere. But at that moment the mood of visions and words was cut short by the third officer, a cheerful and casual youth, coming in with a bang of the door and the exclamation: "You've made it jolly warm in here."

It was warm. I had turned on the steam-heater after placing a tin under the leaky water-cock—for perhaps you do not know that water will leak where steam will not. I am not aware of what my young friend had been doing on deck all that morning, but the hands he rubbed together vigorously were very red and imparted to me a chilly feeling by their mere aspect. He has remained the only banjoist of my acquaintance, and being also a younger son of a retired colonel, the poem of Mr. Kipling, by a strange aberration of associated ideas, always seems to me to have been written with an exclusive view to his person. When he did not play the banjo he loved to sit and look at it. He proceeded to this sentimental inspection, and after meditating a while over the strings under my silent scrutiny, inquired airily:

"What are you always scribbling there, if it's fair to ask?"

It was a fair enough question, but I did not answer him, and simply turned the pad over with a movement of instinctive secrecy: I could not have told him he had put to flight the psychology of Nina Almayer, her opening speech of the tenth chapter and the words of Mrs. Almayer's wisdom which were to follow in the ominous oncoming of a tropical night. I could not have told him that Nina had said: "It has set at last." He would have been extremely surprised and perhaps have dropped his precious banjo. Neither could I have told him that the sun of my sea-going was setting too, even as I wrote the words expressing the impatience of passionate youth bent on its desire. I did not know this myself, and it is safe to say he would not have cared, though he was an excellent young fellow and treated me with more deference than, in our relative positions, I was strictly entitled to.

He lowered a tender gaze on his banjo and I went on looking through the port-hole. The round opening framed in its brass rim a fragment of the quays, with a row of casks ranged on the frozen ground and the tail-end of a great cart. A red-nosed carter in a blouse and a woollen nightcap leaned against the wheel. An idle, strolling custom-house guard, belted over his blue *capote,* had the air of being depressed by exposure to the weather and the monotony of official existence. The background of grimy houses found a place in the picture framed by my port-hole, across a wide stretch of paved quay, brown with frozen mud. The colouring was sombre, and the most conspicuous feature was a little *café* with curtained windows and a shabby front of white woodwork, corresponding with the squalor of these poorer quarters bordering the river. We had been shifted down there from another berth in the neighbourhood of the Opera House, where that same port-hole gave me a view of quite another sort of *café*—the best in the town, I believe, and the very one where the worthy Bovary and his wife, the romantic daughter of old Père Renault, had some refreshment after the memorable performance of an opera which was the tragic story of Lucia di Lammermoor in a setting of light music.

I could recall no more the hallucination of the Eastern Archipelago which I certainly hoped to see again. The story of "Almayer's Folly" got put away under the pillow for that day. I do not know that I had any occupation to keep me away from it; the truth of the matter is, that on board that ship we were leading just then a contemplative life. I will not say anything of my privileged position. I was there "just to oblige," as an actor of standing may take a small part in the benefit performance of a friend.

As far as my feelings were concerned, I did not wish to be in that steamer at that time and in those circumstances. And perhaps I was not even wanted there in the usual sense in which a ship "wants" an officer. It was the first and last instance in my sea life when I served ship-owners who have remained completely shadowy to my apprehension. I do not mean this for the well-known firm of London ship-brokers which had chartered the ship to the, I will not say short-lived, but ephemeral Franco-Canadian Transport Company. A death leaves something behind, but there was never anything tangible left from the F.C.T.C. It flourished no longer than roses live, and unlike the roses, it blossomed in the dead of winter, emitted a sort of faint perfume of adventure, and died before spring set in. But indubitably it was a company, it had even a house-flag, all white with the letters F.C.T.C. artfully tangled up in a complicated monogram. We flew it at our mainmast head, and now I have come to the conclusion that it was the only flag of its kind in existence. All the same, we on board, for many days, had the impression of being a unit of a large fleet with fortnightly departures for Montreal and Quebec as advertised in pamphlets and prospectuses which came aboard in a large package in Victoria Dock, London, just before we started for Rouen, France. And in the shadowy life of the F.C.T.C. lies the secret of that, my last employment in my calling, which in a remote sense interrupted the rhythmical development of Nina Almayer's story.

The then secretary of the London Shipmasters' Society, with its modest rooms in Fenchurch Street, was a man of indefatigable activity and the greatest devotion to his task. He is responsible for what was my last association with a ship. I call it that because it can hardly be called a sea-going experience. Dear Captain Froud—it is impossible not to pay him the tribute of affectionate familiarity at this distance of years—had very sound views as to the advancement of knowledge and status for the whole body of the officers of the mercantile marine. He organised for us courses of professional lectures, St. John Ambulance classes, corresponded industriously with public bodies and members of Parliament on subjects touching the interests of the service; and as to the oncoming of some inquiry or commission relating to matters of the sea and to the work of seamen, it was a perfect godsend to his need of exerting himself on our corporate behalf. Together with this high sense of his official duties he had in him a vein of personal kindness, a strong disposition to do what good he could to the individual members of that craft of which in his time he had been a very excellent master. And what greater kindness can one do to a seaman than to put him in the way of employment? Captain Froud did not see why the Shipmasters' Society, besides its general guardianship of our interests, should not be unofficially an employment agency of the very highest class.

"I am trying to persuade all our great ship-owning firms to come to us for their men. There is nothing of a trade-union spirit about our society and I really don't see why they should not," he said once to me. "I am always telling the captains, too, that all things being equal they ought to give preference to the members of the society. In my position I can generally find for them what they want amongst our members or our associate members."

In my wanderings about London from West to East and back again (I was very idle then), the two little rooms in Fenchurch Street were a sort of resting-place where my spirit, hankering after the sea, could feel itself nearer to the ships, the men, and the life of its choice—nearer there than any other spot of the solid earth. This resting-place used to be, at about five o'clock in the afternoon, full of men and tobacco smoke, but Captain Froud had the smaller room to himself, and there he granted private interviews, whose principal motive was to render service. Thus, one murky November afternoon, he beckoned me in with a crooked finger and that peculiar glance above his spectacles which is perhaps my strongest physical recollection of the man.

"I have had in here a shipmaster this morning," he said, getting back to his desk and motioning me to a chair, "who is in want of an officer. It's for a steamship. You know, nothing pleases me more than to be asked, but unfortunately I do not quite see my way. . . ."

As the outer room was full of men, I cast a wondering glance at the closed door, but he shook his head.

"Oh, yes, I should be only too glad to get that berth for one of them. But the fact of the matter is, the captain of that ship wants an officer who can speak French fluently, and that's not easy to find. I do not know anybody myself but you. It's a second officer's berth, and, of course, you would not care . . . would you now? I know that it isn't what you are looking for."

It was not. I had given myself up to the idleness of a haunted man who looks for nothing but words wherein to capture his visions. But I admit that outwardly I resembled sufficiently a man who could make a second officer for a steamer chartered by a French company. I showed no sign of being haunted by the fate of Nina and by the murmurs of tropical forests; and even my intimate intercourse with Almayer (a person of weak character) had not put a visible mark upon my features. For many years he and the world of his story had been the companions of my imagination without, I hope, impairing my ability to deal with the realities of sea life. I had had the man and his surroundings with me ever since my return from the eastern waters, some four years before the day of which I speak.

It was in the front sitting-room of furnished apartments in a Pimlico square that they first began to live again with a vividness and poignancy quite foreign to our former real intercourse. I had been treating myself to a long stay on shore, and in the necessity of occupying my mornings, Almayer (that old acquaintance) came nobly to the rescue. Before long, as was only proper, his wife and daughter joined him round my table, and then the rest of that Pantai band came full of words and gestures. Unknown to my respectable landlady, it was my practice directly after my breakfast to hold animated receptions of Malays, Arabs and half-castes. They did not clamour aloud for my attention. They came with a silent and irresistible appeal—and the appeal, I affirm here, was not to my self-love or my vanity. It seems now to have had a moral character, for why should the memory of these beings, seen in their obscure sun-bathed existence, demand to express itself in the shape of a novel, except on the ground of that mysterious fellowship which unites in a community of hopes and fears all the dwellers on this earth?

I did not receive my visitors with boisterous rapture as the bearers of any gifts of profit or fame. There was no vision of a printed book before me as I sat writing at that table, situated in a decayed part of Belgravia. After all these years, each leaving its evidence of slowly blackened pages, I can honestly say that it is a sentiment akin to piety which prompted me to render in words assembled with conscientious care the memory of things far distant and of men who had lived.

But, coming back to Captain Froud and his fixed idea of never disappointing ship-owners or ship-captains, it was not likely that I should fail him in his ambition—to satisfy at a few hours' notice the unusual demand for a French-speaking officer. He explained to me that the ship was chartered by a French company intending to establish a regular monthly line of sailings from Rouen, for the transport of French emigrants to Canada. But, frankly, this sort of thing did not interest me very much. I said gravely that if it were really a matter of keeping up the reputation of the Shipmasters' Society, I would consider it. But the consideration was just for form's sake. The next day I interviewed the Captain, and I believe we were impressed favourably with each other. He explained that his chief mate was an excellent man in every respect, and that he could not think of dismissing him so as to give me the higher position; but that if I consented to come as second officer I would be given certain special advantages—and so on.

I told him that if I came at all the rank really did not matter.

"I am sure," he insisted, "you will get on first rate with Mr. Paramor."

I promised faithfully to stay for two trips at least, and it was in those circumstances that what was to be my last connection with a ship began. And after all there was not even one single trip. It may be that it was simply the fulfilment of a fate, of that written word on my forehead which apparently forbade me, through all my sea wanderings, ever to achieve the crossing of the Western

Ocean—using the words in that special sense in which sailors speak of Western Ocean trade, of Western Ocean packets, of Western Ocean hard cases. The new life attended closely upon the old, and the nine chapters of "Almayer's Folly" went with me to the Victoria Dock, whence in a few days we started for Rouen. I won't go so far as saying that the engaging of a man fated never to cross the Western Ocean was the absolute cause of the Franco-Canadian Transport Company's failure to achieve even a single passage. It might have been that, of course; but the obvious, gross obstacle was clearly the want of money. Four hundred and sixty bunks for emigrants were put together in the 'tween decks by industrious carpenters while we lay in the Victoria Dock, but never an emigrant turned up in Rouen—of which, being a humane person, I confess I was glad. Some gentlemen from Paris—I think there were three of them, and one was said to be the Chairman—turned up indeed and went from end to end of the ship, knocking their silk hats cruelly against the deck-beams. I attended them personally, and I can vouch for it that the interest they took in things was intelligent enough, though, obviously they had never seen anything of the sort before. Their faces as they went ashore wore a cheerfully inconclusive expression. Notwithstanding that this inspecting ceremony was supposed to be a preliminary to immediate sailing, it was then, as they filed down our gangway, that I received the inward monition that no sailing within the meaning of our charter-party would ever take place.

It must be said that in less than three weeks a move took place. When we first arrived we had been taken up with much ceremony well towards the centre of the town, and, all the street corners being placarded with the tricolor poster announcing the birth of our company, the *petit bourgeois* with his wife and family made a Sunday holiday from the inspection of the ship. I was always in evidence in my best uniform to give information as though I had been a Cook's tourists' interpreter, while our quarter-masters reaped a harvest of small change from personally conducted parties. But when the move was made—that move which carried us some mile and a half down the stream to be tied up to an altogether muddier and shabbier quay—then indeed the desolation of solitude became our lot. It was a complete and soundless stagnation; for, as we had the ship ready for sea to the smallest detail, as the frost was hard and the days short, we were absolutely idle—idle to the point of blushing with shame when the thought struck us that all the time our salaries went on. Young Cole was aggrieved because, as he said, we could not enjoy any sort of fun in the evening after loafing like this all day: even the banjo lost its charm since there was nothing to prevent his strumming on it all the time between the meals. The good Paramor—he was really a most excellent fellow—became unhappy as far as was possible to his cheery nature, till one dreary day I suggested out of sheer mischief, that he should employ the dormant energies of the crew in hauling both cables up on deck and turning them end for end.

For a moment Mr. Paramor was radiant. "Excellent idea!" but directly his face fell. "Why . . . Yes! But we can't make that job last more than three days," he muttered discontentedly. I don't know how long he expected us to be stuck on the river-side outskirts of Rouen, but I know that the cables got hauled up and turned end for end according to my satanic suggestion, put down again, and their very existence utterly forgotten, I believe, before a French river pilot came on board to take our ship down, empty as she came, into the Havre roads. You may think that this state of forced idleness favoured some advance in the fortunes of Almayer and his daughter. Yet it was not so. As if it were some sort of evil spell, my banjoist cabin-mate's interruption, as related above, had arrested them short at the point of that fateful sunset for many weeks together. It was always thus with this book, begun in '89 and finished in '94—with that shortest of all the novels which it was to be my lot to write. Between its opening exclamation calling Almayer to his dinner in his wife's voice and Abdullah's (his enemy) mental reference to the God of Islam—"The Merciful, the Compassionate"—which closes the book, there were to come several long sea passages, a visit (to use the elevated phraseology suitable to the occasion) to the scenes (some of them) of my childhood and the realization of childhood's vain words, expressing a light-hearted and romantic whim.

It was in 1868, when nine years old or thereabouts, that while looking at a map of Africa of the time and putting my finger on the blank space then representing the unsolved mystery of that continent, I said to myself with absolute assurance and an amazing audacity which are no longer in my character now:

"When I grow up I shall go *there*."

And of course I thought no more about it till after a quarter of a century or so an opportunity offered to go there—as if the sin of childish audacity was to be visited on my mature head. Yes. I did go there: *there* being the region of Stanley Falls which in '68 was the blankest of blank spaces on the earth's figured surface. And the MS. of "Almayer's Folly," carried about me as if it were a talisman or a treasure, went *there* too. That it ever came out of *there* seems a special dispensation of Providence; because a good many of my other properties, infinitely more valuable and useful to me, remained behind through unfortunate accidents of transportation. I call to mind, for instance, a specially awkward turn of the Congo between Kinchassa and Leopoldsville—more particularly when one had to take it at night in a big canoe with only half the proper number of paddlers. I failed in being the second white man on record drowned at that interesting spot through the upsetting of a canoe. The first was a young Belgian officer, but the accident happened some months before my time, and he, too, I believe, was going home; not perhaps quite so ill as myself—but still he was going home. I got round the turn more or less alive, though I was too sick to care whether I did or not, and, always with "Almayer's Folly" amongst my diminishing baggage, I arrived at that delectable capital Boma, where before the departure of the steamer which was to take me home I had the time to wish myself dead over and over again with perfect sincerity. At that date there were in existence only seven chapters of "Almayer's Folly," but the chapter in my history which followed was that of a long, long illness and very dismal convalescence. Geneva, or more precisely the hydropathic establishment of Champel, is rendered for ever famous by the termination of the eighth chapter in the history of Almayer's decline and fall. The events of the ninth are inextricably mixed up with the details of the proper management of a waterside warehouse owned by a certain city firm whose name does not matter. But that work, undertaken to accustom myself again to the activities of a healthy existence, soon came to an end. The earth had nothing to hold me with for very long. And then that memorable story, like a cask of choice Madeira, got carried for three years to and fro upon the sea. Whether this treatment improved its flavour or not, of course I would not like to say. As far as appearance is concerned, it certainly did nothing of the kind. The whole MS. acquired a faded look and an ancient, yellowish complexion. It became at last unreasonable to suppose that anything in the world would ever happen to Almayer and Nina. And yet something most unlikely to happen on the high seas was to wake them up from their state of suspended animation.

What is it that Novalis says? "It is certain my conviction gains infinitely the moment another soul will believe in it." And what is a novel if not a conviction of our fellow-man's existence strong enough to take upon itself a form of imagined life clearer than reality and whose accumulated verisimilitude of selected episodes puts to shame the pride of documentary history? Providence which saved my MS. from the Congo rapids brought it to the knowledge of a helpful soul far out on the open sea. It would be on my part the greatest ingratitude ever to forget the sallow, sunken face and the deep-set, dark eyes of the young Cambridge man (he was a "passenger for his health" on board the good ship *Torrens* outward bound to Australia) who was the first reader of "Almayer's Folly"—the very first reader I ever had. "Would it bore you very much reading a MS. in a handwriting like mine?" I asked him one evening on a sudden impulse at the end of a longish conversation whose subject was Gibbon's History. Jacques (that was his name) was sitting in my cabin one stormy dog-watch below, after bringing me a book to read from his own travelling store.

"Not at all," he answered with his courteous intonation and a faint smile. As I pulled a drawer open his suddenly aroused curiosity gave him a watchful expression. I wonder what he expected to see. A poem, maybe. All that's beyond guessing now. He was not a cold, but a calm man, still more subdued by disease—a man of few words and of an unassuming modesty in general intercourse, but with something uncommon in the whole of his person which set him apart from the undistinguished lot of our sixty passengers. His eyes had a thoughtful introspective look. In his attractive, reserved manner, and in a veiled, sympathetic voice, he asked:

"What is this?" "It is a sort of tale," I answered with an effort. "It is not even finished yet. Nevertheless, I would like to know what you think of it." He put the MS. in the breast-pocket of his jacket; I remember perfectly his thin brown fingers folding it lengthwise. "I will read it to-morrow," he remarked, seizing the door-handle, and then, watching the roll of the ship for a propitious moment, he opened the door and was gone. In the moment of his exit I heard the sustained booming of the wind, the swish of the water on the decks of the *Torrens,* and the subdued, as if distant, roar of the rising sea. I noted the growing disquiet in the great restlessness of the ocean, and responded professionally to it with the thought that at eight o'clock, in another half-hour or so at the furthest, the top-gallant sails would have to come off the ship.

Next day, but this time in the first dog-watch, Jacques entered my cabin. He had a thick, woollen muffler round his throat and the MS. was in his hand. He tendered it to me with a steady look but without a word. I took it in silence. He sat down on the couch and still said nothing. I opened and shut a drawer under my desk, on which a filled-up log-slate lay wide open in its wooden frame waiting to be copied neatly into the sort of book I was accustomed to write with care, the ship's log-book. I turned my back squarely on the desk. And even then Jacques never offered a word. "Well, what do you say?" I asked at last. "Is it worth finishing?" This question expressed exactly the whole of my thoughts.

"Distinctly," he answered in his sedate veiled voice, and then coughed a little.

"Were you interested?" I inquired further, almost in a whisper.

"Very much!"

In a pause I went on meeting instinctively the heavy rolling of the ship, and Jacques put his feet upon the couch. The curtain of my bed-place swung to and fro as if it were a punkah, the bulkhead lamp circled in its gimbals, and now and then the cabin door rattled slightly in the gusts of wind. It was in latitude 40° south, and nearly in the longitude of Greenwich, as far as I can remember, that these quiet rites of Almayer's and Nina's resurrection were taking place. In the prolonged silence it occurred to me that there was a good deal of retrospective writing in the story as far as it went. Was it intelligible in its action, I asked myself, as if already the story-teller were being born into the body of a seaman. But I heard on deck the whistle of the officer of the watch and remained on the alert to catch the order that was to follow this call to attention. It reached me as a faint, fierce shout to "Square the yards." "Aha!" I thought to myself, "a westerly blow coming on." Then I turned to my very first reader, who, alas! was not to live long enough to know the end of the tale.

"Now let me ask you one more thing: Is the story quite clear to you as it stands?"

He raised his dark, gentle eyes to my face and seemed surprised.

"Yes! Perfectly."

This was all I was to hear from his lips concerning the merits of "Almayer's Folly." We never spoke together of the book again. A long period of bad weather set in and I had no thoughts left but for my duties, whilst poor Jacques caught a fatal cold and had to keep close in his cabin. When we arrived at Adelaide the first reader of my prose went at once up-country, and died rather suddenly in the end, either in Australia or it may be on the passage while going home through the Suez Canal. I am not sure which it was now, and I do not think I ever heard precisely; though I made inquiries about him from some of our return passengers who, wandering about to "see the country" during the ship's stay in port, had come upon him here and there. At last we sailed, homeward bound, and still not one line was added to the careless scrawl of the many pages which poor Jacques had had the patience to read with the very shadows of Eternity gathering already in the hollows of his kind, steadfast eyes.

The purpose instilled into me by his simple and final "Distinctly" remained dormant, yet alive to await its opportunity. I dare say I am compelled, unconsciously compelled, now to write volume after volume, as in past years I was compelled to go to sea, voyage after voyage. Leaves must follow upon each other as leagues used to follow in the days gone by, on and on to the appointed end, which, being Truth itself, is One—one for all men and for all occupations.

I do not know which of the two impulses has appeared more mysterious and more wonderful to me. Still, in writing, as in going to sea, I had to wait my opportunity. Let me confess that I was never one of those wonderful fellows that would go afloat in a wash-tub for the sake of the fun, and if I may pride myself upon my consistency it was ever just the same with my writing. Some men, I have heard, write in railway carriages, and could do it, perhaps, sitting cross-legged on a clothes-line; but I must confess that my sybaritic disposition will not consent to write without something at least resembling a chair. Line by line, rather than page by page, was the growth of "Almayer's Folly."

And so it happened that I very nearly lost the MS., advanced now to the first words of the ninth chapter, in the Friedrichstrasse railway station (that's in Berlin, you know) on my way to Poland, or more precisely Ukraine. On an early, sleepy morning, changing trains in a hurry, I left my Gladstone bag in a refreshment-room. A worthy and intelligent *Kofferträger* rescued it. Yet in my anxiety I was not thinking of the MS. but of all the other things that were packed in the bag.

In Warsaw, where I spent two days, those wandering pages were never exposed to the light, except once, to candle-light, while the bag lay open on a chair. I was dressing hurriedly to dine at a sporting club. A friend of my childhood (he had been in the Diplomatic Service, but had turned to growing wheat on paternal acres, and we had not seen each other for over twenty years) was sitting on the hotel sofa waiting to carry me off there.

"You might tell me something of your life while you are dressing," he suggested kindly.

I do not think I told him much of my life-story either then or later. The talk of the select little party with which he made me dine was extremely animated and embraced most subjects under heaven, from big-game shooting in Africa to the last poem published in a very modernist review, edited by the very young and patronised by the highest society. But it never touched upon "Almayer's Folly," and next morning, in uninterrupted obscurity, this inseparable companion went on rolling with me in the south-east direction towards the Government of Kiev.

At that time there was an eight-hours' drive, if not more, from the railway station to the country house which was my destination.

"Dear boy" (these words were always written in English)—so ran the last letter from that house received in London—"Get yourself driven to the only inn in the place, dine as well as you can, and some time in the evening my own confidential servant, factotum and major-domo, a Mr. V. S. (I warn you he is of noble extraction), will present himself before you, reporting the arrival of the small sledge which will take you here on the next day. I send with him my heaviest fur, which I suppose, with such overcoats as you may have with you, will keep you from freezing on the road."

Sure enough, as I was dining, served by a Hebrew waiter, in an enormous barn-like bedroom with a freshly painted floor, the door opened and, in a travelling costume of long boots, big sheep-skin cap and a short coat girt with a leather belt, the Mr. V. S. (of noble extraction), a man of about thirty-five, appeared with an air of perplexity on his open and moustachioed countenance. I got up from the table and greeted him in Polish, with, I hope, the right shade of consideration demanded by his noble blood and his confidential position. His face cleared up in a wonderful way. It appeared that, notwithstanding my uncle's earnest assurances, the good fellow had remained in doubt of our understanding each other. He imagined I would talk to him in some foreign language. I was told that his last words on getting into the sledge to come to meet me shaped an anxious exclamation:

"Well! Well! Here I am going, but God only knows how I am to make myself understood to our master's nephew."

We understood each other very well from the first. He took charge of me as if I were not quite of age. I had a delightful boyish feeling of coming home from school when he muffled me up next morning in an enormous bear-skin travelling-coat and took his seat protectively by my side. The sledge was a very small one and it looked utterly insignificant, almost like a toy behind the four big bays harnessed two and two. We three, counting the coachman, filled it completely. He was a young fellow with clear blue eyes; the high collar of his livery fur coat framed his cheery countenance and stood all round level with the top of his head.

"Now, Joseph," my companion addressed him, "do you think we shall manage to get home before six?" His answer was that we would surely, with God's help, and providing there were no heavy drifts in the long stretch between certain villages whose names came with an extremely familiar sound to my ears. He turned out an excellent coachman with an instinct for keeping the road amongst the snow-covered fields and a natural gift of getting the best out of the horses.

"He is the son of that Joseph that I suppose the Captain remembers. He who used to drive the Captain's late grandmother of holy memory," remarked V. S., busy tucking fur rugs about my feet.

I remembered perfectly the trusty Joseph who used to drive my grandmother. Why! he it was who let me hold the reins for the first time in my life and allowed me to play with the great four-in-hand whip outside the doors of the coach-house.

"What became of him?" I asked. "He is no longer serving, I suppose."

"He served our master," was the reply. "But he died of cholera ten years ago now—that great epidemic we had. And his wife died at the same time—the whole houseful of them, and this is the only boy that was left."

The MS. of "Almayer's Folly" was reposing in the bag under our feet.

I saw again the sun setting on the plains as I saw it in the travels of my childhood. It set, clear and red, dipping into the snow in full view as if it were setting on the sea. It was twenty-three years since I had seen the sun set over that land; and we drove on in the darkness which fell swiftly upon the livid expanse of snows till, out of the waste of a white earth joining a bestarred sky, surged up black shapes, the clumps of trees about a village of the Ukrainian plain. A cottage or two glided by, a low interminable wall and then, glimmering and winking through a screen of fir-trees, the lights of the master's house.

That very evening the wandering MS. of "Almayer's Folly" was unpacked and unostentatiously laid on the writing-table in my room, the guest-room which had been, I was informed in an affectedly careless tone, awaiting me for some fifteen years or so. It attracted no attention from the affectionate presence hovering round the son of the favourite sister.

"You won't have many hours to yourself while you are staying with me, brother," he said—this form of address borrowed from the speech of our peasants being the usual expression of the highest good humour in a moment of affectionate elation. "I shall be always coming in for a chat."

As a matter of fact we had the whole house to chat in and were everlastingly intruding upon each other. I invaded the retirement of his study, where the principal feature was a colossal silver inkstand presented to him on his fiftieth year by a subscription of all his wards then living. He had been guardian of many orphans of land-owning families from the three southern provinces—ever since the year 1860. Some of them had been my schoolfellows and playmates, but not one of them, girls or boys, that I know of, has ever written a novel. One or two were older than myself—considerably older, too. One of them, a visitor I remember in my early years, was the man who first put me on horseback, and his four-horse bachelor turn-out, his perfect horsemanship and general skill in manly exercises was one of my earliest admirations. I seem to remember my mother looking on from a colonnade in front of the dining-room windows as I was lifted upon the pony, held, for all I know, by the very Joseph—the groom attached specially to my grandmother's service—who died of cholera. It was certainly a young man in a dark blue, tail-less coat and huge Cossack trousers, that being the livery of the men about the stables. It must have been in 1864, but reckoning by another mode of calculating time, it was certainly in the year in which my mother obtained permission to travel south and visit her family, from the exile into which she had followed my father. For that, too, she had had to ask permission, and I know that one of the conditions of that favour was that she should be treated exactly as a condemned exile herself. Yet a couple of years later, in memory of her eldest brother who had served in the Guards and dying early left hosts of friends and a loved memory in the great world of St. Petersburg, some influential personages procured for her this permission—it was officially called the "Highest Grace"—of a three months' leave from exile.

This is also the year in which I first begin to remember my mother with more distinctness than a mere loving, wide-browed, silent, protecting presence, whose eyes had a sort of commanding sweetness; and I also remember, the great gathering of all the relations from near and far, and the grey heads of the family friends paying her the homage of respect and love in the house of her favourite brother who, a few years later, was to take the place for me of both my parents.

I did not understand the tragic significance of it all at the time, though indeed I remember that doctors also came. There were no signs of invalidism about her—but I think that already they had pronounced her doom unless perhaps the change to a southern climate could re-establish her declining strength. For me it seems the very happiest period of my existence. There was my cousin, a delightful, quick-tempered little girl, some months younger than myself, whose life, lovingly watched over, as if she were a royal princess, came to an end with her fifteenth year. There were other children too, many of whom are dead now, and not a few whose very names I have forgotten. Over all this hung the oppressive shadow of the great Russian Empire—the shadow lowering with the darkness of a new-born national hatred fostered by the Moscow school of journalists against the Poles after the ill-omened rising of 1863.

This is a far cry back from the MS. of "Almayer's Folly," but the public record of these formative impressions is not the whim of an uneasy egotism. These, too, are things human, already distant in their appeal. It is meet that something more should be left for the novelist's children than the colours and figures of his own hard-won creation. That which in their grown-up years may appear to the world about them as the most enigmatic side of their natures and perhaps must remain for ever obscure even to themselves, will be their unconscious response to the still voice of that inexorable past from which his work of fiction and their personalities are remotely derived.

Only in men's imagination does every truth find an effective and undeniable existence. Imagination, not invention, is the supreme master of art as of life. An imaginative and exact rendering of authentic memories may serve worthily that spirit of piety towards all things human which sanctions the conceptions of a writer of tales, and the emotions of the man reviewing his own experience.

Letters

At some points in the texts below I have supplemented Conrad's manuscript by including brief explanatory notes in brackets; most of these either spell out a title or are translations from the French. The Cambridge edition of Conrad's letters uses brackets for conjectured dates and addresses; I have duplicated them here. Ellipses in brackets indicate cuts in the text. Conrad's punctuation, capitalization, and italicization have been followed throughout.

To Marguerite Poradowska

BELGIAN-BORN ROMANTIC NOVELIST; AUNT BY MARRIAGE; 1848–1937

26 September 1890
Kinshasa

Dearest and best of Aunts!

I received your three letters together on my return from Stanley Falls, where I went as a supernumerary on board the vessel *Roi des Belges* in order to learn about the river. [. . .] I cannot find words sufficiently strong to make you understand the pleasure your charming (and above all kind) letters have given me. They were as a ray of sunshine piercing through the grey clouds of a dreary winter day; for my days here are dreary. No use deluding oneself! Decidedly I regret having come here. I even regret it bitterly. With all of a man's egoism I am going to speak of myself. I cannot stop myself. Before whom can I ease my heart if not before you?! [. . .]

Everything here is repellent to me. Men and things, but men above all. And I am repellent to them, also. From the manager in Africa who has taken the trouble to tell one and all that I offend him supremely, down to the lowest mechanic, they all have the gift of irritating my nerves—so that I am not as agreeable to them perhaps as I should be. The manager is a common ivory dealer with base instincts who considers himself a merchant although he is only a kind of African shop-keeper. His name is Delcommune. He detests the English, and out here I am naturally regarded as such. I cannot hope for either promotion or salary increases while he is here. Besides, he has said that promises made in Europe carry no weight here if they are not in the contract. Those made to me by M. Wauters are not. In addition, I cannot look forward to anything because I don't have a ship to command. The new boat will not be completed until June of next year, perhaps. Meanwhile, my position here is unclear and I am troubled by that. So there you are! As crowning joy, my health is far from good. *Keep it a secret for me*—but the truth is that in going up the river I suffered from fever four times in two months, and then at the Falls (which is its home territory), I suffered an attack of dysentery lasting five days. I feel somewhat weak physically and not a little demoralized; and then, really, I believe that I feel homesick for the sea, the desire to look again on the level expanse of salt water which has so often lulled me, which has smiled at me so frequently under the sparkling sunshine of a lovely day, which many times too has hurled the threat of death in my face with a swirl of white foam whipped by the wind under the dark December sky. I regret all that. But what I regret even more is having tied myself down for three years. The truth is that it is scarcely probable I shall see them through. Either someone in authority will pick a groundless quarrel in order to send me back (and, really, I sometimes find myself wishing for it), or I shall be sent back to Europe by a new attack of dysentery, unless it consigns me to the other world, which would be a final solution to all my distress! And for four pages I have been speaking of myself! I have not told you with what pleasure I have read your descriptions of men and things at home. Indeed, while reading your dear letters I have forgotten Africa, the Congo, the black savages and the white slaves (of whom I am one) who inhabit it. For one hour I have been happy. Know that it is not a small thing (nor an easy thing) to make a human being happy for an entire hour. [. . .]

Seeking a practical remedy to the disagreeable situation which I have made for myself, I conceived of a little plan—still up in the air—in which you could perhaps help me. It appears that this company, or another affiliated with it, will have some ocean-going vessels (or even has one already). Probably that great (or fat?) banker who rules the roost where we are concerned will have a large interest in the other company. If someone could submit my name for the command of one of their ships (whose home port will be Antwerp) I would be able to get away for a day or two in Brussels when you are there. That would be ideal! If they wanted to call me home to take command, I would naturally pay the cost of coming back myself. This is perhaps not a very practicable idea, but if you return to Brussels in the winter, you could learn through M. Wauters what the chances are. Isn't that so, dear little Aunt?

[. . .] I urge you by all the gods to keep secret from *everybody* the state of my health, or else my uncle will certainly hear of it. I must finish. I leave within an hour for Bamou, by canoe, to select trees and have them felled for building operations at the station here. I shall remain encamped in the forest for two or three weeks, unless ill. I like the prospect well enough. I can doubtless have a shot or two at some buffaloes or elephants. I embrace you most warmly. I shall write a long letter by the next mail.

Your affectionate nephew
J.C.K.

[Translated from the French by Frederick R. Karl and Laurence Davies.]

To Karol Zagórski

COUSIN; 1851–98

17, Gillingham Street,
London, S.W.
10th March, 1896.

My dear Karol,

Once again I am posting to you my masterpiece (this time the second one). Last year I sent three copies of my novel to Poland. Two of them reached their destinations. The third one, destined for you and your wife—presumably did not. I am trying again, hoping that this time both the book and the letter will reach you.

At the same time, I announce solemnly (as the occasion demands) to dear Aunt Gabrynia and to you both that I am getting married. No one can be more surprised at it than myself. However, I am not frightened at all, for as you know, I am accustomed to an adventurous life and to facing terrible dangers. Moreover, I have to avow that my betrothed does not give the impression of being at all dangerous. Jessie is her name; George her surname. She is a small, not at all striking-looking person (to tell the truth alas—rather plain!) who nevertheless is very dear to me. When I met her a year and a half ago she was earning her living in the City as a "Typewriter" in an American business office of the "Caligraph" company. Her father died three years ago. There are nine children in the family. The mother is a very decent woman (and I do not doubt very virtuous as well). However, I must confess that it is all the same to me, as vous comprenez?—I am not marrying the whole family. The wedding will take place on the 24th of this month and we shall leave London immediately so as to conceal from people's eyes our happiness (or our stupidity) amidst the wilderness and beauty of the coast of Brittany where I intend to rent a small house in some fishing village—probably in Plouaret or Pervengan (near St. Malo). There I shall start working on my third opus, for one has to write in order to live. A few days ago I was offered the command of a sailing vessel—the idea had pleased my Jessie (who likes the sea) but the terms were so unsatisfactory that in the end I refused. The literary profession is therefore my sole means of support. You will understand, my dear Karol, that if I have ventured into this field it is with the determination to achieve a reputation—in that sense I do not doubt my success. I know what I can do. It is therefore only a question of earning money—"Qui est une chose tout à fait à part du mérite littéraire." ["Which is a matter quite apart from literary merit."] That I do not feel too certain about—but as I need very little I am prepared to wait for it. I feel fairly confident about the future.

I hope that on the day of my wedding all of you—who are my whole family—will join me in your thoughts. I kiss the hands of my dear Aunt and ask for her blessing. I commend myself to your heart and to that of your wife,

Your loving
Konrad Korzeniowski

To R. B. Cunninghame Graham

SCOTTISH WRITER, SOCIALIST, ARISTOCRAT; SOMETIME MEMBER OF PARLIAMENT; 1852–1936

20th Dec. 1897.
Stanford-le-Hope

My dear Sir.

Your letter reached me just as I was preparing to write to you. What I said in my incoherent missive of last week was not for the purpose of arguing really. I did not seek controversy with you—for this reason: I think that we do agree. If I've read you aright (and I have been reading you for some years now) You are a most hopeless idealist—your aspirations are irrealisable. You want from men faith, honour, fidelity to truth in themselves and others. You want them to have all this, to show it every day, to make out of these words their rule of life. The respectable classes which suspect you of such pernicious longings lock you up and would just as soon have you shot—because your personality counts and you can not deny that you are a dangerous man. What makes you dangerous is your unwarrantable belief that your desire may be realized. This is the only point of difference between us. I do not believe. And if I desire the very same things no one cares. Consequently I am not likely to be locked up or shot. Therein is another difference—this time to your manifest advantage.

There is a—let us say—a machine. It evolved itself (I am severely scientific) out of a chaos of scraps of iron and behold!—it knits. I am horrified at the horrible work and stand appalled. I feel it ought to embroider—but it goes on knitting. You come and say: "this is all right; it's only a question of the right kind of oil. Let us use this—for instance—celestial oil and the machine shall embroider a most beautiful design in purple and gold." Will it? Alas no. You cannot by any special lubrication make embroidery with a knitting machine. And the most withering thought is that the infamous thing has made itself; made itself without thought, without conscience, without foresight, without eyes, without heart. It is a tragic accident—and it has happened. You can't interfere with it. The last drop of bitterness is in the suspicion that you can't even smash it. In virtue of that truth one and immortal which lurks in the force that made it spring into existence it is what it is—and it is indestructible!

It knits us in and it knits us out. It has knitted time space, pain, death, corruption, despair and all the illusions—and nothing matters. I'll admit however that to look at the remorseless process is sometimes amusing. [. . .]

Ever Yours faithfully
Jph. Conrad

To Edward Garnett

PUBLISHER'S READER AND MAN OF LETTERS; RECOMMENDED *ALMAYER'S FOLLY* FOR PUBLICATION; 1868–1937

29th March.
[1898]
[Stanford-le-Hope]

My dear Garnett.

I am ashamed of myself. I ought to have written to you before but the fact is I have not written anything at all. When I received your letter together with part IId of *R*[*escue*] I was in bed—this beastly nervous trouble. Since then I've been better but have been unable to write. I sit down religiously every morning, I sit down for eight hours every day—and the sitting down is all. In the course of that working day of 8 hours I write 3 sentences which I erase before leaving the table in despair. There's not a single word to send you. Not one! And time passes—and McClure waits—not to speak of Eternity for which I don't care a damn. Of McClure however I am afraid.

I ask myself sometimes whether I am bewitched, whether I am the victim of an evil eye? But there is no "jettatura" in England—is there? I assure you—speaking soberly and on my word of honour—that sometimes it takes all my resolution and power of self control to refrain from butting my head against the wall. I want to howl and foam at the mouth but I daren't do it for fear of waking that baby and alarming my wife. It's no joking matter. After such crises of despair I doze for hours till half conscious that there is that story I am unable to write. Then I wake up, try again—and at last go to bed completely done-up. So the days pass and nothing is done. At night I sleep. In the morning I get up with the horror of that powerlessness I must face through a day of vain efforts.

In these circumstances as you imagine I feel not much inclination to write letters. As a matter of fact I had a great difficulty in writing the most commonplace note. I seem to have lost all *sense* of style and yet I am haunted, mercilessly haunted by the *necessity* of style. And that story I can't write weaves itself into all I see, into all I speak, into all I think, into the lines of every book I try to read. I haven't read for days. You know how bad it is when one *feels* one's liver, or lungs. Well I feel my brain. I am distinc[t]ly conscious of the contents of my head. My story is there in a fluid—in an evading shape. I can't get hold of it. It is all there—to bursting, yet I Can't get hold of it no more than you can grasp a handful of water.

There! I've told You all and feel better. While I write this I am amazed to see that I can write. It looks as though the spell were broken but I hasten, I hasten lest it should in five minutes or in half an hour be laid again.

I tried to correct Part II according to Your remarks. I did what I could—that is I knocked out a good many paragraphs. It's so much gained. As to alteration, rewriting and so on I haven't attempted it—except here and there a trifle—for the reason I could not think out anything different to what is written. Perhaps when I come to my senses I shall be able to do something before the *book* comes out. As to the serial it must go anyhow. I would be thankful to be able to write anything, anything, any trash, any rotten thing—something to earn dishonestly and by false pretenses the payment promised by a fool.

That's how things stand to-day; and to-morrow would be more mysterious if it were not so black! I write You a nice cheery letter for a good-bye: don't I, dear old fellow. That's how we use our friends. If I hadn't written I would have burst. [. . .]

Vale frater
Yours ever

J.C.

To John Galsworthy

NOVELIST AND FRIEND; 1867–1933

Pent Farm

Sunday Evening
12 March 1899

Dearest Jack

[. . .] I think that to say Henry James does not write from the heart is maybe hasty. He is cosmopolitan, civilised, very much "homme du monde" and the acquired ("educated" if you like) side of his temperament that is—restraint the instinctive, the nurtured, fostered, cherished side is always presented to the reader first. To me even the R[eal]. T[hing]. seems to flow from the heart because and only because the work approaching so near perfection yet does not strike cold. Technical perfection unless there is some real glow to illumine and warm it from within must necessarily be cold. I argue that in H. J. there is such a glow and not a dim one either, but to us used, absolutely accustomed, to unartistic expression of fine, headlong, honest (or dishonest) sentiments the art of H. J. does appear heartless. The outlines are so clear the figures so finished, chiselled, carved and brought out that we exclaim—we, used to the Shades of the contemporary fiction, to the more or less malformed shades—we exclaim—Stone! Not at all. I say flesh and blood—very perfectly presented—perhaps with too much perfection *of method*. The volume of short stories entitled I think *"The lesson of the Master"* contains a tale called "The Pupil" if I remember rightly where the underlying feeling of the man—his really wide sympathy—is seen nearer the surface. Of course he does not deal in primitive emotions. I maintain he is the most civilised of modern writers. He is also an idealiser. His heart shows itself in the delicacy of his handling. Things like *The Middle years* and *The altar of the dead* in the vol entitled *Terminations* would illustrate my meaning. [. . .] I admit he is not forcible—or, let us say, the only forcible thing in his work is his technique. Now a literary intelligence would be naturally struck by the wonderful technique and that is so wonderful in its way that it dominates the bare expression. The more so that the expression is only of delicate shades. He is never in deep gloom or in violent sunshine. But he feels deeply and vividly every delicate shade. We can not ask for more. Not every one is a Turgeniew. Moreover Turg: is not civilised (therein much of his charm for us) in the sense H. J. is civilised. Satis. [. . .]

Ever Yours

Conrad.

To R. B. Cunninghame Graham

Pent Farm

14 Oct 99

[. . .] Now with this idiotic [Boer] war there will be a bad time coming for print. All that's art, thought, idea will have to step back and hide its head before the intolerable war inanities. [. . .] The whole business is inexpressibly stupid—even on general principles; for evidently a war should be a conclusive proceeding while this noble enterprise (no matter what it's first result) must be the beginning of an endless contest. It is always unwise to begin a war which to be effective must be a war of extermination; it is positively imbecile to start it without a clear notion of what it means and to force on questions for immediate solution which are eminently fit to be left to time. From time only one solution could be expected—and that one favourable to this country. The war brings in an element of incertitude which will be not eliminated by military success. There is an appalling fatuity in this business. If I am to believe Kipling this is a war undertaken for the cause of democracy. C'est a crever de rire. [It's enough to make you die laughing.] However, now the fun has commenced, I trust British successes will be crushing from the first—on the same principle that if there's murder being done in the next room and you can't stop it you wish the head of the victim to be bashed in forthwith and the whole thing over for the sake of your own feelings. [. . .]

Ever Yours

Conrad

To William Blackwood

PUBLISHER; 1836–1912

Pent Farm

31 May 1902

Dear Mr Blackwood.

Directly on my return I sit down to thank you for your very kind and patient hearing. That the occasion was painful to me (it is always painful to be "asking") makes your friendly attitude the more valuable: and to say this is the primary object of my letter. But there is something more.

I admit that after leaving you I remained for some time under the impression of my "worthlessness"; but I beg to assure you that I've never fostered any illusions as to my value. You may believe me implicitly when I say that I never work in a self satisfied elation, which to my mind is no better than a state of inebriety unworthy of a man who means to achieve something. That—labouring against an anxious tomorrow, under the stress of an uncertain future, I have been at times consoled, re-assured and uplifted by a finished page—I'll not deny. This however is not intoxication: it is the Grace of God that will not pass by even an unsuccessful novelist. For the rest I am conscious of having pursued with pain and labour a calm conception of a definite ideal in a perfect soberness of spirit.

[. . .] I've rejected the idea of worthlessness and I'll tell you, dear Mr. Blackwood, on what ground mainly. It is this: that, given my talent [. . .] the fundamental and permanent failure could be only the outcome of an inherent worthlessness of character. Now my character is formed: it has been tried by experience. I have looked upon the worst life can do—and I am sure of myself, even against the demoralising effect of straitened circumstances.

I know exactly what I am doing. Mr. George Blackwood's incidental remark in his last letter that the story is not fairly begun yet is in a measure correct but, on a large view, beside the point. For, the writing is as good as I can make it (first duty), and in the light of the final incident, the whole story in all its descriptive detail shall fall into its place—acquire its value and its significance. This is my method based on deliberate conviction. I've never departed from it. I call your own kind self to witness and I beg to instance Karain—Lord Jim (where the method is fully developed)—the last pages of Heart of Darkness where the interview of the man and the girl locks in—as it were—the whole 30000 words of narrative description into one suggestive view of a whole phase of life and makes of that story something quite on another plane than an anecdote of a man who went mad in the Centre of Africa. And *Youth* itself (which I delight to know you like so well) exists only in virtue of my fidelity to the idea and the method. The favourable critics of that story, Q amongst others remarked with a sort of surprise "This after all is a story for boys yet - - - - -"

Exactly. Out of the material of a boys' story I've made Youth by the force of the idea expressed in accordance with a strict conception of my method. And however unfavourably it may affect the business in hand I must confess that I shall not depart from my method. I am at need prepared to explain on what grounds I think it a true method. All my endeavours shall be directed to understand it better, to develop its great possibilities, to acquire greater skill in the handling—to mastery in short.

[. . .] It is not the haphazard business of a mere temperament. There is in it as much intelligent action guided by a deliberate view of the effect to be attained as in any business enterprise. Therefore I am emboldened to say that ultimate and irretrievable failure is not to be my lot. I know that it is not necessary to say to You but I may just as well point out that I must not by any means be taken for a gifted loafer intent on living upon credulous publishers. Pardon this remark—but in a time when Sherlock Holmes looms so big I may be excused my little bit of self-assertion.

I am long in my development. What of that? Is not Thackeray's penny worth of mediocre fact drowned in an ocean of twaddle? And yet he lives. And Sir Walter, himself, was not the writer of concise anecdotes I fancy. And G. Elliot—is she as swift as the present public (incapable of fixing its attention for five consecutive minutes) requires us to be at the cost of all honesty, of all truth, and even the most elementary conception of art? But these are great names. I don't compare myself with them. I am *modern,* and I would rather recall Wagner the musician and Rodin the Sculptor who both had to starve a little in their day—and Whistler the painter who made Ruskin the critic foam at the mouth with scorn and indignation. They too have arrived. They had to suffer for being "new." And I too hope to find my place in the rear of my betters. But still—my place.

Believe me, dear Mr Blackwood in all trust and confidence yours

Jph Conrad

To Roger Casement

CONSULAR OFFICIAL AND CRUSADER FOR HUMAN RIGHTS; EXPOSED BELGIAN ATROCITIES IN THE CONGO, WHERE HE AND CONRAD MET IN 1890; IRISH PATRIOT; BORN 1864, HANGED AS A TRAITOR BY BRITAIN IN 1916

Pent Farm

21st Dec 1903

My dear Casement

[. . .] It is an extraordinary thing that the conscience of Europe which seventy years ago has put down the slave trade on humanitarian grounds tolerates the Congo State to day. It is as if the moral clock had been put back many hours. And yet nowadays if I were to overwork my horse so as to destroy its happiness of physical wellbeing I should be hauled before a magistrate. It seems to me that the black man—say, of Upoto—is deserving of as much humanitarian regard as any animal since he has nerves, feels pain, can be made physically miserable. But as a matter of fact his happiness and misery are much more complex than the misery or happiness of animals and deserving of greater regard. He shares with us the consciousness of the universe in which we live—no small burden. Barbarism per se is no crime deserving of a heavy visitation; and the Belgians are worse than the seven plagues of Egypt insomuch that in that case it was a punishment sent for a definite transgression; but in this the Upoto man is not aware of any transgression, and therefore can see no end to the infliction. It must appear to him very awful and mysterious; and I confess that it appears so to me too. The amenities of the "middle passage" in the old days were as nothing to it. The slave trade has been abolished—and the Congo State exists to-day. This is very remarkable. What makes it more remarkable is this: the slave trade was an old established form of commercial activity; it was not the monopoly of one small country established to the disadvantage of the rest of the civilized world in defiance of international treaties and in brazen disregard of humanitarian declarations. But the Congo State created yesterday is all that and yet it exists. This is very mysterious. One is tempted to exclaim (as poor Thiers did in 1871) "Il n'y a plus d'Europe." But as a matter of fact in the old days England had in her keeping the conscience of Europe. The initiative came from here. But now I suppose we are busy with other things; too much involved in great affairs to take up cudgels for humanity, decency and justice. But what about our commercial interests? These suffer greatly as Morel has very clearly demonstrated in his book. There can be no serious attempt to controvert his facts. Or [it] is impossible to controvert them for the hardest of lying won't do it. That precious pair of African witch-men seem to have cast a spell upon the world of whites—I mean Leopold and Thys of course. This is very funny.

And the fact remains that in 1903, seventy five years or so after the abolition of the slave trade (because it was cruel) there exists in Africa a Congo State, created by the act of European Powers where ruthless, systematic cruelty towards the blacks is the basis of administration, and bad faith towards all the other states the basis of commercial policy.

I do hope we shall meet before you leave. Once more my best wishes go with you on your crusade. Of course You may make any use you like of what I write to you. Cordially Yours

Jph Conrad.

To William Rothenstein

PAINTER; 1872–1945

Pent Farm

3d 1904 Sept

My dear Rothenstein.

The book [*Nostromo*] is finished; it has been finished for a couple of days now, but I have been too tired too flat to write to you at once. The last month I worked practically night and day; going to bed at three and sitting down again at nine. All the time at it, with the tenacity of despair.

What the book is like I don't know. I don't suppose it'll damage me; but I know that it is open to much intelligent criticism. For the other sort I don't care. Personally I am not satisfied. It is something—but not the thing I tried for. There is no exultation, none of that temporary sense of achievement which is so soothing. Even the mere feeling of relief, at having done with it, is wanting. The strain has been too great; had lasted too long.

But I am ready for more. I don't feel empty, exhausted. I am simply joyless—like most men of little faith. [. . .]

Ever yours

J. Conrad.

To J. B. Pinker

LITERARY AGENT; REPRESENTED CONRAD, HENRY JAMES, AND H. G. WELLS, AMONG OTHERS; 1863–1922

30 July 1907
Hotel de la Roseraie
Geneva

My dear Pinker.

Thanks for the money. The book I think is a book to produce some sensation. I don't say it is good but I say it is the best I could do with the subject. In the 2 months of the boy's illness I managed to write into it some 26–28000 words. After that I imagine I can do anything; for you can have no idea of my mental state all that time. Besides the anxiety for the child there was the tearing awful worry of the circumstances.

We must end this damnable outing now as soon as possible. I have been trying to think out everything. I can't come back to the Pent unless all that's owing there is paid, as I told you before. I'll send you a list here. A hundred will do I fancy to cover it all except the income tax.

After getting back to the Pent the great thing will be to get away from there as soon as possible, and make a fresh start.

There will be the house hunting. Perhaps we may get something near Ashford to make the moving less expensive. If You hear of any inexpensive sort of house in the country near London make a note of it for us.

We have been calculating everything and we have arrived at a budget £664 a year counting the house for £50. In this Borys' schooling is included. He can't go yet to Beaumont but perhaps we could place him as day boy somewhere. There is a school in Ashford which would do for six or nine months or so. But these are details. Adding to the above sum £126 for (alas!) the doctor (better be prepared for that infernal side of my existence) we arrive at £800 for the 12 months. If we can do with less so much the better but I dare not say less. [. . .]

I think I can say safely that the *Secret Agent* is *not* the sort of novel to make what comes after more difficult to place. Neither will it I fancy knock my prices down. *Chance* itself will be altogether different in tone and treatment of course, but it will be saleable I believe. By the end of Sept you will have a really considerable lot of it to show. Of course it will not be on popular lines. Nothing of mine can be, I fear. But even Meredith ended by getting his sales. Now, I haven't Meredith's delicacy and that's a point in my favour. I reckon I may make certain of the support of the Press for the next few years. The young men who are coming in to write criticisms are in my favour so far. At least all of whom I've heard are. I don't get in the way of established reputations. One may read everybody and yet in the end want to read me—for a change if for nothing else. For I don't resemble anybody; and yet I am not specialised enough to call up imitators as to matter or style. There is nothing in me but a turn of mind which whether valuable or worthless can not be imitated.

It has been a disastrous time. You must help me settle down now on an economical basis. It will cost something to do that but that once done 3 years of close sitting will do the trick. I'll be then 52 and not worn out yet as a writer. Without exaggeration I may say I feel renovated by my cure here—and considering the adverse circumstances this seems a good sign. I am anxious to get back and drive on.

We could start from here on the 10th. I would like to start on that date. To fetch me home after settling here I will require £80. The sooner you let me have that the better. [. . .]

Always yours

Conrad

To J. B. Pinker

Talbot House,
Arundel Street, Strand, London
W.C.

[16? July 1908]

My dear P.

You must not treat me as a journeyman joiner. Am I to understand that if the book is not finished by say 10–15 then You will drop me on the 15th of Augt. I don't inquire whether it is You *can't* or *won't*. From the practical point of view it amounts to the same thing.

Hall Caine takes two years to write his books. J.C. may be allowed some time. If your idea is that my stuff is unsaleable then all I can say is that I haven't made it so. If I must starve or beg I won't do it *here*. That's all I have to say really. Consider whether it would be good policy (from a practical point of view) to drive me away. This is nothing but a *statement of the case*. Don't take it in any other spirit. I have no vice to prevent me working and I am willing as soon as practicable to get away into a most economical hole imaginable and write there night and day. I can't believe that my reputation has gone to pieces suddenly.

Yours

J.C.

To Edward Garnett

Capel House

27 May 1912

Dearest Edward,

I do hope you are not too disgusted with me for not thanking you for the "Karamazov" before. It was very dear of you to remember me; and of course I was extremely interested. But it's an impossible lump[?] of valuable matter. It's terrifically bad and impressive and exasperating. Moreover, I don't know what D stands for or reveals, but I do know that he is too Russian for me. It sounds to me like some fierce mouthings from prehistoric ages. I understand the Russians have just "discovered" him. I wish them joy.

Of course your wife's translation is wonderful. One almost breaks one's heart merely thinking of it. What courage! What perseverance! What talent of—interpretation let us say. The word "translation" does not apply to your wife's achievements. But indeed the man's art does not deserve this good fortune. Turgeniew (and perhaps Tolstoï) are the only two really worthy of her. Give her please my awestruck and admiring love. One can be nothing less but infinitely grateful to her whatever one may think of or feel about D. himself. [. . .]

Yours ever

J Conrad

To John Quinn

NEW YORK LAWYER AND COLLECTOR; 1870–1924

Capel House

[late January 1917]

My dear Quinn.

My wife wanted to write herself the letter of thanks for the lovely apples; but our boy has just left us after his first leave from France and she does not feel equal to talk about him on paper—and yet she feels that she would have to write of him. So I am deputed to tell you how much we have appreciated your gift and then to tell you something of the boy.

He celebrated his 19th birthday with us. He said to me: "I am a veteran. When we, the first batch of youngsters, were appointed to the heavy batteries as Mechanical Transport Officers it was an altogether new thing. Nobody could teach us then because nobody knew the practical conditions and the way to go about that work. We had to learn all this by ourselves under shell-fire and sometimes under machine-gun fire. And we have all done pretty well."

One could see he was fairly pleased with himself and extremely proud of his men. He had a year of continuous duty all along the line right from Ypres to the Somme. He has been gassed a little in the early days—a sort of welcome from Fritz. He managed to get in as many side-shows as possible—has flown in action, has squatted in observation posts; went sniper-hunting, had a joy ride in a tank the first time they went over the German lines. But what seems to afford him the greatest satisfaction is having been knocked down by the same shell-concussion with General Gough. The boy had just put the last gun of the battery in position, then got his lorry back on the road and was waiting for a bit because the landscape ahead was full of German shells. He saw a general's car come along from the direction of Pozières. It pulled up opposite him and the general got out, apparently to speak to him. Just at that moment a H.Z. shell landed on the car's forewheel blew the whole thing to smithereens and flung the general covered with his drivers blood and shreds of flesh under B's lorry. B had been flung there too; the lorry (an American—Peerless) was half demolished and of the two men with B one was killed and the other had his hand blown off. B and the general crawled from under the wreck together. The Gen: was a horrible sight. He said to B: "For Goodness' sake lets get out of this." And B said: "Certainly Sir" and pointed out to him an enormous shell-crater quite near the road. So they crawled along over there taking the wounded man with them. In that crater there were a good many people some dead and some alive and luckily two stretcher-bearers who bandaged the man's arm. Meantime B wiped the general down with some rags he found lying about, the best way he could; and then they both sat in that hole for an hour and a half shivering and shaking from the shock. Later the Gen. got away down a trench and B went back to his battery where he helped around generally till the evening, when his junior officer arrived with an ammunition convoy with which B returned to the replenishing station. But before daybreak he was back with the battery with another ammunition convoy. And now said B "whenever the Gen: sees me on the roads he waves his hand to me, though I am certain he doesn't know my name."

We found B matured very much. What struck me most was a sort of good-tempered imperturbable serenity in his manner, speech and thoughts—as if nothing in the world could startle or annoy him any more. He looks wonderfully robust and has developed a respectable moustache. He gave us every minute of his leave; wouldn't hear of going to town except for a day and a half with his mother to call on the more intimate of our circle of friends. We got on extremely well together. We talked not only of War but of the other two W's also. Where the fellow got his taste for wine I can't imagine. As to Women, Cunninghame Graham who went on purpose to meet him in the salon of a very distinguished lady (the world says that she is his last flame. About time. C.G. is sixty-five if a day) wrote to me with great glee that he found the boy "très dégourdi" and that he thought he "will be un homme a femmes like You and I, for he has a way with them." My wife who gave a lunch party has also observed that aptitude and was very much amused. She has indeed snatched a fearful joy during these 10 days. Her fortitude is admirable but I am anxious about her health. She sends you her most friendly regards. What a war-letter I have written!

Believe me always

Yours
Joseph Conrad.

To John Quinn

4C Hyde Park Mansions
N.W. 1
Feb. 6th. 1918

My dear Quinn.

I have just read your letter to Jessie, who is immensely flattered and pleased at her friendly correspondence with J.Q. Speaking of that same lady I will tell you that the surgeons entertain good hopes of mending her thoroughly in the course of 6 to 8 months. And meantime a cleverly devised apparatus which she has to wear on her damaged limb has relieved her from the pain from which she has suffered for the last 14 years. She can look forward to the future now with renewed confidence.

My outlook too has been altered for the better in consequence. This thing has been like a nightmare oppressing our life for a long stretch of years.

Thank you very much for the books. Monahan I like. E[zra] P[ound] is certainly a poet but I am afraid I am too old and too wooden-headed to appreciate him as perhaps he deserves. The critics here consider him harmless; but as he has, I believe, a very good opinion of himself I don't suppose he worries his head about the critics very much. Besides he has many women at his feet; which must be immensely comforting. But I am very grateful to you for sending me that bibliographically valuable copy.

Whatever happens Russia is out of the war now. The great thing is to keep the Russian infection, its decomposing power, from the social organism of the rest of the world. In this Poland will have to play its part on whatever lines her future may have to be laid. And at the same time she will have to resist the immense power of germanism which would be death too, but in another shape. Whether that nation over-run, ruined and shaken to the very foundations of its soul will rise to this awful task I really don't know. What assistance she will be able to get from the Western world nobody can tell. Never was there such a darkness over a people's future, and that, don't forget, coming after more than a century of soul grinding oppression in which apart from a few choice spirits the Western world took no interest. Fine words have been given to it before.

And the finer the words the greater was always the deception. One evening in August in 1914 in a dimly lit, big room I spoke to a small group of Poles belonging to the University and the political life of the town of Cracow. One of the things I said was: "Rest assured that whoever makes peace in six months (that was all the talk then—that the war couldn't last) England will go on for ten years if necessary." But I had also the courage to tell them: "Have no illusions. If anybody has got to be sacrificed in this war it will be you. If there is any salvation to be found it is only in your own breasts, it is only by the force of your inner life that you will be able to resist the rottenness of Russia and the soullessness of Germany. And this will be your fate for ever and ever. For nothing in the world can alter the force of facts."

And if I had to speak to them to-morrow I would repeat these very words. I don't remember now what Mr Wilson said in his latest utterance. There is an awful air of unreality in all the words that are being flung about in the fact of such appalling realities. For the closer they are looked into the more appalling they are. And the tragedy of the situation for all the hearts, that are not the Devils' or the Angels' but those of Men truly worthy of the name, is this: that they can't contemplate either Peace or War otherwise than with an equal dread.

That is the tragedy—the inner anguish—the bitterness of lost lives, of unsettled consciences and of spiritual perplexities. Courage, endurance, enthusiasm, the hardest idealism itself, have their limits. And beyond those limits what is there? The eternal ignorance of mankind, the fateful darkness in which only vague forms can be seen which themselves may be no more than illusions.

In this enormous upheaval of Forces and Consciences all Hopes and all Fears are on an equality. Either can lead mankind equally astray. And there is nothing in the world to hold on to but the work that has to be done on each succeeding day. Outside that there is nothing to lay hold of but what each man can find in himself. [. . .]

Believe me dear Quinn

Yours most sincerely

Joseph Conrad

To Hugh Walpole

ENGLISH POPULAR NOVELIST; 1884–1941

Oswalds

10 Feby 22

My dearest Hugh.

It is very much like You to write at once as you have written, and indeed tho' not surprised I am deeply touched by your sympathetic understanding of my actual feelings as to P[inker]'s death.

Gradually since 1914 an intimacy developed between us in a strange way. He seemed to think that he had earned the right of laying his innermost thoughts and feelings before me. A peculiar but in its way a touching assertion of the right of good service and—no other word will do—of devotion.

The notice in the Times is perfectly true. He had a pride in his work and in his power to help people in ways that from a cold business point of view could not be justified to common prudence.

As to the new situation created by his death it may be for me a little awkward for a time. In any case it must be a loss for no one would be able to conduct my affairs as he did. But my affairs too are nearing their end—in a manner of speaking. But I feel that we all in this house have lost a personality that counted in our lives for stability and support.

Our dear love to You.

Ever Yours

J. Conrad

I shall be probably in town on Monday for the night.

To C. K. Scott Moncrieff

TRANSLATOR; 1889–1930

Oswalds

Dec. 17th. 1922.

My dear Moncrieff,

I forgive you your "horrible" letter. (You will notice how characteristic of Conrad is this proceeding of answering letters by the end. That is the fault that critics found with my novels. They called it "indirect method." Funny lot, the critics.)

I am brilliant this morning. Some day I will begin a novel like this—with a word in quotes and then a long parenthesis.

The lack of response from the public does not surprise me. And I don't think it surprises very much Messrs. Chatto & Windus. The more honour to them in risking that shot for which no great prize can be obtained. As to you, it is clear that you have done this for love—and there is no more to be said.

In the volumes you sent me I was much more interested and fascinated by your rendering than by Proust's creation. One has revealed to me something and there is no revelation in the other. I am speaking now of the sheer *maîtrise de langue;* I mean how far it can be pushed—in your case of two languages—by a supreme faculty akin to genius. For to think that such a result could be obtained by mere study and industry would be too depressing. And that is the revelation. As far as the *maîtrise de langue* is concerned there is no revelation in Proust. [. . .]

Now as to Marcel Proust, *créateur,* I don't think he has been written about much in English, and what I have seen of it was rather superficial. I have seen him praised for his "wonderful" pictures of Paris life and provincial life. But that has been done admirably before, for us, either in love, or in hatred, or in mere irony. One critic goes so far as to say that P.'s great art reaches the universal and that in depicting his own past he reproduces for us the general experience of mankind. But I doubt it. I admire him rather for disclosing a past like nobody else's, for enlarging, as it were, the general experience of mankind by bringing to it something that has not been recorded before. However, all that is not of much importance. The important thing is that whereas before we had analysis allied to creative art, great in poetic conception, in observation, or in style, his is a creative art absolutely based on analysis. It is really more than that. He is a writer who has pushed analysis to the point when it became creative. All that crowd of personages in their infinite variety through all the gradations of the social scale are made to stand up, to live, and are rendered visible to us by the force of analysis alone. I don't say P. has got no gift of description or characterization; but to take an example from each end of the scale: Francoise, the devoted servant, and le baron de Charlus—a consummate portrait—how many descriptive lines have they got to themselves in the whole body of that immense work? Perhaps, counting the lines, half a page each. And yet no intelligent person can doubt for a moment their plastic and coloured existence. One would think that method (and P. has no other, because his method is the expression of his temperament) may be pushed too far, but as a matter of fact it is never wearisome. There may be here and there among those thousands of pages a paragraph that one might think over subtle, a bit of analysis pushed so far as to vanish into nothingness. But those are very few, and all minor, instances. The intense interest never flags because one has got the feeling that the last word is being said upon a subject much studied, much written about and of undying interest—the last word of its time. Those that have found beauty in Proust's work are perfectly right. It is there. What amazes one is its inexplicable character. In that prose so full of life there is no reverie, no emotion, no marked irony, no warmth of conviction, not even a marked rhythm to charm our fancy. It appeals to our sense of wonder and gains our assent by its veiled greatness. I don't think there ever has been in the whole of literature such an example of the power of analysis and I feel pretty safe in saying that there will never be another.

This is more or less what I think, or imagine that I think. It is really not half of what I imagine I think. If it is any good to you, you may alter, cut down, expand, twist, turn over and do anything you like with the above lines to make them suitable. [. . .]

Always, my dear Moncrieff, cordially yours

Suggestions for Further Reading

The secondary literature on Conrad is so large that these suggestions must remain selective. That literature is also of a remarkably high quality. His books seem to marry with every critical approach or methodology imaginable—by which I mean that intelligent scholars of many different stripes have found something in him with which to work. Or as one recent critic, Geoffrey Galt Harpham, has put it, "There is a Conrad for all seasons—an earnest moralist, a stylist . . . a modernist, a postmodernist . . . a psychoanalyst, an anarchist, a popular entertainer." And many others too, so that the best of this scholarship rarely seems to repeat itself. That can't be said of all great writers. Lawrence criticism has a more restricted range, perhaps because it must respond to his prophetic streak; Joyceans must engage with his linguistic and technical complications; even Woolf, who matches Conrad in her accessible difficulty and offers some things he does not, nevertheless responds to a narrower range of political and even narratological approaches. To my mind only Shakespeare and Austen can match Conrad's ability to look so good in so many costumes. This, surely, is one mark of his greatness.

Two scholarly works have been on my desk throughout the preparation of this Portable. The first is the Cambridge edition of *The Collected Letters of Joseph Conrad,* whose last volumes appear simultaneously with this one (Frederick R. Karl and Laurence Davies, et al., eds., 9 vols., Cambridge: Cambridge University Press, 1983–2007). This edition prints every extant letter, and its annotations provide just the right level of detail. My other great debt is to the *Oxford Reader's Companion to Conrad,* edited by Owen Knowles and Gene Moore (Oxford: Oxford University Press, 2000), an encyclopedia that includes such things as thumb-nail biographies of all the important people in Conrad's life; a registry of the ships on which he sailed, with his dates of service and ports of call; entries on his publishers, finances, and health; and concise critical histories of his every book.

Some of Conrad's friends and intimates left important memoirs. Ford Madox Ford's many autobiographical volumes can rarely be trusted as to fact. Nevertheless his *Joseph Conrad: A Personal Remembrance* (London: Duckworth, 1924) contains a suggestive account of Conrad's theories of fiction as well as a record of their collaboration. Edward Garnett's *Letters from Conrad, 1895–1924* (London: Nonesuch, 1928) has an invaluable introduction, a portrait of Conrad in his earliest years as a writer by the editor who discovered him. Garnett considered Jessie Conrad's 1935 *Joseph Conrad and his Circle* (New York: Dutton, 1935) to be a self-serving act of betrayal, a verdict with which most of Conrad's biographers have agreed. The most valuable details from that book, her earlier *Joseph Conrad as I Knew Him* (London: Heinemann, 1926), and the separate memoirs of their sons are subsumed in the biographies.

The first of those biographies was by Conrad's French protégé and translator G. Jean-Aubry, *Joseph Conrad: Life and Letters* (2 vols., London: Heinemann, 1927), a work later supplemented by his 1957 *The Sea-Dreamer: A Definitive Biography of Joseph Conrad* (London: Allen and Unwin). But that subtitle's adjective will not stand, and the first comprehensive biography was Jocelyn Baines's *Joseph Conrad: A Critical Biography* (London: Weidenfeld and Nicolson, 1960). Still, Conrad has yet to find his equivalent of Ellmann on Joyce or Edel on James. Some of the problems in Conrad biography are suggested by the subtitle of one major account, Frederick R. Karl's *Joseph Conrad: The Three Lives* (New York: Farrar, Straus and Giroux, 1979). Those lives are as Pole, sailor, and writer, but the result can be schematic. The most authoritative biography to date is Zdzislaw Najder's *Joseph Conrad: A Chronicle* (Halina Carroll Najder, trans., New Brunswick, NJ: Rutgers University Press, 1983), a book that goes well beyond the limits suggested by its subtitle. Najder is leery of psychoanalytic studies, but Conrad has been the subject of many of them. An early account was Gustav Morf's *The Polish Heritage of Joseph Conrad* (New York: Richard R. Smith, 1930), which reads his career in terms of an attempt to deal with his alleged guilt over leaving Poland. A more wide-ranging attempt can be found in Bernard C. Meyer's *Joseph Conrad: A Psychoanalytic Biography* (Princeton, NJ: Princeton University Press 1967). A new full-scale biography by John Stape, based on fresh archival research, is in press at the time of writing: *The Several Lives of Joseph Conrad* (New York: Knopf, 2007).

All Conrad students owe a special debt to the two volumes in which Norman Sherry traces the historical underpinnings of his fiction: *Conrad's Eastern World* and *Conrad's Western World* (1966 and 1971 respectively, both Cambridge University Press). These books reconstitute, among other things, the portside gossip and historical incidents that Conrad drew upon for *Lord Jim*, the world of the London anarchists he describes in *The Secret Agent*, and the narrative of his experiences in the Congo. Sherry has also edited a rich volume in the Critical Heritage Series (London: Routledge and Kegan Paul, 1973) that reprints the most important of Conrad's first reviews. Two significant posthumous assessments are those of John Dozier Gordon, *Joseph Conrad: The Making of a Novelist* (Cambridge, MA: Harvard University Press, 1940), and M. C. Bradbrook, *Joseph Conrad: Poland's English Genius* (New York: Macmillan, 1941).

What my introduction calls the "heroic age" in Conrad criticism was inaugurated by Morton Dauwen Zabel's *The Portable Conrad* (New York: Viking, 1947) and F. R. Leavis's *The Great Tradition* (London: Chatto and Windus, 1948). Zabel's later thoughts on Conrad will be found in the four essays that he collected, along with much else, in *Craft and Character in Modern Fiction* (New York: Viking, 1957). Despite receiving some criticism in my introduction, Albert J. Guerard's *Conrad the Novelist* (Cambridge, MA: Harvard University Press, 1958) remains a suggestive account of Conrad's narrative technique. Thomas C. Moser's influential *Joseph Conrad: Achievement and Decline* (Cambridge, MA: Harvard University Press, 1957) presents a reading with which many critics continue to engage. Several articles from the 1950s have kept their value: Robert Penn Warren's introduction to *Nostromo* (New York: Random House, 1951); Dorothy Van Ghent's chapter on *Lord Jim* in *The English Novel: Form and Function* (New York: Rinehart, 1953); and Irving

Howe's "Conrad: Order and Anarchy" in *Politics and the Novel* (New York: Horizon, 1957). Two important collections of critical essays are R. W. Stallman, ed., *The Art of Joseph Conrad: A Critical Symposium* (East Lansing: Michigan State University Press, 1960), and Marvin Mudrick, ed., *Conrad: A Collection of Critical Essays* (Englewood Cliffs, NJ: Prentice Hall, 1966). Crucial early books on Conrad's politics are Eloise Knapp Hay's lucid *The Political Novels of Joseph Conrad* (Chicago: University of Chicago Press, 1963) and Avrom Fleishman, *Conrad's Politics* (Baltimore: Johns Hopkins Press, 1967), which is especially strong on the writer's Polish origin.

Edward Said's long and rewarding engagement with Conrad began in 1966 with *Joseph Conrad and the Fiction of Autobiography* (Cambridge, MA: Harvard University Press). It continued with sections on both *Lord Jim* and *Nostromo* in *Beginnings: Intention and Method* (New York: Basic Books, 1975); a rich essay on Conrad's narrative procedures in *The World, the Text, and the Critic* (Cambridge, MA: Harvard University Press, 1983); and a chapter on "Heart of Darkness" in *Culture and Imperialism* (New York: Knopf, 1983). He may be said to have brought Conrad into the age of theory, along with Frederic Jameson in *The Political Unconscious* (Ithaca, NY: Cornell University Press, 1981). A good study of Conrad in relation to genre, adventure fiction in particular, is David Thorburn's *Conrad's Romanticism* (New Haven, CT: Yale University Press, 1974); it can be supplemented by the chapter on the writer in Jefferson Hunter's *Edwardian Fiction* (Cambridge, MA: Harvard University Press, 1982). See also John McClure, *Kipling and Conrad* (Cambridge, MA: Harvard University Press, 1981). Ian Watt's *Conrad in the Nineteenth Century* (Berkeley: University of California Press, 1979) parses all the major debates about Conrad's early work. This wise and indeed majestic volume should be supplemented by his *Essays on Conrad* (Cambridge: Cambridge University Press, 2000), which contains his work on the later career. Watt has also edited a casebook on *The Secret Agent* (London: Macmillan, 1973) that includes Thomas Mann's 1926 introduction to the novel's German translation.

Chinua Achebe's "An Image of Africa" was first published in the *Massachusetts Review* 18 (1977) after its delivery as a public lecture in 1975; it has been many times reprinted. V. S. Naipaul's

"Conrad's Darkness" first appeared in the *New York Review of Books* in 1974; it is now most readily available in his *Literary Occasions* (New York: Knopf, 2003). Christopher L. Miller's *Blank Darkness: Africanist Discourse in French* (Chicago: University of Chicago Press, 1985) both provides a methodology and includes a rewarding chapter on "Heart of Darkness."

I would recommend four collections for readers interested in learning the postcolonial terrain on which Conrad studies are now situated—a terrain that emphasizes contextual readings and, increasingly, the study of gender. The first is Robert D. Hamner's *Joseph Conrad: Third World Perspectives* (Washington, DC: Three Continents Press, 1990). J. H. Stape's *Cambridge Companion to Joseph Conrad* (Cambridge: Cambridge University Press, 1976) includes accounts of all the major fiction; see especially the chapters on "Heart of Darkness" by Cedric Watts and that on *Under Western Eyes* by Keith Carabine. *Conrad in the Twenty-First Century,* edited by Carola M. Kaplan, Peter Lancelot Mallios, and Andrea White (New York: Routledge, 2005), illustrates the range of Conrad scholarship today; see especially the editors' introduction, Mallios's interview with Said, and the interesting dissent from J. Hillis Miller, wondering what has been lost in our turn toward context and politics. Finally, Paul B. Armstrong's fourth Norton Critical Edition of "Heart of Darkness" (2006) reprints feminist assessments by Marianna Torgovnick and Jeremy Hawthorn, along with Achebe's essay and Patrick Brantlinger's important chapter on the tale from *Rule of Darkness: British Literature and Imperialism, 1830–1914* (Ithaca, NY: Cornell University Press, 1988). Johanna K. Smith has a useful analysis of "Heart of Darkness" and gender in the second edition of Ross C. Murfin's casebook, *Heart of Darkness: A Case Study in Contemporary Criticism* (Boston and New York: Bedford/St. Martin's, 1996). My account of the waterways in that tale is indebted to Stephen Clingman's argument in his forthcoming *The Grammar of Identity.*

Paul B. Armstrong's own *The Challenge of Bewilderment* (Ithaca, NY: Cornell University Press, 1987) offers one of the most sophisticated postheroic-age accounts of Conrad's narrative technique. See also Mark Wollaeger, *Joseph Conrad and the Fictions of Skepticism* (Stanford, CA: Stanford University Press, 1990). But most of the critical energy has gone another way. Here

I admire Benita Parry, *Conrad and Imperialism* (London: Macmillan, 1983); Chris Bongie, *Exotic Memories: Literature, Colonialism, and the Fin de Siècle* (Stanford, CA: Stanford University Press, 1991); Andrea White, *Joseph Conrad and the Adventure Tradition* (Cambridge: Cambridge University Press, 1993); Michael Valdes Moses, *The Novel and the Globalization of Culture* (New York: Oxford University Press, 1995); and especially Christopher GoGwilt, *The Invention of the West: Joseph Conrad and the Double-Mapping of Europe and Empire* (Stanford, CA: Stanford University Press, 1995). Stephen Ross's *Conrad and Empire* (Columbia and London: University of Missouri Press, 2004) provides a richly detailed reading of Conrad in light of current theories of globalization. The most interesting, and category-breaking, recent work on Conrad is, however, that of Geoffrey Galt Harpham in *One of Us: The Mastery of Joseph Conrad* (Chicago: University of Chicago Press, 1996).

Susan Jones has a detailed account of *Chance* and the other late fiction in *Conrad and Women* (Oxford: Clarendon Press, 1999). One new development, in the study of a writer who created only a few memorable female characters, is the use of the insights provided by feminist and gender studies to account for Conrad's articulation of masculine identity. See Christopher Laner, *The Ruling Passion* (Durham, NC: Duke University Press, 1995), and Andrew Michael Roberts, *Conrad and Masculinity* (New York: St. Martin's, 2000). The major scholarly journals devoted to Conrad's work are *Conradiana,* published at Texas Tech University, and *The Conradian,* produced by the Joseph Conrad Society of the United Kingdom; the latter maintains a useful website at www.josephconradsociety.org.